MURDER FOR
CHRISTMAS
and
THREE OTHER
GREAT MYSTERIES

MURDER FOR CHRISTMAS

and

THREE OTHER GREAT MYSTERIES

by

Agatha Christie

MYSTERY

Garden City, New York

CONTENTS

CONTENTS

MURDER FOR CHRISTMAS

My dear James,

You have always been one of the most faithful and kindly of my readers, and I was therefore seriously perturbed when I received from you a word of criticism.

You complained that my murders were getting too refined—anaemic, in fact! You yearned for a "good violent murder with lots of blood." A murder where there was no doubt about its being murder!

So this is your special story—written for you. I hope it may please.

Your affectionate sister-in-law,

Agatha

CONTENTS

PART I

PART II

PART III

PART IV

PART V

PART VI

PART VII

Yet who would have thought the old man to have had so much blood in him?

MACBETH

PART I

I

STEPHEN PULLED UP the collar of his coat as he walked briskly along the platform. Overhead a dim fog clouded the station. Large engines hissed superbly, throwing off clouds of steam into the cold raw air. Everything was dirty and smoke-grimed.

Stephen thought with revulsion:

"What a foul country—what a foul city!"

His first excited reaction to London—its shops, its restaurants, its well-dressed attractive women—had faded. He saw it now as a glittering rhinestone set in a dingy setting.

Supposing he were back in South Africa now. . . . He felt a quick pang of homesickness. Sunshine—blue skies—gardens of flowers—cool blue flowers—hedges of plumbago—blue convolvulus clinging to every little shanty.

And here—dirt, grime and endless incessant crowds—moving, hurrying, jostling. Busy ants running industriously about their ant hill.

For a moment he thought: "I wish I hadn't come. . . ."

Then he remembered his purpose and his lips set back in a grim line. No, by Hell, he'd go on with it! He'd planned this for years. He'd always meant to do—what he was going to do. Yes, he'd go on with it!

That momentary reluctance, that sudden questioning of himself: "Why? Is it worth it? Why dwell on the past? Why not wipe out the whole thing?" —all that was only weakness. He was not a boy to be turned this way and that by the whim of the moment. He was a man of forty, assured, purposeful. He would get on with it. He would do what he had come to England to do.

He got on the train and passed along the corridor, looking for a place. He had waved aside a porter and was carrying his own rawhide suitcase.

He looked into carriage after carriage. The train was full. It was only three days before Christmas.

Stephen Farr looked distastefully at the crowded carriages.

People! Incessant, innumerable people! And all so—so—what was the word—so *drab* looking! So alike, so horribly alike! Those that hadn't got faces like sheep had faces like rabbits, he thought. Some of them chattered and fussed. Some, heavy middle-aged men, grunted. More like pigs, those. Even the girls, slender egg-faced, scarlet-lipped, were of a depressing uniformity.

He thought with a sudden longing of open veldt, sunbaked and lonely. . . .

And then, suddenly, he caught his breath, looking into a carriage. This girl was different. Black hair, rich creamy pallor—eyes with the depth and darkness of night in them. The sad proud eyes of the South. . . . It was all wrong that this girl should be sitting in this train among these dull drab looking people—all wrong that she should be going into the dreary midlands of England. She should have been on a balcony, a rose between her lips, a piece of black lace draping her proud head, and there should have been dust and heat and the smell of blood—the smell of the bull-ring—in the air. . . . She should be somewhere splendid, not squeezed into the corner of a third class carriage.

He was an observant man. He did not fail to note the shabbiness of her little black coat and skirt, the cheap quality of her fabric gloves, the flimsy shoes and the defiant note of a flame-red handbag. Nevertheless splendour was the quality he associated with her. She *was* splendid, fine, exotic. . . .

What the Hell was she doing in this country of fogs and chills and hurrying industrious ants?

He thought: "I've got to know who she is and what she's doing here. . . . I've got to know. . . ."

II

Pilar sat squeezed up against the window and thought how very odd the English smelled. . . . It was what had struck her so far most forcibly about England—the difference of smell. There was no garlic and no dust and very little perfume. In this carriage now there was a smell of cold stuffiness—the sulphur smell of the trains—the smell of soap and another very unpleasant smell—it came, she thought, from the fur collar of the stout woman sitting beside her. Pilar sniffed delicately, imbibing the odour of moth balls reluctantly. It was a funny scent to choose to put on yourself, she thought.

A whistle blew, a stentorian voice cried out something and the train jerked slowly out of the station. They had started. She was on her way. . . .

Her heart beat a little faster. Would it be all right? Would she be able to accomplish what she had set out to do? Surely—surely—she had thought it all out so carefully. . . . She was prepared for every eventuality. Oh, yes, she would succeed—she must succeed. . . .

The curve of Pilar's red mouth curved upwards. It was suddenly cruel, that mouth. Cruel and greedy—like the mouth of a child or a kitten—a mouth that knew only its own desires and that was as yet unaware of pity.

She looked round her with the frank curiosity of a child. All these people—seven of them—how funny they were, the English! They all seemed so rich, so prosperous—their clothes—their boots— Oh! undoubtedly England was a very rich country as she had always heard. But they were not at all gay—no, decidedly not gay.

That was a handsome man standing in the corridor. . . . Pilar thought he was very handsome. She liked his deeply bronzed face and his high bridged nose and his square shoulders. More quickly than any English girl, Pilar had seen that the man admired her. She had not looked at him once directly, but she knew perfectly how often he had looked at her and exactly how he had looked.

She registered the facts without much interest or emotion. She came from a country where men looked at women as a matter of course and did not disguise the fact unduly. She wondered if he was an Englishman and decided that he was not.

"He is too alive, too real, to be English," Pilar decided. "And yet he is fair. He may be perhaps Americano." He was, she thought, rather like the actors she had seen in Wild West films.

An attendant pushed his way along the corridor.

"First lunch, please. First lunch. Take your seats for first lunch."

The other seven occupants of Pilar's carriage all held tickets for the first lunch. They rose in a body and the carriage was suddenly deserted and peaceful.

Pilar quickly pulled up the window which had been let down a couple of inches at the top by a militant looking grey-haired lady in the opposite corner. Then she sprawled comfortably back on her seat and peered out of the window at the northern suburbs of London. She did not turn her head at the sound of the door sliding back. It was the man from the corridor and Pilar knew, of course, that he had entered the carriage on purpose to talk to her.

She continued to look pensively out of the window.

Stephen Farr said:

"Would you like the window down at all?"

Pilar replied demurely:

"On the contrary. I have just shut it."

She spoke English perfectly, but with a slight accent.

During the pause that ensued Stephen thought:

"A delicious voice. It has the sun in it . . . it is warm like a summer night. . . ."

Pilar thought:

"I like his voice. It is big and strong. He is attractive—yes, he is attractive."

Stephen said:

"The train is very full."

"Oh, yes, indeed. The people go away from London, I suppose, because it is so black there."

Pilar had not been brought up to believe that it was a crime to talk to strange men in trains. She could take care of herself as well as any girl, but she had no rigid taboos.

If Stephen had been brought up in England he might have felt ill at ease at entering into conversation with a young girl. But Stephen was a friendly soul who found it perfectly natural to talk to anyone if he felt like it.

He smiled without any self-consciousness and said:

"London's rather a terrible place, isn't it?"

"Oh, yes. I do not like it at all."

"No more do I."

Pilar said:

"You are not English, no?"

"I'm British, but I come from South Africa."

"Oh, I see; that explains it."

"Have you just come from abroad?"

Pilar nodded.

"I come from Spain."

Stephen was interested.

"From Spain, do you? You're Spanish, then?"

"I am half Spanish. My mother was English. That is why I talk English so well."

"What about this war business?" asked Stephen.

"It is very terrible, yes—very sad. There has been damage done, quite a lot—yes."

"Which side are you on?"

Pilar's politics seemed to be rather vague. In the village where she came from, she explained, nobody had paid very much attention to the war. "It has not been near us, you understand. The Mayor, he is of course an officer of the Government, so he is for the Government, and the priest is for General Franco—but most of the people are so busy with the vines and the land, they have not time to go into these questions."

"So there wasn't any fighting round you?"

Pilar said that there had not been. "But then I drove in a car," she explained, "all across the country and there was much destruction. And I saw a bomb drop and it blew up a car—yes, and another destroyed a house. It was very exciting!"

Stephen Farr smiled a faintly twisted smile.

"So that's how it seemed to you?"

"It was a nuisance, too," explained Pilar. "Because I wanted to get on and the driver of my car, he was killed."

Stephen said, watching her:

"That didn't upset you?"

Pilar's great dark eyes opened very wide.

"Everyone must die! That is so, is it not? If it comes quickly from the sky—bouff—like that, it is as well as any other way. One is alive for a time —yes, and then one is dead. That is what happens in this world."

Stephen Farr laughed.

"I don't think you are a pacifist."

"You do not think I am what?" Pilar seemed puzzled by a word which had not previously entered her vocabulary.

"Do you forgive your enemies, Señorita?"

Pilar shook her head.

"I have no enemies. But if I had—"

"Well?"

He was watching her, fascinated anew by the sweet cruel upward curving mouth.

Pilar said gravely:

"If I had an enemy—if anyone hated me and I hated them—then I would cut my enemy's throat like *this*. . . ."

She made a graphic gesture.

It was so swift and so crude that Stephen Farr was momentarily taken aback. He said:

"You're a bloodthirsty young woman!"

Pilar asked in a matter-of-fact tone:

"What would you do to your enemy?"

He started—stared at her, then laughed aloud.

"I wonder—" he said. "I wonder!"

Pilar said disapprovingly:

"But surely—you know."

He checked his laughter, drew in his breath and said in a low voice:

"Yes. I know. . . ."

Then, with a rapid change of manner, he asked:

"What made you come to England?"

Pilar replied with a certain demureness:

"I am going to stay with my relations—with my English relations."

"I see."

He leaned back in his seat, studying her—wondering what these English relations of whom she spoke were like—wondering what they would make of this Spanish stranger . . . trying to picture her in the midst of some sober British family at Christmas time.

Pilar asked:

"It is nice, South Africa, yes?"

He began to talk to her about South Africa. She listened with the pleased attention of a child hearing a story. He enjoyed her naïve but shrewd questions and amused himself by making a kind of exaggerated fairy story of it all.

The return of the proper occupants of the carriage put an end to this diversion. He rose, smiled into her eyes, and made his way out again into the corridor.

As he stood back for a minute in the doorway, to allow an elderly lady to come in, his eyes fell on the label of Pilar's obviously foreign straw case. He read the name with interest: *Miss Pilar Estravados,* then as his eye caught the address, it widened to incredulity and some other feeling. *Gorston Hall, Longdale, Addlesfield.*

He half turned, staring at the girl with a new expression—puzzled, resentful, suspicious. . . . He went out into the corridor and stood there smoking a cigarette and frowning to himself. . . .

III

In the big blue and gold drawing-room at Gorston Hall, Alfred Lee and Lydia, his wife, sat discussing their plans for Christmas. Alfred was a squarely built man of middle-age with a gentle face and mild brown eyes. His voice when he spoke was quiet and precise with a very clear enunciation. His head was sunk into his shoulders and he gave a curious impression of inertia. Lydia, his wife, was an energetic lean greyhound of a woman. She was amazingly thin, but all her movements had a swift startled grace about them.

There was no beauty in her careless haggard face, but it had distinction. Her voice was charming.

Alfred said:

"Father insists! There's nothing else for it."

Lydia controlled a sudden impatient movement. She said:

"Must you always give in to him?"

"He's a very old man, my dear—"

"Oh, I know—I know!"

"He expects to have his own way."

Lydia said drily:

"Naturally, since he has always had it! But sometime or other, Alfred, you will have to make a stand."

"What do you mean, Lydia?"

He stared at her, so palpably upset and startled, that for a moment she bit her lip and seemed doubtful whether to go on.

Alfred Lee repeated:

"What do you mean, Lydia?"

She shrugged her thin graceful shoulders.

She said, trying to choose her words cautiously:

"Your father is—inclined to be—tyrannical—"

"He's old."

"And will grow older. And consequently more tyrannical. Where will it end? Already he dictates our lives to us completely. We can't make a plan of our own! If we do, it is always liable to be upset."

Alfred said:

"Father expects to come first. He is very good to us, remember."

"Oh! good to us!"

"*Very* good to us."

Alfred spoke with a trace of sternness.

Lydia said calmly:

"You mean financially?"

"Yes. His own wants are very simple. But he never grudges us money. You can spend what you like on dress and on this house and the bills are paid without a murmur. He gave us a new car only last week."

"As far as money goes, your father is very generous, I admit," said Lydia. "But in return he expects us to behave like slaves."

"Slaves?"

"That's the word I used. You *are* his slave, Alfred. If we have planned to go away and Father suddenly wishes us not to go, you cancel the arrangements and remain without a murmur! If the whim takes him to send us away, we go. . . . . We have no lives of our own—no independence."

Her husband said distressfully:

"I wish you wouldn't talk like this, Lydia. It is very ungrateful. My father has done everything for us. . . ."

She bit off a retort that was on her lips. She shrugged those thin graceful shoulders once more.

Alfred said:

"You know, Lydia, the old man is very fond of you—"

His wife said clearly and distinctly:

"I am not at all fond of him."

"Lydia, it distresses me to hear you say things like that. It is so unkind—"

"Perhaps. But sometimes a compulsion comes over one to speak the truth."

"If Father guessed—"

"Your father knows perfectly well that I do not like him! It amuses him, I think."

"Really, Lydia, I am sure you are wrong there. He has often told me how charming your manner to him is."

"Naturally I've always been polite. I always shall be. I'm just letting you know what my real feelings are. I dislike your father, Alfred. I think he is a malicious and tyrannical old man. He bullies you and presumes on your affection for him. You ought to have stood up to him years ago."

Alfred said sharply:

"That will do, Lydia. Please don't say any more."

She sighed.

"I'm sorry. Perhaps I was wrong. . . . Let's talk of our Christmas arrangements. Do you think your brother David will really come?"

"Why not?"

She shook her head doubtfully.

"David is—queer. He's not been inside the house for years, remember. He was so devoted to your mother—he's got some feeling about this place."

"David always got on Father's nerves," said Alfred, "with his music and his dreamy ways. Father was, perhaps, a bit hard on him sometimes. But I think David and Hilda will come all right. Christmas time, you know."

"Peace and good will," said Lydia. Her delicate mouth curved ironically. "I wonder! George and Magdalene are coming. They said they would probably arrive to-morrow. I'm afraid Magdalene will be frightfully bored."

Alfred said with some slight annoyance:

"Why my brother George ever married a girl twenty years younger than himself I can't think! George was always a fool!"

"He's very successful in his career," said Lydia. "His constituents like him. I believe Magdalene works quite hard politically for him."

Alfred said slowly:

"I don't think I like her very much. She is very good-looking—but I sometimes think she is like one of those beautiful pears one gets—they have a rosy flush and a rather waxen appearance—" He shook his head.

"And they're bad inside?" said Lydia. "How funny you should say that, Alfred!"

"Why funny?"

She answered:

"Because—usually—you are such a gentle soul. You hardly ever say an unkind thing about anyone. I get annoyed with you sometimes because you're not sufficiently—oh, what shall I say?—sufficiently suspicious—not worldly enough!"

Her husband smiled.

"The world, I always think, is as you yourself make it."

Lydia said sharply:

"No! Evil is not only in one's mind. Evil exists! *You* seem to have no consciousness of the evil in the world. I have. I can feel it. I've always felt it—here in this house—" She bit her lip and turned away.

Alfred said: "Lydia—"

But she raised a quick admonitory hand, her eyes looking past him at something over his shoulder. Alfred turned.

A dark man with a smooth face was standing there deferentially.

Lydia said sharply:

"What is it, Horbury?"

Horbury's voice was low, a mere deferential murmur.

"It's Mr. Lee, madam. He asked me to tell you that there would be two more guests arriving for Christmas, and would you have rooms prepared for them."

Lydia said, "Two more guests?"

Horbury said smoothly: "Yes, madam, another gentleman and a young lady."

Alfred said wonderingly:

"A young lady?"

"That's what Mr. Lee said, sir."

Lydia said quickly:

"I will go up and see him—"

Horbury made one little step, it was a mere ghost of a movement but it stopped Lydia's rapid progress automatically.

"Excuse me, madam, but Mr. Lee is having his afternoon sleep. He asked specially that he should not be disturbed."

"I see," said Alfred. "Of course we won't disturb him."

"Thank you, sir."

Horbury withdrew.

Lydia said vehemently:

"How I dislike that man! He creeps about the house like a cat! One never hears him going or coming."

"I don't like him very much either. But he knows his job. It's not so easy to get a good male nurse attendant. And Father likes him; that's the main thing."

"Yes, that's the main thing, as you say. Alfred, what is this about a young lady? What young lady?"

Her husband shook his head.

"I can't imagine. I can't even think of anyone it might be likely to be."

They stared at each other. Then Lydia said, with a sudden twist of her expressive mouth:

"Do you know what I think, Alfred?"

"What?"

"I think your father has been bored lately. I think he is planning a little Christmas diversion for himself."

"By introducing two strangers into a family gathering?"

"Oh! I don't know what the details are—but I do fancy that your father is preparing to—amuse himself."

"I hope he *will* get some pleasure out of it," said Alfred gravely. "Poor old chap, tied by the leg, an invalid—after the adventurous life he has led."

Lydia said slowly:

"After the—adventurous life he has led."

The pause she made before the adjective gave it some special though obscure significance. Alfred seemed to feel it. He flushed and looked unhappy.

She cried out suddenly:

"How he ever had a son like you, I can't imagine! You two are poles apart. And he fascinates you—you simply worship him!"

Alfred said with a trace of vexation:

"Aren't you going a little far, Lydia? It's natural, I should say, for a son to love his father. It would be very unnatural not to do so."

Lydia said:

"In that case, most of the members of this family are—unnatural! Oh! don't let's argue! I apologize. I've hurt your feelings, I know. Believe me, Alfred, I really didn't mean to do that. I admire you enormously for your —your—*fidelity*. Loyalty is such a rare virtue in these days. Let us say, shall we, that I am jealous? Women are supposed to be jealous of their mothers-in-law—why not, then, of their fathers-in-law?"

He put a gentle arm round her.

"Your tongue runs away with you, Lydia. There's no reason for you to be jealous."

She gave him a quick remorseful kiss, a delicate caress on the tip of his ear.

"I know. All the same, Alfred, I don't believe I should have been in the least jealous of your mother. I wish I'd known her."

He sighed.

"She was a poor creature," he said.

His wife looked at him interestedly.

"So that's how she struck you . . . as a poor creature. . . . That's interesting."

He said dreamily:

"I remember her as nearly always ill. . . . Often in tears. . . ." He shook his head. "She had no spirit."

Still staring at him, she murmured very softly:

"How odd. . . ."

But as he turned a questioning glance on her, she shook her head quickly and changed the subject.

"Since we are not allowed to know who our mysterious guests are, I shall go out and finish my garden."

"It's very cold, my dear; a biting wind."

"I'll wrap up warmly."

She left the room. Alfred Lee, left alone, stood for some minutes motionless, frowning a little to himself, then he walked over to the big window at the end of the room. Outside was a terrace running the whole length of the house. Here, after a minute or two, he saw Lydia emerge, carrying a flat basket. She was wearing a big blanket coat. She set down the basket and began to work at a square stone sink slightly raised above ground level.

Her husband watched for some time. At last he went out of the room, fetched himself a coat and muffler and emerged onto the terrace by a side door. As he walked along he passed various other stone sinks arranged as miniature gardens, all the products of Lydia's agile fingers.

One represented a desert scene with smooth yellow sand, a little clump of green palm trees in coloured tin, and a procession of camels with one or two little Arab figures. Some primitive mud houses had been constructed of plasticine. There was an Italian garden with terraces and formal beds with flowers in coloured sealing-wax. There was an arctic one, too, with lumps of green glass for icebergs, and a little cluster of penguins. Next came a Japanese garden with a couple of beautiful little stunted trees, looking glass arranged for water, and bridges modeled out of plasticine.

He came at last to stand beside her where she was at work. She had laid down blue paper and covered it over with glass. Round this were lumps of rock piled up. At the moment she was pouring out coarse pebbles from a little bag and forming them into a beach. Between the rocks were some small cactuses.

Lydia was murmuring to herself:

"Yes, that's exactly right—exactly what I want. . . ."

Alfred said:

"What's this latest work of art?"

She started, for she had not heard him come up.

"This? Oh, it's the Dead Sea, Alfred. Do you like it?"

He said: "It's rather arid, isn't it? Oughtn't there to be more vegetation?"

She shook her head.

"It's my idea of the Dead Sea. It *is* dead, you see—"

"It's not so attractive as some of the others."

"It's not meant to be specially attractive."

Footsteps sounded on the terrace. An elderly butler, white-haired and slightly bowed, was coming towards them.

"Mrs. George Lee on the telephone, madam. She says will it be convenient if she and Mr. George arrive by the 5:20 to-morrow?"

"Yes, tell her that will be quite all right."

"Thank you, madam."

The butler hurried away. Lydia looked after him with a softened expression on her face.

"Dear old Tressilian. What a standby he is! I can't imagine what we should do without him."

Alfred agreed.

"He's one of the old school. He's been with us nearly forty years. He's devoted to us all."

Lydia nodded.

"Yes. He's like the faithful old retainers of fiction. I believe he'd lie himself blue in the face if it was necessary to protect one of the family!"

Alfred said:

"I believe he would. . . . Yes, I believe he would. . . ."

Lydia smoothed over the last bit of her shingle.

"There," she said. "That's ready."

"Ready?" Alfred looked puzzled.

She laughed.

"For Christmas, silly! For this sentimental family Christmas we're going to have."

IV

David was rereading the letter. Once he screwed it up into a ball and thrust it away from him. Then, reaching for it, he smoothed it out and read it again.

Quietly, without saying anything, his wife, Hilda, watched him. She noted the jerking muscle (or was it a nerve?) in his temple, the slight tremor of the long delicate hands, the nervous spasmodic movements of his whole body. When he pushed aside the lock of fair hair that always tended to stray down over his forehead and looked across at her with appealing blue eyes she was ready.

"Hilda, what shall we do about it?"

Hilda hesitated a minute before speaking. She had heard the appeal in his voice. She knew how dependent he was upon her—had always been ever since their marriage—knew that she could probably influence his decision finally and decisively. But for just that reason she was chary of pronouncing anything too final.

She said, and her voice had the calm soothing quality that can be heard in the voice of an experienced nannie in a nursery:

"It depends on how you feel about it, David."

A broad woman, Hilda, not beautiful, but with a certain magnetic quality. Something about her like a Dutch picture. Something warming and endearing in the sound of her voice. Something strong about her—the vital hidden strength that appeals to weakness. An overstout dumpy middle-aged woman—not clever—not brilliant—but with *something* about her that you couldn't pass over. Force! Hilda Lee had force!

David got up and began pacing up and down. His hair was practically untouched by grey. He was strangely boyish looking. His face had the mild quality of a Burne-Jones knight. It was, somehow, not very real. . . .

He said, and his voice was wistful:

"You know how I feel about it, Hilda. You must."

"I'm not sure."

"But I've told you—I've told you again and again! How I hate it all— the house and the country round and everything! It brings back nothing but misery. I hated every moment that I spent there! When I think of it— of all that *she* suffered—my mother. . . ."

His wife nodded sympathetically.

"She was so sweet, Hilda, and so patient. Lying there, often in pain, but bearing it—enduring everything. And when I think of my father"—his face darkened—"bringing all that misery into her life—humiliating her—

boasting of his love affairs—constantly unfaithful to her and never troubling to conceal it."

Hilda Lee said:

"She should not have put up with it. She should have left him."

He said with a touch of reproof:

"She was too good to do that. She thought it was her duty to remain. Besides it was her home—where else should she go?"

"She could have made a life of her own."

David said fretfully:

"Not in those days! You don't understand. Women didn't behave like that. They put up with things. They endured patiently. She had us to consider. Even if she had divorced my father, what would have happened? He would probably have married again. There might have been a second family. *Our* interests might have gone to the wall. She had to think of all those considerations."

Hilda did not answer.

David went on:

"No, she did right. She was a saint! She endured to the end—uncomplainingly."

Hilda said: "Not quite uncomplainingly or you would not know so much, David!"

He said softly, his face lighting up:

"Yes—she told me things. . . . She knew how I loved her. When she died—"

He stopped. He ran his hands through his hair.

"Hilda, it was awful—horrible! The desolation! She was quite young still; she *needn't* have died. *He* killed her—my father! He was responsible for her dying. He broke her heart. I decided then that I'd not go on living under his roof. I broke away—got away from it all."

Hilda nodded.

"You were very wise," she said. "It was the right thing to do."

David said:

"Father wanted me to go into the works. That would have meant living at home. I couldn't have stood that. I can't think how Alfred stands it— how he has stood it all these years?"

"Did he never rebel against it?" asked Hilda with some interest. "I thought you told me something about his having given up some other career."

David nodded.

"Alfred was going into the Army. Father arranged it all. Alfred, the eldest, was to go into some cavalry regiment, Harry was to go into the works, so was I. George was to enter politics."

"And it didn't work out like that?"

David shook his head.

"Harry broke all that up! He was always frightfully wild. Got into debt —and all sorts of other troubles. Finally he went off one day with several hundred pounds that didn't belong to him leaving a note behind him saying an office stool didn't suit him and he was going to see the world."

"And you never heard any more of him?"

"Oh, yes, we did!" David laughed. "We heard quite often! He was always cabling for money from all over the world. He usually got it, too!"

"And Alfred?"

"Father made him chuck up the Army and come back and go into the works."

"Did he mind?"

"Very much to begin with. He hated it. But Father could always twist Alfred round his little finger. He's absolutely under Father's thumb still, I believe."

"And you—escaped!" said Hilda.

"Yes. I went to London and studied painting. Father told me plainly that if I went off on a fool's errand like that I'd get a small allowance from him during his lifetime and nothing when he died. I said I didn't care. He called me a young fool, and that was that! I've never seen him since."

Hilda said gently:

"And you haven't regretted it?"

"No, indeed. I realize I sha'n't ever get anywhere with my art. I shall never be a great artist—but we're happy enough in this cottage—we've got everything we want—all the essentials. And if I die, well, my life's insured for you."

He paused and then said:

"And now—*this!*"

He struck the letter with his open hand.

"I am sorry your father ever wrote that letter, if it upsets you so much," said Hilda.

David went on as though he had not heard her:

"Asking me to bring my wife for Christmas, expressing a hope that we may be all together for Christmas, a united family! What can it mean?"

Hilda said:

"Need it mean anything more than it says?"

He looked at her questioningly.

"I mean," she said, smiling, "that your father is growing old. He's beginning to feel sentimental about family ties. That does happen, you know."

"I suppose it does," said David slowly.

"He's an old man and he's lonely."

He gave her a quick look.

"You want me to go, don't you, Hilda?"

She said slowly:

"It seems a pity—not to answer an appeal. I'm old-fashioned, I daresay, but why not have peace and good will at Christmas time?"

"After all I've told you?"

"I know, dear, I know. But all that's in the *past.* It's all done and finished with."

"Not for me."

"No, *because you won't let it die.* You keep the past alive in your own mind."

"I can't forget."

"You *won't* forget—that's what you mean, David."

His mouth set in a firm line.

"We're like that, we Lees. We remember things for years—brood about them, keep memory green."

Hilda said with a touch of impatience:

"Is that anything to be proud of? I do not think so!"

He looked thoughtfully at her, a touch of reserve in his manner.

He said: "You don't attach much value to loyalty, then—loyalty to a memory?"

Hilda said:

"I believe the *present* matters—not the past! The past must go. If we seek to keep the past alive, we end, I think, by *distorting* it. We see it in exaggerated terms—a false perspective."

"I can remember every word and every incident of those days perfectly," said David passionately.

"Yes, but you *shouldn't,* my dear! It isn't natural to do so! You're applying the judgment of a boy to those days instead of looking back on them with the more temperate outlook of a man."

"What difference would that make?" demanded David.

Hilda hesitated. She was aware of unwisdom in going on, and yet there were things she badly wanted to say.

"I think," she said, "that you're seeing your father as a *Bogy!* You're exalting him into a kind of personification of Evil. Probably, if you were to see him now, you would realize that he was only a very ordinary man; a man, perhaps, whose passions ran away with him, a man whose life was far from blameless, but nevertheless merely a *man*—not a kind of inhuman Monster!"

"You don't understand! His treatment of my mother—"

Hilda said gravely:

"There is a certain kind of meekness—of submission—that brings out the worst in a man—whereas that same man, faced by spirit and determination, might be a different creature!"

"So you say it was her fault—"

Hilda interrupted him.

"No, of course I don't! I've no doubt your father treated your mother very badly indeed, but marriage is an extraordinary thing—and I doubt if any outsider—even a child of the marriage—has the right to judge. Besides, all this resentment on your part now cannot help your mother. It is all *gone*—it is behind you! What is left now is an old man, in feeble health, asking his son to come home for Christmas."

"And you want me to go?"

Hilda hesitated, then she suddenly made up her mind.

"Yes," she said, "I do. I want you to go and lay the Bogy once and for all."

V

George Lee, M.P. for Westeringham, was a somewhat corpulent gentleman of forty-one. His eyes were pale blue and slightly prominent with a suspicious expression, he had a heavy jowl, and a slow pedantic utterance.

He said now in a weighty manner:

"I have told you, Magdalene, that I think it my *duty* to go."

His wife shrugged her shoulders impatiently.

She was a slender creature, a platinum blonde with plucked eyebrows and a smooth egg-like face. It could, on occasions, look quite blank and devoid of any expression whatever. She was looking like that now.

"Darling," she said, "it will be perfectly grim, I am sure of it."

"Moreover," said George Lee, and his face lit up as an attractive idea occurred to him, "it will enable us to save considerably. Christmas is always an expensive time. We can put the servants on board wages."

"Oh, well!" said Magdalene. "After all, Christmas is pretty grim anywhere!"

"I suppose," said George, pursuing his own line of thought, "they will expect to have a Christmas dinner? A nice piece of beef, perhaps, instead of a turkey."

"Who? The servants? Oh, George, don't fuss so. You're always worrying about money."

"Somebody has to worry," said George.

"Yes, but it's absurd to pinch and scrape in all these little ways. Why don't you make your father give you some more money?"

"He already gives me a very handsome allowance."

"It's awful to be completely dependent on your father, as you are! He ought to settle some money on you outright."

"That's not his way of doing things."

Magdalene looked at him. Her hazel eyes were suddenly sharp and keen. The expressionless egg-like face showed sudden meaning.

"He's frightfully rich, isn't he, George? A kind of millionaire, isn't he?"

"A millionaire twice over, I believe."

Magdalene gave an envious sigh.

"How did he make it all? South Africa, wasn't it?"

"Yes, he made a big fortune there in his early days. Mainly diamonds."

"Thrilling!" said Magdalene.

"Then he came to England and started in business and his fortune has actually doubled or trebled itself, I believe."

"What will happen when he dies?" asked Magdalene.

"Father's never said much on the subject. Of course one can't exactly *ask*. I should imagine that the bulk of his money will go to Alfred and myself. Alfred, of course, will get the larger share."

"You've got other brothers, haven't you?"

"Yes, there's my brother David. I don't fancy *he* will get much. He went off to do art or some tomfoolery of that kind. I believe Father warned him that he would cut him out of his will and David said he didn't care."

"How silly," said Magdalene with scorn.

"There was my sister Jennifer, too. She went off with a foreigner—a Spanish artist—one of David's friends. But she died just over a year ago. She left a daughter, I believe. Father might leave a little money to her, but nothing much. And of course there's Harry—"

He stopped, slightly embarrassed.

"Harry?" said Magdalene, surprised. "Who is Harry?"

"Ah—er—my brother."

"I never knew you had another brother?"

"My dear, he wasn't a great—er—credit—to us. We don't mention him. His behaviour was disgraceful. We haven't heard anything of him for some years now. He's probably dead."

Magdalene laughed suddenly.

"What is it? What are you laughing at?"

Magdalene said:

"I was only thinking how funny it was that you—*you*, George, should have a disreputable brother! You're so very respectable."

"I should hope so," said George coldly.

Her eyes narrowed.

"Your father isn't—very respectable, George?"

"Really, Magdalene!"

"Sometimes the things he says make me feel quite uncomfortable."

George said: "Really, Magdalene, you surprise me. Does—er—does Lydia feel the same?"

"He doesn't say the same kind of things to Lydia," said Magdalene. She added angrily: "No, he never says them to *her*. I can't think why not."

George glanced at her quickly and then glanced away.

"Oh, well," he said vaguely. "One must make allowances. At Father's age—and with his health being so bad—"

He paused. His wife asked:

"Is he really—pretty ill?"

"Oh, I wouldn't say *that*. He's remarkably tough. All the same, since he wants to have his family round him at Christmas, I think we are quite right to go. It may be his last Christmas."

She said sharply:

"You *say* that, George, but really, I suppose, he may live for years?"

Slightly taken aback, her husband stammered:

"Yes—yes, of course he may."

Magdalene turned away.

"Oh, well," she said, "I suppose we're doing the right thing by going."

"I have no doubt about it."

"But I hate it! Alfred's so dull, and Lydia snubs me."

"Nonsense."

"She does. And I hate that beastly man-servant."

"Old Tressilian?"

"No, Horbury. Sneaking round like a cat and smirking."

"Really, Magdalene, I can't see that Horbury can affect you in any way!"

"He just gets on my nerves, that's all. But don't let's bother. We've got to go, I can see that. Won't do to offend the old man."

"No—no, that's just the point. About the servants' Christmas dinner—"

"Not now, George, some other time. I'll just ring up Lydia and tell her we'll come by the 5:20 to-morrow."

Magdalene left the room precipitately. After telephoning, she went up to her own room and sat down in front of the desk. She let down the flap and rummaged in its various pigeonholes. Cascades of bills came tumbling out. Magdalene sorted through them, trying to arrange them in some kind of order. Finally, with an impatient sigh, she bundled them up and thrust them back whence they had come. She passed a hand over her smooth platinum head.

"What on earth am I to do?" she murmured.

VI

On the first floor of Gorston Hall a long passage led to a big room overlooking the front drive. It was a room furnished in the more flamboyant of old-fashioned styles. It had heavy brocaded wallpaper, rich leather armchairs, large vases embossed with dragons, sculptures in bronze. . . . Everything in it was magnificent, costly and solid.

In a big grandfather armchair, the biggest and most imposing of all the chairs, sat the thin shriveled figure of an old man. His long claw-like hands rested on the arms of the chair. A gold-mounted stick was by his side. He wore an old shabby blue dressing-gown. On his feet were carpet slippers. His hair was white and the skin of his face was yellow.

A shabby insignificant figure, one might have thought. But the nose, aquiline and proud, and the eyes, dark and intensely alive, might cause an observer to alter his opinion. Here was fire and life and vigour. . . .

Old Simeon Lee cackled to himself, a sudden high cackle of amusement. He said:

"You gave my message to Mrs. Alfred, hey?"

Horbury was standing beside his chair. He replied in his soft deferential voice:

"Yes, sir."

"Exactly in the words I told you? Exactly, mind?"

"Yes, sir. I didn't make a mistake, sir."

"No—you don't make mistakes. You'd better not make mistakes either —or you'll regret it! And what did she say, Horbury? What did Mr. Alfred say?"

Quietly, unemotionally, Horbury repeated what had passed.

The old man cackled again and rubbed his hands together.

"Splendid . . . first rate . . . they'll have been thinking and wondering—all the afternoon! Splendid! I'll have 'em up now. Go and get them."

"Yes, sir."

Horbury walked noiselessly across the room and went out.

"And, Horbury—"

The old man looked round, then cursed to himself.

"Fellow moves like a cat. Never know where he is."

He sat quite still in his chair, his fingers caressing his chin till there was a tap on the door and Alfred and Lydia came in.

"Ah, there you are, there you are. Sit here, Lydia, my dear, by me. What a nice colour you've got."

"I've been out in the cold. It makes one's cheeks burn afterwards."

Alfred said:

"How are you, Father? Did you have a good rest this afternoon?"

"First rate—first rate. Dreamed about the old days! That was before I settled down and became a pillar of society."

He cackled with sudden laughter.

His daughter-in-law sat silently smiling with polite attention.

Alfred said:

"What's this, Father, about two extra being expected for Christmas?"

"Ah! that. Yes, I must tell you about that. It's going to be a grand Christmas for me this year—a grand Christmas. Let me see, George is coming and Magdalene—"

Lydia said:

"Yes, they are arriving to-morrow by the 5:20."

Old Simeon said:

"Poor stick, George! Nothing but a gasbag! Still, he *is* my son."

Alfred said:

"His constituents like him."

Simeon cackled again.

"They probably think he's honest. Honest! There never was a Lee who was honest yet."

"Oh, come now, Father."

"I except you, my boy. I except you."

"And David?" asked Lydia.

"David now. I'm curious to see the boy after all these years. He was a namby-pamby youngster. Wonder what his wife is like? At any rate *he* hasn't married a girl twenty years younger than himself, like that fool George!"

"Hilda wrote a very nice letter," said Lydia. "I've just had a wire from her confirming it and saying they are definitely arriving to-morrow."

Her father-in-law looked at her, a keen penetrating glance.

He laughed.

"I never get any change out of Lydia," he said. "I'll say this for you, Lydia, you're a well-bred woman. Breeding tells. I know that well enough. A funny thing, though, heredity. There's only one of you that's taken after me—only one out of all the litter."

His eyes danced.

"Now guess who's coming for Christmas. I'll give you three guesses and I'll bet you a fiver you won't get the answer."

He looked from one face to the other. Alfred said, frowning:

"Horbury said you expected a young lady."

"That intrigued you—yes, I daresay it did. Pilar will be arriving any minute now. I gave orders for the car to go and meet her."

Alfred said sharply:

"*Pilar?*"

Simeon said:

"Pilar Estravados. Jennifer's girl. My granddaughter. I wonder what she'll be like?"

Alfred cried out:

"Good Heavens, Father, you never told me. . . ."

The old man was grinning.

"No, I thought I'd keep it a secret! Got Charlton to write out and fix things."

Alfred repeated, his tone hurt and reproachful:

"You never told me. . . ."

His father said, still grinning wickedly:

"It would have spoiled the surprise! Wonder what it will be like to have young blood under this roof again? I never saw Estravados. Wonder which the girl takes after—her mother or her father?"

"Do you really think it's wise, Father?" began Alfred. "Taking everything into consideration—"

The old man interrupted him.

"Safety—safety—you play for safety too much, Alfred! Always have! That hasn't been my way! Do what you want and be damned to it! That's what I say! The girl's my granddaughter—the only grandchild in the family! I don't care what her father was or what he did! She's my flesh and blood! And she's coming to live here in my house."

Lydia said sharply:

"She's coming to *live* here?"

He darted a quick look at her.

"Do you object?"

She shook her head. She said, smiling:

"I couldn't very well object to your asking someone to your own house, could I? No, I was wondering about—her."

"About her—what d'you mean?"

"Whether she would be happy here."

Old Simeon flung up his head.

"She's not got a penny in the world. She ought to be thankful!"

Lydia shrugged her shoulders.

Simeon turned to Alfred:

"You see? It's going to be a grand Christmas! All my children round me. *All* my children! There, Alfred, there's your clue. Now guess who the other visitor is."

Alfred stared at him.

"All my children! Guess, boy! *Harry*, of course! Your brother Harry!"

Alfred had gone very pale. He stammered:

"Harry—not Harry—"

"Harry himself!"

"But we thought he was dead!"

"Not he!"

"You—you are having him back here? After everything?"

"The prodigal son, eh? You're right! The fatted calf! We must kill the fatted calf, Alfred. We must give him a grand welcome."

Alfred said:

"He treated you—all of us—disgracefully. He—"

"No need to recite his crimes! It's a long list. But Christmas, you'll remember, is the season of forgiveness! We'll welcome the prodigal home."

Alfred rose. He murmured:

"This has been—rather a shock. I never dreamed that Harry would ever come inside these walls again."

Simeon leaned forward.

"You never liked Harry, did you?" he said softly.

"After the way he behaved to you—"

Simeon cackled. He said:

"Ah, but bygones must be bygones. That's the spirit for Christmas, isn't it, Lydia?"

Lydia, too, had gone pale. She said drily:

"I see that you have thought a good deal about Christmas this year."

"I want my family round me. Peace and good will. I'm an old man. Are you going, my dear?"

Alfred had hurried out. Lydia paused a moment before following him. Simeon nodded his head after the retreating figure.

"It's upset him. He and Harry never got on. Harry used to jeer at Alfred. Called him old Slow and Sure."

Lydia's lips parted. She was about to speak, then as she saw the old man's eager expression, she checked herself. Her self-control, she saw, disappointed him. The perception of that fact enabled her to say:

"The hare and the tortoise? Ah, well, the tortoise wins the race."

"Not always," said Simeon. "Not always, my dear Lydia."

She said, still smiling:

"Excuse me, I must go after Alfred. Sudden excitements always upset him."

Simeon cackled.

"Yes, Alfred doesn't like changes. He always was a regular sobersides."

Lydia said:

"Alfred is very devoted to *you.*"

"That seems odd to you, doesn't it?"

"Sometimes," said Lydia, "it does."

She left the room. Simeon looked after her.

He chuckled softly and rubbed his palms together.

"Lots of fun," he said. "Lots of fun still. I'm going to enjoy this Christmas."

With an effort he pulled himself upright and with the help of his stick shuffled slowly across the room.

He went to a big safe that stood at the corner of the room. He twirled the handle of the combination. The door came open and with shaking fingers he felt inside.

He lifted out a small chamois leather bag and opening it let a stream of uncut diamonds pass through his fingers.

"Well, my beauties, well. . . . Still the same—still my old friends. Those were good days—good days. . . . They sha'n't carve you and cut you about, my friends. *You* sha'n't hang round the necks of women or sit on their fingers or hang on their ears. You're *mine!* My old friends! We know a thing or two, you and I. I'm old, they say, and ill, but I'm not done for! Lots of life in the old dog yet. And there's still some fun to be got out of life. Still some fun—"

PART II

DECEMBER 23RD

I

TRESSILIAN WENT TO answer the doorbell. It had been an unusually aggressive peal and now, before he could make his slow way across the hall, it pealed out again.

Tressilian flushed. An ill-mannered, impatient way of ringing the bell at a gentleman's house! If it was a fresh lot of those carol singers he'd give them a piece of his mind.

Through the frosted glass of the upper half of the door he saw a silhouette—a big man in a slouch hat. He opened the door. As he had thought—a cheap flashy stranger—nasty pattern of suit he was wearing—loud! Some impudent begging fellow!

"Blessed if it isn't Tressilian," said the stranger. "How are you, Tressilian?"

Tressilian stared—took a deep breath—stared again. That bold arrogant jaw, the high bridged nose, the rollicking eye. Yes, they had all been there years ago. More subdued then. . . .

He said with a gasp:

"Mr. Harry!"

Harry Lee laughed.

"Looks as though I'd given you quite a shock. Why? I'm expected, aren't I?"

"Yes, indeed, sir. Certainly, sir."

"Then why the surprise act?" Harry stepped back a foot or two and looked up at the house—a good solid mass of red brick, unimaginative but solid.

"Just the same ugly old mansion," he remarked. "Still standing, though, that's the main thing. How's my father, Tressilian?"

"He's somewhat of an invalid, sir. Keeps his room, and can't get about much. But he's wonderfully well, considering."

"The old sinner!"

Harry Lee came inside, let Tressilian remove his scarf and take the somewhat theatrical hat.

"How's my dear brother Alfred, Tressilian?"

"He's very well, sir."

Harry grinned.

"Looking forward to seeing me? Eh?"

"I expect so, sir."

"I don't! Quite the contrary. I bet it's given him a nasty jolt, my turning up! Alfred and I never did get on. Ever read your Bible, Tressilian?"

"Why, yes, sir, sometimes, sir."

"Remember the tale of the prodigal's return? The good brother didn't like it, remember, didn't like it at all! Good old stay-at-home Alfred doesn't like it either, I bet."

Tressilian remained silent looking down his nose. His stiffened back expressed protest. Harry clapped him on the shoulder.

"Lead on, old son," he said. "The fatted calf awaits me! Lead me right to it."

Tressilian murmured:

"If you will come this way into the drawing-room, sir. I am not quite sure where everyone is. . . . They were unable to send to meet you, sir, not knowing the time of your arrival."

Harry nodded. He followed Tressilian along the hall, turning his head to look about him as he went.

"All the old exhibits in their place, I see," he remarked. "I don't believe anything has changed since I went away twenty years ago."

He followed Tressilian into the drawing-room. The old man murmured:

"I will see if I can find Mr. or Mrs. Alfred," and hurried out.

Harry Lee had marched into the room and had then stopped, staring at the figure seated on one of the window sills. His eyes roamed incredulously over the black hair and the creamy exotic pallor.

"Good Lord!" he said. "Are you my father's seventh and most beautiful wife?"

Pilar slipped down and came towards him.

"I am Pilar Estravados," she announced. "And you must be my Uncle Harry, my mother's brother."

Harry said, staring:

"So that's who you are! Jenny's daughter."

Pilar said:

"Why did you ask me if I was your father's seventh wife? Has he really had six wives?"

Harry laughed.

"No, I believe he's only had one official one. Well—Pil—what's your name?"

"Pilar, yes."

"Well, Pilar, it really gives me quite a turn to see something like you blooming in this mausoleum."

"This—maus—please?"

"This museum of stuffed dummies! I always thought this house was lousy! Now I see it again I think it's lousier than ever!"

Pilar said in a shocked voice:

"Oh, no, it is very handsome here! The furniture is good and the carpets —thick carpets everywhere, and there are lots of ornaments. Everything is very good quality and very, very rich!"

"You're right there," said Harry, grinning. He looked at her with amusement. "You know I can't help getting a kick out of seeing you in the midst—"

He broke off as Lydia came rapidly into the room.

She came straight to him.

"How d'you do, Harry? I'm Lydia—Alfred's wife."

"How de do, Lydia?" He shook hands, examining her intelligent mobile face in a swift glance and approving mentally of the way she walked—very few women moved well.

Lydia in her turn took quick stock of him.

She thought:

"He looks a frightful tough—attractive, though. I wouldn't trust him an inch. . . ."

She said, smiling:

"How does it look after all these years? Quite different, or very much the same?"

"Pretty much the same." He looked round him. "This room's been done over."

"Oh! many times."

He said:

"I meant by you. You've made it—different."

"Yes, I expect so. . . ."

He grinned at her, a sudden impish grin that reminded her with a start of the old man upstairs.

"It's got more class about it now! I remember hearing that old Alfred had married a girl whose people came over with the Conqueror."

Lydia smiled.

She said:

"I believe they did. But they've rather run to seed since those days."

Harry said:

"How's old Alfred? Just the same blessed old stick-in-the-mud as ever?"

"I've no idea whether you will find him changed or not."

"How are the others? Scattered all over England?"

"No—they're all here for Christmas you know."

Harry's eyes opened.

"Regular Christmas family reunion? What's the matter with the old man? He used not to give a damn for sentiment. Don't remember his caring much for his family either. He must have changed!"

"Perhaps." Lydia's voice was dry.

Pilar was staring, her big eyes wide and interested.

Harry said:

"How's old George? Still the same skinflint? How he used to howl if he had to part with a halfpenny of his pocket money!"

Lydia said:

"George is in Parliament. He's member for Westeringham."

"What? Popeye in Parliament? Lord, that's good."

Harry threw back his head and laughed.

It was rich stentorian laughter—it sounded uncontrolled and brutal in the confined space of the room. Pilar drew in her breath with a gasp. Lydia flinched a little.

Then, at a movement behind him, Harry broke off his laugh and turned sharply. He had not heard anyone come in, but Alfred was standing there quietly. He was looking at Harry with an odd expression on his face.

Harry stood a minute, then a slow smile crept to his lips. He advanced a step.

"Why," he said, "it's Alfred!"

Alfred nodded.

"Hullo, Harry," he said.

They stood staring at each other. Lydia caught her breath. She thought: "How absurd! Like two dogs—looking at each other. . . ."

Pilar's gaze widened even further. She thought to herself:

"How silly they look standing there . . . why do they not embrace? No, of course, the English do not do that. But they might *say* something. Why do they just *look?*"

Harry said at last:

"Well, well. Feels funny to be here again!"

"I expect so—yes. A good many years since you—got out."

Harry threw up his head. He drew his finger along the line of his jaw. It was a gesture that was habitual with him. It expressed belligerence.

"Yes," he said. "I'm glad to have come—" he paused to bring out the word with greater significance—"*home. . . .*"

II

"I've been, I suppose, a very wicked man," said Simeon Lee.

He was leaning back in his chair. His chin was raised and with one finger he was stroking his jaw reflectively. In front of him a big fire glowed and danced. Beside it sat Pilar, a little screen of papier-mâché held in her hand. With it she shielded her face from the blaze. Occasionally she fanned herself with it, using her wrist in a supple gesture. Simeon looked at her with satisfaction.

He went on talking, perhaps more to himself than to the girl, and yet stimulated by the fact of her presence.

"Yes," he said. "I've been a wicked man. What do you say to that, Pilar?"

Pilar shrugged her shoulders. She said:

"All men are wicked. The nuns say so. That is why one has to pray for them."

"Ah, but I've been more wicked than most." Simeon laughed. "I don't regret it, you know. No, I don't regret anything. I've enjoyed myself . . . every minute! They say you repent when you get old. That's bunkum. I don't repent. And as I tell you, I've done most things . . . all the good old sins! I've cheated and stolen and lied. . . . Lord, yes! And women! Always women! Someone told me the other day of an Arab chief who had a bodyguard of forty of his sons—all roughly the same age! Aha! Forty! I don't know about forty, but I bet I could produce a very fair bodyguard if I went about looking for the brats! Hey, Pilar, what do you think of that? Shocked?"

Pilar stared.

"No, why should I be shocked? Men always desire women. My father, too. That is why wives are so often unhappy and why they go to church and pray."

Old Simeon was frowning.

"I made Adelaide unhappy," he said. He spoke almost under his breath, to himself. "Lord, what a woman! Pink and white and pretty as they make 'em when I married her! And afterwards? Always wailing and weeping. It rouses the devil in a man when his wife is always crying. . . . She'd no guts, that's what was the matter with Adelaide. If she'd stood up to me! But she never did—not once. I believed when I married her that I was going to be able to settle down—raise a family, cut loose from the old life. . . ."

His voice died away. He stared—stared into the glowing heart of the fire.

"Raise a family. . . . God, what a family!" He gave a sudden shrill pipe of angry laughter. "Look at 'em—look at 'em! Not a child among them—to carry on! What's the matter with them? Haven't they got any of my blood in their veins? Not a son among 'em, legitimate or illegitimate. Alfred, for instance. Heavens above, how bored I get with Alfred! Looking at me with his dog's eyes. Ready to do anything I ask. Lord, what a fool! His wife, now—Lydia—I like Lydia. She's got spirit. She doesn't like me, though. No, she doesn't like me. But she has to put up with me for that nincompoop Alfred's sake." He looked over at the girl by the fire. "Pilar—remember—nothing is so boring as devotion."

She smiled at him. He went on, warmed by the presence of youth and strong femininity.

"George? What's George? A stick! A stuffed codfish! A pompous wind-bag with no brains and no guts—and mean about money as well! David? David always was a fool. A fool and a dreamer. His mother's boy. That was always David. Only sensible thing he ever did was to marry that solid comfortable-looking woman." He brought down his hand with a bang on the edge of his chair. "Harry's the best of 'em! Poor old Harry, the wrong 'un! But at any rate he's *alive!*"

Pilar agreed.

"Yes, he is nice. He laughs—laughs out loud—and throws his head back. Oh, yes, I like him very much."

The old man looked at her.

"You do, do you, Pilar? Harry always had a way with the girls. Takes after me there." He began to laugh, a slow wheezy chuckle. "I've had a good life—a very good life. Plenty of everything."

Pilar said:

"In Spain we have a proverb. It is like this: *Take what you like and pay for it, says God.*"

Simeon beat an appreciative hand on the arm of his chair.

"That's good. That's the stuff. Take what you like. . . . I've done that —all my life—taken what I wanted. . . ."

Pilar said, her voice high and clear, and suddenly arresting:

"And have you paid for it?"

Simeon stopped laughing to himself. He sat up and stared at her. He said: "What's that you say?"

"I said, have you paid for it, Grandfather?"

Simeon Lee said slowly:

"I—don't know. . . ."

Then, beating his fist on the arm of the chair, he cried out with sudden anger:

"What makes you say that, girl? What makes you say that?"

Pilar said: "I—wondered."

Her hand, holding the screen, was arrested. Her eyes were dark and mysterious. She sat, her head thrown back, conscious of herself, of her womanhood.

Simeon said: "You devil's brat. . . ."

She said softly:

"But you like me, Grandfather. You like me to sit here with you."

Simeon said:

"Yes, I like it. It's a long time since I've seen anything so young and beautiful . . . it does me good, warms my old bones. . . . And you're my own flesh and blood. . . . Good for Jennifer, she turned out to be the best of the bunch after all!"

Pilar sat there, smiling.

"Mind you, you don't fool me," said Simeon. "I know why you sit here so patiently and listen to me droning on. It's money—it's all money . . . or do you pretend you love your old grandfather?"

Pilar said:

"No, I do not love you. But I like you. I like you very much. You must believe that, for it is true. I think you have been wicked but I like that too. You are more real than the other people in this house. And you have interesting things to say. You have traveled and you have led a life of adventure. If I were a man I would be like that, too."

Simeon nodded.

"Yes, I believe you would. . . . We've gypsy blood in us, so it's always been said. It hasn't shown much in my children—except Harry—but I think it's come out in you. I can be patient, mind you, when it's necessary. I waited once fifteen years to get even with a man who'd done me an injury. That's another characteristic of the Lees. They don't forget! They'll avenge a wrong if they have to wait years to do it. A man swindled me. I waited fifteen years till I saw my chance—and then I struck. I ruined him. Cleaned him right out!"

He laughed softly.

Pilar said:

"That was in South Africa?"

"Yes. A grand country."

"You have been back there, yes?"

"I went back five years after I married. That was the last time."

"But before that? You were there for many years?"

"Yes."

"Tell me about it."

He began to talk. Pilar, shielding her face, listened.

His voice slowed, wearied. . . . He said:

"Wait, I'll show you something."

He pulled himself carefully to his feet. Then, with his stick, he limped slowly across the room. He opened the big safe. Turning, he beckoned her to him.

"There, look at these. Feel them—let them run through your fingers."

He looked into her wandering face and laughed.

"Do you know what they are? Diamonds, child, diamonds."

Pilar's eyes opened. She said as she bent over:

"But they are little pebbles, that is all."

Simeon laughed.

"They are uncut diamonds. That is how they are found—like this."

Pilar asked incredulously:

"And if they were cut they would be real diamonds?"

"Certainly."

"They would flash and sparkle?"

"Flash and sparkle."

Pilar said childishly:

"Oh-o-o, I cannot believe it!"

He was amused.

"It's quite true."

"They are valuable?"

"Fairly valuable. Difficult to say before they are cut—anyway this little lot is worth several thousands of pounds."

Pilar said, with a space between each two words:

"Several—thousands—of—pounds?"

"Say nine or ten thousand—they're biggish stones, you see."

Pilar asked, her eyes opening:

"But why do you not sell them then?"

"Because I like to have them here."

"But all that money?"

"I don't need the money."

"Oh—I see." Pilar looked impressed.

She said:

"But why do you not have them cut and made beautiful?"

"Because I prefer them like this." His face was set in a grim line. He turned away and began speaking to himself. "They take me back—the touch of them, the feel of them through my fingers. . . . It all comes back to me, the sunshine, and the smell of the veldt, the oxen—old Eb—all the boys—the evenings. . . ."

There was a soft tap on the door.

Simeon said:

"Put 'em back in the safe and bang it to."

Then he called: "Come in."

Horbury came in, soft and deferential.

He said:

"Tea is ready downstairs."

III

Hilda said:

"So there you are, David. I've been looking for you everywhere. Don't let's stay in this room, it's so frightfully cold."

David did not answer for a minute. He was standing looking at a chair, a low chair with faded satin upholstery.

He said abruptly:

"That's her chair . . . the chair she always sat in . . . just the same —it's just the same. Only faded, of course."

A little frown creased Hilda's broad forehead. She said:

"I see. Do let's come out of here, David, it's frightfully cold."

David took no notice. Looking round, he said:

"She sat in here mostly. I remember sitting on that stool there while she read to me. *Jack the Giant Killer,* that was it—*Jack the Giant Killer.* I must have been six years old then."

Hilda put a firm hand through his arm.

"Come back to the drawing-room, dear. There's no heating in this room."

He turned obediently, but she felt a little shiver go through him.

"Just the same," he murmured. "Just the same. As though time had stood still."

Hilda looked worried. She said in a cheerful, determined voice:

"I wonder where the others are? It must be nearly teatime."

David disengaged his arm and opened another door.

"There used to be a piano in here . . . oh, yes, here it is! I wonder if it's in tune?"

He sat down and opened the lid, running his hands lightly over the keys.

"Yes, it's evidently kept tuned."

He began to play.

His touch was good, the melody flowed out from under his fingers. Hilda asked:

"What is that? I seem to know it and I can't quite remember."

He said:

"I haven't played it for years. *She* used to play it. One of Mendelssohn's *Songs Without Words.*"

The sweet, over-sweet, melody filled the room. Hilda said:

"Play some Mozart, do."

David shook his head. He began another Mendelssohn.

Then, suddenly, he brought his hands down upon the keys in a harsh discord. He got up. He was trembling all over. Hilda went to him.

She said:

"David—David. . . ."

He said:

"It's nothing—it's nothing. . . ."

IV

The bell pealed aggressively. Tressilian rose from his seat in the pantry and went slowly out and along to the door.

The bell pealed again. Tressilian frowned. Through the frosted glass of the door he saw the silhouette of a man wearing a slouch hat.

Tressilian passed a hand over his forehead. Something worried him. It was as though everything was happening twice.

Surely this had happened before. Surely—

He drew back the latch and opened the door.

Then the spell broke. The man standing there said:

"Is this where Mr. Simeon Lee lives?"

"Yes, sir."

"I'd like to see him, please."

A faint echo of memory awoke in Tressilian. It was an intonation of voice that he remembered from the old days when Mr. Lee was first in England.

Tressilian shook his head dubiously.

"Mr. Lee is an invalid, sir. He doesn't see many people now. If you—"

The stranger interrupted.

He drew out an envelope and handed it to the butler.

"Please give this to Mr. Lee."

"Yes, sir."

V

Simeon Lee took the envelope. He drew out the single sheet of paper it held. He looked surprised. His eyebrows rose, but he smiled.

"By all that's wonderful!" he said.

Then to the butler:

"Show Mr. Farr up here, Tressilian."

"Yes, sir."

Simeon said:

"I was just thinking of old Ebenezer Farr. He was my partner out there in Kimberley. Now here's his son come along!"

Tressilian reappeared. He announced:

"Mr. Farr."

Stephen Farr came in with a trace of nervousness. He disguised it by putting on a little extra swagger. He said—and just for the moment his South African accent was more marked than usual—

"Mr. Lee?"

"I'm glad to see you. So you're Eb's boy."

Stephen Farr grinned rather sheepishly.

He said:

"My first visit to the old country. Father always told me to look you up if I did come."

"Quite right." The old man looked round. "This is my granddaughter, Pilar Estravados."

"How do you do?" said Pilar demurely.

Stephen Farr thought with a touch of admiration:

"Cool little devil. She was surprised to see me, but it only showed for a flash."

He said, rather heavily:

"I'm very pleased to make your acquaintance, Miss Estravados."

"Thank you," said Pilar.

Simeon Lee said:

"Sit down and tell me all about yourself. Are you in England for long?"

"Oh, I sha'n't hurry myself now I've really got here!"

Stephen laughed, throwing his head back.

Simeon Lee said:

"Quite right. You must stay here with us for a while."

"Oh, look here, sir. I can't butt in like that. It's only two days to Christmas."

"You must spend Christmas with us—unless you've got other plans?"

"Well, no, I haven't, but I don't like—"

Simeon said: "That's settled." He turned his head. "Pilar?"

"Yes, Grandfather."

"Go and tell Lydia we shall have another guest. Ask her to come up here."

Pilar left the room. Stephen's eyes followed her. Simeon noted the fact with amusement.

He said:

"You've come straight here from South Africa?"

"Pretty well."

They began to talk of that country.

Lydia entered a few minutes later.

Simeon said:

"This is Stephen Farr, son of my old friend and partner, Ebenezer Farr. He's going to be with us for Christmas if you can find room for him."

Lydia smiled.

"Of course." Her eyes took in the stranger's appearance. His bronzed face and blue eyes and the easy backward tilt of his head.

"My daughter-in-law," said Simeon.

Stephen said:

"I feel rather embarrassed—butting in on a family party like this."

"You're one of the family, my boy," said Simeon. "Think of yourself as that."

"You're too kind, sir."

Pilar reentered the room. She sat down quietly by the fire and picked up the hand screen. She used it as a fan, slowly tilting her wrist to and fro. Her eyes were demure and downcast.

PART III

I

"DO YOU REALLY want me to stay on here, Father?" asked Harry. He tilted his head back. "I'm stirring up rather a hornet's nest you know."

"What do you mean?" asked Simeon sharply.

"Brother Alfred," said Harry. "Good brother Alfred! He, if I may say so, resents my presence here."

"The devil he does!" snapped Simeon. "I'm master in this house."

"All the same, sir, I expect you're pretty dependent on Alfred. I don't want to upset—"

"You'll do as I tell you," snapped his father.

Harry yawned.

"Don't know that I shall be able to stick a stay-at-home life. Pretty stifling to a fellow who's knocked about the world."

His father said:

"You'd better marry and settle down."

Harry said:

"Whom shall I marry? Pity one can't marry one's niece. Young Pilar is devilish attractive."

"You've noticed that?"

"Talking of settling down, fat George has done well for himself as far as looks go. Who was she?"

Simeon shrugged his shoulders.

"How should I know? George picked her up at a mannequin parade, I believe. She says her father was a retired naval officer."

Harry said:

"Probably a second mate of a coasting steamer. George will have a bit of trouble with her if he's not careful."

"George," said Simeon Lee, "is a fool."

Harry said:

"What did she marry him for? His money?"

Simeon shrugged his shoulders.

Harry said:

"Well, you think you can square Alfred all right?"

"We'll soon settle that," said Simeon grimly.

He touched a bell that stood on a table near him.

Horbury appeared promptly. Simeon said:

"Ask Mr. Alfred to come here."

Horbury went out and Harry drawled:

"That fellow listens at doors!"

Simeon shrugged his shoulders.

"Probably."

Alfred hurried in. His face twitched when he saw his brother. Ignoring Harry, he said pointedly:

"You wanted me, Father?"

"Yes, sit down. I was just thinking we must reorganize things a bit now that we have two more people living in the house."

"Two?"

"Pilar will make her home here, naturally. And Harry is home for good."

Alfred said:

"Harry is coming to live here?"

"Why not, old boy?" said Harry.

Alfred turned sharply to him.

"I should think that you yourself would see that!"

"Well, sorry—but I don't."

"After everything that has happened? The disgraceful way you behaved. The scandal—"

Harry waved an easy hand.

"All that's in the past, old boy."

"You behaved abominably to Father after all he'd done for you."

"Look here, Alfred, it strikes me that's Father's business, not yours. If he's willing to forgive and forget—"

"I'm willing," said Simeon. "Harry's my son, after all, you know, Alfred."

"Yes, but—I resent it—for Father's sake."

Simeon said:

"Harry's coming here! I wish it. . . ." He laid a hand gently on the latter's shoulder. "I'm very fond of Harry."

Alfred got up and left the room. His face was white. Harry rose too and went after him laughing.

Simeon sat chuckling to himself. Then he started and looked round.

"Who the devil's that? Oh, it's you, Horbury. Don't creep about that way."

"I beg your pardon, sir."

"Never mind. Listen, I've got some orders for you. I want everybody to come up here after lunch—*everybody.*"

"Yes, sir."

"There's something else. When they come, you come with them. And when you get half-way along the passage *raise your voice,* so that I can hear. Any pretext will do. Understand?"

"Yes, sir."

Horbury went downstairs. He said to Tressilian:

"If you ask me, we *are* going to have a merry Christmas!"

Tressilian said sharply:

"What d'you mean?"

"You wait and see, Mr. Tressilian. It's Christmas Eve to-day and a nice Christmas spirit abroad, I don't think!"

II

They came into the room and paused at the doorway.

Simeon was speaking into the telephone. He waved a hand to them.

"Sit down, all of you, I sha'n't be a minute."

He went on speaking into the telephone.

"Is that Charlton, Hodgkins & Brace? Is that you, Charlton? Simeon Lee speaking. Yes, isn't it? . . . Yes. . . . No, I wanted you to make a new will for me. . . . Yes, it's some time since I made the other. . . . Circumstances have altered. . . . Oh, no, no hurry. Don't want you to spoil your Christmas. Say Boxing Day or the day after. Come along and I'll tell you what I want done. No, that's quite all right. I sha'n't be dying just yet."

He replaced the receiver, then looked round at the eight members of his family. He cackled and said:

"You're all looking very glum. What is the matter?"

Alfred said:

"You sent for us. . . ."

Simeon said quickly:

"Oh, sorry—nothing portentous about it. Did you think it was a family council? No, I'm just rather tired to-day, that's all. None of you need come up after dinner. I shall go to bed. I want to be fresh for Christmas Day."

He grinned at them. George said portentously:

"Of course. . . . Of course. . . ."

Simeon said:

"Grand old institution, Christmas! Promotes solidarity of family feeling. What do *you* think, Magdalene, my dear?"

Magdalene Lee jumped. Her rather silly little mouth flew open and then shut itself. She said:

"Oh— Oh, *yes!*"

Simeon said:

"Let me see, you lived with a retired naval officer"—he paused—"your *father*—don't suppose you made much of Christmas; it needs a big family for that!"

"Well—well—yes, perhaps it does."

Simeon's eyes slid past her.

"Don't want to talk of anything unpleasant at this time of year, but you know, George, I'm afraid I'll have to cut down your allowance a bit. My establishment here is going to cost me a bit more to run in future."

George got very red.

"But look here, Father, you can't do that!"

Simeon said softly:

"Oh, I can't?"

"My expenses are very heavy already. Very heavy. As it is, I don't know how I make both ends meet. It needs the most rigorous economy."

"Let your wife do a bit more of it," said Simeon. "Women are good at that sort of thing. They often think of economies where a man would never have dreamed of them. And a clever woman can make her own clothes. My wife, I remember, was clever with her needle. About all she *was* clever with—a good woman but deadly dull—"

David sprang up. His father said:

"Sit down, boy, you'll knock something over—"

David said:

"My mother—"

Simeon said:

"Your mother had the brains of a louse! And it seems to me she's transmitted those brains to her children." He raised himself up suddenly. A red spot appeared in each cheek. His voice came high and shrill. "You're not worth a penny piece, any of you! I'm sick of you all! You're not *men!* You're weaklings—a set of namby-pamby weaklings—Pilar's worth any two of you put together! I'll swear to Heaven I've got a better son somewhere in the world than any of you even if you are born the right side of the blanket!"

"Here, Father, hold hard," cried Harry.

He had jumped up and stood there, a frown on his usually good-humoured face.

Simeon snapped:

"The same goes for *you!* What have *you* ever done? Whined to me for money from all over the world! I tell you I'm sick of the sight of you all! Get out!"

He leaned back in his chair, panting a little.

Slowly, one by one his family went out. George was red and indignant, Magdalene looked frightened. David was pale and quivering. Harry blustered out of the room. Alfred went like a man in a dream. Lydia followed him with her head held high. Only Hilda paused in the doorway and came slowly back.

She stood over him and he started when he opened his eyes and found her standing there. There was something menacing in the solid way she stood there quite immovably.

He said irritably:

"What is it?"

Hilda said:

"When your letter came I believed what you said—that you wanted your family round you for Christmas. I persuaded David to come."

Simeon said:

"Well, what of it?"

Hilda said slowly:

"You *did* want your family round you—but not for the purpose you said! You wanted them there, didn't you, in order to set them all by the ears? God help you, it's your idea of *fun!*"

Simeon chuckled.

He said:

"I always had rather a specialized sense of humour. I don't expect anyone else to appreciate the joke. *I*'m enjoying it!"

She said nothing. A vague feeling of apprehension came over Simeon Lee. He said sharply:

"What are you thinking about?"

Hilda Lee said slowly:

"I'm afraid. . . ."

Simeon said:

"You're afraid—of me?"

Hilda said:

"Not *of* you. I'm afraid—*for* you!"

Like a judge who has delivered sentence, she turned away. She marched, slowly and heavily, out of the room. . . .

Simeon sat staring at the door.

Then he got to his feet and made his way over to the safe.

He murmured:

"Let's have a look at my beauties. . . ."

III

The doorbell rang about a quarter to eight.

Tressilian went to answer it. He returned to his pantry to find Horbury there, picking up the coffee cups off the tray and looking at the mark on them.

"Who was it?" said Horbury.

"Superintendent of Police—Mr. Sugden—mind what you're doing!"

Horbury had dropped one of the cups with a crash.

"Look at that now," lamented Tressilian. "Eleven years I've had the washing up of those and never one broken and now you come along touching things you've no business to touch and look what happens!"

"I'm sorry, Mr. Tressilian. I am indeed," the other apologized. His face was covered with perspiration. "I don't know how it happened. Did you say a Superintendent of Police had called?"

"Yes, Mr. Sugden."

The valet passed a tongue over pale lips.

"What—what did he want?"

"Collecting for the Police Orphanage."

"Oh!" The valet straightened his shoulders. In a more natural voice he said:

"Did he get anything?"

"I took up the book to old Mr. Lee, and he told me to fetch the Superintendent up and to put the sherry on the table."

"Nothing but begging this time of year," said Horbury. "The old devil's generous, I will say that for him, in spite of his other failings."

Tressilian said with dignity:

"Mr. Lee has always been an open-handed gentleman."

Horbury nodded.

"It's the best thing about him! Well, I'll be off now."

"Going to the pictures?"

"I expect so. Ta ta, Mr. Tressilian."

He went through the door that led to the servants' hall.

Tressilian looked up at the clock hanging on the wall.

He went into the dining-room and laid the rolls in the napkins.

Then, after assuring himself that everything was as it should be, he sounded the gong in the hall.

As the last note died away the Superintendent came down the stairs. Superintendent Sugden was a large, handsome man. He wore a tightly buttoned blue suit and moved with a sense of his own importance!

He said affably:

"I rather think we shall have a frost to-night. Good thing; the weather's been very unseasonable lately."

Tressilian said, shaking his head:

"The damp affects my rheumatism."

The Superintendent said that rheumatism was a painful complaint and Tressilian let him out by the front door.

The old butler refastened the door and came back slowly into the hall. He passed his hand over his eyes and sighed. Then he stretched his back as he saw Lydia pass into the drawing-room. George Lee was just coming down the stairs.

Tressilian hovered ready. When the last guest, Magdalene, had entered the drawing-room, he made his own appearance, murmuring:

"Dinner is served."

In his way Tressilian was a connoisseur of ladies' dress. He always noted and criticized the gowns of the ladies as he circled round the table, decanter in hand.

Mrs. Alfred, he noted, had got on her new flowered black and white taffeta. A bold design, very striking, but she could carry it off, though many ladies couldn't. The dress Mrs. George had on was a model, he was pretty sure of that. Must have cost a pretty penny! He wondered how Mr. George would like paying for it! Mr. George didn't like spending money—he never had. Mrs. David now, a nice lady, but didn't have any idea of how to dress. For her figure, plain black velvet would have been the best. Figured velvet, and crimson at that, was a bad choice. Miss Peela, now, it didn't matter what she wore; with her figure and her hair she looked well in anything. A flimsy cheap little white gown it was, though. Still, Mr. Lee would soon see to that! Taken to her wonderful, he had. Always was the same way when a gentleman was elderly. A young face could do anything with him!

"Hock or claret?" murmured Tressilian in a deferential whisper in Mrs. George's ear. Out of the tail of his eye he noted that Walter, the footman, was handing the vegetables before the gravy again—after all he had been told!

Tressilian went round with the soufflé. It struck him, now that his interest in the ladies' toilets and his misgivings over Walter's deficiencies were a thing of the past, that everyone was very silent to-night. At least, not exactly *silent*—Mr. Harry was talking enough for twenty—no, not Mr. Harry, the South African gentleman. And the others were talking too, but

only, as it were, in spasms. There was something a little—queer about
them.

Mr. Alfred, for instance, he looked downright ill. As though he had had
a shock or something. Quite dazed he looked and just turning over the
food on his plate without eating it. The mistress she was worried about
him. Tressilian could see that. Kept looking down the table towards him—
not noticeably, of course—just quietly. Mr. George was very red in the
face—gobbling his food, he was, without tasting it. He'd get a stroke one
day if he wasn't careful. Mrs. George wasn't eating. Slimming, as likely as
not. Miss Peela seemed to be enjoying her food all right and talking and
laughing up at the South African gentleman. Properly taken with her, he
was. Didn't seem to be anything on *their* minds!

Mr. David? Tressilian felt worried about Mr. David. Just like his
mother, he was, to look at. And remarkably young looking still. But nervous—there, he'd knocked over his glass.

Tressilian whisked it away, mopped up the stream deftly. It was all
over. Mr. David hardly seemed to notice what he had done. Just sat staring in front of him with a white face.

Thinking of white faces, funny the way Horbury had looked in the
pantry just now when he'd heard a police officer had come to the house
. . . almost as though—

Tressilian's mind stopped with a jerk. Walter had dropped a pear off the
dish he was handing. Footmen were no good nowadays! They might be
stable boys the way they went on!

He went round with the port. Mr. Harry seemed a bit distrait to-night.
Kept looking at Mr. Alfred. Never had been any love lost between those
two, not even as boys. Mr. Harry, of course, had always been his father's
favourite and that had rankled with Mr. Alfred. Mr. Lee had never cared
for Mr. Alfred much. A pity, when Mr. Alfred always seemed so devoted
to his father.

There, Mrs. Alfred was getting up now. She swept round the table. Very
nice that design on the taffeta, that cape suited her. A very graceful lady.

He went out to the pantry, closing the dining-room door on the gentlemen with their port.

He took the coffee tray into the drawing-room. The four ladies were
sitting there rather uncomfortably, he thought. They were not talking. He
handed round the coffee in silence.

He went out again. As he went into his pantry he heard the dining-
room door open. David Lee came out and went along the hall to the
drawing-room.

Tressilian went back into his pantry. He read the riot act to Walter.
Walter was nearly, if not quite, impertinent!

Tressilian, alone in his pantry, sat down rather wearily.

He had a feeling of depression. Christmas Eve, and all this strain and tension . . . he didn't like it!

With an effort he roused himself. He went to the drawing-room and collected the coffee cups. The room was empty except for Lydia who was standing half concealed by the window curtain at the far end of the room. She was standing there looking out into the night.

From the next room the piano sounded.

Mr. David playing. But why, Tressilian asked himself, did Mr. David play the *Dead March?* For that's what it was. Oh, indeed, things were very wrong.

He went slowly along the hall and back into his pantry.

It was then he first heard the noise from overhead . . . a crashing of china, the overthrowing of furniture—a series of cracks and bumps.

"Good gracious!" thought Tressilian. "Whatever is the master doing? What's happening up there?"

And then, clear and high, came a scream—a horrible high wailing scream that died away in a choke or gurgle.

Tressilian stood there a moment paralyzed, then he ran out into the hall and up the broad staircase. Others were with him. That scream had been heard all over the house.

They raced up the stairs and round the bend, past a recess with statues gleaming white and eerie, and along the straight passage to Simeon Lee's door. Mr. Farr was there already and Mrs. David. She was leaning back against the wall and he was twisting at the door handle.

"The door's locked," he was saying. "The door's locked!"

Harry Lee pushed past and wrested it from him. He, too, turned and twisted at the handle.

"Father!" he shouted. "Father, let us in."

He held up his hand and in the silence they all listened. There was no answer. No sound from inside the room.

The front doorbell rang but no one paid any attention to it.

Stephen Farr said:

"We've got to break the door down. It's the only way."

Harry said:

"That's going to be a tough job. These doors are good solid stuff. Come on, Alfred."

They heaved and strained. Finally they went and got an oak bench and used it as a battering ram. The door gave at last. Its hinges splintered and the door sank shuddering from its frame.

For a minute they stood there huddled together looking in. What they saw was a sight that no one of them ever forgot. . . .

There had clearly been a terrific struggle. Heavy furniture was overturned. China vases lay splintered on the floor. In the middle of the hearth-
rug in front of the blazing fire, lay Simeon Lee in a great pool of blood
. . . blood was splashed all round. The place was like a shambles.

There was a long shuddering sigh and then two voices spoke in turn.
Strangely enough the words they uttered were both quotations.

David Lee said:

"*The mills of God grind slowly.* . . ."

Lydia's voice came like a fluttering whisper:

"*Who would have thought the old man to have had so much blood in
him?*"

IV

Superintendent Sugden had rung the bell three times. Finally, in desperation he pounded on the knocker.

A scared Walter at length opened the door.

"Oh—er," he said. A look of relief came over his face. "I was just
ringing up the police."

"What for?" said Superintendent Sugden sharply. "What's going on
here?"

Walter whispered:

"It's old Mr. Lee. *He's been done in.* . . ."

The Superintendent pushed past him and ran up the stairs. He came
into the room without anyone being aware of his entrance. As he entered
he saw Pilar bend forward and pick up something from the floor. He saw
David Lee standing with his hands over his eyes.

He saw the others huddled into a little group. Alfred Lee alone had
stepped near his father's body. He stood now quite close, looking down.
His face was blank.

George Lee was saying importantly:

"Nothing must be touched—remember that—*nothing*—till the police
arrive. That is *most* important!"

"Excuse me," said Sugden.

He pushed his way forward, gently thrusting the ladies aside.

Alfred Lee recognized him.

"Ah," he said. "It's you, Superintendent Sugden. You've got here very
quickly."

"Yes, Mr. Lee." Superintendent Sugden did not waste time on explanations. "What's all this?"

"My father," said Alfred Lee, "has been killed—*murdered.* . . ."

His voice broke.

Magdalene began suddenly to sob hysterically.

Superintendent Sugden held up a large official hand.

He said authoritatively:

"Will everybody kindly leave the room except Mr. Lee and—er—Mr. George Lee. . . ."

They moved slowly towards the door, reluctantly, like sheep. Superintendent Sugden intercepted Pilar suddenly.

"Excuse me, miss," he said pleasantly. "Nothing must be touched or disturbed."

She stared at him. Stephen Farr said impatiently:

"Of course not. She understands that."

Superintendent Sugden said, still in the same pleasant manner:

"You picked up something from the floor just now?"

Pilar's eyes opened. She stared and said incredulously:

"*I* did?"

Superintendent Sugden was still pleasant. His voice was just a little firmer.

He said:

"Yes, I saw you. . . ."

"Oh!"

"So please give it to me. It's in your hand now."

Slowly Pilar unclosed her hand. There lay in it a wisp of rubber and a small object made of wood. Superintendent Sugden took them, enclosed them in an envelope and put them away in his breast pocket.

He said:

"Thank you."

He turned away. Just for a minute Stephen Farr's eyes showed a startled respect. It was as though he had underestimated the large handsome superintendent.

They went slowly out of the room. Behind them they heard the Superintendent's voice saying officially:

"And now, if you please—"

V

"Nothing like a wood fire," said Colonel Johnson as he threw on an additional log and then drew his chair nearer to the blaze. "Help yourself," he added, hospitably calling attention to the tantalus and syphon that stood near his guest's elbow.

The guest raised a polite hand in negation. Cautiously, he edged his own chair nearer to the blazing logs, though he was of the opinion that the opportunity for roasting the soles of one's feet (like some medieval torture) did not offset the cold draught that swirled round the back of the shoulders.

Colonel Johnson, Chief Constable of Middleshire, might be of the opinion that nothing could beat a wood fire, but Hercule Poirot was of the opinion that central heating could and did every time!

"Amazing business, that Cartwright case," remarked the host reminiscently. "Amazing man! Enormous charm of manner. Why, when he came here with you, he had us all eating out of his hand."

He shook his head.

"We'll never have anything like that case!" he said. "Nicotine poisoning is rare, fortunately."

"There was a time when you would have considered all poisoning un-English," suggested Hercule Poirot. "A device of foreigners! Unsportsmanlike!"

"I hardly think we could say that," said the Chief Constable. "Plenty of poisoning by arsenic—probably a good deal more than has ever been suspected."

"Possibly, yes."

"Always an awkward business, a poisoning case," said Johnson. "Conflicting testimony of the experts—then doctors are usually so extremely cautious in what they say. Always a difficult case to take to a jury. No, if one *must* have murder (which Heaven forbid) give me a straightforward case. Something where there's no ambiguity about the cause of death."

Poirot nodded.

"The bullet wound, the cut throat, the crushed-in skull? It is there your preference lies?"

"Oh, don't call it a preference, my dear fellow. Don't harbour the idea that I *like* murder cases! Hope I never have another. Anyway, we ought to be safe enough during your visit."

Poirot began modestly:

"My reputation—"

But Johnson had gone on.

"Christmas time," he said. "Peace, good will—and all that kind of thing. Good will all round."

Hercule Poirot leaned back in his chair. He joined his fingertips. He studied his host thoughtfully.

He murmured:

"It is, then, your opinion, that Christmas time is an unlikely season for crime?"

"That's what I said."

"Why?"

"Why?" Johnson was thrown slightly out of his stride. "Well, as I've just said—season of good cheer and all that!"

Hercule Poirot murmured:

"The British, they are so sentimental!"

Johnson said stoutly:

"What if we are? What if we do like the old ways, the old traditional festivities? What's the harm?"

"There is no harm. It is all most charming! But let us for a moment examine *facts*. You have said that Christmas is a season of good cheer. That means, does it not, a lot of eating and drinking? It means, in fact, the *over*eating! And with the overeating there comes the indigestion! And with the indigestion there comes the irritability!"

"Crimes," said Colonel Johnson, "are not committed from irritability."

"I am not so sure! Take another point. There is, at Christmas, a spirit of good will. It is, as you say, 'the thing to do.' Old quarrels are patched up, those who have disagreed, consent to agree once more, even if it is only temporarily."

Johnson nodded.

"Bury the hatchet, that's right."

Poirot pursued his theme.

"And families now, families who have been separated throughout the year assemble once more together. Now under these conditions, my friend, you must admit that there will occur a great amount of *strain*. People who do not *feel* amiable are putting great pressure on themselves to *appear* amiable! There is at Christmas time a great deal of *hypocrisy*, honourable hypocrisy, hypocrisy undertaken *pour le bon motif, c'est entendu,* but nevertheless hypocrisy!"

"Well, I shouldn't put it quite like that myself," said Colonel Johnson doubtfully.

Poirot beamed upon him.

"No, no. It it *I* who am putting it like that, not *you!* I am pointing out to you that under these conditions—mental strain, physical *malaise*—it is highly probable that dislikes that were before merely mild, and disagreements that were trivial, might suddenly assume a more serious character. The result of pretending to be a more amiable, a more forgiving, a more high-minded person than one really is, has sooner or later the effect of causing one to behave as a more disagreeable, a more ruthless and an altogether more unpleasant person than is actually the case! If you dam the stream of natural behaviour, *mon ami,* sooner or later the dam bursts and a cataclysm occurs!"

Colonel Johnson looked at him doubtfully.

"Never know when you're serious and when you're pulling my leg," he grumbled.

Poirot smiled at him.

"I am not serious! Not in the least am I serious! But all the same, it is true what I say—artificial conditions bring about their natural reaction."

Colonel Johnson's man-servant entered the room.

"Superintendent Sugden on the phone, sir."

"Right. I'll come."

With a word of apology the Chief Constable left the room.

He returned some three minutes later. His face was grave and perturbed.

"Damn it all!" he said. "Case of murder! On Christmas Eve, too!"

Poirot's eyebrows rose.

"It is that definitely—murder, I mean?"

"Eh? Oh, no other solution possible! Perfectly clear case. Murder—and a brutal murder at that!"

"Who is the victim?"

"Old Simeon Lee. One of the richest men we've got! Made his money in South Africa originally. Gold—no, diamonds, I believe. He sunk an immense fortune in manufacturing some particular gadget of mining machinery. His own invention, I believe. Anyway, it's paid him hand over fist! They say he's a millionaire twice over."

Poirot said:

"He was well liked, yes?"

Johnson said slowly:

"Don't think anyone liked him. Queer sort of chap. He's been an invalid for some years now. I don't know very much about him myself. But of course he is one of the big figures of the county."

"So this case, it will make a big stir?"

"Yes. I must get over to Longdale as fast as I can."

He hesitated, looking at his guest. Poirot answered the unspoken question.

"You would like that I should accompany you?"

Johnson said awkwardly:

"Seems a shame to ask you. But, well, you know how it is! Superintendent Sugden is a good man, none better; painstaking, careful, thoroughly sound—but—well, he's not an *imaginative* chap in any way. Should like very much, as you are here, benefit of your advice."

He halted a little over the end part of his speech, making it somewhat telegraphic in style. Poirot responded quickly.

"I shall be delighted. You can count on me to assist you in any way I

can. We must not hurt the feelings of the good Superintendent. It will be
his case—not mine. I am only the unofficial consultant."

Colonel Johnson said warmly:

"You're a good fellow, Poirot."

With those words of commendation, the two men started out.

VI

It was a constable who opened the front door to them and saluted.
Behind him, Superintendent Sugden advanced down the hall and said:

"Glad you've got here, sir. Shall we come into this room here on the left
—Mr. Lee's study? I'd like to run over the main outlines. The whole
thing's a rum business."

He ushered them into a small room on the left of the hall. There was a
telephone there and a big desk covered with papers. The walls were lined
with bookcases.

The Chief Constable said:

"Sugden, this is M. Hercule Poirot. You may have heard of him. Just
happened to be staying with me. Superintendent Sugden."

Poirot made a little bow and looked the other man over. He saw a tall
man with square shoulders and a military bearing who had an aquiline
nose, a pugnacious jaw and a large flourishing chestnut coloured moustache. Sugden stared hard at Hercule Poirot after acknowledging the introduction. Hercule Poirot stared hard at Superintendent Sugden's moustache. Its luxuriance seemed to fascinate him.

The Superintendent said:

"Of course I have heard of you, Mr. Poirot. You were in this part of the
world some years ago if I remember rightly. Death of Sir Bartholomew
Strange. Poisoning case. Nicotine. Not my district but of course I heard all
about it."

Colonel Johnson said impatiently:

"Now, then, Sugden, let's have the facts. A clear case, you said."

"Yes, sir, it's murder right enough—not a doubt of that. Mr. Lee's
throat was cut—jugular vein severed I understand from the doctor. But
there's something very odd about the whole matter."

"You mean—"

"I'd like you to hear my story first, sir. These are the circumstances:
This afternoon, about five o'clock, I was rung up by Mr. Lee at Addlesfield
police station. He sounded a bit odd over the phone—asked me to come
and see him at eight o'clock this evening—made a special point of the

time. Moreover, he instructed me to say to the butler that I was collecting subscriptions for some Police charity."

The Chief Constable looked up sharply.

"Wanted some plausible pretext to get you into the house?"

"That's right, sir. Well, naturally, Mr. Lee is an important person, and I acceded to his request. I got here a little before eight o'clock, and represented myself as seeking subscriptions for the Police Orphanage. The butler went away and returned to tell me that Mr. Lee would see me. Thereupon he showed me up to Mr. Lee's room which is situated on the next floor, immediately over the dining-room."

Superintendent Sugden paused, drew a breath and then proceeded in a somewhat official manner with his report.

"Mr. Lee was seated in a chair by the fireplace. He was wearing a dressing-gown. When the butler had left the room and closed the door, Mr. Lee asked me to sit down near him. He then said rather hesitatingly that he wanted to give me particulars of a robbery. I asked him what had been taken. He replied that he had reason to believe that diamonds (uncut diamonds, I think he said) to the value of several thousand pounds had been stolen from his safe."

"Diamonds, eh?" said the Chief Constable.

"Yes, sir. I asked him various routine questions but his manner was very uncertain and his replies were somewhat vague in character. At last he said: 'You must understand, Superintendent, that I may be mistaken in this matter.' I said: 'I do not quite understand, sir. Either the diamonds are missing, or they are not missing—one or the other.' He replied: 'The diamonds are certainly missing, but it is just possible, Superintendent, that their disappearance may be simply a rather foolish kind of practical joke.' Well, that seemed odd to me, but I said nothing. He went on: 'It is difficult for me to explain in detail, but what it amounts to is this: So far as I can see only two persons can possibly have the stones. One of those persons might have done it as a joke. If the other person took them, then they have definitely been stolen.' I said: 'What exactly do you want me to do, sir?' He said quickly: 'I want you, Superintendent, to return here in about an hour —no, make it a little more than that—say, nine-fifteen. At that time I shall be able to tell you definitely whether I have been robbed or not.' I was a little mystified, but I agreed and went away."

Colonel Johnson commented:

"Curious—very curious. What do you say, Poirot?"

Hercule Poirot said:

"May I ask, Superintendent, what conclusions you yourself drew?"

The Superintendent stroked his jaw as he replied carefully:

"Well, various ideas occurred to me, but on the whole, I figured it out this way. There was no question of any practical joke. The diamonds had been stolen all right. But the old gentleman wasn't sure who'd done it. It's my opinion that he was speaking the truth when he said that it might have been one of two people—and of those two people one was a servant and the other was a *member of the family.*"

Poirot nodded appreciatively.

"*Très bien.* Yes, that explains his attitude very well."

"Hence his desire that I should return later. In the interval he meant to have an interview with the person in question. He would tell them that he had already spoken of the matter to the police but that if restitution were promptly made he could hush the matter up."

Colonel Johnson said:

"And if the suspect didn't respond?"

"In that case, he meant to place the investigation in our hands."

Colonel Johnson frowned and twisted his moustache. He demurred.

"Why not take that course *before* calling you in?"

"No, no, sir." The Superintendent shook his head. "Don't you see, if he had done that, it might have been bluff. It wouldn't have been half so convincing. The person might say to himself: 'The old man won't call the police in, no matter what he suspects!' But if the old gentleman says to him, 'I've *already spoken to the Police,* the Superintendent has only just left.' Then the thief asks the butler, say, and the butler confirms that. He says, 'Yes, the Superintendent was here just before dinner.' Then the thief is convinced the old gentleman means business and it's up to him to cough up the stones."

"H'm, yes, I see that," said Colonel Johnson. "Any idea, Sugden, who this 'member of the family' might be?"

"No, sir."

"No indication whatsoever?"

"None."

Johnson shook his head. Then he said:

"Well, let's get on with it."

Superintendent Sugden resumed his official manner.

"I returned to the house, sir, at nine-fifteen precisely. Just as I was about to ring the front doorbell, I heard a scream from inside the house and then a confused sound of shouts and a general commotion. I rang several times and also used the knocker. It was three or four minutes before the door was answered. When the footman at last opened it I could see that something momentous had occurred. He was shaking all over and looked as though he was about to faint. He gasped out that Mr. Lee had been murdered. I ran hastily upstairs. I found Mr. Lee's room in a state of wild confusion. There had evidently been a severe struggle. Mr. Lee himself was lying in a pool of blood in front of the fireplace with his throat cut."

The Chief Constable said sharply:

"He couldn't have done it himself?"

Sugden shook his head.

"Impossible, sir. For one thing there were the chairs and tables overturned and the broken crockery and ornaments and then there was no sign of the razor or knife with which the crime had been committed."

The Chief Constable said thoughtfully:

"Yes, that seems conclusive. Anyone in the room?"

"Most of the family were there, sir. Just standing round."

Colonel Johnson said sharply:

"Any ideas, Sugden?"

The Superintendent said slowly:

"It's a bad business, sir. It looks to me as though one of them must have done it. I don't see how anyone from outside could have done it and got away in that time."

"What about the window? Closed or open?"

"There are two windows in the room, sir. One was closed and locked. The other was open a few inches at the bottom—but it was fixed in that position by a burglar screw and moreover, I've tried it and it's stuck fast—hasn't been opened for years, I should say. Also the wall outside is quite smooth and unbroken—no ivy or creepers. I don't see how anyone could have left that way."

"How many doors in the room?"

"Just one. The room is at the end of a passage. That door was locked on the inside. When they heard the noise of the struggle and the old man's dying scream and rushed upstairs they had to break down the door to get in."

Johnson said sharply:

"And who was in the room?"

Superintendent Sugden replied gravely:

"Nobody was in the room, sir, except the old man who had been killed not more than a few minutes previously."

VII

Colonel Johnson stared at Sugden for some minutes before he spluttered:

"Do you mean to tell me, Superintendent, that this is one of those damned cases you get in detective stories where a man is killed in a locked room by some apparently supernatural agency?"

A very faint smile agitated the Superintendent's moustache as he replied gravely:

"I do not think it's quite as bad as that, sir."

Colonel Johnson said:

"Suicide. It must be suicide!"

"Where's the weapon, if so? No, sir, suicide won't do."

"Then how did the murderer escape? By the window?"

Sugden shook his head.

"I'll take my oath he didn't do that."

"But the door was locked, you say, on the inside."

The Superintendent nodded. He drew a key from his pocket and laid it on the table.

"No fingerprints," he announced. "But just look at that key, sir. Take a look at it with that magnifying glass there."

Poirot bent forward. He and Johnson examined the key together. The Chief Constable uttered an exclamation.

"By Jove, I get you. Those faint scratches on the end of the barrel. You see 'em, Poirot?"

"But, yes, I see. That means, does it not, that the key was turned from outside the door—turned by means of a special implement that went through the keyhole and gripped the barrel—possibly an ordinary pair of pliers would do it."

The Superintendent nodded.

"It can be done all right."

Poirot said:

"The idea being, then, that the death would be thought to be suicide, since the door was locked and no one was in the room?"

"That was the idea, Mr. Poirot, not a doubt of it, I should say."

Poirot shook his head doubtfully.

"But the disorder in the room! As you say, that by itself wiped out the idea of suicide. Surely the murderer would first of all have set the room to rights."

Superintendent Sugden said:

"But he hadn't *time*, Mr. Poirot. That's the whole point. He hadn't time. Let's say he counted on catching the old gentleman unawares. Well, that didn't come off. There was a struggle—a struggle heard plainly in the room underneath and what's more the old gentleman called out for help. Everyone came rushing up. The murderer only had time to nip out of the room and turn the key from the outside."

"That is true," Poirot admitted. "Your murderer, he may have made the bungle. But why, oh, why, did he not at least leave the weapon? For naturally, if there is no weapon, it cannot be suicide! That was an error most grave."

Superintendent Sugden said stolidly:

"Criminals usually make mistakes. That's our experience."

Poirot gave a slight sigh. He murmured:

"But all the same, in spite of his mistakes, he has escaped, this criminal."

"I don't think he has exactly *escaped.*"

"You mean he is in the house still?"

"I don't see where else he can be. It was an inside job."

"But, *tout de même,*" Poirot pointed out gently, "he has escaped to this extent. *You do not know who he is.*"

Superintendent Sugden said gently but firmly:

"I rather fancy that we soon shall. We haven't done any questioning of the household yet."

Colonel Johnson cut in:

"Look here, Sugden, one thing strikes me. Whoever turned that key from the outside must have had some knowledge of the job. That's to say he probably had had criminal experience. Those sort of tools aren't easy to manage."

"You mean it was a professional job, sir?"

"That's what I mean."

"It does look like it," the other admitted. "Following up that, it looks as though there were a professional thief among the servants. That would explain the diamonds being taken and the murder would follow on logically from that."

"Well, anything wrong with that theory?"

"It's what I thought myself to begin with. But it's difficult. There are eight servants in the house, six of them are women and of those six, five have been here for four years and more. Then there's the butler and the footman. The butler has been here for close on forty years—bit of a record that, I should say. The footman's local, son of the gardener and brought up here. Don't see very well how he can be a professional. The only other person is Mr. Lee's valet attendant. He's comparatively new but he was out of the house—still is—went out just before eight o'clock."

Colonel Johnson said:

"Have you got a list of just who exactly was in the house?"

"Yes, sir. I got it from the butler." He took out his notebook. "Shall I read it to you?"

"Please, Sugden."

"Mr. and Mrs. Alfred Lee. Mr. George Lee, M.P., and his wife. Mr.

Henry Lee. Mr. and Mrs. David Lee. Miss" (the Superintendent paused a little, taking the words carefully) "Pillar" (he pronounced it like a piece of architecture) "Estravados. Mr. Stephen Farr. Then for the servants: Edward Tressilian, butler. Walter Champion, footman. Emily Reeves, cook. Queenie Jones, kitchenmaid. Gladys Spent, head housemaid. Grace Best, second housemaid. Beatrice Moscombe, third housemaid. Joan Kench, betweenmaid. Sydney Horbury, valet attendant."

"That's the lot, eh?"

"That's the lot, sir."

"Any idea where everybody was at the time of the murder?"

"Only roughly. As I told you, I haven't questioned anybody yet. According to Tressilian, the gentlemen were in the dining-room still. The ladies had gone to the drawing-room. Tressilian had served coffee. According to his statement he had just got back to his pantry when he heard a noise upstairs. It was followed by a scream. He ran out into the hall and upstairs in the wake of the others."

Colonel Johnson said:

"How many of the family live in the house and who are just staying here?"

"Mr. and Mrs. Alfred Lee live here. The others are just visiting."

Johnson nodded.

"Where are they all?"

"I asked them to stay in the drawing-room until I was ready to take their statements."

"I see. Well, we'd better go upstairs and take a look at the doings."

The Superintendent led the way up the broad stairs and along the passage.

As he entered the room where the crime had taken place Johnson drew a deep breath.

"Pretty horrible," he commented.

He stood for a minute studying the overturned chairs, the smashed china and the blood-bespattered débris.

A thin elderly man stood up from where he had been kneeling by the body and gave a nod.

"Evening, Johnson," he said. "Bit of a shambles, eh?"

"I should say it was. Got anything for us, doctor?"

The doctor shrugged his shoulders. He grinned.

"I'll let you have the scientific language at the inquest! Nothing complicated about it. Throat cut like a pig. He bled to death in less than a minute. No sign of the weapon."

Poirot went across the room to the windows. As the Superintendent had said, one was shut and bolted. The other was open about four inches at the bottom. A thick patent screw of the kind known many years ago as an anti-burglar screw secured it in that position.

Sugden said:

"According to the butler that window was never shut, wet or fine. There's a linoleum mat underneath it in case rain beat in, but it didn't much, as the overhanging roof protects it."

Poirot nodded.

He came back to the body and stared down at the old man.

The lips were drawn back from the bloodless gums in something that looked like a snarl. The fingers were curved like claws.

Poirot said:

"He does not seem a strong man, no."

The doctor said:

"He was pretty tough, I believe. He'd survived several pretty bad illnesses that would have killed most men."

Poirot said:

"I do not mean that. I mean, he was not big, not strong physically."

"No, he's frail enough."

Poirot turned from the dead man. He bent to examine an overturned chair, a big chair of mahogany. Beside it was a round mahogany table and the fragments of a big china lamp. Two other smaller chairs lay near by, also the smashed fragments of a decanter and two glasses, a heavy glass paperweight was unbroken, some miscellaneous books, a big Japanese vase smashed in pieces, and a bronze statuette of a naked girl completed the débris.

Poirot bent over all these exhibits, studying them gravely but without touching them. He frowned to himself as though perplexed.

The Chief Constable said:

"Anything strike you, Poirot?"

Hercule Poirot sighed. He murmured:

"Such a frail shrunken old man—and yet—all this."

Johnson looked puzzled. He turned away and said to the sergeant who was busy at his work:

"What about prints?"

"Plenty of them, sir, all over the room."

"What about the safe?"

"No good. Only prints on that are those of the old gentleman himself."

Johnson turned to the doctor.

"What about bloodstains?" he asked. "Surely whoever killed him must have got blood in him."

The doctor said doubtfully:

"Not necessarily. Bleeding was almost entirely from the jugular vein. That wouldn't spout like an artery."

"No, no. Still, there seems a lot of blood about."

Poirot said:

"Yes, there is a lot of blood—it strikes one, that. A lot of blood."

Superintendent Sugden said respectfully:

"Do you—er—does that suggest anything to you, Mr. Poirot?"

Poirot looked about him. He shook his head perplexedly.

He said:

"There is something here—some violence. . . ." He stopped a minute, then went on. "Yes, that is it—*violence*. . . . And blood—an insistence on *blood*. . . . There is—how shall I put it?—there is *too much blood*. Blood on the chairs, on the tables, on the carpet. . . . The blood ritual? Sacrificial blood? Is that it? Perhaps. Such a frail old man, so thin, so shriveled, so dried up—and yet—in his death—*so much blood*. . . ."

His voice died away. Superintendent Sugden, staring at him with round startled eyes, said in an awed voice:

"Funny—that's what she said—the lady. . . ."

Poirot said sharply:

"What lady? What was it she said?"

Sugden answered:

"Mrs. Lee—Mrs. Alfred. Stood over there by the door and half whispered it. It didn't make sense to me."

"What did she say?"

"Something about who would have thought the old gentleman had so much blood in him. . . ."

Poirot said softly:

"*Yet who would have thought the old man to have had so much blood in him?* The words of Lady Macbeth. She said that. . . . Ah, that is interesting. . . ."

VIII

Alfred Lee and his wife came into the small study where Poirot, Sugden and the Chief Constable were standing waiting. Colonel Johnson came forward.

"How do you do, Mr. Lee? We've never actually met, but as you probably know, I'm Chief Constable of the County. Johnson's my name. I can't tell you how distressed I am by this."

Alfred, his brown eyes like those of a suffering dog, said hoarsely:

"Thank you. It's terrible—quite terrible. I—this is my wife."

Lydia said in her quiet voice:

"It has been a frightful shock to my husband—to all of us—but particularly to him."

Her hand was on her husband's shoulder.

Colonel Johnson said:

"Won't you sit down, Mrs. Lee? Let me introduce M. Hercule Poirot."

Hercule Poirot bowed. His eyes went interestedly from husband to wife.

Lydia's hand pressed gently on Alfred's shoulder.

"Sit down, Alfred."

Alfred sat. He murmured:

"Hercule Poirot. Now who—who—"

He passed his hand in a dazed fashion over his forehead.

Lydia Lee said:

"Colonel Johnson will want to ask you a lot of questions, Alfred."

The Chief Constable looked at her with approval. He was thankful that Mrs. Alfred Lee was turning out to be such a sensible and competent woman.

Alfred said:

"Of course. Of course. . . ."

Johnson said to himself:

"Shock seems to have knocked him out completely. Hope he can pull himself together a bit."

Aloud he said:

"I've got a list here of everybody who was in the house to-night. Perhaps you'll tell me, Mr. Lee, if it is correct?"

He made a slight gesture to Sugden and the latter pulled out his notebook and once more recited the list of names.

The businesslike procedure seemed to restore Alfred Lee to something more like his usual self. He had regained command of himself, his eyes no longer looked dazed and staring. When Sugden finished, he nodded in agreement.

"That's quite right," he said.

"Do you mind telling me a little more about your guests? Mr. and Mrs. George Lee and Mr. and Mrs. David Lee are, I gather, relatives."

"They are my two younger brothers and their wives."

"They are staying here only?"

"Yes, they came to us for Christmas."

"Mr. Henry Lee is also a brother?"

"Yes."

"And your two other guests? Miss Estravados and Mr. Farr?"

"Miss Estravados is my niece. Mr. Farr is the son of my father's one-time partner in South Africa."

"Ah, an old friend."

Lydia intervened.

"No, actually we had never seen him before until yesterday."

"I see. But you invited him to stay with you for Christmas?"

Alfred hesitated, then looked towards his wife. She said clearly:

"Mr. Farr turned up quite unexpectedly yesterday. He happened to be in the neighbourhood and came to call upon my father-in-law. When my father-in-law found he was the son of his old friend and partner he insisted on his remaining with us for Christmas."

Colonel Johnson said:

"I see. That explains the household. As regards the servants, Mrs. Lee, do you consider them all trustworthy?"

Lydia considered for a moment before replying. Then she said:

"Yes, I am quite sure they are all thoroughly reliable. They have mostly been with us for many years. Tressilian, the butler, has been here since my husband was a young child. The only newcomers are the betweenmaid, Joan, and the nurse-valet who attended on my father-in-law."

"What about them?"

"Joan is rather a silly little thing. That is the worst that can be said of her. I know very little about Horbury. He has been here just over a year. He was quite competent at his job and my father-in-law seemed satisfied with him."

Poirot said acutely:

"But you, madam, were not so satisfied?"

Lydia shrugged her shoulders slightly.

"It was nothing to do with me."

"But you are the mistress of the house, madam. The servants are your concern?"

"Oh, yes, of course. But Horbury was my father-in-law's personal attendant. He did not come under my jurisdiction."

"I see."

Colonel Johnson said:

"We come now to the events of to-night. I'm afraid this will be painful for you, Mr. Lee, but I would like your account of what happened."

Alfred said in a low voice:

"Of course."

Colonel Johnson said, prompting him:

"When, for instance, did you last see your father?"

A slight spasm of pain crossed Alfred's face as he replied in a low voice:

"It was after tea. I was with him for a short time. Finally I said good-night to him and left him at—let me see—about a quarter to six."

Poirot observed:

"You said good-night to him? You did not then expect to see him again that evening?"

"No. My father's supper, a light meal, was always brought to him at seven. After that he sometimes went to bed early or sometimes sat up in his chair, but he did not expect to see any members of the family again unless he specially sent for them."

"Did he often send for them?"

"Sometimes. If he felt like it."

"But it was not the ordinary procedure?"

"No."

"Go on, please, Mr. Lee."

Alfred continued:

"We had our dinner at eight o'clock. Dinner was over and my wife and the other ladies had gone into the drawing-room." His voice faltered. His eyes began to stare again. "We were sitting there—at the table . . . . suddenly there was the most astounding noise overhead. Chairs overturning, furniture crashing, breaking glass and china and then— Oh, God" (he shuddered), "I can hear it still—my father screamed—a horrible long-drawn scream—the scream of a man in mortal agony. . . ."

He raised shaking hands to cover his face. Lydia stretched out her hand and touched his sleeve. Colonel Johnson said gently:

"And then?"

Alfred said in a broken voice:

"I think—just for a minute we were *stunned*. Then we sprang up and went out of the door and up the stairs to my father's room. The door was locked. We couldn't get in. It had to be broken open. Then, when we did get in, we saw—"

His voice died away.

Johnson said quickly:

"There's no need to go into that part of it, Mr. Lee. To go back a little, to the time you were in the dining-room. Who was there with you when you heard the cry?"

"Who was there? Why, we were all— No, let me see. My brother was there—my brother Harry."

"Nobody else?"

"No one else."

"Where were the other gentlemen?"

Alfred sighed and frowned in an effort of remembrance.

"Let me see—it seems so long ago—yes, like years—what did happen? Oh, of course, George had gone to telephone. Then we began to talk of family matters and Stephen Farr said something about seeing we wanted to discuss things and he took himself off. He did it very nicely and tactfully."

"And your brother David?"

Alfred frowned.

"David? Wasn't he there? No, of course he wasn't. I don't quite know when he slipped away."

Poirot said gently:

"So you had the family matters to discuss?"

"Er—yes."

"That is to say, you had matters to discuss with *one* member of your family?"

Lydia said:

"What do you mean, M. Poirot?"

He turned quickly to her.

"Madam, your husband says that Mr. Farr left them because he saw they had affairs of the family to discuss. But it was not a *conseil de famille*, since M. David was not there and M. George was not there. It was, then, a discussion between two members of the family only."

Lydia said:

"My brother-in-law, Harry, had been abroad for a great number of years. It was natural that he and my husband should have things to talk over."

"Ah! I see. It was like that."

She shot him a quick glance, then turned her eyes away.

Johnson said:

"Well, that seems clear enough. Did you notice anyone else as you ran upstairs to your father's room?"

"I—really I don't know. I think so. We all came from different directions. But I'm afraid I didn't notice—I was so alarmed. That terrible cry. . . ."

Colonel Johnson passed quickly to another subject.

"Thank you, Mr. Lee. Now there is another point. I understand that your father had some valuable diamonds in his possession."

Alfred looked rather surprised.

"Yes," he said. "That is so."

"Where did he keep them?"

"In the safe in his room."

"Can you describe them at all?"

"They were rough diamonds—that is, uncut stones."

"Why did your father have them there?"

"It was a whim of his. They were stones he had brought with him from South Africa. He never had them cut. He just liked keeping them in his possession. As I say, it was a whim of his."

"I see," said the Chief Constable.

From his tone it was plain that he did not see. He went on:

"Were they of much value?"

"My father estimated their value at about ten thousand pounds."

"In fact they were very valuable stones?"

"Yes."

"It seems a curious idea to keep such stones in a bedroom safe."

Lydia interposed:

"My father-in-law, Colonel Johnson, was a somewhat curious man. His ideas were not the conventional ones. It definitely gave him pleasure to handle those stones."

"They recalled, perhaps, the past to him," said Poirot.

She gave him a quick appreciative look.

"Yes," she said. "I think they did."

"Were they insured?" asked the Chief Constable.

"I think not."

Johnson leaned forward. He asked quietly:

"Did you know, Mr. Lee, that those stones had been stolen?"

"What?" Alfred Lee stared at him.

"Your father said nothing to you of their disappearance?"

"Not a word."

"You did not know that he had sent for Superintendent Sugden here and had reported the loss to him?"

"I hadn't the faintest idea of such a thing!"

The Chief Constable transferred his gaze.

"What about you, Mrs. Lee?"

Lydia shook her head.

"I heard nothing about it."

"As far as you knew the stones were still in the safe?"

"Yes."

She hesitated and then asked:

"Is that why he was killed? For the sake of those stones?"

Colonel Johnson said:

"That is what we are going to find out!"

He went on:

"Have you any idea, Mrs. Lee, who could have engineered such a theft?"

She shook her head.

"No, indeed. I am sure the servants are all honest. In any case it would be very difficult for them to get at the safe. My father-in-law was always in his room. He never came downstairs."

"Who attended to the room?"

"Horbury. He made the bed and dusted. The second housemaid went in to do the grate and lay the fire every morning, otherwise Horbury did everything."

Poirot said:

"So Horbury would be the person with the best opportunity?"

"Yes."

"Do you think that it was he who stole the diamonds, then?"

"It is possible, I suppose . . . he had the best opportunity. Oh! I don't know what to think."

Colonel Johnson said:

"Your husband has given us his account of the evening. Will you do the same, Mrs. Lee? When did you last see your father-in-law?"

"We were all up in his room this afternoon—before tea. That was the last time I saw him."

"You did not see him later to bid him good-night?"

"No."

Poirot said:

"Do you usually go and say good-night to him?"

Lydia said sharply:

"No."

The Chief Constable went on:

"Where were you when the crime took place?"

"In the drawing-room."

"You heard the noise of the struggle?"

"I think I heard something heavy fall. Of course the room is over the dining-room, not the drawing-room, so I wouldn't have heard so much."

"But you heard the cry?"

Lydia shuddered.

"Yes, I heard that . . . it was horrible . . . like—like a soul in Hell. I knew at once something dreadful had happened. I hurried out and followed my husband and Harry up the stairs."

"Who else was in the drawing-room at the time?"

Lydia frowned.

"Really—I can't remember. David was next door in the music room, playing Mendelssohn. I think Hilda had gone to join him."

"And the other two ladies?"

Lydia said slowly:

"Magdalene went to telephone. I can't remember whether she had come back or not. I don't know where Pilar was."

Poirot said gently:

"In fact you may have been quite alone in the drawing-room?"

"Yes—yes—as a matter of fact I believe I was."

Colonel Johnson said:

"About these diamonds. We ought, I think, to make quite sure about them. Do you know the combination of your father's safe, Mr. Lee? I see it is of a somewhat old-fashioned pattern."

"You will find it written down in a small notebook he carried in the pocket of his dressing-gown."

"Good. We will go and look presently. It will be better, perhaps, if we interview the other members of the house party first. The ladies may want to get to bed."

Lydia stood up.

"Come, Alfred." She turned to them. "Shall I send them in to you?"

"One by one, if you wouldn't mind, Mrs. Lee."

"Certainly."

She moved towards the door. Alfred followed her.

Suddenly, at the last moment, he swung round.

"Of course," he said. He came quickly back to Poirot. "You are Hercule Poirot! I don't know where my wits have been. I should have realized at once. . . ."

He spoke quickly, in a low excited voice.

"It's an absolute godsend, your being here! You must find out the truth, M. Poirot. Spare no expense! I will be responsible for any expense. *But find out.* . . . My poor father—killed by someone—killed with the utmost brutality! You *must* find out, M. Poirot. My father has got to be avenged."

Poirot answered quietly:

"I can assure you, M. Lee, that I am prepared to do my utmost to assist Colonel Johnson and Superintendent Sugden."

Alfred Lee said:

"I want you to work for *me*. My father has got to be avenged."

He began to tremble violently. Lydia had come back. She went up to him and drew his arm through hers.

"Come, Alfred," she said. "We must get the others."

Her eyes met Poirot's. They were eyes that kept their own secrets. They did not waver.

Poirot said softly:

"Who would have thought the old man—"

She interrupted him:

"Stop! Don't say that!"

Poirot murmured:

"You said it, madam."

She breathed softly:

"I know . . . I remember . . . it was—so horrible."

Then she went abruptly out of the room, her husband beside her.

IX

George Lee was solemn and correct.

"A terrible business," he said, shaking his head. "A terrible, terrible business. I can only believe that it must—er—have been the work of a *lunatic!*"

Colonel Johnson said politely:

"That is your theory?"

"Yes. Yes, indeed. A homicidal maniac. Escaped, perhaps, from some mental Home in the vicinity."

Superintendent Sugden put in:

"And how do you suggest this—er—lunatic gained admittance to the house, Mr. Lee? And how did he leave it?"

George shook his head.

"That," he said firmly, "is for the police to discover."

Sugden said:

"We made the round of the house at once. All windows were closed and barred. The side door was locked, so was the front door. Nobody could have left by the kitchen premises without being seen by the kitchen staff."

George Lee cried:

"But that's absurd! You'll be saying next that my father was never murdered at all!"

"He was murdered all right," said Superintendent Sugden. "There's no doubt about that."

The Chief Constable cleared his throat and took up the questioning.

"Just where were you, Mr. Lee, at the time of the crime?"

"I was in the dining-room. It was just after dinner. No, I was, I think, in this room. I had just finished telephoning."

"You had been telephoning?"

"Yes. I had put a call through to the Conservative agent in Westeringham—my constituency. Some urgent matters."

"And it was after that that you heard the scream?"

George Lee gave a slight shiver.

"Yes, very unpleasant. It—er—froze my marrow. It died away in a kind of choke or gurgle."

He took out a handkerchief and wiped his forehead where the perspiration had broken out.

"Terrible business," he muttered.

"And then you hurried upstairs?"

"Yes."

"Did you see your brothers, Mr. Alfred and Mr. Harry Lee?"

"No, they must have gone up just ahead of me, I think."

"When did you last see your father, Mr. Lee?"

"This afternoon. We were all up there."

"You did not see him after that?"

"No."

The Chief Constable paused, then he said:

"Were you aware that your father kept a quantity of valuable uncut diamonds in the safe in his bedroom?"

George Lee nodded.

"A most unwise procedure," he said pompously. "I often told him so. He might have been murdered for them—I mean—that is to say—"

Colonel Johnson cut in:

"Are you aware that these stones have disappeared?"

George's jaw dropped. His protuberant eyes stared.

"Then he *was* murdered for them?"

The Chief Constable said slowly:

"He was aware of their loss and reported it to the police some hours before his death."

George said:

"But then—I don't understand—I—"

Hercule Poirot said gently:

"We, too, do not understand. . . ."

X

Harry Lee came into the room with a swagger. For a moment Poirot stared at him, frowning. He had a feeling that somewhere he had seen this man before. He noted the features, the high bridged nose, the arrogant poise of the head, the line of the jaw and he realized that though Harry Lee was a big man and his father had been a man of merely middle height yet there had been a good deal of resemblance between them.

He noted something else, too. For all his swagger, Harry Lee was nervous. He was carrying it off with a swing, but the anxiety underneath was real enough.

"Well, gentlemen," he said, "what can I tell you?"

Colonel Johnson said:

"We shall be glad of any light you can throw on the events of this evening."

Harry Lee shook his head.

"I don't know anything at all. It's all pretty horrible and utterly unexpected."

Poirot said:

"You have recently returned from abroad, I think, Mr. Lee?"

Harry turned to him quickly.

"Yes. Landed in England a week ago."

Poirot said:

"You had been away a long time?"

Harry Lee lifted up his chin and laughed.

"You might as well hear straight away—someone will soon tell you! I'm the prodigal son, gentlemen! It's nearly twenty years since I last set foot in this house."

"But you returned—now. Will you tell us why?" asked Poirot.

With the same appearance of frankness Harry answered readily enough.

"It's the good old parable still. I got tired of the husks that the swine do eat—or don't eat, I forget which. I thought to myself that the fatted calf would be a welcome exchange. I had had a letter from my father suggesting that I come home. I obeyed the summons and came. That's all."

Poirot said:

"You came for a short visit—or a long one?"

Harry said:

"I came home—for good!"

"Your father was willing?"

"The old man was delighted." He laughed again. The corners of his eyes crinkled engagingly. "Pretty boring for the old man living here with Alfred! Alfred's a dull stick—very worthy and all that, but poor company. My father had been a bit of a rip in his time. He was looking forward to my company."

"And your brother and his wife, were they pleased that you were to live here?"

Poirot asked the question with a slight lifting of his eyebrows.

"Alfred? Alfred was livid with rage. Don't know about Lydia. She was probably annoyed on Alfred's behalf. But I've no doubt she'd be quite pleased in the end. I like Lydia. She's a delightful woman. I should have got on with Lydia. But Alfred was quite another pair of shoes." He laughed again. "Alfred's always been as jealous as Hell of me. He's always been the good dutiful stay-at-home stick-in-the-mud son. And what was he going to get for it in the end? What the good boy of the family always gets. A kick in the pants. Take it from me, gentlemen, virtue doesn't pay."

He looked from one face to another.

"Hope you're not shocked by my frankness. But after all, it's the truth you're after. You'll drag out all the family dirty linen into the light of day in the end. I might as well display mine straight away. I'm not particularly broken-hearted by my father's death—after all, I hadn't seen the old devil since I was a boy—but nevertheless he was my father and he was murdered. I'm all out for revenge on the murderer." He stroked his jawbone, watching them. "We're rather hot on revenge in our family. None of the Lees forget easily. I mean to make sure that my father's murderer is caught and hanged."

"I think you can trust us to do our best in that line, Mr. Lee," said Sugden.

"If you don't I shall take the law into my own hands," said Harry Lee.

The Chief Constable said sharply:

"Have you any ideas on the subject of the murderer's identity, then, Mr. Lee?"

Harry shook his head.

"No," he said slowly. "No—I haven't. You know—it's rather a jolt. Because I've been thinking about it—and I don't see that it can have been an outside job. . . ."

"Ah," said Sugden, nodding his head.

"And if so," said Harry Lee. "Then someone here in the house killed him. . . . But who the devil could have done it? Can't suspect the servants. Tressilian has been here since the year one. The half-witted footman? Not on your life. Horbury, now, he's a cool customer, but Tressilian tells me he was out at the pictures. So what do you come to? Passing over Stephen Farr (and why the devil should Stephen Farr come all the way from South Africa and murder a total stranger?) there's only the family. And for the life of me I can't see one of us doing it. Alfred? He adored Father. George? He hasn't got the guts. David? David's always been a moon dreamer. He'd faint if he saw his own finger bleed. The wives? Women don't go and slit a man's throat in cold blood. So who did? Blessed if I know. But it's damned disturbing."

Colonel Johnson cleared his throat—an official habit of his—and said:

"When did you last see your father this evening?"

"After tea. He'd just had a row with Alfred. About your humble servant. The old man was no end bucked with himself. He always liked stirring up trouble. In my opinion that's why he kept my arrival dark from the others. Wanted to see the fur fly when I blew in unexpectedly! That's why he talked about altering his will, too."

Poirot stirred softly. He murmured:

"So your father mentioned his will?"

"Yes. In front of the whole lot of us. Watching us like a cat to see how we reacted. Just told the lawyer chap to come over and see him about it after Christmas."

Poirot asked:

"What changes did he contemplate making?"

Harry Lee grinned.

"He didn't tell us that! Trust the old fox! I imagine—or shall we say I hoped—that the change was to the advantage of your humble servant! I should imagine I'd been cut out of any former wills. Now, I rather fancy, I was to go back. Nasty blow for the others. Pilar, too—he'd taken a fancy to her. She was in for something good, I should imagine. You haven't seen her yet? My Spanish niece. She's a beautiful creature, Pilar—with the lovely warmth of the South—and its cruelty. Wish I wasn't a mere uncle!"

"You say your father took to her?"

Harry nodded.

"She knew how to get round the old man. Sat up there with him a good deal. I bet she knew just what she was after! Well, he's dead now. No wills can be altered in Pilar's favour—nor mine either, worse luck."

He frowned, paused a minute, and then went on with a change of tone.

"But I'm wandering from the point. You wanted to know what was the last time I saw my father? As I've told you it was after tea—might have been a little past six. The old man was in good spirits then—a bit tired perhaps. I went away and left him with Horbury. I never saw him again."

"Where were you at the time of his death?"

"In the dining-room with brother Alfred. Not a very harmonious after dinner session. We were in the middle of a pretty sharp argument when we heard the noise overhead. Sounded as though ten men were wrestling up there. And then poor old Father screamed. It was like killing a pig. The sound of it paralyzed Alfred. He just sat there with his jaw dropping. I fairly shook him back to life and we started off upstairs. The door was locked. Had to break it open. Took some doing, too. How the devil that door came to be locked I can't imagine! There was no one in the room but Father, and I'm damned if anyone could have got away through the windows."

Superintendent Sugden said:

"The door was locked from the outside."

"What?" Harry stared. "But I'll swear the key was on the *inside.*"

Poirot murmured:

"So you noticed that?"

Harry Lee said sharply:

"I do notice things. It's a habit of mine."

He looked sharply from one face to the other.

"Is there anything more you want to know, gentlemen?"

Johnson shook his head.

"Thank you, Mr. Lee, not for the moment. Perhaps you will ask the
next member of the family to come along?"

"Certainly I will."

He walked to the door and went out without looking back.

The three men looked at each other.

Colonel Johnson said:

"What about it, Sugden?"

The Superintendent shook his head doubtfully. He said:

"He's afraid of something. I wonder why. . . ."

XI

Magdalene Lee paused effectively in the doorway. One long slender
hand touched the burnished platinum sheen of her hair. The leaf-green
velvet frock she wore clung to the delicate lines of her figure. She looked
very young and a little frightened.

The three men were arrested for a moment looking at her. Johnson's
eyes showed a sudden surprised admiration. Superintendent Sugden's
showed no animation, merely the impatience of a man anxious to get on
with his job. Hercule Poirot's eyes were deeply appreciative (as she saw)
but the appreciation was not for her beauty but for the effective use she
made of it. She did not know that he was thinking to himself

*"Jolie mannequin, la petite. Elle se pose tout naturellement. Elle a les
yeux dures."*

Colonel Johnson was thinking:

"Damned good-looking girl. George Lee will have trouble with her if he
doesn't look out. Got an eye for a man all right."

Superintendent Sugden was thinking:

"Empty headed, vain piece of goods. Hope we get through with her
quickly."

Colonel Johnson rose.

"Will you sit down, Mrs. Lee? Let me see, you are—?"

"Mrs. George Lee."

She accepted the chair with a warm smile of thanks. "After all," the
glance seemed to say, "although you *are* a man and a policeman, you are
not so dreadful after all."

The tail end of the smile included Poirot. Foreigners were so susceptible
where women were concerned. About Superintendent Sugden she did not
bother.

She murmured, twisting her hands together in a pretty distress:

"It's all so terrible. I feel so frightened."

"Come, come, Mrs. Lee," said Colonel Johnson kindly but briskly. "It's been a shock, I know, but it's all over now. We just want an account from you of what happened this evening."

She cried out:

"But I don't know anything about it—I don't indeed."

For a minute the Chief Constable's eyes narrowed. He said gently:

"No, of course not."

"We only arrived here yesterday. George *would* make me come here for Christmas! I wish we hadn't. I'm sure I shall never feel the same again!"

"Very upsetting—yes."

"I hardly know George's family, you see. I'd only seen Mr. Lee once or twice—at our wedding and once since. Of course I've seen Alfred and Lydia more often, but they're really all quite strangers to me."

Again the wide-eyed frightened child look. Again Hercule Poirot's eyes were appreciative—and again he thought to himself:

"Elle joue très bien la comédie, cette petite. . . ."

"Yes, yes," said Colonel Johnson. "Now just tell me about the last time you saw your father-in-law—Mr. Lee—alive."

"Oh! *that!* That was this afternoon. It was dreadful!"

Johnson said quickly:

"Dreadful? Why?"

"They were so angry!"

"Who was angry?"

"Oh! all of them. . . . I don't mean George. His father didn't say anything to him. But all the others."

"What happened exactly?"

"Well, when we got there—he asked for all of us—he was speaking into the telephone—to his lawyers about his will. And then he told Alfred he was looking very glum. I think that was because of Harry coming home to live. Alfred was very upset about that, I believe. You see years ago Harry did something quite dreadful. And then he said something about his wife (she's dead long ago); she had had the brains of a louse, he said, and David sprang up and looked as though he'd like to murder him— Oh!" She stopped suddenly, her eyes alarmed. "I didn't *mean* that—I didn't mean it at all!"

Colonel Johnson said soothingly:

"Quite—quite; figure of speech, that was all."

"Hilda, that's David's wife, quieted him down and—well, I think that's all. Mr. Lee said he didn't want to see anyone again that evening. So we all went away."

"And that was the last time you saw him?"

"Yes. Until—until—"

She shivered.

Colonel Johnson said:

"Yes, quite so. Now where were you at the time of the crime?"

"Oh—let me see. I think I was in the drawing-room."

"Aren't you sure?"

Magdalene's eyes flickered a little, the lids drooped over them.

She said:

"Of course! How stupid of me. . . . I'd gone to telephone. One gets so mixed up."

"You were telephoning, you say? In this room?"

"Yes; that's the only telephone except the one upstairs in my father-in-law's room."

Superintendent Sugden said:

"Was anybody else in the room with you?"

Her eyes widened.

"Oh, no, I was quite alone."

"Had you been here long?"

"Well—a little time. It takes some time to put a call through in the evening."

"It was a trunk call, then?"

"Yes. To Westeringham."

"I see."

"And then?"

"And then there was that awful scream—and everybody running—and the door being locked and having to break it down. Oh! it was like a *nightmare!* I shall always always remember it!"

"No, no." Colonel Johnson's tone was mechanically kind. He went on:

"Did you know that your father-in-law kept a quantity of valuable diamonds in his safe?"

"No, did he?" Her tone was quite frankly thrilled. "Real diamonds?"

Hercule Poirot said:

"Diamonds worth about ten thousand pounds."

"Oh!" It was a soft gasping sound—holding in it the essence of feminine cupidity.

"Well," said Colonel Johnson, "I think that's all for the present. We needn't bother you any further, Mrs. Lee."

"Oh, thank you."

She stood up—smiled from Johnson to Poirot—the smile of a grateful little girl, then she went out walking with her head held high and her palms a little turned outwards.

Colonel Johnson called:

"Will you ask your brother-in-law, Mr. David Lee, to come here?"

Closing the door after her, he came back to the table.

"Well," he said, "what do you think? We're getting at some of it now! You notice one thing. George Lee was telephoning when he heard the scream! His wife was telephoning when she heard it! That doesn't fit—it doesn't fit at all."

He added:

"What do you think, Sugden?"

The Superintendent said slowly:

"I don't want to speak offensively of the lady, but I should say that though she's the kind who would be first class at getting money out of a gentleman, I don't think she's the kind who'd cut a gentleman's throat. That wouldn't be her line at all."

"Ah, but one never knows, *mon vieux,*" murmured Poirot.

The Chief Constable turned round to him.

"And you, Poirot, what do you think?"

Hercule Poirot leaned forward. He straightened the blotter in front of him, and flicked a minute speck of dust from a candlestick. He answered:

"I would say that the character of the late Mr. Simeon Lee begins to emerge for us. It is there, I think, that the whole importance of this case lies . . . in the character of the dead man."

Superintendent Sugden turned a puzzled face to him.

"I don't quite get you, Mr. Poirot," he said. "What exactly has the character of the deceased got to do with his murder?"

Poirot said dreamily:

"The character of the victim has always something to do with his or her murder. The frank and unsuspicious mind of Desdemona was the direct cause of her death. A more suspicious woman would have seen Iago's machinations and circumvented them much earlier. The uncleanness of Marat directly invited his end in a bath. From the temper of Mercutio's mind came his death at the sword's point."

Colonel Johnson pulled his moustache.

"What exactly are you getting at, Poirot?"

"I am telling you that because Simeon Lee was a certain kind of man, he set in motion certain forces, which forces in the end brought about his death."

"You don't think the diamonds had anything to do with it then?"

Poirot smiled at the honest perplexity in Johnson's face.

"*Mon cher,*" he said. "It was because of Simeon Lee's peculiar character that he kept ten thousand pounds' worth of uncut diamonds in his safe! You have not there the action of every man."

"That's very true, Mr. Poirot," said Superintendent Sugden, nodding his head with the air of a man who at last sees what a fellow conversationalist is driving at. "He was a queer one, Mr. Lee was. He kept those stones there so he could take them out and handle them and get the feeling of the past back. Depend upon it, that's why he never had them cut.'"

Poirot nodded energetically.

"Precisely—precisely. I see you have great acumen, Superintendent."

The Superintendent looked a little doubtful at the compliment, but Colonel Johnson cut in.

"There's something else, Poirot. I don't know whether it has struck you—"

"*Mais oui,* " said Poirot. "I know what you mean. Mrs. George Lee, she let the cat out of the bag more than she knew! She gave us a pretty impression of that last family meeting. She indicates, oh! so naïvely, that Alfred was angry with his father—and that David looked as 'though he could murder him.' Both those statements, I think, were true. But from them we can draw our own reconstruction. What did Simeon Lee assemble his family for—why should they have arrived in time to hear him telephoning to his lawyer? *Parbleu,* it was no error, that. He *wanted* them to hear it! The poor old one, he sits in his chair and he has lost the diversions of his younger days. So he invents a new diversion for himself. He amuses himself by playing upon the cupidity and the greed of human nature—yes, and on its emotions and its passions, too! But from that arises one further deduction. In his game of rousing the greed and emotion of his children, he would not omit anyone. He must, logically and necessarily, have had his dig at Mr. George Lee as well as at the others! His wife is carefully silent about that. At her, too, he may have shot a poisoned arrow or so. We shall find out, I think, from others what Simeon Lee had to say to George Lee and George Lee's wife—"

He broke off. The door opened and David Lee came in.

XII

David Lee had himself well in hand. His demeanour was calm—almost unnaturally so. He came up to them, drew a chair forward and sat down, looking with grave interrogation at Colonel Johnson.

The electric light touched the fair peak of hair that grew on his forehead and showed up the sensitive modeling of the cheek bones. He looked absurdly young to be the son of that shriveled old man who lay dead upstairs.

"Yes, gentlemen," he said, "what can I tell you?"

Colonel Johnson said:

"I understand, Mr. Lee, that there was a kind of family meeting held in your father's room this afternoon?"

"There was. But it was quite informal. I mean, it was not a family council or anything of that kind."

"What took place there?"

David Lee answered calmly:

"My father was in a difficult mood. He was an old man and an invalid; of course, one had to make allowances for him. He seemed to have assembled us there in order to—well—vent his spite upon us."

"Can you remember what he said?"

David said quietly:

"It was really all rather foolish. He said we were no use—any of us—that there wasn't a single man in the family! He said Pilar (that is my Spanish niece) was worth two of any of us. He said—" David stopped.

Poirot said:

"Please, Mr. Lee, the exact words, if you can."

David said reluctantly:

"He spoke rather coarsely—said he hoped that somewhere in the world he had better sons—even if they were born the wrong side of the blanket. . . ."

His sensitive face showed distaste for the words he was repeating. Superintendent Sugden looked up suddenly alert. Leaning forward, he said:

"Did your father say anything in particular to your brother, Mr. George Lee?"

"To George? I don't remember. Oh, yes, I believe he told him he would have to cut down expenses in future, he'd have to reduce his allowance. George was very upset, got as red as a turkey cock. He spluttered and said he couldn't possibly manage with less. My father said quite coolly that he'd have to. He said he'd better get his wife to help him economize—rather a nasty dig that—George has always been the economical one—saves and stints on every penny. Magdalene, I fancy, is a bit of a spender—she has extravagant tastes."

Poirot said:

"So that she, too, was annoyed?"

"Yes. Besides, my father worded something else rather crudely, mentioned her as having lived with a naval officer—of course he really meant her father, but it sounded rather dubious. Magdalene went scarlet. I don't blame her."

Poirot said:

"Did your father mention his late wife, your mother?"

The red blood ran in waves up David's temples. His hands clenched themselves on the table in front of him, trembling slightly.

He said in a low choked voice:

"Yes, he did. He insulted her."

Colonel Johnson said:

"What did he say?"

David said abruptly:

"I don't remember. Just some slighting reference."

Poirot said softly:

"Your mother has been dead some years?"

David said shortly:

"She died when I was a boy."

"She was not—perhaps—very happy in her life here?"

David gave a scornful laugh.

"Who could be happy with a man like my father? My mother was a saint. She died a broken-hearted woman."

Poirot went on:

"Your father was, perhaps, distressed by her death?"

David said abruptly:

"I don't know. I left home."

He paused and then said:

"Perhaps you may not be aware of the fact that when I came on this visit I had not seen my father for nearly twenty years. So you see I can't tell you very much about his habits or his enemies or what went on here."

Colonel Johnson asked:

"Did you know that your father kept a lot of valuable diamonds in the safe in his bedroom?"

David said indifferently:

"Did he? Seems a foolish sort of thing to do."

Johnson said:

"Will you describe briefly your own movements last night?"

"Mine? Oh, I went away from the dinner table fairly quickly. It bores me, this sitting round over port. Besides I could see that Alfred and Harry were working up for a quarrel. I hate rows. I slipped away and went to the music room and played the piano."

Poirot asked:

"The music room, it is next to the drawing-room, is it not?"

"Yes. I played there for some time—till—till the thing happened."

"What did you hear exactly?"

"Oh! a far-off noise of furniture being overturned somewhere upstairs. And then a pretty ghastly cry." He clenched his hands again. "Like a soul in Hell. God, it was awful!"

Johnson said:

"Were you alone in the music room?"

"Eh? No, my wife, Hilda, was there. She'd come in from the drawing-room. We—we went up with the others."

He added quickly and nervously:

"You don't want me, do you, to describe what—what I saw there?"

Colonel Johnson said:

"No, quite unnecessary. Thank you, Mr. Lee, there's nothing more. You can't imagine, I suppose, who would be likely to want to murder your father?"

David Lee said recklessly:

"I should think—quite a lot of people! I don't know of anyone definite."

He went out rapidly, shutting the door loudly behind him.

XIII

Colonel Johnson had had no time to do more than clear his throat when the door opened again and Hilda Lee came in.

Hercule Poirot looked at her with interest. He had to admit to himself that the wives these Lees had married were an interesting study. The swift intelligence and greyhound grace of Lydia, the meretricious airs and graces of Magdalene, and now the solid comfortable strength of Hilda. She was, he saw, younger than her rather dowdy style of hairdressing and unfashionable clothes made her appear. Her mouse brown hair was unflecked with grey and her steady hazel eyes set in the rather podgy face shone out like beacons of kindliness. She was, he thought, a nice woman.

Colonel Johnson was talking in his kindliest tone.

"—a great strain on all of you," he was saying. "I gather from your husband, Mrs. Lee, that this is the first time you have been to Gorston Hall?"

She bowed her head.

"Were you previously acquainted with your father-in-law, Mr. Lee?"

Hilda replied in her pleasant voice:

"No. We were married soon after David left home. He always wanted to have nothing to do with his family. Until now we have not seen any of them."

"How then, did this visit come about?"

"My father-in-law wrote to David. He stressed his age and his desire that all his children should be with him this Christmas."

"And your husband responded to this appeal?"

Hilda said:

"His acceptance was, I am afraid, all my doing. I—misunderstood the situation."

Poirot interposed. He said:

"Will you be so kind as to explain yourself a little more clearly, madam? I think what you can tell us may be of value."

She turned to him immediately.

She said:

"At that time I had never seen my father-in-law. I had no idea what his real motive was. I assumed that he was old and lonely and that he really wanted to be reconciled to all his children."

"And what was his real motive, in your opinion, madam?"

Hilda hesitated a moment. Then she said slowly:

"I have no doubt—no doubt at all—that what my father-in-law really wanted was not to promote peace but to stir up strife."

"In what way?"

Hilda said in a low voice:

"It amused him to—to appeal to the worst instincts in human nature. There was—how can I put it—a kind of diabolical impishness about him. He wished to set every member of the family at loggerheads with each other."

Johnson said sharply:

"And did he succeed?"

"Oh, yes," said Hilda Lee. "He succeeded."

Poirot said:

"We have been told, madam, of a scene that took place this afternoon. It was, I think, rather a violent scene."

She bowed her head.

"Will you describe it to us—as truthfully as possible if you please."

She reflected a minute.

"When we went in my father-in-law was telephoning."

"To his lawyer, I understand?"

"Yes, he was suggesting that Mr.—was it Charlton?—I don't quite remember the name—should come over as he, my father-in-law, wanted to make a new will. His old one, he said, was quite out of date."

Poirot said:

"Think carefully, madam, in your opinion, did your father-in-law deliberately ensure that you should all overhear this conversation, or was it just by *chance* that you overheard it?"

Hilda Lee said:

"I am almost sure that he meant us to overhear."

"With the object of fomenting doubt and suspicion among you?"

"Yes."

"So that, really, he may not have meant to alter his will at all?"

She demurred.

"No, I think that part of it was quite genuine. He probably did wish to make a new will—but he enjoyed underlining the fact."

"Madam," said Poirot. "I have no official standing and my questions, you understand, are not perhaps those that an English officer of the law would ask. But I have a great desire to know what form you think that new will would have taken. I am asking, you perceive, not for your knowledge, but simply for your opinion. *Les femmes,* they are never slow to form opinions, *Dieu merci.*"

Hilda Lee smiled a little.

"I don't mind saying what I think. My husband's sister Jennifer married a Spaniard, Juan Estravados. Her daughter, Pilar, has just arrived here. She is a very lovely girl—and she is, of course, the only grandchild in the family. Old Mr. Lee was delighted with her. He took a tremendous fancy to her. In my opinion he wished to leave her a considerable sum in his new will. Probably he had only left her a small portion or even nothing at all in an old one."

"Did you know your sister-in-law at all?"

"No, I never met her. Her Spanish husband died in tragic circumstances, I believe, soon after the marriage. Jennifer herself died a year ago. Pilar was left an orphan. This is why Mr. Lee sent for her to come and live with him in England."

"And the other members of the family, did they welcome her coming?"

Hilda said quietly:

"I think they all liked her. It was very pleasant to have someone young and alive in the house."

"And she, did she seem to like being here?"

Hilda said slowly:

"I don't know. It must seem cold and strange to a girl brought up in the South—in Spain."

Johnson said:

"Can't be very pleasant being in Spain just at present. Now, Mrs. Lee, we'd like to hear your account of the conversation this afternoon."

Poirot murmured:

"I apologize. I have made the digressions."

Hilda Lee said:

"After my father-in-law finished telephoning, he looked round at us and laughed and said we all looked very glum. Then he said that he was tired and should go to bed early. Nobody was to come up and see him this evening. He said he wanted to be in good form for Christmas Day. Something like that.

"Then—" Her brows knit in an effort of remembrance. "I think he said something about its being necessary to be one of a large family to appreciate Christmas, and then he went on to speak of money. He said it would cost him more to run this house in future. He told George and Magdalene they would have to economize. Told her she ought to make her own clothes. Rather an old-fashioned idea, I'm afraid. I don't wonder it annoyed her. He said his own wife had been clever with her needle."

Poirot said gently:

"Is that all that he said about her?"

Hilda flushed.

"He made a slighting reference to her brains. My husband was very devoted to his mother, and that upset him very much. And then, suddenly, Mr. Lee began shouting at us all. He worked himself up about it. I can understand, of course, how he felt—"

Poirot said gently, interrupting her:

"How did he feel?"

She turned her tranquil eyes upon him.

"He was disappointed, of course," she said. "Because there are no grandchildren—no boys, I mean—no Lees to carry on. I can see that that must have festered for a long time. And suddenly he couldn't keep it in any longer and vented his rage against his sons—saying they were a lot of namby-pamby old women—something like that. I felt sorry for him, then, because I realized how his pride was hurt by it."

"And then?"

"And then," said Hilda slowly, "we all went away."

"That was the last you saw of him?"

She bowed her head.

"Where were you at the time the crime occurred?"

"I was with my husband in the music room. He was playing to me."

"And then?"

"We heard tables and chairs overturned upstairs and china being broken—some terrible struggle. And then that awful scream as his throat was cut. . . ."

Poirot said:

"Was it such an awful scream? Was it"—he paused—*"like a soul in Hell?"*

Hilda Lee said:

"It was worse than that!"

"What do you mean, madam?"

"It was like someone *who had no soul* . . . it was inhuman like a beast. . . ."

Poirot said gravely:

"So—you have judged him, madam?"

She raised a hand in sudden distress. Her eyes fell and she stared down at the floor.

XIV

Pilar came into the room with the wariness of an animal who suspects a trap. Her eyes went quickly from side to side. She looked not so much afraid as deeply suspicious.

Colonel Johnson rose and put a chair for her. Then he said:

"You understand English, I suppose, Miss Estravados?"

Pilar's eyes opened wide. She said:

"Of course. My mother was English. I am really very English indeed."

A faint smile came to Colonel Johnson's lips, as his eyes took in the black gloss of her hair, the proud dark eyes and the curling red lips. Very English! An incongruous term to apply to Pilar Estravados.

He said:

"Mr. Lee was your grandfather. He sent for you to come from Spain. And you arrived a few days ago. Is that right?"

Pilar nodded.

"That is right. I had—oh! a lot of adventures getting out of Spain—there was a bomb from the air and the chauffeur he was killed—where his head had been there was all blood. And I could not drive a car, so for a long way I had to walk—and I do not like walking. I never walk. My feet were sore—but sore—"

Colonel Johnson smiled.

He said:

"At any rate you arrived here. Had your mother spoken to you of your grandfather much?"

Pilar nodded cheerfully.

"Oh, yes, she said he was an old devil."

Hercule Poirot smiled.

He said:

"And what did you think of him when you arrived, mademoiselle?"

Pilar said:

"Of course he was very, very old. He had to sit in a chair—and his face was all dried up. But I liked him all the same. I think that when he was a young man, he must have been handsome—very handsome, like you," said Pilar to Superintendent Sugden. Her eyes dwelt with naïve pleasure on his handsome face which had turned brick red at the compliment.

Colonel Johnson stifled a chuckle. It was one of the few occasions when he had seen the stolid Superintendent taken aback.

"But, of course," Pilar continued regretfully, "he could never have been as big as you."

Hercule Poirot sighed.

"You like, then, big men, señorita?" he inquired.

Pilar agreed enthusiastically.

"Oh, yes, I like a man to be very big, tall, and the shoulders broad and very, very strong."

Colonel Johnson said sharply:

"Did you see much of your grandfather when you arrived here?"

Pilar said:

"Oh, yes. I went to sit with him. He told me things—that he had been a very wicked man, and all the things he did in South Africa."

"Did he ever tell you that he had diamonds in the safe in his room?"

"Yes, he showed them to me. But they were not like diamonds—they were just like pebbles—very ugly—very ugly indeed."

Superintendent Sugden said shortly:

"So he showed them to you, did he?"

"Yes."

"He didn't give you any of them?"

Pilar shook her head.

"No, he did not. I thought that perhaps one day he would—if I were very nice to him and came often to sit with him. Because old gentlemen they like very much young girls."

Colonel Johnson said:

"Do you know that those diamonds have been stolen?"

Pilar opened her eyes very wide.

"Stolen?"

"Yes, have you any idea who might have taken them?"

Pilar nodded her head.

"Oh, yes," she said. "It would be Horbury."

"Horbury? You mean the valet?"

"Yes."

"Why do you think that?"

"Because he has the face of a thief. His eyes go so, from side to side, he walks softly and listens at doors. He is like a cat. And all cats are thieves."

"H'm," said Colonel Johnson. "We'll leave it at that. Now I understand that all the family were up in your grandfather's room this afternoon, and that some—er—angry words passed."

Pilar nodded and smiled.

"Yes," she said. "It was great fun. Grandfather made them, oh! so angry!"

"Oh, you enjoyed it, did you?"

"Yes. I like to see people get angry. I like it very much. But here in England they do not get angry like they do in Spain. In Spain they take out their knives and they curse and shout. In England they do nothing, just get very red in the face and shut up their mouths tight."

"Do you remember what was said?"

Pilar seemed rather doubtful.

"I am not sure. Grandfather said they were no good—that they had not got any children. He said I was better than any of them. He liked me, very much."

"Did he say anything about money or a will?"

"A will—no, I don't think so. I don't remember."

"What happened?"

"They all went away—except Hilda—the fat one, David's wife, she stayed behind."

"Oh, she did, did she?"

"Yes. David looked very funny. He was all shaking and, oh! so white. He looked as though he might be sick."

"And what then?"

"Then I went and found Stephen. We danced to the gramophone."

"Stephen Farr?"

"Yes. He is from South Africa—he is the son of Grandfather's partner. He is very handsome, too. Very brown and big and he has nice eyes."

Johnson asked:

"Where were you when the crime occurred?"

"You ask where I was?"

"Yes."

"I had gone into the drawing-room with Lydia. And then I went up to my room and did my face. I was going to dance again with Stephen. And then, far away, I heard a scream and everyone was running, so I went too. And they were trying to break down Grandfather's door. Harry did it with Stephen, they are both big, strong men."

"Yes?"

"And then—crash—down it went—and we all looked in. Oh, such a sight—everything smashed and knocked over and Grandfather lying in a lot of blood, and his throat was cut like *this*"— she made a vivid, dramatic gesture at her own neck—"right up under his ear."

She paused, having obviously enjoyed her narrative.

Johnson said:

"The blood didn't make you feel ill?"

She stared.

"No, why should it? There is usually blood when people are killed. There was, oh! so much blood everywhere!"

Poirot said:

"Did anyone say anything?"

Pilar said:

"David said such a funny thing—what was it? Oh, yes. The mills of God—that is what he said"—she repeated it with emphasis on each word —"the—mills—of—God—What does that mean? Mills are what make flour, are they not?"

Colonel Johnson said:

"Well, I don't think there is anything more just now, Miss Estravados."

Pilar got up obediently. She flashed a quick, charming smile at each man in turn.

"I will go now then."

She went out.

Colonel Johnson said:

"The mills of God grind slowly, yet they grind exceeding small. And David Lee said that!"

XV

As the door opened once more, Colonel Johnson looked up. For a moment he took the entering figure to be that of Harry Lee, but as Stephen Farr advanced into the room he saw his error.

"Sit down, Mr. Farr," he said.

Stephen sat. His eyes, cool, intelligent eyes, went from one to the other of the three men. He said:

"I'm afraid I sha'n't be of much use to you. But please ask me anything that you think may help. Perhaps I'd better explain to start with exactly who I am. My father, Ebenezer Farr, was Simeon Lee's partner in South Africa in the old days. I'm talking of over forty years ago."

He paused.

"My dad talked to me a lot about Simeon Lee—what a personality he was. He and Dad cleaned up a good bit together. Simeon Lee went home with a fortune and my father didn't do badly either. My father always told me that when I came to this country I was to look up Mr. Lee. I said once that it was a long time ago and that he'd probably not know who I was, but Dad scoffed at the idea. He said, 'When two men have been through what Simeon and I went through, they don't forget.' Well, my father died a couple of years ago. This year I came over to England for the first time, and I thought I'd act on Dad's advice and look up Mr. Lee."

With a slight smile he went on:

"I was just a little nervous when I came along here, but I needn't have been. Mr. Lee gave me a warm welcome and absolutely insisted that I should stay with the family over Christmas. I was afraid I was butting in, but he wouldn't hear of a refusal."

He added rather shyly:

"They were all very nice to me—Mr. and Mrs. Alfred Lee couldn't have been nicer. I'm terribly sorry for them that all this should come upon them."

"How long have you been here, Mr. Farr?"

"Since yesterday."

"Did you see Mr. Lee to-day at all?"

"Yes, I had a chat with him this morning. He was in good spirits then and anxious to hear about a lot of people and places."

"That was the last time you saw him?"

"Yes."

"Did he mention to you that he kept a quantity of uncut diamonds in his safe?"

"No."

He added before the other could speak:

"Do you mean that this business was murder and robbery?"

"We're not sure yet," said Johnson. "Now to come to the events of this evening, will you tell me in your own words what you were doing?"

"Certainly. After the ladies left the dining-room I stayed and had a glass of port. Then I realized that the Lees had family business they wanted to discuss and that my being there was hampering them, so I excused myself and left them."

"And what did you do then?"

Stephen Farr leaned back in his chair. His forefinger caressed his jaw. He said rather woodenly:

"I—er—went along to a big room with parquet floor—kind of ball-room, I fancy. There's a gramophone there and dance records. I put some records on."

Poirot said:

"It was possible, perhaps, that someone might join you there?"

A very faint smile curved Stephen Farr's lips. He answered:

"It was possible, yes. One always hopes."

And he grinned outright.

Poirot said:

"Señorita Estravados is very beautiful."

Stephen answered:

"She's easily the best thing to look at that I've seen since I came to England."

"Did Miss Estravados join you?" asked Colonel Johnson.

Stephen shook his head.

"I was still there when I heard the rumpus. I came out into the hall and ran hell for leather to see what was the matter. I helped Harry Lee to break the door down."

"And that's all you have to tell us?"

"Absolutely all, I'm afraid."

Hercule Poirot leaned forward. He said softly:

"But I think, Monsieur Farr, that you could tell us a good deal if you liked."

Farr said sharply:

"What d'you mean?"

"You can tell us of something that is very important in this case—the character of Mr. Lee. You say that your father talked much of him to you. What manner of a man was it that he described to you?"

Stephen Farr said slowly:

"I think I see what you're driving at. What was Simeon Lee like in his young days? Well—you want me to be frank, I suppose?"

"If you please."

"Well, to begin with, I don't think that Simeon Lee was a highly moral member of society. I don't mean that he was exactly a crook, but he sailed pretty near the wind. His morals were nothing to boast about anyway. He had charm, though, a good deal of it. And he was fantastically generous. No one with a hard luck story ever appealed to him in vain. He drank a bit, but not overmuch; was attractive to women and had a sense of humour. All the same, he had a queer revengeful streak in him. Talk of the elephant never forgets and you talk of Simeon Lee. My father told me of several cases where Lee waited years to get even with someone who'd done him a nasty turn."

Superintendent Sugden said:

"Two might play at that game. You've no knowledge, I suppose, Mr. Farr, of anyone Simeon Lee had done a bad turn to out there? Nothing out of the past that could explain the crime committed here this evening?"

Stephen Farr shook his head.

"He had enemies, of course, must have had, being the man he was. But I know of no specific case. Besides," his eyes narrowed, "I understand (as a matter of fact I've been questioning Tressilian) there have been no strangers in or near the house this evening."

Hercule Poirot said:

"With the exception of yourself, M. Farr."

Stephen Farr swung round upon him.

"Oh, so that's it? Suspicious stranger within the gates! Well, you won't find anything of that kind. No back history of Simeon Lee doing Ebenezer

Farr down, and Eb's son coming over to revenge his dad! No," he shook his head, "Simeon and Ebenezer had nothing against each other. I came here, as I've told you, out of sheer curiosity. And moreover, I should imagine a gramophone is as good an alibi as anything else. I never stopped putting on records—somebody must have heard them. One record wouldn't give me time to race away upstairs—these passages are a mile long, anyway—slit an old man's throat, wash off the blood and get back again before the others came rushing up. The idea's farcical!"

Colonel Johnson said:

"We're not making any insinuations against you, Mr. Farr."

Stephen Farr said:

"I didn't care much for the tone of Mr. Hercule Poirot's voice."

"That," said Hercule Poirot, "is unfortunate!"

He smiled benignly at the other.

Stephen Farr looked angrily at him.

Colonel Johnson interposed quickly:

"Thank you, Mr. Farr. That will be all for the present. You will, of course, not leave this house."

Stephen Farr nodded. He got up and left the room, walking with a freely swinging stride.

As the door closed behind him, Johnson said:

"There goes X, the unknown quantity. His story seems straightforward enough. All the same, he's the dark horse. He *might* have pinched those diamonds—might have come here with a bogus story just to gain admittance. You'd better get his fingerprints, Sugden, and see if he's known."

"I've already got them," said the Superintendent with a dry smile.

"Good man. You don't overlook much. I suppose you're on to all the obvious lines?"

Superintendent Sugden checked off on his fingers:

"Check up on those telephone calls—times, etc. Check up on Horbury. What time he left, who saw him go. Check up all entrances and exits. Check up on staff generally. Check up financial position of members of family. Get on to the lawyers and check up on will. Search house for the weapon and for bloodstains on clothing—also, possibly diamonds hidden somewhere."

"That covers everything, I think," said Colonel Johnson approvingly. "Can you suggest anything, M. Poirot?"

Poirot shook his head. He said:

"I find the Superintendent admirably thorough."

Sugden said gloomily:

"It won't be any joke looking through this house for the missing diamonds. Never saw so many ornaments and knick-knacks in my life."

"The hiding places are certainly abundant," Poirot agreed.

"And there's really nothing you would suggest, Poirot?"

The Chief Constable looked a little disappointed—rather like a man whose dog has refused to do its trick.

Poirot said:

"You will permit that I take a line of my own?"

"Certainly—certainly," said Johnson at the same moment as Superintendent Sugden said rather suspiciously:

"What line?"

"I would like," said Hercule Poirot, "to converse—very often—very frequently—with members of the family."

"You mean you'd like to have another shot at questioning them?" asked the Colonel, a little puzzled.

"No, no, not to question—to converse!"

"Why?" asked Sugden.

Hercule Poirot waved an emphatic hand.

"In conversation, points arise! If a human being converses much, it is impossible for him to avoid the truth!"

Sugden said:

"Then you think someone is lying?"

Poirot sighed.

"*Mon cher,* everyone lies—in parts like the egg of the English curate. It is profitable to separate the harmless lies from the vital ones."

Colonel Johnson said sharply:

"All the same, it's incredible, you know. Here's a particularly crude and brutal murder—and whom have we as suspects? Alfred Lee and his wife—both charming, well-bred, quiet people. George Lee, who's a member of parliament and the essence of respectability. His wife? She's just an ordinary modern lovely. David Lee seems a gentle creature and we've got his brother Harry's word for it that he can't stand the sight of blood. His wife seems a nice, sensible woman—quite commonplace. Remains the Spanish niece and the man from South Africa. Spanish beauties have hot tempers, but I don't see that attractive creature slitting the old man's neck in cold blood, especially as from what has come out she had every reason to keep him alive—at any rate until he had signed a new will. Stephen Farr's a possibility—that is to say, he may be a professional crook and have come here after the diamonds. The old man discovered the loss and Farr slit his throat to keep him quiet. That could have been so—that gramophone alibi isn't too good."

Poirot shook his head.

"My dear friend," he said. "Compare the physique of M. Stephen Farr and old Simeon Lee. If Farr decided to kill the old man he could have done it in a minute—Simeon Lee couldn't possibly have put up that fight against him. Can one believe that that frail old man and that magnificent specimen of humanity struggled for some minutes overturning chairs and breaking china? To imagine such a thing is fantastic!"

Colonel Johnson's eyes narrowed.

"You mean," he said, "that it was a *weak* man who killed Simeon Lee?"

"Or a woman!" said the Superintendent.

XVI

Colonel Johnson looked at his watch.

"Nothing much more that I can do here. You've got things well in hand, Sugden. Oh, just one thing. We ought to see the butler fellow. I know you've questioned him, but we know a bit more about things now. It's important to get confirmation of just where everybody says he was at the time of the murder."

Tressilian came in slowly. The Chief Constable told him to sit down.

"Thank you, sir. I will, if you don't mind. I've been feeling very queer—very queer indeed. My legs, sir, and my head."

Poirot said gently:

"You have had the shock, yes."

The butler shuddered.

"Such—such a violent thing to happen. In this house! Where everything has always gone on so quietly."

Poirot said:

"It was a well-ordered house, yes? But not a happy one?"

"I wouldn't like to say that, sir."

"In the old days when all the family was at home, was it happy then?"

Tressilian said slowly:

"It wasn't, perhaps, what one would call very harmonious, sir."

"The late Mrs. Lee was somewhat of an invalid, was she not?"

"Yes, sir, very poorly she was."

"Were her children fond of her?"

"Mr. David, he was devoted to her. More like a daughter than a son. And after she died, he broke away, couldn't face living here any longer."

Poirot said:

"And Mr. Harry? What was he like?"

"Always rather a wild young gentleman, sir, but good-hearted. Oh, dear, gave me quite a turn it did, when the bell rang—and then again, so impatient like, and I opened the door and there was a strange man and then Mr. Harry's voice said: 'Hullo, Tressilian. Still here, eh? Just the same as ever.' "

Poirot said sympathetically:

"It must have been the strange feeling, yes, indeed."

Tressilian said, a little pink flush showing in his cheek:

"It seems sometimes, sir, as though the past isn't the past! I believe there's been a play on in London about something like that. There's something in it, sir—there really is. There's a feeling comes over you—as though you'd done everything before. It just seems to me as though the bell rings and I go to answer it and there's Mr. Harry—even if it should be Mr. Farr or some other person—I'm just saying to myself—*but I've done this before. . . ."*

Poirot said:

"That is very interesting—very interesting."

Tressilian looked at him gratefully.

Johnson, somewhat impatient, cleared his throat and took charge of the conversation.

"Just want to get various times checked correctly," he said. "Now when the noise upstairs started I understand that only Mr. Alfred Lee and Mr. Harry Lee were in the dining-room. Is that so?"

"I really couldn't tell you, sir. All the gentlemen were there when I served coffee to them—but that would be about a quarter of an hour earlier."

"Mr. George Lee was telephoning. Can you confirm that?"

"I think somebody did telephone, sir. The bell rings in my pantry, and when anybody takes off the receiver to call a number, there's just a faint noise on the bell. I do remember hearing that, but I didn't pay any attention to it."

"You don't know exactly when it was?"

"I couldn't say, sir. It was after I had taken coffee to the gentlemen, that is all I can say."

"Do you know where any of the ladies were at the time I mentioned?"

"Mrs. Alfred was in the drawing-room, sir, when I went for the coffee tray. That was just a minute or two before I heard the cry upstairs."

Poirot asked:

"What was she doing?"

"She was standing by the far window, sir. She was holding the curtain a little back and looking out."

"And none of the other ladies was in the room?"

"No, sir."

"Do you know where they were?"

"I couldn't say at all, sir."

"You don't know where anyone else was?"

"Mr. David, I think, was playing in the music room next to the drawing-room."

"You heard him playing?"

"Yes, sir." Again the old man shivered. "It was like a sign, sir, so I felt afterwards. It was the *Dead March* he was playing. Even at the time, I remember, it gave me the creeps."

"It is curious, yes," said Poirot.

"Now about this fellow, Horbury, the valet," said the Chief Constable. "Are you definitely prepared to swear that he was out of the house by eight o'clock?"

"Oh, yes, sir. It was just after Mr. Sugden arrived. I remember particular because he broke a coffee cup."

Poirot said:

"Horbury broke a coffee cup?"

"Yes, sir—one of the old Worcester ones. Eleven years I've washed them up and never one broken till this evening."

Poirot said:

"What was Horbury doing with the coffee cups?"

"Well, of course, sir, he'd no business to have been handling them at all. He was just holding one up, admiring it like, and I happened to mention that Mr. Sugden had called and he dropped it."

Poirot said:

"Did you say 'Mr. Sugden' or did you mention the word police?"

Tressilian looked a little startled.

"Now I come to think of it, sir, I mentioned that the Police Superintendent had called."

"And Horbury dropped the coffee cup?" said Poirot.

"Seems suggestive, that," said the Chief Constable. "Did Horbury ask any questions about the Superintendent's visit?"

"Yes, sir, asked what he wanted here. I said he'd come collecting for the Police Orphanage and had gone up to Mr. Lee."

"Did Horbury seem relieved when you said that?"

"Do you know, sir, now you mention it, he certainly did. His manner changed at once. Said Mr. Lee was a good old chap and free with his money—rather disrespectfully he spoke—and then he went off."

"Which way?"

"Out through the door to the servants' hall."

Sugden interposed:

"All that's O.K., sir. He passed through the kitchen where the cook and the kitchenmaid saw him, and out through the back door."

"Now listen, Tressilian, and think carefully. Is there any means by which Horbury could return to the house without anyone seeing him?"

The old man shook his head.

"I don't see how he could have done so, sir. All the doors are locked on the inside."

"Supposing he had had a key?"

"The doors are bolted as well."

"How does he get in when he comes?"

"He has a key to the back door, sir. All the servants come in that way."

"He *could* have returned that way, then?"

"Not without passing through the kitchen, sir. And the kitchen would be occupied till well after half-past nine or a quarter to ten."

Colonel Johnson said:

"That seems conclusive. Thank you, Tressilian."

The old man got up and with a bow left the room. He returned, however, a minute or two later.

"Horbury has just returned, sir. Would you like to see him now?"

"Yes, please, send him in at once."

XVII

Sydney Horbury did not present a very prepossessing appearance. He came into the room and stood rubbing his hands together, and darting quick looks from one person to another. His manner was unctuous.

Johnson said:

"You're Sydney Horbury?"

"Yes, sir."

"Valet attendant to the late Mr. Lee?"

"Yes, sir. It's terrible, sir, isn't it? You could have knocked me down with a feather when I heard from Gladys. Poor old gentleman—"

Johnson cut him short.

"Just answer my questions, please."

"Yes, sir, certainly, sir."

"What time did you go out to-night, and where have you been?"

"I left the house just before eight, sir. I went to the 'Superb,' sir, just five minutes' walk away. *Love in Old Seville* was the picture, sir."

"Anyone who saw you there?"

"The young lady in the box office, sir, she knows me. And the Commissionaire at the door. He knows me, too. And—er—as a matter of fact I was with a young lady, sir. I met her there by appointment."

"Oh, you did, did you? What's her name?"

"Doris Buckle, sir. She works in the Combined Dairies, sir, 23 Markham Road."

"Good, we'll look into that. Did you come straight home?"

"I saw my young lady home first, sir. Then I came straight back. You'll find it's quite all right, sir. I didn't have anything to do with this. I was—"

Colonel Johnson said curtly:

"Nobody's accusing you of having anything to do with it."

"No, sir, of course not, sir. But it's not very pleasant when a murder happens in a house."

"Nobody said it was. Now then, how long had you been in Mr. Lee's service?"

"Just over a year, sir."

"Did you like your place here?"

"Yes, sir. I was quite satisfied. The pay was good. Mr. Lee was rather difficult sometimes, but of course I'm used to attending on invalids."

"You've had previous experience?"

"Oh, yes, sir. I was with Major West and with the Honourable Jasper Finch—"

"You can give all these particulars to Sugden later. What I want to know is this—at what time did you last see Mr. Lee this evening?"

"It was about half-past seven, sir. Mr. Lee had a light supper brought to him every evening at seven o'clock. I then prepared him for bed. After that he would sit in front of the fire in his dressing-gown till he felt like going to bed."

"What time was that, usually?"

"It varied, sir. Sometimes he would go to bed as early as eight o'clock—that is, if he felt tired. Sometimes he would sit up till eleven or after."

"What did he do when he did want to go to bed?"

"Usually he rang for me, sir."

"And you assisted him to bed?"

"Yes, sir."

"But this was your evening out—did you always have Friday?"

"Yes, sir, Friday was my regular day."

"What happened then when Mr. Lee wanted to go to bed?"

"He would ring his bell and either Tressilian or Walter would see to him."

"He was not helpless? He could move about?"

"Yes, sir, but not very easily. Rheumatoid arthritis was what he suffered from, sir. He was worse some days than others."

"Did he never go into another room in the daytime?"

"No, sir. He preferred to be in just the one room. Mr. Lee wasn't luxurious in his tastes. It was a big room with plenty of air and light in it."

"Mr. Lee had his supper at seven, you say?"

"Yes, sir. I took the tray away and put out the sherry and two glasses on the bureau."

"Why did you do that?"

"Mr. Lee's orders."

"Was that usual?"

"Sometimes. It was the rule that none of the family came to see Mr. Lee in the evening unless he invited them. Some evenings he liked to be alone. Other evenings he'd send down and ask Mr. Alfred, or Mrs. Alfred, or both of them to come up after dinner."

"But as far as you know he had not done so on this occasion? That is, he had not sent a message to any member of the family requesting their presence?"

"He hadn't sent any message by *me*, sir."

"So that he wasn't expecting any of the family?"

"He might have asked one of them personally, sir."

"Of course."

Horbury continued:

"I saw that everything was in order, wished Mr. Lee good-night and left the room."

Poirot asked:

"Did you make up the fire before you left the room?"

The valet hesitated.

"It wasn't necessary, sir. It was well built up."

"Could Mr. Lee have done that himself?"

"Oh, no, sir. I expect Mr. Harry Lee had done it."

"Mr. Harry Lee was with him when you came in before supper?"

"Yes, sir. He went away when I came."

"What was the relationship between the two as far as you could judge?"

"Mr. Harry Lee seemed in very good spirits, sir. Throwing back his head and laughing a good deal."

"And Mr. Lee?"

"He was quiet, and rather thoughtful."

"I see. Now there's something more I want to know, Horbury. What can you tell us about the diamonds Mr. Lee kept in his safe?"

"Diamonds, sir? I never saw any diamonds."

"Mr. Lee kept a quantity of uncut stones there. You must have seen him handling them."

"Those funny little pebbles, sir? Yes, I did see him with them once or twice. But I didn't know they were diamonds. He was showing them to the foreign young lady only yesterday—or was it the day before?"

Colonel Johnson said abruptly:

"Those stones have been stolen."

Horbury cried out:

"I hope you don't think, sir, that *I* had anything to do with it!"

"I'm not making any accusations," said Johnson. "Now then, is there anything you can tell us that has any bearing on this matter?"

"The diamonds, sir? Or the murder?"

"Both."

Horbury considered. He passed his tongue over his pale lips. At last he looked up with eyes that were a shade furtive.

"I don't think there's anything, sir."

Poirot said softly:

"Nothing you've overheard, say, in the course of your duties, which might be helpful."

The valet's eyelids flickered a little.

"No, sir, I don't think so, sir. There was a little awkwardness between Mr. Lee—and some members of his family."

"Which members?"

"I gathered there was a little trouble over Mr. Harry Lee's return. Mr. Alfred Lee resented it. I understand he and his father had a few words about it—but that was all there was to it. Mr. Lee didn't accuse him for a minute of having taken any diamonds. And I'm sure Mr. Alfred wouldn't do such a thing."

Poirot said quickly:

"His interview with Mr. Alfred was *after* he had discovered the loss of the diamonds, was it not, though?"

"Yes, sir."

Poirot leaned forward.

"I thought, Horbury," he said softly, *"that you did not know of the theft of the diamonds until we informed you of it just now?* How then, do you know that Mr. Lee had discovered his loss *before* he had this conversation with his son?"

Horbury turned brick red.

"No use lying. Out with it," said Sugden. "When did you know?"

Horbury said sullenly:

"I heard him telephoning to someone about it."

"You weren't in the room?"

"No, outside the door. Couldn't hear much—only a word or two."

"What did you hear exactly?" asked Poirot sweetly.

"I heard the words robbery and diamonds and I heard him say, 'I don't know who to suspect'—and I heard him say something about this evening at eight o'clock."

Superintendent Sugden nodded.

"That was to me he was speaking, my lad. About ten after five, was it?"

"That's right, sir."

"And when you went into his room afterwards, did he look upset?"

"Just a bit, sir. Seemed absent-minded and worried."

"So much so that you got the wind up—eh?"

"Look here, Mr. Sugden, I won't have you saying things like that. Never touched any diamonds, I didn't, and you can't prove I did. I'm not a thief."

Superintendent Sugden, unimpressed, said:

"That remains to be seen." He glanced questioningly at the Chief Constable, received a nod and went on: "That'll do for you, my lad. Sha'n't want you again to-night."

Horbury went out gratefully in haste.

Sugden said appreciatively:

"Pretty bit of work, M. Poirot. You trapped him as neatly as I've ever seen it done. He may be a thief or he may not, but he's certainly a first class liar!"

"An unprepossessing person," said Poirot.

"Nasty bit of goods," agreed Johnson. "Question is, what do we think of his evidence?"

Sugden summarized the position neatly.

"Seems to me there are three possibilities: No. 1: Horbury's a thief *and* a murderer. No. 2: Horbury's a thief but *not* a murderer. No. 3: Horbury's an innocent man. Certain amount of evidence for No. 1. He overheard telephone call and knew the theft had been discovered. Gathered from old man's manner that he was suspected. Made his plans accordingly. Went out ostentatiously at eight o'clock and cooked up an alibi. Easy enough to slip out of a theater and return there unnoticed. He'd have to be pretty sure of the girl, though, that she wouldn't give him away. I'll see what I can get out of her to-morrow."

"How, then, did he manage to reenter the house?" asked Poirot.

"That's more difficult," Sugden admitted. "But there might be ways. Say one of the women servants unlocked a side door for him."

Poirot raised his eyebrows quizzically.

"He places then his life at the mercy of two women? With *one* woman it would be taking a big risk—with *two*, *eh bien*—I find the risk fantastic!"

Sugden said:

"Some criminals think they can get away with anything!"

He went on:

"Let's take No. 2: Horbury pinched those diamonds. He took 'em out of the house to-night and has possibly passed them on to some accomplice. That's quite easy going and highly probable. Now we've got to admit that somebody else chose this night to murder Mr. Lee. That somebody being quite unaware of the diamond complication. It's possible, of course, but it's a bit of a coincidence.

"Possibility No. 3: Horbury's innocent. Somebody else both took the diamonds and murdered the old gentleman. There it is; it's up to us to get at the truth."

Colonel Johnson yawned. He looked again at his watch and got up.

"Well," he said, "I think we'll call it a night, eh? Better just have a look in the safe before we go. Odd thing if those wretched diamonds were there all the time."

But the diamonds were not in the safe. They found the combination where Alfred Lee had told them, in the small notebook taken from the dressing-gown pocket of the dead man. In the safe they found an empty chamois leather bag. Among the papers the safe contained, only one was of interest.

It was a will dated some fifteen years previously. After various legacies and bequests, the provisions were simple enough. Half Simeon Lee's fortune went to Alfred Lee. The other half was to be divided in equal shares among his remaining children—Harry, George, David and Jennifer.

PART IV

DECEMBER 25TH

I

IN THE BRIGHT sun of Christmas noon, Poirot walked in the gardens of Gorston Hall. The Hall itself was a large solidly built house with no special architectural pretensions.

Here on the south side was a broad terrace flanked with a hedge of clipped yew. Little plants grew in the interstices of the stone flags and at intervals along the terrace there were stone sinks arranged as miniature gardens.

Poirot surveyed them with benign approval. He murmured to himself:

"C'est bien imaginé, ça!"

In the distance he caught sight of two figures going towards an ornamental sheet of water some three hundred yards away. Pilar was easily recognizable as one of the figures and he thought at first the other was Stephen Farr, then he saw that the man with Pilar was Harry Lee. Harry seemed very attentive to his attractive niece. At intervals he flung his head back and laughed, then bent once more attentively towards her.

"Assuredly, there is one who does not mourn," Poirot murmured to himself.

A soft sound behind him made him turn. Magdalene Lee was standing there. She, too, was looking at the retreating figures of the man and girl. She turned her head and smiled enchantingly at Poirot.

She said:

"It's such a glorious sunny day! One can hardly believe in all the horrors of last night, can one, M. Poirot?"

"It is difficult, truly, madam."

Magdalene sighed.

"I've never been mixed up in tragedy before. I've—I've really only just grown up. I stayed a child too long, I think. . . . That's not a good thing to do."

Again she sighed. She said:

"Pilar, now, seems so extraordinarily self-possessed. . . . I suppose it's the Spanish blood? It's all very odd, isn't it?"

"What is odd, madam?"

"The way she turned up here, out of the blue!"

Poirot said:

"I have learned that Mr. Lee had been searching for her for some time. He had been in correspondence with the Consulate in Madrid and with the Vice-Consul at Aliquara where her mother died."

"He was very secretive about it all," said Magdalene. "Alfred knew nothing about it. No more did Lydia."

"Ah!" said Poirot.

Magdalene came a little nearer to him. He could smell the delicate perfume she used.

"You know, M. Poirot, there's some story connected with Jennifer's husband, Estravados. He died quite soon after the marriage and there's some mystery about it. Alfred and Lydia know. I believe it was something —rather disgraceful. . . ."

"That," said Poirot, "is sad indeed."

Magdalene said:

"My husband feels—and I agree with him—that the family ought to have been told more about the girl's antecedents. After all, if her father was a *criminal*—"

She paused, but Hercule Poirot said nothing. He seemed to be admiring such beauties of nature as could be seen in the winter season in the grounds of Gorston Hall.

Magdalene said:

"I can't help feeling that the manner of my father-in-law's death was somehow *significant.* It—it was so very *un-English."*

Hercule Poirot turned slowly. His grave eyes met hers in innocent inquiry.

"Ah," he said. "The Spanish touch, you think?"

"Well, they *are* cruel, aren't they?" Magdalene spoke with an effect of childish appeal. "All those bull fights and things!"

Hercule Poirot said pleasantly:

"You are saying that in your opinion Señorita Estravados cut her grandfather's throat?"

"Oh! no, M. Poirot!" Magdalene was vehement. She was shocked. "I never said anything of the kind! Indeed I didn't!"

"Well," said Poirot. "Perhaps you did not."

"But I *do* think that she is—well, a suspicious person. The furtive way she picked up something from the floor of that room last night, for instance."

A different note crept into Hercule Poirot's voice. He said sharply:

"She picked up something from the floor last night?"

Magdalene nodded. Her childish mouth curved spitefully.

"Yes, as soon as we got into the room. She gave a quick glance round to see if anyone was looking and then pounced on it. But the Superintendent man saw her, I'm glad to say, and made her give it up."

"What was it that she picked up? Do you know, madam?"

"No. I wasn't near enough to see." Magdalene's voice held regret. "It was something quite small."

Poirot frowned to himself.

"It is interesting, that," he murmured to himself.

Magdalene said quickly:

"Yes, I thought you ought to know about it. After all, we don't know *anything* about Pilar's upbringing and what her life has been like. Alfred is always so unsuspicious and dear Lydia is so casual." Then she murmured: "Perhaps I'd better go and see if I can help Lydia in any way. There may be letters to write."

She left him with a smile of satisfied malice on her lips.

Poirot remained on the terrace, lost in thought.

II

To him there came Superintendent Sugden. The Police Superintendent looked gloomy. He said:

"Good-morning, Mr. Poirot. Doesn't seem quite the right thing to say Merry Christmas, does it?"

"*Mon cher collègue,* I certainly do not observe any traces of merriment on your countenance. If you had said, 'Merry Christmas,' I should not have replied, 'Many of them!'"

"I don't want another one like this one and that's a fact," said Sugden.

"You have made the progress, yes?"

"I've checked up on a good many points. Horbury's alibi is holding water all right. The Commissionaire at the movie theater saw him go in with the girl, and saw him come out with her at the end of the performance, and seems pretty positive he didn't leave and couldn't have left and returned during the performance. The girl swears quite definitely he was with her in the theater all the time."

Poirot's eyebrows rose.

"I hardly see, then, what more there is to say?"

The cynical Sugden said:

"Well, one never knows with girls! Lie themselves black in the face for the sake of a man."

"That does credit to their hearts," said Hercule Poirot.

Sugden growled:

"That's a foreign way of looking at it. It's defeating the ends of justice."

Hercule Poirot said:

"Justice is a very strange thing. Have you ever reflected on it?"

Sugden stared at him. He said:

"You're a queer one, Mr. Poirot."

"Not at all. I follow a logical train of thought. But we will not enter into a dispute on the question. It is your belief, then, that this demoiselle from the milk shop is not speaking the truth?"

Sugden shook his head.

"No," he said. "It's not like that at all. As a matter of fact I think she *is* telling the truth. She's a simple kind of girl and I think if she was telling me a pack of lies, I'd spot it."

Poirot said:

"You have the experience, yes."

"That's just it, Mr. Poirot. One does know, more or less, after a lifetime of taking down statements when a person's lying and when they're not. No, I think the girl's evidence is genuine, and if so Horbury *couldn't* have murdered old Mr. Lee, and that brings us right back to the people in the house."

He drew a deep breath.

"One of 'em did it, Mr. Poirot. One of 'em did it. But *which?*"

"You have no new data?"

"Yes, I've had a certain amount of luck over the telephone calls. Mr. George Lee put through a call to Westeringham at two minutes to nine. That call lasted under six minutes."

"Aha!"

"As you say! Moreover *no other call* was put through—to Westeringham or anywhere else."

"Very interesting," said Poirot, with approval. "M. George Lee says he has just finished telephoning when he hears the noise overhead—but actually he had finished telephoning nearly *ten minutes before that.* Where was he in those ten minutes? Mrs. George Lee says that *she* was telephoning—but actually she never put through a call at all. Where was *she?*"

Sugden said:

"I saw you talking to her, M. Poirot?"

His voice held a question, but Poirot replied:

"You are in error!"

"Eh?"

"I was not talking to *her*—she was talking to *me!"*

"Oh—" Sugden seemed to be about to brush the distinction aside impatiently; then, as its significance sank in, he said:

"She was talking to *you,* you say?"

"Most definitely. She came out here for that purpose."

"What did she have to say?"

"She wished to stress certain points—the un-English character of the crime—the possibly undesirable antecedents of Miss Estravados on the paternal side—the fact that Miss Estravados had furtively picked up something from the floor last night."

"She told you that, did she?" said Sugden with interest.

"Yes. What was it that the señorita picked up?"

Sugden sighed.

"I could give you three hundred guesses! I'll show it to you. It's the sort of thing that solves the whole mystery in detective stories! If you can make anything out of it, I'll retire from the police force!"

"Show it to me."

Sugden took an envelope from his pocket and tilted its contents onto the palm of his hand. A faint grin showed on his face.

"There you are. What do you make of it?"

On the Superintendent's broad palm lay a little triangular piece of pink rubber and a small wooden peg.

His grin broadened, as Poirot picked up the articles and frowned over them.

"Make anything of them, Mr. Poirot?"

"This little piece of stuff might have been cut from a sponge bag?"

"It was. It comes from a sponge bag in Mr. Lee's room. Somebody with sharp scissors just cut a small triangular piece out of it. Mr. Lee may have done it himself for all I know. But it beats me *why* he should do it. Horbury can't throw any light on the matter. As for the peg, it's about the size of a cribbage peg, but they're usually made of ivory. This is just rough wood—whittled out of a bit of deal, I should say."

"Most remarkable," murmured Poirot.

"Keep 'em if you like," said Sugden kindly. *"I* don't want them."

"Mon ami, I would not deprive you of them!"

"They don't mean anything at all to you?"

"I must confess—nothing whatever!"

"Splendid!" said Sugden with heavy sarcasm, returning them to his pocket. "We *are* getting on!"

Poirot said:

"Mrs. George Lee, she recounts that the young lady stooped and picked these bagatelles up in a furtive manner. Should you say that that was true?"

Sugden considered the point.

"N-o," he said hesitatingly. "I shouldn't quite go as far as that. She didn't look guilty—nothing of that kind—but she did set about it rather—well—quickly and quietly—if you know what I mean. *And she didn't know I'd seen her do it!* That I'm sure of—she jumped when I rounded on her."

Poirot said thoughtfully:

"Then there *was* a reason—but what conceivable reason could there have been? That little piece of rubber is quite fresh—it has not been used for anything—it can have no meaning whatsoever and yet—"

Sugden said impatiently:

"Well, you can worry about it if you like, Mr. Poirot. I've got other things to think about."

Poirot asked:

"The case stands—where, in your opinion?"

Sugden took out his notebook.

"Let's get down to *facts*. To begin with there are the people who *couldn't* have done it. Let's get them out of the way first—"

"They are?"

"Alfred and Harry Lee. They've got a definite alibi. Also Mrs. Alfred Lee, since Tressilian saw her in the drawing-room only about a minute before the row started upstairs. Those three are clear. Now for the others. Here's a list. I've put it this way for clearness."

He handed the book to Poirot.

At the time of the crime

George Lee	was	?
Mrs. George Lee	was	?
David Lee	was	playing piano in music room (confirmed by his wife)
Mrs. David Lee	was	in music room (confirmed by husband)
Miss Estravados	was	in her bedroom (no confirmation)
Stephen Farr	was	in ballroom playing gramophone (confirmed by three of staff who could hear the music in servants' hall)

Poirot said, handing back the list:

"And therefore?"

"And therefore," said Sugden, "George Lee could have killed the old man. Mrs. George Lee could have killed him, Pilar Estravados could have killed him and *either Mr. or Mrs. David Lee could have killed him,* but not *both.*"

"You do not, then, accept that alibi?"

Superintendent Sugden shook his head emphatically.

"Not on your life! Husband and wife—devoted to each other! They may be in it together, or if one of them did it, the other is ready to swear to an alibi. I look at it this way. *Someone* was in the music room, playing the piano. It *may* have been David Lee. It probably *was,* since he was an acknowledged musician, but there's nothing to say his wife was there too *except her word and his.* In the same way, it *may* have been Hilda Lee who was playing that piano while David Lee crept upstairs and killed his father! No, it's an absolutely different case from the two brothers in the dining-room. Alfred Lee and Harry Lee don't love each other. Neither of them would perjure himself for the other's sake."

"What about Stephen Farr?"

"He's a possible suspect because that gramophone alibi is a bit thin. On the other hand it's the sort of alibi that's really sounder than a good cast-iron dyed-in-the-wool alibi which ten to one has been faked up before-hand!"

Poirot bowed his head thoughtfully.

"I know what you mean. It is the alibi of a man *who did not know that he would be called upon to provide such a thing.*"

"Exactly! And anyway, somehow, I don't believe a stranger was mixed up in this thing."

Poirot said quickly:

"I agree with you. It is here a *family* affair. It is a poison that works in the blood—it is intimate—it is deep-seated. There is here, I think, *hate* and *knowledge.* . . ."

He waved his hands.

"I do not know—it is difficult!"

Superintendent Sugden had waited respectfully, but without being much impressed. He said:

"Quite so, Mr. Poirot. But we'll get at it, never fear, with elimination and logic. We've got the *possibilities* now—the people with *opportunity.* George Lee, Magdalene Lee, David Lee, Hilda Lee, Pilar Estravados and I'll add Stephen Farr. Now we come to *motive.* Who had a *motive* for putting old Mr. Lee out of the way? There again we can wash out certain people. Miss Estravados, for one. I gather that as the will stands now, she doesn't get anything at all. If Simeon Lee had died before her mother, her mother's share would have come down to her (unless her mother willed it otherwise) but as Jennifer Estravados predeceased Simeon Lee, that particular legacy reverts to the other members of the family. So it was definitely to Miss Estravados' interests to keep the old man alive. He'd taken a fancy to her, it's pretty certain he'd have left her a good slice of money when he made a new will. She had everything to lose and nothing to gain by his murder. You agree to that?"

"Perfectly."

"There remains, of course, the possibility that she cut his throat in the heat of a quarrel but that seems extremely unlikely to me. To begin with, they were on the best of terms, and she hadn't been here long enough to bear him a grudge about anything. It therefore seems highly unlikely that Miss Estravados has anything to do with the crime—except that you might argue that to cut a man's throat is an un-English sort of thing to do, as your friend Mrs. George put it."

"Do not call her *my* friend," said Poirot hastily. "Or I shall speak of *your* friend, Miss Estravados, who finds you such a handsome man!"

He had the pleasure of seeing the Superintendent's official poise upset again. The police officer turned crimson. Poirot looked at him with malicious amusement.

He said, and there was a wistful note in his voice:

"It is true that your moustache is superb. . . . Tell me, do you use for it a special pomade?"

"Pomade? Good Lord, no!"

"What do you use?"

"Use? Nothing at all. It—it just *grows.*"

Poirot sighed.

"You are favoured by nature." He caressed his own well-groomed black moustache, then sighed. "However expensive the preparation," he murmured, "to restore the natural colour does somewhat impoverish the quality of the hair."

Superintendent Sugden, uninterested in hairdressing problems, was continuing in a stolid manner:

"Considering the *motive* for the crime, I should say that we can probably wash out Mr. Stephen Farr. It's just *possible* that there was some hanky-panky between his father and Mr. Lee and the former suffered, but I doubt it. Farr's manner was too easy and assured when he mentioned that subject. He was quite confident—and I don't think he was acting. No, I don't think we'll find anything there."

"I do not think you will," said Poirot.

"And there's one other person with a motive for keeping old Mr. Lee alive. His son Harry. It's true that he benefits under the will, but I don't believe *he was aware of the fact.* Certainly couldn't have been *sure* of it! The general impression seemed to be that Harry had been definitely cut out of his share of the inheritance at the time he cut loose. But now he was on the point of coming back into favour! It was all to his advantage that his father should make a new will. He wouldn't be such a fool as to kill him now. Actually, as we know, he *couldn't* have done it. You see, we're getting on, we're clearing quite a lot of people out of the way."

"How true. Very soon there will be nobody left!"

Sugden grinned.

"We're not going as far as that! We've got George Lee and his wife, and David Lee and Mrs. David. They all benefit by the death, and George Lee, from all I can make out, is grasping about money. Moreover, his father was threatening to cut down supplies. So we've George Lee with motive *and* opportunity!"

"Continue," said Poirot.

"And we've got Mrs. George! As fond of money as a cat is fond of cream, and I'd be prepared to bet she's heavily in debt at the minute! She was jealous of the Spanish girl. She was quick to spot that the other was gaining an ascendency over the old man. She'd heard him say that he was sending for the lawyer. So she struck quickly. You could make out a case."

"Possibly."

"Then there's David Lee and his wife. They inherit under the present will, but I don't believe, somehow, that the money motive would be particularly strong in their case."

"No?"

"No. David Lee seems to be a bit of a dreamer—not a mercenary type. But he's—well, he's *odd*. As I see it, there are three possible motives for this murder. There's the diamond complication, there's the will, and there's—well—just plain *hate.*"

"Ah, you see that, do you?"

Sugden said:

"Naturally. It's been present in my mind all along. *If* David Lee killed his father, I don't think it was for money. And if he was the criminal it might explain the—well, the blood letting!"

Poirot looked at him appreciatively.

"Yes, I wondered when you would take that into consideration. *So much blood*— that is what Mrs. Alfred said. It takes one back to ancient rituals—to blood sacrifice, to the anointing with the blood of the sacrifice. . . ."

Sugden said, frowning:

"You mean whoever did it was mad?"

"*Mon cher*—there are all sorts of deep instincts in man of which he himself is unaware. The craving for blood—the demand for sacrifice!"

Sugden said doubtfully:

"David Lee looks a quiet harmless fellow."

Poirot said:

"You do not understand the psychology. David Lee is a man who lives in the past—a man in whom the memory of his mother is still very much alive. He kept away from his father for many years because he could not forgive his father's treatment of his mother. He came here, let us suppose, to forgive. *But he may not have been able to forgive. . . .* We do know one thing—that when David Lee stood by his father's dead body, some part of him was appeased and satisfied. *The mills of God grind slowly, yet they grind exceeding small.* Retribution! Payment! The wrong wiped out by expiation!"

Sugden gave a sudden shudder. He said:

"Don't talk like that, Mr. Poirot. You give me quite a turn. It may be that it's as you say. If so, Mrs. David knows—and means to shield him all she knows how. I can imagine her doing that. On the other hand I can't imagine her being a murderess. She's such a comfortable commonplace sort of woman."

Poirot looked at him curiously.

"So she strikes you like that?" he murmured.

"Well, yes—a homely body, if you know what I mean!"

"Oh! I know what you mean perfectly!"

Sugden looked at him.

"Come now, Mr. Poirot; you've got ideas about this case, let's have them."

Poirot said slowly:

"I have ideas, yes, but they are rather nebulous. Let me first hear your summing up of the case."

"Well, it's as I said—three possible motives. Hate, gain—and this diamond complication. Take the facts chronologically:

"3:30. Family gathering. Telephone conversation to lawyer overheard by all the family. Then the old man lets loose on his family, tells them where they all get off. They slink out like a lot of scared rabbits."

"Hilda Lee remained behind," said Poirot.

"So she did. But not for long. Then about six Alfred has an interview with his father—unpleasant interview. Harry is to be reinstated. Alfred isn't pleased. Alfred, of course, *ought* to be our principal suspect. He had by far the strongest motive. However, to get on, Harry comes along next. Is in boisterous spirits. Has got the old man just where he wants him. But *before* those two interviews Simeon Lee has discovered the loss of the diamonds and has telephoned to me. He doesn't mention his loss to either of his two sons. Why? In my opinion because he was quite sure neither of them had anything to do with it. Neither of them were under suspicion. I believe, as I've said all along, that the old man suspected Horbury and *one other person*. And I'm pretty sure of what he meant to do. Remember, he said definitely he didn't want anyone to come and sit with him that evening. Why? Because he was preparing the way for two things. First, my visit, and second, *the visit of that other suspected person*. He did ask *someone* to come and see him immediately after dinner. Now who was that person likely to be? Might have been George Lee. Much more likely to have been his wife. And there's another person who comes back into the picture here. Pilar Estravados. He'd shown her the diamonds. He'd told her their value. How do we know that girl isn't a thief? Remember these mysterious hints about the disgraceful behaviour of her father. Perhaps *he* was a professional thief and finally went to prison for it."

Poirot said slowly:

"And so, as you say, Pilar Estravados comes back into the picture. . . ."

"Yes—as a *thief*. No other way. She *may* have lost her head when she was found out. She *may* have flown at her grandfather and attacked him."

Poirot said slowly:

"It is possible—yes. . . ."

Superintendent Sugden looked at him keenly.

"But that's not *your* idea? Come, Mr. Poirot, what *is* your idea?"

Poirot said:

"I go back always to the same thing—*the character of the dead man*. What manner of a man was Simeon Lee?"

"There isn't much mystery about that," said Sugden, staring.

"Tell me then. That is to say, tell me from the local point of view what was known of the man."

Superintendent Sugden drew a doubtful finger along his jawbone. He looked perplexed. He said:

"I'm not a local man myself. I come from Reeveshire, over the border— next county. But of course old Mr. Lee was a well-known figure in these parts. I know all about him by hearsay."

"Yes? And that hearsay was—what?"

Sugden said:

"Well, he was a sharp customer—there weren't many who could get the better of him. But he was generous with his money. Open-handed as they make 'em. Beats me how Mr. George Lee can be the exact opposite and he his father's son."

"Ah! but there are two distinct strains in the family. Alfred, George and

David resemble—superficially at least—their mother's side of the family. I have been looking at some portraits in the gallery this morning."

"He was hot-tempered," continued Superintendent Sugden, "and of course he had a bad reputation with women—that was in his younger days. He's been an invalid for many years now. But even there he always behaved generously. If there was trouble, he always paid up handsomely and got the girl married off as often as not. He may have been a bad lot, but he wasn't mean. He treated his wife badly, ran after other women and neglected her. She died of a broken heart, so they say. It's a convenient term, but I believe she was really very unhappy, poor lady. She was always sickly and never went about much. There's no doubt that Mr. Lee was an odd character. Had a revengeful streak in him, too. If anyone did him a nasty turn he always paid it back, so they say, and didn't mind how long he had to wait to do it."

"The mills of God grind slowly, yet they grind exceeding small," murmured Poirot.

Superintendent Sugden said heavily:

"Mills of the devil, more likely! Nothing saintly about Simeon Lee. The kind of man you might say had sold his soul to the devil and enjoyed the bargain! And he was proud, too, proud as Lucifer."

"Proud as Lucifer!" said Poirot. "It is suggestive, what you say there."

Superintendent Sugden said, looking puzzled:

"You don't mean that he was murdered because he was proud?"

"I mean," said Poirot, "that there is such a thing as inheritance. Simeon Lee transmitted that pride to his sons—"

He broke off. Hilda Lee had come out of the house and was standing looking along the terrace.

<h1 style="text-align:center">III</h1>

Hilda Lee said simply:

"I wanted to find you, Mr. Poirot."

Superintendent Sugden had excused himself and gone back into the house. Looking after him, Hilda said:

"I didn't know he was with you. I thought he was with Pilar. He seems a nice man, quite considerate."

Her voice was pleasant, a low soothing cadence to it.

Poirot asked:

"You wanted to see me, you say?"

She inclined her head.

"Yes. I think you can help me."

"I shall be delighted to do so, madam."

She said:

"You are a very intelligent man, Mr. Poirot. I saw that last night. There are things which you will, I think, find out quite easily. I want you to understand my husband."

"Yes, madam?"

"I shouldn't talk like this to Superintendent Sugden. He wouldn't understand. But you will."

Poirot bowed.

"You honour me, madam."

Hilda went calmly on:

"My husband, for many years, ever since I married him, has been what I can only describe as a mental cripple."

"Ah!"

"When one suffers some great hurt physically, it causes shock and pain, but slowly it mends, the flesh heals, the bone knits. There may be, perhaps, a little weakness, a slight scar, but nothing more. My husband, Mr. Poirot, suffered a great hurt *mentally* at his most susceptible age. He adored his mother and he saw her die. He believed that his father was morally responsible for that death. From that shock he has never quite recovered. His resentment against his father never died down. It was I who persuaded David to come here this Christmas, to be reconciled to his father. I wanted it—for *his* sake—I wanted that mental wound to heal. I realize now that coming here was a mistake. Simeon Lee amused himself by probing into that old wound. It was—a very dangerous thing to do. . . ."

Poirot said:

"Are you telling me, madam, that your husband killed his father?"

"I am telling you, Mr. Poirot, that he easily *might* have done so. . . . And I will also tell you this—that he did *not!* When Simeon Lee was killed, his son David was playing the *Dead March*. The wish to kill was in his heart. It passed out through his fingers and died in waves of sound. . . . That is the truth."

Poirot was silent for a minute or two, then he said:

"And you, madam, what is your verdict on that past drama?"

"You mean the death of Simeon Lee's wife?"

"Yes."

Hilda said slowly:

"I know enough of life to know that you can never judge any case on its outside merits. To all seeming, Simeon Lee was entirely to blame and his wife was abominably treated. At the same time I honestly believe that there is a kind of meekness, a predisposition to martyrdom which does arouse the worst instincts in men of a certain type. Simeon Lee would have admired, I think, spirit and force of character. He was merely irritated by patience and tears."

Poirot nodded. He said:

"Your husband said last night, 'My mother never complained.' Is that true?"

Hilda Lee said impatiently:

"Of course it isn't! She complained the whole time to David! She laid the whole burden of her unhappiness on his shoulders. He was too young —far too young to bear all she gave him to bear!"

Poirot looked thoughtfully at her. She flushed under his gaze and bit her lip.

He said:

"I see."

She said sharply:

"What do you see?"

He answered:

"I see that you have had to be a mother to your husband when you would have preferred to be a wife."

She turned away.

At that moment David Lee came out of the house and along the terrace towards them. He said, and his voice had a clear joyful note in it:

"Hilda, isn't it a glorious day? Almost like spring instead of winter."

He came nearer. His head was thrown back, a lock of fair hair fell across his forehead, his blue eyes shone. He looked amazingly young and boyish. There was about him a youthful eagerness, a carefree radiance. Hercule Poirot caught his breath. . . .

David said:

"Let's go down to the lake, Hilda."

She smiled, put her arm through his and they moved off together.

As Poirot watched them go, he saw her turn and give him a rapid glance. He caught a momentary glimpse of swift anxiety—or was it, he wondered, fear?

Slowly Hercule Poirot walked to the other end of the terrace.

He murmured to himself:

"As I have always said, me, I am the father confessor! And since women come to confession more frequently than men, it is women who have come to me this morning. Will there, I wonder, be another very shortly?"

As he turned at the end of the terrace and paced back again, he knew that his question was answered. Lydia Lee was coming towards him.

IV

Lydia said:

"Good-morning, Mr. Poirot. Tressilian told me I should find you out here with Harry but I am glad to find you alone. My husband has been speaking about you. I know he is very anxious to talk to you."

"Ah! yes? Shall I go and see him now?"

"Not just yet. He got hardly any sleep last night. In the end I gave him a strong sleeping draught. He is still asleep, and I don't want to disturb him."

"I quite understand. That was very wise. I could see last night that the shock had been very great."

She said seriously:

"You see, Mr. Poirot, he really *cared*—much more than the others."

"I understand."

She asked:

"Have you—has the Superintendent—any idea of who can have done this awful thing?"

Poirot said deliberately:

"We have certain ideas, madam, as to who did *not* do it."

Lydia said, almost impatiently:

"It's like a nightmare—so fantastic—I can't believe it's *real!*"

She added:

"What about Horbury? Was he really at the pictures as he said?"

"Yes, madam, his story has been checked. He was speaking the truth."

Lydia stopped and plucked at a bit of yew. Her face went a little paler. She said:

"But that's *awful!* It only leaves—the family!"

"Exactly."

"Mr. Poirot, I *can't* believe it!"

"Madam, you *can* and you *do* believe it!"

She seemed about to protest. Then suddenly she smiled ruefully. She said:

"What a hypocrite one is!"

He nodded.

"If you were to be frank with me, madam," he said, "you would admit that to you it seems quite natural that one of his family should murder your father-in-law!"

Lydia said sharply:

"That's really a fantastic thing to say, Mr. Poirot!"

"Yes, it is. But your father-in-law was a fantastic person!"

Lydia said:

"Poor old man. I can feel sorry for him now. When he was alive, he just annoyed me unspeakably!"

Poirot said:

"So I should imagine!"

He bent over one of the stone sinks.

"They are very ingenious, these. Very pleasing."

"I'm glad you like them. It's one of my hobbies. Do you like this Arctic one with the penguins and the ice?"

"Charming. And this, what is this?"

"Oh, that's the Dead Sea—or going to be. It isn't finished yet. You mustn't look at it. Now this one is supposed to be Piana in Corsica. The rocks there, you know, are quite pink and too lovely where they go down into the blue sea. This desert scene is rather fun, don't you think?"

She led him along. When they had reached the further end she glanced at her wrist-watch.

"I must go and see if Alfred is awake."

When she had gone Poirot went slowly back again to the garden representing the Dead Sea. He looked at it with a good deal of interest. Then he scooped up a few of the pebbles and let them run through his fingers.

Suddenly his face changed. He held up the pebbles close to his face.

"Sapristi!" he said. "This is a surprise! Now what exactly does this mean?"

PART V

I

THE CHIEF CONSTABLE and Superintendent Sugden stared at Poirot incredulously. The latter returned a stream of small pebbles carefully into a small cardboard box and pushed it across to the Chief Constable.

"Oh, yes," he said. "They are the diamonds all right."

"And you found them, where did you say? In the garden?"

"In one of the small gardens constructed by Madam Alfred Lee."

"Mrs. Alfred?" Sugden shook his head. "Doesn't seem likely."

Poirot said:

"You mean, I presume, that you do not consider it likely that Mrs. Alfred cut her father-in-law's throat?"

Sugden said quickly:

"We know she didn't do that. I meant it seemed unlikely that she pinched these diamonds."

Poirot said:

"One would not easily believe her a thief—no."

Sugden said:

"Anybody could have hidden them there."

"That is true. It was convenient that in that particular garden—the Dead Sea as it represents—there happened to be pebbles very similar in shape and appearance."

Sugden said:

"You mean she fixed it like that beforehand? Ready?"

Colonel Johnson said warmly:

"I don't believe it for a moment. Not for a moment. Why should she take the diamonds in the first place?"

"Well, as to that—" Sugden said slowly.

Poirot nipped in quickly:

"There is a possible answer to that. She took the diamonds to suggest a motive for the murder. That is to say she knew that murder was going to be done though she herself took no active part in it."

Johnson frowned.

"That won't hold water for a minute. You're making her out to be an accomplice—but whose accomplice would she be likely to be? Only her husband's. But as we know that he, too, had nothing to do with the murder, the whole theory falls to the ground."

Sugden stroked his jaw reflectively.

"Yes," he said, "that's so. No, if Mrs. Lee took the diamonds—and it's a big if—it was just plain robbery, and it's true she might have prepared that garden specially as a hiding place for them till the hue and cry had died down. Another possibility is that of *coincidence.* That garden, with its similarity of pebbles, struck the thief, whoever he or she was, as an ideal hiding place."

Poirot said:

"That is quite possible. I am always prepared to admit *one* coincidence."

Superintendent Sugden shook his head dubiously.

Poirot said:

"What is your opinion, Superintendent?"

The Superintendent said cautiously:

"Mrs. Lee's a very nice lady. Doesn't seem likely that she'd be mixed up in any business that was fishy. But, of course, one never knows."

Colonel Johnson said testily:

"In any case, whatever the truth is about the diamonds, her being mixed up in the murder is out of the question. The butler saw her in the drawing-room at the actual time of the crime. You remember that, Poirot?"

Poirot said:

"I had not forgotten that."

The Chief Constable turned to his subordinate.

"We'd better get on. What have you got to report? Anything fresh?"

"Yes, sir. I've got hold of some new information. To start with— Horbury. There's a reason why he might be scared of the police."

"Robbery? Eh?"

"No, sir. Extorting money under threats. Modified blackmail. The case couldn't be proved so he got off, but I rather fancy he's got away with a thing or two in that line. Having a guilty conscience he probably thought we were on to something of that kind when Tressilian mentioned a police officer last night and it made him get the wind up."

The Chief Constable said:

"H'm, so much for Horbury! What else?"

The Superintendent coughed:

"Er—Mrs. George Lee, sir. We've got a line on her before her marriage. Was living with a Commander Jones. Passed as his daughter—but she *wasn't* his daughter. . . . I think from what we've been told, that old Mr. Lee summed her up pretty correctly—he was smart where women were concerned, knew a bad lot when he saw one—and was just amusing himself by taking a shot in the dark. *And* he got her on the raw!"

Colonel Johnson said thoughtfully:

"That gives her another possible motive—apart from the money angle. She may have thought he knew something definite and was going to give her away to her husband. That telephone story of hers is pretty fishy. She *didn't* telephone."

Sugden suggested:

"Why not have them in together, sir, and get that telephone business straight? See what we get."

Colonel Johnson said:

"Good idea."

He rang the bell. Tressilian answered it.

"Ask Mr. and Mrs. George Lee to come here."

"Very good, sir."

As the old man turned away Poirot said:

"The date on that wall calendar, has it remained like it is since the murder?"

Tressilian turned back.

"Which calendar, sir?"

"The one on the wall over there."

The three men were sitting once more in Alfred Lee's small sitting-room. The calendar in question was a large one with tear off leaves, a bold date on each leaf.

Tressilian peered across the room, then shuffled slowly across till he was a foot or two away.

He said:

"Excuse me, sir, it has been torn off. It's the twenty-sixth to-day."

"Ah, pardon. Who would have been the person to tear it off?"

"Mr. Lee does, sir, every morning. Mr. Alfred, he's a very methodical gentleman."

"I see. Thank you."

Tressilian went out. Sugden said, puzzled:

"Is there anything fishy about that calendar, Mr. Poirot? Have I missed something there?"

With a shrug of his shoulders, Poirot said:

"The calendar is of no importance. It was just a little experiment I was making."

Colonel Johnson said:

"Inquest to-morrow. There'll be an adjournment, of course."

Sugden said:

"Yes, sir, I've seen the Coroner and it's all arranged for."

II

George Lee came into the room accompanied by his wife.

Colonel Johnson said:

"Good-morning. Sit down, will you? There are a few questions I want to ask you both. Something I'm not quite clear about."

"I shall be glad to give you any assistance I can," said George, somewhat pompously.

Magdalene said faintly:

"Of course!"

The Chief Constable gave a slight nod to Sugden. The latter said:

"About those telephone calls on the night of the crime? You put through a call to Westeringham, I think you said, Mr. Lee?"

George said coldly:

"Yes, I did. To my agent in the constituency. I can refer you to him and—"

Superintendent Sugden held up his hand to stem the flow.

"Quite so—quite so, Mr. Lee. We're not disputing that point. Your call went through at 8:59 exactly."

"Well—I—er—couldn't say as to the exact time."

"Ah," said Sugden. "But we can! We always check up on these things very carefully. Very carefully indeed. The call was put through at 8:59 and it was terminated at 9:04. Your father, Mr. Lee, was killed about 9:15. I must ask you once more for an account of your movements."

"I've told you—I was telephoning!"

"No, Mr. Lee, you weren't."

"Nonsense—you must have made a mistake! Well, I may perhaps have just finished telephoning—I think I debated making another call—was just considering whether it was—er—worth—the expense—when I heard the noise upstairs."

"You would hardly debate whether or not to make a telephone call for ten minutes."

George went purple. He began to splutter.

"What do you mean? What the devil do you mean? Damned impudence! Are you doubting my word? Doubting the word of a man of my position? I—er—why should I have to account for every minute of my time?"

Superintendent Sugden said with a stolidness that Poirot admired:

"It's usual."

George turned angrily on the Chief Constable.

"Colonel Johnson. Do you countenance this—this unprecedented attitude?"

The Chief Constable said crisply:

"In a murder case, Mr. Lee, these questions must be asked—*and answered.*"

"I have answered them! I had finished telephoning and was—er—deliberating a further call."

"You were in this room when the alarm was raised upstairs?"

"I was—yes, I was."

Johnson turned to Magdalene.

"I think, Mrs. Lee," he said, "that you stated that *you* were telephoning when the alarm broke out, and that at the time you were alone in this room?"

Magdalene was flustered. She caught her breath, looked sideways at George—at Sugden, then appealingly at Colonel Johnson. She said:

"Oh, really—I don't know—I don't remember what I said. . . . I was so *upset.* . . ."

Sugden said:

"We've got it all written down, you know."

She turned her batteries on him—wide appealing eyes—quivering mouth. But she met in return the rigid aloofness of a man of stern respectability who didn't approve of her type.

She said uncertainly:

"I—I—of course I telephoned. I can't be quite sure just *when—*"

She stopped.

George said:

"What's all this? Where did you telephone from? Not in here."

Superintendent Sugden said:

"I suggest, Mrs. Lee, that *you didn't telephone at all.* In that case, where were you and what were you doing?"

Magdalene glanced distractedly about her and burst into tears. She sobbed:

"George, don't let them bully me! You know that if anyone frightens me and thunders questions at me, I can't remember anything *at all!* I—I didn't know *what* I was saying that night—it was all so horrible—and I was so upset—and they're being so beastly to me. . . ."

She jumped up and ran sobbing out of the room.

Springing up, George Lee blustered:

"What d'you mean? I won't have my wife bullied and frightened out of her life! She's very sensitive. It's disgraceful! I shall have a question asked in the House about the disgraceful bullying methods of the police. It's absolutely disgraceful!"

He strode out of the room and banged the door.

Superintendent Sugden threw his head back and laughed.

He said:

"We've got them going properly! Now we'll see!"

Johnson said, frowning:

"Extraordinary business! Looks fishy. We must get a further statement out of her."

Sugden said easily:

"Oh! she'll be back in a minute or two. When she's decided what to say. Eh, Mr. Poirot?"

Poirot, who had been sitting in a dream, gave a start.

"Pardon?"

"I said she'll be back."

"Probably—yes, possibly. Oh, yes!"

Sugden said, staring at him:

"What's the matter, Mr. Poirot? Seen a ghost?"

Poirot said slowly:

"You know—I am not sure that I have not done *just exactly that.*"

Colonel Johnson said impatiently:

"Well, Sugden, anything else?"

Sugden said:

"I've been trying to check up on the order in which everyone arrived on the scene of the murder. It's quite clear what must have happened. The murderer slipped out, locked the door with pliers, or something of that kind, and a moment or two later became one of the people hurrying *to* the scene of the crime. Unfortunately it's not easy to check exactly whom everyone has seen because people's memories aren't very accurate on a point like that. Tressilian says he saw Harry and Alfred Lee cross the hall from the dining-room and race upstairs. That lets them out, but we don't suspect them anyway. As far as I can make out Miss Estravados got there late—one of the last. The general idea seems to be that Farr, Mrs. George and Mrs. David were the first. Each of those three says one of the others was just ahead of them. That's what's so difficult, you can't distinguish between a deliberate lie and a genuine haziness of recollection. Everybody ran there—that's agreed—but in what order they ran isn't so easy to get at."

Poirot said slowly:

"You think that important?"

Sugden said:

"It's the time element. The time, remember, was incredibly short."

Poirot said:

"I agree with you that the time element is very important in this case."

Sugden went on:

"What makes it more difficult is that there are two staircases. There's the main one in the hall here about equidistant from the dining-room and the drawing-room doors. Then there's one the other end of the house. Stephen Farr came up by the latter. Miss Estravados came along the upper landing from that end of the house (her room is right at the other end). The others say they went up by this one."

Poirot said:

"It is a confusion, yes."

The door opened and Magdalene came quickly in. She was breathing fast and had a bright spot of colour in each cheek. She came up to the table and said quietly:

"My husband thinks I'm lying down. I slipped out of my room quietly. Colonel Johnson," she appealed to him with wide, distressed eyes, "if I tell you the truth you *will* keep quiet about it, won't you? I mean you don't have to make *everything* public?"

Colonel Johnson said:

"You mean, I take it, Mrs. Lee, something that has no connection with the crime?"

"Yes, no connection at all. Just something in my—my private life."

The Chief Constable said:

"You'd better make a clean breast of it, Mrs. Lee, and leave us to judge."

Magdalene said, her eyes swimming:

"Yes, I will trust you. I know I can. You look so kind. You see it's like this. There's somebody—" She stopped.

"Yes, Mrs. Lee?"

"I wanted to telephone to somebody last night—a man—a friend of mine, and I didn't want George to know about it. I know it was very wrong of me—but, well, it was like that. So I went to telephone after dinner when I thought George would be safely in the dining-room. But when I got here I heard him telephoning, so I waited."

"Where did you wait, madam?" asked Poirot.

"There's a place for coats and things behind the stairs. It's dark there. I slipped back there where I could see George come out from this room. But he didn't come out and then all the noise happened and Mr. Lee screamed and I ran upstairs."

"So your husband did not leave this room until the moment of the murder?"

"No."

The Chief Constable said:

"And you yourself from nine o'clock to nine-fifteen were waiting in the recess behind the stairs?"

"Yes, but I couldn't *say* so, you see! They'd want to know what I was doing there. It's been very, very awkward for me, you *do* see that, *don't* you?"

Johnson said drily:

"It was certainly awkward."

She smiled at him sweetly.

"I'm *so* relieved to have told you the truth. And you *won't* tell my husband, will you? No, I'm sure you won't! I can trust you, all of you."

She included them all in her final pleading look, then she slipped quickly out of the room.

Colonel Johnson drew a deep breath.

"Well," he said. "It *might* be like that! It's a perfectly plausible story. On the other hand—"

"It might not," finished Sugden. "That's just it. We don't know."

III

Lydia Lee stood by the far window of the drawing-room looking out. Her figure was half hidden by the heavy window curtain. A sound in the room made her turn with a start to see Hercule Poirot standing by the door.

She said:

"You startled me, Mr. Poirot."

"I apologize, madam. I walk softly."

She said:

"I thought it was Horbury."

Hercule Poirot nodded.

"It is true, he steps softly, that one—like a cat—or a *thief.*"

He paused a minute, watching her.

Her face showed nothing, but she made a slight grimace of distaste as she said:

"I have never cared for that man. I shall be glad to get rid of him."

"I think you will be wise to do so, madam."

She looked at him quickly. She said:

"What do you mean? Do you know anything against him?"

Poirot said:

"He is a man who collects secrets—and uses them to his advantage."

She said sharply:

"Do you think he knows anything—about the murder?"

Poirot shrugged his shoulders. He said:

"He has quiet feet and long ears. He may have overheard something that he is keeping to himself."

Lydia said clearly:

"Do you mean that he may try to blackmail one of us?"

"It is within the bounds of possibility. But that is not what I came here to say."

"What did you come to say?"

Poirot said slowly:

"I have been talking with Mr. Alfred Lee. He has made to me a proposition, and I wished to discuss it with you before accepting or declining it. But I was so struck by the picture you made—the charming pattern of your jumper against the deep red of the curtains—that I paused to admire."

Lydia said sharply:

"Really, Mr. Poirot, must we waste time in compliments?"

"I beg your pardon, madam. So few English ladies understand *la toilette*. The dress you were wearing the first night I saw you, its bold but simple pattern, it had grace—distinction."

Lydia said impatiently:

"What was it you wanted to see me about?"

Poirot became grave.

"Just this, madam. Your husband, he wishes me to take up the investigation very seriously. He demands that I stay here, in the house, and do my utmost to get to the bottom of the matter."

Lydia said sharply:

"Well?"

Poirot said slowly:

"I would not wish to accept an invitation that was not endorsed by the lady of the house."

She said coldly:

"Naturally I endorse my husband's invitation."

"Yes, madam, but I need more than that. Do you really *want* me to come here?"

"Why not?"

"Let us be more frank. What I ask you is this: do you want the truth to come out, or not?"

"Naturally."

Poirot sighed.

"Must you return me these conventional replies?"

Lydia said:

"I am a conventional woman."

Then she bit her lip, hesitated, and said:

"Perhaps it is better to speak frankly. Of course I understand you! The position is not a pleasant one. My father-in-law has been brutally murdered, and unless a case can be made out against the most likely suspect—Horbury—for robbery and murder—and it seems that it cannot—then it comes to this—*one of his own family killed him.* To bring that person to justice will mean bringing shame and disgrace on us all. . . . If I am to speak honestly I must say that I do *not* want this to happen."

Poirot said:

"You are content for the murderer to escape unpunished?"

"There are probably several undiscovered murderers at large in the world."

"That, I grant you."

"Does one more matter, then?"

Poirot said:

"And what about the other members of the family? The innocent?"

She stared.

"What about them?"

"Do you realize that if it turns out as you hope, *no one will ever know.* The shadow will remain on all alike. . . ."

She said uncertainly:

"I hadn't thought of that. . . ."

Poirot said:

"No one will ever know who the guilty person is. . . ."

He added softly:

"Unless *you* already know, madam?"

She cried out:

"You have no business to say that! It's not true! Oh! if only it could be a stranger—not a member of the family."

Poirot said:

"It might be both."

She stared at him.

"What do you mean?"

"It might be a member of the family—and at the same time a stranger

. . . you do not see what I mean? *Eh bien,* it is an idea that has occurred to the mind of Hercule Poirot."

He looked at her.

"Well, madam, what am I to say to Mr. Lee?"

Lydia raised her hands and let them fall in a sudden, helpless gesture. She said:

"Of course—you must accept."

IV

Pilar stood in the centre of the music room. She stood very straight, her eyes darting from side to side like an animal who fears an attack.

She said:

"I want to get away from here!"

Stephen Farr said gently:

"You're not the only one who feels like that. But they won't let us go, my dear."

"You mean—the police?"

"Yes."

Pilar said very seriously:

"It is not nice to be mixed up with the police. It is a thing that should not happen to respectable people."

Stephen said with a faint smile:

"Meaning yourself?"

Pilar said:

"No, I mean Alfred and Lydia and David and George and Hilda and— yes—Magdalene, too."

Stephen lit a cigarette. He puffed at it for a moment or two before saying:

"Why the exception?"

"What is that, please?"

Stephen said:

"Why leave out brother Harry?"

Pilar laughed, her teeth showing white and even.

"Oh, Harry is different! I think he knows very well what it is to be mixed up with the police."

"Perhaps you are right. He certainly is a little too picturesque to blend well into the domestic picture."

He went on:

"Do you like your English relations, Pilar?"

Pilar said doubtfully:

"They are kind—they are all very kind. But they do not laugh much, they are not gay."

"My dear girl, there's just been a murder in the house!"

"Y-es," said Pilar doubtfully.

"A murder," said Stephen instructively, "is not such an everyday occurrence as your nonchalance seems to imply. In England they take their murders seriously, whatever they may do in Spain."

Pilar said:

"You are laughing at me. . . ."

Stephen said:

"You're wrong. I'm not in a laughing mood."

Pilar looked at him and said:

"Because you, too, wish to get away from here?"

"Yes."

"And the big handsome policeman will not let you go?"

"I haven't asked him. But if I did, I've no doubt he'd say no. I've got to watch my step, Pilar, and be very, very careful."

"That is tiresome," said Pilar, nodding her head.

"It's just a little bit more than tiresome, my dear. Then there's that lunatic foreigner prowling about. I don't suppose he's any good but he makes me feel jumpy."

Pilar was frowning. She said:

"My grandfather was very, very rich, was he not?"

"I should imagine so."

"Where does his money go to now? To Alfred and the others?"

"Depends on his will."

Pilar said thoughtfully:

"He might have left me some money, but I am afraid that perhaps he did not."

Stephen said kindly:

"You'll be all right. After all, you're one of the family. You belong here. They'll have to look after you."

Pilar said with a sigh:

"I—belong here. It is very funny, that. And yet it is not funny at all."

"I can see that you mightn't find it very humorous."

Pilar sighed again. She said:

"Do you think if we put on the gramophone, we could dance?"

Stephen said dubiously:

"It wouldn't look any too good. This is a house of mourning, you callous Spanish baggage."

Pilar said, her big eyes opening very wide:

"But I do not feel sad at all. Because I did not really know my grandfather, and though I liked to talk to him, I do not want to cry and be unhappy because he is dead. It is very silly to pretend."

Stephen said:

"You're adorable!"

Pilar said coaxingly:

"We could put some stockings and some gloves in the gramophone, and then it would not make much noise, and no one would hear."

"Come along then, temptress."

She laughed happily and ran out of the room, going along towards the ballroom at the far end of the house.

Then, as she reached the side passage which led to the garden door she stopped dead. Stephen caught up with her and stopped also.

Hercule Poirot had unhooked a portrait from the wall and was studying it by the light from the terrace. He looked up and saw them.

"Aha!" he said. "You arrive at an opportune moment."

Pilar said:

"What are you doing?"

She came and stood beside him.

Poirot said gravely:

"I am studying something very important, the face of Simeon Lee when he was a young man."

"Oh, is that my grandfather?"

"Yes, mademoiselle."

She stared at the painted face. She said slowly:

"How different—how very different . . . he was so old, so shriveled up. Here he is like Harry, like Harry might have been ten years ago."

Hercule Poirot nodded.

"Yes, mademoiselle. Harry Lee is very much the son of his father. Now here"—he led her a little way along the gallery—"here is madam, your grandmother—a long gentle face, very blond hair, mild blue eyes."

Pilar said:

"Like David."

Stephen said:

"Just a look of Alfred, too."

Poirot said:

"The heredity, it is very interesting. Mr. Lee and his wife were diametrically opposite types. On the whole the children of the marriage took after the mother. See here, mademoiselle."

He pointed to a picture of a girl of nineteen or so, with hair like spun gold and wide, laughing blue eyes. The colouring was that of Simeon Lee's wife, but there was a spirit, a vivacity that those mild blue eyes and placid features had never known.

"Oh!" said Pilar.

The colour came up in her face.

Her hand went to her neck. She drew out a locket on a long gold chain. She pressed the catch and it flew open. The same laughing face looked up at Poirot.

"My mother," said Pilar.

Poirot nodded. On the opposite side of the locket was the portrait of a man. He was young and handsome, with black hair and dark blue eyes.

Poirot said:

"Your father?"

Pilar said:

"Yes, my father. He is very beautiful, is he not?"

"Yes, indeed. Few Spaniards have blue eyes, have they, señorita?"

"Sometimes, in the north. Besides, my father's mother was Irish."

Poirot said thoughtfully:

"So you have Spanish blood, and Irish and English and a touch of gypsy too. Do you know what I think, mademoiselle? With that inheritance, you should make a bad enemy."

Stephen said, laughing:

"Remember what you said in the train, Pilar? That your way of dealing with your enemies would be to cut their throats. Oh!"

He stopped—suddenly realizing the import of his words.

Hercule Poirot was quick to lead the conversation away. He said:

"Ah, yes, there was something, señorita, I had to ask you. Your passport. It is needed by my friend the Superintendent. There are, you know, police regulations—very stupid, very tiresome, but necessary—for a foreigner in this country. And of course by law you are a foreigner."

Pilar's eyebrows rose.

"My passport? Yes, I will get it. It is in my room."

Poirot said apologetically as he walked by her side:

"I am most sorry to trouble you. I am indeed."

They had reached the end of the long gallery. Here was a flight of stairs. Pilar ran up and Poirot followed. Stephen came too. Pilar's bedroom was just at the head of the stairs.

She said as she reached the door:

"I will get it for you."

She went in. Poirot and Stephen Farr remained waiting outside.

Stephen said remorsefully:

"Damn silly of me to say a thing like that. I don't think she noticed, though, do you?"

Poirot did not answer. He held his head a little on one side as though listening.

He said:

"The English are extraordinarily fond of fresh air. Miss Estravados must have inherited that characteristic."

Stephen said, staring:

"Why?"

Poirot said softly:

"Because though it is to-day extremely cold—the black frost you call it (not like yesterday so mild and sunny)—Miss Estravados has just flung up her lower window sash. Amazing to love so much the fresh air."

Suddenly there was an exclamation in Spanish from inside the room and Pilar reappeared laughingly dismayed.

"Ah!" she cried. "But I am stupid—and clumsy. My little case it was on the window-sill, and I was sorting through it so quickly and very stupidly I knock my passport out of the window. It is down on the flower bed below. I will get it."

"I'll get it," said Stephen, but Pilar had flown past him and cried back over her shoulder.

"No, it was my stupidity. You go to the drawing-room with Mr. Poirot and I will bring it to you there."

Stephen Farr seemed inclined to go after her, but Poirot's hand fell gently on his arm and Poirot's voice said:

"Let us go this way."

They went along the corridor towards the other end of the house until they got to the head of the main staircase. Here Poirot said:

"Let us not go down for a minute. If you will come with me to the room of the crime there is something I want to ask you."

They went along the corridor which led to Simeon Lee's room. On their left they passed an alcove which contained two marble statues, stalwart nymphs clasping their draperies in an agony of Victorian propriety.

Stephen Farr glanced at them and murmured:

"Pretty frightful by daylight. I thought there were three of them when I came along the other night, but thank goodness there are only two!"

"They are not what is admired nowadays," admitted Poirot. "But no doubt they cost much money in their time. They look better by night, I think."

"Yes, one sees only a white glimmering figure."

Poirot murmured:

"All cats are grey in the dark!"

They found Superintendent Sugden in the room. He was kneeling by the safe and examining it with a magnifying glass. He looked up as they entered.

"This was opened with the key all right," he said. "By someone who knew the combination. No sign of anything else."

Poirot went up to him, drew him aside and whispered something. The Superintendent nodded and left the room.

Poirot turned to Stephen Farr, who was standing staring at the armchair in which Simeon Lee always sat. His brows were drawn together and the veins showed in his forehead. Poirot looked at him for a minute or two in silence, then he said:

"You have the memories—yes?"

Stephen said slowly:

"Two days ago he sat here alive—and now . . ."

Then, shaking off his absorption, he said:

"Yes, Mr. Poirot, you brought me here to ask me something?"

"Ah, yes. You were, I think, the first person to arrive on the scene that night?"

"Was I? I don't remember. No, I think one of the ladies was here before me."

"Which lady?"

"One of the wives—George's wife or David's—I know they were both here pretty soon."

"You did not hear the scream, I think you said?"

"I don't think I did. I can't quite remember. Somebody did cry out but that may have been someone downstairs."

Poirot said:

"You did not hear a noise like this?"

He threw his head back and suddenly gave vent to a piercing yell.

It was so unexpected that Stephen started backwards and nearly fell over. He said angrily:

"For the Lord's sake, do you want to scare the whole house? No, I didn't hear anything in the least like that! You'll have the whole place by the ears again! They'll think another murder has happened!"

Poirot looked crestfallen. He murmured:

"True . . . it was foolish . . . we must go at once."

He hurried out of the room. Lydia and Alfred were at the foot of the stairs peering up—George came out of the library to join them and Pilar came running, a passport held in her hand.

Poirot cried:

"It is nothing—nothing. Do not be alarmed. A little experiment that I make. That was all."

Alfred looked annoyed and George indignant. Poirot left Stephen to explain and he hurriedly slipped away along the passage to the other end of the house.

At the end of the passage, Superintendent Sugden came quietly out of Pilar's door and met Poirot.

"*Eh bien?*" asked Poirot.

The Superintendent shook his head.

"Not a sound."

His eyes met Poirot's appreciatively and he nodded.

V

Alfred Lee said:

"Then you accept, Mr. Poirot?"

His hand, as it went to his mouth, shook slightly. His mild, brown eyes were alight with a new and feverish expression. He stammered slightly in his speech. Lydia, standing silently by, looked at him with some anxiety.

Alfred said:

"You don't know—you c-c-can't imagine—what it m-m-means to me . . . my father's murderer *must* be f-f-found."

Poirot said:

"Since you have assured me that you have reflected long and carefully —yes, I accept. But you comprehend, Mr. Lee, there can be no drawing back. I am not the dog one sets on to hunt and then recalls because you do not like the game he puts up!"

"Of course . . . of course . . . everything is ready. Your bedroom is prepared. Stay as long as you like—"

Poirot said gravely:

"It will not be long."

"Eh? What's that?"

"I said it will not be long. There is in this crime such a restricted circle that it cannot possibly take long to arrive at the truth. Already, I think, the end draws near."

Alfred stared at him.

"Impossible!" he said.

"Not at all. The facts all point more or less clearly in one direction. There is just some irrelevant matter to be cleared out of the way. When that is done the truth will appear."

Alfred said incredulously:

"You mean you *know?*"

Poirot smiled.

"Oh, yes," he said. "I know."

Alfred said:

"My father—my father—" He turned away.

Poirot said briskly:

"There are, Mr. Lee, two requests that I have to make."

Alfred said in a muffled voice:

"Anything—anything."

"Then, in the first place, I would like the portrait of Mr. Lee as a young man placed in the bedroom you are good enough to allot to me."

Alfred and Lydia stared at him.

The former said:

"My father's portrait—but why?"

Poirot said with a wave of the hand:

"It will—how shall I say—inspire me?"

Lydia said sharply:

"Do you propose, Mr. Poirot, to solve a crime by clairvoyance?"

"Let us say, madam, that I intend to use not only the eyes of the body, but the eyes of the mind."

She shrugged her shoulders.

Poirot continued:

"Next, Mr. Lee, I should like to know of the true circumstances attending the death of your sister's husband, Juan Estravados."

Lydia said:

"Is that necessary?"

"I want all the facts, madam."

Alfred said:

"Juan Estravados, as the result of a quarrel about a woman, killed another man in a café."

"How did he kill him?"

Alfred looked appealingly at Lydia. She said evenly:

"He stabbed him. Juan Estravados was not condemned to death, as there had been provocation. He was sentenced to a term of imprisonment and died in prison."

"Does his daughter know about her father?"

"I think not."

Alfred said:

"No, Jennifer never told her."

"Thank you."

Lydia said:

"You don't think that Pilar— Oh, it's absurd!"

Poirot said:

"Now, Mr. Lee, will you give me some facts about your brother, M. Harry Lee?"

"What do you want to know?"

"I understand that he was considered somewhat of a disgrace to the family. Why?"

Lydia said:

"It is so long ago. . . ."

Alfred said, the colour coming up in his face:

"If you want to know, Mr. Poirot, he stole a large sum of money by forging my father's name to a check. Naturally my father didn't prosecute. Harry's always been crooked. He's been in trouble all over the world. Always cabling for money to get out of a scrape. He's been in and out of gaol here, there and everywhere."

Lydia said:

"You don't really *know* all this, Alfred."

Alfred said angrily, his hands shaking:

"Harry's no good—no good whatever! He never has been!"

Poirot said:

"There is, I see, no love lost between you?"

Alfred said:

"He victimized my father—victimized him shamefully!"

Lydia sighed—a quick, impatient sigh. Poirot heard it and gave her a sharp glance.

She said:

"If only those diamonds could be found. I'm sure the solution lies there."

Poirot said:

"They have been found, madam."

"What?"

Poirot said gently:

"They were found in your little garden of the Dead Sea. . . ."

Lydia cried:

"In my garden? How—how extraordinary!"

Poirot said softly:

"Is it not, madam?"

PART VI

DECEMBER 27TH

I

ALFRED LEE SAID with a sigh:

"That was better than I feared!"

They had just returned from the inquest.

Mr. Charlton, an old-fashioned type of solicitor with a cautious blue eye, had been present and had returned with them. He said:

"Ah—I told you the proceedings would be purely formal—purely formal—there was bound to be an adjournment—to enable the police to gather up additional evidence."

George Lee said vexedly:

"It is all most unpleasant—really *most* unpleasant—a terrible position in which to be placed! I myself am quite convinced that this crime was done by a maniac who somehow or other gained admittance to the house. That man Sugden is obstinate as a mule. Colonel Johnson should enlist the aid of Scotland Yard. These local police are no good. Thick-headed. What about this man Horbury, for instance? I hear his past is definitely unsatisfactory but the police do nothing whatever about it."

Mr. Charlton said:

"Ah—I believe the man Horbury has a satisfactory alibi covering the period of time in question. The police have accepted it."

"Why should they?" George fumed. "If I were they, I should accept such an alibi with reserve—with great reserve. Naturally a criminal always provides himself with an alibi! It is the duty of the police to break down the alibi—that is, if they know their job."

"Well, well," said Mr. Charlton. "I don't think it's quite our business to teach the police their jobs, eh? Pretty competent body of men on the whole."

George shook his head darkly.

"Scotland Yard should be called in. I'm not at all satisfied with Superintendent Sugden—he may be painstaking—but he is certainly far from brilliant."

Mr. Charlton said:

"I don't agree with you, you know. Sugden's a good man. Doesn't throw his weight about, but he gets there."

Lydia said:

"I'm sure the police are doing their best. Mr. Charlton, will you have a glass of sherry?"

Mr. Charlton thanked her politely, but declined. Then, clearing his throat, he proceeded to the reading of the will, all members of the family being assembled.

He read it with a certain relish, lingering over its more obscure phraseology, and savouring its legal technicalities.

He came to the end, took off his glasses, wiped them and looked round on the assembled company inquiringly.

Harry Lee said:

"All this legal stuff's a bit hard to follow. Give us the bare bones of it, will you?"

"Really," said Mr. Charlton. "It's a perfectly simple will."

Harry said:

"My God, what's a difficult will like then?"

Mr. Charlton rebuked him with a cold glance. He said:

"The main provisions of the will are quite simple. Half Mr. Lee's property goes to his son, Mr. Alfred Lee, the remainder is divided among his other children."

Harry laughed unpleasantly. He said:

"As usual, Alfred's struck lucky! Half my father's fortune! Lucky dog, aren't you, Alfred?"

Alfred flushed. Lydia said sharply:

"Alfred was a loyal and devoted son to his father. He's managed the works for years and has had all the responsibility."

Harry said:

"Oh, yes. Alfred was always the good boy."

Alfred said sharply:

"You may consider *yourself* lucky, I think, Harry, that my father left you anything at all!"

Harry laughed, throwing his head back, and said:

"You'd have liked it better if he'd cut me right out, wouldn't you? You've always disliked me."

Mr. Charlton coughed. He was used—only too well used—to the painful scenes that succeeded the reading of a will. He was anxious to get away before the usual family quarrel got too well under way.

He murmured:

"I think—er—that that is all that I need—er—"

Harry said sharply:

"What about Pilar?"

Mr. Charlton coughed again, this time apologetically.

"Er— Miss Estravados is not mentioned in the will."

Harry said:

"Doesn't she get her mother's share?"

Mr. Charlton explained.

"Señora Estravados, if she had lived, would of course have received an equal share with the rest of you, but as she is dead, the portion that would have been hers goes back into the estate to be shared out among you."

Pilar said slowly in her rich Southern voice:

"Then—I—have—nothing?"

Lydia said quickly:

"My dear, the family will see to that, of course."

George Lee said:

"You will be able to make your home here with Alfred—eh, Alfred? We —er—you are our niece—it is our duty to look after you."

Hilda said:

"We shall always be glad to have Pilar with us."

Harry said:

"She ought to have her proper share. She ought to have Jennifer's whack."

Mr. Charlton murmured:

"Must really—er—be going. Good-bye, Mrs. Lee—anything I can do— er—consult me at any time. . . ."

He escaped quickly. His experience enabled him to predict that all the ingredients for a family row were present.

As the door shut behind him Lydia said in her clear voice:

"I agree with Harry. I think Pilar is entitled to a definite share. This will was made many years before Jennifer's death."

"Nonsense," said George. "Very slipshod and illegal way of thinking, Lydia. The law's the law. We must abide by it."

Magdalene said:

"It's hard luck, of course, and we're all very sorry for Pilar, but George is right. As he says, the law is the law."

Lydia got up. She took Pilar by the hand.

"My dear," she said. "This must be very unpleasant for you. Will you please leave us while we discuss the question?"

She led the girl to the door.

"Don't worry, Pilar, dear," she said. "Leave it to me."

Pilar went slowly out of the room. Lydia shut the door behind her and turned back.

There was a moment's pause while everyone drew breath and in another moment the battle was in full swing.

Harry said:

"You've always been a damned skinflint, George."

George retorted:

"At any rate I've not been a sponge and a rotter!"

"You've been just as much of a sponge as I have! You've battened on Father all these years."

"You seem to forget that I hold a responsible and arduous position which—"

Harry said:

"Responsible and arduous my foot! You're only an inflated gas bag!"

Magdalene screamed.

"How dare you?"

Hilda's calm voice, slightly raised, said:

"Couldn't we just discuss this *quietly?*"

Lydia threw her a grateful glance.

David said with sudden violence:

"Must we have all this disgraceful fuss over *money!*"

Magdalene said venomously to him:

"It's all very well to be so high-minded. You're not going to refuse your legacy, are you? *You* want money just as much as the rest of us do! All this unworldliness is just a pose!"

David said in a strangled voice:

"You think I ought to refuse it? I wonder—"

Hilda said sharply:

"Of course you oughtn't. Must we all behave like children? Alfred, you're the head of the family—"

Alfred seemed to wake out of a dream. He said:

"I beg your pardon. All of you shouting at once. It—it confuses me."

Lydia said:

"As Hilda has just pointed out, why must we behave like greedy children? Let us discuss this thing quietly and sanely and—" she added this quickly—"one at a time. Alfred shall speak first because he is the eldest. What do you think, Alfred, we should do about Pilar?"

He said slowly:

"She must make her home here, certainly. And we should make her an allowance. I do not see that she has any legal claim to the money which would have gone to her mother. She's not a Lee, remember. She's a Spanish subject."

"No legal claim, no," said Lydia. "But I think she has a *moral* claim. As I see it, your father, although his daughter had married a Spaniard against his wishes, recognized her to have an equal claim upon him. George, Harry, David and Jennifer were to share equally. Jennifer only died last year. I am sure that when he sent for Mr. Charlton, he meant to make ample provision for Pilar in a new will. He would have allotted her at least her mother's share. It is possible that he might have done much more than that. She was the only grandchild, remember. I think the least *we* can do is to endeavour to remedy an injustice that your father himself was preparing to remedy."

Alfred said warmly:

"Well put, Lydia! I was wrong. I agree with you that Pilar must be given Jennifer's share of my father's fortune."

Lydia said:

"Your turn, Harry."

Harry said:

"As you know, I agree. I think Lydia has put the case very well, and I'd like to say I admire her for it."

Lydia said:

"George?"

George was red in the face. He spluttered:

"Certainly not! Whole thing's preposterous! Give her a home and a decent dress allowance. Quite enough for her!"

"Then you refuse to cooperate?" asked Alfred.

"Yes, I do."

"And he's quite right," said Magdalene. "It's disgraceful to suggest he should do anything of the kind! Considering that George is the *only* member of the family who has done *anything* in the world, I think it's a shame his father left him so little!"

Lydia said:

"David?"

David said vaguely:

"Oh, I think you're right. It's a pity there's got to be so much ugliness and disputing about it all."

Hilda said:

"You're quite right, Lydia. It's only justice!"

Harry looked round. He said:

"Well, that's clear. Of the family, Alfred, David and myself are in favour of the motion. George is against it. The ayes have it."

George said sharply:

"There is no question of ayes or noes. My share of my father's estate is mine absolutely. I shall not part with a penny of it."

"No, indeed," said Magdalene.

Lydia said sharply:

"If you like to stand out, that is your business. The rest of us will make up your share of the total."

She looked round for assent and the others nodded.

Harry said:

"Alfred's got the lion's share. He ought to stand most of the racket."

Alfred said:

"I see that your original disinterested suggestion will soon break down."

Hilda said firmly:

"Don't let's start again! Lydia shall tell Pilar what we've decided. We can settle details later." She added in the hope of making a diversion, "I wonder where Mr. Farr is and Mr. Poirot?"

Alfred said:

"We dropped Poirot in the village on our way to the inquest. He said he had an important purchase to make."

Harry said:

"Why didn't *he* go to the inquest? Surely he ought to have done so."

Lydia said:

"Perhaps he knew it was not going to be important. Who's that out there in the garden? Superintendent Sugden, or Mr. Farr?"

The efforts of the two women were successful. The family conclave broke up.

Lydia said to Hilda privately:

"Thank you, Hilda. It was nice of you to back me up. You know, you really *have* been a comfort in all this."

Hilda said thoughtfully:

"Queer how money upsets people."

The others had all left the room. The two women were alone.

Lydia said:

"Yes—even Harry—although it was his suggestion! And my poor Alfred—he is so British—he doesn't really like Lee money going to a Spanish subject."

Hilda said, smiling:

"Do you think we women are more unworldly?"

Lydia said with a shrug of her graceful shoulders:

"Well, you know, it isn't really our money—not our *own*! That may make a difference."

Hilda said thoughtfully:

"She is a strange child—Pilar, I mean. I wonder what will become of her?"

Lydia sighed.

"I'm glad that she will be independent. To live here, to be given a home and a dress allowance, would not, I think, be very satisfactory to her. She's too proud and, I think, too—too—alien."

She added musingly:

"I once brought some beautiful blue lapis home from Egypt. Out there, against the sun and the sand it was a glorious colour—a brilliant, warm blue. But when I got it home, the blue of it hardly showed any more. It was just a dull, darkish string of beads."

Hilda said:

"Yes, I see. . . ."

Lydia said gently:

"I am so glad to come to know you and David at last. I'm glad you both came here."

Hilda sighed:

"How often I've wished in the last few days that we hadn't!"

"I know. You must have done . . . but you know, Hilda, the shock hasn't affected David nearly as badly as it might have done. I mean he is so sensitive that it might have upset him completely. Actually, since the murder, he's seemed ever so much better—"

Hilda looked slightly disturbed. She said:

"So you've noticed that? It's rather dreadful in a way . . . but, oh! Lydia, it's undoubtedly so!"

She was silent a minute recollecting words that her husband had spoken only the night before. He had said to her, eagerly, his fair hair tossed back from his forehead:

"Hilda, you remember in *Tosca*—when Scarpia is dead and Tosca lights the candles at his head and feet? Do you remember what she says: '*Now* I can forgive him.' That is what I feel—about Father. I see now that all these years I couldn't forgive him and yet I really wanted to. . . . But now— *now*— there's no rancour any more. It's all wiped away. And I feel—oh, I feel as though a great load had been lifted from my back."

She had said, striving to fight back a sudden fear:

"Because he's dead?"

He had answered quickly, stammering in his eagerness:

"No, no, you don't understand. Not because *he* is dead, but because my childish, stupid hate of him is dead. . . ."

Hilda thought of those words now. . . .

She would have liked to repeat them to the woman at her side, but she felt instinctively that it was wiser not.

She followed Lydia out of the drawing-room into the hall.

Magdalene was there standing by the hall table with a little parcel in her hand. She jumped when she saw them. She said:

"Oh, this must be Mr. Poirot's important purchase. I saw him put it down here just now. I wonder what it is."

She looked from one to the other of them, giggling a little, but her eyes were sharp and anxious, belying the affected gaiety of her words.

Lydia's eyebrows rose. She said:

"I must go and get ready for lunch."

Magdalene said, still with that affectation of childishness, but unable to keep the desperate note out of her voice:

"I must just *peep!*"

She unrolled the piece of paper and gave a sharp exclamation. She stared at the thing in her hand.

Lydia stopped and Hilda too. Both women stared.

Magdalene said in a puzzled voice:

"It's a false moustache. But—but—why—?"

Hilda said doubtfully:

"Disguise? But—"

Lydia finished the sentence for her.

"But Mr. Poirot has a very fine moustache of his own!"

Magdalene was wrapping the parcel up again. She said:

"I don't understand. It's—it's *mad. Why* does Mr. Poirot buy a false moustache?"

II

When Pilar left the drawing-room she walked slowly along the hall. Stephen Farr was coming in through the garden door. He said:

"Well? Is the family conclave over? Has the will been read?"

Pilar said, her breath coming fast:

"I have got nothing—nothing at all! It was a will made many years ago. My grandfather left money to my mother, but because she is dead it does not go to me but goes back to *them.*"

Stephen said:

"That seems rather hard lines."

Pilar said:

"If that old man had lived, he would have made another will. He would have left money to *me*—a lot of money! Perhaps in time, he would have left me *all* the money!"

Stephen said, smiling:

"That wouldn't have been very fair either, would it?"

"Why not? He would have liked me best, that is all."

Stephen said:

"What a greedy child you are. A real little gold digger."

Pilar said soberly:

"The world is very cruel to women. They must do what they can for themselves—while they are young. When they are old and ugly no one will help them."

Stephen said slowly:

"That's more true than I like to think. But it isn't *quite* true. Alfred Lee, for instance, was genuinely fond of his father in spite of the old man being thoroughly trying and exacting."

Pilar's chin went up.

"Alfred," she said, "is rather a fool."

Stephen laughed.

Then he said:

"Well, don't worry, lovely Pilar. The Lees are bound to look after you, you know."

Pilar said disconsolately:

"It will not be very amusing, that."

Stephen said slowly:

"No, I'm afraid it won't. I can't see you living here, Pilar. Would you like to come to South Africa?"

Pilar nodded.

Stephen said:

"There's sun there, and space. There's hard work, too. Are you good at work, Pilar?"

Pilar said doubtfully:

"I do not know."

He said:

"You'd rather sit on a balcony and eat sweets all day long? And grow enormously fat and have three double chins?"

Pilar laughed and Stephen said:

"That's better. I've made you laugh."

Pilar said:

"I thought I should laugh this Christmas! In books I have read that an English Christmas is very gay, that one eats burning raisins and there is a plum pudding all in flames and something that is called a Yule log."

Stephen said:

"Ah, but you must have a Christmas uncomplicated by murder. Come in here a minute. Lydia took me in here yesterday. It's her storeroom."

He led her into a small room little bigger than a cupboard.

"Look, Pilar, boxes and boxes of crackers, and preserved fruits and oranges and dates and nuts. And here—"

"Oh!" Pilar clasped her hands. "They are pretty, these gold and silver balls."

"Those were to hang on a tree, with presents for the servants. And here are little snow men all glittering with frost to put on the dinner table. And here are balloons of every colour all ready to blow up!"

"Oh!" Pilar's eyes shone. "Oh! can we blow up one? Lydia would not mind. I do love balloons."

Stephen said:

"Baby! Here, which will you have?"

Pilar said: "I will have a red one."

They selected their balloons and blew, their cheeks distended. Pilar stopped blowing to laugh and her balloon went down again.

She said:

"You look so funny—blowing—with your cheeks puffed out."

Her laugh rang out. Then she fell to, blowing industriously. They tied up their balloons carefully and began to play with them, patting them upwards, sending them to and fro.

Pilar said:

"Out in the hall, there would be more room."

They were sending the balloons to each other and laughing when Poirot came along the hall. He regarded them indulgently.

"So you play *les jeux d'enfants?* It is pretty, that!"

Pilar said breathlessly:

"Mine is the red one. It is bigger than his. Much bigger. If we took it outside it would go right up in the sky."

"Let's send them up and wish," said Stephen.

"Oh, yes, that is a good idea."

Pilar ran to the garden door, Stephen followed. Poirot came behind, still looking indulgent.

"I will wish for a great deal of money," announced Pilar.

She stood on tiptoe, holding the string of the balloon. It tugged gently as a puff of wind came. Pilar let go and it floated along, taken by the breeze.

Stephen laughed:

"You mustn't tell your wish."

"No, why not?"

"Because it doesn't come true. Now, I'm going to wish."

He released his balloon. But he was not so lucky. It floated sideways, caught on a holly bush and expired with a bang.

Pilar ran to it.

She announced tragically:

"It is gone. . . ."

Then, as she stirred the little limp wisp of rubber with her toe, she said: "So that was what I picked up in Grandfather's room. He, too, had had a balloon, only his was a pink one."

Poirot gave a sharp exclamation. Pilar turned inquiringly. Poirot said:

"It is nothing. I stabbed—no, stubbed—the toe."

He wheeled round and looked at the house.

He said:

"So many windows! A house, mademoiselle, has its eyes—and its ears. It is indeed regrettable that the English are so fond of open windows."

Lydia came out on the terrace.

She said:

"Lunch is just ready. Pilar, my dear, everything has been settled quite satisfactorily. Alfred will explain the exact details to you after lunch. Shall we come in?"

They went into the house. Poirot came last. He was looking grave.

III

Lunch was over.

As they came out of the dining-room, Alfred said to Pilar:

"Will you come into my room? There is something I want to talk over with you."

He led her across the hall and into his study, shutting the door after him. The others went on into the drawing-room. Only Hercule Poirot remained in the hall, looking thoughtfully at the closed study door.

He was aware suddenly of the old butler hovering uneasily near him.

Poirot said:

"Yes, Tressilian, what is it?"

The old man seemed troubled. He said:

"I wanted to speak to Mr. Lee. But I don't like to disturb him now."

Poirot said:

"Something has occurred?"

Tressilian said slowly:

"It's such a queer thing. It doesn't make sense."

"Tell me," said Hercule Poirot.

Tressilian hesitated. Then he said:

"Well, it's this, sir. You may have noticed that each side of the front door there was a cannon ball. Big heavy stone things. Well, sir, *one of them's gone.*"

Hercule Poirot's eyebrows rose. He said:

"Since when?"

"They were both there this morning, sir. I'll take my oath on that."

"Let us see."

Together they went outside the front door. Poirot bent and examined the remaining cannon ball. When he straightened himself, his face was very grave.

Tressilian quavered.

"Who'd want to steal a thing like that, sir? It doesn't make *sense*."

Poirot said:

"I do not like it. I do not like it at all. . . ."

Tressilian was watching him anxiously. He said slowly:

"What's come to the house, sir? Ever since the master was murdered it doesn't seem like the same place. I feel the whole time as though I am going about in a dream. I mix things up, and I sometimes feel I can't trust my own eyes."

Hercule Poirot shook his head. He said:

"You are wrong. Your own eyes are just what you must trust."

Tressilian said, shaking his head:

"My sight's bad—I can't see like I used to do. I get things mixed up—and people. I'm getting too old for my work."

Hercule Poirot clapped him on the shoulder and said:

"Courage."

"Thank you, sir. You mean it kindly, I know. But there it is, I am too old. I'm always going back to the old days and the old faces. Miss Jenny and Master David and Master Alfred. I'm always seeing them as young gentlemen and ladies. Ever since that night when Mr. Harry came home—"

Poirot nodded.

"Yes," he said, "that is what I thought. You said just now 'ever since the master was murdered'—but it began before that. It is *ever since Mr. Harry came home,* is it not, that things have altered and seemed unreal?"

The butler said:

"You're quite right, sir. It was then. Mr. Harry always brought trouble into the house, even in the old days."

His eyes wandered back to the empty stone base.

"Who can have taken it, sir?" he whispered. "And why? It's—it's like a madhouse."

Hercule Poirot said:

"It is not madness I am afraid of. It is sanity! Somebody, Tressilian, is in great danger."

He turned and reentered the house.

At that moment Pilar came out from the study. A red spot shone on either cheek. She held her head high and her eyes glittered.

As Poirot came up to her, she suddenly stamped her foot and said: "I will not take it."

Poirot raised his eyebrows. He said:

"What is this that you will not take, mademoiselle?"

Pilar said:

"Alfred has just told me that I am to have my mother's share of the money my grandfather left."

"Well?"

"I could not get it by law, he said. But he and Lydia and the others consider it should be mine. They say it is a matter of justice. And so they will hand it over to me."

Poirot said again:

"Well?"

Pilar stamped once more with her foot.

"Do you not understand? They are giving it to me—*giving* it to me."

"Need that hurt your pride? Since what they say is true—that it should in justice be yours?"

Pilar said:

"You do not understand. . . ."

Poirot said:

"On the contrary—I understand very well."

"Oh! . . ." She turned away pettishly.

There was a ring at the bell. Poirot glanced over his shoulder. He saw the silhouette of Superintendent Sugden outside the door. He said hurriedly to Pilar:

"Where are you going?"

She said sulkily:

"To the drawing-room. To the others."

Poirot said quickly:

"Good. Stay with them there. Do not wander about the house alone, especially after dark. Be on your guard. You are in great danger, mademoiselle. You will never be in greater danger than you are to-day."

He turned away from her and went to meet Sugden.

The latter waited till Tressilian had gone back into his pantry.

Then he shoved a cable form under Poirot's nose.

"Now we've got it!" he said. "Read that. It's from the South African Police."

The cable said:

"Ebenezer Farr's only son died two years ago."

Sugden said:

"So now we know! Funny—I was on a different tack altogether. . . ."

IV

Pilar marched into the drawing-room, her head held high.

She went straight up to Lydia, who was standing in the window with some knitting.

Pilar said:

"Lydia, I have come to tell you that I will not take that money. I am going away—at once. . . ."

Lydia looked astonished. She laid down her knitting.

She said:

"My dear child, Alfred must have explained very badly! It is not in the least a matter of charity, if that is what you feel. Really, it is not a question of kindness or generosity on our part. It is a plain matter of right and wrong. In the ordinary course of events your mother would have inherited this money, and you would have come into it from her. It is your right— your blood right. It is a matter, not of charity, but of *justice!*"

Pilar said fiercely:

"And that is why I cannot do it—not when you speak like that—not when you are like that! I enjoyed coming here. It was fun! It was an adventure, but now you have spoiled it all! I am going away now, at once —you will never be bothered by me again. . . ."

Tears choked her voice. She turned and ran blindly out of the room.

Lydia stared. She said helplessly:

"I'd no idea she would take it like that!"

Hilda said:

"The child seems quite upset. . . ."

George cleared his throat and said portentously:

"Er—as I pointed out this morning—the principle involved is wrong. Pilar has the wit to see that for herself. She refuses to accept charity—"

Lydia said sharply:

"It is *not* charity. It is her right!"

George said:

"She does not seem to think so!"

Superintendent Sugden and Hercule Poirot came in. The former looked round and asked:

"Where's Mr. Farr? I want a word with him."

Before anyone had time to answer, Hercule Poirot said sharply:

"Where is the señorita Estravados?"

George Lee said with a trace of malicious satisfaction:

"Going to clear out, so she says. Apparently she has had enough of her English relations."

Poirot wheeled round.

He said to Sugden:

"Come!"

As the two men emerged into the hall, there was the sound of a heavy crash and a faraway shriek.

Poirot cried:

"Quick . . . come. . . ."

They raced along the hall and up the far staircase. The door of Pilar's room was open and a man stood in the doorway. He turned his head as they ran up. It was Stephen Farr.

He said:

"She's alive. . . ."

Pilar stood crouched against the wall of her room. She was staring at the floor where a big stone cannon ball was lying.

She said breathlessly:

"It was on top of my door, balanced there. It would have crashed down on my head when I came in, but my skirt caught on a nail and jerked me back just as I was coming in."

Poirot knelt down and examined the nail. On it was a thread of purple tweed. He looked up and nodded gravely:

"That nail, mademoiselle," he said, "saved your life."

The Superintendent said, bewildered:

"Look here, what's the meaning of all this?"

Pilar said:

"Someone tried to kill me!"

She nodded her head several times.

Superintendent Sugden glanced up at the door.

"Booby trap," he said. "An old-fashioned booby trap—and its purpose was murder! That's the second murder planned in this house. But this time it didn't come off!"

Stephen Farr said huskily:

"Thank God you're safe."

Pilar flung out her hands in a wide, appealing gesture.

"*Madre de Dios!*" she cried. "Why should anyone wish to kill *me?* What have I done?"

Hercule Poirot said slowly:

"You should rather ask, mademoiselle, *what do I know?*"

She stared.

"Know? I do not know anything."

Hercule Poirot said:

"That is where you are wrong. Tell me, Mademoiselle Pilar, where were you at the time of the murder? You were not in this room."

"I was. I have told you so!"

Superintendent Sugden said with deceptive mildness:

"Yes, but you weren't speaking the truth when you said that, you know. You told us you heard your grandfather scream—you couldn't have heard that if you were in here—Mr. Poirot and I tested that yesterday."

"Oh!" Pilar caught her breath.

Poirot said:

"You were somewhere very much nearer his room. I will tell you where you were, mademoiselle. You were in the recess with the statues quite close to your grandfather's door."

Pilar said, startled:

"Oh . . . how did you know?"

Poirot said with a faint smile:

"Mr. Farr saw you there."

Stephen said sharply:

"I did not. That's an absolute lie!"

Poirot said:

"I ask your pardon, Mr. Farr, but you *did* see her. Remember your impression that there were *three* statues in that recess, not *two*. Only one person wore a white dress that night, Mademoiselle Estravados. *She* was the third white figure you saw. That is so, is it not, mademoiselle?"

Pilar said after a moment's hesitation:

"Yes, it is true."

Poirot said gently:

"Now tell us, mademoiselle, the whole truth. *Why* were you there?"

Pilar said:

"I left the drawing-room after dinner and I thought I would go and see my grandfather. I thought he would be pleased. But when I turned into the passage I saw someone else was there at his door. I did not want to be seen because I knew my grandfather had said he did not want to see anyone that night. I slipped into the recess in case the person at the door turned round.

"Then, all at once, I heard the most terrible sounds—tables—chairs—" she waved her hands—"everything falling and crashing. I did not move. I do not know why. I was frightened. And then there was a terrible scream—" she crossed herself—"and my heart, it stopped beating, and I said: *'Someone is dead. . . .'* "

"And then?"

"And then people began coming running along the passage and I came out at the end and joined them."

Superintendent Sugden said sharply:

"You said nothing of all this when we first questioned you. Why not?"

Pilar shook her head. She said with an air of wisdom:

"It is not good to tell too much to the police. I thought, you see, that if I said I was near there, you might think that *I* had killed him. So I said I was in my room."

Sugden said sharply:

"If you tell deliberate lies all that it ends in is that you're bound to come under suspicion."

Stephen Farr said:

"Pilar?"

"Yes."

"Who did you see standing at the door when you turned into the passage? Tell us."

Sugden said:

"Yes—tell us."

For a moment the girl hesitated. Her eyes opened, then narrowed. She said slowly:

"I don't know who it was. It was too dimly lit to see. But it was a woman. . . ."

V

Superintendent Sugden looked round at the circle of faces. He said with something as near irritation as he had yet shown:

"This is very irregular, Mr. Poirot."

Poirot said:

"It is a little idea of mine. I wish to share with everyone the knowledge that I have acquired. I shall then invite their cooperation, and so we shall get at the truth."

Sugden murmured under his breath:

"Monkey tricks."

He leaned back in his chair.

Poirot said:

"To begin with, you have, I think, an explanation to ask of Mr. Farr."

Sugden's mouth tightened.

"I should have chosen a less public moment," he said. "However, I've no objection." He handed the cable to Stephen Farr. "Now, Mr. *Farr,* as you call yourself, perhaps you can explain *this?"*

Stephen Farr took it. Raising his eyebrows, he read it slowly out loud. Then, with a bow, he handed it back to the Superintendent.

"Yes," he said. "It's pretty damning, isn't it?"

Sugden said:

"Is that all you've got to say about it? You quite understand there is no obligation on you to make a statement—"

Stephen Farr interrupted. He said:

"You needn't caution me, Superintendent. I can see it trembling on your tongue! Yes, I'll give you an explanation. It's not a very good one, but it's the truth."

He paused. Then he began:

"I'm not Ebenezer Farr's son. But I knew both father and son quite well. Now try and put yourself in my place—(my name is Stephen Grant, by the way). I arrived in this country for the first time in my life. I was disappointed. Everything and everybody seemed drab and lifeless. Then I was traveling by train and I saw a girl. I've got to say it straight out! I fell for that girl! She was the loveliest and most unlikely creature in the world! I talked to her for a while in the train and I made up my mind then and there not to lose sight of her. As I was leaving the compartment I caught sight of the label on her suitcase. Her name meant nothing to me, but the address to which she was traveling did. I'd heard of Gorston Hall and I knew all about its owner. He was Ebenezer Farr's one-time partner and old Eb often talked about him and said what a personality he was.

"Well, the idea came to me to go to Gorston Hall and pretend I was Eb's son. He had died, as this cable says, two years ago, but I remembered old Eb saying that he had not heard from Simeon Lee now for many years and I judged that Lee would not know of the death of Eb's son. Anyway, I felt it was worth trying."

Sugden said:

"You didn't try it on at once, though. You stayed in the King's Arms at Addlesfield for two days."

Stephen said:

"I was thinking it over—whether to try it or not. At last I made up my mind I would. It appealed to me as a bit of an adventure. Well, it worked like a charm! The old man greeted me in the friendliest manner and at once asked me to come and stay in the house. I accepted. There you are, Superintendent, there's my explanation. If you don't fancy it, cast your mind back to your courting days and see if you don't remember some bit of foolishness you indulged in then. As for my real name, as I say, it's Stephen Grant. You can cable to South Africa and check up on me, but I'll tell you this, you'll find I'm a perfectly respectable citizen. I'm not a crook or a jewel thief."

Poirot said softly:

"I never believed you were."

Superintendent Sugden stroked his jaw cautiously.

He said:

"I'll have to check up on that story. What I'd like to know is this: Why didn't you come clean after the murder instead of telling us a pack of lies?"

Stephen said disarmingly:

"Because I was a fool! I thought I could get away with it! I thought it would look fishy if I admitted to being here under a false name. If I hadn't been a complete idiot I would have realized you were bound to cable to Jo'burg."

Sugden said:

"Well, Mr. Farr—er—Grant—I'm not saying I disbelieve your story. It will be proved or disproved soon enough."

He looked across inquiringly at Poirot. The latter said:

"I think Miss Estravados has something to say."

Pilar had gone very white. She said in a breathless voice:

"It is true. I would never have told you, but for Lydia and the money. To come here and pretend and cheat and act—that was fun, but when Lydia said the money was mine and that it was only justice, that was different. It was not fun any longer."

Alfred Lee said with a puzzled face:

"I do not understand, my dear, what you are talking about?"

Pilar said:

"You think I am your niece, Pilar Estravados? But that is not so! Pilar was killed when I was traveling with her in a car in Spain. A bomb came and it hit the car and she was killed, but I was not touched. I did not know her very well, but she had told me all about herself and how her grandfather had sent for her to England and that he was very rich. And I had no money at all and I did not know where to go or what to do. And I thought suddenly: 'Why should not I take Pilar's passport and go to England and become very rich?' " Her face lit up with its sudden wide smile. "Oh, it was fun wondering if I could get away with it! Our faces on the photograph were not unlike. But when they wanted my passport here I opened the window and threw it out and ran down to get it, and then I rubbed some earth just over the face a little because at a barrier traveling they do not look very closely, but here they might—"

Alfred Lee said angrily:

"Do you mean to say that you represented yourself to my father as his granddaughter, and played on his affection for you?"

Pilar nodded. She said complacently:

"Yes, I saw at once I could make him like me very much."

George Lee broke out:

"Preposterous!" he spluttered. "Criminal! Attempting to get money by false pretences."

Harry Lee said:

"She didn't get any from *you*, old boy! Pilar, I'm on your side! I've got a profound admiration for your daring. And, thank goodness, I'm not your uncle any more! That gives me a much freer hand."

Pilar said to Poirot:

"*You* knew? When did you know?"

Poirot smiled.

"Mademoiselle, if you had studied the laws of Mendel you would know that two blue-eyed people are not likely to have a brown-eyed child. Your mother was, I was sure, a most chaste and respectable lady. It followed then, that you were not Pilar Estravados at all. When you did your trick with the passport, I was quite sure of it. It was ingenious, but not, you understand, quite ingenious enough."

Superintendent Sugden said unpleasantly:

"The whole thing's not quite ingenious enough."

Pilar stared at him. She said:

"I don't understand. . . ."

Sugden said:

"You've told us a story—but I think there's a good deal more you haven't told."

Stephen said:

"You leave her alone!"

Superintendent Sugden took no notice. He went on:

"You've told us that you went up to your grandfather's room after dinner. You said it was an impulse on your part. I'm going to suggest something else. It was you who stole those diamonds. You'd handled them. On occasion, perhaps, you'd put them away in the safe and the old man hadn't watched you do it! When he found the stones were missing, he saw at once that only two people could have taken them. One was Horbury, who might have got to know the combination and have crept in and stolen them during the night. The other person was *you*.

"Well, Mr. Lee at once took measures. He rang me up and had me come to see him. Then he sent word to you to come and see him immediately after dinner. You did so and he accused you of the theft. You denied it, you pressed the charge. I don't know what happened next—perhaps he tumbled to the fact that you weren't his granddaughter but a very clever little professional thief. Anyway the game was up, exposure loomed over you and you slashed at him with a knife. There was a struggle and he screamed. You were properly up against it then. You hurried out of the room, turned the key from the outside and then, knowing you could not get away, before the others came, *you slipped into the recess by the statues.*"

Pilar cried shrilly:

"It is not true! It is not true! I did not steal the diamonds! I did not kill him. I swear it by the Blessed Virgin."

Sugden said sharply:

"Then who did? You say you saw a figure standing outside Mr. Lee's door. According to your story, *that person must have been the murderer. No one else* passed the recess! But we've only *your* word for it *that there was a figure there at all.* In other words, *you made that up* to exculpate yourself!"

George Lee said sharply:

"Of course she's guilty! It's all clear enough! I always *said* an outsider killed my father! Preposterous nonsense to pretend one of his family would do a thing like that! It—it wouldn't be natural!"

Poirot stirred in his seat. He said:

"I disagree with you. Taking into consideration the character of Simeon Lee, it would be a very natural thing to happen."

"Eh?" George's jaw dropped. He stared at Poirot.

Poirot went on:

"And in my opinion that very thing *did* happen. Simeon Lee was killed by his own flesh and blood, for what seemed to the murderer a very good and sufficient reason."

George cried:

"One of us? I deny—"

Poirot's voice broke in hard as steel.

"There is a case against every person here. We will, Mr. George Lee, begin with the case against *you. You* had no love for your father! You kept on good terms with him for the sake of money. On the day of his death *he threatened to cut down your allowance.* You knew that on his death you would probably inherit a very substantial sum. There is the motive. After dinner you went, as you say, to telephone. You *did* telephone—but the call lasted only *five minutes.* After that, you could easily have gone to your father's room, chatted with him, and then attacked him and killed him. You left the room and turned the key from outside, for you hoped the affair would be put down to a burglar. You omitted, in your panic, to make sure that the window was fully open so as to support the burglar theory. That was stupid, but you are, if you will pardon my saying so, rather a stupid man!

"However," said Poirot, after a brief pause during which George tried to speak and failed, "many stupid men have been criminals!"

He turned his eyes on Magdalene.

"Madam, too, she also had a motive. She is, I think, in debt, and the tone of certain of your father's remarks may—have caused her uneasiness. She, too, has no alibi. She went to telephone, but she did *not* telephone, and we have *only her word for* what she did do. . . .

"Then"—he paused—"there is Mr. David Lee. We have heard, not once but many times of the revengeful tempers and long memories that went with the Lee blood. Mr. David Lee did not forgive or forget the way his father had treated his mother. A final jibe directed at the dead lady may have been the last straw. David Lee is said to have been playing the piano at the time of the murder. By a coincidence he was playing the *Dead March*. But suppose *somebody else* was playing that *Dead March*, somebody who knew what he was going to do and who approved his action."

Hilda Lee said quietly:

"That is an infamous suggestion."

Poirot turned to her.

"I will offer you another, madam. It was *your* hand that did the deed. It was *you* who crept upstairs to execute judgment on a man you considered beyond human forgiveness. You are of those, madam, who can be terrible in anger. . . ."

Hilda said:

"I did not kill him."

Superintendent Sugden said brusquely:

"Mr. Poirot's quite right. There is a possible case against everyone except Mr. Alfred Lee, Mr. Harry Lee and Mrs. Alfred Lee."

Poirot said gently:

"I should not even except those three. . . ."

The Superintendent protested.

"Oh, come now, Mr. Poirot!"

Lydia Lee said:

"And what is the case against me, Mr. Poirot?"

She smiled a little as she spoke, her brows raised ironically.

Poirot bowed. He said:

"Your motive, madam, I pass over. It is sufficiently obvious. As to the rest, you were wearing last night a flowered taffeta dress of a very distinctive pattern with a cape. I will remind you of the fact that Tressilian, the butler, is shortsighted. Objects at a distance are dim and vague to him. I will also point out that your drawing-room is big and lighted by heavily shaded lamps. On that night, a minute or two before the cries were heard, Tressilian came into the drawing-room to take away the coffee cups. He saw you, *as he thought,* in a familiar attitude by the far window half concealed by the heavy curtains."

Lydia Lee said:

"He did see me."

Poirot went on:

"I suggest that it is possible that *what Tressilian saw was the cape of your dress,* arranged to show by the window curtain, as though you yourself were standing there."

Lydia said:

"I was standing there. . . ."

Alfred said:

"How dare you suggest—"

Harry interrupted him.

"Let him go on, Alfred. It's our turn next. How do you suggest that dear Alfred killed his beloved father since we were both together in the dining-room at the time?"

Poirot beamed at him.

"That," he said, "is very simple. An alibi gains in force accordingly as it is unwillingly given. You and your brother are on bad terms. It is well known. *You* jibe at *him* in public. *He* has not a good word to say for *you!* But *supposing that were all part of a very clever plot.* Supposing that Alfred Lee is tired of dancing attendance upon an exacting taskmaster. Supposing that you and he have got together some time ago. Your plan is laid. You come home. Alfred appears to resent your presence. He shows jealousy and dislike of you. You show contempt for him. And then comes the night of the murder you have so cleverly planned together. One of you remains in the dining-room, talking and perhaps quarreling aloud as though two people were there. *The other goes upstairs and commits the crime.* . . ."

Alfred sprang to his feet.

"You devil," he said. His voice was inarticulate. "You inhuman devil. . . ."

Sugden was staring at Poirot. He said:

"Do you really mean—?"

Poirot said, with a sudden ring of authority in his voice:

"I have had to show you the *possibilities!* These are the things that *might* have happened! Which of them actually *did* happen we can only tell by passing from the outside appearance to the inside reality. . . ."

He paused and then said slowly:

"We must come back, as I said before, to the character of Simeon Lee himself. . . ."

VI

There was a momentary pause. Strangely enough, all indignation and all rancour had died down. Hercule Poirot held his audience under the spell of his personality. They watched him, fascinated, as he began slowly to speak.

"It is all there, you see. The dead man is the focus and centre of the mystery! We must probe deep into the heart and mind of Simeon Lee and see what we find there. For a man does not live and die to himself alone. That which he has, he hands on—to those who come after him. . . .

"What had Simeon Lee to bequeath to his sons and daughter? Pride, to begin with—a pride which in the old man was frustrated in his disappointment over his children. Then there was the quality of patience. We have been told that Simeon Lee waited patiently for years in order to revenge himself upon someone who had done him an injury. We see that that aspect of his temperament was inherited by the son who resembled him least in face. David Lee also could remember and continue to harbour resentment through long years. In *face*, Harry Lee was the only one of his children who closely resembled him. That resemblance is quite striking when we examine the portrait of Simeon Lee as a young man. There is the same high-bridged aquiline nose, the long sharp line of the jaw, the backward poise of the head. I think, too, that Harry inherited many of his father's mannerisms—that habit, for instance, of throwing back his head and laughing and another habit of drawing his finger along the line of his jaw.

"Bearing all these things in mind and being convinced that the murder was committed by a person closely connected with the dead man, I studied the family from the psychological standpoint. That is, I tried to decide which of them were *psychologically possible criminals*. And in my judgment only two persons qualified in that respect. They were Alfred Lee and Hilda Lee, David's wife. David himself I rejected as a possible murderer. I do not think a person of his delicate susceptibilities could have faced the actual bloodshed of a cut throat. George Lee and his wife I likewise rejected. Whatever their desires I did not think they had the temperament to take a *risk*. They were both essentially cautious. Mrs. Alfred Lee I felt sure was quite incapable of an act of violence. She has too much irony in her nature. About Harry Lee I hesitated. He had a certain coarse truculence of aspect, but I was nearly sure that Harry Lee, in spite of his bluff and his bluster, was essentially a weakling. That, I now know, was also his father's opinion. Harry, he said, was worth no more than the rest. That left me with the two people I have already mentioned. Alfred Lee was a person capable of a great deal of selfless devotion. He was a man who had controlled and subordinated himself to the will of another person for many long years. It is always possible under these conditions for something to snap. Moreover he might quite possibly have harboured a secret grudge against his father which might gradually have grown in force through never being expressed in any way. It is the quietest and meekest people who are often capable of the most sudden and unexpected violences for the reason that when their control does snap, it goes entirely! The other person I considered was capable of the crime was Hilda Lee. She is the kind of individual who is capable on occasions of taking the law into her own hands—though never through selfish motives. Such people judge and also execute. Many Old Testament characters are of this type. Jael and Judith for example.

"And now having got so far I examined the circumstances of the crime itself. And the first thing that arises—that strikes one in the face as it were —is the extraordinary conditions under which that crime took place! Take your minds back to that room where Simeon Lee lay dead. If you remember, there was both a heavy table and a heavy chair overturned, a lamp, crockery, glasses, etc. But the chair and the table were especially surprising. They were of solid mahogany. It was hard to see how *any* struggle between that frail old man and his opponent could result in so much solid furniture being overturned and knocked down. The whole thing seemed *unreal.* And yet surely no one in their senses would stage such an effect if it had not really occurred—unless possibly Simeon Lee had been killed by a powerful man and the idea was to suggest that the assailant was a woman or somebody of weak physique.

"But such an idea was unconvincing in the extreme since the noise of the furniture falling would give the alarm and the murderer would thereby have very little time to make his exit. It would surely be to *anyone's* advantage to cut Simeon Lee's throat as *quietly* as possible.

"Another extraordinary point was the turning of the key in the lock from the outside. Again there seemed no *reason* for such a proceeding. It could not suggest suicide, since nothing in the death itself accorded with suicide. It was not to suggest escape through the windows—for those windows were so arranged that escape that way was impossible! Moreover, once again, it involved *time.* Time which *must* be precious to the murderer!

"There was one other incomprehensible thing—a piece of rubber cut from Simeon Lee's sponge bag and a small wooden peg shown to me by Superintendent Sugden. These had been picked up from the floor by one of the persons who first entered that room. There again—*these things did not make sense!* They meant exactly nothing at all! Yet they had been there.

"The crime, you perceive, is becoming increasingly incomprehensible. It has no order, no method—*enfin*, it is not *reasonable!*

"And now we come to a further difficulty. Superintendent Sugden was sent for by the dead man—a robbery was reported to him and he was asked to return an hour and a half later. *Why?* If it is because Simeon Lee suspected his granddaughter or some other member of his family, why does he not ask Superintendent Sugden to wait downstairs while he has his interview straightaway with the suspected party? With the Superintendent actually in the house, his lever over the guilty person would have been much stronger.

"So now we arrive at the point where not only the behaviour of the murder is extraordinary but the behaviour of Simeon Lee also is extraordinary!

"And I say to myself: 'This thing is all wrong!' Why? Because we are looking at it *from the wrong angle*. We are looking at it *from the angle that the murderer wants us to look at it*. . . .

"We have three things that do not make sense—the struggle, the turned key, and the snip of rubber. But there *must* be some way of looking at those three things which *would* make sense! And I empty my mind blank and forget the circumstances of the crime and take these things *on their own merits*. I say—a *struggle*—what does *that* suggest? Violence—breakage—noise. . . . The *key? Why* does one turn a key? So that no one shall enter? But the key did not prevent that since the door was broken down almost immediately. To keep someone *in?* To keep someone *out?* A snip of rubber? I say to myself: 'A little piece of a sponge bag is a little piece of a sponge bag and that is all!'

"So you would say there is nothing there—and yet that is not strictly true, for three impressions remain. Noise—seclusion—blankness. . . .

"Do they fit with either of my two possibles? No, they do not. To both Alfred Lee and Hilda Lee a *quiet* murder would have been infinitely preferable, to have wasted time in locking the door from the outside is absurd, and the little piece of sponge bag means yet once more—nothing at all!

"And yet I have very strongly the feeling that there is nothing absurd about this crime—that it is on the contrary very well planned and admirably executed. That it has, in fact, *succeeded!* Therefore that everything that has happened was *meant*. . . .

"And then, going over it again, I got my first glimmer of light. . . .

"Blood—*so much blood*—blood everywhere. . . . An insistence on blood—fresh wet gleaming blood . . . so much blood—*too much blood.* . . .

"And a second thought comes with that. This is a crime of *blood*— it is *in* the blood. *It is Simeon Lee's own blood that rises up against him.* . . ." Hercule Poirot leaned forward.

"The two most valuable clues in this case were uttered quite unconsciously by two different people. The first was when Mrs. Alfred Lee quoted a line from Macbeth: *Who would have thought the old man to have had so much blood in him?* The other was a phrase uttered by Tressilian, the butler. He described how he felt dazed and things seemed to be happening that had happened before. It was a very simple occurrence that gave him that strange feeling. He heard a ring at the bell and went to open the door to Harry Lee, and the next day he did the same thing to Stephen Farr.

"Now *why* did he have that feeling? Look at Harry Lee and Stephen Farr *and you will see why.* They are astoundingly alike! *That* was why *opening the door to Stephen Farr was just like opening the door to Harry Lee.* It might almost have been the same man standing there. And then, only to-day, Tressilian mentioned that he was always getting muddled between people. No wonder! Stephen Farr has a high-bridged nose, a habit of throwing his head back when he laughs and a trick of stroking his jaw with his forefinger. Look long and earnestly at the portrait of Simeon Lee as a young man and you see *not only Harry Lee, but Stephen Farr.* . . ."

Stephen moved. His chair creaked. Poirot said:

"Remember that outburst of Simeon Lee's, his tirade against his family. He said, if you remember, that he would swear he had better sons *born the wrong side of the blanket.* We are back again at the character of Simeon Lee. Simeon Lee who was successful with women and who broke his wife's heart! Simeon Lee who boasted to Pilar that he might have a bodyguard of sons almost the same age! So I came to this conclusion. Simeon Lee had not only his legitimate family in the house *but an unacknowledged and unrecognized son of his own blood.*"

Stephen got to his feet. Poirot said:

"That was your real reason, wasn't it? Not that pretty romance of the girl you met in the train! You were coming here *before you met her.* Coming to see *what kind of a man your father was.* . . ."

Stephen had gone dead white. He said, and his voice was broken and husky:

"Yes, I've always wondered. . . . Mother spoke about him sometimes. It grew into a kind of obsession with me—to see what he was like! I made a bit of money and I came to England. I wasn't going to let him know who I was. I pretended to be old Eb's son. I came here for one reason only—to see the man who was my father. . . ."

Superintendent Sugden said in almost a whisper:

"Lord, I've been blind. . . . I can see it now. Twice I've taken you for Mr. Harry Lee and then seen my mistake, and yet I never guessed!"

He turned on Pilar:

"That was it, wasn't it? It was Stephen Farr you saw standing outside that door? You hesitated, I remember, and looked at him before you said it was a woman. It was Farr you saw, *and you weren't going to give him away.*"

There was a gentle rustle. Hilda Lee's deep voice spoke.

"No," she said. "You're wrong. It was *I* whom Pilar saw. . . ."

Poirot said:

"You, madam? Yes, I thought so. . . ."

Hilda said quietly:

"Self-preservation is a curious thing. I wouldn't believe I could be such a coward. To keep silence just because I was afraid!"

Poirot said:

"You will tell us now?"

She nodded.

"I was with David in the music room. He was playing. He was in a very queer mood. I was a little frightened and I felt my responsibility very keenly because it was I who had insisted on coming here. David began to play the *Dead March* and suddenly I made up my mind. However odd it might seem, I determined that we would both leave at once—that night. I went quietly out of the music room and upstairs, I meant to go to old Mr. Lee and tell him quite plainly why we were going. I went along the corridor to his room and knocked on the door. There was no answer. I knocked again a little louder. There was still no answer. Then I tried the door-handle. The door was locked. And then, as I stood hesitating, *I heard a sound inside the room—*"

She stopped.

"You won't believe me, but it's true! *Someone was in there—*assaulting Mr. Lee. I heard tables and chairs overturned and the crash of glass and china and then I heard that one last horrible cry that died away to nothing and then silence.

"I stood there paralyzed! I couldn't move! And then Mr. Farr came running along and Magdalene and all the others and Mr. Farr and Harry began to batter on the door. It went down and we saw the room *and there was no one in it*—except Mr. Lee lying dead in all that blood."

Her quiet voice rose higher. She cried:

"There was no one else there—no one, you understand! And *no one had come out of the room. . . ."*

VII

Superintendent Sugden drew a deep breath. He said:

"Either I'm going mad or everybody else is! What you've said, Mrs. Lee, is just plumb impossible. It's crazy!"

Hilda Lee cried:

"I tell you I heard them fighting in there and I heard the old man scream when his throat was cut—and no one came out and no one was in the room!"

Hercule Poirot said:

"And all this time you have said nothing?"

Hilda Lee's face was white, but she said steadily:

"No, because if I told you what had happened there's only one thing you could say or think—that it was *I* who killed him. . . ."

Poirot shook his head.

"No," he said. "You did not kill him. His son killed him."

Stephen Farr said:

"I swear before God I never touched him!"

"Not you," said Poirot. "He had other sons!"

Harry said:

"What the Hell—"

George stared. David drew his hand across his eyes. Alfred blinked twice.

Poirot said:

"The very first night I was here—the night of the murder I saw a ghost. *It was the ghost of the dead man.* When I first saw Harry Lee I was puzzled. I felt I had seen him before. Then I noted his features carefully and I realized how like his father he was, and I told myself that that was what caused the feeling of familiarity.

"But yesterday a man sitting opposite me threw back his head and laughed—*and I knew who it was Harry Lee reminded me of.* And I traced again, in another face, the features of the dead man.

"No wonder poor old Tressilian felt confused when he had answered the door not to two, but to *three* men who resembled each other closely. No wonder he confessed to getting muddled about people when there were three men in the house who, at a little distance, could pass for each other! The same build, the same gestures (one in particular, a trick of stroking the jaw), the same habit of laughing with the head thrown back, the same

distinctive high-bridged nose. Yet the similarity was not always easy to see
—*for the third man had a moustache.*"

He leaned forward.

"One forgets sometimes that police officers are men, that they have
wives and children, mothers"—he paused—"and *fathers.* . . . Remember
Simeon Lee's local reputation: A man who broke his wife's heart because
of his affairs with women. A son, born the wrong side of the blanket, may
inherit many things. He may inherit his father's features and even his
gestures. He may inherit his pride and his patience and his revengeful
spirit!"

His voice rose.

"All your life, Sugden, you've resented the wrong your father did you. I
think you determined long ago to kill him. You come from the next
county, not very far away. Doubtless your mother, with the money Simeon
Lee so generously gave her, was able to find a husband who would stand
father to her child. Easy for you to enter the Middleshire Police Force and
wait your opportunity. A Police Superintendent has a grand opportunity
of committing a murder and getting away with it."

Sugden's face had gone white as paper.

He said:

"You're mad! I was outside the house when he was killed."

Poirot shook his head.

"No, you killed him before you left the house the first time. No one saw
him alive after you left. It was all so easy for you. Simeon Lee expected
you, yes, *but he never sent for you.* It was *you* who rang him up and spoke
vaguely about an attempt at robbery. You said you would call upon him
just before eight that night and would pretend to be collecting for a Police
Charity. Simeon Lee had no suspicions. He did not know you were his son.
You came and told him a tale of substituted diamonds. He opened the safe
to show you that the real diamonds were safe in his possession. You apologized, came back to the hearth with him, and catching him unawares you
cut his throat, holding your hand over his mouth so that he shouldn't cry
out. Child's play to a man of your powerful physique.

"Then you set the scene. You took the diamonds. You piled up tables
and chairs, lamps and glasses, and twined a very thin rope or cord which
you had brought in coiled round your body, in and out between them. You
had with you a bottle of some freshly killed animal's blood to which you
had added a quantity of sodium citrate. You sprinkled this about freely
and added more sodium citrate to the pool of blood which flowed from
Simeon Lee's wound. You made up the fire so that the body should keep its
warmth. Then you passed the two ends of the cord out through the narrow
slit at the bottom of the window and let them hang down the wall. You left

the room and turned the key from the outside. That was vital, *since no one must by any chance enter that room.*

"Then you went out and hid the diamonds in the stone sink garden. If, sooner or later, they were discovered there, they would only focus suspicion more strongly where you wanted it—on the members of Simeon Lee's legitimate family. A little before nine-fifteen you returned and going up to the wall underneath the window you pulled on the cord. That dislodged the carefully piled up structure you had arranged. Furniture and china fell with a crash. You pulled on one end of the cord and rewound it round your body under your coat and waistcoat.

"You had one further device!"

He turned to the others.

"Do you remember, all of you, how each of you described the dying scream of Mr. Lee in a different way. You, Mr. Lee, described it as the cry of a man in mortal agony. Your wife and David Lee both used the expression, a soul in Hell. Mrs. David Lee, on the contrary, said it was the cry of someone who had *no* soul. She said it was inhuman like a beast. It was Harry Lee who came nearest to the truth. He said it sounded like killing a pig.

"Do you know those long pink bladders that are sold at fairs with faces painted on them called 'Dying Pigs'? As the air rushes out they give forth an inhuman wail. That, Sugden, was your final touch. You arranged one of those in the room. The mouth of it was stopped up with a peg, but that peg was connected to the cord. When you pulled on the cord the peg came out and the pig began to deflate. On top of the falling furniture came the scream of the Dying Pig."

He turned once more to the others.

"You see now what it was that Pilar Estravados picked up? The Superintendent had hoped to get there in time to retrieve that little wisp of rubber before anyone noticed it. However, he took it from Pilar quickly enough in his most official manner. But remember *he never mentioned that incident to anyone.* In itself that was a singularly suspicious fact. I heard of it from Magdalene Lee and tackled him about it. He was prepared for that eventuality. He had snipped a piece from Mr. Lee's rubber sponge bag and produced that together with a wooden peg. Superficially it answered to the same description—a fragment of rubber and a piece of wood. It meant, as I realized at the time, absolutely nothing! But fool that I was, I did not at once say: 'This means nothing, *so it cannot have been there and Superintendent Sugden is lying. . . .*' No, I foolishly went on trying to find an explanation for it. It was not until Mademoiselle Estravados was playing with a balloon that burst, and she cried out that it must have been a burst balloon she picked up in Simeon Lee's room, that I saw the truth.

"You see now how everything fits in? The improbable struggle *which is necessary to establish a false time of death.* The locked door—so that nobody shall find the body too soon. The dying man's scream. The crime is now logical and reasonable.

"But from the moment that Pilar Estravados cried aloud her discovery about the balloon, she was a source of danger to the murderer. And if that remark had been heard by him from the house (which it well might, for her voice was high and clear and the windows were open) she herself was in considerable danger. Already she had given the murderer one very nasty moment. She had said, speaking of old Mr. Lee: 'He must have been very good-looking when he was young.' And had added, speaking directly to Sugden—*'like you.'* She meant that literally and Sugden knew it. No wonder Sugden went purple in the face and nearly choked. It was so unexpected and so deadly dangerous. He hoped after that to fix the guilt on her but it proved unexpectedly difficult, since as the old man's granddaughter she had obviously no motive for the crime. Later, when he overheard from the house, her clear high voice calling out its remark about the balloon, he decided on desperate measures. He set that booby trap when we were at lunch. Luckily, almost by a miracle, it failed. . . ."

There was dead silence. Then Sugden said quietly:

"When were you sure?"

Poirot said:

"I was not quite sure till I brought home a false moustache and tried it on Simeon Lee's picture. Then—the face that looked at me was yours."

Sugden said:

"God rot his soul in Hell! I'm glad I did it!"

PART VII

DECEMBER 28TH

I

LYDIA LEE SAID:

"Pilar, I think you had better stay with us until we can arrange something definite for you."

Pilar said meekly:

"You are very good, Lydia. You are nice. You forgive people quite easily without making a fuss about it."

Lydia said, smiling:

"I still call you Pilar, though I know your name is something else."

"Yes, I am really Conchita Lopez."

"Conchita is a pretty name, too."

"You are really almost too nice, Lydia. But you don't need to be bothered by me. I am going to marry Stephen and we are going to South Africa."

Lydia said, smiling:

"Well, that rounds off things very nicely."

Pilar said timidly:

"Since you have been so kind, do you think, Lydia, that one day we might come back and stay with you—perhaps for Christmas and then we could have the crackers and the burning raisins and those shiny things on a tree and the little snow men?"

"Certainly you shall come and have a real English Christmas."

"That will be lovely. You see, Lydia, I feel that this year it was not a nice Christmas at all."

Lydia caught her breath. She said:

"No, it was not a nice Christmas. . . ."

II

Harry said:

"Well, good-bye, Alfred. Don't suppose you'll be troubled by seeing much of me. I'm off to Hawaii. Always meant to live there if I had a bit of money."

Alfred said:

"Good-bye, Harry. I expect you'll enjoy yourself. I hope so."

Harry said rather awkwardly:

"Sorry I riled you so much, old man. Rotten sense of humour I've got. Can't help trying to pull a fellow's leg."

Alfred said with an effort:

"Suppose I must learn to take a joke."

Harry said with relief:

"Well—so long."

III

Alfred said:

"David, Lydia and I have decided to sell up this place. I thought perhaps you'd like some of the things that were our mother's—her chair and that footstool. You were always her favourite."

David hesitated a minute. Then he said slowly:

"Thanks for the thought, Alfred, but do you know, I don't think I will. I don't want anything out of the house. I feel it's better to break with the past altogether."

Alfred said:

"Yes, I understand. Maybe you're right."

IV

George said:

"Well, good-bye, Alfred. Good-bye, Lydia. What a terrible time we have been through. There's the trial coming on, too. I suppose the whole disgraceful story is bound to come out? Sugden being—er—my father's son. One couldn't arrange for it to be put to him, I suppose, that it would be better if he pleaded advanced Communist views and dislike of my father as a Capitalist—something of that kind?"

Lydia said:

"My dear George, do you really imagine that a man like Sugden would tell lies to soothe *our* feelings?"

George said:

"Er—perhaps not. No, I see your point. All the same, the man must be mad. Well, good-bye again."

Magdalene said:

"*Good*-bye. Next year do let's all go to the Riviera or somewhere for Christmas and be really gay."

George said:

"Depends on the Exchange."

Magdalene said:

"Darling, don't be *mean.*"

V

Alfred came out on the terrace. Lydia was bending over a stone sink. She straightened up when she saw him.

He said with a sigh:

"Well—they've all gone."

Lydia said:

"Yes—what a blessing."

"It is rather."

Alfred said:

"You'll be glad to leave here."

She asked:

"Will you mind very much?"

"No, I shall be glad. There are so many interesting things we can do together. To live on here would be to be constantly reminded of that nightmare. Thank God, it's all over!"

Lydia said:

"Thanks to Hercule Poirot."

"Yes. You know, it was really amazing the way everything fell into place when he explained it."

"I know. Like when you finish a jig-saw puzzle and all the queer shaped bits you swear won't fit in anywhere find their places quite naturally."

Alfred said:

"There's one little thing that never fitted in. What *was* George doing *after* he telephoned. Why wouldn't he say?"

Lydia laughed.

"Don't you know? I knew all the time. He was having a look through your papers on your desk."

"Oh! no, Lydia, no one would do a thing like that!"

"George would. He's frightfully curious about money matters. But of course he couldn't say so. He'd have had to be actually in the dock before he'd have owned up to that."

Alfred said:

"Are you making another garden?"

"Yes."

"What is it this time?"

"I think," said Lydia, "it's an attempt at the Garden of Eden. A new version—without any serpent—and Adam and Eve are definitely middle-aged."

Alfred said gently:

"Dear Lydia, how patient you have been all these years. You have been very good to me."

Lydia said:

"But you see, Alfred, I love you. . . ."

VI

Colonel Johnson said:

"God bless my soul!" Then he said: "Upon my word!" and finally once more, "God bless my soul!"

He leaned back in his chair and stared at Poirot. He said plaintively:

"My best man! What's the police coming to?"

Poirot said:

"Even policemen have private lives! Sugden was a very proud man."

Colonel Johnson shook his head.

To relieve his feelings he kicked at the logs in the grate. He said jerkily:

"I always say—nothing like a wood fire."

Hercule Poirot, conscious of the draughts round his neck, thought to himself:

"Pour moi, every time the central heating. . . ."

THE HOLLOW

For Larry and Dande
With apologies for using their swimming pool
as the scene of a murder

Chapter I

AT 6:13 A.M. ON a Friday morning Lucy Angkatell's big blue eyes opened upon another day, and as always, she was at once wide awake and began immediately to deal with the problems conjured up by her incredibly active mind. Feeling urgently the need of consultation and conversation, and selecting for the purpose her young cousin Midge Hardcastle, who had arrived at The Hollow the night before, Lady Angkatell slipped quickly out of bed, threw a negligee round her still graceful shoulders, and went along the passage to Midge's room. Since she was a woman of disconcertingly rapid thought processes, Lady Angkatell, as was her invariable custom, commenced the conversation in her own mind, supplying Midge's answers out of her own fertile imagination.

The conversation was in full swing when Lady Angkatell flung open Midge's door.

"—And so, darling, you really must agree that the weekend *is* going to present difficulties!"

"Eh? Hwah?" Midge grunted inarticulately, aroused thus abruptly from a satisfying and deep sleep.

Lady Angkatell crossed to the window, opening the shutters and jerking up the blind with a brisk movement, letting in the pale light of a September dawn.

"Birds!" she observed, peering with kindly pleasure through the pane. "So sweet."

"What?"

"Well, at any rate, the weather isn't going to present difficulties. It looks as though it had set in fine. That's something. Because if a lot of discordant personalities are boxed up indoors, I'm sure you will agree with me that it makes it ten times worse. Round games perhaps, and that would be like last year when I shall never forgive myself about poor Gerda. I said to Henry afterwards it was most thoughtless of me—and one *has* to have her, of course, because it would be so rude to ask John without her, but it really does make things difficult—and the worst of it is that she is so nice—really it seems odd sometimes that anyone so nice as Gerda is should be so devoid of any kind of intelligence, and if that is what they mean by the law of compensation I don't really think it is at all fair."

"What *are* you talking about, Lucy?"

"The week-end, darling. The people who are coming tomorrow. I have been thinking about it all night and I have been dreadfully bothered about it. So it really is a relief to talk it over with you, Midge. You are always so sensible and practical."

"Lucy," said Midge sternly, "do you know what time it is?"

"Not exactly, darling. I never do, you know."

"It's quarter past six."

"Yes, dear," said Lady Angkatell, with no signs of contrition.

Midge gazed sternly at her. How maddening, how absolutely impossible Lucy was! Really, thought Midge, I don't know why we put up with her!

Yet, even as she voiced the thought to herself, she was aware of the answer. Lucy Angkatell was smiling, and as Midge looked at her, she felt the extraordinary pervasive charm that Lucy had wielded all her life and that even now, at over sixty, had not failed her. Because of it, people all over the world, foreign potentates, A.D.Cs, Government officials, had endured inconvenience, annoyance and bewilderment. It was the childlike pleasure and delight in her own doings that disarmed and nullified criticism. Lucy had but to open those wide blue eyes and stretch out those fragile hands, and murmur: "Oh! but I'm so *sorry* . . ." and resentment immediately vanished.

"Darling," said Lady Angkatell, "I'm so *sorry*. You should have told me!"

"I'm telling you now—but it's too late! I'm thoroughly awake."

"What a shame. But you *will* help me, won't you?"

"About the week-end? Why? What's wrong with it?"

Lady Angkatell sat down on the edge of the bed. It was not, Midge thought, like anyone else sitting on your bed. It was as unsubstantial as though a fairy had poised itself there for a minute.

Lady Angkatell stretched out fluttering white hands in a lovely, helpless gesture.

"All the wrong people coming—the wrong people to be *together,* I mean—not in themselves. They're all charming really."

"Who *is* coming?"

Midge pushed thick, wiry black hair back from her square forehead with a sturdy brown arm. Nothing unsubstantial or fairylike about her.

"Well, John and Gerda. That's all right by itself. I mean John is delightful—*most* attractive. And as for poor Gerda—well, I mean, we must all be very kind. Very, very kind."

Moved by an obscure instinct of defence, Midge said:

"Oh, come now, she's not as bad as that."

"Oh, darling, she's pathetic. Those *eyes.* And she never seems to understand a single word one says."

"She doesn't," said Midge. "Not what you say—but I don't know that I blame her. Your mind, Lucy, goes so fast, that to keep pace with it your conversation takes the most amazing leaps. All the connecting links are left out."

"Just like a monkey," said Lady Angkatell vaguely.

"But who else is coming beside the Christows? Henrietta, I suppose?"

Lady Angkatell's face brightened.

"Yes—and I really do feel that she will be a tower of strength. She always is. Henrietta, you know, is really kind—kind all through, not just on top. She will help a lot with poor Gerda. She was simply wonderful last year. That was the time we played limericks, or wordmaking, or quotations—or one of those things, and we had all finished and were reading them out when we suddenly discovered that poor dear Gerda hadn't even begun. She wasn't even sure what the game was. It was dreadful, wasn't it, Midge?"

"Why anyone ever comes to stay with the Angkatells, I don't know," said Midge. "What with the brainwork, and the round games, and your peculiar style of conversation, Lucy."

"Yes, darling, we must be trying—and it must always be hateful for Gerda, and I often think that if she had any spirit she would stay away—but, however, there it was, and the poor dear looked so bewildered and—well—mortified, you know. And John looked so dreadfully impatient. And I simply couldn't think of how to make things all right again—and it was then that I felt so grateful to Henrietta. She turned right round to Gerda and asked about the pullover she was wearing—really a dreadful affair in faded lettuce green—too depressing and jumble sale, darling—and Gerda brightened up at once; it seems that she had knitted it herself, and Henrietta asked her for the pattern, and Gerda looked so happy and proud. And that is what I mean about Henrietta. She can always *do* that sort of thing. It's a kind of knack."

"She takes trouble," said Midge slowly.

"Yes, and she knows what to say."

"Ah," said Midge. "But it goes further than saying. Do you know, Lucy, that Henrietta actually knitted that pullover."

"Oh, my dear." Lady Angkatell looked grave. "And *wore* it?"

"And wore it. Henrietta carries things through."

"And was it very dreadful?"

"No. On Henrietta it looked very nice."

"Well, of course, it would. That's just the difference between Henrietta and Gerda. Everything Henrietta does she does well and it turns out right. She's clever about nearly everything, as well as in her own line. I must say, Midge, that if anyone carries us through this week-end, it will be Henrietta. She will be nice to Gerda and she will amuse Henry, and she'll keep John in a good temper and I'm sure she'll be most helpful with David—"

"David Angkatell?"

"Yes. He's just down from Oxford—or perhaps Cambridge. Boys of that age are so difficult—especially when they are intellectual. David is very intellectual. One wishes that they could put off being intellectual until they were rather older. As it is, they always glower at one so and bite their nails and seem to have so many spots and sometimes an Adam's apple as well. And they either won't speak at all, or else are very loud and contradictory. Still, as I say, I am trusting to Henrietta. She is very tactful and asks the right kind of questions, and being a sculptress they respect her, especially as she doesn't just carve animals or children's heads but does advanced things like that curious affair in metal and plaster that she exhibited at the New Artists last year. It looked rather like a Heath Robinson step ladder. It was called Ascending Thought—or something like that. It is the kind of thing that would impress a boy like David . . . I thought myself it was just silly."

"Dear Lucy!"

"But some of Henrietta's things I think are quite lovely. That Weeping Ash tree figure for instance."

"Henrietta has a touch of real genius, I think. And she is a very lovely and satisfying person as well," said Midge.

Lady Angkatell got up and drifted over to the window again. She played absentmindedly with the blind cord.

"Why acorns, I wonder?" she murmured.

"Acorns?"

"On the blind cord. Like pineapples on gates. I mean, there must be a *reason.* Because it might just as easily be a fir cone or a pear, but it's always an acorn. Mash, they call it in crosswords—you know, for pigs. So curious, I always think."

"Don't ramble off, Lucy. You came in here to talk about the week-end and I can't see why you are so anxious about it. If you manage to keep off round games, and try to be coherent when you're talking to Gerda, and put Henrietta on to tame the intellectual David, where is the difficulty?"

"Well, for one thing, darling, Edward is coming."

"Oh, Edward." Midge was silent for a moment after saying the name. Then she asked quietly:

"What on earth made you ask Edward for this week-end?"

"I didn't, Midge. That's just it. He asked himself. Wired to know if we could have him. You know what Edward is. How sensitive. If I'd wired back 'No,' he'd probably never have asked himself again. He's like that."

Midge nodded her head slowly.

Yes, she thought, Edward was like that. For an instant she saw his face clearly, that very dearly loved face. A face with something of Lucy's insubstantial charm; gentle, diffident, ironic . . .

"Dear Edward," said Lucy, echoing the thought in Midge's mind.

She went on impatiently:

"If only Henrietta would make up her mind to marry him. She is really fond of him, I know she is. If they had been here some week-end without the Christows . . . As it is, John Christow has always the most unfortunate effect on Edward. John, if you know what I mean, becomes so much *more* so and Edward becomes so much *less* so. You understand?"

Again Midge nodded.

"And I can't put the Christows off because this week-end was arranged long ago, but I do feel, Midge, that it is all going to be difficult, with David glowering and biting his nails, and with trying to keep Gerda from feeling out of it, and with John being so positive and dear Edward so negative—"

"The ingredients of the pudding are not promising," murmured Midge.

Lucy smiled at her.

"Sometimes," she said meditatively, "things arrange themselves quite simply. I've asked the crime man to lunch on Sunday. It will make a distraction, don't you think so?"

"Crime man?"

"Like an egg," said Lady Angkatell. "He was in Baghdad, solving something, when Henry was High Commissioner. Or perhaps it was afterwards? We had him to lunch with some other duty people. He had on a white duck suit, I remember, and a pink flower in his buttonhole, and black patent leather shoes. I don't remember much about it because I never think it's very interesting who killed who. I mean once they are dead it doesn't seem to matter why, and to make a fuss about it all seems so silly . . ."

"But have you any crimes down here, Lucy?"

"Oh, no, darling. He's in one of those funny new cottages—you know, beams that bump your head and a lot of very good plumbing and quite the wrong kind of garden. London people like that sort of thing. There's an actress in the other, I believe. They don't live in them all the time like we do. Still," Lady Angkatell moved vaguely across the room, "I daresay it pleases them. Midge darling, it's sweet of you to have been so helpful."

"I don't think I have been so very helpful."

"Oh, haven't you?" Lucy Angkatell looked surprised. "Well, have a

nice sleep now and don't get up to breakfast, and when you do get up, do
be as rude as ever you like."

"Rude?" Midge looked surprised. "Why? Oh!" she laughed. "I see!
Penetrating of you, Lucy. Perhaps I'll take you at your word."

Lady Angkatell smiled and went out. As she passed the open bathroom
door and saw the kettle and gas ring, an idea came to her.

People were fond of tea, she knew—and Midge wouldn't be called for
hours. She would make Midge some tea. She put the kettle on and then
went on down the passage.

She paused at her husband's door and turned the handle, but Sir Henry
Angkatell, that able administrator, knew his Lucy. He was extremely fond
of her but he liked his morning sleep undisturbed. The door was locked.

Lady Angkatell went on into her own room. She would have liked to
have consulted Henry but later would do. She stood by her open window,
looking out for a moment or two, then she yawned. She got into bed, laid
her head on the pillow and in two minutes was sleeping like a child.

In the bathroom the kettle came to the boil and went on boiling . . .

"Another kettle gone, Mr. Gudgeon," said Simmons, the housemaid.

Gudgeon, the butler, shook his grey head.

He took the burnt-out kettle from Simmons and, going into the pantry,
produced another kettle from the bottom of the plate cupboard where he
had a stock of half a dozen.

"There you are, Miss Simmons. Her ladyship will never know."

"Does her ladyship often do this kind of thing?" asked Simmons.

Gudgeon sighed.

"Her ladyship," he said, "is at once kind-hearted and very forgetful, if
you know what I mean. But in this house," he continued, "I see to it that
everything possible is done to spare her ladyship annoyance or worry."

Chapter II

HENRIETTA SAVERNAKE ROLLED up a little strip of clay and patted it into place. She was building up the clay head of a girl with swift practised skill.

In her ears, but penetrating only to the edge of her understanding, was the thin whine of a slightly common voice:

"And I do think, Miss Savernake, that I was quite right! 'Really,' I said, 'if *that's* the line you're going to take!' Because I do think, Miss Savernake, that a girl owes it to herself to make a stand about these sort of things—if you know what I mean. 'I'm not accustomed,' I said, 'to having things like that said to me, and I can only say that you must have a very nasty imagination!' One does hate unpleasantness, but I do think I was right to make a stand, don't you, Miss Savernake?"

"Oh, absolutely," said Henrietta with a fervour in her voice which might have led someone who knew her well to suspect that she had not been listening very closely.

"'And if your wife says things of that kind,' I said, 'well, I'm sure *I* can't help it!' I don't know how it is, Miss Savernake, but it seems to be trouble wherever I go, and I'm sure it's not *my* fault. I mean, men are so susceptible, aren't they?" The model gave a coquettish little giggle.

"Frightfully," said Henrietta, her eyes half closed.

"Lovely," she was thinking. "Lovely that plane just below the eyelid— and the other plane coming up to meet it. That angle by the jaw's wrong . . . I must scrape off there and build up again. It's tricky."

Aloud she said in her warm, sympathetic voice:

"It must have been *most* difficult for you."

"I do think jealousy's so unfair, Miss Savernake, and so *narrow,* if you know what I mean. It's just envy, if I may say so, because someone's better looking and younger than they are."

Henrietta, working on the jaw, said absently, "Yes, of course."

She had learned the trick, years ago, of shutting her mind into watertight compartments. She could play a game of bridge, conduct an intelligent conversation, write a clearly constructed letter, all without giving more than a fraction of her essential mind to the task. She was now completely intent on seeing the head of Nausicaa build itself up under her fingers, and the thin, spiteful stream of chatter issuing from those very lovely childish lips penetrated not at all into the deeper recesses of her mind. She kept the conversation going without effort. She was used to models who wanted to talk. Not so much the professional ones—it was the amateurs who, uneasy at their forced inactivity of limb, made up for it by bursting into garrulous self-revelation. So an inconspicuous part of Henrietta listened and replied, and, very far and remote, the real Henrietta commented: "Common, mean, spiteful little piece—but what eyes . . . Lovely, lovely, lovely eyes . . ."

Whilst she was busy on the eyes, let the girl talk. She would ask her to keep silent when she got to the mouth. Funny when you came to think of it, that that thin stream of spite should come out through those perfect curves.

"Oh, damn," thought Henrietta with sudden frenzy, "I'm ruining that eyebrow arch! What the hell's the matter with it? I've over-emphasized the bone—it's sharp, not thick . . ."

She stood back again, frowning from the clay to the flesh and blood sitting on the platform.

Doris Sanders went on:

" 'Well,' I said, 'I really don't see why your husband shouldn't give me a present if he likes, and I don't think,' I said, 'you ought to make insinuations of that kind.' It was ever such a nice bracelet, Miss Savernake, *reely* quite lovely—and, of course, I daresay the poor fellow couldn't really afford it, but I do think it was nice of him, and I certainly wasn't going to give it back!"

"No, no," murmured Henrietta.

"And it's not as though there was anything between us—anything *nasty,* I mean—there was nothing of *that* kind."

"No," said Henrietta, "I'm sure there wouldn't be."

Her brow cleared. For the next half hour she worked in a kind of fury. Clay smeared itself on her forehead, clung to her hair, as she pushed an impatient hand through it. Her eyes had a blind intense ferocity. It was coming . . . she was getting it . . .

Now, in a few hours, she would be out of her agony—the agony that had been growing upon her for the last ten days.

Nausicaa—she had been haunted by Nausicaa, she had got up with Nausicaa and had breakfasted with Nausicaa and had gone out with Nausicaa. She had tramped the streets in a nervous, excitable restlessness, unable to fix her mind on anything but a beautiful blind face somewhere just beyond her mind's eye—hovering there just not able to be clearly seen.

She had interviewed models, hesitated over Greek types, felt profoundly dissatisfied . . .

She wanted something—something to give her the start—something that would bring her own already partially realized vision alive. She had walked long distances, getting physically tired out and welcoming the fact. And driving her, harrying her, was that urgent incessant longing—to *see*—

There was a blind look in her own eyes as she walked. She saw nothing of what was around her. She was straining—straining the whole time to make that face come nearer . . . She felt sick, ill, miserable . . .

And then, suddenly, her vision had cleared and with normal human eyes she had seen opposite her in the bus which she had boarded absent-mindedly and with no interest in its destination—she had seen—yes, *Nausicaa!*

A foreshortened childish face, half parted lips and eyes—lovely, vacant, blind eyes.

The girl rang the bell and got out; Henrietta followed her.

She was now quite calm and businesslike. She had got what she wanted —the agony of baffled search was over.

"Excuse me for speaking to you. I'm a professional sculptor and, to put it frankly, your head is just what I have been looking for."

She was friendly, charming and compelling, as she knew how to be when she wanted something.

Doris Sanders had been doubtful, alarmed, flattered.

"Well, I don't know, I'm sure. If it's just the *head*. Of course, I've never *done* that sort of thing!"

Suitable hesitations, delicate financial inquiry.

"Of course, I should insist on your accepting the proper professional fee."

And so here was Nausicaa, sitting on the platform, enjoying the idea of her attractions being immortalized (though not liking very much the examples of Henrietta's work which she could see in the studio!) and enjoying also the revelation of her personality to a listener whose sympathy and attention seemed to be so complete.

On the table beside the model were her spectacles—the spectacles that she put on as seldom as possible, owing to vanity, preferring to feel her way almost blindly sometimes, since she admitted to Henrietta that without them she was so short-sighted that she could hardly see a yard in front of her.

Henrietta had nodded comprehendingly. She understood now the physical reason for that blank and lovely stare.

Time went on. Henrietta suddenly laid down her modelling tools and stretched her arms widely.

"All right," she said, "I've finished. I hope you're not too tired?"

"Oh, no, thank you, Miss Savernake. It's been very interesting, I'm sure. Do you mean it's really done—so soon?"

Henrietta laughed.

"Oh, no, it's not actually finished. I shall have to work on it quite a bit. But it's finished as far as you're concerned. I've got what I wanted—built up the planes."

The girl came down slowly from the platform. She put on her spectacles and at once the blind innocence and vague confiding charm of the face vanished. There remained now an easy, cheap prettiness.

She came to stand by Henrietta and look at the clay model.

"Oh," she said doubtfully, disappointment in her voice, "it's not very like me, is it?"

Henrietta smiled.

"Oh, no, it's not a portrait."

There was, indeed, hardly a likeness at all. It was the setting of the eyes —the line of the cheekbone—that Henrietta had seen as the essential keynote of her conception of Nausicaa. This was not Doris Sanders; it was a blind girl about whom a poem could be made. The lips were parted as Doris's were parted, but they were not Doris's lips. They were lips that would speak another language and would utter thoughts that were not Doris's thoughts—

None of the features were clearly defined. It was Nausicaa remembered, not seen . . .

"Well," said Miss Sanders doubtfully, "I suppose it'll look better when you've got on with it a bit . . . And you *reely* don't want me any more?"

"No, thank you," said Henrietta. ("And thank God I don't!" said her inner mind.) "You've been simply splendid. I'm very grateful."

She got rid of Doris expertly and returned to make herself some black coffee. She was tired—she was horribly tired . . . But happy—happy and at peace.

"Thank goodness," she thought, "now I can be a human being again."

And at once her thoughts went to John . . .

John, she thought. Warmth crept into her cheeks, a sudden quick lifting of the heart made her spirits soar.

Tomorrow, she thought, I'm going to The Hollow . . . I shall see John . . .

She sat quite still, sprawled back on the divan, drinking down the hot strong liquid. She drank three cups of it . . . She felt vitality surging back . . .

It was nice, she thought, to be a human being again—and not that other thing. Nice to have stopped feeling restless and miserable and driven. Nice to be able to stop walking about the streets unhappily, looking for something, and feeling irritable and impatient because, really, you didn't know what you were looking for! Now, thank goodness, there would be only hard work—and who minded hard work?

She put down the empty cup and got up and strolled back to Nausicaa. She looked at the face for some time, and slowly a little frown crept between her brows.

It wasn't—it wasn't quite—

What was it that was wrong . . .

Blind eyes . . .

Blind eyes that were more beautiful than any eyes that could see . . . Blind eyes that tore at your heart because they were blind . . . Had she got that or hadn't she?

She'd got it, yes—but she'd got something else as well. Something that she hadn't meant or thought about . . . The structure was all right—yes, surely. But where did it come from—that faint insidious suggestion . . .

The suggestion, somewhere, of a common spiteful mind . . .

She hadn't been listening, not really listening. Yet, somehow, in through her ears and out at her fingers, it had worked its way into the clay.

And she wouldn't, she knew she wouldn't, be able to get it out again . . .

Henrietta turned away sharply. Perhaps it was fancy. Yes, surely it was fancy. She would feel quite differently about it in the morning. She thought with dismay, how vulnerable one is.

She walked, frowning, up to the end of the studio. She stopped in front of her figure of The Worshipper.

That was all right—a lovely bit of pearwood, graining just right. She'd saved it up for ages, hoarding it.

She looked at it critically. Yes, it was good, No doubt about that. The best thing she had done for a long time—it was for the International Group. Yes, quite a worthy exhibit.

She'd *got* it all right; the humility, the strength in the neck muscles, the bowed shoulders, the slightly upraised face—a featureless face, since worship drives out personality.

—Yes, submission, adoration—and that final devotion that is beyond, not this side, idolatry.

Henrietta sighed. If only, she thought, John had not been so angry . . .

It had startled her, that anger. It had told her something about him that he did not, she thought, know himself.

He had said flatly, "You can't exhibit that!"

And she had said, as flatly, "I shall."

She went slowly back to Nausicaa. There was nothing there, she thought, that she couldn't put right. She sprayed it and wrapped it up in the damp cloths. It would have to stand over until Monday or Tuesday. There was no hurry now. The urgency had gone—all the essential planes were there. It only needed patience.

Ahead of her were three happy days with Lucy and Henry and Midge—and John!

She yawned, stretched herself like a cat stretches itself with relish and abandon, pulling out each muscle to its fullest extent. She knew suddenly how very tired she was.

She had a hot bath and went to bed. She lay on her back staring at a star or two through the skylight. Then from there her eyes went to the one light she always left on, the small bulb that illuminated the glass mask that had been one of her earliest bits of work. Rather an obvious piece, she thought now. Conventional in its suggestion.

Lucky, thought Henrietta, that one outgrew oneself . . .

And now, sleep! The strong black coffee that she had drunk did not bring wakefulness in its train unless she wished it to do so. Long ago she had taught herself the essential rhythm that could bring oblivion at call.

You took thoughts, choosing them out of your store, and then, not dwelling on them, you let them slip through the fingers of your mind, never clutching at them, never dwelling on them, no concentration . . . just letting them drift gently past . . .

Outside in the Mews a car was being revved up—somewhere there was hoarse shouting and laughing. She took the sounds into the stream of her semi-consciousness—

The car, she thought, was a tiger roaring . . . yellow and black . . . striped like the striped leaves—leaves and shadows—a hot jungle . . . and then down the river—a wide tropical river . . . to the sea and the liner starting . . . and hoarse voices calling good-bye—and John beside her on the deck . . . she and John starting—blue sea and down into the dining saloon—smiling at him across the table—like dinner at the Maison Dorée—poor John, so angry! . . . out into the night air—and the car, the feeling of sliding in the gears—effortless, smooth, racing out of London . . . up over Shovel Down . . . the trees . . . tree worship . . . The Hollow . . . Lucy . . . John . . . John . . . Ridgeway's Disease . . . dear John . . .

Passing into unconsciousness now, into a happy beatitude . . .

And then some sharp discomfort, some haunting sense of guilt pulling her back. Something she ought to have done . . . Something that she had shirked . . .

Nausicaa?

Slowly, unwillingly, Henrietta got out of bed. She switched on the lights, went across to the stand and unwrapped the cloths.

She took a deep breath.

Not Nausicaa—Doris Sanders!

A pang went through Henrietta. She was pleading with herself, "I can get it right—I can get it right . . ."

"Stupid," she said to herself. "You know quite well what you've got to do."

Because if she didn't do it now, at once—tomorrow she wouldn't have the courage. It was like destroying your flesh and blood. It hurt—yes, it hurt . . .

Perhaps, thought Henrietta, cats feel like this when one of their kittens has something wrong with it and they kill it . . .

She took a quick sharp breath, then she seized the clay, twisting it off the armature, carrying it, a large heavy lump, to dump it in the clay bin.

She stood there, breathing deeply, looking down at her clay-smeared hands, still feeling the wrench to her physical and mental self. She cleaned the clay off her hands slowly.

She went back to bed feeling a curious emptiness, yet a sense of peace.

Nausicaa, she thought sadly, would not come again. She had been born, had been contaminated and had died . . .

Queer, thought Henrietta, how things can seep into you without your knowing it . . .

She hadn't been listening—not really listening—and yet knowledge of Doris's cheap, spiteful little mind had seeped into her mind and had, unconsciously, influenced her hands.

And now the thing that had been Nausicaa—Doris—was only—clay— just the raw material that would soon be fashioned into something else.

Henrietta thought dreamily, Is that, then, what *death* is? Is what we call personality just the shaping of it—the impress of somebody's thought? Whose thought? God's?

That was the idea, wasn't it, of *Peer Gynt?* Back into the Button Moulder's ladle. *Where am I, myself, the whole man, the true man? Where am I with God's mark upon my brow?*

Did John feel like that? He had been so tired the other night—so disheartened. Ridgeway's Disease . . . Not one of those books told you who Ridgeway was! Stupid, she thought, she would like to know . . . Ridgeway's Disease . . . John . . .

Chapter III

JOHN CHRISTOW SAT in his consulting room seeing his last patient but one for that morning. His eyes, sympathetic and encouraging, watched her as she described—explained—went into details. Now and then he nodded his head understandingly. He asked questions, gave directions. A gentle glow pervaded the sufferer. Dr. Christow was really wonderful! He was so interested—so truly concerned. Even talking to him made one feel stronger.

John Christow drew a sheet of paper towards him and began to write. Better give her a laxative, he supposed. That new American proprietary—nicely put up in cellophane and attractively coated in an unusual shade of salmon pink. Very expensive, too, and difficult to get—not every chemist stocked it. She'd probably have to go to that little place in Wardour Street. That would be all to the good—probably buck her up no end for a month or two, then he'd have to think of something else. There was nothing he could do for her. Poor physique and nothing to be done about it! Nothing to get your teeth into. Not like old Mother Crabtree . . .

A boring morning. Profitable financially—but nothing else. God, he was tired! Tired of sickly women and their ailments. Palliation, alleviation—nothing to it but that. Sometimes he wondered if it was worth it . . . but always then he remembered St. Christopher's, and the long row of beds in the Margaret Russell Ward, and Mrs. Crabtree grinning up at him with her toothless smile.

He and she understood each other! She was a fighter, not like that limp slug of a woman in the next bed. She was on his side, she wanted to live—though God knew why, considering the slum she lived in, with a husband who drank and a brood of unruly children, and she herself obliged to work day in day out, scrubbing endless floors of endless offices. Hard, unremitting drudgery and few pleasures! But she wanted to live—she enjoyed life —just as he, John Christow, enjoyed life! It wasn't the circumstances of life they enjoyed, it was life itself—the zest of existence. Curious—a thing one couldn't explain. He thought to himself that he must talk to Henrietta about that.

He got up to accompany his patient to the door. His hand took hers in a warm clasp, friendly, encouraging. His voice was encouraging, too, full of interest and sympathy. She went away revived, almost happy. Dr. Christow took such an interest!

As the door closed behind her, John Christow forgot her, he had really been hardly aware of her existence even when she had been there. He had just done his stuff. It was all automatic. Yet, though it had hardly ruffled the surface of his mind, he had given out strength. His had been the automatic response of the healer and he felt the sag of depleted energy.

God, he thought again, I'm tired . . .

Only one more patient to see and then the clear space of the week-end. His mind dwelt on it gratefully. Golden leaves tinged with red and brown, the soft moist smell of Autumn—the road down through the woods—the wood fires. Lucy, most unique and delightful of creatures—with her curious, elusive, will-o'-the-wisp mind. He'd rather have Henry and Lucy than any other host and hostess in England. And The Hollow was the most delightful house he knew. On Sunday he'd walk through the woods with Henrietta—up onto the crest of the hill and along the ridge. Walking with Henrietta he'd forget that there were any sick people in the world. Thank goodness, he thought, there's never anything the matter with Henrietta.

And then with a sudden quick twist of humour, she'd never let on to me if there was!

One more patient to see. He must press the bell on his desk . . . Yet, unaccountably, he delayed. Already he was late. Lunch would be ready upstairs in the dining room. Gerda and the children would be waiting. He must get on . . .

Yet he sat there motionless. He was so tired—so very tired.

It had been growing on him lately, this tiredness. It was at the root of the constantly increasing irritability which he was aware of but could not check. Poor Gerda, he thought, she has a lot to put up with . . . If only she was not so submissive—so ready to admit herself in the wrong when, half the time, it was *he* who was to blame! There were days when everything that Gerda said or did conspired to irritate him, and mainly, he thought ruefully, it was her virtues that irritated him. It was her patience, her unselfishness, her subordination of her wishes to his, that aroused his ill humour. And she never resented his quick bursts of temper, never stuck to her own opinion in preference to his, never attempted to strike out a line of her own.

(Well, he thought, that's why you married her, isn't it? What are you complaining about? After that Summer at San Miguel.)

Curious, when you came to think of it, that the very qualities that irritated him in Gerda, were the qualities he wanted so badly to find in

Henrietta. What irritated him in Henrietta—(no, that was the wrong word
—it was anger, not irritation, that she inspired)—what angered him there
was Henrietta's unswerving rectitude where he was concerned. It was so at
variance with her attitude to the world in general. He had said to her once:
  "I think you are the greatest liar I know."
  "Perhaps."
  "You are always willing to say anything to people if only it pleases
them."
  "That always seems to me more important."
  "More important than speaking the truth?"
  "Much more."
  "Then why, in God's name, can't you lie a little more to *me?*"
  "Do you want me to?"
  "Yes."
  "I'm sorry, John, but I can't."
  "You must know so often what I want you to say—"
  Come now, he mustn't start thinking of Henrietta. He'd be seeing her
this very afternoon. The thing to do now was to get on with things! Ring
the bell and see this last damned woman. Another sickly creature! One
tenth genuine ailment and nine tenths hypochondria! Well, why shouldn't
she enjoy ill health if she cared to pay for it? It balanced the Mrs. Crab-
trees of this world.
  But still he sat there motionless.
  He was tired—he was so very tired. It seemed to him that he had been
tired for a very long time. There was something he wanted—wanted badly.
  And there shot into his mind the thought: *I want to go home.*
  It astonished him. Where had that thought come from? And what did it
mean? Home? He had never had a home. His parents had been Anglo-
Indians, he had been brought up, bandied about from aunt to uncle, one
set of holidays with each. The first permanent home he had had, he sup-
posed, was this house in Harley Street.
  Did he think of this house as home? He shook his head. He knew that
he didn't.
  But his medical curiosity was aroused. What had he meant by that
phrase that had flashed out suddenly in his mind?
  I want to go home . . .
  There must be something—some image . . .
  He half closed his eyes—there must be some *background.*
  And very clearly, before his mind's eye, he saw the deep blue of the
Mediterranean Sea, the palms, the cactus and the prickly pear; he smelt
the hot Summer dust, and remembered the cool feeling of the water after
lying on the beach in the sun. *San Miguel!*

He was startled—a little disturbed. He hadn't thought of San Miguel for years. He certainly didn't want to go back there. All of that belonged to a past chapter in his life.

That was twelve—fourteen—fifteen years ago. And he'd done the right thing! His judgment had been absolutely right! He'd been madly in love with Veronica but it wouldn't have done. Veronica would have swallowed him body and soul. She was the complete egoist and she had made no bones about admitting it! Veronica had grabbed most things that she wanted but she hadn't been able to grab him! He'd escaped. He had, he supposed, treated her badly from the conventional point of view. In plain words, he had jilted her! But the truth was that he intended to live his own life, and that was a thing that Veronica would not have allowed him to do. She intended to live *her* life and carry John along as an extra.

She had been astonished when he had refused to come with her to Hollywood.

She had said disdainfully:

"If you really want to be a doctor you can take a degree over there, I suppose, but it's quite unnecessary. You've got enough to live on, and *I* shall be making heaps of money."

And he had replied vehemently:

"But I'm *keen* on my profession. I'm going to work with *Radley.*"

His voice—a young, enthusiastic voice—was quite awed.

Veronica sniffed.

"That funny snuffy old man?"

"That funny snuffy old man," John had said angrily, "has done some of the most valuable research work on Pratt's disease—"

She had interrupted: Who cared for Pratt's disease? California, she said, was an enchanting climate. And it was fun to see the world. She added: "I shall hate it without you. I want you, John—I *need* you."

And then he had put forward the, to Veronica, amazing suggestion that she should turn down the Hollywood offer and marry him and settle down in London.

She was amused and quite firm! She was going to Hollywood, and she loved John, and John must marry her and come, too. She had had no doubts of her beauty and of her power.

He had seen that there was only one thing to be done and he had done it. He had written to her breaking off the engagement.

He had suffered a good deal, but he had had no doubts as to the wisdom of the course he had taken. He'd come back to London and started work with Radley and a year later he had married Gerda, who was as unlike Veronica in every way as it was possible to be.

The door opened and his secretary, Beryl Collier, came in.

"You've still got Mrs. Forrester to see."

He said shortly, "I know."

"I thought you might have forgotten."

She crossed the room and went out at the farther door. Christow's eyes followed her calm withdrawal. A plain girl, Beryl, but damned efficient. He'd had her six years. She never made a mistake, she was never flurried or worried or hurried. She had black hair and a muddy complexion and a determined chin. Through strong glasses, her clear grey eyes surveyed him and the rest of the universe with the same dispassionate attention.

He had wanted a plain secretary with no nonsense about her, and he had got a plain secretary with no nonsense about her, but sometimes, illogically, John Christow felt aggrieved! By all the rules of stage and fiction, Beryl should have been hopelessly devoted to her employer. But he had always known that he cut no ice with Beryl. There was no devotion, no self-abnegation—Beryl regarded him as a definitely fallible human being. She remained unimpressed by his personality, uninfluenced by his charm. He doubted sometimes whether she even *liked* him.

He had heard her once speaking to a friend on the telephone.

"No," she had been saying, "I don't really think he is *much* more selfish than he was. Perhaps rather more thoughtless and inconsiderate."

He had known that she was speaking of him, and for quite twenty-four hours he had been annoyed about it!

Although Gerda's indiscriminate enthusiasm irritated him, Beryl's cool appraisal irritated him too. In fact, he thought, nearly everything irritates me.

Something wrong there. Overwork? Perhaps— No, that was the excuse. This growing impatience, this irritable tiredness, it had some deeper significance. He thought, This won't do. I can't go on this way. What's the matter with me? If I could get *away* . . .

There it was again—the blind idea rushing up to meet the formulated idea of escape.

I want to go home . . .

Damn it all, 404 Harley Street *was* his home!

And Mrs. Forrester was sitting in the waiting room. A tiresome woman, a woman with too much money and too much spare time to think about her ailments.

Someone had once said to him: "You must get very tired of these rich patients always fancying themselves ill. It must be so satisfactory to get to the Poor who come only when there is something *really* the matter with them!" He had grinned! Funny the things people believed about the Poor with a capital P. They should have seen old Mrs. Pearstock, on five different clinics, up every week, taking away bottles of medicine, liniment for

her back, linctus for her cough, aperients, digestive mixtures! "Fourteen
years I've 'ad the brown medicine, doctor, and it's the only thing does me
any good. That young doctor last week writes me down a *white* medicine.
No good at all! It stands to reason, doesn't it, doctor? I mean, I've 'ad me
brown medicine for fourteen years and if I don't 'ave me liquid paraffin
and them brown pills. . . ."

He could hear the whining voice now—excellent physique, sound as a
bell—even all the physic she took couldn't really do her any harm!

They were the same, sisters under the skin, Mrs. Pearstock from Tottenham and Mrs. Forrester of Park Lane Court. You listened and you wrote
scratches with your pen on a piece of stiff expensive notepaper, or on a
hospital card as the case might be. . . .

God, he was tired of the whole business. . . .

Blue sea, the faint, sweet smell of mimosa, hot dust. . . .

*Fifteen years ago. All that was over and done with—yes, done with, thank
Heaven! He'd had the courage to break off the whole business—*

"Courage?" said a little imp somewhere. "Is *that* what you call it?"

Well, he'd done the sensible thing, hadn't he? It had been a wrench.
Damn it all, it had hurt like hell! But he'd gone through with it, cut loose,
come home, and married Gerda.

He'd got a plain secretary and he'd married a plain wife. That was what
he wanted, wasn't it? He'd had enough of beauty, hadn't he? He'd seen
what someone like Veronica could do with her beauty—seen the effect it
had had on every male within range. After Veronica, he'd wanted safety.
Safety and peace and devotion and the quiet enduring things of life. He'd
wanted, in fact, Gerda! He'd wanted someone who'd take her ideas of life
from him, who would accept his decisions and who wouldn't have, for one
moment, any ideas of her own.

*Who was it who had said that the real tragedy of life was that you got
what you wanted?*

Angrily he pressed the buzzer on his desk.

He'd deal with Mrs. Forrester.

It took him a quarter of an hour to deal with Mrs. Forrester. Once
again it was easy money. Once again he listened, asked questions, reassured, sympathized, infused something of his own healing energy. Once
more he wrote out a prescription for an expensive proprietary.

The sickly neurotic woman who had trailed into the room left it with a
firmer step, with colour in her cheeks, with a feeling that life might possibly, after all, be worth while . . .

John Christow leant back in his chair. He was free now—free to go upstairs to join Gerda and the children—free from the preoccupations of illness and suffering for a whole week-end.

But he still felt that strange disinclination to move, that new queer lassitude of the will.

He was tired—tired—tired. . . .

Chapter IV

IN THE DINING room of the flat above the consulting room, Gerda Christow was staring at a joint of mutton.

Should she or should she not send it back to the kitchen to be kept warm?

If John was going to be much longer it would be cold—congealed, and that would be dreadful . . .

But, on the other hand, the last patient had gone, John would be up in a moment, if she sent it back there would be delay—John was so impatient. "But surely you knew I was just coming . . ." There would be that tone of suppressed exasperation in his voice that she knew and dreaded. Besides, it would get overcooked, dried up—John hated overcooked meat.

But on the other hand he disliked cold food very much indeed.

At any rate the dish was nice and hot . . .

Her mind oscillated to and fro and her sense of misery and anxiety deepened.

The whole world had shrunk to a leg of mutton getting cold on a dish.

On the other side of the table her son Terence, aged twelve, said:

"Boracic salts burn with a green flame, sodium salts are yellow."

Gerda looked distractedly across the table at his square freckled face. She had no idea what he was talking about.

"Did you know that, Mother?"

"Know what, dear?"

"About salts."

Gerda's eyes flew distractedly to the salt cellar. Yes, salt and pepper were on the table. That was all right. Last week Lewis had forgotten them and that had annoyed John. There was always something . . .

"It's one of the chemical tests," said Terence in a dreamy voice. "Jolly interesting, _I_ think."

Zena, aged nine, with a pretty, vacuous face, whimpered:

"I want my dinner. Can't we start, Mother?"

"In a minute, dear; we must wait for Father."

"We could start," said Terence. "Father wouldn't mind. You know how fast he eats."

Gerda shook her head.

Carve the mutton? But she never could remember which was the right side to plunge the knife in. Of course, perhaps Lewis had put it the right way on the dish—but sometimes she didn't—and John was always annoyed if it was done the wrong way. And, Gerda reflected desperately, it always *was* the wrong way when she did it. Oh, dear, how cold the gravy was getting—a skin was forming on the top of it—she *must* send it back—but then if John were just coming—and surely he would be coming now—

Her mind went round and round unhappily . . . like a trapped animal.

Sitting back in his consulting room chair, tapping with one hand on the table in front of him, conscious that upstairs lunch must be ready, John Christow was nevertheless unable to force himself to get up . . .

San Miguel . . . blue sea . . . smell of mimosa . . . a scarlet tritoma upright against green leaves . . . the hot sun . . . the dust . . . that desperation of love and suffering . . .

He thought, Oh, God, not that. Never that again! That's over . . .

He wished suddenly that he had never known Veronica, never married Gerda, never met Henrietta . . .

Mrs. Crabtree, he thought, was worth the lot of them . . . That had been a bad afternoon last week. He'd been so pleased with the reactions. She could stand .005 by now. And then had come that alarming rise in toxicity and the D.L. reaction had been negative instead of positive.

The old bean had lain there, blue, gasping for breath—peering up at him with malicious, indomitable eyes.

"Making a bit of a guinea pig out of me, ain't you, dearie? Experimenting—that kinder thing."

"We want to get you well," he had said, smiling down at her.

"Up to your tricks, yer mean!" She had grinned suddenly. "I don't mind, bless yer. You carry on, doctor! Someone's got to be first, that's it, ain't it? 'Ad me 'air permed, I did, when I was a kid. It wasn't 'alf a difficult business then! Looked like a nigger, I did. Couldn't get a comb through it. But there—I enjoyed the fun. You can 'ave yer fun with me. *I* can stand it."

"Feel pretty bad, don't you?" His hand was on her pulse. Vitality passed from him to the panting old woman on the bed.

"Orful, I feel. You're about right! 'Asn't gone according to plan—that's it, isn't it? Never you mind. Don't you lose 'eart. I can stand a lot, I can!"

John Christow said appreciatively:

"You're fine. I wish all my patients were like you."

"I wanter get well . . . that's why! I wanter get well . . . Mum, she lived to be eighty-eight—and old grandma was ninety when she popped off. We're long livers in our family, we are."

He had come away miserable, racked with doubt and uncertainty. He'd been so sure he was on the right track. Where had he gone wrong? How diminish the toxicity and keep up the hormone content and at the same time neutralize the pantratin . . .

He'd been too cock-sure—he'd taken it for granted that he'd circumvented all the snags.

And it was then, on the steps of St. Christopher's, that a sudden desperate weariness had overcome him—a hatred of all this long, slow, wearisome clinical work, and he'd thought of Henrietta. Thought of her suddenly, not as herself, but of her beauty and her freshness, her health and her radiant vitality—and the faint smell of primroses that clung about her hair.

And he had gone to Henrietta straight away, sending a curt telephone message home about being called away. He had strode into the studio and taken Henrietta in his arms, holding her to him with a fierceness that was new in their relationship.

There had been a quick startled wonder in her eyes. She had freed herself from his arms and had made him coffee. And as she moved about the studio she had thrown out desultory questions. Had he come, she asked, straight from the hospital?

He didn't want to talk about the hospital. He wanted to make love to Henrietta and forget that the hospital and Mrs. Crabtree and Ridgeway's Disease and all the rest of the caboodle existed.

But, at first unwillingly, then more fluently, he answered her questions. And presently he was striding up and down, pouring out a spate of technical explanations and surmises. Once or twice he paused, trying to simplify —to explain.

"You see, you have to get a reaction—"

Henrietta said quickly:

"Yes, yes, the D.L. reaction has to be positive. I understand that. Go on."

He said sharply, "How do *you* know about the D.L. reaction?"

"I got a book—"

"What book? Whose?"

She motioned towards the small book table. He snorted.

"Scobell? Scobell's no good. He's fundamentally unsound. Look here, if you want to read—don't—"

She interrupted him.

"I only want to understand some of the terms you use—enough so as to understand you without making you stop to explain everything the whole time. Go on. I'm following you all right."

"Well," he said doubtfully, "remember Scobell's unsound." He went on talking. He talked for two hours and a half. Reviewing the set-backs, analyzing the possibilities, outlining possible theories. He was hardly conscious of Henrietta's presence. And yet, more than once, as he hesitated, her quick intelligence took him a step on the way, seeing, almost before he did, what he was hesitating to advance. He was interested now, and his belief in himself was creeping back. He had been right—the main theory was correct—and there were ways, more ways than one, of combatting the toxic symptoms . . .

And then, suddenly, he was tired out. He'd got it all clear now. He'd get on to it tomorrow morning. He'd ring up Neill, tell him to combine the two solutions and try that. Yes—try that. By God, he wasn't going to be beaten!

"I'm tired," he said abruptly. "My God, I'm tired."

And he had flung himself down and slept—slept like the dead.

He had wakened to find Henrietta smiling at him in the morning light and making tea and he had smiled back at her.

"Not at all according to plan," he said.

"Does it matter?"

"No. No. You are rather a nice person, Henrietta." His eyes went to the bookcase. "If you're interested in this sort of thing, I'll get you the proper stuff to read."

"I'm not interested in this sort of thing. I'm interested in you, John."

"You can't read Scobell." He took up the offending volume. "The man's a charlatan."

And she had laughed. He could not understand why his strictures on Scobell amused her so.

But that was what, every now and then, startled him about Henrietta. The sudden revelation, disconcerting to him, that she was able to laugh at him . . .

He wasn't used to it. Gerda took him in deadly earnest. And Veronica had never thought about anything but herself. But Henrietta had a trick of throwing her head back, of looking at him through half-closed eyes, with a sudden, tender, half-mocking little smile, as though she were saying: "Let me have a good look at this funny person called John . . . Let me get a long way away and look at him. . . ."

It was, he thought, very much the same as the way she screwed up her eyes to look at her work—or a picture. It was—damn it all—it was *detached*. He didn't want Henrietta to be detached. He wanted Henrietta to think only of him, never to let her mind stray away from him.

("Just what you object to in Gerda, in fact," said his private imp, bobbing up again.)

The truth of it was that he was completely illogical. He didn't know what he wanted.

(*I want to go home* . . . What an absurd, what a ridiculous phrase. It didn't *mean* anything.)

In an hour or so at any rate he'd be driving out of London—forgetting about sick people with their faint, sour, "wrong" smell . . . sniffing wood smoke and pines and soft wet Autumn leaves. . . . The very motion of the car would be soothing—that smooth, effortless increase of speed . . .

But it wouldn't, he reflected suddenly, be at all like that because owing to a slightly strained wrist, Gerda would have to drive, and Gerda, God help her, had never been able to begin to drive a car! Every time she changed gear, he would sit silent, grinding his teeth together, managing not to say anything because he knew, by bitter experience, that when he did say anything Gerda became immediately worse. Curious that no one had ever been able to teach Gerda to change gear—not even Henrietta. He'd turned her over to Henrietta, thinking that Henrietta's enthusiasm might do better than his own irritability.

For Henrietta loved cars. She spoke of cars with the lyrical intensity that other people gave to Spring, or the first snowdrop.

"Isn't he a beauty, John? Doesn't he just purr along? (For Henrietta's cars were always masculine.) He'll do Bale Hill in third—not straining at all—quite effortlessly. Listen to the even way he ticks over."

Until he had burst out suddenly and furiously:

"Don't you think, Henrietta, you could pay *some* attention to me and forget the damned car for a minute or two!"

He was always ashamed of these outbursts.

He never knew when they would come upon him out of a blue sky.

It was the same thing over her work. He realized that her work was good. He admired it—and hated it—at the same time.

The most furious quarrel he had had with her had arisen over that.

Gerda had said to him one day:

"Henrietta has asked me to sit for her."

"What?" His astonishment had not, if he came to think of it, been flattering. *"You?"*

"Yes, I'm going over to the studio tomorrow."

"What on earth does she want you for?"

No, he hadn't been very polite about it. But luckily Gerda hadn't realized that fact. She had looked pleased about it. He suspected Henrietta of one of those insincere kindnesses of hers—Gerda, perhaps, had hinted that she would like to be modelled. Something of that kind.

Then, about ten days later, Gerda had shown him triumphantly a small plaster statuette.

It was a pretty thing—technically skilful like all of Henrietta's work. It idealized Gerda—and Gerda herself was clearly pleased about it.

"I really think it's rather charming, John."

"Is that Henrietta's work? It means nothing—nothing at all. I don't see how she came to do a thing like that."

"It's different, of course, from her abstract work—but I think it's good, John, I really do."

He had said no more—after all, he didn't want to spoil Gerda's pleasure. But he tackled Henrietta about it at the first opportunity.

"What did you want to make that silly thing of Gerda for? It's unworthy of you. After all, you usually turn out decent stuff."

Henrietta said slowly:

"I didn't think it was bad. Gerda seemed quite pleased."

"Gerda was delighted. She would be. Gerda doesn't know art from a coloured photograph."

"It wasn't bad art, John. It was just a portrait statuette—quite harmless and not at all pretentious."

"You don't usually waste your time doing that kind of stuff—"

He broke off, staring at a wooden figure about five feet high.

"Hullo, what's this?"

"It's for the International Group. Pearwood. The Worshipper."

She watched him. He stared and then—suddenly, his neck swelled and he turned on her furiously.

"So that's what you wanted Gerda for? How dare you?"

"I wondered if you'd see. . . ."

"See it? Of course I see it. It's *here.*" He placed a finger on the broad, heavy neck muscles.

Henrietta nodded.

"Yes, it's the neck and shoulders I wanted—and that heavy forward slant—the submission—that bowed look. It's wonderful!"

"Wonderful? Look here, Henrietta, I won't have it. You're to leave Gerda alone."

"Gerda won't know. Nobody will know. You know Gerda would never recognize herself here—nobody else would either. And it *isn't* Gerda. It isn't *anybody.*"

"*I* recognized it, didn't I?"

"You're different, John. You—see things."

"It's the damned cheek of it! I won't have it, Henrietta! I won't have it. Can't you see that it was an indefensible thing to do?"

"Was it?"

"Don't you know it was? Can't you *feel* it was? Where's your usual sensitiveness?"

Henrietta said slowly:

"You don't understand, John. I don't think I could ever make you understand . . . You don't know what it is to want something—to look at it day after day—that line of the neck—those muscles—the angle where the head goes forward—that heaviness round the jaw. I've been looking at them, wanting them—every time I saw Gerda . . . In the end I just had to have them!"

"Unscrupulous!"

"Yes, I suppose just that. But when you want things in that way you just have to take them."

"You mean you don't care a damn about anybody else. You don't care about Gerda—"

"Don't be stupid, John. That's why I made that statuette thing. To please Gerda and make her happy. I'm not inhuman!"

"Inhuman is exactly what you are."

"Do you think—honestly—that Gerda would ever recognize herself in this?"

John looked at it unwillingly. For the first time his anger and resentment became subordinated to his interest. A strange submissive figure, a figure offering up worship to an unseen deity—the face raised—blind, dumb, devoted—terribly strong, terribly fanatical. . . . He said:

"That's rather a terrifying thing that you have made, Henrietta!"

Henrietta shivered slightly.

She said: "Yes—*I* thought that. . . ."

John said sharply:

"What's she looking at—who is it?—there in front of her?"

Henrietta hesitated. She said, and her voice had a queer note in it—

"I don't know. But I *think*— she might be looking at *you*, John."

Chapter V

IN THE DINING room the child Terence made another scientific statement.

"Lead salts are more soluble in cold water than in hot."

He looked expectantly at his mother but without any real hope. Parents, in the opinion of young Terence, were sadly disappointing.

"Did you know that, Mother?"

"I don't know anything about chemistry, dear."

"You could read about it in a book," said Terence.

It was a simple statement of fact but there was a certain wistfulness behind it.

Gerda did not hear the wistfulness. She was caught in the trap of her anxious misery. Round and round and round . . . She had been miserable ever since she woke up this morning and realized that at last this long-dreaded week-end with the Angkatells was upon her. Staying at The Hollow was always a nightmare to her. She always felt bewildered and forlorn. Lucy Angkatell with her sentences that were never finished, her swift inconsequences, and her obvious attempt at kindliness was the figure she dreaded most. But the others were nearly as bad. For Gerda it was two days of sheer martyrdom—to be endured for John's sake.

For John, that morning, as he stretched himself, had remarked in tones of unmitigated pleasure:

"Splendid to think we'll be getting into the country this week-end. It will do you good, Gerda; just what you need."

She had smiled mechanically and had said with unselfish fortitude, "It will be delightful."

Her unhappy eyes had wandered round the bedroom. The wallpaper, cream striped with a black mark just by the wardrobe, the mahogany dressing table with the glass that swung too far forward, the cheerful, bright blue carpet, the water colours of the Lake district. All dear familiar things and she would not see them again until Monday.

Instead, tomorrow a housemaid who rustled would come into the strange bedroom and put down a little dainty tray of early tea by the bed and pull up the blinds and would then rearrange and fold Gerda's clothes —a thing which made Gerda feel hot and uncomfortable all over. She would lie miserably, enduring these things, trying to comfort herself by thinking, Only one morning more . . . Like being at school and counting the days.

Gerda had not been happy at school. At school there had been even less reassurance than elsewhere. Home had been better. But even home had not been very good. For they had all, of course, been quicker and more clever than she was. Their comments, quick, impatient, not quite unkind, had whistled about her ears like a hailstorm: "Oh, do be quick, Gerda." "Butterfingers, give it to me!" "Oh, don't let Gerda do it, she'll be *ages.*" "Gerda never takes in anything. . . ."

Hadn't they seen, all of them, that that was the way to make her slower and more stupid still? She'd got worse and worse, more clumsy with her fingers, more slow-witted, more inclined to stare vacantly when something was said to her.

Until, suddenly, she had reached the point where she had found a way out . . . Almost accidentally, really, she found her weapon of defence.

She had grown slower still, her puzzled stare had become even more blank. But now, when they said impatiently, "Oh, Gerda, how stupid you are, don't you understand *that?*" she had been able, behind her blank expression, to hug herself a little in her secret knowledge . . . For she wasn't quite as stupid as they thought . . . Often, when she pretended not to understand, she *did* understand. And often, deliberately, she slowed down in her task of whatever it was, smiling to herself when someone's impatient fingers snatched it away from her.

For, warm and delightful, was a secret knowledge of superiority. She began to be, quite often, a little amused. . . . Yes, it was amusing to know more than they thought you knew. To be able to do a thing, but not let anybody know that you could do it.

And it had the advantage, suddenly discovered, that people often did things for you. That, of course, saved you a lot of trouble. And, in the end, if people got into the habit of doing things for you, you didn't have to do them at all, and then people didn't know that you did them badly. And so, slowly, you came round again almost to where you started. To feeling that you could hold your own on equal terms with the world at large.

(But that wouldn't, Gerda feared, hold good with the Angkatells; the Angkatells were always so far ahead that you didn't feel even in the same street with them. How she hated the Angkatells! It was good for John— John liked it there. He came home less tired—and sometimes less irritable.)

Dear John! she thought. John was wonderful. Everyone thought so!

Such a clever doctor, so terribly kind to his patients. Wearing himself out —and the interest he took in his hospital patients—all that side of his work that didn't pay at all. John was so *disinterested*— so truly noble.

She had always known, from the very first, that John was brilliant and was going to get to the top of the tree. And he had chosen her, when he might have married somebody far more brilliant. He had not minded her being slow and rather stupid and not very pretty. "I'll look after you," he had said. Nicely, rather masterfully. "Don't worry about things, Gerda, I'll take care of you . . ."

Just what a man ought to be. Wonderful to think John should have chosen her.

He had said, with that sudden, very attractive, half pleading smile of his, "I like my own way, you know, Gerda."

Well, that was all right. She had always tried to give in to him in everything. Even lately when he had been so difficult and nervy—when nothing seemed to please him. When, somehow, nothing she did was right. One couldn't blame him. He was so busy, so unselfish—

Oh, dear, that mutton! She ought to have sent it back! Still no sign of John . . . Why couldn't she, sometimes, decide right. Again those dark waves of misery swept over her. The mutton! This awful week-end with the Angkatells! She felt a sharp pain through both temples. Oh, dear, now she was going to have one of her headaches. And it did so annoy John when she had headaches. He never would give her anything for them, when surely it would be so easy, being a doctor. Instead, he always said, "Don't think about it. No use poisoning yourself with drugs. Take a brisk walk."

The mutton! Staring at it, Gerda felt the words repeating themselves in her aching head, "The mutton, the MUTTON, *THE MUTTON. . . .*"

Tears of self-pity sprang to her eyes. Why, she thought, does nothing *ever* go right for me?

Terence looked across the table at his mother and then at the joint. He thought, Why can't *we* have our dinner? How stupid grown up people are. They haven't any sense!

Aloud he said in a careful voice:

"Nicholson Minor and I are going to make nitro-glycerine in his father's shrubbery. They live at Streatham."

"Are you, dear! That will be very nice," said Gerda.

There was still time. If she rang the bell and told Lewis to take the joint down now—

Terence looked at her with faint curiosity. He had felt instinctively that the manufacture of nitro-glycerine was not the kind of occupation that would be encouraged by parents. With base opportunism he had selected a moment when he felt tolerably certain that he had a good chance of getting away with his statement. And his judgment had been justified. If, by any chance, there should be a fuss—if, that is, the properties of nitro-glycerine should manifest themselves too evidently, he would be able to say in an injured voice, "I *told* Mother . . ."

All the same, he felt vaguely disappointed.

Even *Mother*, he thought, ought to know about nitro-glycerine.

He sighed. There swept over him that intense sense of loneliness that only childhood can feel. His father was too impatient to listen, his mother was too inattentive. Zena was only a silly kid . . .

Pages of interesting chemical tests. And who cared about them? Nobody!

Bang! Gerda started. It was the door of John's consulting room. It was John running upstairs.

John Christow burst into the room, bringing with him his own particular atmosphere of intense energy. He was good-humoured, hungry, impatient. . . .

"God," he exclaimed as he sat down and energetically sharpened the carving knife against the steel, "how I hate sick people!"

"Oh, John." Gerda was quickly reproachful. "Don't say things like that. *They'* ll think you mean it."

She gestured slightly with her head towards the children.

"I do mean it," said John Christow. "Nobody ought to be ill."

"Father's joking," said Gerda quickly to Terence.

Terence examined his father with the dispassionate attention he gave to everything.

"I don't think he is," he said.

"If you hated sick people, you wouldn't be a doctor, dear," said Gerda, laughing gently.

"That's exactly the reason," said John Christow. "No doctors like sickness. Good God, this meat's stone cold. Why on earth didn't you have it sent down to keep hot?"

"Well, dear, I didn't know. You see, I thought you were just coming—"

John Christow pressed the bell, a long, irritated push. Lewis came promptly.

"Take this down, and tell cook to warm it up."

He spoke curtly.

"Yes, sir." Lewis, slightly impertinent, managed to convey in the two innocuous words exactly her opinion of a mistress who sat at the dining table watching a joint of meat grow cold.

Gerda went on rather incoherently:

"I'm so sorry, dear, it's all my fault, but first, you see, I thought you were coming, and then I thought, well, if I did send it back . . ."

John interrupted her impatiently.

"Oh, what does it matter? It isn't important. Not worth making a song and dance about."

Then he asked:

"Is the car here?"

"I think so. Collie ordered it."

"Then we can get away as soon as lunch is over."

Across Albert Bridge, he thought, and then over Clapham Common—the short cut by the Crystal Palace—Croydon—Purley Way, then avoid the main road—take that right-hand fork up Metherly Hill—along Haverston Ridge—get suddenly right out of the suburban belt, through Cormerton, and then up Shovel Down—trees golden red—woodland below one everywhere—the soft Autumn smell, and down over the crest of the hill . . .

Lucy and Henry . . . Henrietta . . .

He hadn't seen Henrietta for four days. When he had last seen her, he'd been angry. She'd had that look in her eyes . . . Not abstracted, not inattentive—he couldn't quite describe it—that look of *seeing* something—something that wasn't there—something (and that was the crux of it) something that wasn't John Christow!

He said to himself, "I know she's a sculptor. I know her work's good. But, damn it all, can't she put it aside sometimes? Can't she sometimes think of me—and nothing else?"

He was unfair. He knew he was unfair. Henrietta seldom talked of her work—was indeed less obsessed by it than most artists he knew. It was only on very rare occasions that her absorption with some inner vision spoiled the completeness of her interest in him. But it always roused his furious anger.

Once he had said, his voice sharp and hard, "Would you give all this up if I asked you to?"

"All—what?" Her warm voice held surprise.

"All—this." He waved a comprehensive hand round the studio.

And immediately he thought to himself, Fool! Why did you ask her that? And again, Let her say "Of course." Let her lie to me! If she'll only say, "Of course I will." It doesn't matter if she means it or not! But let her say it. I *must* have peace.

Instead, she had said nothing for some time. Her eyes had gone dreamy and abstracted. She had frowned a little.

Then she had said slowly:

"I suppose so. If it was *necessary . . .*"

"Necessary! What do you mean by necessary?"

"I don't really know what I mean by it, John. Necessary, as an amputation might be necessary . . ."

"Nothing short of a surgical operation, in fact!"

"You are angry. What did you want me to say?"

"You know well enough. One word would have done. *Yes.* Why couldn't you say it? You say enough things to other people to please them, without caring whether they're true or not. Why not to me? For God's sake, why not to me?"

And still, very slowly, she had answered:

"I don't know . . . really, I don't know, John. I can't—that's all. I can't."

He had walked up and down for a minute or two. Then he had said:

"You will drive me mad, Henrietta. I never feel that I have any influence over you at all."

"Why should you want to have?"

"I don't know, but I do."

He threw himself down on a chair.

"I want to come first."

"You do, John."

"No. If I were dead, the first thing you'd do, with the tears streaming down your face, would be to start modeling some damned mourning woman or some figure of grief. . . ."

"I wonder. I believe—yes, perhaps I would. It's rather horrible . . ."

She had sat there looking at him with dismayed eyes—

The pudding was burnt. Christow raised his eyebrows over it and Gerda hurried into apologies.

"I'm so sorry, dear. I can't think *why* that should happen! It's my fault. Give me the top and you take the underneath."

The pudding was burnt because he, John Christow, had stayed sitting in his consulting room for a quarter of an hour after he needed to, thinking about Henrietta and Mrs. Crabtree and letting ridiculous nostalgic feelings about San Miguel sweep over him. The fault was his. It was idiotic of Gerda to try and take the blame, maddening of her to try and eat the burnt part herself. Why did she always have to make a martyr of herself? Why did Terence stare at him in that slow, interested way? Why, oh, why, did Zena have to sniff so continually? Why were they all so damned irritating?

His wrath fell on Zena.

"Why on earth don't you blow your nose?"

"She's got a little cold, I think, dear."

"No, she hasn't. You're always thinking they have colds! She's all right."

Gerda sighed. She had never been able to understand why a doctor, who spent his time treating the ailments of others, could be so indifferent to the health of his own family. He always ridiculed any suggestion of illness.

"I sneezed eight times before lunch," said Zena importantly.

"Heat sneeze!" said John.

"It's not hot," said Terence. "The thermometer in the hall is fifty-five." John got up.

"Have we finished? Good, let's get on. Ready to start, Gerda?"

"In a minute, John; I've just a few things to put in."

"Surely you could have done that *before*. What have you been doing all the morning?"

He went out of the dining room fuming. Gerda had hurried off into her bedroom. Her anxiety to be quick would make her much slower. But why couldn't she have been ready? His own suit-case was packed and in the hall. Why on earth—

Zena was advancing on him, clasping some rather sticky cards.

"Can I tell your fortune, Daddy? I know how. I've told Mother's and Terry's and Lewis's and Jane's and Cook's."

"All right—"

He wondered how long Gerda was going to be. He wanted to get away from this horrible house and this horrible street and this city full of ailing, sniffling, diseased people. He wanted to get to woods and wet leaves—and the graceful aloofness of Lucy Angkatell who always gave you the impression she hadn't even got a body.

Zena was importantly dealing out cards.

"That's you in the middle, Father, the King of Hearts. The person whose fortune's told is always the King of Hearts. And then I deal the others face down. Two on the left of you and two on the right of you and one over your head—that has power over you, and one under your feet— you have power over it. And this one—covers you!

"Now!" Zena drew a deep breath. "We turn them over. On the right of you is the Queen of Diamonds—quite close."

Henrietta, he thought, momentarily diverted and amused by Zena's solemnity.

"And the next one is the Knave of Clubs—he's some quite young man—

"On the left of you is the eight of spades—that's a secret enemy. Have you got a secret enemy, Father?"

"Not that I know of."

"And beyond is the Queen of Spades—that's a much older lady."

"Lady Angkatell," he said to himself.

"Now this is what's over your head and has power over you—the Queen of Hearts. . . ."

Veronica, he thought. *Veronica!* And then: What a fool I am! Veronica doesn't mean a thing to me now.

"And this is under your feet and you have power over it—the Queen of Clubs . . ."

Gerda hurried into the room.

"I'm quite ready now, John."

"Oh, wait, Mother, wait, I'm telling Daddy's fortune. Just the last card, Daddy—the most important of all. The one that covers you."

Zena's small sticky fingers turned it over. She gave a gasp.

"Oo—it's the Ace of Spades! That's usually a *death*—but—"

"Your mother," said John, "is going to run over someone on the way out of London. Come on, Gerda. Goodbye, you two. Try and behave."

Chapter VI

MIDGE HARDCASTLE CAME downstairs about eleven on Saturday morning. She had had breakfast in bed and had read a book and dozed a little and then got up.

It was nice lazing this way. About time she had a holiday! No doubt about it, Madame Alfrege's got on your nerves.

She came out of the front door into the pleasant Autumn sunshine. Sir Henry Angkatell was sitting on a rustic seat reading *The Times*. He looked up and smiled. He was fond of Midge.

"Hullo, my dear."

"Am I very late?"

"You haven't missed lunch," said Sir Henry, smiling.

Midge sat down beside him and said with a sigh:

"It's nice being here."

"You're looking rather peaked."

"Oh, I'm all right. How delightful to be somewhere where no fat women are trying to get into clothes several sizes too small for them!"

"Must be dreadful!" Sir Henry paused and then said, glancing down at his wrist-watch, "Edward's arriving by the 12:15."

"Is he?" Midge paused, then said, "I haven't seen Edward for a long time . . ."

"He's just the same," said Sir Henry. "Hardly ever comes up from Ainswick."

Ainswick, thought Midge. *Ainswick!* Her heart gave a sick pang. Those lovely days at Ainswick. Visits looked forward to for months! *I'm going to Ainswick* . . . Lying awake for nights beforehand thinking about it . . . And at last—the day! The little country station at which the train—the big London express—had to stop if you gave notice to the guard! The Daimler waiting outside. The drive—the final turn in through the gate and up through the woods till you came out into the open and there the house was —big and white and welcoming. Old Uncle Geoffrey in his patchwork tweed coat . . .

"Now then, youngsters—enjoy yourselves." And how they had enjoyed themselves. Henrietta, over from Ireland. Edward, home from Eton. She herself, from the North country grimness of a manufacturing town. How like heaven it had been.

But always centering about Edward. Edward, tall and gentle and diffident and always kind. But never, of course, noticing her very much because Henrietta was there. . . .

Edward, always so retiring, so very much of a visitor that she had been startled one day when Tremlet the head gardener had said:

"The place will be Mr. Edward's some day."

"But why, Tremlet? He's not Uncle Geoffrey's son?"

"He's the *heir,* Miss Midge. Entailed, that's what they call it. Miss Lucy, she's Mr. Geoffrey's only child, but she can't inherit because she's a female and Mr. Henry, her husband, he's only a second cousin. Not so near as Mr. Edward."

And now Edward lived at Ainswick. Lived there alone and very seldom came away. Midge wondered, sometimes, if Lucy minded. Lucy always looked as though she never minded about anything.

Yet Ainswick had been her home, and Edward was only her first cousin once removed and over twenty years younger than she was. Her father, old Geoffrey Angkatell, had been a great "character" in the county. He had had considerable wealth as well, most of which had come to Lucy, so that Edward was a comparatively poor man, with enough to keep the place up, but not much over when that was done.

Not that Edward had expensive tastes. He had been in the diplomatic service for a time, but when he inherited Ainswick he had resigned and come to live on his property. He was of a bookish turn of mind, collected first editions, and occasionally wrote rather hesitating, ironical little articles for obscure reviews. He had asked his second cousin, Henrietta Savernake, three times to marry him.

Midge sat in the Autumn sunshine thinking of these things. She could not make up her mind whether she was glad she was going to see Edward or not. It was not as though she were what is called "getting over it." One simply did not get over anyone like Edward. Edward at Ainswick was just as real to her as Edward rising to greet her from a restaurant table in London. She had loved Edward ever since she could remember . . .

Sir Henry's voice recalled her:

"How do you think Lucy is looking?"

"Very well. She's just the same as ever." Midge smiled a little. "More so."

"Ye-es." Sir Henry drew on his pipe. He said unexpectedly:

"Sometimes, you know, Midge, I get worried about Lucy."

"Worried?" Midge looked at him in surprise. "Why?"

Sir Henry shook his head.

"Lucy," he said, "doesn't realize that there are things that she can't do."

Midge stared. He went on:

"She gets away with things. She always has." He smiled. "She's flouted the traditions of Government House—she's played merry hell with precedence at dinner parties (and that, Midge, is a black crime!). She's put deadly enemies next to each other at the dinner table, and run riot over the Colour question! And instead of raising one big almighty row and setting everyone at loggerheads and bringing disgrace on the British Raj—I'm damned if she hasn't got away with it! That trick of hers—smiling at people and looking as though she couldn't help it! Servants are the same—she gives them any amount of trouble and they adore her."

"I know what you mean," said Midge thoughtfully. "Things that you wouldn't stand from anyone else, you feel are all right if Lucy does them. What is it, I wonder? Charm? Magnetism?"

Sir Henry shrugged his shoulders.

"She's always been the same from a girl—only sometimes I feel it's growing on her. . . . I mean that she doesn't realize that there *are* limits. Why, I really believe, Midge," he said, amused, "that Lucy would feel she could get away with murder!"

Henrietta got the Delage out from the garage in the Mews, and after a wholly technical conversation with her friend Albert, who looked after the Delage's health, she started off.

"Running a treat, Miss," said Albert.

Henrietta smiled. She shot away down the Mews, savouring the unfailing pleasure she always felt when setting off in the car alone. She much preferred to be alone when driving. In that way she could realize to the full the intimate personal enjoyment that driving a car brought to her.

She enjoyed her own skill in traffic, she enjoyed nosing out new short cuts out of London. She had routes of her own and when driving in London itself had as intimate a knowledge of its streets as any taxi driver.

She now took her own newly discovered way southwest, turning and twisting through intricate mazes of suburban streets.

When she finally came to the long ridge of Shovel Down it was half past twelve. Henrietta had always loved the view from that particular place. She paused now just at the point where the road began to descend. All around and below her were trees, trees whose leaves were turning from gold to brown. It was a world incredibly golden and splendid in the strong Autumn sunlight.

Henrietta thought, I love Autumn. It's so much richer than Spring.

And suddenly one of those moments of intense happiness came to her—a sense of the loveliness of the world—of her own intense enjoyment of that world.

She thought, I shall never be as happy again as I am now . . . never. . . .

She stayed there a minute, gazing out over that golden world that seemed to swim and dissolve into itself, hazy and blurred with its own beauty. . . .

Then she came down over the crest of the hill, down through the woods, down the long steep road to The Hollow.

When Henrietta drove in, Midge was sitting on the low wall of the terrace, and waved to her cheerfully. Henrietta was pleased to see Midge whom she liked.

Lady Angkatell came out of the house, and said:

"Oh! there you are, Henrietta. When you've taken your car into the stables and given it a bran mash, lunch will be ready."

"What a penetrating remark of Lucy's," said Henrietta as she drove round the house, Midge accompanying her on the running board. "You know, I always prided myself on having completely escaped the horsy taint of my Irish forebears. When you've been brought up amongst people who talk nothing but horse, you go all superior about not caring for them. And now Lucy has just shown me that I treat my car exactly like a horse. It's quite true. I do."

"I know," said Midge. "Lucy is quite devastating. She told me this morning that I was to be as rude as I liked whilst I was here."

Henrietta considered this for a moment and then nodded.

"Of course," she said. "The *shop!*"

"Yes. When one has to spend every day of one's life in a damnable little box, being polite to rude women, calling them Madam, pulling frocks over their heads, smiling and swallowing their damned cheek whatever they like to say to one—well, one does want to cuss! You know, Henrietta, I always wonder why people think it's so humiliating to go 'into service' and that it's grand and independent to be in a shop. One puts up with far more insolence in a shop than Gudgeon or Simmons or any decent domestic does."

"It must be foul, darling. I wish you weren't so grand and proud and insistent on earning your own living . . ."

"Anyway, Lucy's an angel. I shall be gloriously rude to everyone this week-end."

"Who's here?" said Henrietta as she got out of the car.

"The Christows are coming." Midge paused and then went on: "Edward's just arrived."

"Edward? How nice! I haven't seen Edward for ages. Anybody else?"

"David Angkatell. That, according to Lucy, is where you are going to come in useful. You're going to stop him biting his nails."

"It sounds very unlike me," said Henrietta. "I hate interfering with people and I wouldn't dream of checking their personal habits. What did Lucy really say?"

"It amounted to that! He's got an Adam's apple, too!"

"I'm not expected to do anything about that, am I?" asked Henrietta, alarmed.

"And you're to be kind to Gerda."

"How I should hate Lucy if I were Gerda!"

"And someone who solves crimes is coming to lunch tomorrow."

"We're not going to play the Murder Game, are we?"

"I don't think so. I think it is just neighbourly hospitality."

Midge's voice changed a little.

"Here's Edward coming out to hunt us."

"Dear Edward," thought Henrietta with a sudden rush of warm affection.

Edward Angkatell was very tall and thin. He was smiling now as he came towards the two young women.

"Hullo, Henrietta. I haven't seen you for over a year."

"Hullo, Edward."

How nice Edward was! That gentle smile of his, the little creases at the corners of his eyes. And all his nice knobbly bones . . . I believe it's his *bones* I like so much, thought Henrietta. The warmth of her affection for Edward startled her. She had forgotten that she liked Edward so much. . . .

After lunch Edward said, "Come for a walk, Henrietta."

It was Edward's kind of walk—a stroll.

They went up behind the house, taking a path that zigzagged up through the trees. Like the woods at Ainswick, thought Henrietta . . . Dear Ainswick, what fun they had had there! She began to talk to Edward about Ainswick. They revived old memories.

"Do you remember our squirrel? The one with the broken paw? And we kept it in a cage and it got well?"

"Of course. It had a ridiculous name—what was it now?"

"Cholmondeley-Marjoribanks!"

"That's it."

They both laughed.

"And old Mrs. Bondy, the housekeeper—she always *said* it would go up the chimney one day."

"And we were so indignant . . ."

"And then it *did* . . ."

"She made it," said Henrietta positively. "She put the thought into the squirrel's head."

She went on:

"Is it all the same, Edward? Or is it changed? I always imagine it as just the same."

"Why don't you come and see, Henrietta? It's a long, long time since you've been there."

"I know. . . ."

Why, she thought, had she let so long a time go by? One got busy—interested—tangled up with people . . .

"You know you're always welcome there at any time."

"How sweet you are, Edward!"

Dear Edward, she thought, with his *nice* bones . . .

He said presently:

"I'm glad you're fond of Ainswick, Henrietta."

She said dreamily, "Ainswick is the loveliest place in the world. . . ."

A long-legged girl, with a mane of untidy brown hair . . . a happy girl with no idea at all of the things that life was going to do to her . . . a girl who loved trees . . .

To have been so happy and not to have known it! *If I could go back,* she thought . . .

And aloud she said suddenly:

"Is Ygdrasil still there?"

"It was struck by lightning."

"Oh, no, not *Ygdrasil!*"

She was distressed. Ygdrasil—her own special name for the big oak tree. If the gods could strike down Ygdrasil, then nothing was safe! Better not go back . . .

"Do you remember your special sign, the Ygdrasil sign?" Edward asked.

"The funny tree like no tree that ever was I used to draw on bits of paper? I still do, Edward! On blotters, and on telephone books, and on bridge scores. I doodle it all the time. Give me a pencil."

He handed her a pencil and note-book, and laughing, she drew the ridiculous tree.

"Yes," he said, "that's Ygdrasil . . ."

They had come almost to the top of the path. Henrietta sat on a fallen tree trunk. Edward sat down beside her.

She looked down through the trees.

"It's a little like Ainswick here—a kind of pocket Ainswick. I've sometimes wondered—Edward, do you think that that is why Lucy and Henry came here?"

"It's possible."

"One never knows," said Henrietta slowly, "what goes on in Lucy's head." Then she asked, "What have you been doing with yourself, Edward, since I saw you last?"

"Nothing, Henrietta."

"That sounds very peaceful."

"I've never been very good at—doing things."

She threw him a quick glance. There had been something in his tone. . . . But he was smiling at her quietly.

And again she felt that rush of deep affection.

"Perhaps," she said, "you are wise."

"Wise?"

"Not to do things . . ."

Edward said slowly, "That's an odd thing for you to say, Henrietta. You, who've been so successful."

"Do you think of me as successful? How funny."

"But you are, my dear. You're an artist. You must be proud of yourself —you can't help being."

"I know," said Henrietta. "A lot of people say that to me. They don't understand—they don't understand the first thing about it! *You* don't, Edward. Sculpture isn't a thing you set out to do and succeed in. It's a thing that gets *at* you, that nags at you—and haunts you—so that, sooner or later, you've got to make terms with it. And then, for a bit, you get some peace—until the whole thing starts over again."

"Do you want to be peaceful, Henrietta?"

"Sometimes I think I want to be peaceful more than anything in the world, Edward!"

"You could be peaceful at Ainswick . . . I think you could be happy there. Even—even if you had to put up with *me.* What about it, Henrietta? Won't you come to Ainswick and make it your home? It's always been there, you know, waiting for you."

Henrietta turned her head slowly. She said in a low voice:

"I wish I wasn't so dreadfully fond of you, Edward. It makes it so very much harder to go on saying no."

"It *is* no, then?"

"I'm sorry."

"You've said no before—but this time—well, I thought it might be different. You've been happy this afternoon, Henrietta. You can't deny that."

"I've been very happy."

"Your face even—it's younger than it was this morning."

"I know."

"We've been happy together, talking about Ainswick, thinking about Ainswick. Don't you see what that means, Henrietta?"

"It's *you* who don't see what it means, Edward! We've been living all this afternoon in the past."

"The past is sometimes a very good place to live."

"One can't go back. That's the one thing one can't do—go back."

He was silent for a minute or two. Then he said in a quiet, pleasant and quite unemotional voice:

"What you really mean is that you won't marry me because of John Christow."

Henrietta did not answer, and Edward went on:

"That's it, isn't it? If there were no John Christow in the world you would marry me."

Henrietta said harshly, "I can't imagine a world in which there was no John Christow! That's what *you*'ve got to understand."

"If it's like that, why on earth doesn't the fellow get a divorce from his wife and then you could marry?"

"John doesn't want to get a divorce from his wife. And I don't know that I should want to marry John if he did. It isn't—it isn't in the least like you think."

Edward said in a thoughtful, considering way:

"John Christow . . . There are too many John Christows in this world . . ."

"You're wrong," said Henrietta. "There are very few people like John . . ."

"If that's so—it's a good thing! At least, that's what I think!"

He got up. "We'd better go back again."

Chapter VII

AS THEY GOT into the car and Lewis shut the front door of the Harley Street house, Gerda felt the pang of exile go through her. That shut door was so final. She was barred out—this awful week-end was upon her. And there were things, quite a lot of things, that she ought to have done before leaving. Had she turned off that tap in the bathroom? And that note for the laundry—she'd put it—where had she put it? Would the children be all right with Mademoiselle? Mademoiselle was so—so— Would Terence, for instance, ever do anything that Mademoiselle told him to? French governesses never seemed to have any authority.

She got into the driving seat, still bowed down by misery, and nervously pressed the starter. She pressed it again and again. John said, "The car will start better, Gerda, if you switch on the engine."

"Oh, dear, how stupid of me." She shot a quick alarmed glance at him. If John was going to become annoyed straight away— But to her relief he was smiling.

That's because, thought Gerda, with one of her flashes of acumen, he's so pleased to be going to the Angkatells'.

Poor John, he worked so hard! His life was so unselfish, so completely devoted to others. No wonder he looked forward to this long week-end. And, her mind harking back to the conversation at lunch, she said, as she let in the clutch rather too suddenly so that the car leapt forward from the curb:

"You know, John, you really shouldn't make jokes about hating sick people. It's wonderful of you to make light of all you do, and *I* understand. But the children don't. Terry, in particular, has such a very literal mind."

"There are times," said John Christow, "when Terry seems to me almost human—not like Zena! How long do girls go on being a mass of affectation?"

Gerda gave a little, quite sweet laugh. John, she knew, was teasing her. She stuck to her point. Gerda had an adhesive mind.

"I really think, John, that it's *good* for children to realize the unselfishness and devotion of a doctor's life."

"Oh, God!" said Christow.

Gerda was momentarily deflected. The traffic lights she was approaching had been green for a long time. They were almost sure, she thought, to change before she got to them. She began to slow down . . . Still green . . .

John Christow forgot his resolutions of keeping silent about Gerda's driving and said, "What are you stopping for?"

"I thought the lights might change—"

She pressed her foot on the accelerator, the car moved forward a little, just beyond the lights, then, unable to pick up, the engine stalled. The lights changed.

The cross traffic hooted angrily.

John said, but quite pleasantly:

"You really are the worst driver in the world, Gerda!"

"I always find traffic lights so worrying. One doesn't know just when they are going to change."

John cast a quick sideways look at Gerda's anxious unhappy face.

Everything worries Gerda, he thought, and tried to imagine what it must feel like to live in that state. But since he was not a man of much imagination, he could not picture it at all.

"You see," Gerda stuck to her point, "I've always impressed on the children just what a doctor's life is—the self-sacrifice, the dedication of oneself to helping pain and suffering—the desire to serve others. It's such a noble life—and I'm so proud of the way you give your time and energy and never spare yourself—"

John Christow interrupted her.

"Hasn't it ever occurred to you that I *like* doctoring—that it's a pleasure, not a sacrifice! Don't you realize that the damned thing's *interesting!*"

But, no, he thought, Gerda would never realize a thing like that! If he told her about Mrs. Crabtree and the Margaret Russell Ward she would only see him as a kind of angelic helper of the Poor with a capital P.

"Drowning in treacle," he said under his breath.

"What?" Gerda leaned towards him.

He shook his head.

If he were to tell Gerda that he was trying to "find a cure for cancer," she would respond—she could understand a plain sentimental statement. But she would never understand the peculiar fascination of the intricacies of Ridgeway's Disease—he doubted if he could even make her understand what Ridgeway's Disease actually was. (Particularly, he thought with a grin, as we're not really quite sure ourselves! We don't really know *why* the cortex degenerates!)

But it occurred to him suddenly that Terence, child though he was, might be interested in Ridgeway's Disease. He had liked the way that Terence had eyed him appraisingly before stating: "I think Father does mean it . . ."

Terence had been out of favour the last few days for breaking the Cona coffee machine—some nonsense about trying to make ammonia . . . Ammonia? Funny kid, why should he want to make ammonia? Interesting in a way . . .

Gerda was relieved at John's silence. She could cope with driving better if she were not distracted by conversation. Besides, if John was absorbed in thought, he was not so likely to notice that jarring noise of her occasional forced changes of gear. (She never changed down if she could help it.)

There were times, Gerda knew, when she changed gear quite well (though never with confidence), but it never happened if John were in the car. Her nervous determination to do it right this time was always disastrous, her hand fumbled, she accelerated too much or not enough, and then she pushed the gear lever quickly and clumsily so that it shrieked in protest.

"Stroke it in, Gerda, stroke it in," Henrietta had pleaded once, years ago. Henrietta had demonstrated. "Can't you *feel* the way it wants to go— it wants to slide in—keep your hand flat till you get the feeling of it—don't just push it anywhere—*feel* it."

But Gerda had never been able to feel anything about a gear lever. If she was pushing it more or less in the proper direction it ought to go in! Cars ought to be made so that you didn't have that horrible grinding noise.

On the whole, thought Gerda, as she began the ascent of Mersham Hill, this drive wasn't going too badly. John was still absorbed in thought—and he hadn't noticed rather a bad crashing of gears in Croydon. Optimistically, as the car gained speed, she changed up into third, and immediately the car slackened. John, as it were, woke up.

"What on earth's the point of changing up just when you're coming to the steep bit?"

Gerda set her jaw. Not very much farther now. Not that she wanted to get there. No, indeed, she'd much rather drive on for hours and hours, even if John *did* lose his temper with her!

But now they were driving along Shovel Down—flaming Autumn woods all round them.

"Wonderful to get out of London into this," exclaimed John. "Think of it, Gerda, most afternoons we're stuck in that dingy drawing room having tea—sometimes with the light on."

The image of the somewhat dark drawing room of the flat rose up before Gerda's eyes with the tantalizing delight of a mirage. Oh! if only she could be sitting there now.

"The country looks lovely," she said heroically.

Down the steep hill—no escape now . . . That vague hope that something, she didn't know what, might intervene to save her from the nightmare, was unrealized. They were there.

She was a little comforted, as she drove in, to see Henrietta sitting on a wall with Midge and a tall thin man. She felt a certain reliance on Henrietta who would sometimes unexpectedly come to the rescue if things were getting very bad.

John was glad to see Henrietta, too . . . It seemed to him exactly the fitting journey's end to that lovely panorama of Autumn, to drop down from the hilltop and find Henrietta waiting for him . . .

She had on the green tweed coat and skirt that he liked her in and which he thought suited her so much better than London clothes. Her long legs were stuck out in front of her, ending in well-polished brown brogues.

They exchanged a quick smile—a brief recognition of the fact that each was glad of the other's presence. John didn't want to talk to Henrietta now. He just enjoyed feeling that she was there—knowing that without her the week-end would be barren and empty.

Lady Angkatell came out from the house and greeted them. Her conscience made her more effusive to Gerda than she would have been normally to any guest.

"But how *very* nice to see you, Gerda! It's been such a *long* time. *And* John!"

The idea was clearly that Gerda was the eagerly awaited guest, and John the mere adjunct. It failed miserably of its object, making Gerda stiff and uncomfortable.

Lucy said, "You know Edward? Edward Angkatell?"

John nodded to Edward and said, "No, I don't think so."

The afternoon sun lighted up the gold of John's hair and the blue of his eyes. So might a Viking look who had just come ashore on a conquering mission. His voice, warm and resonant, charmed the ear, and the magnetism of his whole personality took charge of the scene.

That warmth and that objectiveness did no damage to Lucy. It set off, indeed, that curious elfin elusiveness of hers. It was Edward who seemed, suddenly, by contrast with the other man, bloodless—a shadowy figure, stooping a little . . .

Henrietta suggested to Gerda that they should go and look at the kitchen garden.

"Lucy is sure to insist on showing us the rock garden and the Autumn border," she said as she led the way, "but I always think kitchen gardens are nice and peaceful. One can sit on the cucumber frames, or go inside a greenhouse if it's cold, and nobody bothers one and sometimes there's something to eat."

They found, indeed, some late peas, which Henrietta ate raw, but which Gerda did not much care for. She was glad to have got away from Lucy Angkatell whom she had found more alarming than ever.

She began to talk to Henrietta with something like animation. The questions Henrietta asked always seemed to be questions to which Gerda knew the answers. After ten minutes Gerda felt very much better and began to think that perhaps the week-end wouldn't be so bad after all.

Zena was going to dancing class now and had just had a new frock. Gerda described it at length. Also, she had found a very nice new leather-craft shop. Henrietta asked whether it would be difficult to make herself a handbag; Gerda must show her.

It was really very easy, she thought, to make Gerda look happy, and what an enormous difference it made to her when she did look happy!

"She only wants to be allowed to curl up and purr," thought Henrietta.

They sat happily on the corner of the cucumber frames where the sun, now low in the sky, gave an illusion of a Summer day.

Then a silence fell. Gerda's face lost its expression of placidity. Her shoulders drooped. She sat there, the picture of misery. She jumped when Henrietta spoke.

"Why do you come," said Henrietta, "if you hate it so much?"

Gerda hurried into speech.

"Oh, I don't! I mean, I don't know why you should think—"

She paused, then went on:

"It is really delightful to get out of London, and Lady Angkatell is so *very* kind—"

"Lucy? She's not a bit kind."

Gerda looked faintly shocked.

"Oh, but she *is*. She's so very nice to me always."

"Lucy has good manners and she can be gracious. But she is rather a cruel person. I think really because she isn't quite human—she doesn't know what it's like to feel and think like ordinary people. And you *are* hating being here, Gerda! You know you are. And why should you come if you feel like that?"

"Well, you see, John likes it—"

"Oh, John likes it all right. But you could let him come by himself."

"He wouldn't like that. He wouldn't enjoy it without me. John is so unselfish. He thinks it is good for me to get out into the country."

"The country is all right," said Henrietta, "but there's no need to throw in the Angkatells."

"I—I—don't want you to feel that I'm ungrateful."

"My dear Gerda, why should you like us? I always have thought the Angkatells were an odious family. We all like getting together and talking an extraordinary language of our own. I don't wonder outside people want to murder us."

Then she added:

"I expect it's about teatime. Let's go back."

She was watching Gerda's face as the latter got up and started to walk towards the house.

It's interesting, thought Henrietta, one portion of whose mind was always detached, to see exactly what a female Christian martyr's face looked like before she went into the Arena. . . .

As they left the walled kitchen garden, they heard shots and Henrietta remarked:

"Sounds as though the massacre of the Angkatells had begun!"

It turned out to be Sir Henry and Edward discussing firearms and illustrating their discussion by firing revolvers. Henry Angkatell's hobby was firearms and he had quite a collection of them.

He had brought out several revolvers and some target cards and he and Edward were firing at them.

"Hullo, Henrietta. Want to try if you could kill a burglar?"

Henrietta took the revolver from him.

"That's right—yes, so, aim like this."

Bang!

"Missed him," said Sir Henry.

"You try, Gerda."

"Oh, I don't think I—"

"Come on, Mrs. Christow. It's quite simple."

Gerda fired the revolver, flinching, and shutting her eyes. The bullet went even wider than Henrietta's had done.

"Oo, I want to do it," said Midge, strolling up.

"It's more difficult than you'd think," she remarked after a couple of shots. "But it's rather fun."

Lucy came out from the house. Behind her came a tall, sulky young man with an Adam's apple.

"Here's David," she announced.

She took the revolver from Midge as her husband greeted David Angkatell, reloaded it and without a word put three holes close to the centre of the target.

"Well done, Lucy," exclaimed Midge. "I didn't know shooting was one of your accomplishments."

"Lucy," said Sir Henry gravely, "always kills her man!"

Then he added reminiscently, "Came in useful once. Do you remember, my dear, those thugs that set upon us that day on the Asian side of the Bosporus? I was rolling about with two of them on top of me, feeling for my throat."

"And what did Lucy do?" asked Midge.

"Fired two shots into the mêlée. I didn't even know she had the pistol with her. Got one bad man through the leg and the other in the shoulder. Nearest escape in the world *I've* ever had. I can't think how she didn't hit me."

Lady Angkatell smiled at him.

"I think one always has to take some risk," she said gently. "And one should do it quickly and not think too much about it."

"An admirable sentiment, my dear," said Sir Henry. "But I have always felt slightly aggrieved that *I* was the risk you took!"

Chapter VIII

AFTER TEA JOHN said to Henrietta, "Come for a walk," and Lady Angkatell said that she *must* show Gerda the rock garden though of course it was quite the wrong time of year.

Walking with John, thought Henrietta, was as unlike walking with Edward as anything could be.

With Edward one seldom did more than potter. Edward, she thought, was a born potterer. Walking with John, it was all she could do to keep up, and by the time they got up to Shovel Down she said breathlessly, "It's not a Marathon, John!"

He slowed down and laughed.

"Am I walking you off your feet?"

"I can do it—but is there any need? We haven't got a train to catch. Why do you have this ferocious energy? Are you running away from yourself?"

He stopped dead. "Why do you say that?"

Henrietta looked at him curiously.

"I didn't mean anything particular by it."

John went on again, but walking more slowly.

"As a matter of fact," he said, "I'm tired. I'm very tired."

She heard the lassitude in his voice.

"How's the Crabtree?"

"It's early days to say, but I think, Henrietta, that I've got the hang of things. If I'm right"—his footsteps began to quicken—"a lot of our ideas will be revolutionised—we'll have to reconsider the whole question of hormone secretion—"

"You mean that there will be a cure for Ridgeway's Disease? That people won't die?"

"That, incidentally."

What odd people doctors were, thought Henrietta. Incidentally!

"Scientifically, it opens up all sorts of possibilities!"

He drew a deep breath. "But it's good to get down here—good to get some air into your lungs—good to see you." He gave her one of his sudden quick smiles, "And it will do Gerda good."

"Gerda, of course, simply loves coming to The Hollow!"

"Of course she does. By the way, have I met Edward Angkatell before?"

"You've met him twice," said Henrietta dryly.

"I couldn't remember. He's one of those vague, indefinite people."

"Edward's a dear. I've always been very fond of him."

"Well, don't let's waste time on Edward! None of these people count." Henrietta said in a low voice:

"Sometimes, John—I'm afraid for you!"

"Afraid for me—what do you mean?"

He turned an astonished face upon her.

"You are so oblivious—so—yes, *blind.*"

"Blind?"

"You don't know—you don't see—you're curiously insensitive! You don't know what other people are feeling and thinking."

"I should have said just the opposite."

"You see what you're looking *at,* yes. You're—you're like a search-light. A powerful beam turned onto the one spot where your interest is, and behind it and each side of it, darkness!"

"Henrietta, my dear, what is all this?"

"It's *dangerous,* John. You assume that everyone likes you, that they mean well to you. People like Lucy, for instance."

"Doesn't Lucy like me?" he said, surprised. "I've always been extremely fond of her."

"And so you assume that she likes you. But I'm not sure . . . And Gerda and Edward—and Midge and Henry? How do you know what they feel towards you?"

"And Henrietta? Do I know how she feels?" He caught her hand for a moment. "At least—I'm sure of you."

She took her hand away.

"You can be sure of no one in this world, John."

His face had grown grave.

"No, I won't believe that. I'm sure of you and I'm sure of myself. At least—" His face changed.

"What is it, John?"

"Do you know what I found myself saying today? Something quite ridiculous. *'I want to go home.'* That's what I said and I haven't the least idea what I meant by it."

Henrietta said slowly, "You must have had some picture in your mind . . ."

He said sharply, "Nothing. Nothing at all!"

At dinner that night, Henrietta was put next to David and from the end of the table Lucy's delicate eyebrows telegraphed—not a command—Lucy never commanded—but an appeal.

Sir Henry was doing his best with Gerda and succeeding quite well. John, his face amused, was following the leaps and bounds of Lucy's discursive mind. Midge talked in rather a stilted way to Edward who seemed more absentminded than usual.

David was glowering and crumbling his bread with a nervous hand.

David had come to The Hollow in a spirit of considerable unwillingness. Until now, he had never met either Sir Henry or Lady Angkatell, and disapproving of the Empire generally, he was prepared to disapprove of these relatives of his. Edward, whom he did know, he despised as a dilettante. The remaining four guests he examined with a critical eye. Relations, he thought, were pretty awful, and one was expected to talk to people, a thing which he hated doing.

Midge and Henrietta he discounted as empty-headed. This Dr. Christow was just one of these Harley Street charlatans—all manner and social success—his wife obviously did not count.

David shifted his neck in his collar and wished fervently that all these people could know how little he thought of them! They were really all quite negligible.

When he had repeated that three times to himself he felt rather better. He still glowered but he was able to leave his bread alone.

Henrietta, though responding loyally to the eyebrows, had some difficulty in making headway. David's curt rejoinders were snubbing in the extreme. In the end she had recourse to a method she had employed before with the tongue-tied young.

She made, deliberately, a dogmatic and quite unjustifiable pronouncement on a modern composer, knowing that David had much technical musical knowledge.

To her amusement the plan worked. David drew himself up from his slouching position where he had been more or less reclining on his spine. His voice was no longer low and mumbling. He stopped crumbling his bread.

"That," he said in loud, clear tones, fixing a cold eye on Henrietta, "shows that you don't know the first thing about the subject!"

From then on until the end of dinner he lectured her in clear and biting accents, and Henrietta subsided into the proper meekness of one instructed.

Lucy Angkatell sent a benignant glance down the table, and Midge grinned to herself.

"So clever of you, darling," murmured Lady Angkatell as she slipped an arm through Henrietta's on the way to the drawing-room. "What an awful thought it is that if people had less in their heads they would know better what to do with their hands! Do you think hearts or bridge or rummy or something terribly, terribly simple like animal grab?"

"I think David would be rather insulted by animal grab."

"Perhaps you are right. Bridge, then. I am sure he will feel that bridge is rather worthless and then he can have a nice glow of contempt for us."

They made up two tables. Henrietta played with Gerda against John and Edward. It was not her idea of the best grouping. She had wanted to segregate Gerda from Lucy and if possible from John also—but John had shown determination. And Edward had then forestalled Midge.

The atmosphere was not, Henrietta thought, quite comfortable, but she did not quite know from whence the discomfort arose. Anyway, if the cards gave them anything like a break, she intended that Gerda should win. Gerda was not really a bad bridge player—away from John she was quite average—but she was a nervous player with bad judgment and with no real knowledge of the value of her hand. John was a good, if slightly over-confident player. Edward was a very good player indeed.

The evening wore on and at Henrietta's table they were still playing the same rubber. The scores rose above the line on either side. A curious tensity had come into the play of which only one person was unaware.

To Gerda, this was just a rubber of bridge which she happened for once to be quite enjoying. She felt, indeed, a pleasurable excitement. Difficult decisions had been unexpectedly eased by Henrietta's over-calling her own bids and playing the hand.

Those moments when John, unable to refrain from that critical attitude which did more to undermine Gerda's self-confidence than he could possibly have imagined, exclaimed, "Why on earth did you lead that club, Gerda?" were countered almost immediately by Henrietta's swift, "Nonsense, John, of course she had to lead the club! It was the only possible thing to do."

Finally, with a sigh, Henrietta drew the score towards her.

"Game and rubber, but I don't think we shall make much out of it, Gerda."

John said, "A lucky finesse," in a cheerful voice.

Henrietta looked up sharply. She knew his tone. She met his eyes and her own dropped.

She got up and went to the mantelpiece and John followed her. He said conversationally, "You don't *always* look deliberately into people's hands, do you?"

Henrietta said calmly, "Perhaps I was a little obvious. How despicable it is to want to win at games!"

"You wanted Gerda to win the rubber, you mean. In your desire to give pleasure to people, you don't draw the line at cheating."

"How horribly you put things! And you are always quite right."

"Your wishes seemed to be shared by my partner."

So he *had* noticed, thought Henrietta. She had wondered, herself, if she had been mistaken. Edward was so skilful—there was nothing you could have taken hold of. A failure, once, to call the game. A lead that had been sound and obvious—but when a less obvious lead would have assured success.

It worried Henrietta . . . . Edward, she knew, would never play his cards in order that she, Henrietta, might win. He was far too imbued with English sportsmanship for that. No, she thought, it was just any more success for John Christow that he was unable to endure . . .

She felt suddenly keyed up, alert. She didn't like this party of Lucy's.

And then dramatically, unexpectedly, with the unreality of a stage entrance, Veronica Cray came through the window!

The French windows had been pushed to, not closed, for the evening was warm. Veronica pushed them wide, came through them and stood there framed against the night, smiling, a little rueful, wholly charming, waiting just that infinitesimal moment before speaking so that she might be sure of her audience.

"You must forgive me—bursting in upon you this way. I'm your neighbour, Lady Angkatell—from that ridiculous cottage Dovecotes—and the most frightful catastrophe has occurred!"

Her smile broadened—became more humorous.

"Not a match! Not a single match in the house! And Saturday evening. So stupid of me. But what could I do? I came along here to beg help from my only neighbour within miles."

Nobody spoke for a moment, for Veronica had rather that effect. She was lovely—not quietly lovely, not even dazzlingly lovely—but so efficiently lovely that it made you gasp! The waves of pale shimmering hair, the curving mouth—the platinum foxes that swathed her shoulders and the long sweep of white velvet underneath them. . . .

She was looking from one to the other of them, humorous, charming!

"And I smoke," she said, "like a chimney! And my lighter won't work! And besides, there's breakfast—gas stoves—" She thrust out her hands. "I do feel such a complete fool."

Lucy came forward, gracious, faintly amused.

"Why, of course—" she began, but Veronica Cray interrupted.

She was looking at John Christow. An expression of utter amazement, of incredulous delight, was spreading over her face. She took a step towards him, hands outstretched.

"Why, surely—*John!* It's John Christow! Now isn't that too extraordinary? I haven't seen you for years and years and years! And suddenly—to find you *here!*"

She had his hands in hers by now. She was all warmth and simple eagerness. She half turned her head to Lady Angkatell.

"This is just the most wonderful surprise. John's an old, old friend of mine. Why, John's the first man I ever loved! I was crazy about you, John."

She was half laughing now—a woman moved by the ridiculous remembrance of young love.

"I always thought John was just wonderful!"

Sir Henry, courteous and polished, had moved forward to her.

She must have a drink. He manoeuvred glasses. Lady Angkatell said: "Midge dear, ring the bell."

When Gudgeon came, Lucy said:

"A box of matches, Gudgeon—at least has cook got plenty?"

"A new dozen came in today, m'lady."

"Then bring in half a dozen, Gudgeon."

"Oh, no, Lady Angkatell—just one!"

Veronica protested, laughing; she had her drink now and was smiling round at everyone. John Christow said:

"This is my wife, Veronica."

"Oh, but how lovely to meet you." Veronica beamed upon Gerda's air of bewilderment.

Gudgeon brought in the matches, stacked on a silver salver.

Lady Angkatell indicated Veronica Cray with a gesture and he brought the salver to her.

"Oh, dear Lady Angkatell, not all these!"

Lucy's gesture was negligently royal.

"It's so tiresome having only one of a thing. We can spare them quite easily."

Sir Henry was saying pleasantly:

"And how do you like living at Dovecotes?"

"I adore it. It's wonderful here, near London, and yet one feels so beautifully isolated."

Veronica put down her glass. She drew the platinum foxes a little closer round her. She smiled on them all.

"Thank you *so* much! You've been so kind—" the words floated between Sir Henry and Lady Angkatell, and for some reason, Edward. "I shall now carry home the spoils. John," she gave him an artless, friendly smile, "you must see me safely back, because I want dreadfully to hear all you've been doing in the years and years since I've seen you. It makes me feel, of course, dreadfully *old* . . ."

She moved to the window and John Christow followed her. She flung a last brilliant smile at them all.

"I'm so dreadfully sorry to have bothered you in this stupid way . . . Thank you *so* much, Lady Angkatell."

She went out with John. Sir Henry stood by the window looking after them.

"Quite a fine warm night," he said.

Lady Angkatell yawned.

"Oh, dear," she murmured, "we must go to bed. Henry, we must go and see one of her pictures. I'm sure, from tonight, she must give a lovely performance."

They went upstairs. Midge, saying good night, asked Lucy:

"A lovely performance?"

"Didn't you think so, darling?"

"I gather, Lucy, that you think it's just possible she may have some matches in Dovecotes all the time."

"Dozens of boxes, I expect, darling. But we mustn't be uncharitable. And it *was* a lovely performance!"

Doors were shutting all down the corridor, voices were murmuring good nights. Sir Henry said, "I'll leave the window for Christow." His own door shut.

Henrietta said to Gerda, "What fun actresses are. They make such marvellous entrances and exits!" She yawned and added, "I'm frightfully sleepy."

Veronica Cray moved swiftly along the narrow path through the chestnut woods.

She came out from the woods to the open space by the swimming pool. There was a small pavilion here where the Angkatells sat on days that were sunny but when there was a cold wind.

Veronica Cray stood still. She turned and faced John Christow.

Then she laughed. With her hand she gestured towards the leaf-strewn surface of the swimming pool.

"Not quite like the Mediterranean, is it, John?" she said.

He knew then what he had been waiting for—knew that in all those fifteen years of separation from Veronica, she had still been with him. *The blue sea, the scent of mimosa, the hot dust—* pushed down, thrust out of sight, but never really forgotten . . . They all meant one thing—Veronica. He was a young man of twenty-four, desperately and agonizingly in love and this time he was not going to run away. . . .

Chapter IX

JOHN CHRISTOW CAME out from the chestnut woods onto the green slope by the house. There was a moon and the house basked in the moonlight with a strange innocence in its curtained windows. He looked down at the wrist-watch he wore.

It was three o'clock. He drew a deep breath and his face was anxious. He was no longer, even remotely, a young man of twenty-four in love. He was a shrewd practical man of just on forty and his mind was clear and level-headed.

He'd been a fool, of course, a complete damned fool, but he didn't regret that! For he was, he now realized, completely master of himself. It was as though, for years, he had dragged a weight upon his leg—and now the weight was gone. He was free.

He was free and himself, John Christow—and he knew that to John Christow, successful Harley Street specialist, Veronica Cray meant nothing whatsoever. All that had been in the past—and because that conflict had never been resolved, because he had always suffered humiliatingly from the fear that he had, in plain language, "run away," Veronica's image had never completely left him. She had come to him tonight out of a dream . . . and he had accepted the dream, and now, thank God, he was delivered from it for ever. He was back in the present—and it was 3:00 a.m., and it was just possible that he had mucked up things rather badly.

He'd been with Veronica for three hours. She had sailed in like a frigate, and cut him out of the circle and carried him off as her prize, and he wondered now what on earth everybody had thought about it.

What, for instance, would Gerda think?

And Henrietta? (But he didn't care quite so much about Henrietta. He could, he felt, at a pinch explain to Henrietta. He could never explain to Gerda.)

And he didn't, definitely he didn't, want to lose anything.

All his life he had been a man who took a justifiable amount of risks. Risks with patients, risks with treatment, risks with investments. Never a fantastic risk—only the kind of risk that was just beyond the margin of safety.

If Gerda guessed—if Gerda had the least suspicion.

But would she have? How much did he really know about Gerda? Normally, Gerda would believe white was black if he told her so. But over a thing like this . . .

What had he looked like when he followed Veronica's tall, triumphant figure out of that window? What had he shown in his face? Had they seen a boy's dazed, love-sick face? Or had they only observed a man doing a polite duty? He didn't know! He hadn't the least idea.

But he was afraid—afraid for the ease and order and safety of his life. He'd been mad—quite mad, he thought with exasperation—and then took comfort in that very thought. Nobody would believe, surely, he could have been as mad as that?

Everybody was in bed and asleep, that was clear. The French window of the drawing-room stood half open, left for his return. He looked up again at the innocent sleeping house. It looked, somehow, too innocent.

Suddenly he started. He had heard, or he had imagined he heard, the faint closing of a door.

He turned his head sharply. If someone had come down to the pool, following him there. If someone had waited and followed him back, that someone could have taken a higher path and so gained entrance to the house again by the side garden door and the soft closing of the garden door would have made just the sound that he had heard.

He looked up sharply at the windows. Was that curtain moving, had it been pushed aside for someone to look out, and then allowed to fall? Henrietta's room . . .

Henrietta! Not Henrietta, his heart cried in a sudden panic. I can't lose Henrietta!

He wanted suddenly to fling up a handful of pebbles at her window, to cry out to her.

"Come out, my dear love. Come out to me now and walk with me up through the woods to Shovel Down and there listen—listen to everything that I now know about myself and that you must know, too, if you do not know it already . . ."

He wanted to say to Henrietta:

"I am starting again. A new life begins from today. The things that crippled and hindered me from living have fallen away. You were right this afternoon when you asked me if I was running away from myself. That is what I have been doing for years. Because I never knew whether it was strength or weakness that took me away from Veronica, I have been afraid of myself, afraid of life, afraid of you."

If he were to wake Henrietta and make her come out with him now—
up through the woods to where they could watch, together, the sun come
up over the rim of the world . . .

"You're mad," he said to himself. He shivered. It was cold now, late
September after all. "What the devil is the matter with you?" he asked
himself. "You've behaved quite insanely enough for one night. If you get
away with it as it is, you're damned lucky!" What on earth would Gerda
think if he stayed out all night and came home with the milk?

What, for the matter of that, would the Angkatells think?

But that did not worry him for a moment. The Angkatells took Green-
wich time, as it were, from Lucy Angkatell. And to Lucy Angkatell, the
unusual always appeared perfectly reasonable.

But Gerda, unfortunately, was not an Angkatell.

Gerda would have to be dealt with, and he'd better go in and deal with
Gerda as soon as possible.

Supposing it had been Gerda who had followed him tonight—

No good saying people didn't do such things. As a doctor, he knew only
too well what people, high-minded, sensitive, fastidious, honourable people
constantly did. They listened at doors, and opened letters and spied and
snooped—not because for one moment they approved of such conduct, but
because, before the sheer necessity of human anguish, they were rendered
desperate.

Poor devils, he thought, poor suffering human devils . . . John Christow knew a good deal about human suffering. He had not very much pity
for weakness, but he had for suffering, for it was, he knew, the strong who
suffer . . .

If Gerda knew—

"Nonsense," he said to himself, "why should she? She's gone up to bed
and she's fast asleep. She's no imagination, never has had."

He went in through the French windows, switched on a lamp, closed
and locked the windows. Then, switching off the light, he left the room,
found the switch in the hall, went quickly and lightly up the stairs. A
second switch turned off the hall light. He stood for a moment by the
bedroom door, his hand on the doorknob, then he turned it, and went in.

The room was dark and he could hear Gerda's even breathing. She
stirred as he came in and closed the door. Her voice came to him, blurred
and indistinct with sleep:

"Is that you, John?"

"Yes,"

"Aren't you very late? What time is it?"

He said easily,

"I've no idea. Sorry I woke you up. I had to go in with the woman and have a drink."

He made his voice sound bored and sleepy.

Gerda murmured, "Oh? Good night, John."

There was a rustle as she turned over in bed.

It was all right! As usual, he'd been lucky . . . As *usual*—just for a moment it sobered him, the thought of how often his luck had held! Time and again there had been a moment when he'd held his breath and said, "If *this* goes wrong . . ." And it hadn't gone wrong! But some day, surely, his luck would change. . . .

He undressed quickly and got into bed. Funny, that kid's fortune telling. *And this one is over your head and has power over you* . . . Veronica! and she *had* had power over him all right.

But not any more, my girl, he thought with a kind of savage satisfaction. All that's over. I'm quit of you now!

Chapter X

IT WAS TEN o'clock the next morning when John came down. Breakfast was on the sideboard. Gerda had had her breakfast sent up to her in bed and had been rather perturbed since perhaps she might be "giving trouble."

Nonsense, John had said. People like the Angkatells, who still managed to have butlers and servants, might just as well give them something to do.

He felt very kindly towards Gerda this morning. All that nervous irritation that had so fretted him of late seemed to have died down and disappeared.

Sir Henry and Edward had gone out shooting, Lady Angkatell told him. She herself was busy with a gardening basket and gardening gloves. He stayed talking to her for a while until Gudgeon approached him with a letter on a salver.

"This has just come by hand, sir."

He took it with slightly raised eyebrows.

Veronica!

He strolled into the library, tearing it open.

> *Please come over this morning. I must see you.*
> *Veronica.*

Imperious as ever, he thought! He'd a good mind not to go. Then he thought he might as well and get it over. He'd go at once.

He took the path opposite the library window, passed by the swimming pool which was a kind of nucleus with paths radiating from it in every direction, one up the hill to the woods proper, one from the flower walk above the house, one from the farm and the one that led on to the lane which he took now.

A few yards up the lane was the cottage called Dovecotes.

Veronica was waiting for him. She spoke from the window of the pretentious half-timbered building.

"Come inside, John. It's cold this morning."

There was a fire lit in the sitting room which was furnished in off-white with pale cyclamen cushions.

Looking at her this morning with an appraising eye, he saw the differences there were from the girl he remembered, as he had not been able to see them last night.

Strictly speaking, he thought, she was more beautiful now than then. She understood her beauty better, and she cared for it and enhanced it in every way. Her hair which had been deep golden was now a silvery platinum colour. Her eyebrows were different, giving much more poignancy to her expression.

Hers had never been a mindless beauty. Veronica, he remembered, had qualified as one of our "intellectual actresses." She had a university degree and had had views on Strindberg and on Shakespeare.

He was struck now with what had been only dimly apparent to him in the past—that she was a woman whose egoism was quite abnormal. Veronica was accustomed to getting her own way and beneath the smooth, beautiful contours of flesh he seemed to sense an ugly iron determination.

"I sent for you," said Veronica as she handed him a box of cigarettes, "because we've got to talk. We've got to make arrangements. For our future, I mean."

He took a cigarette and lighted it. Then he said quite pleasantly:

"But have we a future?"

She gave him a sharp glance.

"What do you mean, John? Of course we have got a future. We've wasted fifteen years. There's no need to waste any more time."

He sat down.

"I'm sorry, Veronica. But I'm afraid you've got all this taped out wrong. I've—enjoyed meeting you again very much. But your life and mine don't touch anywhere. They are quite divergent."

"Nonsense, John. I love you and you love me. We've always loved each other. You were incredibly obstinate in the past! But never mind that now. Our lives needn't clash. I don't mean to go back to the States. When I've finished this picture I'm working on now, I'm going to play a straight part on the London stage. I've got a wonderful play—Elderton's written it for me. It will be a terrific success."

"I'm sure it will," he said politely.

"And you can go on being a doctor." Her voice was kind and condescending. "You're quite well known, they tell me."

"My dear girl, I'm married. I've got children."

"I'm married myself at the moment," said Veronica. "But all these things are easily arranged. A good lawyer can fix up everything." She smiled at him dazzlingly. "I always did mean to marry you, darling. I can't think why I have this terrible passion for you, but there it is!"

"I'm sorry, Veronica, but no good lawyer is going to fix up anything. Your life and mine have nothing to do with each other."

"Not after last night?"

"You're not a child, Veronica. You've had a couple of husbands, and by all accounts, several lovers. What does last night mean actually? Nothing at all, and you know it."

"Oh, my dear John—" she was still amused, indulgent. "If you'd seen your face—there in that stuffy drawing-room! You might have been in San Miguel again!"

John sighed. He said:

"I *was* in San Miguel . . . Try to understand, Veronica. You came to me out of the past. Last night I, too, was in the past, but today—today's different. I'm a man fifteen years older. A man you don't even know—and whom, I daresay, you wouldn't like much if you did know."

"You prefer your wife and children to me?"

She was genuinely amazed.

"Odd as it may seem to you, I do."

"Nonsense, John, you love me."

"I'm sorry, Veronica."

She said incredulously:

"You don't love me?"

"It's better to be quite clear about these things. You are an extraordinarily beautiful woman, Veronica, but I don't love you."

She sat so still that she might have been a waxwork. That stillness of hers made him just a little uneasy.

When she spoke it was with such venom that he recoiled.

"Who is she?"

"She? Who do you mean?"

"That woman by the mantelpiece last night?"

Henrietta! he thought. How the devil did she get on to Henrietta? Aloud he said:

"Who are you talking about? Midge Hardcastle?"

"Midge? That's the square dark girl, isn't it? No, I don't mean her. And I don't mean your wife. I mean that insolent devil who was leaning against the mantelpiece! It's because of *her* that you're turning me down! Oh, don't pretend to be so moral about your wife and children. It's that other woman."

She got up and came towards him.

"Don't you understand, John, that ever since I came back to England, eighteen months ago, I've been thinking about you? Why do you imagine I took this idiotic place here? Simply because I found out that you often came down for week-ends with the Angkatells!"

"So last night was all planned, Veronica?"

"You *belong* to me, John. You always have!"

"I don't belong to anyone, Veronica! Hasn't life taught you even now that you can't own other human beings body and soul? I loved you when I was a young man. I wanted you to share my life. You wouldn't do it!"

"*My* life and career were much more important than *yours!* Anyone can be a doctor!"

He lost his temper a little.

"Are you *quite* as wonderful as you think you are?"

"You mean that I haven't got to the top of the tree. I shall! *I shall!*"

John Christow looked at her with a sudden quite dispassionate interest.

"I don't believe, you know, that you will . . . There's a *lack* in you, Veronica. You're all grab and snatch—no real generosity—I think that's it . . ."

Veronica got up. She said in a quiet voice:

"You turned me down fifteen years ago . . . You've turned me down again today. I'll make you sorry for this."

John got up and went to the door.

"I'm sorry, Veronica, if I've hurt you. You're very lovely, my dear, and I once loved you very much. Can't we leave it at that?"

"Good-bye, John. We're not leaving it at that. You'll find that out all right. I think—I think I hate you more than I believed I could hate anyone."

He shrugged his shoulders.

"I'm sorry. Good-bye."

John walked back slowly through the wood. When he got to the swimming pool he sat down on the bench there. He had no regrets for his treatment of Veronica. Veronica, he thought dispassionately, was a nasty bit of work. She always had been a nasty bit of work and the best thing he had ever done was to get clear of her in time. God alone knew what would have happened to him by now if he hadn't!

As it was, he had that extraordinary sensation of starting a new life, unfettered and unhampered by the past. He must have been extremely difficult to live with for the last year or two. Poor Gerda, he thought, with her unselfishness and her continual anxiety to please him. He would be kinder in future.

And perhaps now he would be able to stop trying to bully Henrietta. Not that one could really bully Henrietta—she wasn't made that way. Storms broke over her and she stood there, meditative, her eyes looking at you from very far away . . .

He thought, I shall go to Henrietta and tell her—

He looked up sharply, disturbed by some small unexpected sound. There had been shots in the woods higher up, and there had been the usual small noises of woodlands, birds, and the faint melancholy dropping of leaves. But this was another noise—a very faint businesslike click . . .

And suddenly, John was acutely conscious of danger. How long had he been sitting here? Half an hour? An hour? There was someone watching him. Someone—

And that click was—of course it was—

He turned sharply, a man very quick in his reactions. But he was not quick enough. His eyes widened in surprise, but there was no time for him to make a sound.

The shot rang out and he fell, awkwardly, sprawled out by the edge of the swimming pool . . .

A dark stain welled up slowly on his left side and trickled slowly onto the concrete of the pool edge and from there dripped red into the blue water . . .

Chapter XI

HERCULE POIROT FLICKED a last speck of dust from his shoes. He had dressed carefully for his luncheon party and he was satisfied with the result.

He knew well enough the kind of clothes that were worn in the country on a Sunday in England, but he did not choose to conform to English ideas. He preferred his own standards of urban smartness. He was not an English country gentleman and he would not dress like an English country gentleman. He was Hercule Poirot!

He did not, he confessed it to himself, really like the country. The week-end cottage—so many of his friends had extolled it—he had allowed himself to succumb, and had purchased Resthaven, though the only thing he had liked about it was its shape which was quite square like a box. The surrounding landscape he did not care for, though it was, he knew, supposed to be a beauty spot. It was, however, too wildly asymmetrical to appeal to him. He did not care much for trees at any time—they had that untidy habit of shedding their leaves! He could endure poplars and he approved of a monkey puzzle—but this riot of beech and oak left him unmoved. Such a landscape was best enjoyed from a car on a fine afternoon. You exclaimed, *"Quel beau paysage!"* and drove back to a good hotel.

The best thing about Resthaven, he considered, was the small vegetable garden neatly laid out in rows by his Belgian gardener, Victor. Meanwhile, Françoise, Victor's wife, devoted herself with tenderness to the care of her employer's stomach.

Hercule Poirot passed through the gate, sighed, glanced down once more at his shining black shoes, adjusted his pale grey Homburg hat, and looked up and down the road.

He shivered slightly at the aspect of Dovecotes. Dovecotes and Resthaven had been erected by rival builders, each of whom had acquired a small piece of land. Further enterprise on their part had been swiftly curtailed by a National Trust for preserving the beauties of the country-side. The two houses remained representative of two schools of thought.

Resthaven was a box with a roof, severely modern and a little dull. Dove-cotes was a riot of half-timbering and Olde Worlde packed into as small a space as possible.

Hercule Poirot debated within himself as to how he should approach The Hollow. There was, he knew, a little higher up the lane, a small gate and a path. This, the unofficial way, would save a half mile detour by the road. Nevertheless, Hercule Poirot, a stickler for etiquette, decided to take the longer way round and approach the house correctly by the front entrance.

This was his first visit to Sir Henry and Lady Angkatell. One should not, he considered, take short cuts uninvited, especially when one was the guest of people of social importance. He was, it must be admitted, pleased by their invitation.

"Je suis un peu snob," he murmured to himself.

He had retained an agreeable impression of the Angkatells from the time in Baghdad, particularly of Lady Angkatell. *"Une originale!"* he thought to himself.

His estimation of the time required for walking to The Hollow by road was accurate. It was exactly one minute to one when he rang the front door bell. He was glad to have arrived and felt slightly tired. He was not fond of walking.

The door was opened by the magnificent Gudgeon of whom Poirot approved. His reception, however, was not quite as he had hoped.

"Her ladyship is in the pavilion by the swimming pool, sir. Will you come this way?"

The passion of the English for sitting out of doors irritated Hercule Poirot. Though one had to put up with this whimsy in the height of Summer, surely, Poirot thought, one should be safe from it by the end of September! The day was mild, certainly, but it had, as Autumn days always had, a certain dampness. How infinitely pleasanter to have been ushered into a comfortable drawing-room with, perhaps, a small fire in the grate. But no, here he was being led out through French windows across a slope of lawn, past a rockery and then, through a small gate and along a narrow track between closely planted young chestnuts.

It was the habit of the Angkatells to invite guests for one o'clock, and on fine days they had cocktails and sherry in the small pavilion by the swimming pool. Lunch itself was scheduled for one-thirty, by which time, the most unpunctual of guests should have managed to arrive, which permitted Lady Angkatell's excellent cook to embark on soufflés and such accurately timed delicacies without too much trepidation.

To Hercule Poirot, the plan did not commend itself.

"In a little minute," he thought, "I shall be almost back where I started."

With an increasing awareness of his feet in his shoes he followed Gudgeon's tall figure.

It was at that moment from just ahead of him that he heard a little cry. It increased, somehow, his dissatisfaction. It was incongruous, in some way unfitting. He did not classify it, nor indeed think about it. When he thought about it afterwards he was hard put to it to remember just what emotions it had seemed to convey. Dismay? Surprise? Horror? He could only say that it suggested, very definitely, the unexpected.

Gudgeon stepped out from the chestnuts. He was moving to one side, deferentially, to allow Poirot to pass and at the same time clearing his throat preparatory to murmuring, "M. Poirot, m' lady," in the proper subdued and respectful tones when his suppleness became suddenly rigid. He gasped. It was an unbutlerlike noise.

Hercule Poirot stepped out onto the open space surrounding the swimming pool, and immediately he too stiffened, but with annoyance.

It was too much—it was really too much! He had not suspected such cheapness of the Angkatells. The long walk by the road, the disappointment at the house—and now *this!* The misplaced sense of humour of the English!

He was annoyed and he was bored—oh! how he was bored! Death was not, to him, amusing. And here they had arranged for him, by way of a joke, a set piece.

For what he was looking at was a highly artificial murder scene. By the side of the pool was the body, artistically arranged with an outflung arm and even some red paint dripping gently over the edge of the concrete into the pool. It was a spectacular body, that of a handsome fair-haired man. Standing over the body, revolver in hand, was a woman, a short, powerfully built, middle-aged woman with a curiously blank expression.

And there were three other actors. On the far side of the pool was a tall young woman whose hair matched the Autumn leaves in its rich brown; she had a basket in her hand full of dahlia heads. A little further off was a man, a tall inconspicuous man in a shooting coat carrying a gun. And immediately on his left, with a basket of eggs in her hand, was his hostess, Lady Angkatell.

It was clear to Hercule Poirot that several different paths converged here at the swimming pool and that these people had each arrived by a different path.

It was all very mathematical and artificial.

He sighed. *Enfin,* what did they expect him to do? Was he to pretend to believe in this "crime"? Was he to register dismay—alarm? Or was he to bow, to congratulate his hostess—"Ah! but it is very charming, what you arrange for me here."

Really, the whole thing was very stupid—not *spirituel* at all! Was it not Queen Victoria who had said, "We are not amused"? He felt very inclined to say the same. "I, Hercule Poirot, am not amused."

Lady Angkatell had walked towards the body. He followed, conscious of Gudgeon, still breathing hard, behind him. He is not in the secret, that one, Hercule Poirot thought to himself. From the other side of the pool, the other two people joined them. They were all quite close now, looking down on that spectacular sprawling figure by the pool's edge.

And suddenly, with a terrific shock, with that feeling as of blurring on a cinematograph screen before the picture comes into focus, Hercule Poirot realized that this artificially set scene had a point of reality.

For what he was looking down at was, if not a dead, at least a dying man . . .

It was not red paint dripping off the edge of the concrete, it was blood. This man had been shot, and shot a very short time ago.

He darted a quick glance at the woman who stood there, revolver in hand. Her face was quite blank, without feeling of any kind. She looked dazed and rather stupid.

Curious, he thought.

Had she, he wondered, drained herself of all emotion, all feeling, in the firing of the shot? Was she now, all passion spent, nothing but an exhausted shell? It might be so, he thought.

Then he looked down on the shot man, and he started. For the dying man's eyes were open. They were intensely blue eyes and they held an expression that Poirot could not read but which he described to himself as a kind of intense awareness.

And suddenly, or so it felt to Poirot, there seemed to be in all this group of people only one person who was really alive—the man who was at the point of death.

Poirot had never received so strong an impression of vivid and intense vitality. The others were pale, shadowy figures, actors in a remote drama, but this man was *real*.

John Christow opened his mouth and spoke. His voice was strong, unsurprised and urgent.

"*Henrietta—*" he said.

Then his eyelids dropped, his head jerked sideways . . .

Hercule Poirot knelt down, made sure, then rose to his feet, mechanically dusting the knees of his trousers.

"Yes," he said. "He is dead . . ."

The picture broke up, wavered, refocussed itself. There were individual reactions now—trivial happenings. Poirot was conscious of himself as a kind of magnified eyes and ears—recording. Just that, *recording.*

He was aware of Lady Angkatell's hand relaxing its grip on her basket and Gudgeon springing forward, quickly taking it from her.

"Allow me, m' lady . . ."

Mechanically, quite naturally, Lady Angkatell murmured:

"Thank you, Gudgeon."

And then, hesitantly, she said:

"Gerda—"

The woman holding the revolver stirred for the first time. She looked round at them all. When she spoke, her voice held what seemed to be pure bewilderment.

"John's dead," she said. "John's *dead.* . . ."

With a kind of swift authority the tall young woman with the leaf brown hair, came swiftly to her.

"Give that to me, Gerda," she said.

And dexterously, before Poirot could protest or intervene, she had taken the revolver out of Gerda Christow's hand.

Poirot took a quick step forwards.

"You should not do that, Mademoiselle—"

The young woman started nervously at the sound of his voice. The revolver slipped through her fingers. She was standing by the edge of the pool and the revolver fell with a splash into the water.

Her mouth opened and she uttered an "Oh" of consternation, turning her head to look at Poirot apologetically.

"What a fool I am," she said. "I'm sorry."

Poirot did not speak for a moment. He was staring into a pair of clear hazel eyes. They met his quite steadily and he wondered if his momentary suspicion had been unjust.

He said quietly:

"Things should be handled as little as possible. Everything must be left exactly as it is for the police to see."

There was a little stir then—very faint, just a ripple of uneasiness.

Lady Angkatell murmured distastefully, "Of course. I suppose—yes, the police—"

In a quiet pleasant voice, tinged with fastidious repulsion, the man in the shooting coat said, "I'm afraid, Lucy, it's inevitable."

Into that moment of silence and realization, there came the sound of footsteps and voices, assured, brisk footsteps and cheerful, incongruous voices.

Along the path from the house came Sir Henry Angkatell and Midge Hardcastle, talking and laughing together.

At the sight of the group round the pool, Sir Henry stopped short, and exclaimed in astonishment:

"What's the matter? What's happened?"

His wife answered. "Gerda has—" she broke off sharply. "I mean—John is—"

Gerda said in her flat, bewildered voice:

"John has been shot . . . he's dead. . . ."

They all looked away from her, embarrassed.

Then Lady Angkatell said quickly:

"My dear, I think you'd better go and—and lie down . . . Perhaps we had better all go back to the house? Henry, you and M. Poirot can stay here and—and wait for the police."

"That will be the best plan, I think," said Sir Henry. He turned to Gudgeon. "Will you ring up the police station, Gudgeon? Just state exactly what has occurred. When the police arrive, bring them straight out here."

Gudgeon bent his head a little and said, "Yes, Sir Henry." He was looking a little white about the gills, but he was still the perfect servant.

The tall young woman said, "Come, Gerda," and putting her hand through the other woman's arm, she led her unresistingly away and along the path towards the house. Gerda walked as though in a dream. Gudgeon stood back a little to let them pass and then followed, carrying the basket of eggs.

Sir Henry turned sharply to his wife.

"Now, Lucy, what is all this? What happened exactly?"

Lady Angkatell stretched out vague hands, a lovely helpless gesture. Hercule Poirot felt the charm of it and the appeal.

"My dear, I hardly know . . . I was down by the hens. I heard a shot that seemed very near, but I didn't really think anything about it. After all," she appealed to them all, "one *doesn't!* And then I came up the path to the pool and there was John lying there and Gerda standing over him with the revolver. Henrietta and Edward arrived almost at the same moment—from over there."

She nodded towards the farther side of the pool, where two paths ran up into the woods.

Hercule Poirot cleared his throat.

"Who were they, this John and this Gerda? If I may know," he added apologetically.

"Oh, of course." Lady Angkatell turned to him in quick apology. "One forgets—but then one doesn't exactly *introduce* people—not when somebody has just been killed. John is John Christow, Dr. Christow. Gerda Christow is his wife."

"And the lady who went with Mrs. Christow to the house?"

"My cousin, Henrietta Savernake."

There was a movement, a very faint movement from the man on Poirot's left.

Henrietta Savernake, thought Poirot, and he does not like that she should say it—but it is, after all, inevitable that I should know . . .

("Henrietta!" the dying man had said. He had said it in a very curious way. A way that reminded Poirot of something—of some incident . . . now, what was it? No matter, it would come to him.)

Lady Angkatell was going on, determined now on fulfilling her social duties.

"And this is another cousin of ours, Edward Angkatell. And Miss Hardcastle."

Poirot acknowledged the introductions with polite bows. Midge felt suddenly that she wanted to laugh hysterically; she controlled herself with an effort.

"And now, my dear," said Sir Henry, "I think that, as you suggested, you had better go back to the house . . . I will have a word or two here with M. Poirot."

Lady Angkatell looked thoughtfully at them.

"I do hope," she said, "that Gerda *is* lying down. Was that the right thing to suggest? I really couldn't think what to say. I mean, one has no *precedent.* What *does* one say to a woman who has just killed her husband?"

She looked at them as though hoping that some authoritative answer might be given to her question.

Then she went along the path towards the house. Midge followed her. Edward brought up the rear.

Poirot was left with his host.

Sir Henry cleared his throat. He seemed a little uncertain what to say.

"Christow," he observed at last, "was a very able fellow—a *very* able fellow."

Poirot's eyes rested once more on the dead man. He still had the curious impression that the dead man was more alive than the living.

He wondered what gave him that impression.

He responded politely to Sir Henry:

"Such a tragedy as this is very unfortunate," he said.

"This sort of thing is more in your line than mine," said Sir Henry. "I don't think I have ever been at close quarters with a murder before. I hope I've done the right thing so far?"

"The procedure has been quite correct," said Poirot. "You have summoned the police and until they arrive and take charge, there is nothing for us to do—except to make sure that nobody disturbs the body or tampers with the evidence."

As he said the last word he looked down into the pool where he could see the revolver lying on the concrete bottom slightly distorted by the blue water.

The evidence, he thought, had perhaps already been tampered with before he, Hercule Poirot, had been able to prevent it . . .

But no—that had been an accident.

Sir Henry murmured distastefully:

"Think we've got to stand about? A bit chilly. It would be all right, I should think, if we went inside the pavilion?"

Poirot, who had been conscious of damp feet and a disposition to shiver, acquiesced gladly. The pavilion was at the side of the pool farthest from the house and through its open door they commanded a view of the pool and the body and the path to the house along which the police would come.

The pavilion was luxuriously furnished with comfortable settees and gay native rugs. On a painted iron table a tray was set with glasses and a decanter of sherry.

"I'd offer you a drink," said Sir Henry, "but I suppose I'd better not touch anything until the police come—not, I should imagine, that there's anything to interest them in here. Still, it is better to be on the safe side. Gudgeon hadn't brought out the cocktails yet, I see. He was waiting for you to arrive."

The two men sat down rather gingerly in two wicker chairs near the door so that they could watch the path from the house.

A constraint settled over them. It was an occasion on which it was difficult to make small talk.

Poirot glanced round the pavilion, noting anything that struck him as unusual. An expensive cape of platinum fox had been flung carelessly across the back of one of the chairs. He wondered whose it was. Its rather ostentatious magnificence did not harmonize with any of the people he had seen up to now. He could not, for instance, imagine it round Lady Angkatell's shoulders.

It worried him. It breathed a mixture of opulence and self-advertisement—and those characteristics were lacking in anyone he had seen so far.

"I suppose we can smoke," said Sir Henry, offering his case to Poirot.

Before taking the cigarette, Poirot sniffed the air.

French perfume . . . an expensive French perfume . . .

Only a trace of it lingered, but it was there, and again the scent was not the scent that associated itself in his mind with any of the occupants of The Hollow . . .

As he leaned forward to light his cigarette at Sir Henry's lighter, Poirot's glance fell on a little pile of match-boxes—six of them—stacked on a small table near one of the settees.

It was a detail that struck him as definitely odd.

Chapter XII

"HALF PAST TWO," said Lady Angkatell.

She was in the drawing-room with Midge and Edward. From behind the closed door of Sir Henry's study came the murmur of voices. Hercule Poirot, Sir Henry and Inspector Grange were in there.

Lady Angkatell sighed.

"You know, Midge, I still feel one ought to do something about lunch . . . It seems, of course, quite heartless to sit down round the table as though nothing had happened. But after all, M. Poirot was asked to lunch —and he is probably hungry. And it can't be upsetting to *him* that poor John Christow has been killed, like it is to us . . . And I must say that though I really do not feel like eating myself, Henry and Edward must be extremely hungry after being out shooting all the morning—"

Edward Angkatell said, "Don't worry on my account, Lucy dear."

"You are always considerate, Edward. And then there is David—I noticed that he ate a great deal at dinner last night. Intellectual people always seem to need a good deal of food. Where *is* David, by the way?"

"He went up to his room," said Midge, "after he had heard what had happened."

"Yes—well, that was rather tactful of him. I daresay it made him feel awkward . . . Of course, say what you like, a murder *is* an awkward thing —it upsets the servants and puts the general routine out—we were having ducks for lunch—fortunately they are quite nice eaten cold . . . What does one do about Gerda, do you think? Something on a tray? A little strong soup, perhaps?"

Really, thought Midge, Lucy is inhuman! And then with a qualm she reflected that it was perhaps because Lucy was too human that it shocked one so! Wasn't it the plain unvarnished truth that all catastrophes were hedged round with these little trivial wonderings and surmises? Lucy merely gave utterance to the thoughts which most people did not acknowledge. One *did* remember the servants, and worry about meals, and one did even feel hungry. She felt hungry herself at this very moment! Hungry, she thought, and at the same time, rather sick . . . A curious mixture.

And there was, undoubtedly, just plain awkward embarrassment in not knowing how to react to a quiet commonplace woman whom one had referred to, only yesterday, as "poor Gerda" and who was now, presumably, shortly to be standing in the dock accused of murder.

"These things happen to other people," thought Midge. "They can't happen to *us*."

She looked across the room at Edward. They oughtn't, she thought, to happen to people like Edward. People who are so very *un*violent . . . She took comfort in looking at Edward. Edward, so quiet, so reasonable, so kind and calm . . .

Gudgeon entered, inclined himself confidentially and spoke in a suitably muted voice.

"I have placed sandwiches and some coffee in the dining room, m' lady."

"Oh, *thank* you, Gudgeon!"

"Really," said Lady Angkatell as Gudgeon left the room. "Gudgeon is wonderful! I don't know what I should do without Gudgeon. He always knows the right thing to do. Some really substantial sandwiches are as good as lunch—and nothing *heartless* about them if you know what I mean!"

"Oh, Lucy, *don't* . . ."

Midge suddenly felt warm tears running down her cheeks. Lady Angkatell looked surprised, murmured:

"Poor darling. It's all been too much for you."

Edward crossed to the sofa and sat down by Midge. He put his arm round her.

"Don't worry, little Midge," he said.

Midge buried her face on his shoulder and sobbed there comfortably. She remembered how nice Edward had been to her when her rabbit had died at Ainswick one Easter holidays.

Edward said gently, "It's been a shock. Can I get her some brandy, Lucy?"

"On the sideboard in the dining room. I don't think—"

She broke off as Henrietta came into the room. Midge sat up. She felt Edward stiffen and sit very still.

What, thought Midge, does Henrietta feel? She felt almost reluctant to look at her cousin—but there was nothing to see. Henrietta looked, if anything, belligerent. She had come in with her chin up, her colour high, and with a certain swiftness.

"Oh, there you are, Henrietta," cried Lady Angkatell. "I have been wondering. The police are with Henry and M. Poirot. What have you given Gerda? Brandy? Or tea and an aspirin?"

"I gave her some brandy—and a hot water bottle."

"Quite right," said Lady Angkatell approvingly. "That's what they tell you in First Aid classes—the hot water bottle, I mean, for shock—*not* the brandy; there is a reaction nowadays against stimulants. But I think that is only a fashion. We always gave brandy for shock when I was a girl at Ainswick. Though, really, I suppose, it can't be exactly *shock* with Gerda. I don't know really *what* one would feel if one had killed one's husband—it's the sort of thing one just can't begin to imagine—but it wouldn't exactly give one a *shock*. I mean there wouldn't be any element of *surprise*."

Henrietta's voice, icy cold, cut into the placid atmosphere.

She said, "Why are you all so sure that Gerda killed John?"

There was a moment's pause—and Midge felt a curious shifting in the atmosphere—there was confusion, strain and, finally, a kind of slow watchfulness.

Then Lady Angkatell said, her voice quite devoid of any inflection:

"It seemed—self-evident. What else do you suggest?"

"Isn't it possible that Gerda came along to the pool, that she found John—lying there, and that she had just picked up the revolver when—when we came upon the scene?"

Again there was that silence. Then Lady Angkatell asked:

"Is that what Gerda says?"

"Yes."

It was not a simple assent. It had force behind it. It came out like a revolver shot.

Lady Angkatell raised her eyebrows, then she said with apparent irrelevancy:

"There are sandwiches and coffee in the dining room."

She broke off with a little gasp as Gerda Christow came through the open door. Gerda said hurriedly and apologetically:

"I—I really didn't feel I could lie down any longer. One is—one is so terribly restless."

Lady Angkatell cried:

"You must sit down—you must sit down *at once*."

She displaced Midge from the sofa, settled Gerda there, put a cushion at her back.

"You poor dear," said Lady Angkatell.

She spoke with emphasis, but the words seemed quite meaningless.

Edward walked to the window and stood there looking out.

Gerda pushed back the untidy hair from her forehead. She spoke in a worried bewildered tone:

"I—I really am only just beginning to realize it. You know I haven't

been able to feel—I still can't feel—that it's *real*—that John—is *dead."*
She began to shake a little. "Who can have killed him? Who can possibly
have killed him?"

Lady Angkatell drew a deep breath—then she turned her head sharply.
Sir Henry's door had opened. He came in accompanied by Inspector
Grange who was a large heavily built man with a down-drooping pessimis-
tic moustache.

"This is my wife—Inspector Grange."

Grange bowed and said:

"I was wondering, Lady Angkatell, if I could have a few words with
Mrs. Christow—"

He broke off as Lady Angkatell indicated the figure on the sofa.

"Mrs. Christow?"

Gerda said eagerly:

"Yes, I am Mrs. Christow."

"I don't want to distress you, Mrs. Christow, but I would like to ask
you a few questions. You can, of course, have your solicitor present if you
prefer it—"

Sir Henry put in:

"It is sometimes wiser, Gerda—"

She interrupted:

"A solicitor? Why a solicitor? Why should a solicitor know anything
about John's death?"

Inspector Grange coughed. Sir Henry seemed about to speak. Henrietta
put in:

"The Inspector only wants to know just what happened this morning."

Gerda turned to him. She spoke in a wondering voice,

"It seems all like a bad dream—not real. I—I haven't been able to cry
or anything. One just doesn't feel anything at all."

Grange said soothingly:

"That's the shock, Mrs. Christow."

"Yes, yes—I suppose it is . . . But you see it was all so *sudden.* I went
out from the house and along the path to the swimming pool—"

"At what time, Mrs. Christow?"

"It was just before one o'clock—about two minutes to one. I know,
because I looked at that clock. And when I got there—there was John,
lying there—and blood on the edge of the concrete . . ."

"Did you hear a shot, Mrs. Christow?"

"Yes—no—I don't know. I knew Sir Henry and Mr. Angkatell were out
shooting . . . I—I just saw John—"

"Yes, Mrs. Christow?"

"John—and blood—and a revolver. I picked up the revolver—"

"Why?"

"I beg your pardon?"

"Why did you pick up the revolver, Mrs. Christow?"

"I—I don't know."

"You shouldn't have touched it, you know."

"Shouldn't I?" Gerda was vague, her face vacant. "But I did. I held it in my hand . . ."

She looked down now at her hands as though she was, in fancy, seeing the revolver lying in them.

She turned sharply to the Inspector. Her voice was suddenly sharp—anguished.

"Who could have killed John? Nobody could have wanted to kill him. He was—he was the best of men. So kind, so unselfish—he did everything for other people. Everybody loved him, Inspector. He was a wonderful doctor. The best and kindest of husbands. It must have been an accident—it must—*it must!*"

She flung out a hand to the room.

"Ask anyone, Inspector. Nobody could have wanted to kill John, could they?"

She appealed to them all.

Inspector Grange closed up his note-book.

"Thank you, Mrs. Christow," he said in an unemotional voice. "That will be all for the present."

Hercule Poirot and Inspector Grange went together through the chestnut woods to the swimming pool. The thing that had been John Christow but which was now "the body" had been photographed and measured and written about and examined by the police surgeon and had now been taken away to the mortuary. The swimming pool, Poirot thought, looked curiously innocent— Everything about today, he thought, had been strangely fluid. Except John Christow—he had not been fluid. Even in death he had been purposeful and objective. The swimming pool was not now preeminently a swimming pool, it was the place where John Christow's body had lain and where his life blood had welled away over concrete into artificially blue water . . .

Artificial—for a moment Poirot grasped at the word . . . Yes, there had been something artificial about it all. As though—

A man in a bathing suit came up to the Inspector.

"Here's the revolver, sir," he said.

Grange took the dripping object gingerly.

"No hope of finger-prints now," he remarked, "but luckily it doesn't matter in this case. Mrs. Christow was actually holding the revolver when you arrived, wasn't she, M. Poirot?"

"Yes."

"Identification of the revolver is the next thing," said Grange. "I should imagine Sir Henry will be able to do that for us. She got it from his study, I should say."

He cast a glance around the pool.

"Now, let's have that again to be quite clear. The path below the pool comes up from the farm and that's the way Lady Angkatell came— The other two, Mr. Edward Angkatell and Miss Savernake, came down from the woods—but not together. He came by the left-hand path, and she by the right-hand one which leads out of the long flower walk above the house. But they were both standing on the far side of the pool when you arrived?"

"Yes."

"And this path here beside the pavilion leads on to Podder's Lane. Right—we'll go along it."

As they walked, Grange spoke, without excitement, just with knowledge and quiet pessimism.

"Never like these cases much," he said. "Had one last year—down near Ashridge. Retired military man he was—distinguished career. Wife was the nice, quiet, old-fashioned kind, sixty-five, grey hair—rather pretty hair with a wave in it. Did a lot of gardening. One day she goes up to his room, gets out his service revolver, and walks out into the garden and shoots him. Just like that! A good deal behind it, of course, that one had to dig out. Sometimes they think up some fool story about a tramp! We pretend to accept it, of course, keep things quiet whilst we're making inquiries, but we know what's what."

"You mean," said Poirot, "that you have decided that Mrs. Christow shot her husband?"

Grange gave him a look of surprise.

"Well, don't you think so?"

Poirot said slowly, "It could all have happened as she said."

Inspector Grange shrugged his shoulders.

"It *could* have—yes. But it's a thin story. And *they* all think she killed him! They know something we don't." He looked curiously at his companion. "You thought she'd done it all right, didn't you, when you arrived on the scene?"

Poirot half closed his eyes. Coming along the path . . . Gudgeon stepping aside . . . Gerda Christow standing over her husband with the revolver in her hand and that blank look on her face. Yes, as Grange had said, he *had* thought she had done it . . . had thought, at least, that that was the impression he was meant to have . . .

Yes, but that was not the same thing . . .

A scene staged—set to deceive . . .

Had Gerda Christow looked like a woman who had just shot her husband? That was what Inspector Grange wanted to know.

And with a sudden shock of surprise, Hercule Poirot realized that in all his long experience of deeds of violence he had never actually come face to face with a woman who had just killed her husband . . . What would a woman look like in such circumstances? Triumphant, horrified, satisfied, dazed, incredulous, empty?

Any one of these things, he thought . . .

Inspector Grange was talking. Poirot caught the end of his speech.

"—once you get all the facts behind the case, and you can usually get all that from the servants."

"Mrs. Christow is going back to London?"

"Yes. There're a couple of kids there. Have to let her go. Of course, we keep a sharp eye on her, but she won't know that. She thinks she's got away with it all right. Looks rather a stupid kind of woman to me . . ."

Did Gerda Christow realize, Poirot wondered, what the police thought —and what the Angkatells thought? She had looked as though she did not realize anything at all—she had looked like a woman whose reactions were slow and who was completely dazed and heartbroken by her husband's death. . . .

They had come out into the lane.

Poirot stopped by his gate. Grange said:

"This your little place? Nice and snug. Well, good-bye for the present, M. Poirot. Thanks for your cooperation. I'll drop in sometime and give you the lowdown on how we're getting on."

His eye travelled up the lane.

"Who's your neighbour? That's not where our new celebrity hangs out, is it?"

"Miss Veronica Cray, the actress, comes there for week-ends, I believe."

"Of course. Dovecotes. I liked her in *Lady Rides on Tiger* but she's a bit highbrow for my taste. Give me Deanna Durbin or Hedy Lamarr."

He turned away.

"Well, I must get back to the job. So long, M. Poirot."

"You recognize this, Sir Henry?"

Inspector Grange laid the revolver on the desk in front of Sir Henry and looked at him expectantly.

"I can handle it?" Sir Henry's hand hesitated over the revolver as he asked the question.

Grange nodded.

"It's been in the pool. Destroyed whatever finger-prints there were on it. A pity, if I may say so, that Miss Savernake let it slip out of her hand."

"Yes, yes—but, of course, it was a very tense moment for all of us. Women are apt to get flustered and—er—drop things."

Again Inspector Grange nodded. He said:

"Miss Savernake seems a cool, capable young lady on the whole."

The words were devoid of emphasis, yet something in them made Sir Henry look up sharply. Grange went on:

"Now, do you recognize it, sir?"

Sir Henry picked up the revolver and examined it. He noted the number and compared it with a list in a small leather-bound book. Then, closing the book with a sigh, he said:

"Yes, Inspector, this comes from my collection here."

"When did you see it last?"

"Yesterday afternoon. We were doing some shooting in the garden with a target, and this was one of the firearms we were using."

"Who actually fired this revolver on that occasion?"

"I think everybody had at least one shot with it."

"Including Mrs. Christow?"

"Including Mrs. Christow."

"And after you had finished shooting?"

"I put the revolver away in its usual place. Here."

He pulled out the drawer of a big bureau. It was half full of guns.

"You've got a big collection of firearms, Sir Henry."

"It's been a hobby of mine for many years."

Inspector Grange's eyes rested thoughtfully on the ex-Governor of the Hollowene Islands. A good-looking distinguished man, the kind of man he would be quite pleased to serve under himself—in fact, a man he would much prefer to his own present Chief Constable. Inspector Grange did not think much of the Chief Constable of Wealdshire—a fussy despot and a tuft-hunter—he brought his mind back to the job in hand.

"The revolver was not, of course, loaded when you put it away, Sir Henry?"

"Certainly not."

"And you keep your ammunition—where?"

"Here." Sir Henry took a key from a pigeonhole and unlocked one of the lower drawers of the desk.

Simple enough, thought Grange. The Christow woman had seen where it was kept. She'd only got to come along and help herself. Jealousy, he thought, plays the dickens with women. He'd lay ten to one it *was* jealousy. The thing would come clear enough when he'd finished the routine here and got onto the Harley Street end. But you'd got to do things in their proper order.

He got up and said:

"Well, thank you, Sir Henry. I'll let you know about the inquest."

Chapter XIII

THEY HAD THE cold ducks for supper. After the ducks there was a caramel custard which, Lady Angkatell said, showed just the right feeling on the part of Mrs. Medway.

Cooking, she said, really gave great scope to delicacy of feeling.

"We are only, as she knows, moderately fond of caramel custard. There would be something very gross, just after the death of a friend, in eating one's favourite pudding. But caramel custard is so easy—slippery if you know what I mean—and then one leaves a little on one's plate."

She sighed and said that she hoped they had done right in letting Gerda go back to London.

"But quite correct of Henry to go with her."

For Sir Henry had insisted on driving Gerda to Harley Street.

"She will come back here for the inquest, of course," went on Lady Angkatell, meditatively eating caramel custard. "But, naturally, she wanted to break it to the children—they might see it in the papers and with only a French-woman in the house—one knows how excitable—a *crise de nerfs,* possibly. But Henry will deal with her, and I really think Gerda will be quite all right. She will probably send for some relations—sisters perhaps. Gerda is the sort of person who is sure to have sisters—three or four, I should think, probably living at Tunbridge Wells."

"What extraordinary things you do say, Lucy," said Midge.

"Well, darling, Torquay if you prefer it—no, not Torquay. They would be at least sixty-five if they were living at Torquay—Eastbourne, perhaps, or St. Leonard's."

Lady Angkatell looked at the last spoonful of caramel custard, seemed to condole with it, and laid it down very gently uneaten.

David, who liked only savouries, looked down gloomily at his empty plate.

Lady Angkatell got up.

"I think we shall all want to go to bed early tonight," she said. "So much has happened, hasn't it? One has no idea, from reading about these things in the paper, how *tiring* they are. I feel, you know, as though I had walked about fifteen miles . . . instead of actually having done nothing but sit about—but that is tiring, too, because one does not like to read a book or a newspaper, it looks so heartless. Though I think perhaps the leading article in the *Observer* would have been all right—but *not* the *News of the World*. Don't you agree with me, David? I like to know what the young people think; it keeps one from losing touch."

David said in a gruff voice that he never read the *News of the World*.

"I always do," said Lady Angkatell. "We pretend we get it for the servants, but Gudgeon is very understanding and never takes it out until after tea. It is a most interesting paper, all about women who put their heads in gas ovens—an incredible number of them!"

"What will they do in the houses of the future which are all electric?" asked Edward Angkatell with a faint smile.

"I suppose they will just have to decide to make the best of things—so much more sensible."

"I disagree with you, sir," said David, "about the houses of the future being all electric. There can be communal heating laid on from a central supply. Every working-class house should be completely labour-saving—"

Edward Angkatell said hastily that he was afraid that was a subject he was not very well up in. David's lip curled with scorn.

Gudgeon brought in coffee on a tray, moving a little slower than usual to convey a sense of mourning.

"Oh, Gudgeon," said Lady Angkatell, "about those eggs. I meant to write the date in pencil on them as usual. Will you ask Mrs. Medway to see to it?"

"I think you will find, m' lady, that everything has been attended to quite satisfactorily." He cleared his throat. "I have seen to things myself."

"Oh, thank you, Gudgeon."

As Gudgeon went out she murmured, "Really, Gudgeon is wonderful. The servants are all being marvellous. And one does so sympathize with them having the police here—it must be dreadful for them. By the way, are there any left?"

"Police, do you mean?" asked Midge.

"Yes. Don't they usually leave one standing in the hall? Or perhaps he's watching the front door from the shrubbery outside."

"Why should he watch the front door?"

"I don't know, I'm sure. They do in books. And then somebody else is murdered in the night."

"Oh, Lucy, don't," said Midge.

Lady Angkatell looked at her curiously.

"Darling, I am so sorry. Stupid of me. And, of course, nobody else could be murdered. Gerda's gone home—I mean, oh, Henrietta dear, I am sorry. I didn't mean to say *that*."

But Henrietta did not answer. She was standing by the round table staring down at the bridge score she had kept last night.

She said, rousing herself, "Sorry, Lucy, what did you say?"

"I wondered if there were any police left over?"

"Like remnants in a sale? I don't think so. They've all gone back to the police station, to write out what we said in proper police language."

"What are you looking at, Henrietta?"

"Nothing."

Henrietta moved across to the mantelpiece.

"What do you think Veronica Cray is doing tonight?" she asked.

A look of dismay crossed Lady Angkatell's face.

"My dear! You don't think she might come over here again? She must have heard by now."

"Yes," said Henrietta thoughtfully. "I suppose she's heard . . ."

"Which reminds me," said Lady Angkatell, "I really must telephone to the Careys. We can't have them coming to lunch tomorrow just as though nothing had happened."

She left the room.

David, hating his relations, murmured that he wanted to look up something in the *Encyclopaedia Britannica*. The library, he thought, would be a peaceful place.

Henrietta went to the French windows, opened them, and passed through. After a moment's hesitation Edward followed her.

He found her standing outside looking up at the sky. She said:

"Not so warm as last night, is it?"

In his pleasant voice, Edward said, "No, distinctly chilly."

She was standing looking up at the house. Her eyes were running along the windows. Then she turned and looked towards the woods. He had no clue to what was in her mind.

He made a movement towards the open window.

"Better come in. It's cold."

She shook her head.

"I'm going for a stroll. To the swimming pool."

"Oh, my dear—" He took a quick step towards her. "I'll come with you."

"No, thank you, Edward." Her voice cut sharply through the chill of the air. "I want to be alone with my dead."

"Henrietta! My dear—I haven't said anything. But you do know how—how sorry I am."

"Sorry? That John Christow is dead?"

There was still the brittle sharpness in her tone.

"I meant—sorry for you, Henrietta. I know it must have been a—a great shock."

"Shock? Oh, but I'm very tough, Edward! I can stand shocks. Was it a shock to you? What did you feel when you saw him lying there? Glad, I suppose . . . You didn't like John Christow."

Edward murmured, "He and I—hadn't much in common."

"How nicely you put things! In such a restrained way. But, as a matter of fact, you did have one thing in common. Me! You were both fond of me, weren't you? Only that didn't make a bond between you—quite the opposite."

The moon came fitfully through a cloud and he was startled as he suddenly saw her face looking at him. Unconsciously he always saw Henrietta as a projection of the Henrietta he had known at Ainswick. To him she was always a laughing girl, with dancing eyes full of eager expectation. The woman he saw now seemed to him a stranger, with eyes that were brilliant but cold and which seemed to look at him inimically.

He said earnestly:

"Henrietta, dearest, do believe this—that I do sympathize with you—in —in your grief, your loss."

"*Is* it grief?"

The question startled him. She seemed to be asking it, not of him, but of herself.

She said in a low voice:

"So quick—it can happen so quickly . . . One moment living, breathing, and the next—dead—gone—emptiness. Oh! the emptiness! And here we are, all of us, eating caramel custard and calling ourselves alive—and John, who was more alive than any of us, is dead. I say the word, you know, over and over again to myself. Dead—dead—dead—dead—*dead* . . . And soon it hasn't got any meaning—not any meaning at all . . . It's just a funny little word like the breaking off of a rotten branch. *Dead— dead—dead—dead—* It's like a tom-tom, isn't it, beating in the jungle? Dead—dead—dead—dead—dead—dead—"

"Henrietta, stop! For God's sake, stop!"

She looked at him curiously.

"Didn't you know I'd feel like this? What did you think? That I'd sit gently crying into a nice little pocket handkerchief while you held my hand. That it would all be a great shock but that presently I'd begin to get over it. And that you'd comfort me very nicely. You *are* nice, Edward. You're very nice, but you're so—so inadequate."

He drew back. His face stiffened. He said in a dry voice:

"Yes, I've always known that."

She went on fiercely:

"What do you think it's been like all the evening, sitting round, with John dead and nobody caring but me and Gerda! With you glad, and David embarrassed and Midge distressed and Lucy delicately enjoying the *News of the World* come from print into real life! Can't you *see* how like a fantastic nightmare it all is?"

Edward said nothing. He stepped back a pace, into shadows.

Looking at him, Henrietta said:

"Tonight—nothing seems real to me, nobody *is* real—but John!"

Edward said quietly, "I know . . . I am not very real. . . ."

"What a brute I am, Edward! But I can't help it. I can't help resenting that John who was so alive is dead."

"And that I who am half dead am alive . . ."

"I didn't mean that, Edward."

"I think you did, Henrietta . . . I think, perhaps, you are right."

But she was saying, thoughtfully, harking back to an earlier thought:

"But it is not grief. Perhaps I cannot feel grief . . . Perhaps I never shall . . . And yet—I would like to grieve for John . . ."

Her words seemed to him fantastic. Yet he was even more startled when she added, suddenly, in an almost businesslike voice:

"I must go to the swimming pool."

She glided away through the trees.

Walking stiffly, Edward went through the open window.

Midge looked up as Edward came through the window with unseeing eyes. His face was grey and pinched. It looked bloodless.

He did not hear the little gasp that Midge stifled immediately.

Almost mechanically he walked to a chair and sat down. Aware of something expected of him, he said:

"It's cold . . ."

"Are you very cold, Edward? Shall we—shall I—light a fire?"

"What?"

Midge took a box of matches from the mantelpiece. She knelt down and set a match to the fire. She looked cautiously sideways at Edward. He was quite oblivious, she thought, of everything.

She said, "A fire is nice. It warms one . . ."

How cold he looks, she thought. But it can't be as cold as that outside. It's Henrietta! What has she said to him?

"Bring your chair nearer, Edward. Come close to the fire."

"What?"

"Your chair. To the fire."

She was talking to him now, loudly and slowly, as though to a deaf person.

And suddenly, so suddenly that her heart turned over with relief, Edward, the real Edward, was there again. Smiling at her gently.

"Have you been talking to me, Midge? I'm sorry. I'm afraid I was—thinking of something."

"Oh, it was nothing. Just the fire."

The sticks were crackling and some fir cones were burning with a bright clear flame. Edward looked at them. He said:

"It's a nice fire."

He stretched out his long thin hands to the blaze, aware of relief from tension.

Midge said, "We always had fir cones at Ainswick . . ."

"I still do. A basket of them is brought in every day and put by the grate."

Edward at Ainswick . . . Midge half closed her eyes, picturing it. He would sit, she thought, in the library, on the west side of the house. There was a magnolia that almost covered one window and which filled the room with a golden green light in the afternoons. Through the other window you looked out on the lawn and a tall Wellingtonia stood up like a sentinel. And to the right was the big copper beech.

Oh, Ainswick—Ainswick . . .

She could smell the soft air that drifted in from the magnolia which would still, in September, have some great, white, sweet-smelling, waxy flowers on it . . . And the pine cones on the fire . . . and a faintly musty smell from the kind of book that Edward was sure to be reading . . . He would be sitting in the saddle-back chair, and occasionally, perhaps, his eyes would go from the book to the fire, and he would think, just for a minute, of Henrietta . . .

Midge stirred and asked:

"Where is Henrietta?"

"She went to the swimming pool."

Midge stared. "Why?"

Her voice, abrupt and deep, roused Edward a little.

"My dear Midge, surely you knew—oh, well—guessed. She knew Christow pretty well. . . ."

"Oh, of course, one knew *that!* But I don't see why she should go mooning off to where he was shot. That's not at all like Henrietta. She's never melodramatic."

"Do any of us know what anyone else is like? Henrietta, for instance. . . ."

Midge frowned. She said:

"After all, Edward, you and I have known Henrietta all our lives."

"She has changed."

"Not really. I don't think one changes."

"Henrietta has changed."

Midge looked at him curiously.

"More than we have, you and I?"

"Oh, I have stood still, I know that well enough. And you—"

His eyes, suddenly focussing, looked at her where she knelt by the fender. It was as though he was looking at her from a long way off, taking in the square chin, the dark eyes, the resolute mouth. He said:

"I wish I saw you more often, Midge my dear."

She smiled up at him. She said:

"I know. It isn't easy, these days, to keep touch."

There was a sound outside and Edward got up.

"Lucy was right," he said. "It has been a tiring day—one's first introduction to murder! I shall go to bed. Good night."

He had left the room when Henrietta came through the window.

Midge turned on her.

"What have you done to Edward?"

"Edward?" Henrietta was vague. Her forehead was puckered. She seemed to be thinking of something far away.

"Yes, Edward. He came in looking dreadful—so cold and grey."

"If you care about Edward so much, Midge, why don't you do something about him?"

"Do something? What do you mean?"

"I don't know. Stand on a chair and shout! Draw attention to yourself. Don't you know that's the only hope with a man like Edward?"

"Edward will never care about anyone but you, Henrietta. He never has."

"Then it's very unintelligent of him." She threw a quick glance at Midge's white face. "I've hurt you. I'm sorry. But I hate Edward tonight—"

"Hate Edward? You *can't* . . ."

"Oh, yes, I can! You don't know—"

"What?"

Henrietta said slowly:

"He reminds me of such a lot of things I would like to forget."

"What things?"

"Well, Ainswick, for instance."

"Ainswick? You want to forget Ainswick?"

Midge's tone was incredulous.

"Yes, yes, *yes!* I was happy there. I can't stand, just now, being reminded of happiness . . . Don't you understand? A time when one didn't know what was coming. When one said confidently, everything is going to be lovely! Some people are wise—they never expect to be happy. I did."

She said abruptly:

"I shall never go back to Ainswick."

Midge said slowly:

"I wonder . . ."

Chapter XIV

MIDGE WOKE UP abruptly on Monday morning.

For a moment she lay there bemused, her eyes going confusedly towards the door, for she half expected Lady Angkatell to appear— What was it Lucy had said when she came drifting in that first morning?

A difficult week-end? She had been worried . . . had thought that something unpleasant might happen.

Yes, and something unpleasant had happened—something that was lying now upon Midge's heart and spirits like a thick black cloud. Something that she didn't want to think about—didn't want to remember. Something, surely, that *frightened* her. . . . Something to do with Edward . . .

Memory came with a rush. One ugly stark word—*murder!*

Oh, no, thought Midge, it can't be true. It's a dream I've been having. John Christow, murdered, shot—lying there by the pool. Blood and blue water—like the jacket of a detective story . . . Fantastic, unreal . . . The sort of thing that doesn't happen to oneself . . . If we were at Ainswick, now. It couldn't have happened at Ainswick.

The black weight moved from her forehead. It settled instead in the pit of her stomach, making her feel slightly sick.

It was not a dream. It was a real happening—a *News of the World* happening—and she and Edward and Lucy and Henry and Henrietta were all mixed up with it.

Unfair—surely unfair—since it was nothing to do with them if Gerda had shot her husband.

Midge stirred uneasily.

Quiet, stupid, slightly pathetic Gerda—you couldn't associate Gerda with melodrama—with violence.

Gerda, surely, couldn't shoot *anybody.*

Again that inward uneasiness rose. No, no, one mustn't think like that . . . Because who else *could* have shot John? And Gerda had been standing there by his body with the revolver in her hand. The revolver she had taken from Henry's study.

Gerda had said that she had found John dead and picked up the revolver . . . Well, what else could she say? She'd have to say *something*, poor thing . . .

All very well for Henrietta to defend her—to say that Gerda's story was perfectly possible. Henrietta hadn't considered the impossible alternatives.

Henrietta had been very odd last night. . . .

But that, of course, had been the shock of John Christow's death.

Poor Henrietta—who had cared so terribly for John!

But she would get over it in time—one got over everything. And then she would marry Edward and live at Ainswick—and Edward would be happy at last. . . .

Henrietta had always loved Edward very dearly. It was only the aggressive, dominant personality of John Christow that had come in the way. He had made Edward look so—so *pale* by comparison.

It struck Midge, when she came down to breakfast that morning, that already Edward's personality, freed from John Christow's dominance, had begun to assert itself. He seemed more sure of himself, less hesitant and retiring.

He was talking pleasantly to the glowering and unresponsive David.

"You must come more often to Ainswick, David. I'd like you to feel at home there and to get to know all about the place."

Helping himself to marmalade, David said coldly:

"These big estates are completely farcical. They should be split up."

"That won't happen in my time, I hope," said Edward, smiling. "My tenants are a contented lot."

"They shouldn't be," said David. "Nobody should be contented."

"If apes had been content with tails—" murmured Lady Angkatell from where she was standing by the sideboard, looking vaguely at a dish of kidneys. "That's a poem I learnt in the nursery, but I simply can't remember how it goes on. I must have a talk with you, David, and learn all the new ideas. As far as I can see, one must hate everybody but at the same time give them free medical attention and a lot of extra education, poor things! All those helpless little children herded into schoolhouses every day —and cod liver oil forced down babies' throats whether they like it or not —such nasty-smelling stuff."

Lucy, Midge thought, was behaving very much as usual.

And Gudgeon, when she passed him in the hall, also looked just as usual. Life at The Hollow seemed to have resumed its normal course. With the departure of Gerda, the whole business seemed like a dream.

Then there was a scrunch of wheels on the gravel outside and Sir Henry drew up in his car. He had stayed the night at his club and driven down early.

"Well, dear," said Lucy, "was everything all right?"

"Yes. The secretary was there—competent sort of girl—She took charge of things. There's a sister it seems. The secretary telegraphed to her."

"I knew there would be," said Lady Angkatell. "At Tunbridge Wells?"

"Bexhill, I think," said Sir Henry, looking puzzled.

"I daresay—" Lucy considered Bexhill. "Yes—quite probably."

Gudgeon approached.

"Inspector Grange telephoned, Sir Henry. The inquest will be at eleven o'clock on Wednesday."

Sir Henry nodded. Lady Angkatell said:

"Midge, you'd better ring up your shop."

Midge went slowly to the telephone.

Her life had always been so entirely normal and commonplace that she felt she lacked the phraseology to explain to her employer that after four days' holiday she was unable to return to work owing to the fact that she was mixed up in a murder case.

It did not sound credible. It did not even feel credible.

And Madame Alfrege was not a very easy person to explain things to at any time.

Midge set her chin resolutely and picked up the receiver.

It was all just as unpleasant as she had imagined it would be. The raucous voice of the vitriolic little Jewess came angrily over the wires.

"What ith that, Mith Hardcathtle? A death? A funeral? Do you not know very well I am short-handed. Do you think I am going to stand for these excutheth? Oh, yeth, you are having a good time, I darethay!"

Midge interrupted, speaking sharply and distinctly.

"The poleeth? The poleeth, you thay?" It was almost a scream. "You are mixed up with the poleeth?"

Setting her teeth, Midge continued to explain. Strange how sordid that woman at the other end made the whole thing seem. A vulgar police case. What alchemy there was in human beings!

Edward opened the door and came in, then seeing that Midge was telephoning, he was about to go out. She stopped him.

"Do stay, Edward. Please. Oh, I *want* you to."

The presence of Edward in the room gave her strength—counteracted the poison.

She took her hand from where she had laid it over the receiver.

"What? Yes. I am sorry, Madam . . . But, after all, it is hardly my fault—"

The ugly raucous voice was screaming angrily:

"Who are thethe friendth of yourth? What thort of people are they to have the poleeth there and a man shot. I've a good mind not to have you back at all! I can't have the tone of my ethtablishment lowered."

Midge made a few submissive noncommittal replies. She replaced the receiver at last, with a sigh of relief. She felt sick and shaken.

"It's the place I work," she explained. "I had to let them know that I wouldn't be back until Thursday because of the inquest and the—the police."

"I hope they were decent about it? What is it like, this dress shop of yours? Is the woman who runs it pleasant and sympathetic to work for?"

"I should hardly describe her as that! She's a White-chapel Jewess with dyed hair and a voice like a corncrake."

"But, my dear Midge—"

Edward's face of consternation almost made Midge laugh. He was so concerned.

"But, my dear child—you can't put up with that sort of thing. If you must have a job, you must take one where the surroundings are harmonious and where you like the people you are working with."

Midge looked at him for a moment without answering.

How explain, she thought, to a person like Edward? What did Edward know of the labour market, of jobs?

And suddenly a tide of bitterness rose in her. Lucy, Henry, Edward—yes, even Henrietta—they were all divided from her by an impassable gulf—the gulf that separates the leisured from the working.

They had no conception of the difficulties of getting a job, and, once you had got it, of keeping it! One might say, perhaps, that there was no need, actually, for her to earn her living. Lucy and Henry would gladly give her a home—they would with equal gladness have made her an allowance. Edward would also willingly have done the latter.

But something in Midge rebelled against the acceptance of ease offered her by her well-to-do relations. To come on rare occasions and sink into the well-ordered luxury of Lucy's life was delightful. She could revel in that. But some sturdy independence of spirit held her back from accepting that life as a gift. The same feeling had prevented her from starting a business on her own with money borrowed from relations and friends. She had seen too much of that.

She would borrow no money—use no influence. She had found a job for herself at four pounds a week and if she had actually been given the job because Madame Alfrege hoped that Midge would bring her "smart" friends to buy, Madame Alfrege was disappointed. Midge sternly discouraged any such notion on the part of her friends.

She had no particular illusions about working. She disliked the shop, she disliked Madame Alfrege, she disliked the eternal subservience to ill-tempered and impolite customers, but she doubted very much whether she could obtain any other job which she would like better, since she had none of the necessary qualifications.

Edward's assumption that a wide range of choice was open to her was simply unbearably irritating this morning. What right had Edward to live in a world so divorced from reality?

They were Angkatells, all of them! And she—was only half an Angkatell! And sometimes, like this morning, she did not feel like an Angkatell at all! She was all her father's daughter.

She thought of her father with the usual pang of love and compunction, a grey-haired, middle-aged man with a tired face. A man who had struggled for years, running a small family business that was bound, for all his care and efforts, to go slowly down the hill. It was not incapacity on his part—it was the march of progress.

Strangely enough, it was not to her brilliant Angkatell mother but to her quiet tired father that Midge's devotion had always been given. Each time, when she came back, from those visits to Ainswick, which were the wild delight of her life, she would answer the faint deprecating question in her father's tired face by flinging her arms round his neck and saying, "I'm *glad* to be home—I'm glad to be *home."*

Her mother had died when Midge was thirteen. Sometimes, Midge realized that she knew very little about her mother. She had been vague, charming, gay. Had she regretted her marriage, the marriage that had taken her outside the circle of the Angkatell clan? Midge had no idea. Her father had grown greyer and quieter after his wife's death. His struggles against the extinction of his business had grown more unavailing. He had died quietly and inconspicuously when Midge was eighteen.

Midge had stayed with various Angkatell relations, had accepted presents from the Angkatells, had had good times with the Angkatells, but she had refused to be financially dependent on their good will. And much as she loved them, there were times such as these, when she felt suddenly and violently divergent from them.

She thought with rancour, they don't know *anything!*

Edward, sensitive as always, was looking at her with a puzzled face. He asked gently:

"I've upset you? Why?"

Lucy drifted into the room. She was in the middle of one of her conversations.

"—you see, one doesn't really know whether she'd *prefer* the White Hart to us or not."

Midge looked at her blankly—then at Edward.

"It's no use looking at Edward," said Lady Angkatell. "Edward simply wouldn't know; you, Midge, are always so practical."

"I don't know what you are talking about, Lucy."

Lucy looked surprised.

"The *inquest,* darling. Gerda has to come down for it. Should she stay here? Or go to the White Hart? The associations here are painful, of course —but then at the White Hart there will be people who will stare and quantities of reporters. . . . Wednesday, you know, at eleven, or is it eleven-thirty?" A smile lit up Lady Angkatell's face. "I have never been to an inquest! I thought my grey—and a hat, of course, like church—but *not* gloves—

"You know," went on Lady Angkatell, crossing the room and picking up the telephone receiver and gazing down at it earnestly, "I don't believe I've *got* any gloves except gardening gloves nowadays! And, of course, lots of long evening ones put away from the Government House days. Gloves are rather stupid, don't you think so?"

"Their only use is to avoid finger-prints in crimes," said Edward, smiling.

"Now, it's very interesting that you should say that, Edward— Very interesting—what am I doing with this thing?" Lady Angkatell looked at the telephone receiver with faint distaste.

"Were you going to ring up someone?"

"I don't think so." Lady Angkatell shook her head vaguely and put the receiver back on its stand very gingerly.

She looked from Edward to Midge.

"I don't think, Edward, that you ought to upset Midge. Midge minds sudden deaths more than we do."

"My dear Lucy," exclaimed Edward. "I was only worrying about this place where Midge works. It sounds all wrong to me."

"Edward thinks I ought to have a delightful, sympathetic employer who would appreciate me," said Midge drily.

"Dear Edward," said Lucy with complete appreciation.

She smiled at Midge and went out again.

"Seriously, Midge," said Edward, "I am worried—"

She interrupted him:

"The damned woman pays me four pounds a week. That's all that matters."

She brushed past him and went out into the garden.

Sir Henry was sitting in his usual place on the low wall but Midge turned away and walked up towards the flower walk.

Her relatives were charming but she had no use for their charm this morning.

David Angkatell was sitting on the seat at the top of the path.

There was no overdone charm about David and Midge made straight for him and sat down by him, noting with malicious pleasure his look of dismay.

How extraordinarily difficult it was, thought David, to get away from people.

He had been driven from his bedroom by the brisk incursion of housemaids, purposeful with mops and dusters.

The library (and the *Encyclopaedia Britannica)* had not been the sanctuary he had hoped optimistically it might be. Twice Lady Angkatell had drifted in and out, addressing him kindly with remarks to which there seemed no possible intelligent reply.

He had come out here to brood upon his position. The mere week-end, to which he had unwillingly committed himself, had now lengthened out, owing to the exigencies connected with sudden and violent death.

David, who preferred the contemplation of an Academic Past or the earnest discussion of a Left Wing Future, had no aptitude for dealing with a violent and realistic present. As he had told Lady Angkatell, he did not read the *News of the World.* But now the *News of the World* seemed to have come to The Hollow.

Murder! David shuddered distastefully. What would his friends think! How did one, so to speak, *take* murder? What was one's attitude? Bored? Disgusted? Lightly amused?

Trying to settle these problems in his mind, he was by no means pleased to be disturbed by Midge. He looked at her uneasily as she sat beside him.

He was rather startled by the defiant stare with which she returned his look. A disagreeable girl of no intellectual value.

She said, "How do you like your relations?"

David shrugged his shoulders. He said:

"Does one really *think* about relations?"

Midge said:

"Does one really think about anything?"

Doubtless, David thought, *she* didn't. He said almost graciously:

"I was analyzing my reactions to murder."

"It is certainly odd," said Midge, "to be *in* one."

David sighed and said:

"Wearisome. . . ." That was quite the best attitude. "All the clichés that one thought existed only in the pages of detective fiction!"

"You must be sorry you came," said Midge.

David sighed.

"Yes, I might have been staying with a friend of mine in London." He added: "He keeps a Left Wing bookshop."

"I expect it's more comfortable here," said Midge.

"Does one really care about being comfortable?" David asked scornfully.

"There are times," said Midge, "when I feel I don't care about anything else."

"The pampered attitude to life," said David. "If you were a worker—"

Midge interrupted him.

"I *am* a worker. That's just why being comfortable is so attractive. Box beds, down pillows—early morning tea softly deposited beside the bed—a porcelain bath with lashings of hot water—and delicious bath salts. The kind of easy chair you really sink into . . ."

Midge paused in her catalogue.

"The workers," said David, "should have all these things."

But he was a little doubtful about the softly deposited early morning tea which sounded impossibly sybaritic for an earnestly organised world.

"I couldn't agree with you more," said Midge heartily.

Chapter XV

HERCULE POIROT, ENJOYING a mid-morning cup of chocolate, was interrupted by the ringing of the telephone. He got up and lifted the receiver.

" 'Allo?"

"M. Poirot?"

"Lady Angkatell?"

"How nice of you to know my voice. Am I disturbing you?"

"But not at all. You are, I hope, none the worse for the distressing events of yesterday?"

"No, indeed. Distressing, as you say, but one feels, I find, quite *detached.* I rang you up to know if you could possibly come over—an imposition, I know, but I am really in great distress . . ."

"But certainly, Lady Angkatell. Did you mean now?"

"Well, yes, I did mean now. As quickly as you can. That's very sweet of you."

"Not at all. I will come by the woods, then?"

"Oh, of course—the shortest way. Thank you so much, dear M. Poirot."

Pausing only to brush a few specks of dust off the lapels of his coat and to slip on a thin overcoat, Poirot crossed the lane and hurried along the path through the chestnuts. The swimming pool was deserted—the police had finished their work and gone. It looked innocent and peaceful in the soft, misty Autumnal light.

Poirot took a quick look into the pavilion. The platinum fox cape, he noted, had been removed. But the six boxes of matches still stood upon the table by the settee. He wondered more than ever about those matches.

"It is not a place to keep matches—here in the damp. One box, for convenience, perhaps—but not six."

He frowned down on the painted iron table. The tray of glasses had been removed. Someone had scrawled with a pencil on the table—a rough design of a nightmarish tree. It pained Hercule Poirot. It offended his tidy mind.

He clicked his tongue, shook his head, and hurried on towards the house, wondering at the reason for this urgent summons.

Lady Angkatell was waiting for him at the French windows and swept him into the empty drawing-room.

"It was nice of you to come, M. Poirot."

She clasped his hand warmly.

"Madame, I am at your service."

Lady Angkatell's hands floated out expressively. Her wide beautiful eyes opened.

"You see, it's all so difficult. The Inspector person is interviewing, no, questioning—taking a statement—what *is* the term they use?—*Gudgeon.* And really, our whole life here depends on Gudgeon, and one does so sympathize with him. Because, naturally, it is terrible for him to be questioned by the police—even Inspector Grange, who I do feel is really nice and probably a family man—boys, I think, and he helps them with Meccano in the evenings—and a wife who has everything spotless but a little overcrowded . . ."

Hercule Poirot blinked as Lady Angkatell developed her imaginary sketch of Inspector Grange's home life.

"By the way his moustache droops," went on Lady Angkatell—"I think that a home that is too spotless might be sometimes depressing—like soap on hospital nurses' faces. Quite a *shine!* But that is more abroad where things lag behind—in London nursing homes they have lots of powder and really *vivid* lipstick. But I was saying, M. Poirot, that you really must come to lunch *properly* when all this ridiculous business is over."

"You are very kind."

"I do not mind the police myself," said Lady Angkatell. "I really find it all quite interesting. 'Do let me help you in any way I can,' I said to Inspector Grange. He seems rather a bewildered sort of person, but methodical.

"Motive seems so important to policemen," she went on. "Talking of hospital nurses just now, I believe that John Christow—a nurse with red hair and an upturned nose—quite attractive. But, of course, it was a long time ago and the police might not be interested. One doesn't really know how much poor Gerda had to put up with. She is the loyal type, don't you think? Or possibly she believes what is told her. I think if one has not a great deal of intelligence, it is wise to do that."

Quite suddenly, Lady Angkatell flung open the study door and ushered Poirot in, crying brightly, "Here is M. Poirot." She swept round him and out, shutting the door. Inspector Grange and Gudgeon were sitting by the desk. A young man with a note-book was in a corner. Gudgeon rose respectfully to his feet.

Poirot hastened into apologies.

"I retire immediately. I assure you I had no idea that Lady Angkatell—"

"No, no, you wouldn't have." Grange's moustache looked more pessimistic than ever this morning. Perhaps, thought Poirot, fascinated by Lady Angkatell's recent sketch of Grange, there has been too much cleaning or perhaps a Benares brass table has been purchased so that the good Inspector he really cannot have space to move.

Angrily he dismissed these thoughts. Inspector Grange's clean but overcrowded home, his wife, his boys and their addiction to Meccano were all figments of Lady Angkatell's busy brain.

But the vividness with which they assumed concrete reality interested him. It was quite an accomplishment.

"Sit down, M. Poirot," said Grange. "There's something I want to ask you about, and I've nearly finished here."

He turned his attention back to Gudgeon, who deferentially and almost under protest resumed his seat and turned an expressionless face towards his interlocutor.

"And that's all you can remember?"

"Yes, sir. Everything, sir, was very much as usual. There was no unpleasantness of any kind."

"There's a fur cape thing—out in that summer house by the pool. Which of the ladies did it belong to?"

"Are you referring, sir, to a cape of platinum fox? I noticed it yesterday when I took out the glasses to the pavilion. But it is not the property of anyone in this house, sir."

"Whose is it, then?"

"It might possibly belong to Miss Cray, sir. Miss Veronica Cray, the motion picture actress. She was wearing something of the kind."

"When?"

"When she was here the night before last, sir."

"You didn't mention her as having been a guest here."

"She was not a guest, sir. Miss Cray lives at Dovecotes, the—er—cottage up the lane, and she came over after dinner, having run out of matches, to borrow some."

"Did she take away six boxes?" asked Poirot.

Gudgeon turned to him.

"That is correct, sir. Her ladyship, after having inquired if we had plenty, insisted on Miss Cray's taking half a dozen boxes."

"Which she left in the pavilion," said Poirot.

"Yes, sir, I observed them there yesterday morning."

"There is not much that that man does not observe," remarked Poirot as Gudgeon departed, closing the door softly and deferentially behind him.

Inspector Grange merely remarked that servants were the devil!

"However," he said with a little renewed cheerfulness, "there's always the kitchen maid. Kitchen maids *talk*—not like these stuck-up upper servants."

"I've put a man on to make inquiries at Harley Street," he went on, "and I shall be there myself later in the day. We ought to get something there. Daresay, you know, that wife of Christow's had a good bit to put up with. Some of these fashionable doctors and their lady patients—well, you'd be surprised! And I gather from Lady Angkatell that there was some trouble over a hospital nurse. Of course, she was very vague about it."

"Yes," Poirot agreed. "She would be vague. . . ."

A skilfully built up picture . . . John Christow and amorous intrigues with hospital nurses . . . the opportunities of a doctor's life . . . plenty of reasons for Gerda Christow's jealousy which had culminated at last in murder. . . .

Yes, a skilfully suggested picture . . . drawing attention to a Harley Street background—away from The Hollow—away from the moment when Henrietta Savernake, stepping forward, had taken the revolver from Gerda Christow's unresisting hand . . . away from that other moment when John Christow, dying, had said *Henrietta.* . . .

Suddenly opening his eyes, which had been half closed, Hercule Poirot demanded with irresistible curiosity:

"Do your boys play with Meccano?"

"Eh, what?" Inspector Grange came back from a frowning reverie to stare at Poirot. "Why, what on earth? As a matter of fact, they're a bit young—but I was thinking of giving Teddy a Meccano set for Christmas. What made you ask?"

Poirot shook his head.

What made Lady Angkatell dangerous, he thought, was the fact that those intuitive wild guesses of hers might often be right . . . With a careless (seemingly careless) word she built up a picture—and if part of the picture was right, wouldn't you, in spite of yourself, believe in the other half of the picture . . .

Inspector Grange was speaking.

"There's a point I want to put to you, M. Poirot. This Miss Cray, the actress—she traipses over here borrowing matches. If she wanted to borrow matches why didn't she come to your place only a step or two away? Why come about half a mile?"

Hercule Poirot shrugged his shoulders.

"There might be reasons. Snob reasons, shall we say? My little cottage, it is small, unimportant. I am only a week-ender but Sir Henry and Lady Angkatell are important—they live here—they are what is called gentry in the county. This Miss Veronica Cray, she may have wanted to get to know them—and after all, this was a way."

Inspector Grange got up.

"Yes," he said, "that's perfectly possible, of course, but one doesn't want to overlook anything. Still, I've no doubt that everything's going to be plain sailing. Sir Henry has identified the gun as one of his collection. It seems they were actually practising with it the afternoon before. All Mrs. Christow had to do was to go into the study and get it from where she'd seen Sir Henry put it and the ammunition away. It's all quite simple."

"Yes," Poirot murmured. "It seems all quite simple."

Just so, he thought, would a woman like Gerda Christow commit a crime. Without subterfuge or complexity—driven suddenly to violence by the bitter anguish of a narrow but deeply loving nature . . .

And yet surely—*surely,* she would have had *some* sense of self-preservation. Or had she acted in that blindness—that darkness of the spirit—when reason is entirely laid aside?

He recalled her blank dazed face.

He did not know—he simply did not know.

But he felt that he ought to know.

Chapter XVI

GERDA CHRISTOW PULLED the black dress up over her head and let it fall on a chair.

Her eyes were piteous with uncertainty.

She said, "I don't know . . . I really don't know . . . Nothing seems to matter."

"I know, dear, I know." Mrs. Patterson was kind but firm. She knew exactly how to treat people who had had a bereavement. "Elsie is *wonderful* in a crisis," her family said of her.

At the present moment she was sitting in her sister Gerda's bedroom in Harley Street, being wonderful. Elsie Patterson was tall and spare with an energetic manner. She was looking now at Gerda with a mixture of irritation and compassion.

Poor dear Gerda—tragic for her to lose her husband in such an awful way—and really, even now, she didn't seem to take in the—well, the *implications* properly! Of course, Mrs. Patterson reflected, Gerda always was terribly slow. And there was shock, too, to take into account.

She said in a brisk voice, "I think I should decide on that black marocain at twelve guineas."

One always did have to make up Gerda's mind for her.

Gerda stood motionless, her brow puckered. She said hesitantly:

"I don't really know if John liked mourning. I think I once heard him say he didn't . . ."

John, she thought. If only John were here to tell me what to do.

But John would never be there again. Never—never—never . . . Mutton getting cold—congealing on the table . . . the bang of the consulting room door, John running up two steps at a time, always in a hurry, so vital, so alive . . .

Alive . . .

Lying on his back by the swimming pool . . . the slow drip of blood over the edge . . . the feel of the revolver in her hand . . .

A nightmare, a bad dream, presently she would wake up and none of it would be true . . .

Her sister's crisp voice came cutting through her nebulous thoughts.

"You *must* have something black for the inquest. It would look most odd if you turned up in bright blue."

Gerda said, "That awful inquest!" and half shut her eyes.

"Terrible for you, darling," said Elsie Patterson quickly. "But after it is all over you will come straight down to us and we shall take great care of you."

The nebulous blur of Gerda Christow's thoughts hardened. She said, and her voice was frightened, almost panic-stricken:

"What am I going to do without John?"

Elsie Patterson knew the answer to that one. "You've got your children. You've got to live for *them.*"

Zena, sobbing and crying . . . "My Daddy's dead!" Throwing herself on her bed. Terry, pale, inquiring, shedding no tears . . .

An accident with a revolver, she had told them—poor Daddy has had an accident.

Beryl Collins (so thoughtful of her) had confiscated the morning papers so that the children should not see them. She had warned the servants, too. Really, Beryl had been most kind and thoughtful . . .

Terence coming to his mother in the dim drawing-room. His lips pursed close together, his face almost greenish in its odd pallor.

"Why was Father shot?"

"An accident, dear. I—I can't talk about it."

"It wasn't an accident. Why do you say what isn't true? Father was killed. It was murder. The paper says so."

"Terry, how did you get hold of a paper? I told Miss Collins—"

He had nodded—queer repeated nods like a very old man.

"I went out and bought one, of course. I knew there must be something in them that you weren't telling us, or else why did Miss Collins hide them?"

It was never any good hiding truth from Terence. That queer, detached, scientific curiosity of his had always to be satisfied.

"*Why* was he killed, Mother?"

She had broken down then, becoming hysterical.

"Don't ask me about it—don't talk about it—I can't talk about it . . . it's all too dreadful."

"But they'll find out, won't they? I mean they have to find out. It's necessary."

So reasonable, so detached . . . It made Gerda want to scream and laugh and cry. She thought, He doesn't care—he can't care—he just goes on asking questions. Why, he hasn't cried, even.

Terence had gone away, evading his Aunt Elsie's ministrations, a lonely little boy with a stiff pinched face. He had always felt alone. But it hadn't mattered until today.

Today, he thought, was different. If only there was someone who would answer questions reasonably and intelligently.

Tomorrow, Tuesday, he and Nicholson Minor were going to make nitroglycerine. He had been looking forward to it with a thrill. The thrill had gone. He didn't care if he never made nitroglycerine.

Terence felt almost shocked at himself. Not to care any more about scientific experiment! But when a chap's father had been murdered . . . He thought, My father—murdered . . .

And something stirred—took root—grew . . . a slow anger.

Beryl Collier tapped on the bedroom door and came in. She was pale, composed, efficient. She said:

"Inspector Grange is here." And as Gerda gasped and looked at her piteously, Beryl went on quickly, "He said there was no need for him to worry you. He'll have a word with you before he goes, but it is just routine questions about Dr. Christow's practice and I can tell him everything he wants to know."

"Oh, thank you, Collie."

Beryl made a rapid exit and Gerda sighed out:

"Collie is such a help. She's so practical."

"Yes, indeed," said Mrs. Patterson. "An excellent secretary, I'm sure. Very plain, poor girl, isn't she? Oh, well, I always think that's just as well. Especially with an attractive man like John was."

Gerda flamed out at her:

"What do you mean, Elsie? John would never—he never—you talk as though John would have flirted or something horrid if he had had a pretty secretary. John wasn't like that at all."

"Of course not, darling," said Mrs. Patterson. "But after all, one knows what men are *like!*"

In the consulting room Inspector Grange faced the cool, belligerent glance of Beryl Collier. It *was* belligerent, he noted that. Well, perhaps that was only natural.

Plain bit of goods, he thought. Nothing between her and the doctor, I shouldn't think. *She* may have been sweet on *him*, though. It works that way sometimes.

But not this time, he came to the conclusion, when he leaned back in his chair a quarter of an hour later. Beryl Collier's answers to his questions had been models of clearness. She replied promptly, and obviously had every detail of the doctor's practice at her fingertips. He shifted his ground and began to probe gently into the relations existing between John Christow and his wife.

They had been, Beryl said, on excellent terms.

"I suppose they quarrelled every now and then like most married couples?" The Inspector sounded easy and confidential.

"I do not remember any quarrels. Mrs. Christow was quite devoted to her husband—really quite slavishly so."

There was a faint edge of contempt in her voice. Inspector Grange heard it.

Bit of a feminist, this girl, he thought.

Aloud he said:

"Didn't stand up for herself at all?"

"No. Everything revolved round Dr. Christow."

"Tyrannical, eh?"

Beryl considered.

"No, I wouldn't say that . . . But he was what I should call a very selfish man. He took it for granted that Mrs. Christow would always fall in with *his* ideas."

"Any difficulties with patients—women, I mean? You needn't mind about being frank, Miss Collier. One knows doctors have their difficulties in that line."

"Oh, that sort of thing!" Beryl's voice was scornful. "Dr. Christow was quite equal to dealing with any difficulties in *that* line. He had an excellent manner with patients." She added, "He was really a wonderful doctor."

There was an almost grudging admiration in her voice.

Grange said, "Was he tangled up with any woman? Don't be loyal, Miss Collier, it's important that we should know."

"Yes, I can appreciate that. Not to my knowledge."

A little too brusque, he thought. She doesn't know, but perhaps she guesses . . .

He said sharply, "What about Miss Henrietta Savernake?"

Beryl's lips closed tightly.

"She was a close friend of the family's."

"No—trouble between Dr. and Mrs. Christow on her account?"

"Certainly not."

The answer was emphatic. (Overemphatic?)

The Inspector shifted his ground.

"What about Miss Veronica Cray?"

"Veronica Cray?"

There was pure astonishment in Beryl's voice.

"She was a friend of Dr. Christow's, was she not?"

"I never heard of her. At least, I seem to know the *name*—"

"The motion picture actress."

Beryl's brow cleared.

"Of course! I wondered why the name was familiar. But I didn't even know that Dr. Christow knew her."

She seemed so positive on the point that the Inspector abandoned it at once. He went on to question her about Dr. Christow's manner on the preceding Saturday. And here, for the first time, the confidence of Beryl's replies wavered. She said, slowly:

"His manner *wasn't* quite as usual."

"What was the difference?"

"He seemed distrait. There was quite a long gap before he rang for his last patient—and yet normally he was always in a hurry to get through when he was going away. I thought—yes, I definitely thought he had something on his mind."

But she could not be more definite.

Inspector Grange was not very satisfied with his investigations. He'd come nowhere near establishing motive—and motive had to be established before there was a case to go to the Public Prosecutor.

He was quite certain in his own mind that Gerda Christow had shot her husband. He suspected jealousy as the motive—but so far he had found nothing to go on. Sergeant Coombes had been working on the maids but they all told the same story. Mrs. Christow worshipped the ground her husband walked on.

Whatever happened, he thought, must have happened down at The Hollow. And remembering The Hollow, he felt a vague disquietude. They were an odd lot down there.

The telephone on the desk rang and Miss Collier picked up the receiver.

She said, "It's for you, Inspector," and passed the instrument to him.

"Hullo, Grange here. . . . What's that? . . ." Beryl heard the alteration in his tone and looked at him curiously. The wooden-looking face was impassive as ever. He was grunting—listening—

"Yes . . . yes, I've got that. . . . That's absolutely certain, is it? . . . No margin of error . . . Yes . . . yes . . . yes, I'll be down. I've about finished here . . . Yes."

He put the receiver back and sat for a moment motionless. Beryl looked at him curiously.

He pulled himself together and asked in a voice that was quite different from the voice of his previous questions:

"You've no ideas of your own, I suppose, Miss Collier, about this matter?"

"You mean—"

"I mean no ideas as to who it was killed Dr. Christow?"

She said flatly:

"I've absolutely no idea at all, Inspector."

Grange said slowly:

"When the body was found, Mrs. Christow was standing beside it with the revolver in her hand—"

He left it purposely as an unfinished sentence.

Her reaction came promptly. Not heated, cool and judicial.

"If you think Mrs. Christow killed her husband, I am quite sure you are wrong. Mrs. Christow is not at all a violent woman. She is very meek and submissive and she was entirely under the doctor's thumb. It seems to me quite ridiculous that anyone could imagine for a moment that she shot him, however much appearances may be against her."

"Then if she didn't, who did?" he asked sharply.

Beryl said slowly, "I've no idea . . ."

The Inspector moved to the door. Beryl asked:

"Do you want to see Mrs. Christow before you go?"

"No—yes, perhaps I'd better."

Again Beryl wondered; this was not the same man who had been questioning her before the telephone rang. What news had he got that had altered him so much?

Gerda came into the room nervously. She looked unhappy and bewildered. She said in a low, shaky voice:

"Have you found out any more about who killed John?"

"Not yet, Mrs. Christow."

"It's so impossible—so absolutely impossible."

"But it happened, Mrs. Christow."

She nodded, looking down, screwing a handkerchief into a little ball. He said quietly:

"Had your husband any enemies, Mrs. Christow?"

"John? Oh, no. He was wonderful. Everyone adored him."

"You can't think of anyone who had a grudge against him," he paused, "or against you?"

"Against me?" She seemed amazed. "Oh, no, Inspector."

Inspector Grange sighed.

"What about Miss Veronica Cray?"

"Veronica Cray? Oh, you mean the one who came that night to borrow matches?"

"Yes, that's the one. You knew her?"

Gerda shook her head.

"I'd never seen her before. John knew her years ago—or so she said."

"I suppose she might have had a grudge against him that you didn't know about?"

Gerda said with dignity:

"I don't believe anybody could have had a grudge against John. He was the kindest and most unselfish—oh, and one of the noblest men."

"H'm," said the Inspector. "Yes. Quite so. Well, good morning, Mrs. Christow. You understand about the inquest? Eleven o'clock Wednesday in Market Depleach. It will be very simple—nothing to upset you—probably be adjourned for a week so that we can make further inquiries."

"Oh, I see. Thank you."

She stood there staring after him. He wondered whether, even now, she had grasped the fact that she was the principal suspect.

He hailed a taxi—justifiable expense in view of the piece of information he had just been given over the telephone. Just where that piece of information was leading him, he did not know. On the face of it, it seemed completely irrelevant—crazy. It simply did not make sense. But in some way that he could not yet see, it must make sense.

The only inference to be drawn from it was that the case was not quite the simple straightforward one that he had hitherto assumed it to be.

Chapter XVII

SIR HENRY STARED curiously at Inspector Grange.

He said slowly, "I'm not quite sure that I understand you, Inspector."

"It's quite simple, Sir Henry. I'm asking you to check over your collection of firearms. I presume they are catalogued and indexed?"

"Naturally. But I have already identified the revolver as part of my collection."

"It isn't quite so simple as that, Sir Henry." Grange paused a moment. His instincts were always against giving out any information, but his hand was being forced in this particular instance. Sir Henry was a person of importance. He would doubtless comply with the request that was being made to him, but he would also require a reason. The Inspector decided that he had got to give him the reason.

He said quietly:

"Dr. Christow was not shot with the revolver you identified this morning."

Sir Henry's eyebrows rose.

"Remarkable!" he said.

Grange felt vaguely comforted. Remarkable was exactly what he felt himself. He was grateful to Sir Henry for saying so, and equally grateful for his not saying any more. It was as far as they could go at the moment. The thing was remarkable—and beyond that simply did not make sense.

Sir Henry asked:

"Have you any reason to believe that the weapon from which the fatal shot was fired comes from my collection?"

"No reason at all. But I have got to make sure, shall we say, that it doesn't."

Sir Henry nodded his head in confirmation.

"I appreciate your point. Well, we will get to work. It will take a little time."

He opened the desk and took out a leather-bound volume.

As he opened it he repeated:

"It will take a little time to check up—"

Grange's attention was held by something in his voice. He looked up sharply. Sir Henry's shoulders sagged a little—he seemed suddenly an older and more tired man.

Inspector Grange frowned.

He thought, Devil if I know what to make of these people down here . . .

"Ah—"

Grange spun round. His eyes noted the time by the clock, thirty minutes—twenty minutes—since Sir Henry had said, "It will take a little time . . ."

Grange said sharply:

"Yes, sir?"

"A .38 Smith & Wesson is missing. It was in a brown leather holster and was at the end of the rack in this drawer."

"Ah!" The Inspector kept his voice calm, but he was excited. "And when, sir, to your certain knowledge, did you last see it in its proper place?"

Sir Henry reflected for a moment or two.

"That is not very easy to say, Inspector. I last had this drawer open about a week ago and I think—I am almost certain—that if the revolver had been missing then I should have noticed the gap. But I should not like to swear definitely that I *saw* it there."

Inspector Grange nodded his head.

"Thank you, sir, I quite understand . . . Well, I must be getting on with things—"

He left the room—a busy, purposeful man.

Sir Henry stood motionless for a while after the Inspector had gone, then he went out slowly through the French windows onto the terrace. His wife was busy with a gardening basket and gloves. She was trimming some rare shrubs with a pair of scissors.

She waved to him brightly.

"What did the Inspector want? I hope he is not going to worry the servants again. You know, Henry, they *don't* like it. They can't see it as amusing or as a novelty like we do."

"Do we see it like that?"

His tone attracted her attention. She smiled up at him sweetly.

"How tired you look, Henry. Must you let all this worry you so much?"

"Murder *is* worrying, Lucy."

Lady Angkatell considered a moment, absently clipping off some branches, then her face clouded over.

"Oh, dear—that is the worst of scissors, they are so fascinating—one can't stop and one always clips off more than one means. What was it you were saying—something about murder being worrying? But, really, Henry, I have never seen *why*. I mean if one has to die, it may be cancer, or tuberculosis in one of those dreadful bright sanatoriums, or a stroke—horrid, with one's face all on one side—or else one is shot or stabbed or strangled perhaps—but the whole thing comes to the same in the end. There one is; I mean, dead! Out of it all. And all the worry over. And the relations have all the difficulties—money quarrels and whether to wear black or not—and who was to have Aunt Selina's writing desk—things like that!"

Sir Henry sat down on the stone coping. He said:

"This is all going to be more upsetting than we thought, Lucy."

"Well, darling, we shall have to bear it. And when it's all over we might go away somewhere. Let's not bother about present troubles but look forward to the future. I really *am* happy about that. I've been wondering whether it would be nice to go to Ainswick for Christmas—or leave it until Easter. What do you think?"

"Plenty of time to make plans for Christmas."

"Yes, but I like to *see* things in my mind. Easter, perhaps . . . Yes," Lucy smiled happily, "she will certainly have got over it by then."

"Who?" Sir Henry was startled.

Lady Angkatell said calmly:

"Henrietta . . . I think if they were to have the wedding in October—October of next year, I mean, then we could go and stop for *that* Christmas. I've been thinking, Henry—"

"I wish you wouldn't, my dear. You think too much."

"You know the barn? It will make a perfect studio. And Henrietta will need a studio. She has real talent, you know. Edward, I am sure, will be immensely proud of her. Two boys and a girl would be nice—or two boys and two girls—"

"Lucy—Lucy! How you run on."

"But, darling," Lady Angkatell opened wide beautiful eyes, "Edward will never marry anyone but Henrietta—he is very, *very* obstinate. Rather like my father in that way. He gets an idea in his head! So, of course, Henrietta *must* marry him—and she *will* now that John Christow is out of the way. He was really the greatest misfortune that could possibly have happened to her."

"Poor devil!"

"Why? Oh, you mean because he's dead? Oh, well, everyone has to die sometime. I never worry over people dying . . ."

He looked at her curiously.

"I always thought you liked Christow, Lucy?"

"I found him amusing. And he had charm. But I never think one ought to attach too much importance to *anybody.*"

And gently, with a smiling face, Lady Angkatell clipped remorselessly at a vine.

Chapter XVIII

HERCULE POIROT LOOKED out of his window and saw Henrietta Savernake walking up the path to the front door. She was wearing the same green tweeds that she had worn on the day of the tragedy. There was a spaniel with her.

He hastened to the front door and opened it. She stood smiling at him.

"May I come in and see your house? I like looking at people's houses. I'm just taking the dog for a walk."

"But most certainly. How English it is to take the dog for a walk!"

"I know," said Henrietta. "I thought of that. Do you know that nice poem: 'The days passed slowly one by one. I fed the ducks, reproved my wife, played Handel's *Largo* on the fife, And took the dog a run.' "

Again she smiled—a brilliant, unsubstantial smile.

Poirot ushered her into his sitting room. She looked round its neat and prim arrangement and nodded her head.

"Nice," she said, "two of everything. How you would hate my studio."

"Why should I hate it?"

"Oh, a lot of clay sticking to things—and here and there just one thing that I happen to like and which would be ruined if there were two of them."

"But I can understand that, Mademoiselle. You are an artist."

"Aren't you an artist too, M. Poirot?"

Poirot put his head on one side.

"It is a question, that. But, on the whole, I would say no. I have known crimes that were artistic—they were, you understand, supreme exercises of imagination—but the solving of them—no, it is not the creative power that is needed. What is required is a passion for the truth."

"A passion for the truth," said Henrietta meditatively. "Yes, I can see how dangerous that might make you. Would the truth satisfy you?"

He looked at her curiously.

"What do you mean, Miss Savernake?"

"I can understand that you would want to *know*. But would knowledge be enough? Would you have to go a step further and translate knowledge into action?"

He was interested in her approach.

"You are suggesting that if I knew the truth about Dr. Christow's death —I might be satisfied to keep that knowledge to myself. Do *you* know the truth about his death?"

Henrietta shrugged her shoulders.

"The obvious answer seems to be Gerda. How cynical it is that a wife or a husband is always the first suspect."

"But you do not agree?"

"I always like to keep an open mind."

Poirot said quietly:

"Why did you come here, Miss Savernake?"

"I must admit that I haven't your passion for truth, M. Poirot. Taking the dog for a walk was such a nice English countryside excuse. But, of course, the Angkatells haven't got a dog—as you may have noticed the other day."

"The fact had not escaped me."

"So I borrowed the gardener's spaniel. I am not, you must understand, M. Poirot, very truthful."

Again that brilliant, brittle smile flashed out. He wondered why he should suddenly find it unendurably moving. He said quietly:

"No, but you have integrity."

"Why on earth do you say that?"

She was startled—almost, he thought, dismayed.

"Because I believe it to be true."

"Integrity," Henrietta repeated thoughtfully. "I wonder what that word really means. . . ."

She sat very still, staring down at the carpet, then she raised her head and looked at him steadily.

"Don't you want to know why I did come?"

"You find a difficulty, perhaps, in putting it into words."

"Yes, I think I do . . . The inquest, M. Poirot, is tomorrow. One has to make up one's mind just how much—"

She broke off. Getting up, she wandered across to the mantelpiece, displaced one or two of the ornaments and moved a vase of Michaelmas daisies from its position in the middle of a table, to the extreme corner of the mantelpiece. She stepped back, eyeing the arrangement with her head on one side.

"How do you like that, M. Poirot?"

"Not at all, Mademoiselle."

"I thought you wouldn't." She laughed, moved everything quickly and deftly back to their original positions. "Well, if one wants to say a thing one has to say it! You are, somehow, the sort of person one can talk to. Here goes. Is it necessary, do you think, that the police should know that I was John Christow's mistress?"

Her voice was quite dry and unemotional. She was looking, not at him, but at the wall over his head. With one forefinger she was following the curve of the jar that held the purple flowers. He had an idea that in the touch of that finger was her emotional outlet.

Hercule Poirot said precisely and also without emotion:

"I see. You were lovers?"

"If you prefer to put it like that."

He looked at her curiously.

"It was not how you put it, Mademoiselle."

"No."

"Why not?"

Henrietta shrugged her shoulders. She came and sat down by him on the sofa. She said slowly:

"One likes to describe things as—as accurately as possible."

His interest in Henrietta Savernake grew stronger. He said:

"You had been Dr. Christow's mistress—for how long?"

"About six months."

"The police will have, I gather, no difficulty in discovering the fact?"

Henrietta considered.

"I imagine not. That is, if they are looking for something of that kind?"

"Oh, they will be looking, I can assure you of that."

"Yes, I rather thought they would." She paused, stretched out her fingers on her knee and looked at them, then gave him a swift friendly glance. "Well, M. Poirot, what does one do? Go to Inspector Grange and say— what does one say to a moustache like that? It's such a domestic family moustache."

Poirot's hand crawled upwards to his own proudly borne adornment.

"Whereas mine, Mademoiselle?"

"Your moustache, M. Poirot, is an artistic triumph. It has no associations with anything but itself. It is, I am sure, unique."

"Absolutely."

"And it is probably the reason why I am talking to you as I am. Granted that the police have to know the truth about John and myself, will it necessarily have to be made public?"

"That depends," said Poirot. "If the police think it has no bearing on the case, they will be quite discreet. You—are very anxious on this point?"

Henrietta nodded. She stared down at her fingers for a moment or two, then suddenly lifted her head and spoke. Her voice was no longer dry and light.

"Why should things be made worse than they are for poor Gerda? She adored John and he's dead. She's lost him. Why should she have to bear an added burden?"

"It is for her that you mind?"

"Do you think that is hypocritical? I suppose you're thinking that if I cared at all about Gerda's peace of mind, I would never have become John's mistress. But you don't understand—it was not like that. I did not break up his married life. I was only one—of a procession."

"Ah, it was like that?"

She turned on him sharply:

"No, no, *no!* Not what you are thinking. That's what I mind most of all! The false idea that everybody will have of what John was like. That's why I'm here talking to you—because I've got a vague foggy hope that I can make you understand. Understand, I mean, the sort of person John was! I can see so well what will happen—the headlines in the papers—*A Doctor's Love Life*—Gerda, myself, Veronica Cray. John wasn't like that—he wasn't, actually, a man who thought much about women. It wasn't *women* who mattered to him most, it was his *work!* It was in his work that his interest and his excitement—yes, and his sense of adventure really lay! If John had been taken unawares at any moment and asked to name the woman who was most in his mind, do you know who he would have said —Mrs. Crabtree."

"Mrs. Crabtree?" Poirot was surprised. "Who, then, is this Mrs. Crabtree?"

There was something between tears and laughter in Henrietta's voice as she went on.

"She's an old woman—ugly, dirty, wrinkled, quite indomitable. John thought the world of her. She's a patient in St. Christopher's Hospital. She's got Ridgeway's Disease. That's a disease that's very rare but if you get it, you're bound to die—there just isn't any cure. But John was finding a cure—I can't explain technically—it was all very complicated—some question of hormone secretion. He'd been making experiments and Mrs. Crabtree was his prize patient—you see, she's got *guts,* she *wants* to live— and she was fond of John. She and he were fighting on the same side. Ridgeway's Disease and Mrs. Crabtree is what has been uppermost in John's mind for months—night and day—nothing else really counted. That's what being the kind of doctor John was really means—not all the Harley Street stuff and the rich fat women, that was only a sideline—it's the intense scientific curiosity and achievement. I—oh, I wish I could make you understand."

Her hands flew out in a curiously despairing gesture and Hercule Poirot thought how very lovely and sensitive those hands were.

He said:

"*You* seem to understand very well."

"Oh, yes, I understood. John used to come and talk, do you see? Not quite to me—partly I think to himself. He got things clear that way. Sometimes he was almost despairing—he couldn't see how to overcome the heightened toxicity—and then he'd get an idea for varying the treatment. I can't explain to you what it was like—it was like, yes, a *battle*. You can't imagine the—the fury of it and the concentration—and yes, sometimes the agony. And sometimes the sheer tiredness . . ."

She was silent for a minute or two, her eyes dark with remembrance.

Poirot said curiously:

"You must have a certain technical knowledge yourself?"

She shook her head.

"Not really. Only enough to understand what John was talking about. I got books and read about it."

She was silent again, her face softened, her lips half parted. She was, he thought, remembering.

With a sigh, her mind came back to the present. She looked at him wistfully.

"If I could only make you see—"

"But you have, Mademoiselle."

"Really?"

"Yes. One recognizes authenticity when one hears it."

"Thank you. But it won't be so easy to explain to Inspector Grange."

"Probably not. He will concentrate on the personal angle."

Henrietta said vehemently:

"And that was so unimportant—so completely unimportant."

Poirot's eyebrows rose slowly. She answered his unspoken protest.

"But it was! You see—after a while—I got between John and what he was thinking of. I affected him, as a woman . . . He couldn't concentrate as he wanted to concentrate—because of me. He began to be afraid that he was beginning to love me—he didn't want to love anyone. He—he made love to me because he didn't want to think about me too much. He wanted it to be light, easy, just an affair like other affairs that he had had."

"And you—" Poirot was watching her closely. "You were content to have it—like that?"

Henrietta got up. She said and once more it was her dry voice:

"No, I wasn't—content. After all, one is human. . . ."

Poirot waited a minute, then he said:

"Then why, Mademoiselle—"

"Why?" she whirled round on him. "I wanted John to be satisfied, I wanted *John* to have what he wanted. I wanted him to be able to go on with the thing he cared about—his work. If he didn't want to be hurt—to be vulnerable again—why—why, then, that was all right by me!"

Poirot rubbed his nose.

"Just now, Miss Savernake, you mentioned Veronica Cray. Was she also a friend of John Christow's?"

"Until last Saturday night, he hadn't seen her for fifteen years."

"He knew her fifteen years ago?"

"They were engaged to be married." Henrietta came back and sat down. "I see I've got to make it all clearer. John loved Veronica desperately. Veronica was, and is, a bitch of the first water. She's the supreme egoist. Her terms were that John was to chuck everything he cared about and become Miss Veronica Cray's little tame husband. John broke up the whole thing—quite rightly. But he suffered like hell. His one idea was to marry someone as unlike Veronica as possible. He married Gerda whom you might describe inelegantly as a first class chump. That was all very nice and safe, but, as anyone could have told him, the day came when being married to a chump irritated him. He had various affairs—none of them important. Gerda, of course, never knew about them. But I think, myself, that for fifteen years there has been something wrong with John— something connected with Veronica. He never really got over her. And then last Saturday he met her again."

After a long pause, Poirot recited dreamily:

"He went out with her that night to see her home and returned to The Hollow at 3:00 a.m."

"How do you know?"

"A housemaid had the toothache."

Henrietta said irrelevantly, "Lucy has far too many servants."

"But you yourself knew that, Mademoiselle."

"Yes."

"How did you know?"

Again there was an infinitesimal pause. Then Henrietta replied slowly:

"I was looking out of my window and saw him come back to the house."

"The toothache, Mademoiselle?"

She smiled at him.

"Quite another kind of ache, M. Poirot."

She got up and moved towards the door and Poirot said:

"I will walk back with you, Mademoiselle."

They crossed the lane and went through the gate into the chestnut plantation.

Henrietta said:

"We need not go past the pool. We can go up to the left and along the top path to the flower walk."

A track led steeply up hill towards the woods. After a while they came to a broader path at right angles across the hillside above the chestnut trees. Presently they came to a bench and Henrietta sat down, Poirot beside her. The woods were above and behind them and below were the closely planted chestnut groves. Just in front of the seat a curving path led downwards, to where just a glimmer of blue water could be seen.

Poirot watched Henrietta without speaking. Her face had relaxed, the tension had gone. It looked rounder and younger. He realized what she must have looked like as a young girl.

He said very gently at last:

"Of what are you thinking, Mademoiselle?"

"Of Ainswick. . . ."

"What is Ainswick?"

"Ainswick? It's a place." Almost dreamily, she described Ainswick to him. The white graceful house—the big magnolia—growing up it—the whole set in an amphitheatre of wooded hills.

"It was your home?"

"Not really. I lived in Ireland. It was where we came, all of us, for holidays. Edward and Midge and myself. It was Lucy's home actually. It belonged to her father. After his death it came to Edward."

"Not to Sir Henry? But it is he who has the title."

"Oh, that's a K.C.B.," she explained. "Henry was only a distant cousin."

"And after Edward Angkatell, to whom does it go, this Ainswick?"

"How odd. I've never really thought. If Edward doesn't marry—" She paused. A shadow passed over her face. Hercule Poirot wondered exactly what thought was passing through her mind.

"I suppose," said Henrietta slowly, "it will go to David. So that's why—"

"Why what?"

"Why Lucy asked him here . . . David and Ainswick?" She shook her head. "They don't fit somehow."

Poirot pointed to the path in front of them.

"It is by that path, Mademoiselle, that you went down to the swimming pool yesterday?"

She gave a quick shiver.

"No, by the one nearer the house. It was Edward who came this way." She turned on him suddenly. "Must we talk about it any more? I hate the swimming pool. . . . I even hate The Hollow."

> *"I hate the dreadful Hollow behind the little wood.*
> *Its lips in the field above are dabbled with blood-red heath;*
> *The red-ribb'd ledges drip with a silent horror of blood,*
> *And Echo there, whatever is ask'd her, answers 'Death.' "*

Henrietta turned an astonished face on him.

"Tennyson," said Hercule Poirot, nodding his head proudly. "The poetry of your Lord Tennyson."

Henrietta was repeating.

"And Echo there, whatever is asked her . . ." She went on, almost to herself. "But, of course—I see—that's what it is—Echo!"

"How do you mean, Echo?"

"This place—The Hollow itself! I almost saw it before—on Saturday when Edward and I walked up to the ridge. An echo of Ainswick . . . And that's what we are, we Angkatells. Echoes! We're not real—not real as John was real." She turned to Poirot. "I wish you had known him, M. Poirot. We're all shadows compared with John. John was really alive."

"I knew that even when he was dying, Mademoiselle."

"I know. One felt it . . . And John is dead, and we, the echoes, are alive. . . . It's like, you know, a very bad joke. . . ."

The youth had gone from her face again. Her lips were twisted, bitter with sudden pain.

When Poirot spoke, asking a question, she did not, for a moment, take in what he was saying.

"I am sorry. What did you say, M. Poirot?"

"I was asking whether your aunt, Lady Angkatell, liked Dr. Christow."

"Lucy? She is a cousin, by the way, not an aunt. Yes, she liked him very much."

"And your—also a cousin?—Mr. Edward Angkatell—did he like Dr. Christow?"

Her voice was, he thought, a little constrained, as she replied:

"Not particularly—but then he hardly knew him."

"And your—yet another cousin?—Mr. David Angkatell?"

Henrietta smiled.

"David, I think, hates all of us. He spends his time immured in the library reading the *Encyclopaedia Britannica.*"

"Ah, a serious temperament."

"I am sorry for David. He has had a difficult home life—his mother was unbalanced—an invalid. Now his only way of protecting himself is to try to feel superior to everyone. It's all right as long as it works, but now and then it breaks down and the vulnerable David peeps through."

"Did he feel himself superior to Dr. Christow?"

"He tried to—but I don't think it came off. I suspect that John Christow was just the kind of man that David would like to be— He disliked John in consequence."

Poirot nodded his head thoughtfully.

"Yes—self-assurance, confidence, virility—all the intensive male qualities. It is interesting—very interesting."

Henrietta did not answer.

Through the chestnuts, down by the pool, Hercule Poirot saw a man stooping, searching for something, or so it seemed.

He murmured, "I wonder—"

"I beg your pardon?"

Poirot said, "That is one of Inspector Grange's men. He seems to be looking for something."

"Clues, I suppose. Don't policemen look for clues? Cigarette ash, footprints, burnt matches?"

Her voice held a kind of bitter mockery. Poirot answered seriously:

"Yes, they look for these things—and sometimes they find them. But the real clues, Miss Savernake, in a case like this, usually lie in the personal relationships of the people concerned."

"I don't think I understand you."

"Little things," said Poirot, his head thrown back, his eyes half closed. "Not cigarette ash, or a rubber heel mark—but a gesture, a look, an unexpected action . . ."

Henrietta turned her head sharply to look at him. He felt her eyes but he did not turn his head. She said:

"Are you thinking of—anything in particular?"

"I was thinking of how you stepped forward and took the revolver out of Mrs. Christow's hand and then dropped it in the pool."

He felt the slight start she gave. But her voice was quite normal and calm.

"Gerda, M. Poirot, is rather a clumsy person. In the shock of the moment, and if the revolver had had another cartridge in it, she might have fired it and—and hurt someone."

"But it was rather clumsy of *you,* was it not, to drop it in the pool?"

"Well—I had had a shock, too." She paused. "What are you suggesting, M. Poirot?"

Poirot sat up, turned his head, and spoke in a brisk matter-of-fact way:

"If there were finger-prints on that revolver, that is to say, finger-prints made *before Mrs. Christow handled it,* it would be interesting to know whose they were—and that we shall never know now."

Henrietta said quietly, but steadily:

"Meaning that you think they were *mine* . . . You are suggesting that I shot John and then left the revolver beside him so that Gerda could come along and pick it up and be left holding the baby—(that is what you are suggesting, isn't it?) But surely, if I did that, you will give me credit for enough intelligence to have wiped off my own finger-prints first!"

"But surely *you* are intelligent enough to see, Mademoiselle, that if you had done so and if the revolver had had *no finger-prints on it but Mrs. Christow's, that* would have been very remarkable! For you were all shooting with that revolver the day before. Gerda Christow would hardly have wiped the revolver clean of finger-prints *before* using it—why should she?"

Henrietta said slowly:

"So you think I killed John?"

"When Dr. Christow was dying, he said, *'Henrietta.'* "

"And you think that that was an accusation? It was not."

"What was it then?"

Henrietta stretched out her foot and traced a pattern with the toe. She said in a low voice:

"Aren't you forgetting—what I told you not very long ago? I mean— the terms we were on?"

"Ah, yes—he was your lover—and so, as he is dying, he says Henrietta. That is very touching."

She turned blazing eyes upon him.

"Must you sneer?"

"I am not sneering. But I do not like being lied to—and that, I think, is what you are trying to do."

Henrietta said quietly:

"I have told you that I am not very truthful—but when John said *'Henrietta,'* he was not accusing me of having murdered him. Can't you understand that people of my kind, who *make* things, are quite incapable of taking life? I don't kill people, M. Poirot. I *couldn't* kill anyone. That's the plain stark truth. You suspect me simply because my name was murmured by a dying man who hardly knew what he was saying."

"Dr. Christow knew perfectly what he was saying. His voice was as alive and conscious as that of a doctor doing a vital operation who says sharply and urgently, 'Nurse, the forceps, please.' "

"But—" She seemed at a loss, taken aback. Hercule Poirot went on rapidly:

"And it is not just on account of what Dr. Christow said when he was dying. I do not believe for one moment that you are capable of premeditated murder—that, no. But you might have fired that shot in a sudden moment of fierce resentment—and if so—*if* so, Mademoiselle, you have the creative imagination and ability to cover your tracks."

Henrietta got up. She stood for a moment, pale and shaken, looking at him. She said with a sudden rueful smile:

"And I thought you liked me."

Hercule Poirot sighed. He said sadly:

"That is what is so unfortunate for me. I do."

Chapter XIX

WHEN HENRIETTA HAD left him, Poirot sat on until he saw below him Inspector Grange walk past the pool with a resolute easy stride and take the path on past the pavilion.

The Inspector was walking in a purposeful way.

He must be going, therefore, either to Resthaven or to Dovecotes. Poirot wondered which.

He got up and retraced his steps along the way he had come. If Inspector Grange was coming to see him, he was interested to hear what the Inspector had to say.

But when he got back to Resthaven there was no sign of a visitor. Poirot looked thoughtfully up the lane in the direction of Dovecotes. Veronica Cray had not, he knew, gone back to London.

He found his curiosity rising about Veronica Cray. The pale, shining fox furs, the heaped boxes of matches, that sudden imperfectly explained invasion on the Saturday night, and, finally, Henrietta Savernake's revelations about John Christow and Veronica.

It was, he thought, an interesting pattern. . . . Yes, that was how he saw it: a pattern.

A design of intermingled emotions and the clash of personalities. A strange involved design, with dark threads of hate and desire running through it.

Had Gerda Christow shot her husband? Or was it not quite so simple as that?

He thought of his conversation with Henrietta and decided that it was not so simple.

Henrietta had jumped to the conclusion that he suspected her of the murder, but actually he had not gone nearly as far as that in his mind. No further indeed than the belief that Henrietta knew something. Knew something or was concealing something—which?

He shook his head, dissatisfied.

The scene by the pool. A set scene. A stage scene.

Staged by whom?

Staged *for* whom?

The answer to the second question was, he strongly suspected, Hercule Poirot. He had thought so at the time. But he had thought then that it was an impertinence—a joke.

It was still an impertinence—but not a joke.

And the answer to the first question?

He shook his head. He did not know. He had not the least idea.

But he half closed his eyes and conjured them up—all of them—seeing them clearly in his mind's eye. Sir Henry, upright, responsible, trusted administrator of Empire. Lady Angkatell, shadowy, elusive, unexpectedly and bewilderingly charming, with that deadly power of inconsequent suggestion. Henrietta Savernake who had loved John Christow better than she loved herself. The gentle and negative Edward Angkatell. The dark, positive girl called Midge Hardcastle. The dazed, bewildered face of Gerda Christow clasping a revolver in her hand. The offended, adolescent personality of David Angkatell.

There they all were, caught and held in the meshes of the law. Bound together for a little while in the relentless aftermath of sudden and violent death. Each of them had his or her own tragedy and meaning, his or her own story.

And somewhere in that interplay of characters and emotions lay the truth . . .

To Hercule Poirot there was only one thing more fascinating than the study of human beings, and that was the pursuit of truth . . .

He meant to know the truth of John Christow's death.

"But, of course, Inspector," said Veronica. "I'm only too anxious to help you."

"Thank you, Miss Cray."

Veronica Cray was not, somehow, at all what the Inspector had imagined.

He had been prepared for glamour, for artificiality, even possibly, for heroics. He would not have been at all surprised if she had put on an act of some kind.

In fact, she was, he shrewdly suspected, putting on an act. But it was not the kind of act he had expected.

There was no overdone feminine charm—glamour was not stressed.

Instead, he felt that he was sitting opposite to an exceedingly good-looking and expensively dressed woman who was also a good business woman. Veronica Cray, he thought, was no fool.

"We just want a clear statement, Miss Cray. You came over to The Hollow on Saturday evening?"

"Yes, I'd run out of matches. One forgets how important these things are in the country."

"You went all the way to The Hollow? Why not to your next door neighbour, M. Poirot?"

She smiled—a superb confident camera smile.

"I didn't know who my next door neighbour was—otherwise I should have. I just thought he was some little foreigner and I thought, you know, he might become a bore—living so near."

Yes, thought Grange, quite plausible. She'd worked that one out ready for the occasion.

"You got your matches," he said. "And you recognized an old friend in Dr. Christow, I understand?"

She nodded.

"Poor John. Yes, I hadn't seen him for fifteen years."

"Really?" There was polite disbelief in the Inspector's tone.

"Really." Her tone was firmly assertive.

"You were pleased to see him?"

"Very pleased. It's always delightful, don't you think, Inspector, to come across an old friend?"

"It can be on some occasions."

Veronica Cray went on without waiting for further questioning:

"John saw me home. You'll want to know if he said anything that could have a bearing on the tragedy, and I've been thinking over our conversation very carefully—but really there wasn't a pointer of any kind."

"What did you talk about, Miss Cray?"

"Old days. 'Do you remember this, that and the other?' " She smiled pensively. "We had known each other in the South of France. John had really changed very little—older, of course, and more assured. I gather he was quite well known in his profession. He didn't talk about his personal life at all. I just got the impression that his married life wasn't perhaps frightfully happy—but it was only the vaguest impression. I suppose his wife, poor thing, was one of those dim, jealous women—probably always making a fuss about his better-looking lady patients."

"No," said Grange. "She doesn't really seem to have been that way."

Veronica said quickly:

"You mean—it was all *underneath?* Yes—yes, I can see that that would be far more dangerous."

"I see you think Mrs. Christow shot him, Miss Cray?"

"I oughtn't to have said that! One mustn't comment—is that it—before a trial? I'm extremely sorry, Inspector. It was just that my maid told me she'd been found actually standing over the body with the revolver still in her hand. You know how in these quiet country places everything gets so exaggerated and servants do pass things on."

"Servants can be very useful sometimes, Miss Cray."

"Yes, I suppose you get a lot of your information that way."

Grange went on stolidly:

"It's a question, of course, of who had a motive—"

He paused. Veronica said with a faint rueful smile:

"And a wife is always the first suspect? How cynical! But there's usually what's called 'the other woman.' I suppose *she* might be considered to have a motive, too?"

"You think there was another woman in Dr. Christow's life?"

"Well—yes, I did rather imagine there might be. One just gets an impression, you know."

"Impressions can be very helpful sometimes," said Grange.

"I rather imagined—from what he said—that that sculptress woman was, well, a very close friend. But I expect you know all about that already?"

"We have to look into all these things, of course."

Inspector Grange's voice was strictly non-committal, but he saw, without appearing to see, a quick, spiteful flash of satisfaction in those large blue eyes.

He said, making the question very official:

"Dr. Christow saw you home, you say. What time was it when you said good night to him?"

"Do you know, I really can't remember! We talked for some time, I do know that. It must have been quite late."

"He came in?"

"Yes, I gave him a drink."

"I see. I imagined your conversation might have taken place in the—er—pavilion by the swimming pool."

He saw her eyelids flicker. There was hardly a moment's hesitation before she said:

"You really *are* a detective, aren't you? Yes, we sat there and smoked and talked for some time. How did you know?"

Her face bore the pleased, eager expression of a child asking to be shown a clever trick.

"You left your furs behind there, Miss Cray." He added just without emphasis, "And the matches."

"Yes, of course, I did."

"Dr. Christow returned to The Hollow at 3:00 a.m.," announced the Inspector, again without emphasis.

"Was it really as late as that?" Veronica sounded quite amazed.

"Yes, it was, Miss Cray."

"Of course, we had so much to talk over—not having seen each other for so many years."

"Are you sure it was quite so long since you had seen Dr. Christow?"

"I've just told you I hadn't seen him for fifteen years."

"Are you quite sure you're not making a mistake? I've got the impression you might have been seeing quite a lot of him."

"What on earth makes you think that?"

"Well, this note for one thing." Inspector Grange took out a letter from his pocket, glanced down at it, cleared his throat and read:

"Please come over this morning. I must see you, Veronica."

"Ye-es." She smiled. "It *is* a little peremptory, perhaps. I'm afraid Hollywood makes one—well, rather arrogant."

"Dr. Christow came over to your house the following morning in answer to that summons. You had a quarrel. Would you care to tell me, Miss Cray, what that quarrel was about?"

The Inspector had unmasked his batteries. He was quick to seize the flash of anger, the ill-tempered tightening of the lips. She snapped out:

"We didn't quarrel."

"Oh, yes, you did, Miss Cray. Your last words were, 'I think I hate you more than I believed I could hate anyone.' "

She was silent now. He could feel her thinking—thinking quickly and warily. Some women might have rushed into speech. But Veronica Cray was too clever for that.

She shrugged her shoulders and said lightly:

"I see. More servants' tales. My little maid has rather a lively imagination. There are different ways of saying things, you know. I can assure you that I wasn't being melodramatic. It was really a mildly flirtatious remark. We had been sparring together."

"Those words were not intended to be taken seriously?"

"Certainly not. And I can assure you, Inspector, that it *was* fifteen years since I had last seen John Christow. You can verify that for yourself."

She was poised again, detached, sure of herself.

Grange did not argue or pursue the subject. He got up.

"That's all for the moment, Miss Cray," he said pleasantly.

He went out of Dovecotes and down the lane and turned in at the gate of Resthaven.

Hercule Poirot stared at the Inspector in the utmost surprise. He repeated incredulously:

"The revolver that Gerda Christow was holding and which was subsequently dropped into the pool was not the revolver that fired the fatal shot? But that is extraordinary."

"Exactly, M. Poirot. Put bluntly, it just doesn't make sense."

Poirot murmured softly:

"No, it does not make sense . . . But all the same, Inspector, it has got to make sense, eh?"

The Inspector said heavily, "That's just it, M. Poirot. We've got to find some way that it does make sense—but at the moment I can't see it. The truth is that we shan't get much further until we've found the gun that *was* used. It came from Sir Henry's collection all right—at least there's one missing—and that means that the whole thing is still tied up with The Hollow."

"Yes," murmured Poirot. "It is still tied up with The Hollow."

"It seemed a simple, straightforward business," went on the Inspector. "Well, it isn't so simple or so straightforward."

"No," said Poirot, "it is not simple."

"We've got to admit the possibility that the thing was a frame-up—that's to say that it was all set to implicate Gerda Christow. But if that was so, why not leave the right revolver lying by the body for her to pick up?"

"She might not have picked it up."

"That's true, but even if she didn't, so long as nobody else's fingerprints were on the gun—that's to say if it was wiped after use—she would probably have been suspected all right. And that's what the murderer wanted, wasn't it?"

"Was it?"

Grange stared.

"Well, if you'd done a murder, you'd want to plant it good and quick on someone else, wouldn't you? That would be a murderer's normal reaction."

"Ye-es," said Poirot. "But then perhaps we have here a rather unusual type of murderer. It is possible that *that* is the solution of our problem."

"What is the solution?"

Poirot said thoughtfully:

"An unusual type of murderer."

Inspector Grange stared at him curiously. He said:

"But then—what *was* the murderer's idea? What was he or she getting at?"

Poirot spread out his hands with a sigh.

"I have no idea—I have no idea at all. But it seems to me—dimly—"

"Yes?"

"That the murderer is someone who wanted to kill John Christow but who did not want to implicate Gerda Christow."

"Hm! Actually we suspected her right away."

"Ah, yes, but it was only a matter of time before the facts about the gun came to light, and that was bound to give a new angle. In the interval the murderer has had time—"

Poirot came to a full stop.

"Time to do what?"

"Ah, *mon ami,* there you have me. Again I have to say I do not know."

Inspector Grange took a turn or two up and down the room. Then he stopped and came to a stand in front of Poirot.

"I've come to you this afternoon, M. Poirot, for two reasons. One is because I know—it's pretty well known in the Force—that you're a man of wide experience who's done some very tricky work on this type of problem. That's reason Number One. But there's another reason. You were there. You were an eye-witness. You *saw* what happened."

Poirot nodded.

"Yes, I *saw* what happened—but the eyes, Inspector Grange, are very unreliable witnesses."

"What do you mean, M. Poirot?"

"The eyes see, sometimes, what they are *meant* to see."

"You think that it was planned out beforehand?"

"I suspect it. It was exactly, you understand, like a stage scene. What I *saw* was clear enough. A man who had just been shot and the woman who had shot him holding in her hand the gun she had just used. That is what I *saw* and already we know that in one particular the picture is wrong. That gun had *not* been used to shoot John Christow."

"Hm," the Inspector pulled his drooping moustache firmly downwards. "What you are getting at is that some of the other particulars of the picture may be wrong, too?"

Poirot nodded. He said:

"There were three other people present—three people who had *apparently* just arrived on the scene. But that may not be true either. The pool is surrounded by a thick grove of young chestnuts. From the pool, five paths lead away: one to the house, one up to the woods, one up to the flower walk, one down from the pool to the farm, and one to the lane here.

"Of those three people, each one came along a different path, Edward Angkatell from the woods above, Lady Angkatell up from the farm, and Henrietta Savernake from the flower border above the house. Those three arrived upon the scene of the crime almost simultaneously, and a few minutes after Gerda Christow.

"But one of those three, Inspector, could have been at the pool *before* Gerda Christow, could have shot John Christow, and could have retreated up or down one of the paths and then, turning round, could have arrived at the same time as the others."

Inspector Grange said:

"Yes, it's possible."

"And another possibility, not envisaged at the time: someone could have come along the path from the lane, could have shot John Christow, and could have gone back the same way, unseen."

Grange said, "You're dead right. There are two other possible suspects besides Gerda Christow. We've got the same motive—jealousy—it's definitely a *crime passionel*—there were two other women mixed up with John Christow."

He paused and said:

"Christow went over to see Veronica Cray that morning. They had a row. She told him that she'd make him sorry for what he'd done and she said she hated him more than she believed she could hate anyone."

"Interesting," murmured Poirot.

"She's straight from Hollywood—and by what I read in the papers they do a bit of shooting each other out there sometimes. She could have come along to get her furs which she'd left in the pavilion the night before. They could have met—the whole thing could have flared up—she fired at him—and then, hearing someone coming, she could have dodged back the way she came."

He paused a moment and added irritably:

"And now we come to the part where it all goes haywire. That damned gun! Unless," his eyes brightened, "she shot him with her own gun and dropped one that she'd pinched from Sir Henry's study so as to throw suspicion on the crowd at The Hollow. She mightn't know about our being able to identify the gun used from the marks on the rifling."

"How many people do know that, I wonder?"

"I put the point to Sir Henry. He said he thought quite a lot of people would know—on account of all the detective stories that are written. Quoted a new one, *The Clue of the Dripping Fountain*, which he said John Christow himself had been reading on Saturday and which emphasized that particular point."

"But Veronica Cray would have had to get the gun somehow from Sir Henry's study."

"Yes, it would mean premeditation . . ." The Inspector took another tug at his moustache, then he looked at Poirot. "But you've hinted yourself at another possibility, M. Poirot. There's Miss Savernake. And here's where your eye-witness stuff, or rather I should say ear-witness stuff, comes in again. Dr. Christow said 'Henrietta' when he was dying. You

heard him—they all heard him, though Mr. Angkatell doesn't seem to
have caught what he said—"

"Edward Angkatell did not hear? That is interesting."

"But the others did. Miss Savernake herself says he tried to speak to
her. Lady Angkatell says he opened his eyes, saw Miss Savernake, and said
'Henrietta.' She doesn't, I think, attach any importance to it."

Poirot smiled. "No—she would not attach importance to it."

"Now, M. Poirot, what about you? You were there—you saw—you
heard. Was Dr. Christow trying to tell you all that it was Henrietta who
had shot him? In short, was that word an *accusation?*"

Poirot said slowly:

"I did not think so at the time."

"But now, M. Poirot? What do you think *now?*"

Poirot sighed. Then he said slowly:

"It may have been so. I cannot say more than that. It is an impression
only for which you are asking me, and when the moment is past there is a
temptation to read into things a meaning which was not there at the time."

Grange said hastily:

"Of course, this is all off the record. What M. Poirot thought isn't
evidence—I know that. It's only a pointer I'm trying to get."

"Oh, I understand you very well—and an impression from an eye-
witness can be a very useful thing. But I am humiliated to have to say that
my impressions are valueless. I was under the misconception, induced by
the visual evidence, that Mrs. Christow had just shot her husband, so that
when Dr. Christow opened his eyes and said 'Henrietta,' I never thought
of it as being an accusation. It is tempting now, looking back, to read into
that scene something that was not there."

"I know what you mean," said Grange. "But it seems to me that since
'Henrietta' was the last word Christow spoke, it must have meant one of
two things. It was either an accusation of murder or else it was—well,
purely emotional. She's the woman he was in love with and he was dying.
Now, bearing everything in mind, which of the two did it sound like to
you?"

Poirot sighed, stirred, closed his eyes, opened them again, stretched out
his hands in acute vexation. He said:

"His voice was urgent—that is all I can say—*urgent*. It seemed to me
neither accusing nor emotional—but urgent, yes! And of one thing I am
sure. He was in full possession of his faculties. He spoke—yes, he spoke
like a doctor—a doctor who has, say, a sudden surgical emergency on his
hands—a patient who is bleeding to death, perhaps. . . ." Poirot
shrugged his shoulders. "That is the best I can do for you."

"Medical, eh?" said the Inspector. "Well, yes, that *is* a third way of looking at it. He was shot, he suspected he was dying, he wanted something done for him quickly. And if, as Lady Angkatell says, Miss Savernake was the first person he saw when his eyes opened, then he would appeal to her . . . It's not very satisfactory, though."

"Nothing about this case is satisfactory," said Poirot with some bitterness.

A murder scene, set and staged to deceive Hercule Poirot—and which *had* deceived him! No, it was not satisfactory.

Inspector Grange was looking out of the window.

"Hullo," he said, "here's Coombes, my Sergeant. Looks as though he's got something. He's been working on the servants—the friendly touch. He's a nice-looking chap, got a way with women."

Sergeant Coombes came in a little breathlessly. He was clearly pleased with himself, though subduing the fact under a respectful official manner.

"Thought I'd better come and report, sir, since I knew where you'd gone."

He hesitated, shooting a doubtful glance at Poirot, whose exotic foreign appearance did not commend itself to his sense of official reticence.

"Out with it, my lad," said Grange. "Never mind M. Poirot here. He's forgotten more about this game than you'll know for many years to come."

"Yes, sir. It's this way, sir. I got something out of the kitchen maid—"

Grange interrupted. He turned to Poirot triumphantly.

"What did I tell you? There's always hope where there's a kitchen maid. Heaven help us when domestic staffs are so reduced that nobody keeps a kitchen maid any more. Kitchen maids talk, kitchen maids babble. They're so kept down and in their place by the cook and the upper servants that it's only human nature to talk about what they know to someone who wants to hear it. Go on, Coombes."

"This is what the girl says, sir. That on Sunday afternoon she saw Gudgeon, the butler, walking across the hall with a revolver in his hand."

"Gudgeon?"

"Yes, sir." Coombes referred to a note-book. "There are her own words. 'I don't know what to do, but I think I ought to say what I saw that day. I saw Mr. Gudgeon; he was standing in the hall with a revolver in his hand. Mr. Gudgeon looked very peculiar indeed.'

"I don't suppose," said Coombes, breaking off, "that the part about looking peculiar means anything. She probably put that in out of her head. But I thought you ought to know about it at once, sir."

Inspector Grange rose, with the satisfaction of a man who sees a task ahead of him which he is well fitted to perform.

"*Gudgeon?*" he said. "I'll have a word with Mr. Gudgeon right away."

Chapter XX

SITTING ONCE MORE in Sir Henry's study, Inspector Grange stared at the impassive face of the man in front of him.

So far, the honours lay with Gudgeon.

"I am very sorry, sir," he repeated. "I suppose I ought to have mentioned the occurrence, but it had slipped my memory."

He looked apologetically from the Inspector to Sir Henry.

"It was about 5:30 if I remember rightly, sir. I was crossing the hall to see if there were any letters for the post when I noticed a revolver lying on the hall table. I presumed it was from the master's collection, so I picked it up and brought it in here. There was a gap on the shelf by the mantelpiece where it had come from, so I replaced it where it belonged."

"Point it out to me," said Grange.

Gudgeon rose and went to the shelf in question, the Inspector close beside him.

"It was this one, sir." Gudgeon's finger indicated a small Mauser pistol at the end of the row.

It was a .25—quite a small weapon. It was certainly not the gun that had killed John Christow.

Grange, with his eyes on Gudgeon's face, said:

"That's an automatic pistol, not a revolver."

Gudgeon coughed.

"Indeed, sir? I'm afraid that I am not at all well up in firearms. I may have used the term revolver rather loosely, sir."

"But you are quite sure that that is the gun you found in the hall and brought in here?"

"Oh, yes, sir, there can be no possible doubt about that."

Grange stopped him as he was about to stretch out a hand.

"Don't touch it, please. I must examine if for finger-prints and to see if it is loaded."

"I don't think it is loaded, sir. None of Sir Henry's collection is kept loaded. And as for finger-prints, I polished it over with my handkerchief before replacing it, sir, so there will only be my finger-prints on it."

"Why did you do that?" asked Grange sharply.

But Gudgeon's apologetic smile did not waver.

"I fancied it might be dusty, sir."

The door opened and Lady Angkatell came in. She smiled at the Inspector.

"How nice to see you, Inspector Grange. What is all this about a revolver and Gudgeon? That child in the kitchen is in floods of tears. Mrs. Medway has been bullying her—but, of course, the girl was quite right to say what she saw if she thought she ought to do so. I always find right and wrong so bewildering myself—easy, you know, if right is unpleasant and wrong is agreeable, because then one knows where one is—but confusing when it is the other way about—and I think, don't you, Inspector, that everyone must do what they think right themselves. What have you been telling them about that pistol, Gudgeon?"

Gudgeon said with respectful emphasis:

"The pistol was in the hall, m' lady, on the centre table. I have no idea where it came from. I brought it in here and put it away in its proper place. That is what I have just told the Inspector and he quite understands."

Lady Angkatell shook her head. She said gently:

"You really shouldn't have said that, Gudgeon. I'll talk to the Inspector myself."

Gudgeon made a slight movement and Lady Angkatell said very charmingly:

"I do appreciate your motives, Gudgeon. I know how you always try to save us trouble and annoyance." She added in gentle dismissal, "That will be all now."

Gudgeon hesitated, threw a fleeting glance towards Sir Henry and then at the Inspector, then bowed and moved towards the door.

Grange made a motion as though to stop him, but for some reason he was not able to define to himself, he let his arm fall again. Gudgeon went out and closed the door.

Lady Angkatell dropped into a chair and smiled at the two men. She said conversationally:

"You know, I really do think that was very charming of Gudgeon. Quite feudal, if you know what I mean. Yes, feudal is the right word."

Grange said stiffly:

"Am I to understand, Lady Angkatell, that you yourself have some further knowledge about the matter?"

"Of course. Gudgeon didn't find it in the hall at all. He found it when he took the eggs out."

"The eggs?" Inspector Grange stared at her.

"Out of the basket," said Lady Angkatell.

She seemed to think that everything was now quite clear. Sir Henry said gently:

"You must tell us a little more, my dear. Inspector Grange and I are still at sea."

"Oh!" Lady Angkatell set herself to be explicit. "The pistol you see was *in* the basket, *under* the eggs."

"What basket and what eggs, Lady Angkatell?"

"The basket I took down to the farm. The pistol was in it, and then I put the eggs in on top of the pistol and forgot all about it. And when we found poor John Christow dead by the pool, it was such a shock I let go of the basket and Gudgeon just caught it in time (because of the eggs, I mean. If I'd dropped it they would have been broken), and he brought it back to the house. And later I asked him about writing the date on the eggs—a thing I always do—otherwise one eats the fresher eggs sometimes before the older ones—and he said all that had been attended to—and now that I remember, he was rather emphatic about it. And that is what I mean by being feudal. He found the pistol and put it back in here—I suppose really because there were police in the house. Servants are always so worried by police, I find. Very nice and loyal—but also quite stupid, because, of course, Inspector, it's the truth you want to hear, isn't it?"

And Lady Angkatell finished up by giving the Inspector a beaming smile.

"The truth is what I mean to get," said Grange rather grimly.

Lady Angkatell sighed.

"It all seems such a fuss, doesn't it?" she said. "I mean, all this hounding people down. I don't suppose whoever it was that shot John Christow really meant to shoot him—not seriously, I mean. If it was Gerda, I'm sure she didn't. In fact, I'm really surprised that she didn't miss—it's the sort of thing that one would expect of Gerda. And she's really a very nice, kind creature. And if you go and put her in prison and hang her, what on earth is going to happen to the children? If she did shoot John, she's probably dreadfully sorry about it now. It's bad enough for children to have a father who's been murdered—but it will make it infinitely worse for them to have their mother hanged for it. Sometimes I don't think you policemen *think* of these things."

"We are not contemplating arresting anyone at present, Lady Angkatell."

"Well, that's sensible at any rate. But I have thought all along, Inspector Grange, that you were a very sensible sort of man."

Again that charming, almost dazzling smile.

Inspector Grange blinked a little. He could not help it, but he came firmly to the point at issue.

"As you said just now, Lady Angkatell, it's the truth I want to get at. You took the pistol from here—which gun was it, by the way?"

Lady Angkatell nodded her head towards the shelf by the mantelpiece. "The second from the end. The Mauser .25." Something in the crisp, technical way she spoke jarred on Grange. He had not, somehow, expected Lady Angkatell, whom up to now he had labelled in his own mind as "vague" and "just a bit batty," to describe a firearm with such technical precision.

"You took the pistol from here and put it in your basket. Why?"

"I knew you'd ask me that," said Lady Angkatell. Her tone, unexpectedly, was almost triumphant. "And, of course, there must be some reason. Don't you think so, Henry?" She turned to her husband. "Don't you think I must have had a reason for taking a pistol out that morning?"

"I should certainly have thought so, my dear," said Sir Henry stiffly.

"One does things," said Lady Angkatell, gazing thoughtfully in front of her, "and then one doesn't remember why one has done them. But I think, you know, Inspector, that there always is a reason if one can only get at it. I must have had *some* idea in my head when I put the Mauser into my egg basket." She appealed to him. "What do you think it can have been?"

Grange stared at her. She displayed no embarrassment—just a childlike eagerness. It beat him. He had never yet met anyone like Lucy Angkatell and just for the moment he didn't know what to do about it.

"My wife," said Sir Henry, "is extremely absentminded, Inspector."

"So it seems, sir," said Grange. He did not say it very nicely.

"Why *do* you think I took that pistol?" Lady Angkatell asked him confidentially.

"I have no idea, Lady Angkatell."

"I came in here," mused Lady Angkatell. "I had been talking to Simmons about the pillow cases—and I dimly remember crossing over to the fireplace—and thinking we must get a new poker—the curate, not the rector—"

Inspector Grange stared. He felt his head going round.

"And I remember picking up the Mauser—it was a nice handy little gun, I've always liked it—and dropping it into the basket—I'd just got the basket from the flower room—But there were so many things in my head —Simmons, you know, and the bindweed in the Michaelmas daisies—and hoping Mrs. Medway would make a really *rich* Nigger in his Shirt—"

"A nigger in his shirt?" Inspector Grange had to break in.

"Chocolate, you know, and eggs—and then covered with whipped cream. Just the sort of sweet a foreigner would like for lunch."

Inspector Grange spoke fiercely and brusquely, feeling like a man who brushes away fine spiders' webs which are impairing his vision.

"Did you load the pistol?"

He had hoped to startle her—perhaps even to frighten her a little, but Lady Angkatell only considered the question with a kind of desperate thoughtfulness.

"Now did I? That's so stupid. I can't remember. But I should think I must have, don't you, Inspector? I mean, what's the good of a pistol without ammunition? I wish I could remember exactly what was in my head at the time."

"My dear Lucy," said Sir Henry. "What goes on or does not go on in your head has been for years the despair of everyone who knows you well."

She flashed him a very sweet smile.

"I *am* trying to remember, Henry dear. One does such curious things. I picked up the telephone receiver the other morning and found myself looking down at it quite bewildered. I couldn't imagine what I wanted with it."

"Presumably you were going to ring someone up," said the Inspector coldly.

"No, funnily enough, I wasn't. I remembered afterwards—I'd been wondering why Mrs. Mears, the gardener's wife, held her baby in such an odd way, and I picked up the telephone receiver to try, you know, just how one would hold a baby and of course I realized that it had looked odd because Mrs. Mears was left-handed and had its head the other way round."

She looked triumphantly from one to the other of the two men.

Well, thought the Inspector, I suppose it's possible that there are people like this. . . .

But he did not feel very sure about it.

The whole thing, he realized, might be a tissue of lies. The kitchen maid, for instance, had distinctly stated that it was a revolver Gudgeon had been holding. Still, you couldn't set much store by that. The girl knew nothing of firearms. She had heard a revolver talked about in connection with the crime and revolver or pistol would be all one to her.

Both Gudgeon and Lady Angkatell had specified the Mauser pistol—but there was nothing to prove their statements. It might actually have been the missing revolver that Gudgeon had been handling and he might have returned it, not to the study, but to Lady Angkatell herself. The servants all seemed absolutely besotted about the damned woman.

Supposing it was actually she who had shot John Christow? (But why should she? He couldn't see why.) Would they still back her up and tell lies for her? He had an uncomfortable feeling that that was just what they would do.

And now this fantastic story of hers about not being able to remember —surely she could think up something better than that. And looking so natural about it—not in the least embarrassed or apprehensive. Damn it all, she gave you the impression that she was speaking the literal truth.

He got up.

"When you remember a little more, perhaps you'll tell me, Lady Angkatell," he said dryly.

She answered, "Of course I will, Inspector. Things come to one quite suddenly sometimes."

Grange went out of the study. In the hall he put a finger round the inside of a collar and drew a deep breath.

He felt all tangled up in thistledown. What he needed was his oldest and foulest pipe, a pint of ale and a good steak and chips. Something plain and objective.

Chapter XXI

IN THE STUDY, Lady Angkatell flitted about, touching things here and there with a vague forefinger. Sir Henry sat back in his chair watching her. He said at last:

"Why did you take the pistol, Lucy?"

Lady Angkatell came back and sank down gracefully into a chair.

"I'm not really quite sure, Henry. I suppose I had some vague ideas of an accident."

"Accident?"

"Yes. All those roots of trees, you know," said Lady Angkatell vaguely, "sticking out—so easy, just to trip over one . . . One might have had a few shots at the target and left one shot in the magazine—careless, of course—but then people *are* careless. I've always thought, you know, that accident would be the simplest way to do a thing of that kind. One would be dreadfully sorry, of course, and blame oneself. . . ."

Her voice died away. Her husband sat very still without taking his eyes off her face. He spoke again in the same quiet careful voice:

"Who was to have had—the accident?"

Lucy turned her head a little, looking at him in surprise.

"John Christow, of course."

"Good God, Lucy—" He broke off.

She said earnestly:

"Oh, Henry, I've been so dreadfully worried. About Ainswick."

"I see. It's Ainswick. You've always cared too much about Ainswick, Lucy. Sometimes I think it's the only thing you do care for. . . ."

"Edward and David are the last—the last of the Angkatells. And David won't do, Henry. He'll never marry—because of his mother and all that. He'll get the place when Edward dies, and he won't marry, and you and I will be dead long before he's even middle-aged. He'll be the last of the Angkatells and the whole thing will die out."

"Does it matter so much, Lucy?"

"Of course it matters! *Ainswick!*"

"You should have been a boy, Lucy."

But he smiled a little—for he could not imagine Lucy being anything but feminine.

"It all depends on Edward's marrying—and Edward's so obstinate—that long head of his, like my father's. I hoped he'd get over Henrietta and marry some nice girl—but I see now that that's hopeless. Then I thought that Henrietta's affair with John would run the usual course. John's affairs were never, I imagined, very permanent. But I saw him looking at her the other evening. He really *cared* about her. If only John were out of the way I felt that Henrietta would marry Edward. She's not the kind of person to cherish a memory and live in the past. So, you see, it all came to that—get rid of John Christow."

"Lucy. You didn't— What did you do, Lucy?"

Lady Angkatell got up again. She took two dead flowers out of a vase.

"Darling," she said, "you don't imagine for a moment, do you, that *I* shot John Christow? I did have that silly idea about an accident. But then, you know, I remembered that we'd asked John Christow here—it's not as though he proposed himself. One can't ask someone to be a guest and then arrange accidents. Even Arabs are most particular about hospitality. So don't worry, will you, Henry?"

She stood looking at him with a brilliant, affectionate smile. He said heavily:

"I always worry about you, Lucy. . . ."

"There's no need, darling. And you see, everything has actually turned out all right. John has been got rid of without our doing anything about it. It reminds me," said Lady Angkatell reminiscently, "of that man in Bombay who was so frightfully rude to me. He was run over by a tram three days later."

She unbolted the French window and went out into the garden.

Sir Henry sat still, watching her tall slender figure wander down the path. He looked old and tired and his face was the face of a man who lives at close quarters with fear.

In the kitchen a tearful Doris Emmott was wilting under the stern reproof of Mr. Gudgeon. Mrs. Medway and Miss Simmons acted as a kind of Greek Chorus.

"Putting yourself forward and jumping to conclusions in a way only an inexperienced girl would do."

"That's right," said Mrs. Medway.

"If you see me with a pistol in my hand, the proper thing to do is to come to me and say, 'Mr. Gudgeon, will you be so kind as to give me an explanation?' "

"Or you could have come to me," put in Mrs. Medway. *"I'm* always willing to tell a young girl what doesn't know the world what she ought to think."

"What you should *not* have done," said Gudgeon severely, "is to go babbling off to a policeman—and only a Sergeant at that! Never get mixed up with the police more than you can help. It's painful enough having them in the house at all."

"Inexpressibly painful," murmured Miss Simmons. "Such a thing never happened to *me* before."

"We all know," went on Gudgeon, "what her ladyship is like. Nothing her ladyship does would ever surprise me—but the police don't know her ladyship the way we do, and it's not to be thought of that her ladyship should be worried with silly questions and suspicions just because she wanders about with firearms. It's the sort of thing she would do, but the police have the kind of minds that just see murder and nasty things like that. Her ladyship is the kind of absentminded lady who wouldn't hurt a fly but there's no denying that she puts things in funny places. I shall never forget," added Gudgeon with feeling, "when she brought back a live lobster and put it in the card tray in the hall. Thought I was seeing things!"

"That must have been before my time," said Simmons with curiosity.

Mrs. Medway checked these revelations with a glance at the erring Doris.

"Some other time," she said. "Now then, Doris, we've only been speaking to you for your own good. It's *common* to be mixed up with the police, and don't you forget it. You can get on with the vegetables now and be more careful with the runner beans than you were last night."

Doris sniffed.

"Yes, Mrs. Medway," she said and shuffled over to the sink.

Mrs. Medway said forebodingly:

"I don't feel as I'm going to have a light hand with my pastry. That nasty inquest tomorrow. Gives me a turn every time I think of it. A thing like that—happening to *us.*"

Chapter XXII

THE LATCH OF the gate clicked and Poirot looked out of the window in time to see the visitor who was coming up the path to the front door. He knew at once who she was. He wondered very much what brought Veronica Cray to see him.

She brought a delicious faint scent into the room with her, a scent that Poirot recognized. She wore tweeds and brogues as Henrietta had done—but she was, he decided, very different from Henrietta.

"M. Poirot." Her tone was delighted, a little thrilled. "I've only just discovered who my neighbour is. And I've always wanted so much to know you."

He took her outstretched hands, bowed over them.

"Enchanted, Madame."

She accepted the homage smilingly, refused his offer of tea, coffee or cocktail.

"No, I've just come to talk to you. To talk seriously. I'm worried."

"You are worried? I am sorry to hear that."

Veronica sat down and sighed.

"It's about John Christow's death. The inquest's tomorrow. You know that?"

"Yes, yes, I know."

"And the whole thing has really been so extraordinary—"

She broke off.

"Most people really wouldn't believe it. But you would, I think, because you know something about human nature."

"I know a little about human nature," admitted Poirot.

"Inspector Grange came to see me. He'd got it into his head that I'd quarrelled with John—which is true in a way, though not in the way he meant— I told him that I hadn't seen John for fifteen years—and he simply didn't believe me. But it's true, M. Poirot."

Poirot said, "Since it is true, it can easily be proved, so why worry?"

She returned his smile in the friendliest fashion.

"The real truth is that I simply haven't dared to tell the Inspector what actually happened on Saturday evening. It's so absolutely fantastic that he certainly wouldn't believe it. But I felt I must tell someone. That's why I have come to you."

Poirot said quietly, "I am flattered."

That fact, he noted, she took for granted. She was a woman, he thought, who was very sure of the effect she was producing. So sure that she might, occasionally, make a mistake.

"John and I were engaged to be married fifteen years ago. He was very much in love with me—so much so that it rather—alarmed me sometimes. He wanted me to give up acting—to give up having any mind or life of my own. He was so possessive and masterful that I felt I couldn't go through with it, and I broke off the engagement. I'm afraid he took that very hard."

Poirot clicked a discreet and sympathetic tongue.

"I didn't see him again until last Saturday night. He walked home with me. I told the Inspector that we talked about old times—that's true in a way. But there was far more than that."

"Yes?"

"John went mad—quite mad. He wanted to leave his wife and children, he wanted me to get a divorce from my husband and marry him. He said he'd never forgotten me—that the moment he saw me time stood still . . ."

She closed her eyes, she swallowed. Under her make-up her face was very pale.

She opened her eyes again and smiled almost timidly at Poirot.

"Can you believe that a—a feeling like that is possible?" she asked.

"I think it is possible, yes," said Poirot.

"Never to forget—to go on waiting—planning—hoping—to determine with all one's heart and mind to get what one wants in the end. . . . There are men like that, M. Poirot."

"Yes—and women."

She gave him a hard stare.

"I'm talking about men—about John Christow. Well, that's how it was. I protested at first, laughed, refused to take him seriously. Then I told him he was mad . . . It was quite late when he went back to the house. We'd argued and argued. . . . He was still—just as determined."

She swallowed again.

"That's why I sent him a note the next morning. I couldn't leave things like that. I had to make him realize that what he wanted was—impossible."

"It *was* impossible?"

"Of course it was impossible! He came over. He wouldn't listen to what I had to say. He was just as insistent. I told him that it was no good, that I didn't love him, that I hated him. . . ." She paused, breathing hard. "I had to be brutal about it. So we parted in anger. . . . And now—he's dead."

He saw her hands creep together, saw the twisted fingers and the knuckles stand out. They were large, rather cruel hands.

The strong emotion that she was feeling communicated itself to him. It was not sorrow, not grief—no, it was anger. The anger, he thought, of a baffled egoist.

"Well, M. Poirot?" Her voice was controlled and smooth again. "What am I to do? Tell the story, or keep it to myself. It's what happened—but it takes a bit of believing."

Poirot looked at her, a long considering gaze.

He did not think that Veronica Cray was telling the truth, and yet there was an undeniable undercurrent of sincerity. It happened, he thought, but it did not happen like that. . . .

And suddenly he got it. It was a true story, inverted. It was she who had been unable to forget John Christow. It was she who had been baffled and repulsed. And now, unable to bear in silence the furious anger of a tigress deprived of what she considered her legitimate prey, she had invented a version of the truth that should satisfy her wounded pride and feed a little the aching hunger for a man who had gone beyond the reach of her clutching hands. Impossible to admit that she, Veronica Cray, could not have what she wanted! So she had changed it all round.

Poirot drew a deep breath and spoke:

"If all this had any bearing on John Christow's death, you would have to speak out, but if it has not—and I cannot see why it should have—then I think you are quite justified in keeping it to yourself."

He wondered if she was disappointed. He had a fancy that in her present mood, she would like to hurl her story into the printed page of a newspaper. She had come to him—why? To try out her story? To test his reaction? Or to use him—to induce him to pass the story on.

If his mild response disappointed her, she did not show it. She got up and gave him one of those long, well-manicured hands.

"Thank you, M. Poirot. What you say seems eminently sensible. I'm so glad I came to you. I—I felt I wanted somebody to know."

"I shall respect your confidence, Madame."

When she had gone, he opened the windows a little. Scents affected him. He did not like Veronica's scent. It was expensive but cloying, over-powering like her personality.

He wondered, as he flapped the curtains, whether Veronica Cray had killed John Christow.

She would have been willing to kill him—he believed that. She would have enjoyed pressing the trigger—would have enjoyed seeing him stagger and fall.

But behind that vindictive anger was something cold and shrewd, something that appraised chances, a cool, calculating intelligence. However much Veronica Cray wished to kill John Christow, he doubted whether she would have taken the risk.

Chapter XXIII

THE INQUEST WAS over. It had been the merest formality of an affair, and though warned of this beforehand, yet nearly everyone had a resentful sense of anti-climax.

Adjourned for a fortnight at the request of the police.

Gerda had driven down with Mrs. Patterson from London in a hired Daimler. She had on a black dress and an unbecoming hat and looked nervous and bewildered.

Preparatory to stepping back into the Daimler, she paused as Lady Angkatell came up to her.

"How are you, Gerda dear? Not sleeping too badly, I hope. I think it went off as well as we could hope for, don't you? So sorry we haven't got you with us at The Hollow, but I quite understand how distressing that would be."

Mrs. Patterson said in her bright voice, glancing reproachfully at her sister for not introducing her properly:

"This was Miss Collier's idea—to drive straight down and back. Expensive, of course, but we thought it was worth it."

"Oh, I do so agree with you."

Mrs. Patterson lowered her voice.

"I am taking Gerda and the children straight down to Bexhill. What she needs is rest and quiet. The reporters! You've no idea! Simply swarming round Harley Street."

A young man snapped off a camera, and Elsie Patterson pushed her sister into the car and they drove off.

The others had a momentary view of Gerda's face beneath the unbecoming hat brim. It was vacant, lost—she looked for the moment like a half-witted child.

Midge Hardcastle muttered under her breath, "Poor devil."

Edward said irritably:

"What did everybody see in Christow? That wretched woman looks completely heartbroken."

"She was absolutely wrapped up in him," said Midge.

"But why? He was a selfish sort of fellow, good company in a way—but—" He broke off. Then he asked, "What did you think of him, Midge?"

"I?" Midge reflected. She said at last, rather surprised at her own words, "I think I respected him."

"Respected him? For what?"

"Well, he knew his job."

"You're thinking of him as a doctor?"

"Yes."

There was no time for more.

Henrietta was driving Midge back to London in her car. Edward was returning to lunch at The Hollow and going up by the afternoon train with David. He said vaguely to Midge, "You must come out and lunch one day?" and Midge said that that would be very nice but that she couldn't take more than an hour off. Edward gave her his charming smile and said:

"Oh, it's a special occasion. I'm sure they'll understand."

Then he moved towards Henrietta. "I'll ring you up, Henrietta."

"Yes, do, Edward. But I may be out a good deal."

"Out?"

She gave him a quick mocking smile.

"Drowning my sorrow. You don't expect me to sit at home and mope, do you?"

He said slowly, "I don't understand you nowadays, Henrietta. You are quite different."

Her face softened. She said unexpectedly, "Darling Edward," and gave his arm a quick squeeze.

Then she turned to Lucy Angkatell. "I can come back if I want to, can't I, Lucy?"

Lady Angkatell said, "Of course, darling. And anyway there will be the inquest again in a fortnight."

Henrietta went to where she had parked the car in the market square. Her suit-cases and Midge's were already inside.

They got in and drove off.

The car climbed the long hill and came out on the road over the ridge. Below them the brown and golden leaves shivered a little in the chill of a grey Autumn day.

Midge said suddenly, "I'm glad to get away—even from Lucy. Darling as she is, she gives me the creeps sometimes."

Henrietta was looking intently into the small driving mirror.

She said rather inattentively:

"Lucy has to give the coloratura touch—even to murder."

"You know, I'd never thought about murder before."

"Why should you? It isn't a thing one thinks about. It's a six-letter word in a crossword, or a pleasant entertainment between the covers of a book. But the real thing—"

She paused. Midge finished:

"*Is* real! That is what startles one."

Henrietta said:

"It needn't be startling to you. *You* are outside it. Perhaps the only one of us who is."

Midge said:

"We're all outside it now. We've got away."

Henrietta murmured, "Have we?"

She was looking in the driving mirror again. Suddenly she put her foot down on the accelerator. The car responded. She glanced at the speedometer. They were doing over fifty. Presently the needle reached sixty . . .

Midge looked sideways at Henrietta's profile. It was not like Henrietta to drive recklessly. She liked speed, but the winding road hardly justified the pace they were going. There was a grim smile hovering round Henrietta's mouth.

She said, "Look over your shoulder, Midge. See that car way back there?"

"Yes."

"It's a Ventnor 10."

"Is it?" Midge was not particularly interested.

"They're useful little cars, low petrol consumption, keep the road well, but they're not fast."

"No?"

Curious, thought Midge, how fascinated Henrietta always was by cars and their performance.

"As I say, they're not fast—but that car, Midge, has managed to keep its distance, although we've been going over sixty."

Midge turned a startled face to her.

"Do you mean that—"

Henrietta nodded. "The police, I believe, have special engines in very ordinary-looking cars."

Midge said:

"You mean they're still keeping an eye on us all?"

"It seems rather obvious."

Midge shivered.

"Henrietta, can you understand the meaning of this second gun business?"

"No, it lets Gerda out. But beyond that it just doesn't seem to add up to anything."

"But, if it was one of Henry's guns—"

"We don't know that it was. It hasn't been found yet, remember."

"No, that's true. It could be someone outside altogether. Do you know who I'd like to think killed John, Henrietta? That woman."

"Veronica Cray?"

"Yes."

Henrietta said nothing. She drove on with her eyes fixed sternly on the road ahead of her.

"Don't you think it's possible?" persisted Midge.

"*Possible,* yes," said Henrietta slowly.

"Then you don't think—"

"It's no good thinking a thing because you *want* to think it. It's the perfect solution—letting all of us out!"

"Us? But—"

"We're in it—all of us. Even you, Midge darling—though they'd be hard put to it to find a motive for your shooting John! Of course, I'd *like* it to be Veronica. Nothing would please me better than to see her giving a lovely performance, as Lucy would put it, in the dock!"

Midge shot a quick look at her.

"Tell me, Henrietta, does it all make you feel vindictive?"

"You mean"—Henrietta paused a moment—"because I loved John?"

"Yes."

As she spoke, Midge realized with a slight sense of shock that this was the first time the bald fact had been put into words. It had been accepted by them all, by Lucy and Henry, by Midge, by Edward even, that Henrietta loved John Christow, but nobody had ever so much as hinted at the fact in words before.

There was a pause whilst Henrietta seemed to be thinking. Then she said in a thoughtful voice:

"I can't explain to you what I feel. Perhaps I don't know myself."

They were driving now over Albert Bridge.

Henrietta said:

"You'd better come to the studio, Midge. We'll have tea and I'll drive you to your digs afterwards."

Here in London the short afternoon light was already fading. They drew up at the studio door and Henrietta put her key into the door. She went in and switched on the light.

"It's chilly," she said. "We'd better light the gas fire. Oh, bother—I meant to get some matches on the way."

"Won't a lighter do?"

"Mine's no good and anyway it's difficult to light a gas fire with one. Make yourself at home. There's an old blind man stands on the corner. I usually get my matches off him. I shan't be a minute or two."

Left alone in the studio, Midge wandered round, looking at Henrietta's work. It gave her an eerie feeling to be sharing the empty studio with these creations of wood and bronze.

There was a bronze head with high cheekbones and a tin hat, possibly a Red Army soldier, and there was an airy structure of twisted, ribbon-like aluminum which intrigued her a good deal. There was a vast static frog in pinkish granite, and at the end of the studio she came to an almost life-sized wooden figure.

She was staring at it when Henrietta's key turned in the lock and Henrietta herself came in slightly breathless.

Midge turned.

"What's this, Henrietta? It's rather frightening."

"That? That's The Worshipper. It's going to the International Group."

Midge repeated, staring at it:

"It's frightening . . ."

Kneeling to light the gas fire, Henrietta said over her shoulder:

"It's interesting your saying that. Why do you find it frightening?"

"I think—because it hasn't any face. . . ."

"How right you are, Midge. . . ."

"It's very good, Henrietta."

Henrietta said lightly: "It's a nice bit of pear wood . . ."

She rose from her knees. She tossed her big satchel bag and her furs on to the divan, and threw down a couple of boxes of matches on the table.

Midge was struck by the expression on her face—it had a sudden quite inexplicable exultation.

"Now for tea," said Henrietta, and in her voice was the same warm jubilation that Midge had already glimpsed in her face.

It struck an almost jarring note—but Midge forgot it in a train of thought aroused by the sight of the two boxes of matches.

"You remember those matches Veronica Cray took away with her?"

"When Lucy insisted on foisting a whole half dozen on her? Yes."

"Did anyone ever find out whether she had matches in her cottage all the time?"

"I expect the police did. They're very thorough."

A faintly triumphant smile was curving Henrietta's lips. Midge felt puzzled and almost repelled.

She thought, Can Henrietta really have cared for John? Can she? Surely not.

And a faint desolate chill struck through her as she reflected:

Edward will not have to wait very long. . . .

Ungenerous of her not to let that thought bring warmth. She wanted Edward to be happy, didn't she? It wasn't as though she could have Edward herself. To Edward she would be always "little Midge." Never more than that. Never a woman to be loved.

Edward, unfortunately, was the faithful kind. Well, the faithful kind usually got what they wanted in the end.

Edward and Henrietta at Ainswick . . . that was the proper ending to the story. Edward and Henrietta living happy ever afterwards . . .

She could see it all very clearly. . . .

"Cheer up, Midge," said Henrietta. "You mustn't let murder get you down. Shall we go out later and have a spot of dinner together?"

But Midge said quickly that she must get back to her rooms. She had things to do—letters to write. In fact, she'd better go as soon as she'd finished her cup of tea.

"All right. I'll drive you there."

"I could get a taxi."

"Nonsense. Let's use the car as it's here."

They went out into damp evening air. As they drove past the end of the Mews, Henrietta pointed out a car drawn in to the side.

"A Ventnor 10. Our shadow. You'll see. He'll follow us."

"How beastly it all is!"

"Do you think so? I don't really mind."

Henrietta dropped Midge at her rooms and came back to the Mews and put her car away in the garage.

Then she let herself into the studio once more.

For some minutes she stood abstractedly drumming with her fingers on the mantelpiece. Then she sighed and murmured to herself:

"Well—to work . . . Better not waste time."

She threw off her tweeds and got into her overall.

An hour and a half later she drew back and studied what she had done. There were dabs of clay on her cheek and her hair was dishevelled, but she nodded approval at the model on the stand.

It was the rough similitude of a horse. The clay had been slapped on in great irregular lumps. It was the kind of horse that would have given the Colonel of a Cavalry Regiment apoplexy, so unlike was it to any flesh and blood horse that had ever been foaled. It would also have distressed Henrietta's Irish hunting forebears. Nevertheless, it was a horse—a horse conceived in the abstract.

Henrietta wondered what Inspector Grange would think of it if he ever saw it, and her mouth widened a little in amusement as she pictured his face.

Chapter XXIV

EDWARD ANGKATELL STOOD hesitantly in the swirl of foot traffic in Shaftesbury Avenue. He was nerving himself to enter the establishment which bore the gold-lettered sign "Madame Alfrege."

Some obscure instinct had prevented him from merely ringing up and asking Midge to come out and lunch. That fragment of telephone conversation at The Hollow had disturbed him—more, had shocked him. There had been in Midge's voice a submission, a subservience that had outraged all his feelings.

For Midge, the free, the cheerful, the outspoken, to have to adopt that attitude. To have to submit, as she clearly was submitting, to rudeness and insolence on the other end of the wire. It was all wrong—the whole thing was wrong! And then, when he had shown his concern, she had met him pointblank with the unpalatable truth that one had to keep one's job, that jobs weren't easy to get, and that the holding down of a job entailed more unpleasantnesses than the mere performing of a stipulated task.

Up till then Edward had vaguely accepted the fact that a great many young women had "jobs" nowadays. If he had thought about it at all, he had thought that, on the whole, they had jobs because they liked jobs—that it flattered their sense of independence and gave them an interest of their own in life.

The fact that a working day of nine to six, with an hour off for lunch, cut a girl off from most of the pleasures and relaxations of a leisured class had simply not occurred to Edward. That Midge, unless she sacrificed her lunch hour, could not drop into a picture gallery, that she could not go to an afternoon concert, drive out of town on a fine summer's day, lunch in a leisurely way at a distant restaurant, but had instead to relegate her excursions into the country to Saturday afternoons and Sundays and to snatch her lunch in a crowded Lyons or a snack bar was a new and unwelcome discovery. He was very fond of Midge. Little Midge—that was how he thought of her. Arriving shy and wide-eyed at Ainswick for the holidays, tongue-tied at first, then opening up into enthusiasm and affection.

Edward's tendency to live exclusively in the past, and to accept the present dubiously as something as yet untested, had delayed his recognition of Midge as a wage-earning adult.

It was on that evening at The Hollow when he had come in cold and shivering from that strange upsetting clash with Henrietta and when Midge had knelt to build up the fire, that he had been first aware of a Midge who was not an affectionate child but a woman. It had been an upsetting vision—he had felt for a moment that he had lost something—something that was a precious part of Ainswick. And he had said impulsively, speaking out of that suddenly aroused feeling, "I wish I saw you more often, Midge my dear. . . ."

Standing outside in the moonlight, speaking to a Henrietta who has no longer, suddenly, the familiar Henrietta he had loved for so long—he had known sudden panic. And he had come in to a further disturbance of the set pattern which was his life. Little Midge was also a part of Ainswick—and this was no longer Little Midge—but a courageous and sad-eyed adult whom he did not know.

Ever since then he had been troubled in his mind, and had indulged in a good deal of self-reproach for the unthinking way in which he had never bothered about Midge's happiness or comfort. The idea of her uncongenial job at Madame Alfrege's had worried him more and more, and he had determined at last to see for himself just what this dress shop of hers was like.

Edward peered suspiciously into the show window at a little black dress with a narrow gold belt, some rakish-looking, skimpy jumper suits, and an evening gown of rather tawdry coloured lace.

Edward knew nothing about women's clothes except by instinct but had a shrewd idea that all these exhibits were somehow of a meretricious order. No, he thought, this place was not worthy of her. Someone—Lucy Angkatell, perhaps—must do something about it.

Overcoming his shyness with an effort, Edward straightened his slightly stooping shoulders and walked in.

He was instantly paralyzed with embarrassment. Two platinum blonde little minxes with shrill voices were examining dresses in a show-case, with a dark saleswoman in attendance. At the back of the shop a small woman with a thick nose, henna-red hair and a disagreeable voice was arguing with a stout and bewildered customer over some alterations to an evening gown. From an adjacent cubicle a woman's fretful voice was raised.

"Frightful—perfectly frightful—can't you bring me anything *decent* to try?"

In response he heard the soft murmur of Midge's voice—a deferential persuasive voice:

"This wine model is really very smart. And I think it would suit you. If you'd just slip it on—"

"I'm not going to waste my time trying on things that I can see are no good. Do take a little trouble. I've told you I don't want reds. If you'd just listen to what you are told—"

The colour surged up into Edward's neck. He hoped Midge would throw the dress in the odious woman's face. Instead she murmured:

"I'll have another look. You wouldn't care for green, I suppose, Madam? Or this peach?"

"Dreadful—perfectly dreadful! No, I won't see anything more. Sheer waste of time—"

But now Madame Alfrege, detaching herself from the stout customer, had come down to Edward, and was looking at him inquiringly.

He pulled himself together.

"Is—could I speak—is Miss Hardcastle here?"

Madame Alfrege's eyebrows went up—but she took in the Savile Row cut of Edward's clothes, and she produced a smile whose graciousness was rather more unpleasant than her bad temper would have been.

From inside the cubicle the fretful voice rose sharply:

"Do be careful! How clumsy you are. You've torn my hair net."

And Midge, her voice unsteady:

"I'm very sorry, Madam."

"Stupid clumsiness." (The voice disappeared, muffled.) "No, I'll do it myself. My belt, please."

"Miss Hardcastle will be free in a minute," said Madame Alfrege. Her smile was now a leer.

A sandy-haired, bad-tempered-looking woman emerged from the cubicle, carrying several parcels, and went out into the street. Midge, in a severe black dress, opened the door for her. She looked pale and unhappy.

"I've come to take you out to lunch," said Edward without preamble.

Midge gave a harried glance up at the clock.

"I don't get off until quarter past one," she began.

It was ten past one.

Madame Alfrege said graciously:

"You can go off now if you like, Miss Hardcastle, as your *friend* has called for you."

Midge murmured, "Oh, thank you, Madame Alfrege," and to Edward, "I'll be ready in a minute," and disappeared into the back of the shop.

Edward, who had winced under the impact of Madame Alfrege's heavy emphasis on *friend*, stood helplessly waiting.

Madame Alfrege was just about to enter into arch conversation with him when the door opened and an opulent-looking woman with a Pekingese came in and Madame Alfrege's business instincts took her forward to the newcomer.

Midge reappeared with her coat on and, taking her by the elbow, Edward steered her out of the shop into the street.

"My God," he said, "is that the sort of thing you have to put up with? I heard that damned woman talking to you behind the curtain. How can you stick it, Midge? Why didn't you throw the damned frocks at her head?"

"I'd soon lose my job if I did things like that."

"But don't you want to fling things at a woman of that kind?"

Midge drew a deep breath.

"Of course I do. And there are times, especially at the end of a hot week during the summer sales, when I am afraid that one day I shall let go and just tell everyone exactly where they get off—instead of 'Yes, Madam, no, Madam—I'll see if we have anything else, Madam.' "

"Midge, dear little Midge, you can't put up with all this!"

Midge laughed a little shakily.

"Don't be so upset, Edward. Why on earth did you have to come here? Why not ring up?"

"I wanted to see for myself. I've been worried . . ." He paused and then broke out. "Why, Lucy wouldn't talk to a scullery maid the way that woman talked to you. It's all wrong that you should have to put up with insolence and rudeness. Good God, Midge, I'd like to take you right out of it all down to Ainswick. I'd like to hail a taxi, bundle you into it, and take you down to Ainswick now by the 2:15."

Midge stopped. Her assumed nonchalance fell from her. She had had a long, tiring morning with trying customers and Madame at her most bullying. She turned on Edward with a sudden flare of resentment.

"Well, then, why don't you? There are plenty of taxis!"

He stared at her, taken aback by her sudden fury. She went on, her anger flaming up:

"Why do you have to come along and *say* these things? You don't mean them. Do you think it makes it any easier after I've had the hell of a morning to be reminded that there are places like Ainswick? Do you think I'm grateful to you for standing there and babbling about how much you'd like to take me out of it all? All very sweet and insincere. You don't really mean a word of it. Don't you know that I'd sell my soul to catch the 2:15 to Ainswick and get away from everything? I can't bear even to *think* of Ainswick, do you understand? You mean well, Edward, but you're cruel! Saying things—just *saying* things. . . ."

They faced each other, seriously incommoding the lunchtime crowd in

Shaftesbury Avenue. Yet they were conscious of nothing but each other. Edward was staring at her like a man suddenly aroused from sleep.

He said, "All right then, damn it. You're coming to Ainswick by the 2:15!"

He raised his stick and hailed a passing taxi. It drew into the curb. Edward opened the door and Midge, slightly dazed, got in. Edward said "Paddington Station" to the driver and followed her in.

They sat in silence. Midge's lips were set together. Her eyes were defiant and mutinous. Edward stared straight ahead of him.

As they waited for the traffic lights in Oxford Street, Midge said disagreeably:

"I seem to have called your bluff."

Edward said shortly:

"It wasn't bluff."

The taxi started forward again with a jerk.

It was not until the taxi turned left in Edgware Road into Cambridge Terrace that Edward suddenly regained his normal attitude to life.

He said, "We can't catch the 2:15," and tapping on the glass he said to the driver, "Go to the Berkeley."

Midge said coldly, "Why can't we catch the 2:15? It's only twenty-five past one now."

Edward smiled at her.

"You haven't got any luggage, little Midge. No nightgowns or toothbrushes or country shoes. There's a 4:15, you know. We'll have some lunch now and talk things over."

Midge sighed.

"That's so like you, Edward. To remember the practical side. Impulse doesn't carry you very far, does it? Oh, well, it was a nice dream while it lasted."

She slipped her hand into his and gave him her old smile.

"I'm sorry I stood on the pavement and abused you like a fishwife," she said. "But you know, Edward, you *were* irritating."

"Yes," he said, "I must have been."

They went into the Berkeley happily side by side. They got a table by the window and Edward ordered an excellent lunch.

As they finished their chicken, Midge sighed and said, "I ought to hurry back to the shop. My time's up."

"You're going to take decent time over your lunch today, even if I have to go back and buy half the clothes in the shop!"

"Dear Edward, you are really rather sweet."

They ate crêpes suzette and then the waiter brought them coffee. Edward stirred his sugar in with his spoon.

He said gently:

"You really do love Ainswick, don't you?"

"Must we talk about Ainswick? I've survived not catching the 2:15—and I quite realize that there isn't any question of the 4:15—but don't rub it in."

Edward smiled.

"No, I'm not proposing that we catch the 4:15. But I am suggesting that you come to Ainswick, Midge. I'm suggesting that you come there for good—that is, if you can put up with me."

She stared at him over the rim of her coffee cup—put it down with a hand that she managed to keep steady.

"What do you really mean, Edward?"

"I'm suggesting that you should marry me, Midge. I don't suppose that I'm a very romantic proposition. I'm a dull dog, I know that, and not much good at anything—I just read books and potter around. But although I'm not a very exciting person, we've known each other a long time and I think that Ainswick itself would—well, would compensate. I think you'd be happy at Ainswick, Midge. Will you come?"

Midge swallowed once or twice—then she said:

"But I thought—Henrietta—" and stopped.

Edward said, his voice level and unemotional:

"Yes, I've asked Henrietta three times to marry me. Each time she has refused. Henrietta knows what she doesn't want."

There was a silence, and then Edward said:

"Well, Midge dear, what about it?"

Midge looked up at him. There was a catch in her voice. She said:

"It seems so extraordinary—to be offered heaven on a plate as it were, at the Berkeley!"

His face lighted up. He laid his hand over hers for a brief moment.

"Heaven on a plate," he said. "So you feel like that about Ainswick . . . Oh, Midge, I'm glad."

They sat there happily. Edward paid the bill and added an enormous tip.

The people in the restaurant were thinning out. Midge said with an effort:

"We'll have to go . . . I suppose I'd better go back to Madame Alfrege. After all, she's counting on me. I can't just walk out."

"No, I suppose you'll have to go back and resign, or hand in your notice, or whatever you call it. You're not to go on working there, though. I won't have it. But first I thought we'd better go to one of those shops in Bond Street where they sell rings."

"Rings?"

"It's usual, isn't it?"

Midge laughed.

In the dimmed lighting of the jeweller's shop, Midge and Edward bent over trays of sparkling engagement rings, whilst a discreet salesman watched them benignantly.

Edward said, pushing away a velvet-covered tray:

"Not emeralds."

Henrietta in green tweeds—Henrietta in an evening dress like Chinese jade . . .

No, not emeralds . . .

Midge pushed away the tiny stabbing pain at her heart.

"Choose for me," she said to Edward.

He bent over the tray before them. He picked out a ring with a single diamond. Not a very large stone, but a stone of beautiful colour and fire.

"I like this."

Midge nodded. She loved this display of Edward's unerring and fastidious taste. She slipped it on her finger as Edward and the shopman drew aside.

Edward wrote out a check for three hundred and forty-two pounds and came back to Midge smiling.

He said, "Let's go and be rude to Madame Alfrege. . . ."

Chapter XXV

"BUT, DARLINGS, I *am* so delighted!"

Lady Angkatell stretched out a fragile hand to Edward and touched Midge softly with the other.

"You did quite right, Edward, to make her leave that horrid shop and to bring her right down here. She'll stay here, of course, and be married from here—St. George's, you know, three miles by the road, though only a mile through the woods, but then one doesn't go to a wedding through woods. And I suppose it will have to be the Vicar—poor man, he has such dreadful colds in the head every Autumn—the Curate, now, has one of those high Anglican voices, and the whole thing would be far more impressive—and more religious, too, if you know what I mean. It is so hard to keep one's mind reverent when somebody is saying things through the nose."

It was, Midge decided, a very Lucyish reception. It made her want to both laugh and cry.

"I'd love to be married from here, Lucy," she said.

"Then that's settled, darling. Off-white satin, I think, and an ivory prayer book—*not* a bouquet. Bridesmaids?"

"No. I don't want a fuss. Just a very quiet wedding."

"I know what you mean, darling—and I think perhaps you are right. With an Autumn wedding it's nearly always chrysanthemums—such an uninspiring flower, I always think. And unless one takes a lot of time to choose them carefully, bridesmaids never *match* properly and there's nearly always one terribly plain one who ruins the whole effect—but one has to have her because she's usually the bridegroom's sister. But, of course—" Lady Angkatell beamed. "Edward hasn't got any sisters."

"That seems to be one point in my favour," said Edward, smiling.

"But children are really the worst at weddings," went on Lady Angkatell, happily pursuing her own train of thought. "Everyone says 'How sweet!' but, my dear, the *anxiety!* They step on the train, or else they howl for Nannie, and quite often they're sick. I always wonder how a girl can go up the aisle in a proper frame of mind, while she's so uncertain about what is happening behind her."

"There needn't be anything behind me," said Midge cheerfully. "Not even a train. I can be married in a coat and skirt."

"Oh, no, Midge, that's so like a widow. No, off-white satin and *not* from Madame Alfrege's."

"Certainly not from Madame Alfrege's," said Edward.

"I shall take you to Mireille," said Lady Angkatell.

"My dear Lucy, I can't possibly afford Mireille."

"Nonsense, Midge. Henry and I are going to give you your trousseau. And Henry, of course, will give you away. I do hope the band of his trousers won't be too tight. It's nearly two years since he last went to a wedding. And I shall wear—"

Lady Angkatell paused and closed her eyes.

"Yes, Lucy?"

"Hydrangea blue," announced Lady Angkatell in a rapt voice. "I suppose, Edward, you will have one of your own friends for best man; otherwise, of course, there is David. I cannot help feeling it would be frightfully good for David. It would give him poise, you know, and he would feel we all *liked* him. That, I am sure, is very important with David. It must be so disheartening, you know, to feel you are clever and intellectual and yet nobody likes you any the better for it! But, of course, it would be rather a risk. He would probably lose the ring, or drop it at the last minute. I expect it would worry Edward too much. But it would be nice in a way to keep it to the same people we've had here for the murder."

Lady Angkatell uttered the last few words in the most conversational of tones.

"Lady Angkatell has been entertaining a few friends for a murder this Autumn," Midge could not help saying.

"Yes," said Lucy meditatively. "I suppose it *did* sound like that. A party for the shooting . . . You know, when you come to think of it, that's just what it has been!"

Midge gave a faint shiver and said:

"Well, at any rate, it's over now."

"It's not exactly over—the inquest was only adjourned. And that nice Inspector Grange has got men all over the place simply crashing through the chestnut woods and startling all the pheasants, and springing up like jacks-in-the-box in the most unlikely places."

"What are they looking for?" asked Edward. "The revolver that Christow was shot with?"

"I imagine that must be it. They even came to the house with a search warrant—the Inspector was most apologetic about it, quite *shy*—but, of course, I told him we should be delighted. It was really most interesting. They looked absolutely *everywhere*. I followed them round, you know, and I suggested one or two places which even they hadn't thought of. But they didn't find anything. It was most disappointing. Poor Inspector Grange, he is growing quite thin and he pulls and pulls at that moustache of his. His wife ought to give him specially nourishing meals with all this worry he is having—but I have a vague idea that she must be one of those women who care more about having the linoleum really well-polished than in cooking a tasty little meal. Which reminds me, I must go and see Mrs. Medway. Funny how servants cannot bear the police. Her cheese soufflé last night was quite uneatable. Soufflés and pastry always show if one is off balance. If it weren't for Gudgeon keeping them all together, I really believe half the servants would leave. Why don't you two go and have a nice walk and help the police look for the revolver?"

Hercule Poirot sat on the bench overlooking the chestnut groves above the pool. He had no sense of trespassing since Lady Angkatell had very sweetly begged him to wander where he would at any time. It was Lady Angkatell's sweetness which Hercule Poirot was considering at this moment.

From time to time he heard the cracking of twigs in the woods above or caught sight of a figure moving through the chestnut groves below him.

Presently, Henrietta came along the path from the direction of the lane. She stopped for a moment when she saw Poirot, then she came and sat down by him.

"Good morning, M. Poirot. I have just been to call upon you. But you were out. You look very Olympian. Are you presiding over the hunt? The Inspector seems very active. What are they looking for? The revolver?"

"Yes, Miss Savernake."

"Will they find it, do you think?"

"I think so. Quite soon now, I should say?"

She looked at him inquiringly.

"Have you an idea, then, where it is?"

"No. But I *think* it will be found soon. It is *time* for it to be found."

"You do say odd things, M. Poirot!"

"Odd things happen here. You have come back very soon from London, Mademoiselle."

Her face hardened. She gave a short, bitter laugh.

"The murderer returns to the scene of the crime? That is the old superstition, isn't it? So you *do* think that I—did it! You don't believe me when I tell you that I wouldn't—that I *couldn't* kill anybody?"

Poirot did not answer at once. At last he said thoughtfully:

"It has seemed to me from the beginning that either this crime was very simple—so simple that it was difficult to believe its simplicity (and simplicity, Mademoiselle, can be strangely baffling) or else it was extremely complex—that is to say, we were contending against a mind capable of intricate and ingenious inventions, so that every time we seemed to be heading for the truth, we were actually being led on a trail that twisted away from the truth and led us to a point which—ended in nothingness. This apparent futility, this continual barrenness, is not *real*—it is artificial, it is *planned*. A very subtle and ingenious mind is plotting against us the whole time—and succeeding."

"Well?" said Henrietta. "What has that to do with me?"

"The mind that is plotting against us is a creative mind, Mademoiselle."

"I see—that's where I come in?"

She was silent, her lips set together bitterly. From her jacket pocket she had taken a pencil and now she was idly drawing the outline of a fantastic tree on the white painted wood of the bench, frowning down as she did so.

Poirot watched her. Something stirred in his mind—standing in Lady Angkatell's drawing-room on the afternoon of the crime, looking down at a pile of bridge markers, standing by a painted iron table in the pavilion the next morning and a question that he had put to Gudgeon.

He said:

"That is what you drew on your bridge marker—a tree."

"Yes." Henrietta seemed suddenly aware of what she was doing. "Ygdrasil, M. Poirot." She laughed.

"Why do you call it Ygdrasil?"

She explained the origin of Ygdrasil.

"And so—when you 'doodle' (that is the word, is it not?)—it is always Ygdrasil you draw?"

"Yes. Doodling is a funny thing, isn't it?"

"Here on the seat . . . on the bridge marker on Saturday evening . . . in the pavilion on Sunday morning . . ."

The hand that held the pencil stiffened and stopped. She said in a tone of careless amusement:

"In the pavilion?"

"Yes, on the round iron table there."

"Oh, that must have been on—on Saturday afternoon."

"It was not on Saturday afternoon. When Gudgeon brought the glasses out to the pavilion about twelve o'clock on Sunday morning, there was nothing drawn on the table. I asked him and he is quite definite about that."

"Then it must have been"—she hesitated for just a moment—"of course, on Sunday afternoon."

But, still smiling pleasantly, Hercule Poirot shook his head.

"I think not. Grange's men were at the pool all Sunday afternoon, photographing the body, getting the revolver out of the water. They did not leave until dusk. They would have seen anyone go into the pavilion."

Henrietta said slowly:

"I remember now—I went along there quite late in the evening—after dinner—"

Poirot's voice came sharply:

"People do not 'doodle' in the dark, Miss Savernake. Are you telling me that you went into the pavilion at night and stood by a table and drew a tree without being able to see what you were drawing?"

Henrietta said calmly:

"I am telling you the truth. Naturally, you don't believe it. You have your own ideas— What is your idea, by the way?"

"I am suggesting that you were in the pavilion on *Sunday morning after* twelve o'clock when Gudgeon brought the glasses out. That you stood by that table watching someone, or waiting for someone, and unconsciously took out a pencil and drew Ygdrasil without being fully aware of what you were doing."

"I was not in the pavilion on Sunday morning. I sat out on the terrace for a while, then I got the gardening basket and went up to the dahlia border and cut off heads and tied up some of the Michaelmas daisies that were untidy. Then, just on one o'clock, I went along to the pool. I've been through it all with Inspector Grange. I never came near the pool until one o'clock, just after John had been shot."

"That," said Hercule Poirot, "is your story. But Ygdrasil, Mademoiselle, testifies against you."

"I was in the pavilion and I shot John; that's what you mean?"

"You were there and you shot Dr. Christow, or you were there and you saw who shot Dr. Christow—or someone else was there who knew about Ygdrasil and deliberately drew it on the table to put suspicion on *you*".

Henrietta got up. She turned on him with her chin lifted.

"You still think that I shot John Christow. You think that you can prove I shot him. Well, I will tell you this. You will never prove it. *Never!*"

"You think that you are cleverer than I am?"

"You will never prove it," said Henrietta, and turning, she walked away down the winding path that led to the swimming pool.

Chapter XXVI

GRANGE CAME INTO Resthaven to drink a cup of tea with Hercule Poirot. The tea was exactly what he had had apprehensions it might be—extremely weak and China tea at that.

"These foreigners," thought Grange, "don't know how to make tea—you can't teach 'em." But he did not mind much. He was in a condition of pessimism when one more thing that was unsatisfactory actually afforded him a kind of grim satisfaction.

He said, "The adjourned inquest's the day after tomorrow and where have we got? Nowhere at all. What the hell, that gun must be *somewhere!* It's this damned country—miles of woods. It would take an army to search them properly. Talk of a needle in a haystack. It may be anywhere. The fact is, we've got to face up to it—we may *never* find that gun."

"You will find it," said Poirot confidently.

"Well, it won't be for want of trying!"

"You will find it, sooner or later. And I should say sooner. Another cup of tea?"

"I don't mind if I do—no, no hot water."

"It is not too strong?"

"Oh, no, it's not too strong." The Inspector was conscious of understatement.

Gloomily he sipped at the pale straw-coloured beverage.

"This case is making a monkey of me, M. Poirot—a monkey of me! I can't get the hang of these people. They *seem* helpful—but everything they tell you seems to lead you away on a wild-goose chase."

"Away?" said Poirot. A startled look came into his eyes. "Yes, I see. *Away . . .*"

The Inspector was developing his grievance.

"Take the gun now. Christow was shot—according to the medical evidence—only a minute or two before your arrival. Lady Angkatell had that egg basket, Miss Savernake had a gardening basket full of dead flower heads, and Edward Angkatell was wearing a loose shooting coat with large pockets stuffed with cartridges. Any one of them could have carried the revolver away with them. It wasn't hidden anywhere near the pool—my men have raked the place, so that's definitely out."

Poirot nodded. Grange went on:

"Gerda Christow was framed—by whom? That's where every clue I follow seems to vanish into thin air."

"Their stories of how they spent the morning are satisfactory?"

"The *stories* are all right. Miss Savernake was gardening. Lady Angkatell was collecting eggs. Edward Angkatell and Sir Henry were shooting and separated at the end of the morning—Sir Henry coming back to the house and Edward Angkatell coming down here through the woods. The young fellow was up in his bedroom reading. (Funny place to read on a nice day, but he's the indoor bookish kind.) Miss Hardcastle took a book down to the orchard. All sounds very natural and likely, and there's no means of checking up on it. Gudgeon took a tray of glasses out to the pavilion about twelve o'clock. He can't say where any of the house party were or what they were doing. In a way, you know, there's something against almost all of them?"

"Really?"

"Of course, the most obvious person is Veronica Cray; she had quarrelled with Christow, she hated his guts, she's quite likely to have shot him —but I can't find the least iota of proof that she did shoot him. No evidence as to her having had any opportunity to pinch the revolvers from Sir Henry's collection, no one who saw her going to or from the pool that day. And the missing revolver definitely isn't in her possession now."

"Ah, you have made sure of that?"

"What do you think? The evidence would have justified a search warrant but there was no need. She was quite gracious about it. It's not anywhere in that tin-pot bungalow. After the inquest was adjourned, we made a show of letting up on Miss Cray and Miss Savernake, and we've had a tail on them to see where they went and what they'd do. We've had a man on at the film studios, watching Veronica—no sign of her trying to ditch the gun there."

"And Henrietta Savernake?"

"Nothing there either. She went straight back to Chelsea and we've kept an eye on her ever since. The revolver isn't in her studio or in her possession. She was quite pleasant about the search—seemed amused. Some of her fancy stuff gave our man quite a turn. He said it beat him why people wanted to do that kind of thing—statues all lumps and swellings, bits of brass and aluminum twisted into fancy shapes, horses that you wouldn't know were horses—"

Poirot stirred a little.

"Horses, you say?"

"Well, *a* horse. If you'd call it a horse! If people want to model a horse why don't they go and *look* at a horse!"

"A *horse,*" repeated Poirot.

Grange turned his head.

"What is there about that that interests you so, M. Poirot? I don't get it."

"Association—a point of the psychology."

"Word association? Horse and cart. Rocking horse? Clothes-horse. No, I don't get it. Anyway, after a day or two, Miss Savernake packs up and comes down here again. You know that?"

"Yes, I have talked with her and I have seen her walking in the woods."

"Restless, yes. Well, she was having an affair with the doctor all right, and his saying 'Henrietta' as he died is pretty near to an accusation. But it's not quite near enough, M. Poirot."

"No," said Poirot thoughtfully, "it is not near enough."

Grange said heavily:

"There's something in the atmosphere here—it gets you all tangled up! It's as though they all *knew* something. Lady Angkatell now—she's never been able to put out a decent reason *why* she took out a gun with her that day. It's a crazy thing to do—sometimes I think she is crazy."

Poirot shook his head very gently.

"No," he said, "she is not crazy."

"Then there's Edward Angkatell. I thought I was getting something on *him.* Lady Angkatell said—no, hinted—that he'd been in love with Miss Savernake for years. Well, that gives him a motive. And now I find it's the *other* girl—Miss Hardcastle—that he's engaged to. So bang goes the case against *him.*"

Poirot gave a sympathetic murmur.

"Then there's the young fellow," pursued the Inspector. "Lady Angkatell let slip something about him—his mother, it seems, died in an asylum—persecution mania—thought everybody was conspiring to kill her. Well, you can see what that might mean. If the boy had inherited that particular strain of insanity, he might have got ideas into his head about Dr. Christow—might have fancied the doctor was planning to certify him. Not that Christow was that kind of doctor. Nervous affections of the alimentary canal and diseases of the Super—Super-something—that was Christow's line. But if the boy was a bit touched, he *might* imagine Christow was here to keep him under observation. He's got an extraordinary manner, that young fellow, nervous as a cat."

Grange sat unhappily for a moment or two.

"You see what I mean? All vague suspicions—leading *nowhere.*"

Poirot stirred again. He murmured softly:

"*Away*—not *towards*. *From*, not *to*. *Nowhere* instead of *somewhere*. . . . Yes, of course, that *must* be it."

Grange stared at him. He said:

"They're queer, all these Angkatells. I'd swear, sometimes, that they know all about it. . . ."

Poirot said quietly:

"*They do.*"

"You mean, they know, all of them, who did it?" the Inspector asked incredulously.

Poirot nodded.

"Yes—they know. I have thought so for some time. I am quite sure now."

"I see." The Inspector's face was grim. "And they're hiding it up among them? Well, I'll beat them yet. *I'm going to find that gun.*"

It was, Poirot reflected, quite the Inspector's theme song.

Grange went on with rancour:

"I'd give anything to get even with them—"

"With—"

"All of them! Muddling me up! Suggesting things! Hinting! Helping my men—*helping* them! All gossamer and spiders' webs; nothing tangible. What I want is a good solid *fact!*"

Hercule Poirot had been staring out of the window for some moments. His eye had been attracted by an irregularity in the symmetry of his domain.

He said now:

"You want a solid fact? *Eh bien,* unless I am much mistaken there is a solid fact in the hedge by my gate."

They went down the garden path. Grange went down on his knees, coaxed the twigs apart till he disclosed more fully the thing that had been thrust between them. He drew a deep sigh as something black and steel was revealed.

He said: "It's a revolver all right."

Just for a moment his eye rested doubtfully on Poirot.

"No, no, my friend," said Poirot. "*I* did not shoot Dr. Christow and I did not put the revolver in my own hedge."

"Of course you didn't, M. Poirot! Sorry! Well, we've got it. Looks like the one missing from Sir Henry's study. We can verify that as soon as we get the number. Then we'll see if it was the gun that shot Christow. Easy does it now."

With infinite care and the use of a silk handkerchief, he eased the gun out of the hedge.

"To give us a break, we want finger-prints. I've a feeling, you know, that our luck's changed at last."

"Let me know—"

"Of course I will, M. Poirot. I'll ring you up."

Poirot received two telephone calls. The first came through that same evening. The Inspector was jubilant.

"That you, M. Poirot? Well, here's the dope. It's the gun all right. The gun missing from Sir Henry's collection *and* the gun that shot John Christow! That's definite. And there is a good set of prints on it. Thumb, first finger, part of the middle finger. Didn't I tell you our luck had changed?"

"You have identified the finger-prints?"

"Now yet. They're certainly not Mrs. Christow's. We took hers. They look more like a man's than a woman's for size. Tomorrow I'm going along to The Hollow to speak my little piece and get a sample from everyone. And then, M. Poirot, *we shall know where we are!*"

"I hope so, I am sure," said Poirot, politely.

The second telephone call came through on the following day and the voice that spoke was no longer jubilant. In tones of unmitigated gloom, Grange said:

"Want to hear the latest? Those finger-prints aren't the prints of anybody connected with the case! No, sir! They're not Edward Angkatell's, nor David's, nor Sir Henry's. They're not Gerda Christow's, nor the Savernake's, nor our Veronica's, nor her ladyship's, nor the little dark girl's! They're not even the kitchen maid's—let alone any of the other servants!"

Poirot made condoling noises. The sad voice of Inspector Grange went on:

"So it looks as though, after all, it *was* an outside job. Someone, that is to say, who had a down on Dr. Christow, and who we don't know anything about! Someone invisible and inaudible who pinched the guns from the study, and who went away after the shooting by the path to the lane. Someone who put the gun in your hedge and then vanished into thin air!"

"Would you like *my* finger-prints, my friend?"

"I don't mind if I do! It strikes me, M. Poirot, that you were on the spot, and that taking it all round you're far and away the most suspicious character in the case!"

Chapter XXVII

THE CORONER CLEARED his throat and looked expectantly at the foreman of the jury.

The latter looked down at the piece of paper he held in his hand. His Adam's apple wagged up and down excitedly. He read out in a careful voice:

"We find that the deceased came to his death by wilful murder by some person or persons unknown."

Poirot nodded his head quietly in his corner by the wall.

There could be no other possible verdict.

Outside, the Angkatells stopped a moment to speak to Gerda and her sister. Gerda was wearing the same black clothes as before. Her face had the same dazed, unhappy expression. This time there was no Daimler. The train service, Elsie Patterson explained, was really very good. A fast train to Waterloo and they could easily catch the 1:20 to Bexhill.

Lady Angkatell, clasping Gerda's hand, murmured:

"You must keep in touch with us, my dear. A little lunch, perhaps, one day in London? I expect you'll come up to do shopping occasionally?"

"I—I don't know," said Gerda.

Elsie Patterson said:

"We must hurry, dear, our train," and Gerda turned away with an expression of relief.

Midge said:

"Poor Gerda. The only thing John's death has done for her is to set her free from your terrifying hospitality, Lucy."

"How unkind you are, Midge. Nobody could say I didn't try."

"You are much worse when you try, Lucy."

"Well, it's very nice to think it's all over, isn't it?" said Lady Angkatell, beaming at them. "Except, of course, for poor Inspector Grange. I do feel so sorry for him. Would it cheer him up, do you think, if we asked him back to lunch? As a *friend*, I mean."

"I should let well alone, Lucy," said Sir Henry.

"Perhaps you are right," said Lady Angkatell meditatively. "And anyway it isn't the right kind of lunch today. Partridges au Choux—and that delicious soufflé surprise that Mrs. Medway makes so well. Not at all Inspector Grange's kind of lunch. A really good steak, a little underdone, and a good old-fashioned apple tart with no nonsense about it—or perhaps apple dumplings—that's what I should order for Inspector Grange."

"Your instincts about food are always very sound, Lucy. I think we had better get home to those partridges—they sound delicious."

"Well, I thought we ought to have *some* celebration! It's wonderful, isn't it, how everything always seems to turn out for the best?"

"Ye-es—"

"I know what you're thinking, Henry, but don't worry. I shall attend to it this afternoon."

"What are you up to now, Lucy?"

Lady Angkatell smiled at him.

"It's quite all right, darling. Just tucking in a loose end."

Sir Henry looked at her doubtfully.

When they reached The Hollow, Gudgeon came out to open the door of the car.

"Everything went off very satisfactorily, Gudgeon," said Lady Angkatell. "Please tell Mrs. Medway and the others. I know how unpleasant it has been for you all, and I should like to tell you now how much Sir Henry and I have appreciated the loyalty you have all shown."

"We have been deeply concerned for you, m'lady," said Gudgeon.

"Very sweet of Gudgeon," said Lucy as she went into the drawing-room, "but really quite wasted. I have really almost *enjoyed* it all—so different, you know, from what one is accustomed to. Don't you feel, David, that an experience like this has broadened your mind? It must be so different from Cambridge."

"I am at Oxford," said David coldly.

Lady Angkatell said vaguely, "The dear boat race. So English, don't you think?" and went towards the telephone.

She picked up the receiver and holding it in her hand she went on:

"I do hope, David, that you will come and stay with us again. It's so difficult, isn't it, to get to know people when there is a murder? And quite impossible to have any really intellectual conversation."

"Thank you," said David. "But when I come down I am going to Athens—to the British School."

Lady Angkatell turned to her husband.

"Who's got the Embassy now? Oh, of course—Hope-Remmington. No, I don't think David would like them. Those girls of theirs are so terribly hearty. They play hockey and cricket and the funny game where you catch the thing in a net."

She broke off, looking down at the telephone receiver.

"Now what am I doing with this thing?"

"Perhaps you were going to ring someone up," said Edward.

"I don't think so." She replaced it. "Do you like telephones, David?"

It was the sort of question, David reflected irritably, that she would ask; one to which there could be no intelligent answer. He replied coldly that he supposed they were useful.

"You mean," said Lady Angkatell, "like mincing machines? Or elastic bands? All the same, one wouldn't—"

She broke off as Gudgeon appeared in the doorway to announce lunch.

"But you like partridges," said Lady Angkatell to David anxiously.

David admitted that he liked partridges.

"Sometimes I think Lucy really is a bit touched," said Midge, as she and Edward strolled over from the house and up towards the woods.

The partridges and the soufflé surprise had been excellent and with the inquest over a weight had lifted from the atmosphere.

Edward said thoughtfully:

"I always think Lucy has a brilliant mind that expresses itself like a missing word competition. To mix metaphors—the hammer jumps from nail to nail and never fails to hit each one squarely on the head."

"All the same," Midge said soberly, "Lucy frightens me sometimes." She added, with a tiny shiver, "This place has frightened me lately."

"The Hollow?"

Edward turned an astonished face to her.

"It always reminds me a little of Ainswick," he said. "It's not, of course, the real thing—"

Midge interrupted:

"That's just it, Edward—I'm frightened of things that aren't the real thing . . . You don't know, you see, what's *behind* them . . . It's like— oh, it's like a *mask.*"

"You mustn't be fanciful, little Midge."

It was the old tone, the indulgent tone he had used years ago. She had liked it then, but now it disturbed her. She struggled to make her meaning clearer—to show him that behind what he called fancy, was some shape of dimly apprehended reality.

"I got away from it in London, but now I get back here it all comes over me again. I feel that everyone knows who killed John Christow . . . That the only person who doesn't know—is *me.*"

Edward said irritably:

"Must we think and talk about John Christow? He's dead. Dead and gone."

Midge murmured:

"He is dead and gone, lady,
He is dead and gone;
At his head a grass-green turf
At his heels a stone."

She put her hand on Edward's arm. "Who *did* kill him, Edward? We thought it was Gerda—but it wasn't Gerda. Then who was it? Tell me what *you* think? Was it someone we've never heard of?"

He said irritably:

"All this speculation seems to me quite unprofitable. If the police can't find out, or can't get sufficient evidence, then the whole thing will have to be allowed to drop—and we shall be rid of it."

"Yes—but it's the not knowing—"

"Why should we want to know? What has John Christow to do with us?"

With *us,* she thought, with Edward and me? Nothing! Comforting thought—she and Edward, linked, a dual entity. And yet—and yet—John Christow, for all that he had been laid in his grave and the words of the burial service read over him, was not buried deep enough. *He is dead and gone, lady* . . . But John Christow was not dead and gone—for all that Edward wished him to be . . . John Christow was still here at The Hollow.

Edward said, "Where are we going?"

Something in his tone surprised her. She said:

"Let's walk up onto the top of the ridge. Shall we?"

"If you like."

For some reason, he was unwilling. She wondered why. It was usually his favourite walk. He and Henrietta used nearly always— Her thought snapped and broke off . . . *He and Henrietta*—She said, "Have you been this way yet this Autumn?"

He said stiffly:

"Henrietta and I walked up here that first afternoon."

They went on in silence.

They came at last to the top and sat on the fallen tree.

Midge thought: *"He and Henrietta sat here, perhaps . . ."*

She turned the ring on her finger round and round. The diamond flashed coldly at her . . . *("Not emeralds,"* he had said.)

She said with a slight effort:

"It will be lovely to be at Ainswick again for Christmas."

He did not seem to hear her. He had gone far away.

She thought, He is thinking of Henrietta and of John Christow.

Sitting here he had said something to Henrietta or she had said something to him . . . Henrietta might know what she didn't want but he belonged to Henrietta still. He always would, Midge thought, belong to Henrietta. . . .

Pain swooped down upon her. The happy bubble world in which she had lived for the last week quivered and broke.

She thought, I can't live like that—with Henrietta always there in his mind. I can't face it. I can't bear it . . .

The wind sighed through the trees—the leaves were falling fast now—there were hardly any gold ones left, only brown.

She said, "Edward!"

The urgency of her voice aroused him. He turned his head.

"Yes?"

"I'm sorry, Edward." Her lips were trembling but she forced her voice to be quiet and self-controlled. "I've got to tell you. It's no use. I can't marry you. It wouldn't work, Edward."

He said, "But, Midge—surely Ainswick—"

She interrupted:

"I can't marry you just for Ainswick, Edward. You—you must see that."

He sighed then, a long, gentle sigh. It was like an echo of the dead leaves slipping gently off the branches of the trees.

"I see what you mean," he said. "Yes, I suppose you are right."

"It was dear of you to ask me, dear and sweet. But it wouldn't do, Edward. It wouldn't *work.*"

She had had a faint hope, perhaps, that he would argue with her, that he would try to persuade her—but he seemed, quite simply, to feel just as she did about it. Here, with the ghost of Henrietta close beside him, he, too, apparently, saw that it couldn't work . . .

"No," he said, echoing her words, "it wouldn't work."

She slipped the ring off her finger and held it out to him.

She would always love Edward and Edward would always love Henrietta and life was just plain unadulterated hell . . .

She said, with a little catch in her voice:

"It's a lovely ring, Edward."

"I wish you'd keep it, Midge. I'd like you to have it."

She shook her head.

"I couldn't do that."

He said, with a faint humorous twist of the lips:

"I shan't give it to anyone else, you know."

It was all quite friendly. He didn't know—he would never know—just what she was feeling . . . Heaven on a plate—and the plate was broken and Heaven had slipped between her fingers or had, perhaps, never been there.

That afternoon, Poirot received his third visitor.

He had been visited by Henrietta Savernake and by Veronica Cray. This time it was Lady Angkatell. She came floating up the path with her usual appearance of insubstantiality.

He opened the door and she stood smiling at him.

"I have come to see you," she announced.

So might a fairy confer a favour on a mere mortal.

"I am enchanted, Madame."

He led the way into the sitting room. She sat down on the sofa and once more, she smiled.

Hercule Poirot thought: "She is old—her hair is grey—there are lines in her face. Yet she has magic—she will always have magic . . ."

Lady Angkatell said softly:

"I want you to do something for me."

"Yes, Madame?"

"To begin with, I must talk to you—about John Christow."

"About Dr. Christow?"

"Yes. It seems to me that the only thing to do is to put a full stop to the whole thing. You understand what I mean, don't you?"

"I am not sure that I do know what you mean, Lady Angkatell."

She gave him her lovely dazzling smile again and she put one long white hand on his sleeve.

"Dear M. Poirot, you know perfectly. The police will have to hunt about for the owner of those finger-prints and they won't find him and in the end they'll have to let the whole thing drop. But I'm afraid, you know, that *you* won't let it drop."

"No, I shall not let it drop," said Hercule Poirot.

"That is just what I thought . . . And that is why I came. It's the truth you want, isn't it?"

"Certainly I want the truth."

"I see I haven't explained myself very well. I'm trying to find out just *why* you won't let things drop. It isn't because of your prestige—or because you want to hang a murderer (such an unpleasant kind of death, I've always thought—so *mediaeval)* It's just, I think, that you want to *know*. You do see what I mean, don't you? If you were to know the truth—if you were to be *told* the truth, I think—I think perhaps that might satisfy you? Would it satisfy you, M. Poirot?"

"You are offering to tell me the truth, Lady Angkatell?"

She nodded:

"You yourself know the truth, then?"

Her eyes opened very wide.

"Oh, yes, I've known for a long time. I'd *like* to tell you. And then we could agree that—well, that it was all over and done with."

She smiled at him.

"Is it a bargain, M. Poirot?"

It was quite an effort for Hercule Poirot to say:

"No, Madame, it is not a bargain."

He wanted—he wanted, very badly, to let the whole thing drop . . . simply because Lucy Angkatell asked him to do so.

Lady Angkatell sat very still for a moment. Then she raised her eyebrows.

"I wonder," she said. . . . "I wonder if you really know what you are doing?"

Chapter XXVIII

MIDGE, LYING DRY eyed and awake in the darkness, turned restlessly on her pillows.

She heard a door unlatch, a footstep in the corridor outside passing her door . . .

It was Edward's door and Edward's step . . .

She switched on the lamp by her bed and looked at the clock that stood by the lamp on the table.

It was ten minutes to three.

Edward passing her door and going down the stairs at this hour in the morning. It was odd.

They had all gone to bed early, at half past ten. She herself had not slept, had lain there with burning eyelids and with a dry aching misery racking her feverishly.

She had heard the clock strike downstairs—had heard owls hoot outside her bedroom window. Had felt that depression that reaches its nadir at 2:00 a.m. Had thought to herself, "I can't bear it—I can't bear it. Tomorrow coming—another day . . . Day after day to be got through."

Banished by her own act from Ainswick—from all the loveliness and dearness of Ainswick which might have been her very own possession.

But better banishment, better loneliness, better a drab and uninteresting life, than life with Edward and Henrietta's ghost. Until that day in the wood she had not known her own capacity for bitter jealousy.

And after all, Edward had never told her that he loved her. Affection, kindliness, he had never pretended to more than that. She had accepted the limitation, and not until she had realized what it would mean to live at close quarters with an Edward whose mind and heart had Henrietta as a permanent guest, did she know that for her Edward's affection was not enough.

Edward walking past her door, down the front stairs . . .

It was odd—very odd—where was he going?

Uneasiness grew upon her. It was all part and parcel of the uneasiness that The Hollow gave her nowadays. What was Edward doing downstairs in the small hours of the morning? Had he gone out?

Inactivity at last became too much for her. She got up, slipped on her dressing gown and taking a flashlight, she opened her door and came out into the passage.

It was quite dark, no lights had been switched on. Midge turned to the left and came to the head of the staircase. Below all was dark too. She ran down the stairs and after a moment's hesitation switched on the light in the hall. Everything was silent. The front door was closed and locked. She tried the side door but that too was locked.

Edward, then, had not gone out. Where could he be?

And suddenly she raised her head and sniffed.

A whiff—a very faint whiff of gas.

The baize door to the kitchen quarters was just ajar. She went through it—a faint light was shining from the open kitchen door. The smell of gas was much stronger.

Midge ran along the passage and into the kitchen. Edward was lying on the floor with his head inside the gas oven which was turned on full.

Midge was a quick practical girl. Her first act was to swing open the shutters. She could not unlatch the window and winding a glass cloth round her arm, she smashed it. Then, holding her breath, she stooped down and tugged and pulled Edward out of the gas oven and switched off the taps.

He was unconscious and breathing queerly, but she knew that he could not have been unconscious long. He could only just have gone under. The wind sweeping through from the window to the open door was fast dispelling the gas fumes. Midge dragged Edward to a spot near the window where the air would have full play. She sat down and gathered him into her strong young arms.

She said his name, first softly, then with increasing desperation: "Edward, Edward, Edward, Edward. . . ."

He stirred, groaned, opened his eyes and looked up at her.

He said very faintly, "Gas oven . . ." and his eyes went round to the gas stove.

"I know, darling, but why—*why?*"

He was shivering now, his hands were cold and lifeless.

He said, "Midge?"

There was a kind of wondering surprise and pleasure in his voice.

She said, "I heard you pass my door . . . I didn't know . . . I came down."

He sighed—a very long sigh as though from very far away.

"Best way out," he said. And then, inexplicably, until she remembered Lucy's conversation on the night of the tragedy, "News of the World."

"But, Edward, why—*why?*"

He looked up at her and the blank, cold darkness of his stare frightened her.

"Because I know now I've never been any good. Always a failure. Always ineffectual. It's men like Christow who do things. They get there and women admire them. I'm nothing—I'm not even quite alive. I inherited Ainswick and I've enough to live on—otherwise I'd have gone under. No good at a career—never much good as a writer. Henrietta didn't want me. No one wanted me. That day—at the Berkeley—I thought—but it was the same story. You couldn't care either, Midge. Even for Ainswick you couldn't put up with me . . . So I thought better get out altogether."

Her words came with a rush.

"Darling, darling. You don't understand. It was because of Henrietta— because I thought you still loved Henrietta so much."

"Henrietta?" He murmured it vaguely, as though speaking of someone infinitely remote. "Yes, I loved her very much."

And from even farther away she heard him murmur:

"It's so cold . . ."

"Edward—my darling."

Her arms closed round him firmly. He smiled at her, murmuring:

"You're so warm, Midge—you're so warm. . . ."

Yes, she thought, that was what despair was. A cold thing—a thing of infinite coldness and loneliness. She'd never understood until now that despair was a cold thing. She had thought of it as something hot and passionate, something violent, a hot-blooded desperation. But that was not so. *This* was despair—this utter outer darkness of coldness and loneliness. And the sin of despair, that priests talked of, was a cold sin, the sin of cutting oneself off from all warm and living human contacts. . . .

Edward said again, "You're so warm, Midge." And suddenly, with a glad proud confidence, she thought, But that's what he *wants*—that's what I can give him! They were all cold, the Angkatells; even Henrietta had something in her of the will-o'-the-wisp, of the elusive fairy coldness in the Angkatell blood. Let Edward love Henrietta as an intangible and unpossessable dream. It was warmth, permanence, stability that was his real need. It was daily companionship and love and laughter at Ainswick.

She thought, What Edward needs is someone to light a fire on his hearth—and *I* am the person to do that.

Edward looked up. He saw Midge's face bending over him, the warm colouring of the skin, the generous mouth, the steady eyes and the dark hair that lay back from her forehead like two wings.

He saw Henrietta always as a projection from the Past. In the grown woman he sought and wanted only to see the seventeen-year-old girl he had first loved. But now, looking up at Midge, he had a queer sense of seeing a continuous Midge—he saw the schoolgirl with her winged hair springing back into two pigtails, he saw its dark waves framing her face now and he saw exactly how those wings would look when the hair was not dark any longer but grey. . . .

Midge, he thought, is *real* . . . the only real thing I have ever known . . . He felt the warmth of her, and the strength—dark, positive, alive, *real!* Midge, he thought, is the rock on which I can build my life . . .

He said, "Darling Midge, I love you so, never leave me again . . ."

She bent down to him and he felt the warmth of her lips on his, felt her love enveloping him, shielding him, and happiness flowered in that cold desert where he had lived alone so long . . .

Suddenly Midge said, with a shaky laugh—

"Look, Edward, a black beetle has come out to look at us. Isn't he a *nice* black beetle! I never thought I could like a black beetle so much!"

She added dreamily:

"How odd life is. Here we are sitting on the floor in a kitchen that still smells of gas all amongst the black beetles and feeling that it's heaven."

He murmured dreamily:

"I could stay here forever."

"We'd better go and get some sleep. It's four o'clock. How on earth are we to explain that broken window to Lucy?"

Fortunately, Midge reflected, Lucy was an extraordinarily easy person to explain things to.

Taking a leaf out of Lucy's own book, Midge went into her room at six o'clock.

She made a bald statement of fact:

"Edward went down and put his head in the gas oven in the night," she said. "Fortunately I heard him and went down after him. I broke the window because I couldn't get it open quickly."

Lucy, Midge had to admit, was wonderful.

She smiled sweetly with no sign of surprise.

"Dear Midge," she said, "you are always so practical. I'm sure you will always be the greatest comfort to Edward."

After Midge had gone Lady Angkatell lay thinking. Then she got up and went into her husband's room, which for once was unlocked.

"Henry."

"My dear Lucy! It's not cock-crow yet."

"No, but listen, Henry, this is really important. We must have electricity installed to cook by and get rid of that gas stove."

"Why, it's quite satisfactory, isn't it?"

"Oh, yes, dear. But it's the sort of thing that gives people ideas, and everybody mightn't be as practical as dear Midge."

She flitted elusively away. Sir Henry turned over with a grunt. Presently he awoke with a start just as he was dozing off.

"Did I dream it," he murmured, "or did Lucy come in and start talking about gas stoves?"

Outside in the passage, Lady Angkatell went into the bathroom and put a kettle on the gas ring. Sometimes, she knew, people liked an early cup of tea . . . Fired with self-approval, she returned to bed and lay back on her pillows, pleased with life and with herself.

Edward and Midge at Ainswick—the inquest over— She would go and talk to M. Poirot again. A nice little man . . .

Suddenly another idea flashed into her head. She sat upright in bed.

"I wonder now," she speculated, "if she has thought of *that?*"

She got out of bed and drifted along the passage to Henrietta's room, beginning her remarks as usual long before she was within earshot.

"—and it suddenly came to me, dear, that you *might* have overlooked that."

Henrietta murmured sleepily:

"For heaven's sake, Lucy, the birds aren't up yet!"

"Oh, I know, dear, it *is* rather early, but it seems to have been a very disturbed night—Edward and the gas stove, and Midge and the kitchen window—and thinking of what to say to M. Poirot and everything—"

"I'm sorry, Lucy, but everything you say sounds like complete gibberish . . . Can't it wait?"

"It was only the holster, dear. I thought, you know, that you might not have thought about the holster."

"Holster?" Henrietta sat up in bed. She was suddenly wide awake. "What's this about a holster?"

"That revolver of Henry's was in a holster, you know. And the holster hasn't been found. And, of course, nobody may think of it—but on the other hand somebody might—"

Henrietta swung herself out of bed. She said:

"One always forgets something—that's what they say! And it's true!"

Lady Angkatell went back to her room.

She got into bed and quickly went fast asleep.

The kettle on the gas ring boiled and went on boiling . . .

Chapter XXIX

GERDA ROLLED OVER to the side of the bed and sat up.

Her head felt a little better now but she was still glad that she hadn't gone with the others on the picnic. It was peaceful and almost comforting to be alone in the house for a bit.

Elsie, of course, had been very kind—very kind—especially at first. To begin with, Gerda had been urged to stay in bed for breakfast, trays had been brought up to her. Everybody urged her to sit in the most comfortable armchair, to put her feet up, not to do anything at all strenuous.

They were all so sorry for her about John. She had stayed, cowering gratefully in that protective dim haze. She hadn't wanted to think, or to feel, or to remember.

But now, every day, she felt it coming nearer—she'd have to start living again, to decide what to do, where to live. Already Elsie was showing a shade of impatience in her manner. "Oh, Gerda, don't be so *slow!*"

It was all the same as it had been—long ago, before John came and took her away. They all thought her slow and stupid. There was nobody to say, as John had said, "I'll look after you."

Her head ached and Gerda thought, I'll make myself some tea.

She went down to the kitchen and put the kettle on. It was nearly boiling when she heard a ring at the front door.

The maids had been given the day out. Gerda went to the door and opened it. She was astonished to see Henrietta's rakish-looking car drawn up to the curb and Henrietta herself standing on the doorstep.

"Why, Henrietta!" she exclaimed. She fell back a step or two. "Come in. I'm afraid my sister and the children are out but—"

Henrietta cut her short.

"Good. I'm glad. I wanted to get you alone. Listen, Gerda, *what did you do with the holster?*"

Gerda stopped. Her eyes looked suddenly vacant and uncomprehending. She said, "Holster?"

"You'd better come in here. I'm afraid it's rather dusty. You see, we haven't had much time this morning—"

Henrietta interrupted again urgently.

She said, "Listen, Gerda, you've got to tell me. Apart from the holster everything's all right—absolutely watertight. There's nothing to connect you with the business. I found the revolver where you'd shoved it into that thicket by the pool. I hid it in a place where you couldn't possibly have put it—and there are finger-prints on it which they'll never identify. So there's only the holster; I must know what you did with that"

She paused, praying desperately that Gerda would react quickly.

She had no idea why she had this vital sense of urgency, but it was there. Her car had not been followed—she had made sure of that. She had started on the London road, had filled up at a garage and had mentioned that she was on her way to London. Then, a little further on, she had swung across country until she had reached a main road leading south to the coast.

Gerda was still staring at her. The trouble with Gerda, thought Henrietta, was that she was so slow.

"If you've still got it, Gerda, you must give it to me. I'll get rid of it somehow. It's the only possible thing, you see, that can connect you now with John's death. *Have* you got it?"

There was a pause and then Gerda slowly nodded her head.

"Didn't you know it was madness to keep it?" Henrietta could hardly conceal her impatience.

"I forgot about it. It was up in my room."

She added, "When the police came up to Harley Street I cut it in two and put it in the bag with my leather work."

Henrietta said, "That was clever of you."

Gerda said, "I'm not quite so stupid as everybody thinks."

She put her hand up to her throat. She said, "John—*John*—" Her voice broke.

Henrietta said, "I know, my dear, I know."

Gerda said, "But you can't know . . . John wasn't—he wasn't—" She stood there, dumb and strangely pathetic. She raised her eyes suddenly to Henrietta's face. "It was all a lie—everything! All the things I thought he was! I saw his face when he followed that woman out that evening. Veronica Cray! I knew he'd cared for her, of course, years ago, before he married me, but I thought it was all over."

Henrietta said gently:

"But it *was* all over."

Gerda shook her head.

"No. She came there and pretended that she hadn't seen John for years —but I saw John's face . . . He went out with her. I went up to bed. I lay there trying to read—I tried to read that detective story that John was reading. And John didn't come. And at last I went out . . ."

Her eyes seemed to be turning inwards seeing the scene.

"It was moonlight. I went along the path to the swimming pool. There was a light in the pavilion. They were *there*—John and that woman . . ."

Henrietta made a faint sound.

Gerda's face had changed—it had none of its usual slightly vacant amiability. It was remorseless, implacable.

"I'd trusted John. I'd believed in him—as though he were God. I thought he was the noblest man in the world—I thought he was everything that was fine and noble . . . And it was all a *lie!* I was left with nothing—nothing at all. I—I'd *worshipped* John!"

Henrietta was gazing at her fascinated. For here, before her eyes, was what she had guessed at and brought to life, carving it out of wood. Here was The Worshipper—blind devotion thrown back on itself, disillusioned —dangerous. . . .

Gerda said, "I couldn't bear it! I had to kill him! I *had* to—you do see that, Henrietta?"

She said it quite conversationally, in an almost friendly tone.

"And I knew I must be careful because the police are very clever. But then I'm not really as stupid as people think! If you're very slow and just stare, people think you don't take things in—and sometimes, underneath, you're laughing at them! I knew I could kill John and nobody would know because I'd read in that detective story about the police being able to tell which gun a bullet has been fired from. Sir Henry had shown me how to load and fire a revolver that afternoon. I'd take *two* revolvers. I'd shoot John with one and then hide it and let people find me holding the other and first they'd think *I'd* shot him and then they'd find he couldn't have been killed with that revolver and so they'd say I hadn't done it after all!"

She nodded her head triumphantly.

"But I forgot about the leather thing. It was in the drawer in my bedroom. What do you call it, a holster? Surely the police won't bother about that *now?*"

"They might," said Henrietta. "You'd better give it to me, and I'll take it away with me. Once it's out of your hands, you're quite safe."

She sat down. She felt suddenly unutterably weary.

Gerda said, "You don't look well. I was just making tea."

She went out of the room. Presently she came back with a tray. On it was a teapot, milk jug and two cups. The milk jug had slopped over because it was overfull. Gerda put the tray down and poured out a cup of tea and handed it to Henrietta.

"Oh, dear," she said, dismayed, "I don't believe the kettle can have been boiling."

"It's quite all right," said Henrietta. "Go and get that holster, Gerda."

Gerda hesitated and then went out of the room. Henrietta leant forward and put her arms on the table and her head down on them. She was so tired, so dreadfully tired . . . But it was nearly done now. Gerda would be safe . . . as John had wanted her to be safe.

She sat up, pushed the hair off her forehead and drew the teacup towards her. Then at a sound in the doorway she looked up. Gerda had been quite quick for once.

But it was Hercule Poirot who stood in the doorway.

"The front door was open," he remarked as he advanced to the table, "so I took the liberty of walking in."

"You!" said Henrietta. "How did you get here?"

"When you left The Hollow so suddenly, naturally I knew where you would go. I hired a very fast car and came straight here."

"I see." Henrietta sighed. "You would."

"You should not drink that tea," said Poirot, taking the cup from her and replacing it on the tray. "Tea that has not been made with boiling water is not good to drink."

"Does a little thing like boiling water really matter?"

Poirot said gently, "Everything matters."

There was a sound behind him and Gerda came into the room. She had a workbag in her hands. Her eyes went from Poirot's face to Henrietta's.

Henrietta said quickly:

"I'm afraid, Gerda, I'm rather a suspicious character. M. Poirot seems to have been shadowing me. He thinks that I killed John—but he can't prove it."

She spoke slowly and deliberately. So long as Gerda did not give herself away—

Gerda said vaguely, "I'm so sorry. Will you have some tea, M. Poirot?"

"No, thank you, Madame."

Gerda sat down behind the tray. She began to talk in her apologetic conversational way.

"I'm so sorry that everybody is out. My sister and the children have all gone for a picnic. I didn't feel very well, so they left me behind."

"I am sorry, Madame."

Gerda lifted a teacup and drank.

"It is all so very worrying. Everything is so worrying. . . . You see, John always arranged *everything* and now John is gone . . ." Her voice tailed off. "Now John is gone . . ."

Her gaze, piteous, bewildered, went from one to the other.

"I don't know what to do without John. John looked after me . . . He took care of me. Now he is gone, everything is gone . . . And the children —they ask me questions and I can't answer them properly. I don't know what to say to Terry. He keeps saying, 'Why was Father killed?' Some day, of course, he will find out why . . . Terry always has to *know*. What puzzles me is that he always asks *why*, not *who!*"

Gerda leaned back in her chair. Her lips were very blue.

She said stiffly:

"I feel—not very well—if John—John—"

Poirot came round the table to her and eased her sideways down in the chair. Her head dropped forward. He bent and lifted her eyelid. Then he straightened up.

"An easy and comparatively painless death."

Henrietta stared at him.

"Heart? No." Her mind leaped forward. "Something in the tea . . . Something she put there herself. She chose that way out?"

Poirot shook his head gently.

"Oh, no, it was meant for *you*. It was in *your* teacup."

"For *me?*" Henrietta's voice was incredulous. "But I was trying to help her."

"That did not matter. Have you not seen a dog caught in a trap—it sets its teeth into anyone who touches it. She saw only that you knew her secret and so you too must die."

Henrietta said slowly:

"And you made me put the cup back on the tray—you meant—you meant *her*—"

Poirot interrupted her quietly.

"No, no, Mademoiselle. I did not *know* that there was anything in your teacup. I only knew that there *might* be. And when the cup was on the tray it was an even chance if she drank from that or the other—if you call it chance. I say myself that an end such as this is merciful. For her—and for two innocent children . . . ."

He said gently to Henrietta, "You are very tired, are you not?"

She nodded. She asked him, "When did you guess?"

"I do not know exactly. The scene was set; I felt that from the first. But I did not realize for a long time that it was set *by Gerda Christow*—that her attitude was stagy because she was, actually, acting a part. I was puzzled by the simplicity and at the same time the complexity. I recognized fairly soon that it was *your* ingenuity that I was fighting against, and that you were being aided and abetted by your relations as soon as they understood what you wanted done!" He paused and added, "Why did *you* want it done?"

"Because John asked me to! That's what he meant when he said '*Henrietta.*' It was all there in that one word. He was asking me to protect Gerda. You see, he loved Gerda . . . I think he loved Gerda much better than he ever knew he did. Better than Veronica Cray—better than me. Gerda *belonged* to him, and John liked things that belonged to him . . . He knew that if anyone could protect Gerda from the consequences of what she'd done, I could— And he knew that I would do anything he wanted, because I loved him."

"And you started at once," said Poirot grimly.

"Yes, the first thing I could think of was to get the revolver away from her and drop it in the pool. That would obscure the finger-print business. When I discovered later that he had been shot with a different gun, I went out to look for it, and naturally found it at once because I knew just the sort of place Gerda would have put it— I was only a minute or two ahead of Inspector Grange's men."

She paused and then went on:

"I kept it with me in that satchel bag of mine until I could take it up to London. Then I hid it in the studio until I could bring it back, and put it where the police would find it."

"The clay horse," murmured Poirot.

"How did you know? Yes, I put it in a sponge bag and wired the armature round it and then slapped up the clay model round it. After all, the police couldn't very well destroy an artist's masterpiece, could they? What made you know where it was?"

"The fact that you chose to model a horse. The horse of Troy was the unconscious association in your mind. But the finger-prints— How did you manage the finger-prints?"

"An old blind man who sells matches in the street. He didn't know what it was I asked him to hold for a moment while I got some money out!"

Poirot looked at her for a moment.

"*C'est* formidable!" he murmured. "You are one of the best antagonists, Mademoiselle, that I have ever had."

"It's been dreadfully tiring always trying to keep one move ahead of *you!*"

"I know. I began to realize the truth as soon as I saw that the pattern was always designed not to implicate any one person but to implicate *everyone*—other than Gerda Christow. Every indication always pointed *away* from her. You deliberately planted Ygdrasil to catch my attention and bring yourself under suspicion. Lady Angkatell, who knew perfectly what you were doing, amused herself by leading poor Inspector Grange in one direction after another. David, Edward, herself.

"Yes, there is only one thing to do if you want to clear a person from suspicion who is actually guilty. You must suggest guilt elsewhere but never localize it. That is why every clue *looked* promising and then petered out and ended in nothing."

Henrietta looked at the figure huddled pathetically in the chair. She said, "Poor Gerda."

"Is that what you have felt all along?"

"I think so . . . Gerda loved John terribly—but she didn't want to love him for what he was. She built up a pedestal for him and attributed every splendid and noble and unselfish characteristic to him. And if you cast down an idol, *there's nothing left . . .*" She paused and then went on. "But John was something much finer than an idol on a pedestal. He was a real, living, vital human being. He was generous and warm and alive, and he was a great doctor—yes, a *great* doctor! And he's dead, and the world has lost a very great man. And I have lost the only man I shall ever love . . ."

Poirot put his hand gently on her shoulder. He said:

"But you are of those who can live with a sword in their hearts—who can go on and smile—"

Henrietta looked up at him. Her lips twisted into a bitter smile. "That's a little melodramatic, isn't it?"

"It is because I am a foreigner and I like to use fine words."

Henrietta said suddenly:

"You have been very kind to me. . . ."

"That is because I have admired you always very much."

"M. Poirot, what are we going to do? About Gerda, I mean."

Poirot drew the raffia workbag towards him. He turned out its contents, scraps of brown suède and other coloured leathers. There were three fragments of thick, shiny brown leather. Poirot fitted them together.

"The holster. I take this. And poor Madame Christow, she was overwrought, her husband's death was too much for her. It will be brought in that she took her life whilst of unsound mind—"

Henrietta said slowly:

"And no one will ever know what really happened?"

"I think one person will know. Dr. Christow's son. I think that one day he will come to me and ask me for the truth."

"But you won't tell him," cried Henrietta.

"Yes, I shall tell him."

"Oh, *no!*"

"You do not understand. To you it is unbearable that anyone should be hurt. But to some minds there is something more unbearable still—not to *know*. You heard that poor woman just a little while ago say, 'Terry always has to *know*. . . .' To the scientific mind, truth comes first. Truth, however bitter, can be accepted, and woven into a design for living."

Henrietta got up.

"Do you want me here, or had I better go?"

"It would be better if you went, I think."

She nodded. Then she said, more to herself than to him:

"Where shall I go? What shall I do—without John?"

"You are speaking like Gerda Christow. You will know where to go and what to do."

"Shall I? I'm so tired, M. Poirot, so tired. . . ."

He said gently:

"Go, my child. Your place is with the living. I will stay here with the dead . . ."

Chapter XXX

AS SHE DROVE towards London, the two phrases echoed through Henrietta's mind— What shall I do? Where shall I go?

For the last few weeks she had been strung up, excited, never relaxing for a moment. She had had a task to perform—a task laid on her by John. But now that was over—had she failed—or succeeded? One could look at it either way . . . But however one looked at it, the task was over. And she experienced the terrible weariness of the reaction.

Her mind went back to the words she had spoken to Edward that night on the terrace—the night of John's death—the night when she had gone along to the pool and into the pavilion and had deliberately, by the light of a match, drawn Ygdrasil upon the iron table. Purposeful, planning—not yet able to sit down and mourn—mourn for her dead. "I should like," she had said to Edward, "to grieve for John . . ."

But she had not dared to relax then—not dared to let sorrow take command over her . . .

But now she could grieve . . . Now she had all the time there was . . .

She said under her breath, "John . . . John . . ."

Bitterness and black rebellion broke over her . . .

She thought, I wish I'd drunk that cup of tea . . .

Driving the car soothed her, gave her strength for the moment . . . But soon she would be in London. Soon she would put the car in the garage and go along to the empty studio . . . Empty since John would never sit there again bullying her, being angry with her, loving her more than he wanted to love her, telling her eagerly about Ridgeway's Disease—about his triumphs and despairs, about Mrs. Crabtree and St. Christopher's . . .

And suddenly, with a lifting of the dark pall that lay over her mind, she said aloud:

"Of course. That's where I will go. To St. Christopher's . . ."

Lying in her narrow hospital bed, old Mrs. Crabtree peered up at her visitor out of rheumy twinkling eyes.

She was exactly as John had described her, and Henrietta felt a sudden warmth, a lifting of the spirit. This was real—this would last! Here, for a little space, she had found John again . . .

"The pore doctor. Orful, ain't it?" Mrs. Crabtree was saying. There was relish in her voice as well as regret, for Mrs. Crabtree loved life; and sudden deaths, particularly murders or deaths in childbed, were the richest parts of the tapestry of life. "Getting 'imself bumped off like that! Turned my stomach right over it did, when I 'eard. I read all about it in the papers —Sister let me 'ave all she could get 'old of—*reely* nice about it, she was. There was pictures and everythink . . . That swimming pool and all. 'Is wife leaving the inquest, pore thing, and that Lady Angkatell what the swimming pool belonged to! Lots of pictures. Real mystery the 'ole thing, weren't it?"

Henrietta was not repelled by her ghoulish enjoyment. She liked it because she knew that John himself would have liked it. If he had to die he would much prefer old Mrs. Crabtree to get a kick out of it, than to sniff and shed tears.

"All I 'ope is that they catch 'ooever done it and 'ang 'im," continued Mrs. Crabtree vindictively. "They don't 'ave 'angings in public like they used to once—more's the pity. I've always thought I'd like to go to an 'anging . . . And I'd go double quick, if you understand me, to see 'ooever killed the doctor 'anged! Real wicked, 'e must 'ave been. Why, the doctor was one in a thousand! Ever so clever, 'e was! And a nice way with 'im! Got you laughing whether you wanted to or not. The things 'e used to say sometimes! I'd 'ave done anythink for the doctor, I would!"

"Yes," said Henrietta. "He was a very clever man. He was a great man."

"Think the world of 'im in the 'orspital, they do! All them nurses. *And* 'is patients! Always felt you were going to get well when 'e'd been along."

"So you are going to get well," said Henrietta.

The little shrewd eyes clouded for a moment.

"I'm not so sure about that, ducky. I've got that mealy-mouthed young fellow with the spectacles now. Quite different to Dr. Christow. Never a laugh! 'E was a one, Dr. Christow was—always up to 'is jokes! Given me some norful times, 'e 'as, with this treatment of 'is. 'I carn't stand any more of it, doctor,' I'd say to 'im and, 'Yes, you can, Mrs. Crabtree,' 'e'd say to me. 'You're tough, you are. You can take it. Going to make medical 'istory, you and I are.' And 'e'd jolly me along like. Do anythink for the doctor, I would 'ave! Expected a lot of you, 'e did, but you felt you couldn't let 'im down, if you know what I mean."

"I know," said Henrietta.

The little sharp eyes peered at her.

"Excuse me, dearie, you're not the doctor's wife by any chance?"

"No," said Henrietta, "I'm just a friend."

"*I* see," said Mrs. Crabtree.

Henrietta thought that she did see.

"What made you come along if you don't mind me arsking?"

"The doctor used to talk to me a lot about you—and about his new treatment. I wanted to see how you were."

"I'm slipping back—that's what I'm doing."

Henrietta cried:

"But you mustn't slip back! You've *got* to get well."

Mrs. Crabtree grinned.

"*I* don't want to peg out, don't you think it!"

"Well, fight then! Dr. Christow said you were a fighter."

"Did 'e now?" Mrs. Crabtree lay still a minute, then she said slowly:

" 'Ooever shot 'im it's a wicked shame! There aren't many of 'is sort. . . ."

We shall not see his like again . . . the words passed through Henrietta's mind. Mrs. Crabtree was regarding her keenly.

"Keep your pecker up, dearie," she said. She added, " 'E 'ad a nice funeral, I 'ope."

"He had a lovely funeral," said Henrietta obligingly.

"Ar! Wish I could of gorn to it!"

Mrs. Crabtree sighed.

"Be going to me own funeral next, I expect."

"No," cried Henrietta. "You mustn't let go. You said just now that Dr. Christow told you that you and he were going to make medical history. Well, you've got to carry on by yourself. The treatment's just the same. You've got to have the guts for two—you've got to make medical history by yourself—for him."

Mrs. Crabtree looked at her for a moment or two.

"Sounds a bit grand! I'll do my best, ducky. Carn't say more than that."

Henrietta got up and took her hand.

"Good-bye. I'll come and see you again if I may."

"Yes, do. It'll do me good to talk about the doctor a bit." The bawdy twinkle came into her eye again. "Proper man in every kind of way, Dr. Christow."

"Yes," said Henrietta. "He was . . ."

The old woman said:

"Don't fret, ducky—what's gorn's gorn. You can't 'ave it back . . ."

Mrs. Crabtree and Hercule Poirot, Henrietta thought, expressed the same idea in different language.

She drove back to Chelsea, put away the car in the garage and walked slowly to the studio.

Now, she thought, it has come. The moment I have been dreading—the moment when I am alone . . .

Now I can put it off no longer . . . Now grief is here with me.

What had she said to Edward? "I should like to grieve for John . . ."

She dropped down on a chair and pushed back the hair from her face.

Alone—empty—destitute . . .

This awful emptiness.

The tears pricked at her eyes, flowed slowly down her cheeks.

Grief, she thought, grief for John . . .

Oh, John—John. . . .

Remembering—remembering. . . . His voice, sharp with pain:

If I were dead, the first thing you'd do, with the tears streaming down your face, would be to start modelling some damned mourning woman or some figure of grief.

She stirred uneasily . . . Why had that thought come into her head?

Grief. . . . Grief. . . . A veiled figure . . . its outline barely perceptible—its head cowled . . .

Alabaster . . .

She could see the lines of it—tall, elongated . . . its sorrow hidden, revealed only by the long mournful lines of the drapery . . .

Sorrow, emerging from clear transparent alabaster.

If I were dead . . .

And suddenly bitterness came over her full tide!

She thought, *That's what I am!* John was right. I cannot love—I cannot mourn—not with the whole of me . . . It's Midge, it's people like Midge who are the salt of the earth.

Midge and Edward at Ainswick . . .

That was reality—strength—warmth . . .

But I, she thought, am not a whole person. I belong not to myself, but to something outside me. . . .

I cannot grieve for my dead . . .

Instead I must take my grief and make it into a figure of alabaster . . .

"Exhibit N. 58 *Grief,* Alabaster. Miss Henrietta Savernake."

She said under her breath:

"John, forgive me . . . forgive me . . . for what I can't help doing . . ."

MURDER IN RETROSPECT

Chapter I

HERCULE POIROT LOOKED with interest and appreciation at the young woman who was being ushered into the room.

There had been nothing distinctive in the letter she had written. It had been a mere request for an appointment, with no hint of what lay behind that request. It had been brief and businesslike. Only the firmness of the handwriting had indicated that Carla Lemarchant was a young woman.

And now here she was in the flesh—a tall, slender young woman in the early twenties. The kind of young woman that one definitely looked at twice. Her clothes were good: an expensive, well-cut coat and skirt and luxurious furs. Her head was well poised on her shoulders, she had a square brow, a sensitively cut nose and a determined chin. She looked very much alive. It was her aliveness, more than her beauty, that struck the predominant note.

Before her entrance, Hercule Poirot had been feeling old—now he felt rejuvenated, alive—keen!

As he came forward to greet her, he was aware of her dark gray eyes studying him attentively. She was very earnest in that scrutiny.

She sat down and accepted the cigarette that he offered her. After it was lit she sat for a minute or two smoking, still looking at him with that earnest, thoughtful scrutiny.

Poirot said gently, "Yes, it has to be decided, does it not?"

She started. "I beg your pardon?" Her voice was attractive, with a faint, agreeable huskiness in it.

"You are making up your mind—are you not?—whether I am a mere mountebank or the man you need."

She smiled. She said, "Well, yes—something of that kind. You see, M. Poirot, you—you don't look exactly the way I pictured you."

"And I am old, am I not? Older than you imagined?"

"Yes, that too." She hesitated. "I'm being frank, you see. I want—I've got to have—the best."

"Rest assured," said Hercule Poirot, "I *am* the best!"

Carla said, "You're not modest. . . . All the same, I'm inclined to take you at your word."

Poirot said placidly, "One does not, you know, employ merely the muscles. I do not need to bend and measure the footprints and pick up the cigarette ends and examine the bent blades of grass. It is enough for me to sit back in my chair and *think.* It is this"—he tapped his egg-shaped head —"*this,* that functions!"

"I know," said Carla Lemarchant. "That's why I've come to you. I want you, you see, to do something fantastic!"

"That," said Hercule Poirot, "promises well!"

He looked at her in encouragement.

Carla Lemarchant drew a deep breath. "My name," she said, "isn't Carla. It's Caroline. The same as my mother's. I was called after her." She paused. "And though I've always gone by the name of Lemarchant—ever since I can remember almost—that isn't my real name. My real name is Crale."

Hercule Poirot's forehead creased a moment perplexedly. He murmured, "Crale—I seem to remember . . ."

She said, "My father was a painter—rather a well-known painter. Some people say he was a great painter. *I* think he was."

"Amyas Crale?"

"Yes."

She paused, then she went on: "And my mother, Caroline Crale, was tried for murdering him!"

"Aha," said Poirot. "I remember now—but only vaguely. I was abroad at the time. It was a long time ago."

"Sixteen years," said the girl. Her face was very white now and her eyes were two burning lights. "Do you understand? *She was tried and convicted.* . . . She wasn't hanged because they felt that there were extenuating circumstances, so the sentence was commuted to penal servitude for life. But she died only a year after the trial. You see? It's all over—done—finished with."

Poirot said quietly, "And so?"

The girl called Carla Lemarchant pressed her hands together. She spoke slowly and haltingly but with an odd, pointed emphasis:

"You've got to understand—exactly—where I come in. I was five years old at the time it—happened. Too young to know anything about it. I remember my mother and my father, of course, and I remember leaving home suddenly—being taken to the country. I remember the pigs and a nice fat farmer's wife—and everybody being very kind—and I remember, quite clearly, the funny way they used to look at me—everybody—a sort of furtive look. I knew, of course, children do, that there was something wrong—but I didn't know what.

"And then I went on a ship—it was exciting—it went on for days and then I was in Canada and Uncle Simon met me, and I lived in Montreal with him and with Aunt Louise, and when I asked about Mummy and Daddy they said they'd be coming soon. And then—and then I think I forgot—only I sort of knew that they were dead without remembering anyone actually telling me so. Because by that time, you see, I didn't think about them any more. I was very happy, you know. Uncle Simon and Aunt Louise were sweet to me, and I went to school and had a lot of friends, and I'd quite forgotten that I'd ever had another name, not Lemarchant. Aunt Louise, you see, told me that that was my name in Canada and that seemed quite sensible to me at the time—it was just my Canadian name—but as I say I forgot in the end that I'd ever had any other."

She flung up her defiant chin. She said:

"Look at me. You'd say—wouldn't you?—if you met me: 'There goes a girl who's got nothing to worry about!' I'm well off, I've got splendid health, I'm sufficiently good to look at, I can enjoy life. At twenty, there wasn't a girl anywhere I'd have changed places with.

"But already, you know, I'd begun to ask questions. About my own mother and father. Who they were and what they did. I'd have been bound to find out in the end.

"As it was, they told me the truth. When I was twenty-one. They had to then, because for one thing I came into my own money. And then, you see, there was the letter. The letter my mother left for me when she died."

Her expression changed, dimmed. Her eyes were no longer two burning points—they were dark, dim pools. She said, "That's when I learned the truth. That my mother had been convicted of murder. It was—rather horrible."

She paused.

"There's something else I must tell you. I was engaged to be married. They said we must wait—that we couldn't be married until I was twenty-one. When I knew, I understood why."

Poirot stirred and spoke for the first time. He said, "And what was your fiancé's reaction?"

"John? John didn't care. He said it made no difference—not to him. He and I were John and Carla—and the past didn't matter."

She leaned forward.

"We're still engaged. But all the same, you know, it *does* matter. It matters to me. And it matters to John too. . . . It isn't the past that matters to us—it's the future." She clenched her hands. "We want children, you see. We both want children. And we don't want to watch our children growing up and be afraid."

"Do you not realize," Poirot said, "that among everyone's ancestors there has been violence and evil?"

"You don't understand. That's so, of course. But, then, one doesn't usually know about it. We do. It's very near to us. And—sometimes—I've seen John just—look at me. Such a quick glance—just a flash. Supposing we were married and we'd quarreled—and I saw him look at me and—and *wonder?*"

Hercule Poirot said, "How was your father killed?"

Carla's voice came clear and firm: "He was poisoned."

Hercule Poirot said, "I see."

There was a silence.

Then the girl said in a calm, matter-of-fact voice, "Thank goodness you're sensible. You see that it does matter—and what it involves. You don't try to patch it up and trot out consoling phrases."

"I understand very well," said Poirot. "What I do *not* understand is what you want of *me?*"

"I want to marry John!" Carla Lemarchant said simply. "And I mean to marry John! And I want to have at least two girls and two boys. And you're going to make that possible!"

"You mean—you want me to talk to your fiancé? Ah, no, it is idiocy what I say there! It is something quite different that you are suggesting. Tell me what is in your mind."

"Listen, M. Poirot. Get this—and get it clearly. I'm hiring you to investigate a case of murder."

"Do you mean—"

"Yes, I do mean. A case of murder is a case of murder whether it happened yesterday or sixteen years ago."

"But my dear young lady—"

"Wait, M. Poirot. You haven't got it all yet. There's a very important point."

"Yes?"

"My mother was innocent," said Carla Lemarchant.

Hercule Poirot rubbed his nose. He murmured, "Well, naturally—I comprehend that—"

"It isn't sentiment. There's her letter. She left it for me before she died. It was to be given to me when I was twenty-one. She left it for that one reason—that I should be quite sure. That's all that was in it. That she hadn't done it—that she was innocent—that I could be sure of that always."

Hercule Poirot looked thoughtfully at the young, vital face staring so earnestly at him. He said slowly, *"Tout de même—"*

Carla smiled. "No, mother wasn't like that! You're thinking that it might be a lie—a sentimental lie." She leaned forward earnestly: "Listen, M. Poirot, there are some things that children know quite well. I can remember my mother—a patchy remembrance, of course, but I remember quite well the *sort* of person she was. She didn't tell lies—kind lies. If a thing was going to hurt she always told you so. Dentists, or thorns in your finger—all that sort of thing. Truth was a—a natural impulse to her. I wasn't, I don't think, specially fond of her—but I trusted her. I *still* trust her! If she says she didn't kill my father, then she didn't kill him! She wasn't the sort of person who would solemnly write down a lie when she knew she was dying."

Slowly, almost reluctantly, Hercule Poirot bowed his head.

Carla went on: "That's why it's all right for *me* to marry John. *I* know it's all right. *But he doesn't.* He feels that naturally I would think my mother was innocent. It's got to be cleared up, M. Poirot. And *you're* going to do it!"

Hercule Poirot said slowly, "Granted that what you say is true, mademoiselle, sixteen years have gone by!"

Carla Lemarchant said, "Oh, of course it's going to be *difficult!* Nobody but *you* could do it!"

Hercule Poirot's eyes twinkled slightly. "You give me the best butter—hein?" he said.

"I've heard about you," Carla said. "The things you've done. The *way* you have done them. It's psychology that interests you, isn't it? Well, that doesn't change with time. The tangible things are gone—the cigarette end and the footprints and the bent blades of grass. You can't look for those any more. But you can go over all the facts of the case, and perhaps talk to the people who were there at the time—they're all alive still—and then—and then, as you said just now, you can lie back in your chair and *think. And you'll know what really happened.* . . ."

Hercule Poirot rose to his feet. One hand caressed his mustache. He said, "Mademoiselle, I am honored! I will justify your faith in me. I will investigate your case of murder. I will search back into the events of sixteen years ago and I will find out the truth."

Carla got up. Her eyes were shining. But she only said, "Good."

Hercule Poirot shook an eloquent forefinger. "One little moment. I have said I will find out the truth. I do not, you understand, have the bias. I do not accept your assurance of your mother's innocence. If she was guilty—*eh bien,* what then?"

Carla's head went back. "I'm her daughter," she said. "I want the truth!" Hercule Poirot said, *"En avant,* then. Though it is not that, that I should say. On the contrary. *En arrière. . . ."*

"Do I remember the Crale case?" asked Sir Montague Depleach. "Certainly I do. Remember it very well. Most attractive woman. But unbalanced, of course. No self-control." He glanced sideways at Poirot. "What makes you ask me about it?"

"I am interested."

"Not really tactful of you, my dear man," said Depleach, showing his teeth in his sudden famous "wolf's smile," which had been reputed to have such a terrifying effect upon witnesses. "Not one of my successes, you know. I didn't get her off."

"I know that."

Sir Montague shrugged his shoulders. He said:

"Of course, I hadn't quite as much experience then as I have now. All the same, I think I did all that could humanly be done. One can't do much without *co-operation.* We *did* get it commuted to penal servitude. Provocation, you know. Lots of respectable wives and mothers got up a petition. There was a lot of sympathy for her."

He leaned back, stretching out his long legs. His face took on a judicial, appraising look.

"If she'd shot him, you know, or even knifed him—I'd have gone all out for manslaughter. But poison—no, you can't play tricks with that. It's tricky—very tricky."

"What was the defense?" asked Hercule Poirot.

He knew because he had already read the newspaper files but he saw no harm in playing completely ignorant to Sir Montague.

"Oh, suicide. Only thing you *could* go for. But it didn't go down well. Crale simply wasn't that kind of man! You never met him, I suppose? No? Well, he was a great blustering, vivid sort of chap. Great beer drinker. Went in for the lusts of the flesh and enjoyed them. You can't persuade a jury that a man like that is going to sit down and quietly do away with himself. It just doesn't fit. No, I was afraid I was up against a losing proposition from the first. And she wouldn't play up! I knew we'd lost as soon as she went into the box. No fight in her at all. But there it is—if you *don't* put your client into the box, the jury draw their own conclusions."

Poirot said, "Is that what you meant when you said just now that one cannot do much without co-operation?"

"Absolutely, my dear fellow. We're not magicians, you know. Half the battle is the impression the accused makes on the jury. I've known juries time and again bring in verdicts dead against the judge's summing up. ' 'E did it, all right'—that's the point of view. Or '*He* never did a thing like that —don't tell me!' Caroline Crale didn't even *try* to put up a fight."

"Why was that?"

Sir Montague shrugged his shoulders. "Don't ask me. Of course, she was fond of the fellow. Broke her all up when she came to and realized what she'd done. Don't believe she ever rallied from the shock."

"So in your opinion she was guilty?"

Depleach looked rather startled. He said, "Er—well, I thought we were taking that for granted."

"Did she ever admit to you that she was guilty?"

Depleach looked shocked. "Of course not—of course not. We have our code, you know. Innocence is always—er—assumed. If you're so interested it's a pity you can't get hold of old Mayhew. Mayhews were the solicitors who briefed me. Old Mayhew could have told you more than I can. But there—he's joined the great majority. There's young George Mayhew, of course, but he was only a boy at the time. It's a long time ago, you know."

"Yes, I know. It is fortunate for me that you remember so much. You have a remarkable memory."

Depleach looked pleased. He murmured, "Oh, well, one remembers the main headings, you know. Especially when it's a capital charge. And, of course, the Crale case got a lot of publicity from the press. Lot of sex interest and all that. The girl in the case was pretty striking. Hard-boiled piece of goods, I thought."

"You will forgive me if I seem too insistent," said Poirot, "but I repeat once more, you had no doubt of Caroline Crale's guilt?"

Depleach shrugged his shoulders.

"Frankly, as man to man," he said, "I don't think there's much doubt about it. Oh, yes, she did it all right."

"What was the evidence against her?"

"Very damning indeed. First of all, there was motive. She and Crale had led a kind of cat-and-dog life for years—interminable rows. He was always getting mixed up with some woman or other. Couldn't help it. He was that kind of man. She stood it pretty well on the whole. Made allowances for him on the score of temperament—and the man really was a first-class painter, you know. His stuff's gone up enormously in price—enormously. Don't care for that style of painting myself—ugly, forceful stuff, but it's *good*—no doubt of that.

"Well, as I say, there had been trouble about women from time to time. Mrs. Crale wasn't the meek kind who suffers in silence. There were rows all right. But he always came back to her in the end. These affairs of his blew over. But this final affair was rather different. It was a girl, you see—and quite a young girl. She was only twenty.

"Elsa Greer, that was her name. She was the only daughter of some Yorkshire manufacturer. She had money and determination and she knew what she wanted. What she wanted was Amyas Crale. She got him to paint her—he didn't paint regular society portraits, 'Mrs. Blinkety Blank in pink satin and pearls,' but he painted figures. I don't know that most women would have cared to be painted by him—he didn't spare them! But he painted the Greer girl, and he ended by falling for her good and proper. He was getting on for forty, you know, and he'd been married a good many years. He was just ripe for making a fool of himself over some chit of a girl. Elsa Greer was the girl. He was crazy about her and his idea was to get a divorce from his wife and marry Elsa.

"Caroline Crale wasn't standing for that. She threatened him. She was overheard by two people to say that if he didn't give the girl up she'd kill him. And she meant it all right! The day before it happened, they'd been having tea with a neighbor. He was by way of dabbling in herbs and home-brewed medicines. Among his patent brews was one of coniine—spotted hemlock. There was some talk about it and its deadly properties.

"The next day he noticed that half the contents of the bottle were gone. Got the wind up about it. They found an almost empty bottle of it in Mrs. Crale's room, hidden away at the bottom of a drawer."

Hercule Poirot moved uncomfortably. He said, "Somebody else might have put it there."

"Oh, she admitted it to the police. Very unwise, of course, but she didn't have a solicitor to advise her at that stage. When they asked her about it, she admitted quite frankly that she had taken it."

"For what reason?"

"She made out that she'd taken it with the idea of doing herself in. She couldn't explain how the bottle came to be empty—nor how it was that there were only her fingerprints on it. That part of it was pretty damning. She contended, you see, that Amyas Crale had committed suicide. But if he'd taken the coniine from the bottle she'd hidden in her room, *his* fingerprints would have been on the bottle as well as hers."

"It was given him in beer, was it not?"

"Yes. She got out the bottle from the refrigerator and took it down herself to where he was painting in the garden. She poured it out and gave it to him and watched him drink it. Everyone went up to lunch and left him—he often didn't come in to meals. Afterward she and the governess found him there dead. Her story was that the beer *she* gave him was all right. Our theory was that he suddenly felt so worried and remorseful that he slipped the poison in himself. All poppycock—he wasn't that kind of man! And the fingerprint evidence was the most damning of all."

"They found her fingerprints on the beer bottle?"

"No, they didn't—they found only *his*—and they were phony ones. She was alone with the body, you see, while the governess went to call up a doctor. And what she must have done was to wipe the bottle and glass and then press his fingers on them. She wanted to pretend, you see, that she'd never even handled the stuff. Well, that didn't work. Old Rudolph, who was prosecuting, had a lot of fun with that—proved quite definitely by demonstration in court that a man *couldn't* hold a bottle with his fingers in that position! Of course *we* did our best to prove that he *could*—that his hands would take up a contorted attitude when he was dying—but frankly our stuff wasn't very convincing."

"The coniine in the beer bottle," Poirot said, "must have been put there before she took it down to the garden."

"There was no coniine in the bottle at all. Only in the glass."

Depleach paused—his large, handsome face suddenly altered—he turned his head sharply.

"Hullo," he said, "Now then, Poirot, *what are you driving at?*"

Poirot said, *"If* Caroline Crale was innocent, how did that coniine get into the beer? The defense said at the time that Amyas Crale himself put it there. But you say to me that that was in the highest degree unlikely—and for my part I agree with you. He was not that kind of man. Then, if Caroline Crale did not do it, *someone else did."*

Depleach said with almost a splutter, "Oh, damn it all, man, you can't flog a dead horse. It's all over and done with years ago. Of course she did it. You'd know that well enough if you'd seen her at the time. It was written all over her! I even fancy that the verdict was a relief to her. She wasn't frightened. No nerves at all. Just wanted to get through the trial and have it over. A very brave woman, really. . . ."

"And yet," said Hercule Poirot, "when she died she left a letter to be given to her daughter in which she swore solemnly that she was innocent. Now her daughter wants the truth."

"H'm—I'm afraid she'll find the truth unpalatable. Honestly, Poirot, I don't think there's any doubt about it. She killed him."

"You will forgive me, my friend, but I must satisfy myself on that point."

"Well, I don't know what more you can do. You can read up the newspaper accounts of the trial. Humphrey Rudolph appeared for the Crown. He's dead—let me see, who was his junior? Young Fogg, I think. Yes, Fogg. You can have a chat with him. And then there are the people who were there at the time. Don't suppose they'll enjoy your butting in and raking the whole thing up, but I dare say you'll get what you want out of them. You're a plausible devil."

"Ah, yes, the people concerned. That is very important. You remember, perhaps, who they were?"

Depleach considered: "Let me see—it's a long time ago. There were only five people who were really in it, so to speak—I'm not counting the servants—a couple of faithful old things, scared-looking creatures—they didn't know anything about anything. No one could suspect them."

"There are five people, you say. Tell me about them."

"Well, there was Philip Blake. He was Crale's greatest friend—had known him all his life. He was staying in the house at the time. *He's* alive. I see him now and again on the links. Lives at St. George's Hill. Stockbroker. Plays the markets and gets away with it. Successful man, running to fat a bit."

"Yes. And who next?"

"Then there was Blake's elder brother. Country squire—stay-at-home sort of chap."

A jingle ran through Poirot's head. He repressed it. He must *not* always be thinking of nursery rhymes. It seemed an obsession with him lately. And yet the jingle persisted:

"This little pig went to market, this little pig stayed at home . . ."

He murmured, "He stayed at home—yes?"

"He's the fellow I was telling you about—messed about with drugs—and herbs—bit of a chemist. His hobby. What was his name now? Literary sort of name—I've got it. Meredith. Meredith Blake. Don't know whether he's alive or not."

"And who next?"

"Next? Well, there's the cause of all the trouble. The girl in the case: Elsa Greer."

"This little pig ate roast beef," murmured Poirot.

Depleach stared at him. "They've fed her meat all right," he said. "She's been a go-getter. She's had three husbands since then. In and out of the divorce court as easy as you please. And every time she makes a change, it's for the better. Lady Dittisham—that's who she is now. Open any *Tatler* and you're sure to find her."

"And the other two?"

"There was the governess woman. I don't remember her name. Nice, capable woman. Thompson—Jones—something like that. And there was the child. Caroline Crale's half sister. She must have been about fifteen. She's made rather a name for herself. Digs up things and goes trekking to the back of beyond. Warren—that's her name. Angela Warren. Rather an alarming young woman nowadays. I met her the other day."

"She is not, then, the little pig who cried 'wee-wee-wee' . . . ?"

Sir Montague Depleach looked at him rather oddly. He said dryly, "She's had something to cry wee-wee about in her life! She's disfigured, you know. Got a bad scar down one side of her face. She—oh, well, you'll hear all about it, I dare say."

Poirot stood up. He said, "I thank you. You have been very kind. If Mrs. Crale did *not* kill her husband—"

Depleach interrupted him: "But she did, old boy, she did. Take my word for it."

Poirot continued without taking any notice of the interruption: "Then it seems logical to suppose that one of these five people must have done so."

"One of them *could* have done it, I suppose," said Depleach doubtfully. "But I don't see why any of them *should*. No reason at all! In fact, I'm quite sure none of them *did* do it. Do get this bee out of your bonnet, old boy!"

But Hercule Poirot only smiled and shook his head.

"Guilty as hell," said Mr. Fogg succinctly.

Hercule Poirot looked meditatively at the thin, clearcut face of the barrister.

Quentin Fogg, K.C., was a very different type from Montague Depleach. Depleach had force, magnetism, an overbearing and slightly bullying personality. He got his effects by a rapid and dramatic change of manner. Handsome, urbane, charming, one minute—then an almost magical transformation, lips back, snarling smile—out for your blood.

Quentin Fogg was thin, pale, singularly lacking in what is called personality. His questions were quiet and unemotional, but they were steadily persistent.

Hercule Poirot eyed him meditatively. "So that," he said, "was how it struck you?"

Fogg nodded. He said, "You should have seen her in the box. Old Humpie Rudolph (he was leading, you know) simply made mincemeat of her. Mincemeat!" He paused and then said unexpectedly, "On the whole, you know, it was rather too much of a good thing."

"I am not sure," said Hercule Poirot, "that I quite understand you."

Fogg drew his delicately marked brows together. His sensitive hand stroked his bare upper lip. "How shall I put it?" he said. "It's a very English point of view. 'Shooting the sitting bird' describes it best. Is that intelligible to you?"

"It is, as you say, a very English point of view, but I think I understand you. In the Assize Court, as on the playing fields of Eton, and in the hunting country, the Englishman likes the victim to have a sporting chance."

"That's it, exactly. Well, in this case, the accused *didn't* have a chance. Humpie Rudolph did as he liked with her. It started with her examination by Depleach. She stood up there, you know—as docile as a little girl at a party, answering Depleach's questions with the answers she'd learned off by heart. Quite docile, word-perfect—and absolutely unconvincing! She'd been told what to say, and she said it. It wasn't Depleach's fault. That old mountebank played his part perfectly—but in any scene that needs two actors, one alone can't carry it. She didn't play up to him. It made the worst possible effect on the jury. And then old Humpie got up. I expect you've seen him? He's a great loss. Hitching his gown up, swaying back on his feet, and then—straight off the mark!

"As I tell you, he made mincemeat of her! Led up to this and that—and she fell into the pitfall every time. He got her to admit the absurdities of her own statements, he got her to contradict herself, she floundered in deeper and deeper. And then he wound up with his usual stuff. Very compelling—very convinced: 'I suggest to you, Mrs. Crale, that this story of yours about stealing coniine in order to commit suicide is a tissue of falsehood. I suggest that you took it in order to administer it to your husband, who was about to leave you for another woman, and that you *did* deliberately administer it to him.' And she looked at him—such a pretty creature, graceful, delicate—and she said, 'Oh, no—no, I didn't.' It was the flattest thing you ever heard, the most unconvincing. I saw old Depleach squirm in his seat. He knew it was all up then."

Fogg paused a minute, then he went on: "The jury were only out just over half an hour. They brought her in: Guilty with a recommendation to mercy.

"Actually, you know, she made a good contrast to the other woman in the case. The girl. The jury were unsympathetic to *her* from the start. She never turned a hair. Very good-looking, hard-boiled, modern. To the women in the court she stood for a type—type of the home breaker. Homes weren't safe when girls like that were wandering abroad. Girls full of sex and contemptuous of the rights of wives and mothers. She didn't spare herself, I will say. She was honest. Admirably honest. She'd fallen in love with Amyas Crale and he with her and she'd no scruples at all about taking him away from his wife and child.

"I admired her in a way. She had guts. Depleach put in some nasty stuff in cross-examination and she stood up well to it. But the court was unsympathetic. And the judge didn't like her. Old Avis, it was. Been a bit of a rip himself when young—but he's very hot on morality when he's presiding in his robes. His summing up against Caroline Crale was mildness itself. He couldn't deny the facts but he threw out pretty strong hints as to provocation and all that."

Hercule Poirot asked, "He did not support the suicide theory of the defense?"

Fogg shook his head. *"That* never really had a leg to stand upon. Mind you, I don't say Depleach didn't do his best with it. He was magnificent. He painted a most moving picture of a greathearted, pleasure-loving, temperamental man, suddenly overtaken by a passion for a lovely young girl, conscience-stricken, yet unable to resist. Then his recoil, his disgust with himself, his remorse for the way he was treating his wife and child and his sudden decision to end it all! The honorable way out.

"I can tell you, it was a most moving performance; Depleach's voice brought tears to your eyes. You saw the poor wretch torn by his passions and his essential decency. The effect was terrific. Only—when it was all over—and the spell was broken, you couldn't quite square that mythical figure with Amyas Crale.

"Everybody knew too much about Crale. He wasn't at all that kind of man. And Depleach hadn't been able to get hold of any evidence to show that he was. I should say Crale came as near as possible to being a man without even a rudimentary conscience. He was a ruthless, selfish, good-tempered, happy egoist. Any ethics he had would have applied to painting. He wouldn't, I'm convinced, have painted a sloppy, bad picture—no matter what the inducement. But for the rest, he was a full-blooded man and he loved life—he had a zest for it. Suicide? Not he!"

"Not, perhaps, a very good defense to have chosen?"

Fogg shrugged his thin shoulders. "What else was there?" he said. "Couldn't sit back and plead that there was no case for the jury—that the prosecution had got to prove their case against the accused. There was a great deal too much proof. She'd handled the poison—admitted pinching it, in fact. There were means, motive, opportunity—everything."

"One might have attempted to show that these things were artificially arranged?"

Fogg said bluntly, "She admitted most of them. And in any case, it's too farfetched. You're implying, I presume, that somebody else murdered him and fixed it up to look as though she had done it."

"You think that quite untenable?"

"I'm afraid I do," Fogg said slowly. "You're suggesting the mysterious X. Where do we look for him?"

Poirot said, "Obviously in a close circle. There were five people—were there not?—who *could* have been concerned."

"Five? Let me see. There was the old duffer who messed about with his herb brewing. A dangerous hobby—but an amiable creature. Vague sort of person. Don't see him as X. There was the girl—she might have polished off Caroline, but certainly not Amyas. Then there was the stockbroker—Crale's best friend. That's popular in detective stories, but I don't believe in it in real life. There's no one else—oh, yes, the kid sister, but one doesn't seriously consider her. That's four."

Hercule Poirot said, "You forget the governess."

"Yes, that's true. Wretched people, governesses, one never does remember them. I do remember her dimly though: Middle-aged, plain, competent. I suppose a psychologist would say that she had a guilty passion for Crale and therefore killed him. The repressed spinster! It's no good—I just don't believe it. As far as my dim remembrance goes she wasn't the neurotic type."

"It is a long time ago."

"Fifteen or sixteen years, I suppose. Yes, quite that. You can't expect my memories of the case to be very acute."

Hercule Poirot said, "But on the contrary, you remember it amazingly well. That astounds me. You can see it, can you not? When you talk, the picture is there before your eyes."

"Yes, you're right," Fogg said slowly. "I do see it—quite plainly."

Poirot said, "It would interest me very much if you would tell me *why?*"

"Why?" Fogg considered the question. His thin, intellectual face was alert and interested, "Yes, now *why?*"

Poirot asked, *"What* do you see so plainly? The witnesses? The counsel? The judge? The accused standing in the dock?"

Fogg said quietly: "That's the reason, of course! You've put your finger on it. I shall always see *her.* . . . Funny thing, romance. She had the quality of it. I don't know if she was really beautiful. . . . She wasn't very young—tired-looking—circles under her eyes. But it all centered round her. The interest, the drama. And yet, half the time, *she wasn't there.* She'd gone away somewhere, quite far away—just left her body there, quiescent, attentive, with the little polite smile on her lips. She was all half tones—you know, lights and shades. And yet, with it all, she was more alive than the other—that girl with the perfect body, and the beautiful face, and the crude young strength.

"I admired Elsa Greer because she had guts, because she could fight, because she stood up to her tormentors and never quailed! But I admired Caroline Crale because she didn't fight, because she retreated into her world of halflights and shadows. She was never defeated because she never gave battle."

He paused. "I'm only sure of one thing. She loved the man she killed. Loved him so much that half of her died with him. . . ."

Mr. Fogg, K.C., paused again and polished his glasses. "Dear me," he said. "I seem to be saying some very strange things! I was quite a young man at the time, you know. Just an ambitious youngster. These things make an impression. But all the same I'm sure that Caroline Crale was a very remarkable woman. I shall never forget her. No—I shall never forget her. . . ."

George Mayhew was cautious and noncommittal. He remembered the case, of course, but not at all clearly. His father had been in charge of the case—he himself had been only nineteen at the time.

Yes, the case had made a great stir. Because of Crale's being such a well-known man. His pictures were very fine—very fine indeed. Two of them were in the Tate. Not that *that* meant anything.

M. Poirot would excuse him, but he didn't see quite what M. Poirot's interest was in the matter—Oh, the *daughter!* Really? Indeed? Canada? He had always heard it was New Zealand.

George Mayhew became less rigid. He unbent.

A shocking thing in a girl's life. He had the deepest sympathy for her. Really it would have been better if she had never learned the truth. Still, it was no use saying that *now.*

She wanted to know? Yes, but what *was* there to know? There were the reports of the trial, of course. He himself didn't really know anything.

No, he was afraid there wasn't much doubt as to Mrs. Crale's being guilty. There was a certain amount of excuse for her. These artists—difficult people to live with. With Crale, he understood, it had always been some woman or other.

And she herself had probably been the possessive type of woman. Unable to accept facts. Nowadays she'd simply have divorced him and got over it. He added cautiously: "Let me see—er—Lady Dittisham, I believe, was the girl in the case."

Poirot said he believed that that was so.

"The newspapers bring it up from time to time," said Mayhew. "She's been in the divorce court a good deal. She's a very rich woman, as I expect you know. She was married to that explorer fellow before Dittisham. She's always more or less in the public eye. The kind of woman who likes notoriety, I should imagine."

"Or possibly a hero worshiper," suggested Poirot.

The idea was upsetting to George Mayhew. He accepted it dubiously: "Well, possibly—yes, I suppose that might be so."

Poirot said, "Had your firm acted for Mrs. Crale for a long period of years?"

George Mayhew shook his head: "On the contrary. Johnathan and Johnathan were the Crale solicitors. Under the circumstances, however,

Mr. Johnathan felt that he could not very well act for Mrs. Crale and he arranged with us—with my father—to take over her case. You would do well, I think, M. Poirot, to arrange a meeting with old Mr. Johnathan. He has retired from active work—he is over seventy—but he knew the Crale family intimately, and he could tell you far more than I can. Indeed, I myself can tell you nothing at all. I was a boy at the time. I don't think I was even in court."

Poirot rose and George Mayhew, rising too, added: "You might like to have a word with Edmunds, our managing clerk. He was with the firm then and took a great interest in the case."

Chapter II

EDMUNDS WAS A man of slow speech. His eyes gleamed with legal caution. He took his time in sizing up Poirot before he let himself be betrayed into speech. He said, "Aye, I mind the Crale case." He added severely, "It was a disgraceful business."

His shrewd eyes rested appraisingly on Hercule Poirot. He said, "It's a long time since to be raking things up again."

"A court verdict is not always an ending."

Edmunds' square head nodded slowly. "I'd not say that you weren't in the right of it there."

Hercule Poirot went on: "Mrs. Crale left a daughter."

"Aye, I mind there was a child. Sent abroad to relatives, was she not?"

"That daughter believes firmly in her mother's innocence."

The bushy eyebrows of Mr. Edmunds rose. "That's the way of it, is it?"

Poirot asked, "Is there anything you can tell me to support that belief?"

Edmunds reflected. Then, slowly, he shook his head.

"I could not conscientiously say there was. I admired Mrs. Crale. Whatever else she was, she was a lady! Not like the other. A hussy—no more, no less. Bold as brass! Jumped-up trash—that's what *she* was—and showed it! Mrs. Crale was quality."

"But none the less a murderess?"

Edmunds frowned. He said, with more spontaneity than he had yet shown, "That's what I used to ask myself, day after day. Sitting there in the dock so calm and gentle. 'I'll not believe it,' I used to say to myself. But, if you take my meaning, Mr. Poirot, there wasn't anything else to believe. That hemlock didn't get into Mr. Crale's beer by accident. It was put there. And if Mrs. Crale didn't put it there, who did?"

"That is the question," said Poirot. "Who did?"

Again those shrewd old eyes searched his face.

"So that's your idea?" said Mr. Edmunds.

"What do you think yourself?"

There was a pause before the other answered. Then he said, "There was nothing that pointed that way—nothing at all."

Poirot said, "You were in court during the hearing of the case?"

"Every day."

"You heard the witnesses give evidence?"

"I did."

"Did anything strike you about them—any abnormality, and insincerity?"

"Was one of them lying, do you mean?" Edmunds said bluntly. "Had one of them a reason to wish Mr. Crale dead? If you'll excuse me, Mr. Poirot, that's a very *melodramatic* idea."

"At least consider it," Poirot urged.

He watched the shrewd face, the screwed-up, thoughtful eyes. Slowly, regretfully, Edmunds shook his head.

"That Miss Greer," he said, "she was bitter enough, *and* vindictive! I'd say she overstepped the mark in a good deal she said, but it was Mr. Crale alive she wanted. He was no use to her dead. She wanted Mrs. Crale hanged all right—but that was because death had snatched her man away from her. Like a balked tigress she was! But, as I say, it was Mr. Crale alive she'd wanted. Mr. Philip Blake, *he* was against Mrs. Crale too. Prejudiced. Got his knife into her whenever he could. But I'd say he was honest according to his lights. He'd been Mr. Crale's great friend. His brother, Mr. Meredith Blake, a bad witness he was—vague, hesitating, never seemed sure of his answers."

"I've seen many witnesses like that. Look as though they're lying when all the time they're telling the truth. Didn't want to say anything more than he could help, Mr. Meredith Blake didn't. Counsel got all the more out of him on that account. One of those quiet gentlemen who get easily flustered. The governess now, she stood up well to them. Didn't waste words and answered pat and to the point. You couldn't have told, listening to her, which side she was on. Got all her wits about her, she had. The brisk kind." He paused. "Knew a lot more than she ever let on about the whole thing, I shouldn't wonder."

"I, too, should not wonder," said Hercule Poirot.

He looked sharply at the wrinkled, shrewd face of Mr. Alfred Edmunds. It was quite bland and impassive. But Hercule Poirot wondered if he had been vouchsafed a hint.

Mr. Caleb Johnathan lived in Essex. After a courteous exchange of letters, Hercule Poirot received an invitation, almost royal in its character, to dine and sleep. The old gentleman was decidedly a character. After the insipidity of young George Mayhew, Mr. Johnathan was like a glass of his own vintage port.

He had his own methods of approach to a subject, and it was not until well on toward midnight, when sipping a glass of fragrant old brandy, that Mr. Johnathan really unbent. In Oriental fashion he had appreciated Hercule Poirot's courteous refusal to rush him in any way. Now, in his own good time, he was willing to elaborate the theme of the Crale family:

"Our firm, of course, has known many generations of the Crales. I knew Amyas Crale and his father, Richard Crale, and I can remember Enoch Crale—the grandfather. Country squires, all of them, thought more of horses than human beings. They rode straight, liked women, and had no truck with ideas. They distrusted ideas. But Richard Crale's wife was cram full of ideas—more ideas than sense. She was poetical and musical—she played the harp, you know. She enjoyed poor health and looked very picturesque on her sofa. She was an admirer of Kingsley. That's why she called her son Amyas. His father scoffed at the name—but he gave in.

"Amyas Crale profited by this mixed inheritance. He got his artistic trend from his weakly mother, and his driving power and ruthless egoism from his father. All the Crales were egoists. They never by any chance saw any point of view but their own."

Tapping with a delicate finger on the arm of his chair, the old man shot a shrewd glance at Poirot. "Correct me if I am wrong, M. Poirot, but I think you are interested in—character, shall we say?"

"That, to me," Poirot replied, "is the principal interest of all my cases."

"I can conceive of it. To get under the skin, as it were, of your criminal. How interesting! How absorbing! Our firm, of course, has never had a criminal practice. We should not have been competent to act for Mrs. Crale, even if taste had allowed. Mayhews, however, were a very adequate firm. They briefed Depleach—they didn't perhaps show much imagination there—still, he was very expensive, and, of course, exceedingly dramatic! What they hadn't the wits to see was that Caroline would never play up in the way he wanted her to. She wasn't a very dramatic woman."

"What was she?" asked Poirot. "It is that that I am chiefly anxious to know."

"Yes, yes—of course. How did she come to do what she did? That is the really vital question. I knew her, you know, before she married. Caroline Spalding, she was. A turbulent, unhappy creature. Very alive. Her mother was left a widow early in life and Caroline was devoted to her mother. Then the mother married again—there was another child. Yes—yes, very sad, very painful. These young, ardent, adolescent jealousies."

"She was jealous?"

"Passionately so. There was a regrettable incident. Poor child, she blamed herself bitterly afterward. But you know, M. Poirot, these things happen. There is an inability to put on the brakes. It comes—it comes with maturity."

"But what really happened?" asked Poirot.

"She struck the child—the baby—flung a paperweight at her. The child lost the sight of one eye and was permanently disfigured."

Mr. Johnathan sighed. He said, "You can imagine the effect a simple question on that point had at the trial." He shook his head. "It gave the impression that Caroline Crale was a woman of ungovernable temper. That was not true. No, that was not true."

He paused and then resumed:

"Caroline Spalding came often to stay at Alderbury. She rode well, and was keen. Richard Crale was fond of her. She waited on Mrs. Crale and was deft and gentle—Mrs. Crale also liked her. The girl was not happy at home. She was happy at Alderbury. Diana Crale, Amyas' sister and she were by way of being friends. Philip and Meredith Blake, boys from the adjoining estate, were frequently at Alderbury. Philip was always a nasty, money-grubbing little brute. I must confess I have always had a distaste for him. But I am told that he tells a very good story and that he has the reputation of being a stanch friend.

"Meredith was what my contemporaries used to call namby-pamby. Liked botany and butterflies and observing birds and beasts. Nature study, they call it nowadays. Ah, dear—all the young people were a disappointment to their parents. None of them ran true to type—huntin', shootin', fishin'. Meredith preferred watching birds and animals to shootin' or huntin' them. Philip definitely preferred town to country and went into the business of money-making. Diana married a fellow who wasn't a gentleman—one of the temporary officers in the war. And Amyas, strong, handsome, virile Amyas, blossomed into being a painter, of all things in the world. It's my opinion that Richard Crale died of the shock.

"And in due course Amyas married Caroline Spalding. They'd always fought and sparred, but it was a love match all right. They were both crazy about each other. And they continued to care. But Amyas was like all the Crales, a ruthless egoist. He loved Caroline but he never once considered her in any way. He did as he pleased. It's my opinion that he was as fond of her as he could be of anybody—but she came a long way behind his art. That came first. And I should say at no time did his art give place to a woman.

"He had affairs with women—they stimulated him—but he left them high and dry when he'd finished with them. He wasn't a sentimental man, nor a romantic one. And he wasn't entirely a sensualist, either. The only woman he cared a button for was his own wife. And because she knew that, she put up with a lot. He was a very fine painter, you know. She realized that, and respected it. He chased off on his amorous pursuits and came back again—usually with a picture to show for it.

"It might have gone on like that if it hadn't come to Elsa Greer. Elsa Greer—"

Mr. Johnathan shook his head.

Poirot said, "What of Elsa Greer?"

"She was, I believe, a crude young woman—with a crude outlook on life. Not, I think, an interesting character. *Rose-white youth, passionate, pale,* etc. Take that away and what remains? Only a somewhat mediocre young woman seeking for another life-sized hero to put on an empty pedestal."

Poirot said, "If Amyas Crale had not been a famous painter—"

Mr. Johnathan agreed quickly:

"Quite—quite. You have taken the point admirably. The Elsas of this world are hero worshipers. A man must have *done* something, must *be* somebody. . . . Caroline Crale, now, could have recognized quality in a bank clerk or an insurance agent! Caroline loved Amyas Crale the man, not Amyas Crale the painter. Caroline Crale was not crude—Elsa Greer was." He added, "But she was young and beautiful and to my mind infinitely pathetic."

Ex-superintendent Hale pulled thoughtfully at his pipe. He said, "This is a funny fancy of yours, M. Poirot."

"It is, perhaps, a little unusual," Poirot agreed cautiously.

"You see," said Hale, "it's all such a long time ago."

Hercule Poirot foresaw that he was going to get a little tired of that particular phrase. He said mildly, "That adds to the difficulty, of course."

"Raking up the past," mused the other. "If there were an *object* in it, now . . ."

"There is an object."

"What is it?"

"One can enjoy the pursuit of truth for its own sake. I do. And you must not forget the young lady."

Hale nodded.

"Yes, I see *her* side of it. But—you'll excuse me, M. Poirot—you're an ingenious man. You could cook her up a tale."

Poirot replied, "You do not know the young lady."

"Oh, come now—a man of your experience!"

Poirot drew himself up. "I may be, *mon cher,* an artistic and competent liar—you seem to think so. But it is not my idea of ethical conduct. I have my standards."

"Sorry, M. Poirot. I didn't mean to hurt your feelings. But it would be all in a good cause, so to speak."

"Oh, I wonder, would it really?"

Hale said slowly:

"It's tough luck on a happy, innocent girl who's just going to get married to find that her mother was a murderess. If I were you I'd go to her and say that, after all, suicide was what it was. Say the case was mishandled by Depleach. Say that there's no doubt in *your* mind that Crale killed himself."

"But there is every doubt in my mind! I do not believe for one minute that Crale killed himself. Do you consider it even reasonably possible yourself?"

Slowly Hale shook his head.

"You see? No, it is the truth I must have—not a plausible or not very plausible lie."

Hale turned and looked at Poirot. He said, "You talk about the *truth*. I'd like to make it plain to you that we think we *got* the truth in the Crale case."

"That pronouncement from you means a great deal," Poirot said quickly. "I know you for what you are—an honest and capable man. Now tell me this, was there no doubt at any time in your mind as to the guilt of Mrs. Crale?"

The superintendent's answer came promptly: "No doubt at all, M. Poirot. The circumstances pointed to her straight away and every single fact that we uncovered supported that view."

"You can give me an outline of the evidence against her?"

"I can. When I received your letter I looked up the case." He picked up a small notebook. "I've jotted down all the salient facts here."

"Thank you, my friend. I am all eagerness to hear."

Hale cleared his throat. A slight official intonation made itself heard in his voice. He said:

"At two-forty-five on the afternoon of September 18th, Inspector Conway was rung up by Dr. Andrew Faussett. Dr. Faussett stated that Mr. Amyas Crale of Alderbury had died suddenly and that in consequence of the circumstances of that death and also of a statement made to him by a Mr. Blake, a guest staying in the house, he considered that it was a case for the police.

"Inspector Conway, in company with a sergeant and the police surgeon, came over to Alderbury straight away. Dr. Faussett was there and took him to where the body of Mr. Crale had not been disturbed.

"Mr. Crale had been painting in a small enclosed garden, known as the Battery Garden, from the fact that it overlooked the sea, and had some miniature cannon placed in embattlements. It was situated at about four minutes' walk from the house. Mr. Crale had not come up to the house for lunch, as he wanted to get certain effects of light on the stone—and the sun would have been wrong for this later. He had therefore remained alone in the Battery Garden painting. This was stated not to be an unusual occurrence. Mr. Crale took very little notice of mealtimes. Sometimes a sandwich would be sent down to him, but more often he preferred to remain undisturbed.

"The last people to see him alive were Miss Elsa Greer (staying in the house) and Mr. Meredith Blake (a near neighbor). These two went up together to the house and went with the rest of the household into lunch. After lunch, coffee was served on the terrace. Mrs. Crale finished drinking her coffee and then observed that she would 'go down and see how Amyas was getting on.' Miss Cecilia Williams, governess, got up and accompanied her. She was looking for a pull-over belonging to her pupil, Miss Angela Warren, sister of Mrs. Crale, which the latter had mislaid, and she thought it possible it might have been left down on the beach.

"These two started off together. The path led downward, through some woods until it emerged at the door leading into the Battery Garden. You could either go into the Battery Garden or you could continue on the same path which led down to the seashore.

"Miss Williams continued on down and Mrs. Crale went into the Battery Garden. Almost at once, however, Mrs. Crale screamed and Miss Williams hurried back. Mr. Crale was reclining on a seat and he was dead.

"At Mrs. Crale's urgent request Miss Williams left the Battery Garden and hurried up to the house to telephone for a doctor. On her way, however, she met Mr. Meredith Blake and entrusted her errand to him, herself returning to Mrs. Crale, who she felt might be in need of someone. Dr. Faussett arrived on the scene a quarter of an hour later. He saw at once that Mr. Crale had been dead for some time—he placed the probable time of death at between one and two o'clock. There was nothing to show what had caused death. There was no sign of any wound and Mr. Crale's attitude was a perfectly natural one. Nevertheless, Dr. Faussett, who was well acquainted with Mr. Crale's state of health, and who knew positively that there was no disease or weakness of any kind, was inclined to take a grave view of the situation. It was at this point that Mr. Philip Blake made a certain statement to Dr. Faussett."

Inspector Hale paused, drew a deep breath and passed, as it were, to Chapter Two:

"Subsequently Mr. Blake repeated this statement to Inspector Conway. It was to this effect: He had that morning received a telephone message from his brother, Mr. Meredith Blake (who lived at Handcross Manor, a mile and a half away). Mr. Meredith Blake was an amateur chemist—or perhaps herbalist would describe it best. On entering his laboratory that morning, Mr. Meredith Blake had been startled to note that a bottle con·

taining a distillation of hemlock, which had been quite full the day before, was now nearly empty.

"Worried and alarmed by this fact he had rung up his brother to ask his advice as to what he should do about it. Mr. Philip Blake had urged his brother to come over to Alderbury at once and they would talk the matter over. He himself walked part way to meet his brother and they had come up to the house together. They had come to no decision as to what course to adopt and had left the matter in order to consult again after lunch.

"As a result of further inquiries, Inspector Conway ascertained the following facts: On the preceding afternoon, five people had walked over from Alderbury to tea at Handcross Manor. There were Mr. and Mrs. Crale, Miss Angela Warren, Miss Elsa Greer and Mr. Philip Blake. During the time spent there, Mr. Meredith Blake had given quite a dissertation on his hobby and had taken the party into his little laboratory and shown them around. In the course of this tour, he had mentioned certain specific drugs—one of which was coniine, the active principle of the spotted hemlock. He had explained its properties, had lamented the fact that it had now disappeared from the pharmacopoeia and boasted that he had known small doses of it to be very efficacious in whooping cough and asthma. Later he had mentioned its lethal properties and had actually read to his guests some passage from a Greek author describing its effects."

Superintendent Hale paused, refilled his pipe and passed on to Chapter Three:

"Colonel Frère, the chief constable, put the case into my hands. The result of the autopsy put the matter beyond any doubt. Coniine, I understand, leaves no definite post-mortem appearances, but the doctors knew what to look for and an ample amount of the drug was recovered. The doctor was of the opinion that it had been administered two or three hours before death. In front of Mr. Crale, on the table, there had been an empty glass and an empty beer bottle. The dregs of both were analyzed. There was no coniine in the bottle, but there was in the glass. I made inquiries and learned that, although a case of beer and glasses were kept in a small summerhouse in the Battery Garden in case Mr. Crale should feel thirsty when painting, on this particular morning Mrs. Crale had brought down from the house a bottle of freshly iced beer. Mr. Crale was busy painting when she arrived and Miss Greer was posing for him, sitting on one of the battlements.

"Mrs. Crale opened the beer, poured it out and put the glass into her husband's hand as he was standing before the easel. He tossed it off in one draught—a habit of his, I learned. Then he made a grimace, set down the glass on the table and said, 'Everything tastes foul to me today!' Miss

Greer upon that laughed and said, 'Liver!' Mr. Crale said, 'Well, at any rate it was *cold.* ' "

Hale paused.

"At what time did this take place?" Poirot asked.

"At about a quarter past eleven. Mr. Crale continued to paint. According to Miss Greer, he later complained of stiffness in the limbs and grumbled that he must have got a touch of rheumatism. But he was the type of man who hates to admit to illness of any kind and he undoubtedly tried not to admit that he was feeling ill. His irritable demand that he should be left alone and the others go up to lunch was quite characteristic of the man, I should say."

Poirot nodded.

Hale continued:

"So Crale was left alone in the Battery Garden. No doubt he dropped down on the seat and relaxed as soon as he was alone. Muscular paralysis would then set in. No help was at hand, and death supervened."

Again Poirot nodded.

Hale said:

"Well, I proceeded according to routine. There wasn't much difficulty in getting down to the facts. On the preceding day there had been a set-to between Mrs. Crale and Miss Greer. The latter had pretty insolently described some change in the arrangement of the furniture 'when I am living here.' Mrs. Crale took her up and said, 'What do you mean? When *you* are living here.' Miss Greer replied, 'Don't pretend you don't know what I mean, Caroline. You're just like an ostrich that buries its head in the sand. You know perfectly well that Amyas and I care for each other and are going to be married.' Mrs. Crale said, 'I know nothing of the kind.' Miss Greer then said, 'Well, you know it now.' Whereupon, it seems, Mrs. Crale turned to her husband, who had just come into the room, and said, 'Is it true, Amyas, that you are going to marry Elsa?' "

Poirot said with interest, "And what did Mr. Crale say to that?"

"Apparently he turned on Miss Greer and shouted at her, 'What the devil do you mean by blurting that out? Haven't you got the sense to hold your tongue?'

"Miss Greer said, 'I think Caroline ought to recognize the truth.'

"Mrs. Crale said to her husband, 'Is it true, Amyas?'

"He wouldn't look at her, it seems, turned his face away and mumbled something.

"She said, 'Speak out. I've got to know.' Whereupon he said, 'Oh, it's true enough—but I don't want to discuss it now.'

"Then he flounced out of the room again and Miss Greer said:

" 'You see!' and went on with something about its being no good for

Mrs. Crale to adopt a dog-in-the-manger attitude about it. They must all behave like rational people. She herself hoped that Caroline and Amyas would always remain good friends."

"And what did Mrs. Crale say to that?" asked Poirot curiously.

"According to the witnesses she laughed. She said, 'Over my dead body, Elsa.'

"She went to the door and Miss Greer called after her, 'What do you mean?'

"Mrs. Crale looked back and said, 'I'll kill Amyas before I give him up to *you*.' "

Hale paused.

"Pretty damning—eh?"

"Yes." Poirot seemed thoughtful. "Who overhead this scene?"

"Miss Williams was in the room, and Philip Blake. Very awkward for them."

"Their accounts of the scene agree?"

"Near enough—you never get two witnesses to remember a thing exactly alike. *You* know that as well as I do, M. Poirot."

Poirot nodded. He said thoughtfully, "Yes, it will be interesting to see—" He stopped with the sentence unfinished.

Hale went on: "I instituted a search of the house. In Mrs. Crale's bedroom I found in a bottom drawer, tucked away underneath some winter stockings, a small bottle labeled jasmine scent. It was empty. I fingerprinted it. The only prints on it were those of Mrs. Crale. On analysis it was found to contain faint traces of oil of jasmine and a strong solution of coniine.

"I cautioned Mrs. Crale and showed her the bottle. She replied readily. She had, she said, been in a very unhappy state of mind. After listening to Mr. Meredith Blake's description of the drug she had slipped back to the laboratory, had emptied out a bottle of jasmine scent which was in her bag and had filled the bottle up with coniine solution. I asked her why she had done this and she said, 'I don't want to speak of certain things more than I can help, but I had received a bad shock. My husband was proposing to leave me for another woman. If that was so, I didn't want to live. That is why I took it.' "

Hale paused.

Poirot said, "After all, it is likely enough."

"Perhaps, M. Poirot. But it doesn't square with what she was overheard to say. And then there was a further scene on the following morning. Mr. Philip Blake overheard a portion of it. Miss Greer overheard a different portion of it. It took place in the library between Mr. and Mrs. Crale. Mr.

Blake was in the hall and caught a fragment or two. Miss Greer was sitting outside near the open library window and heard a good deal more."

"And what did they hear?"

"Mr. Blake heard Mrs. Crale say, 'You and your women. I'd like to kill you. Some day I will kill you.' "

"No mention of suicide?"

"Exactly. None at all. No words like 'If you do this thing, I'll kill myself.' Miss Greer's evidence was much the same. According to her, Mr. Crale said, 'Do try and be reasonable about this, Caroline. I'm fond of you and will always wish you well—you and the child. But I'm going to marry Elsa. We've always agreed to leave each other free.' Mrs. Crale answered to that, 'Very well, don't say I haven't warned you.' He said, 'What do you mean?' And she said, 'I mean that I love you and I'm not going to lose you. I'd rather kill you than let you go to that girl.' "

Poirot made a slight gesture. "It occurs to me," he murmured, "that Miss Greer was singularly unwise to raise this issue. Mrs. Crale could easily have refused her husband a divorce."

"We had some evidence bearing on that point," said Hale. "Mrs. Crale, it seems, confided partly in Mr. Meredith Blake. He was an old and trusted friend. He was very distressed and managed to get a word with Mr. Crale about it. This, I may say, was on the preceding afternoon. Mr. Blake remonstrated delicately with his friend, said how distressed he would be if the marriage between Mr. and Mrs. Crale was to break up so disastrously. He also stressed the point that Miss Greer was a very young girl and that it was a very serious thing to drag a young girl through the divorce court. To this Mr. Crale replied, with a chuckle (callous sort of brute he must have been), 'That isn't Elsa's idea at all. *She* isn't going to appear. We shall fix it up in the usual way.' "

"Therefore," Poirot said, "even more imprudent of Miss Greer to have broken out the way she did."

Superintendent Hale said, "Oh, you know what women are! Have to get at one another's throats. It must have been a difficult situation anyhow. I can't understand Mr. Crale allowing it to happen. According to Mr. Meredith Blake he wanted to finish his picture. Does that make sense to you?"

"Yes, my friend, I think it does."

"It doesn't to me. The man was asking for trouble!"

"He was probably seriously annoyed with his young woman for breaking out the way she did."

"Oh, he was. Meredith Blake said so. If he had to finish the picture I don't see why he couldn't have taken some photographs and worked from them. I know a chap—does water colors of places—*he* does that."

Poirot shook his head. "No—I can understand Crale the artist. You must realize, my friend, that at that moment, probably, his picture was all that mattered to Crale. However much he wanted to marry the girl, the picture came first. That's why he hoped to get through her visit without its coming to an open issue. The girl, of course, didn't see it that way. With women, love always comes first."

"Don't I know it," said Superintendent Hale with feeling.

"Men," continued Poirot, "and especially artists, are different."

"Art!" said the superintendent with scorn. "All this talk about *art!* I never *have* understood it and I never shall! You should have seen that picture Crale was painting. All lopsided. He'd made the girl look as though she had a toothache and the battlements were all cockeyed. Unpleasant-looking, the whole thing. I couldn't get it out of my mind for a long time afterward. I even dreamed about it. And, what's more, it affected my eyesight—I began to see battlements and walls and things all out of drawing. Yes, and women too!"

Poirot smiled. He said, "Although you do not know it, you are paying a tribute to the greatness of Amyas Crale's art."

"Nonsense. Why can't a painter paint something nice and cheerful to look at? Why go out of your way to look for ugliness?"

"Some of us, *mon cher,* see beauty in curious places."

"The girl was a good-looker, all right," said Hale. "Lots of make-up and next to no clothes on. It isn't decent the way these girls go about. And that was sixteen years ago, mind you. Nowadays one wouldn't think anything of it. But then—well, it shocked me. Trousers and one of those sports shirts, open at the neck—and not another thing, I should say!"

"You seem to remember these points very well," murmured Poirot slyly.

Superintendent Hale blushed. "I'm just passing on the impression I got," he said austerely.

"Quite—quite," said Poirot soothingly. He went on: "So it would seem that the principal witnesses against Mrs. Crale were Philip Blake and Elsa Greer?"

"Yes. Vehement, they were, both of them. But the governess was called by the prosecution too, and what she said carried more weight than the other two. She was on Mrs. Crale's side entirely, you see. Up in arms for her. But she was an honest woman and gave her evidence truthfully, without trying to minimize it in any way."

"And Meredith Blake?"

"He was very distressed by the whole thing, poor gentleman. As well he might be! Blamed himself for his drug brewing—and the chief constable blamed him for it too. Coniine, I understand, was in Schedule I of the Poison Act. He was a friend of both parties, and it hit him very hard—

besides being the kind of country gentleman who shrinks from notoriety and being in the public eye."

"Did not Mrs. Crale's young sister give evidence?"

"No. It wasn't necessary. She wasn't there when Mrs. Crale threatened her husband, and there was nothing she could tell us that we couldn't get from someone else equally well. She saw Mrs. Crale go to the refrigerator and get the iced beer out and, of course, the defense could have subpoenaed her to say that Mrs. Crale took it straight down without tampering with it in any way. But that point wasn't relevant because we never claimed that the coniine was in the beer bottle."

"How did she manage to put it in the glass with those two looking on?"

"Well, first of all, they weren't looking on. That is to say, Mr. Crale was painting—looking at his canvas and at the sitter. And Miss Greer was posed, sitting with her back almost to where Mrs. Crale was standing and her eyes looking over Mr. Crale's shoulder."

Poirot nodded.

"As I say, neither of the two was looking at Mrs. Crale. She had the stuff in one of those pipette things—one used to fill fountain pens with them. We found it crushed to splinters on the path up to the house."

"You have an answer to everything," Poirot murmured.

"Well, come now, M. Poirot! Without prejudice. *She* threatens to kill him. *She* takes the stuff from the laboratory. The empty bottle is found in *her* room and *nobody has handled it but her.* She deliberately takes down iced beer to him—a funny thing, anyway, when you realize that they weren't on speaking terms—"

"A very curious thing. I had already remarked on it."

"Yes. Bit of a giveaway. *Why* was she so amiable all of a sudden? He complains of the taste of the stuff—and coniine *has* a nasty taste. She arranges to find the body and sends the other woman off to telephone. Why? So that she can wipe that bottle and glass and then press *his* fingers on it. After that she can pipe up and say that it was remorse and that he committed suicide. A likely story."

"It was certainly not very well imagined."

"No. If you ask me, she didn't take the trouble to *think.* She was so eaten up with hate and jealousy. All she thought of was doing him in. And then, when it's over, when she sees him there dead—well, *then,* I should say, she suddenly comes to herself and realizes that what she's done is murder—and that you get hanged for murder. And desperately she goes bald-headed for the only thing she can think of—which is suicide."

Poirot said, "It is very sound what you say there—yes. Her mind might work that way."

"In a way it was a premeditated crime and in a way it wasn't," said Superintendent Hale. "I don't believe she really thought it out, you know. Just went on with it blindly."

Poirot murmured, "I wonder . . . ."

Chapter III

HALE LOOKED AT Poirot curiously.

"Have I convinced you that it was a straightforward case?" he said.

"Almost. Not quite. There are one or two peculiar points."

"Can you suggest an alternative solution that will hold water?"

Poirot said, "What were the movements of the other people on that morning?"

"We went into them, I can assure you. We checked up on everybody. Nobody had what you could call an alibi—you can't have with poisoning. Why, there's nothing to prevent a would-be murderer from handing his victim some poison in a capsule the day before, telling him it's a specific cure for indigestion and he must take it just before lunch—and then going away to the other end of England."

"But you don't think that happened in this case?"

"Mr. Crale didn't suffer from indigestion. And in any case I can't see that kind of thing happening. It's true that Mr. Meredith Blake was given to recommending quack nostrums of his own concocting, but I don't see Mr. Crale trying any of them. And if he did he'd probably talk and joke about it. Besides, why *should* Mr. Meredith Blake want to kill Mr. Crale? Everything goes to show that he was on very good terms with him. They all were.

"Mr. Philip Blake was his best friend. Miss Greer was in love with him. Miss Williams disapproved of him, I imagine, very strongly—but moral disapprobation doesn't lead to poisoning. Little Miss Warren scrapped with him a lot, she was at a tiresome age—just off to school, I believe—but he was quite fond of her and she of him. She was treated, you know, with particular tenderness and consideration in that house. You may have heard why. She was badly injured when she was a child—injured by Mrs. Crale in a kind of maniacal fit of rage. That rather shows—doesn't it?—that she was a pretty uncontrolled sort of person. To go for a child—and maim her for life!"

"It might show," said Poirot, "that Angela Warren had good reason to bear a grudge against Caroline Crale."

"Perhaps, but not against Amyas Crale. And, anyway, Mrs. Crale was devoted to her young sister—gave her a home when her parents died and, as I say, treated her with special affection—spoiled her badly, so they say. The girl was obviously very fond of Mrs. Crale. She was kept away from the trial and sheltered from it all as far as possible—Mrs. Crale was very insistent about that, I believe. But the child was terribly upset and longed to be taken to see her sister in prison. Caroline Crale wouldn't agree. She said that sort of thing might injure a girl's mentality for life. She arranged for her to go to school abroad."

He added, "Miss Warren turned out to be a very distinguished woman. Traveler to weird places. Lectures at the Royal Geographical—all that sort of thing."

"And no one remembers the trial?"

"Well, it's a different name for one thing. They hadn't even the same maiden name. They had the same mother but different fathers. Mrs. Crale's name was Spalding."

"This Miss Williams, was she the child's governess or Angela Warren's?"

"Angela's. There was a nurse for the child, but she used to do a few little lessons with Miss Williams every day, I believe."

"Where was the child at the time?"

"She'd gone with the nurse to pay a visit to her godmother. A Lady Tressillian. A widow lady who'd lost her own two little girls and who was devoted to this kid."

Poirot nodded. "I see."

Hale continued: "As to the movements of the other people on the day of the murder, I can give them to you. Miss Greer sat on the terrace near the library window after breakfast. There, as I say, she overheard the quarrel between Crale and his wife. After that she accompanied Crale down to the Battery and sat for him until lunchtime, with a couple of breaks to ease her muscles.

"Philip Blake was in the house after breakfast and overheard part of the quarrel. After Crale and Miss Greer went off, he read the paper until his brother telephoned him. Thereupon, he went down to the shore to meet his brother. They walked together up the path again past the Battery Garden. Miss Greer had just gone up to the house to fetch a pull-over, as she felt chilly, and Mrs. Crale was with her husband discussing arrangements for Angela's departure to school."

"Ah, an amicable interview," said Poirot.

"Well, no, not amicable. Crale was fairly shouting at her, I understand. Annoyed at being bothered with domestic details. I suppose she wanted to get things straightened up if there *was* going to be a break."

Poirot nodded.

Hale went on:

"The two brothers exchanged a few words with Amyas Crale. Then Miss Greer reappeared and took up her position, and Crale picked up his brush again, obviously wanting to get rid of them. They took the hint and went up to the house. It was when they were at the Battery, by the way, that Amyas Crale complained that all the beer down there was hot, and his wife promised to send him down some iced beer."

"Aha!"

"Exactly—aha! Sweet as sugar she was about it. They went up to the house and sat on the terrace outside. Mrs. Crale and Angela Warren brought them beer out there.

"Later, Angela Warren went down to bathe and Philip Blake went with her.

"Meredith Blake went down to a clearing with a seat just above the Battery Garden. He could just see Miss Greer as she posed on the battlements, and could hear her voice and Crale's as they talked. He sat there and thought over the coniine business. He was still very worried about it and didn't know quite what to do. Elsa Greer saw him and waved her hand to him. When the bell went for lunch he came down to the battery, and Elsa Greer and he went back to the house together. He noticed then that Crale was looking, as he put it, very queer, but he didn't really think anything of it at the time. Crale was the kind of man who is never ill—and so one didn't imagine he would be. On the other hand, he *did* have moods of fury and despondency according as to whether his painting was not going as he liked it. On those occasions one left him alone and said as little as possible to him. That's what these two did on this occasion.

"As to the others, the servants were busy with housework and cooking lunch. Miss Williams was in the schoolroom part of the morning, correcting some exercise books. Afterward, she took some household mending to the terrace. Angela Warren spent most of the morning wandering about the garden, climbing trees and eating things—you know what a girl of fifteen is—plums, sour apples, hard pears, etc. After that she came back to the house and, as I say, went down with Philip Blake to the beach and had a swim before lunch."

Superintendent Hale paused. "Now, then," he said belligerently, "do you find anything phony about that?"

"Nothing at all," Poirot said.

"Well, then!"

The two words expressed volumes.

"But all the same," said Hercule Poirot, "I am going to satisfy myself. I—"

"What are you going to do?"

"I am going to visit these five people—and from each one I am going to get his or her own story."

Superintendent Hale sighed with a deep melancholy. He said, "Man, you're nuts! None of their stories are going to agree. Don't you grasp that elementary fact? No two people remember a thing in the same order anyway. And after all this time! Why, you'll hear five accounts of five separate murders!"

"That," said Poirot, "is what I am counting upon. It will be very instructive."

Philip Blake was recognizably like the description given of him by Depleach—a prosperous, shrewd, jovial-looking man—slightly running to fat.

Hercule Poirot had timed his appointment for half past six on a Saturday afternoon. Philip Blake had just finished his eighteen holes, and he had been on his game—winning a fiver from his opponent. He was in the mood to be friendly and expansive.

Hercule Poirot explained himself and his errand. On this occasion at least, he showed no undue passion for unsullied truth. It was a question, Blake gathered, of a series of books dealing with famous crimes.

Philip Blake frowned. He said, "Why rake up these things?"

Hercule Poirot shrugged his shoulders. He was at his most foreign today. He was out to be despised but patronized. "It is the public," he murmured. "They eat it up—yes, eat it up."

"Ghouls," said Philip Blake. But he said it good-humoredly—not with the fastidiousness and the distaste that a more sensitive man might have displayed.

Hercule Poirot said with a shrug of the shoulders, "It is human nature. You and I, Mr. Blake, who know the world, have no illusions about our fellow human beings. Not bad people, most of them, but certainly not to be idealized."

Blake said heartily, "I've parted with my illusions long ago."

"Instead, you tell a very good story, so I have been told."

"Ah!" Blake's eyes twinkled. "Heard this one?"

Poirot's laugh came at the right place. It was not an edifying story, but it was funny.

Philip Blake lay back in his chair, his muscles relaxed, his eyes creased with good humor. Hercule Poirot thought suddenly that he looked rather like a contented pig. A pig. *This little pig went to market* . . .

What was he like, this man, this Philip Blake? A man, it would seem, without cares. Prosperous, contented. No remorseful thoughts, no uneasy twinges of conscience from the past, no haunting memories here. No, a well-fed pig who had gone to market—and fetched the full market price. . . .

But once, perhaps, there had been more to Philip Blake. He must have been, when young, a handsome man. Eyes always a shade too small, a fraction too near together, perhaps—but otherwise a well-made, well-set-up young man. How old was he now? At a guess between fifty and sixty. Nearing forty, then, at the time of Crale's death. Less stultified, then, less sunk in the gratifications of the minute. Asking more of life, perhaps, and receiving less. . . .

Poirot murmured as a mere catch phrase, "You comprehend my position."

"No, really, you know, I'm hanged if I do." The stockbroker sat upright again; his glance was once more shrewd. "Why *you?* You're not a writer."

"Not precisely—no. Actually I am a detective."

The modesty of this remark had probably not been equaled before in Poirot's conversation.

"Of course you are. We all know that. The famous Hercule Poirot!"

But his tone held a subtly mocking note. Intrinsically, Philip Blake was too much of an Englishman to take the pretensions of a foreigner seriously. To his cronies he would have said, "Quaint little mountebank. Oh, well, I expect his stuff goes down with the women all right."

And although that derisive, patronizing attitude was exactly the one which Hercule Poirot had aimed at inducing, nevertheless he found himself annoyed by it.

This man, this successful man of affairs, was unimpressed by Hercule Poirot! It was a scandal.

"I am gratified," said Poirot untruly, "that I am so well known to you. My success, let me tell you, has been founded on the psychology—the eternal *why* of human behavior. That, M. Blake, is what interests the world in crime today. It used to be romance. Famous crimes were retold from one angle only—the love story connected with them. Nowadays it is very different. People read with interest that Dr. Crippen murdered his wife because she was a big, bouncing woman and he was little and insignificant and therefore she made him feel inferior. They read of some famous woman criminal that she killed because she'd been snubbed by her father when she was three years old. It is, as I say, the *why* of crime that interests nowadays."

Philip Blake said, with a slight yawn, "The why of most crimes is obvious enough, I should say. Usually money."

"Ah, but my dear sir," Poirot cried, "the why must never be obvious. That is the whole point!"

"And that's where *you* come in?"

"And that, as you say, is where I come in! It is proposed to rewrite the stories of certain bygone crimes—from the psychological angle. Psychology in crime, it is my specialty. I have accepted the commission."

Philip Blake grinned. "Pretty lucrative, I suppose?"

"I hope so; I certainly hope so."

"Congratulations. Now, perhaps, you'll tell me where *I* come in?"

"Most certainly. The Crale case, monsieur."

Philip Blake did not look startled. But he looked thoughtful. He said, "Yes, of course, the Crale case . . ."

Hercule Poirot said anxiously, "It is not displeasing to you, Mr. Blake?"

"Oh, as to that." Philip Blake shrugged his shoulders. "It's no use resenting a thing that you've no power to stop. The trial of Caroline Crale is public property. Anyone can go ahead and write it up. It's no use *my* objecting. In a way—I don't mind telling you—I do dislike it a good deal. Amyas Crale was one of my best friends. I'm sorry the whole unsavory business has to be raked up again. But these things happen."

"You are a philosopher, Mr. Blake."

"No, no. I just know enough not to start kicking against the pricks. I daresay you'll do it less offensively than many others."

"I hope, at least, to write with delicacy and good taste," said Poirot.

Philip Blake gave a loud guffaw but without any real amusement. "Makes me chuckle to hear you say that."

"I assure you, Mr. Blake, I am really interested. It is not just a matter of money with me. I genuinely want to recreate the past—to feel and see the events that took place, to see behind the obvious and to visualize the thoughts and feelings of the actors in the drama."

"I don't know that there was much subtlety about it," Philip Blake said. "It was a pretty obvious business. Crude female jealousy, that was all there was to it."

"It would interest me enormously, Mr. Blake, if I could have your own reactions to the affair."

Philip Blake said with sudden heat, his face deepening in color, "Reactions! Reactions! Don't speak so pedantically. I didn't just stand there and react! You don't seem to understand that my friend—*my friend,* I tell you —had been killed—poisoned! And that if I'd acted quicker I could have saved him."

"How do you make that out, Mr. Blake?"

"Like this. I take it that you've already read up the facts of the case?"

Poirot nodded. "Very well. Now on that morning my brother Meredith called me up. He was in a pretty good stew. One of his hell brews was missing, and it was a fairly deadly hell brew. What did I do? I told him to come along and we'd talk it over. Decide what was best to be done. 'Decide what was best.' It beats me now how I could have been such a hesitating fool! I ought to have realized that there was no time to lose. I ought to have gone to Amyas straight away and warned him. I ought to have said, 'Caroline's pinched one of Meredith's patent poisons, and you and Elsa had better look out for yourselves.' "

Blake got up. He strode up and down in his excitement.

"Do you suppose I haven't gone over it in my mind again and again? I *knew.* I had the chance to have him and I dallied about—waiting for Meredith! Why hadn't I the sense to realize that Caroline wasn't going to have any qualms or hesitancies? She'd taken that stuff to use—and she'd use it at the very first opportunity. She wouldn't wait till Meredith discovered his loss. I knew—of course I knew—that Amyas was in deadly danger and I did nothing!"

"I think you reproach yourself unduly, monsieur. You had not much time—"

The other interrupted him:

"Time? I had plenty of time. Any amount of courses were open to me. I could have gone to Amyas, as I say; but there was the chance, of course, that he wouldn't believe me. Amyas wasn't the sort of man who'd believe easily in his own danger. He'd have scoffed at the notion. And he never thoroughly understood the sort of devil Caroline was. But I could have gone to her. I could have said, 'I know what you're up to. I know what you're planning to do. But if Amyas or Elsa dies of coniine poisoning, you'll be hanged by your neck!' That would have stopped her. Or I might have rung up the police. Oh, there were things that could have been done —and, instead, I let myself be influenced by Meredith's slow, cautious methods! 'We must be sure—talk it over—make quite certain who could have taken it. . . .' Old fool—never made a quick decision in his life! A good thing for him he was the eldest son and has an estate to live on. If he'd ever tried to *make* money he'd have lost every penny he had."

"You had no doubt yourself who had taken the poison?" Poirot asked.

"Of course not. I knew at once it must be Caroline. You see, I knew Caroline very well."

"That is very interesting," Poirot said. "I want to know, Mr. Blake, what kind of a woman Caroline Crale was."

Philip Blake said sharply, "She wasn't the injured that innocent people thought she was at the time of the trial!"

"What was she, then?"

Blake sat down again. He said seriously, "Would you really like to know?"

"I would like to know very much indeed."

"Caroline was a rotter. She was a rotter through and through. Mind you, she had charm. She had that kind of sweetness of manner that deceives people utterly. She had a frail, helpless look about her that appealed to people's chivalry. Sometimes, when I've read a bit of history, I think Mary Queen of Scots must have been a bit like her. Always sweet and unfortunate and magnetic—and actually a cold, calculating woman, a scheming woman who planned the murder of Darnley and got away with it. Caroline was like that—a cold, calculating planner. And she had a wicked temper.

"I don't know whether they've told you—it isn't a vital point of the trial, but it shows her up—what she did to her baby sister? She was jealous, you know. Her mother had married again, and all the notice and affection went to little Angela. Caroline couldn't stand that. She tried to kill the baby—smash its head in. Luckily the blow wasn't fatal. But it was a pretty ghastly thing to do."

"Yes, indeed!"

"Well, that was the real Caroline. She had to be first. That was the thing she simply could not stand—not being first. And there was a cold, egotistical devil in her that was capable of being stirred to murderous lengths."

He paused.

"You'll say that I'm bitter—that I'm unduly prejudiced against Caroline. She *had* charm—I've felt it. But I knew—I always knew—the real woman behind. And that woman, M. Poirot, was evil. She was cruel and malignant and a grabber!"

"And yet it has been told me that Mrs. Crale put up with many hard things in her married life."

"Yes, and didn't she let everybody know about it? Always the martyr! Poor old Amyas. His married life was one long hell—or rather it would have been if it hadn't been for his exceptional quality. His art, you see—he always had that. It was an escape. When he was painting he didn't care; he shook off Caroline and her nagging and all the ceaseless rows and quarrels. They were endless, you know. Not a week passed without a thundering row over one thing or another.

"*She* enjoyed it. Having rows stimulated her, I believe. It was an outlet. She could say all the hard, bitter, stinging things she wanted to say. She'd positively purr after one of those set-tos—go off looking as sleek and well-fed as a cat. But it took it out of *him*. *He* wanted peace, rest, a quiet life. Of course, a man like that ought never to marry; he isn't cut out for domesticity. A man like Crale should have affairs but no binding ties. They're bound to chafe him."

"He confided in you?"

"Well—he knew that I was a pretty devoted pal. He let me see things. He didn't complain. He wasn't that kind of man. Sometimes he'd say, 'Damn all women.' Or he'd say, 'Never get married, old boy. Wait for hell till after this life.' "

"You knew about his attachment to Miss Greer?"

"Oh, yes—at least I saw it coming on. He told me he'd met a marvelous girl. She was different, he said, from anything or anyone he'd ever met before. Not that I paid much attention to that. Amyas was always meeting one woman or other who was 'different.' Usually, a month later, he'd stare at you if you mentioned them, and wonder who you were talking about! But this Elsa Greer really was different. I realized that when I came down to Alderbury to stay. She'd got him, you know—hooked him good and proper. The poor mutt fairly ate out of her hand."

"You did not like Elsa Greer either?"

"No, I didn't like her. She was definitely a predatory creature. She, too, wanted to own Crale body and soul. But I think, all the same, that she'd have been better for him than Caroline. She might conceivably have let him alone once she was sure of him. Or she might have got tired of him and moved on to someone else. The best thing for Amyas would have been to be quite free of female entanglements."

"But that, it would seem, was not to his taste."

Philip Blake said with a sigh, "The fool was always getting himself involved with some woman or other. And yet, in a way, women really meant very little to him. The only two women who really made any impression on him at all in his life were Caroline and Elsa."

"Was he fond of the child?" Poirot asked.

"Angela? Oh, we all liked Angela. She was such a sport. She was always game for anything. What a life she led that wretched governess of hers! Yes, Amyas liked Angela all right; but sometimes she went too far, and then he used to get really mad with her, and then Caroline would step in— Caro was always on Angela's side and that would finish Amyas altogether. He hated it when Caro sided with Angela against him. There was a bit of jealousy all round, you know.

"Amyas was jealous of the way Caro always put Angela first and would do anything for her. And Angela was jealous of Amyas and rebelled against his overbearing ways."

He paused.

"In the interests of truth, Mr. Blake," Poirot said, "I am going to ask you to do something."

"What is it?"

"I am going to beg that you will write me out an exact account of what happened on those days at Alderbury. That is to say, I am going to ask you to write me out a full account of the murder and its attendant circumstances."

"But, my dear fellow, after all this time? I should be hopelessly inaccurate."

"Not necessarily."

"Surely."

"No, Mr. Blake; for one thing, with the passage of time, the mind retains a hold on essentials and rejects superficial matters."

"Oh, you mean a mere broad outline?"

"Not at all. I mean a detailed, conscientious account of each event as it occurred and every conversation you can remember."

"And supposing I remember them wrong?"

"You can give the wording at least to the best of your recollection. There may be gaps, but that cannot be helped."

Blake looked at him curiously. "But what's the idea? The police files will give you the whole thing far more accurately."

"No, Mr. Blake. We are speaking now from the psychological point of view. I do not want bare *facts. I want your own selection of facts.* Time and your memory are responsible for that selection. There may have been things done, words spoken, that I should seek for in vain in the police files. Things and words that you never mentioned because, maybe, you judged them irrelevant, or because you preferred not to repeat them."

Blake said sharply, "Is this account of mine for publication?"

"Certainly not. It is for my eye only. To assist me to draw my own deductions."

"And you won't quote from it without my consent?"

"Certainly not."

"H'm," said Philip Blake. "I'm a very busy man, M. Poirot."

"I appreciate that there will be time and trouble involved. I should be happy to agree to a—reasonable fee."

There was a moment's pause. Then Philip Blake said suddenly, "No, if I do it I'll do it for nothing."

"And you will do it?"

Philip Blake said warningly, "Remember, I can't vouch for the accuracy of my memory."

"That is perfectly understood."

"Then I think," said Philip Blake, "that I should *like* to do it. I feel I owe it—in a way—to Amyas Crale."

Hercule Poirot was not a man to neglect details.

His advance toward Meredith Blake was carefully thought out. Meredith Blake was, he already felt sure, a very different proposition from Philip Blake. Rush tactics would not succeed here. The assault must be leisurely.

Hercule Poirot knew that there was only one way to penetrate the stronghold. He must approach Meredith Blake with the proper credentials. Those credentials must be social, not professional. Fortunately, in the course of his career, Hercule Poirot had made friends in many counties. Devonshire was no exception. He sat down to review what resources he had in Devonshire. As a result he discovered two people who were acquaintances or friends of Mr. Meredith Blake. He descended upon him, therefore, armed with two letters—one from Lady Mary Lytton-Gore, a gentle widow lady of restricted means, the most retiring of creatures; and the other from a retired admiral, whose family had been settled in the county for four generations.

Meredith Blake received Poirot in a state of some perplexity.

As he had often felt lately, things were not what they used to be. Dash it all, private detectives used to be private detectives—fellows you got to guard wedding presents at country receptions, fellows you went to, rather shamefacedly, when there was some dirty business afoot and you had to get the hang of it.

But here was Lady Mary Lytton-Gore writing: "Hercule Poirot is a very old and valued friend of mine. Please do all you can to help him, won't you?" And Mary Lytton-Gore wasn't—no, decidedly she wasn't— the sort of woman you associate with private detectives and all that they stand for. And Admiral Cronshaw wrote: "Very good chap—absolutely sound. Grateful if you will do what you can for him. Most entertaining fellow—can tell you lots of good stories."

And now here was the man himself. Really a most impossible person— the wrong clothes, button boots, an incredible mustache! Not his, Meredith Blake's, kind of fellow at all. Didn't look as though he'd ever hunted or shot—or even played a decent game. A foreigner.

Slightly amused, Hercule Poirot read accurately these thoughts passing through the other's head. He had felt his own interest rising considerably as the train brought him into the west country. He would see now, with his own eyes, the actual place where these long-past events happened.

It was here, at Handcross Manor, that two young brothers had lived and gone over to Alderbury and joked and played tennis and fraternized with a young Amyas Crale and a girl called Caroline. It was from here that Meredith had started out to Alderbury on that fatal morning. That had been sixteen years ago. Hercule Poirot looked with interest at the man who was confronting him with somewhat uneasy politeness.

Very much what he had expected. Meredith Blake resembled superficially every other English country gentleman of straitened means and outdoor tastes.

A shabby old coat of tweed, a weather-beaten, pleasant, middle-aged face with somewhat faded blue eyes, rather a weak mouth, half hidden by a rather straggly mustache. Poirot found Meredith Blake a great contrast to his brother. He had a hesitating manner; his mental processes were obviously leisurely. It was as though his tempo had slowed down with the years just as his brother Philip's had been accelerated.

As Poirot had already guessed, he was a man whom you could not hurry. The leisurely life of the English countryside was in his bones.

He looked, the detective thought, a good deal older than his brother, though, from what Mr. Johnathan had said, it would seem that only a couple of years separated them.

Hercule Poirot prided himself on knowing how to handle an "old-school tie." It was no moment for trying to seem English. No, one must be a foreigner—frankly a foreigner—and be magnanimously forgiven for the fact. "Of course these foreigners don't quite know the ropes. *Will* shake hands at breakfast. Still, a decent fellow really. . . ."

Poirot set about creating this impression of himself. The two men talked, cautiously, of Lady Mary Lytton-Gore and of Admiral Cronshaw. Other names were mentioned. Fortunately, Poirot knew someone's cousin and had met somebody else's sister-in-law. He could see a kind of warmth dawning in the squire's eyes. The fellow seemed to know the right people.

Gracefully, insidiously, Poirot slid into the purpose of his visit. He was quick to counteract the inevitable recoil. This book was, alas, going to be written. Miss Crale—Miss Lemarchant, as she was now called—was anxious for him to exercise a judicious editorship. The facts, unfortunately, were public property. But much could be done in their presentation to avoid wounding susceptibilities. Poirot murmured that before now he had been able to use discreet influence to avoid certain sensational passages in a book of memoirs.

Meredith Blake flushed angrily. His hand shook a little as he filled a pipe. He said, a slight stammer in his voice, "It's—it's g-ghoulish the way they dig these things up. S-sixteen years ago. Why can't they let it be?"

Poirot shrugged his shoulders. "I agree with you," he said. "But what will you? There is a demand for such things. And anyone is at liberty to reconstruct a proved crime and to comment on it."

"Seems disgraceful to me."

Poirot murmured, "Alas, we do not live in a delicate age. . . . You would be surprised, Mr. Blake, if you knew the unpleasant publications I have succeeded in—shall we say—softening? I am anxious to do all I can to save Miss Crale's feeling in the matter."

Blake murmured, "Little Carla! That child! A grown-up woman. One can hardly believe it."

"I know. Time flies swiftly, does it not?"

Meredith Blake sighed. He said, "Too quickly."

Poirot said, "As you will have seen in the letter I handed you from Miss Crale, she is very anxious to know everything possible about the sad events of the past."

"Why?" Meredith Blake said with a touch of irritation. "Why rake up everything again? How much better to let it all be forgotten."

"You say that, Mr. Blake, because you know all the past too well. Miss Crale, remember, knows nothing. That is to say, she knows only the story as she has learned it from the official accounts."

Meredith Blake winced. He said, "Yes, I forgot. Poor child! What a detestable position for her. The shock of learning the truth. And then— those soulless, callous reports of the trial."

"The truth," said Hercule Poirot, "can never be done justice to in a mere legal recital. It is the things that are left out that are the things that matter. The emotions, the feelings, the characters of the actors in the drama, the extenuating circumstances—"

He paused and the other man spoke eagerly, like an actor who had received his cue:

"Extenuating circumstances! That's just it. If ever there were extenuating circumstances, there were in this case. Amyas Crale was an old friend —his family and mine had been friends for generations, but one has to admit that his conduct was, frankly, outrageous. He was an artist, of course, and presumably that explains it. But there it is—he allowed a most extraordinary set of affairs to arise. The position was one that no ordinary decent man could have contemplated for a moment."

Hercule Poirot said, "I am interested that you should say that. It had puzzled me—that situation. Not so does a well-bred man, a man of the world, go about his affairs."

Blake's thin, hesitating face had lit up with animation. He said:

"Yes, but the whole point is that Amyas never was an ordinary man! He was a painter, you see, and with him painting came first—really, some-times, in the most extraordinary way! I don't understand these so-called artistic people myself—never have. I understood Crale a little because, of course, I'd known him all my life. His people were the same sort as my people. And in many ways Crale ran true to type—it was only where art came in that he didn't conform to the usual standards. He wasn't, you see, an amateur in any way. He was first class—really first class.

"Some people say he was a genius. They may be right. But, as a result, he was always what I should describe as unbalanced. When he was painting a picture, nothing else mattered, nothing could be allowed to get in the way. He was like a man in a dream—completely obsessed by what he was doing. Not till the canvas was finished did he come out of this absorption and start to pick up the threads of ordinary life again."

He looked questioningly at Poirot and the latter nodded.

"You understand, I see. Well, that explains, I think, why this particular situation arose. He was in love with this girl. He wanted to marry her. He was prepared to leave his wife and child for her. But he'd started painting her down here, and he wanted to finish that picture. Nothing else mattered to him. He didn't *see* anything else. And the fact that the situation was a perfectly impossible one for the two women concerned didn't seem to have occurred to him."

"Did either of them understand his point of view?"

"Oh, yes—in a way. Elsa did, I suppose. She was terrifically enthusiastic about his painting. But it was a difficult position for her—naturally. And as for Caroline—"

He stopped. Poirot said, "For Caroline—*yes?*"

Chapter IV

MEREDITH BLAKE SAID, speaking with a little difficulty, "Caroline—I had always—well, I had always been very fond of Caroline. There was a time when—when I hoped to marry her. But that was soon nipped in the bud. Still, I remained, if I may say so, devoted to—to her service."

Poirot nodded thoughtfully. That slightly old-fashioned phrase expressed, he felt, the man before him very typically. Meredith Blake was the kind of man who would devote himself readily to a romantic and honorable devotion. He would serve his lady faithfully and without hope of reward. Yes, it was all very much in character.

He said, carefully weighing the words, "You must have resented this—attitude—on *her* behalf?"

"I did. Oh, I did. I—I actually remonstrated with Crale on the subject."

"When was this?"

"Actually the day before—before it all happened. They came over to tea here, you know. I got Crale aside and put it to him. I even said, I remember, that it wasn't fair to either of them."

"Ah, you said that?"

"Yes. I didn't think, you see, that he realized."

"Possibly not."

"I said to him that it was putting Caroline in a perfectly unendurable position. If he meant to marry this girl, he ought not to have her staying in the house and—well—more or less flaunt her in Caroline's face. It was, I said, an unendurable insult."

"What did he answer?" Poirot asked curiously.

Meredith Blake replied with distaste, "He said, 'Caroline must lump it.' "

Hercule Poirot's eyebrow rose. "Not," he said, "a very sympathetic reply."

"I thought it abominable. I lost my temper. I said that no doubt, not caring for his wife, he didn't mind how much he made her suffer, but what, I said, about the girl? Hadn't he realized it was a pretty rotten position for *her?* His reply to that was that Elsa must lump it too!

"Then he went on: 'You don't seem to understand, Meredith, that this thing I'm painting is the best thing I've done. It's *good,* I tell you. And a couple of jealous, quarreling women aren't going to upset it—no, by hell, they're not.'

"It was hopeless talking to him. I said he seemed to have taken leave of all ordinary decency. Painting, I said, wasn't everything. He interrupted there. He said, 'Ah, but it is to *me.'*

"I was still very angry. I said it was perfectly disgraceful the way he had always treated Caroline. She had had a miserable life with him. He said he knew that and he was sorry about it. Sorry! He said, 'I know, Merry, you don't believe that—but it's the truth. I've given Caroline the hell of a life and she's been a saint about it. But she did know, I think, what she might be letting herself in for. I told her candidly the sort of damnable, egotistical, loose-living kind of chap I was.'

"I put it to him then very strongly that he ought not to break up his married life. There was the child to be considered, and everything. I said that I could understand that a girl like Elsa could bowl a man over, but that even for her sake he ought to break off the whole thing. She was very young. She was going into this bald-headed, but she might regret it bitterly afterward. I said couldn't he pull himself together, make a clean break and go back to his wife?"

"And what did he say?"

Blake said: "He just looked—embarrassed. He patted me on the shoulder and said, 'You're a good chap, Merry. But you're too sentimental. You wait till the picture's finished and you'll admit that I was right.'

"I said, 'Damn your picture.' And he grinned and said all the neurotic women in England couldn't do that. Then I said that it would have been more decent to have kept the whole thing from Caroline until after the picture was finished. He said that that wasn't *his* fault. It was Elsa who had insisted on spilling the beans. I said, 'Why?' And he said that she had had some idea that it wasn't straight otherwise. She wanted everything to be clear and above-board. Well, of course, in a way, one could understand that and respect the girl for it. However badly she was behaving, she did at least want to be honest."

"A lot of additional pain and grief is caused by honesty," remarked Hercule Poirot.

Meredith Blake looked at him doubtfully. He did not quite like the sentiment. He sighed: "It was a—a most unhappy time for us all."

"The only person who does not seem to have been affected by it was Amyas Crale," said Poirot.

"And why? Because he was a rank egoist. I remember him now. Grinning at me as he went off saying, 'Don't worry, Merry. Everything's going to pan out all right!' "

"The incurable optimist," murmured Poirot.

"He was the kind of man who didn't take women seriously," Meredith Blake said. "*I* could have told him that Caroline was desperate."

"Did she tell you so?"

"Not in so many words. But I shall always see her face as it was that afternoon—white and strained with a kind of desperate gaiety. She talked and laughed a lot. But her eyes—there was a kind of anguished grief in them that was the most moving thing I have ever known. Such a gentle creature, too."

Hercule Poirot looked at him for a minute or two without speaking. Clearly the man in front of him felt no incongruity in speaking thus of a woman who, on the day after, had deliberately killed her husband.

Meredith Blake went on. He had by now quite overcome his first suspicious hostility. Hercule Poirot had the gift of listening. To men such as Meredith Blake the reliving of the past has a definite attraction. He spoke now almost more to himself than to his famous guest:

"I ought to have suspected something, I suppose. It was Caroline who turned the conversation to—to my little hobby. It was, I must confess, an enthusiasm of mine. The old English herbalists, you know, are a very interesting study. There are so many plants that were formerly used in medicine and which have now disappeared from the official pharmacopoeia. And it's astonishing, really, how a simple decoction of something or other will really work wonders. No need for doctors half the time. The French understand these things—some of their tisanes are first-rate."

He was well away now on his hobby:

"Dandelion tea, for instance, marvelous stuff. And a decoction of hips —I saw the other day somewhere that that's coming into fashion with the medical profession again. Oh, yes, I must confess, I got a lot of pleasure out of my brews. Gathering the plants at the right time, drying them, macerating them—all the rest of it. I've even dropped to superstition sometimes and gathered my roots at the full of the moon or whatever it was the ancients advised. On that day I gave my guests, I remember, a special disquisition on the spotted hemlock. It flowers biennially. You gather the fruits when they're ripening, just before they turn yellow. Coniine, you know, is a drug that's dropped right out—I don't believe there's any official preparation of it in the last pharmacopoeia—but I've proved the usefulness of it in whooping cough, and in asthma too, for that matter—"

"You talked of all this in your laboratory?"

"Yes, I showed them around, explained the various drugs to them—

valerian and the way it attracts cats—one sniff at that was enough for them! Then they asked about deadly nightshade, and I told them about belladonna and atropine. They were very much interested."

"They? What is comprised in that word?"

Meredith Blake looked faintly surprised as though he had forgotten that his listener had no firsthand knowledge of the scene.

"Oh, the whole party. Let me see—Philip was there, and Amyas, and Caroline, of course. Angela. And Elsa Greer."

"That was all?"

"Yes! I think so. Yes, I am sure of it." Blake looked at him curiously. "Who else should there be?"

"I thought perhaps the governess—"

"Oh, I see. No, she wasn't there that afternoon. I believe I've forgotten her name now. Nice woman. Took her duties very seriously. Angela worried her a good deal, I think."

"Why was that?"

"Well, she was a nice kid, but she was inclined to run wild. Always up to something or other. Put a slug or something down Amyas' back one day when he was hard at work painting. He went up in smoke. Cursed her up and down dale. It was after that that he insisted on this school idea."

"Sending her to school?"

"Yes. I don't mean he wasn't fond of her, but he found her a bit of a nuisance sometimes. And I think—I've always thought—"

"Yes?"

"That he was a bit jealous. Caroline, you see, was a slave to Angela. In a way, perhaps, Angela came first with her—and Amyas didn't like that. There was a reason for it, of course. I won't go into that, but—"

Poirot interrupted: "The reason being that Caroline Crale reproached herself for an action that had disfigured the girl."

Blake exclaimed, "Oh, you know that? I wasn't going to mention it. All over and done with. But, yes, that was the cause of her attitude, I think. She always seemed to feel that there was nothing too much she could do—to make up, as it were."

Poirot nodded thoughtfully. "And Angela?" he asked. "Did she bear a grudge against her half sister?"

"Oh, no; don't run away with that idea. Angela was devoted to Caroline. She never gave that old business a thought, I'm sure. It was just Caroline who couldn't forgive herself."

"Did Angela take kindly to the idea of boarding school?"

"No, she didn't. She was furious with Amyas. Caroline took her side, but Amyas had absolutely made his mind up about it. In spite of a hot temper, Amyas was an easy man in most respects, but when he really got his back up everyone had to give in. Both Caroline and Angela knuckled under."

"She was to go to school—when?"

"The autumn term—they were getting her kit together, I remember. I suppose, if it hadn't been for the tragedy she would have gone off a few days later. There was some talk of her packing on the morning of that day."

"And the governess?" Poirot asked.

"What do you mean—the governess?"

"How did she like the idea? It deprived her of a job, did it not?"

"Yes—well, I suppose it did in a way. Little Carla used to do a few lessons, but of course she was only—what? Six or thereabouts. She had a nurse. They wouldn't have kept Miss Williams on for her. Yes, that's the name—Williams. Funny how things come back to you when you talk them over."

"Yes, indeed. You are back now—are you not?—in the past. You relive the scenes—the words that people said, their gestures, the expressions on their faces?"

Meredith Blake said slowly:

"In a way—yes . . . but there are gaps, you know . . . great chunks missed out. I remember, for instance, the shock it was to me when I first learned that Amyas was going to leave Caroline, but I can't remember whether it was he who told me or Elsa. I do remember arguing with Elsa on the subject—trying to show her, I mean, that it was a pretty rotten thing to do. And she only laughed at me in that cool way of hers and said I was old-fashioned. Well, I dare say I *am* old-fashioned, but I still think I was right. Amyas had a wife and child—he ought to have stuck to them."

"But Miss Greer thought that point of view out of date?"

"Yes, Mind you, sixteen years ago, divorce wasn't looked on quite so much as a matter of course as it is now. But Elsa was the kind of girl who went in for being modern. Her point of view was that when two people weren't happy together it was better to make a break. She said that Amyas and Caroline never stopped having rows and that it was far better for the child that she shouldn't be brought up in an atmosphere of disharmony."

"And her argument did not impress you?" asked Poirot.

"I felt, all the time," Meredith Blake said slowly, "that she didn't really know what she was talking about. She was rattling these things off—things she'd read in books or heard from her friends—it was like a parrot. She was—it's a queer thing to say—pathetic somehow. So young and so self-confident." He paused. "There is something about youth, M. Poirot, that is—that can be—terribly moving."

Hercule Poirot said, looking at him with some interest, "I know what you mean."

Blake went on, speaking more to himself than to Poirot: "That's partly, I think, why I tackled Crale. He was nearly twenty years older than the girl. It didn't seem fair."

"Alas, how seldom one makes any effect," Poirot murmured. "When a person has determined on a certain course—especially when there is a woman concerned—it is not easy to turn them from it."

Meredith Blake said, "That is true enough." His tone was a shade bitter: "I certainly did no good by my interference. But, then, I am not a very convincing person. I never have been."

Poirot threw him a quick glance. He read into that slight acerbity of tone the dissatisfaction of a sensitive man with his own lack of personality. And he acknowledged to himself the truth of what Blake had just said. Meredith Blake was not the man to persuade anyone into or out of any course. His well-meaning attempts would always be set aside—indulgently usually, without anger, but definitely set aside. They would not carry weight. He was essentially an ineffective man.

Poirot said, with an appearance of changing a painful subject, "You still have your laboratory of medicines and cordials, yes?"

"No."

The word came sharply—with an almost anguished rapidity Meredith Blake said, his face flushing: "I abandoned the whole thing—dismantled it. I couldn't go on with it—how could I after what had happened? The whole thing, you see, might have been said to be *my* fault."

"No, no, Mr. Blake, you are too sensitive."

"But don't you see? If I hadn't collected those damned drugs; if I hadn't laid stress on them—boasted about them—forced them on those people's notice that afternoon. . . . But I never thought—I never dreamed—how could I—"

"How indeed?"

"But I went bumbling on about them. Pleased with my little bit of knowledge. Blind, conceited fool. I pointed out that damned coniine. I even—fool that I was—took them back into the library and read them out that passage from the Phaedo describing Socrates' death. A beautiful piece of writing—I've always admired it—but it's haunted me ever since."

Poirot said, "Did they find any fingerprints on the coniine bottle?"

Blake answered with one poignant word: "Hers."

"Caroline Crale's?"

"Yes."

"Not yours?"

"No. I didn't handle the bottle, you see. Only pointed to it."

"But at some time, surely, you had handled it?"

"Oh, of course, but I gave the bottles a periodic dusting from time to time—I never allowed the servants in there, of course—and I had done that about four or five days previously."

"You kept the room locked up?"

"Invariably."

"When did Caroline Crale take the coniine from the bottle?"

"She was the last to leave," Meredith Blake replied reluctantly. "I called her, I remember, and she came hurrying out. Her cheeks were just a little pink, and her eyes wide and excited. I can see her now—"

Poirot said: "Did you have any conversation with her at all that afternoon? I mean by that, did you discuss the situation as between her and her husband at all?"

"Not directly," Blake said slowly in a low voice. "She was looking, as I've told you, very upset. I said to her at a moment when we were more or less by ourselves, 'Is anything the matter, my dear?' She said, 'Everything's the matter. . . .' I wish you could have heard the desperation in her voice. Those words were the absolute literal truth. There's no getting away from it—Amyas Crale was Caroline's whole world. She said: 'Everything's gone —finished. I'm finished, Meredith.' And then she laughed and turned to the others and was suddenly wildly and very unnaturally gay."

Hercule Poirot nodded his head slowly. He looked very like a china mandarin. He said, "Yes—I see—it was like that . . ."

Meredith Blake pounded suddenly with his fist. His voice rose. It was almost a shout: "And I'll tell you this, M. Poirot—when Caroline Crale said at the trial that she took the stuff for herself, I'll swear she was speaking the truth! There was no thought in her mind of murder at that time. I swear there wasn't. That came later."

"Are you sure that it *did* come later?" Poirot asked.

Blake stared. "I beg your pardon?" he said. "I don't quite understand—"

Poirot said: "I ask you whether you are sure that the thought of murder ever did come? Are you perfectly convinced in your own mind that Caroline Crale did deliberately commit murder?"

Meredith Blake's breath came unevenly. He said, "But if not—if not— are you suggesting an—well, accident of some kind?"

"Not necessarily."

"That's a very extraordinary thing to say."

"Is it? You have called Caroline Crale a gentle creature. Do gentle creatures commit murder?"

"She was a gentle creature, but all the same—well, there were very violent quarrels, you know."

"Not such a gentle creature, then?"

"But she was— Oh, how difficult these things are to explain."

"I am trying to understand."

"Caroline had a quick tongue—a vehement way of speaking. She might say, 'I hate you. I wish you were dead,' but it wouldn't mean—it wouldn't entail—*action.*"

"So, in your opinion, it was highly uncharacteristic of Mrs. Crale to commit murder?"

"You have the most extraordinary ways of putting things, M. Poirot. I can only say that—yes, it does seem to me uncharacteristic of her. I can only explain it by realizing that the provocation was extreme. She adored her husband. Under those circumstances a woman might—well, kill."

Poirot nodded. "Yes, I agree. . . ."

"I was dumbfounded at first. I didn't feel it *could* be true. And it wasn't true—if you know what I mean—it wasn't the real Caroline who did that."

"But you are quite sure that, in the legal sense, Caroline Crale did do it?"

Again Meredith Blake stared at him. "My dear man, if she didn't—"

"Well, if she didn't?"

"I can't imagine any alternative solution. Accident? Surely impossible."

"Quite impossible, I should say."

"And I can't believe in the suicide theory. It had to be brought forward, but it was quite unconvincing to anyone who knew Crale."

"Quite."

"So what remains?" asked Meredith Blake.

Poirot said coolly, "There remains the possibility of Amyas Crale having been killed by somebody else."

"But that's absurd! *Nobody* could have killed him but his wife. But he drove her to it. And so, in a way, it was suicide after all, I suppose."

"Meaning that he died by the result of his own actions, though not by his own hand?"

"Yes, it's a fanciful point of view, perhaps. But—well, cause and effect, you know."

Hercule Poirot said, "Have you ever reflected, Mr. Blake, that the reason for murder is nearly always to be found by a study of the person murdered?"

"I hadn't exactly—yes, I suppose I see what you mean."

Poirot said, "Until you know exactly *what sort of a person the victim was,* you cannot begin to see the circumstances of a crime clearly." He added, "That is what I am seeking for—and what you and your brother have helped to give me—a reconstruction of the man Amyas Crale."

Meredith Blake passed the main point of the remark over. His attention had been attracted by a single word. He said quickly, "Philip?"

"Yes."

"You have talked with him also?"

"Certainly."

Meredith Blake said sharply, "You should have come to me first."

Smiling a little, Poirot made a courteous gesture. "As your brother lives near London, it was easier to visit him first."

Meredith Blake repeated, "You should have come to me first."

This time Poirot did not answer. He waited. And presently Meredith Blake went on. "Philip," he said, "is prejudiced."

"Yes?"

"As a matter of fact, he's a mass of prejudices—always has been." He shot a quick, uneasy glance at Poirot. "He'll have tried to put you against Caroline."

"Does that matter, so long—after?"

Meredith Blake gave a sharp sigh.

"I know. I forget that it's so long ago—that it's all over. Caroline is beyond being harmed. But, all the same, I shouldn't like you to get a false impression."

"And you think your brother might give me a false impression?"

"Frankly, I do. You see, there was always a certain—how shall I put it? —antagonism between him and Caroline."

"Why?"

The question seemed to irritate Blake. He said, "Why? How should I know *why?* These things are so. Philip always crabbed her whenever he could. He was annoyed, I think, when Amyas married her. He never went near them for over a year. And yet Amyas was almost his best friend. That was the reason really, I suppose. He didn't feel that any woman was good enough. And he probably felt that Caroline's influence would spoil their friendship."

"And did it?"

"No, of course it didn't. Amyas was always just as fond of Philip—right up to the end. Used to twit him with being a moneygrubber and with growing a corporation and being a Philistine generally. Philip didn't care. He just used to grin and say it was a good thing Amyas had one respectable friend."

"How did your brother react to the Elsa Greer affair?"

"Do you know, I find it rather difficult to say. His attitude wasn't really easy to define. He was annoyed, I think, with Amyas for making a fool of himself over the girl. He said more than once that it wouldn't work and that Amyas would live to regret it. At the same time I have a feeling—yes, very definitely I have a feeling that he was just faintly pleased at seeing Caroline let down."

There was a silence. Then Blake said with the irritable plaintiveness of a weak man, "It was all over—forgotten—and now *you* come, raking it all up. . . ."

"Not I. Caroline Crale."

Meredith stared at him: "Caroline? What do you mean?"

Poirot said, watching him, "Caroline Crale the second."

Meredith's face relaxed. "Ah, yes, the child. Little Carla. I—I misunderstood you for a moment."

"You thought I meant the original Caroline Crale? You thought that it was she who would not—how shall I say it?—rest easy in her grave."

Blake shivered. "Don't, man."

"You know that she wrote to her daughter—the last words she ever wrote—that she was innocent?"

Meredith stared at him. He said—and his voice sounded utterly incredulous, "Caroline wrote *that?*"

"Yes." Poirot paused and said, "It surprises you?"

"It would surprise you if you'd seen her in court. Poor, hunted, defenseless creature. Not even struggling."

"A defeatist?"

"No, no. She wasn't that. It was, I think, the knowledge that she'd killed the man she loved—or I thought it was that."

"You are not so sure now?"

"To write a thing like that—solemnly—when she was dying."

Poirot said, "A pious lie, perhaps?"

"Perhaps?" But Meredith was dubious. "That's not—that's not like Caroline. . . ."

Hercule Poirot nodded. Carla Lemarchant had said that. Carla had only a child's obstinate memory. But Meredith Blake had known Caroline well. It was the first confirmation Poirot had got that Carla's belief was to be depended upon.

Meredith Blake looked up at him. He said slowly, "If—*if* Caroline was innocent—why, the whole thing's madness! I don't see—any other possible solution. . . ." He turned sharply on Poirot: "And you? What do you think?"

There was a silence.

"As yet," said Poirot at last, "I think nothing. I collect only the impressions: What Caroline Crale was like. What Amyas Crale was like. What the other people who were there at the time were like. What happened exactly on those two days. *That* is what I need. To go over the facts

laboriously one by one. Your brother is going to help me there. He is
sending me an account of the events as he remembers them."

"You won't get much from that," Meredith Blake said sharply.
"Philip's a busy man. Things slip his memory once they're past and done
with. Probably he'll remember things all wrong."

"There will be gaps, of course. I realize that."

"I tell you what" —Meredith paused abruptly, then went on, reddening
a little as he spoke: "If you like, I—I could do the same. I mean, it would
be a kind of check, wouldn't it?"

Hercule Poirot said warmly: "It would be most valuable. An idea of the
first excellence!"

"Right. I will. I've got some old diaries somewhere. Mind you," he
laughed awkwardly, "I'm not much of a hand at literary language. Even
my spelling's not too good. You—you won't expect too much?"

"Ah, it is not the style I demand. Just a plain recital of everything you
can remember: What everyone said, how they looked—just what happened. Never mind if it doesn't seem relevant. It all helps with the atmosphere, so to speak."

"Yes, I can see that. It must be difficult visualizing people and places
you have never seen."

Poirot nodded. "That is another thing I wanted to ask you. Alderbury
is the adjoining property to this, is it not? Would it be possible to go there
—to see with my own eyes where the tragedy occurred?"

Meredith Blake said slowly: "I can take you over there right away. But,
of course, it is a good deal changed."

"It has not been built over?"

"No, thank goodness—not quite so bad as that. But it's a kind of hostel
now—it was bought by some society. Hordes of young people come down
to it in the summer, and, of course, all the rooms have been cut up and
partitioned into cubicles, and the grounds have been altered a good deal."

"You must reconstruct it for me by your explanations."

"I'll do my best. I wish you could have seen it in the old days. It was
one of the loveliest properties I know."

He led the way out and began walking down a slope of lawn.

"Who was responsible for selling it?"

"The executors on behalf of the child. Everything Crale had came to
her. He hadn't made a will, so I imagine that it would be divided automatically between his wife and the child. Caroline's will left what she had to
the child also."

"Nothing to her half sister?"

"Angela had a certain amount of money of her own left her by her
father."

Poirot nodded. "I see." Then he uttered an exclamation: "But where is it that you take me? This is the seashore ahead of us!"

"Ah, I must explain our geography to you. You'll see for yourself in a minute. There's a creek, you see, Camel Creek, they call it, runs right inland—looks almost like a river mouth, but it isn't—it's just sea. To get to Alderbury by land, you have to go right inland and around the creek, but the shortest way from one house to the other is to row across this narrow bit of the creek. Alderbury is just opposite—there, you can see the house through the trees."

They had come out on a little beach. Opposite them was a wooded headland, and a white house could just be distinguished high up among the trees.

Two boats were drawn up on the beach. Meredith Blake, with Poirot's somewhat awkward assistance, dragged one of them down to the water and presently they were rowing across to the other side.

"We always went this way in the old days," Meredith explained. "Unless there was a storm or it was raining, and then we'd take the car. But it's nearly three miles if you go around that way."

He ran the boat neatly alongside a stone quay on the other side. He cast a disparaging eye on a collection of wooden huts and some concrete terraces.

"All new, this. Used to be a boathouse—tumble-down old place, and nothing else. And one walked along the shore and bathed off those rocks over there."

He assisted his guest to alight, made fast the boat, and led the way up a steep path.

"Don't suppose we'll meet anyone," he said over his shoulder. "Nobody here in April—except for Easter. Doesn't matter if we do. I'm on good terms with my neighbors. Sun's glorious today. Might be summer. It was a wonderful day then. More like July than September. Brilliant sun, but a chilly little wind."

The path came out of the trees and skirted an outcrop of rock. Meredith pointed up with his hand: "That's what they called the Battery. We're underneath it now—skirting round it."

They plunged into trees again and then the path took another sharp turn and they emerged by a door set in a high wall. The path itself continued to zigzag upward, but Meredith opened the door and the two men passed through it.

For a moment Poirot was dazzled, coming in from the shade outside. The Battery was an artificially cleared plateau with battlements set with cannon. It gave one the impression of overhanging the sea. There were trees above it and behind it, but on the sea side there was nothing but the dazzling blue water below.

"Attractive spot," said Meredith. He nodded contemptuously toward a kind of pavilion set back against the back wall. "That wasn't there, of course—only an old tumble-down shed where Amyas kept his painting muck and some bottled beer and a few deck chairs. It wasn't concreted then, either. There used to be a bench and a table—painted iron ones. That was all. Still—it hasn't changed much."

His voice held an unsteady note.

Poirot said, "And it was here that it happened?"

Meredith nodded. "The bench was there—up against the shed. He was sprawled on that. He used to sprawl there sometimes when he was painting —just fling himself down and stare and stare, and then suddenly up he'd jump and start laying the paint on the canvas like mad."

He paused.

"That's why, you know, he looked—almost natural. As though he might be asleep—just have dropped off. But his eyes were open—and he'd —just stiffened up. Stuff sort of paralyzes you, you know. There isn't any pain. . . . I've—I've always been glad of that. . . ."

Poirot asked a thing that he already knew: "Who found him here?"

"She did. Caroline. After lunch. Elsa and I, I suppose, were the last ones to see him alive. It must have been coming on then. He—looked queer. I'd rather not talk about it. I'll write it to you. Easier that way."

He turned abruptly and went out of the Battery. Poirot followed him without speaking.

The two men went on up the zigzag path. At a higher level than the Battery, there was another small plateau. It was overshadowed with trees and there was a bench there and a table. Meredith said: "They haven't changed this much. But the bench used not to be Ye Olde Rustic. It was just a painted iron business. A bit hard for sitting, but a lovely view."

Poirot agreed. Through a framework of trees one looked down over the Battery to the creek mouth.

"I sat up here part of the morning," Meredith explained. "Trees weren't quite so overgrown then. One could see the battlements of the Battery quite plainly. That's where Elsa was posing, you know. Sitting on one, with her head twisted around."

He gave a slight twitch of his shoulders. "Trees grow faster than one thinks," he muttered. "Oh, well, suppose I'm getting old. Come on up to the house."

They continued to follow the path till it emerged near the house. It had been a fine old house, Georgian in style. It had been added to, and on a green lawn near it were set some fifty little wooden bathing hutches.

"Young men sleep there, girls in the house," Meredith explained. "I don't suppose there's anything you want to see here. All the rooms have been cut about. Used to be a little conservatory tacked on here. These people have built a loggia. Oh, well—I suppose they enjoy their holidays. Can't keep everything as it used to be—more's the pity."

He turned away abruptly. "We'll go down another way. It—it all comes back to me, you know. Ghosts. *Ghosts everywhere!*"

Chapter V

THEY RETURNED TO the quay by a somewhat longer and more rambling route. Poirot did not speak; nor did Blake. When they reached Handcross Manor once more, Blake said abruptly:

"I bought that picture, you know. The one that Amyas was painting. I just couldn't stand the idea of its being sold for—well, publicity value—a lot of dirty-minded brutes gaping at it. It was a fine piece of work. Amyas said it was the best thing he'd ever done. I shouldn't be surprised if he was right. It was practically finished. He only wanted to work on it another day or so. Would—would you care to see it?"

Hercule Poirot said quickly, "Yes, indeed."

Blake led the way across the hall and took a key from his pocket. He unlocked a door and they went into a fair-sized, dusty-smelling room. It was closely shuttered. Blake went across to the windows and opened the wooden shutters. Then, with a little difficulty, he flung up a window and a breath of fragrant spring air came wafting into the room.

Meredith said, "That's better."

He stood by the window inhaling the air and Poirot joined him. There was no need to ask what the room had been. The shelves were empty, but there were marks upon them where bottles had once stood. Against one wall was some derelict chemical apparatus and a sink. The room was thick in dust.

Meredith Blake was looking out of the window. He said: "How easily it all comes back. Standing here, smelling the jasmine, and talking—talking, like the damned fool I was, about my precious potions and distillations!"

Absently, Poirot stretched a hand through the window. He pulled off a spray of jasmine leaves just breaking from their woody stem.

Meredith Blake moved resolutely across the floor. On the wall was a picture covered with a dust sheet. He jerked the dust sheet away.

Poirot caught his breath. He had seen, so far, four pictures of Amyas Crale's—two at the Tate; one at a London dealer's; one, the still life of roses. But now he was looking at what the artist himself had called his best picture, and Poirot realized at once what a superb artist the man had been.

The painting had an odd, superficial smoothness. At first sight it might have been a poster, so seemingly crude were its contrasts. A girl, a girl in a canary-yellow shirt and dark blue slacks, sitting on a gray wall in full sunlight against a background of violent blue sea. Just the kind of subject for a poster.

But the first appearance was deceptive: there was a subtle distortion—an amazing brilliance and clarity in the light. And the girl—

Yes, here was life. All there was, all there could be, of life, of youth, of sheer blazing vitality. The face was alive and the eyes . . .

So much life! Such passionate youth! That, then, was what Amyas Crale had seen in Elsa Greer, which had made him blind and deaf to the gentle creature, his wife. Elsa *was* life. Elsa was youth.

A superb, slim, straight creature, arrogant, her head turned, her eyes insolent with triumph. Looking at you, watching you—waiting . . .

Hercule Poirot spread out his hands. He said, "It is a great—yes, it is great."

Meredith Blake said, a catch in his voice, "She was so young—"

Poirot nodded. He thought to himself, "What do most people mean when they say that? So *young.* Something innocent, something appealing, something helpless. But youth is not that! Youth is crude, youth is strong, youth is powerful—yes, and cruel! And one thing more—youth is vulnerable."

Poirot followed his host to the door. His interest was quickened now in Elsa Greer, whom he was to visit next. What would the years have done to that passionate, triumphant, crude child?

He looked back at the picture.

Those eyes. Watching him . . . watching him . . . telling him something. . . .

Supposing he couldn't understand what they were telling him? Would the real woman be able to tell him? Or were those eyes saying something that the real woman did not know?

Such arrogance, such triumphant anticipation—

And then death had stepped in and taken the prey out of those eager, clutching young hands . . .

And the light had gone out of those passionately anticipating eyes. What were the eyes of Elsa Greer like now?

He went out of the room with one last look.

He thought, "She was too much alive."

He felt—a little—frightened. . . .

The house in Brook Street had Darwin tulips in the window boxes. Inside the hall a great vase of white lilacs sent eddies of perfume toward the open front door.

A middle-aged butler relieved Poirot of his hat and stick. A footman appeared to take them and the butler murmured deferentially, "Will you come this way, sir?"

Poirot followed him along the hall and down three steps. A door was opened, the butler pronounced his name with every syllable correct.

Then the door closed behind him and a tall, thin man got up from a chair by the fire and came toward him.

Lord Dittisham was a man just under forty. He was not only a peer of the realm; he was a poet. Two of his fantastical poetic dramas had been staged at vast expense and had had a *succès d'estime*. His forehead was rather prominent, his chin was eager, and his eyes and his mouth unexpectedly beautiful.

He said, "Sit down, M. Poirot."

Poirot sat down and accepted a cigarette from his host. Lord Dittisham shut the box, struck a match and held it for Poirot to light his cigarette, then he himself sat down and looked thoughtfully at his visitor.

"It is my wife you have come to see, I know," he said.

Poirot answered, "Lady Dittisham was so kind as to give me an appointment."

"Yes."

There was a pause.

"You do not, I hope, object, Lord Dittisham?" Poirot hazarded.

The thin, dreamy face was transformed by a sudden, quick smile. "The objections of husbands, M. Poirot, are never taken seriously in these days."

"Then you do object?"

"No. I cannot say that. But I am, I must confess it, a little fearful of the effect upon my wife. Let me be quite frank. A great many years ago, when my wife was only a young girl, she passed through a terrible ordeal. She has, I hope, recovered from the shock. I have come to believe that she has forgotten it. Now you appear and necessarily your questions will reawaken these old memories."

"It is regrettable," said Hercule Poirot politely.

"I do not know quite what the result will be."

"I can only assure you, Lord Dittisham, that I shall be as discreet as possible, and do all I can not to distress Lady Dittisham. She is, no doubt, of a delicate and nervous temperament."

Then, suddenly and surprisingly, the other laughed. He said: "Elsa? Elsa's as strong as a horse!"

"Then—" Poirot paused diplomatically. The situation intrigued him.

Lord Dittisham said: "My wife is equal to any amount of shocks. I wonder if you know her reason for seeing you?"

Poirot replied placidly, "Curiosity?"

A kind of respect showed in the other man's eyes. "Ah, you realize that?"

"It is inevitable," Hercule Poirot said. "Women will *always* see a private detective. Men will tell him to go to the devil."

"Some women might tell him to go to the devil too."

"After they have seen him—not before."

"Perhaps." Lord Dittisham paused. "What is the idea behind this book?"

Hercule Poirot shrugged his shoulders. "One resurrects the old tunes, the old stage turns, the old costumes. One resurrects, too, the old murders."

"Faugh!" said Lord Dittisham.

"Faugh! if you like. But you will not alter human nature by saying faugh. Murder is a drama. The desire for drama is very strong in the human race."

Lord Dittisham murmured, "I know—I know . . ."

He rose and rang the bell. "My wife will be waiting for you," he said brusquely.

The door opened.

"You rang, my lord?"

"Take M. Poirot up to her ladyship."

Up two flights of stairs, feet sinking into soft-pile carpets. Subdued flood lighting. Money, money everywhere. Of taste, not so much. There had been a somber austerity in Lord Dittisham's room. But here, in the house, there was only a solid lavishness. The best. Not necessarily the showiest nor the most startling. Merely "expense no object," allied to a lack of imagination.

It was not a large room into which Poirot was shown. The big drawing room was on the first floor. This was the personal sitting room of the mistress of the house, and the mistress of the house was standing against the mantelpiece as Poirot was announced and shown in.

A phrase leaped into his startled mind and refused to be driven out: *She died young. . . .*

That was his thought as he looked at Elsa Dittisham who had been Elsa Greer.

He would never have recognized her from the picture Meredith Blake had shown him. That had been, above all, a picture of youth, a picture of vitality. Here there was no youth—there might never have been youth. And yet he realized, as he had not realized from Crale's picture, that Elsa was beautiful. Yes, it was a very beautiful woman who came forward to meet him. And certainly not old. After all, what was she? Not more than thirty-six now, if she had been twenty at the time of the tragedy.

He felt a strange pang. It was, perhaps, the fault of old Mr. Johnathan, speaking of Juliet . . . No Juliet here—unless perhaps one could imagine Juliet a survivor—living on, deprived of Romeo. . . . Was it not an essential part of Juliet's make-up that she should die young?

Elsa Greer had been left alive. . . .

She was greeting him in a level, rather monotonous voice: "I am so interested, M. Poirot! Sit down and tell me what you want me to do?"

He thought: "But she isn't interested. Nothing interests her."

Big gray eyes—like dead lakes.

Poirot became, as was his way, a little obviously foreign. He exclaimed, "I am confused, madame, veritably I am confused."

"Oh, no; why?"

"Because I realize that this—this reconstruction of a past drama must be excessively painful to you."

She looked amused. Yes, it was amusement. Quite genuine amusement. She said: "I suppose my husband put that idea into your head. He saw you when you arrived. Of course, he doesn't understand in the least. He never has. I'm not at all the sensitive sort of person he imagines I am."

Poirot thought to himself: "Yes, that is true. A thin-skinned person would not have come to stay in Caroline Crale's house."

Lady Dittisham said, "What is it you want me to do?"

"You are sure, madame, that to go over the past would not be painful to you?"

She considered a minute, and it struck Poirot suddenly that Lady Dittisham was a very frank woman. She might lie from necessity but never from choice.

Elsa Dittisham said slowly: "No, not *painful*. In a way, I wish it were." "Why?"

She said impatiently, "It's so stupid—never to feel anything. . . ."

And Hercule Poirot thought, "Yes, Elsa Greer is dead." Aloud he said, "At all events, Lady Dittisham, it makes my task very much easier. Have you a good memory?"

"Reasonably good, I think."

"And you are sure it will not pain you to go over those days in detail?"

"It won't pain me at all. Things can only pain you when they are happening."

"It is so with some people, I know."

Lady Dittisham said: "That's what Edward, my husband, can't understand. He thinks the trial and all that was a terrible ordeal for me."

"Was it not?"

Elsa Dittisham said, "No, I enjoyed it." There was a reflective, satisfied quality in her voice. She went on: "God, how that old brute Depleach went for me! He's a devil, if you like. I enjoyed fighting him. He didn't get me down."

She looked at Poirot with a smile. "I hope I'm not upsetting your illusions. A girl of twenty, I ought to have been prostrated, I suppose— agonized with shame or something. I wasn't. I didn't care what they said to me. I only wanted one thing."

"What?"

"To get her hanged, of course," said Elsa Dittisham.

He noticed her hands—beautiful hands but with long, curving nails. Predatory hands.

She said: "You're thinking me vindictive? So I am vindictive—to anyone who has injured me. That woman was to my mind the lowest kind of woman there is. She knew that Amyas cared for me—that he was going to leave her—and she killed him so that *I* shouldn't have him."

She looked across at Poirot.

"Don't you think that's pretty mean?"

"You do not understand or sympathize with jealousy?"

"No, I don't think I do. If you've lost, you've lost. If you can't keep your husband, let him go with a good grace. It's possessiveness I don't understand."

"You might have understood it if you had ever married him."

"I don't think so. We weren't—" She smiled suddenly at Poirot. Her smile was, he felt, a little frightening. It was so far removed from any real feeling. "I'd like you to get this right," she said. "Don't think that Amyas Crale seduced an innocent young girl. It wasn't like that at all! Of the two of us, *I* was responsible. I met him at a party and I fell for him. I knew I had to have him—"

"Although he was married?"

"Trespassers will be prosecuted? It takes more than a printed notice to keep you from reality. If he was unhappy with his wife and could be happy with me, then why not? We've only one life to live."

"But it has been said he was happy with his wife."

Elsa shook her head. "No. They quarreled like cat and dog. She nagged at him. She was—oh, she was a horrible woman!"

She got up and lit a cigarette. She said with a little smile: "Probably I'm unfair to her. But I really *do* think she was rather hateful."

Poirot said slowly, "It was a great tragedy."

"Yes, it was a great tragedy." She turned on him suddenly; into the dead, monotonous weariness of her face something came quiveringly alive.

"It killed *me*, do you understand? It killed me. Ever since, there's been nothing—nothing at all." Her voice dropped: "Emptiness!" She waved her hands impatiently. "Like a stuffed fish in a glass case!"

"Did Amyas Crale mean so much to you?"

She nodded. It was a queer, confiding little nod—oddly pathetic. She said, "I think I've always had a single-track mind." She mused somberly. "I suppose—really—one ought to put a knife into oneself—like Juliet. But —but to do that is to acknowledge that you're done for—that life's beaten you."

"And instead?"

"There ought to be everything—just the same—once one has got over it. I *did* get over it. It didn't mean anything to me any more. I thought I'd go on to the next thing."

Yes, the next thing. Poirot saw her plainly trying so hard to fulfill that crude determination. Saw her beautiful and rich, seductive to men, seeking with greedy, predatory hands to fill up a life that was empty. Hero worship —a marriage to a famous aviator; then an explorer, that big giant of a man Arnold Stevensen, possibly not unlike Amyas Crale physically—a reversion to the creative arts; Dittisham!

Elsa Dittisham said, "I've never been a hypocrite! There's a Spanish proverb I've always liked. *Take what you want and pay for it, says God.* Well, I've done that. I've taken what I wanted—but I've always been willing to pay the price."

"What you do not understand," Poirot said, "is that there are things that cannot be bought."

She stared at him. "I don't mean just money."

Poirot said: "No, no; I understand what you meant. But it is not everything in life that has its ticket, so much. There are things that are *not for sale.*"

"Nonsense!"

He smiled very faintly. In her voice was the arrogance of the successful mill hand who had risen to riches.

Hercule Poirot felt a sudden wave of pity. He looked at the ageless smooth face, the weary eyes, and he remembered the girl whom Amyas Crale had painted.

Elsa Dittisham said: "Tell me all about this book. What is the purpose of it? Whose idea is it?"

"Oh, my dear lady, what other purpose is there but to serve up yesterday's sensation with today's sauce?"

"But *you're* not a writer?"

"No, I am an expert on crime."

"You mean, they consult you on crime books?"

"Not always. In this case, I have a commission."

"From whom?"

"I am—what do you say?—working on this publication on behalf of an interested party."

"What party?"

"Miss Carla Lemarchant."

"Who is she?"

"She is the daughter of Amyas and Caroline Crale."

Elsa stared for a minute. Then she said: "Oh, of course, there *was* a child. I remember. I suppose she's grown up now?"

"Yes, she is twenty-one."

"What is she like?"

"She is tall and dark and, I think, beautiful. And she has courage and personality."

Elsa said thoughtfully, "I should like to see her."

"She might not care to see you."

Elsa looked surprised. "Why? Oh, I see. But what nonsense! She can't possibly remember anything about it. She can't have been more than six."

"She knows that her mother was tried for her father's murder."

"And she thinks it's my fault?"

"It is a possible interpretation."

Elsa shrugged her shoulders. "How stupid!" she said. "If Caroline had behaved like a reasonable human being—"

"So you take no responsibility?"

"Why should I? *I've* nothing to be ashamed of. I loved him. I would have made him happy." She looked across at Poirot. Her face broke up—suddenly, incredibly, he saw the girl of the picture. She said: "If I could make you see. If you could see it from my side. If you knew—"

Poirot leaned forward. "But that is what I want. See, Mr. Philip Blake, who was there at the time, he is writing me a meticulous account of everything that happened. Mr. Meredith Blake the same. Now if you—"

Elsa Dittisham took a deep breath. She said contemptuously: "Those two! Philip was always stupid. Meredith used to trot around after Caroline —but he was quite a dear. But you won't have *any* real idea from *their* accounts."

He watched her, saw the animation rising in her eyes, saw a living woman take shape from a dead one. She said quickly and almost fiercely: "Would you like the *truth?* Oh, not for publication. But just for your-self—"

"I will undertake not to publish without your consent."

"I'd like to write down the truth. . . ." She was silent a minute or two, thinking. He saw the smooth hardness of her cheeks falter and take on a younger curve; he saw life flowing into her as the past claimed her again.

"To go back—to write it all down. . . . To show you what she was—"

Her eyes flashed. Her breast heaved passionately. "She killed him. She killed Amyas. Amyas, who wanted to live—who enjoyed living. Hate oughtn't to be stronger than love—but her hate was. And my hate for her is—I hate her—I hate her—I hate her. . . ."

She came across to him. She stopped, her hand clutched at his sleeve. She said urgently: "You must understand—you *must*—how we felt about each other. Amyas and I, I mean. There's something—I'll show you."

She whirled across the room. She was unlocking a little desk, pulling out a drawer concealed inside a pigeonhole.

Then she was back. In her hand was a creased letter, the ink faded. She thrust it on him and Poirot had a sudden poignant memory of a child he had known who had thrust on him one of her treasures—a special shell picked up on the seashore and zealously guarded. Just so had that child stood back and watched him. Proud, afraid, keenly critical of his reception of her treasure.

He unfolded the faded sheets, and read:

"Elsa—you wonderful child! There never was anything as beautiful. And yet I'm afraid—I'm too old—a middle-aged, ugly-tempered devil with no stability in me. Don't trust me, don't believe in me—I'm no good, apart from my work. The best of me is in that. There, don't say you haven't been warned.

"But, my lovely, I'm going to have you all the same. I'd go to the devil for you, and you know it. And I'll paint a picture of you that will make the fat-headed world hold its sides and gasp! I'm crazy about you—I can't sleep, I can't eat. Elsa—Elsa—Elsa—I'm yours forever; yours till death. AMYAS."

Sixteen years ago. Faded ink, crumbling paper. But the words still alive, still vibrating. . . .

He looked across at the woman to whom they had been written.

But it was no longer a woman at whom he looked.

It was a young girl in love.

He thought again of Juliet. . . .

"May I ask why, M. Poirot?"

Hercule Poirot considered his answer to the question. He was aware of a pair of very shrewd gray eyes watching him out of the small, wizened face.

He had climbed to the top floor of the bare building and knocked on the door of No. 584 Gillespie Buildings, which had come into existence to provide so-called "flatlets" for workingwomen.

Here, in a small cubic space, existed Miss Cecilia Williams, in a room that was bedroom, sitting room, dining room and, by judicious use of the gas ring, kitchen—a kind of cubbyhole attached to it contained a quarter-length bath and the usual offices.

Meager though these surroundings might be, Miss Williams had contrived to impress upon them her stamp of personality.

The walls were distempered an ascetic pale gray, and various reproductions hung upon them. Danté meeting Beatrice on a bridge, and that picture once described by a child as a "blind girl sitting on an orange and called, I don't know why, Hope." There were also two water colors of Venice and a sepia copy of Botticelli's Primavera. On the top of the low chest of drawers were a large quantity of faded photographs, mostly, by their style of hairdressing, dating from twenty to thirty years ago.

The square of carpet was threadbare, the furniture battered and of poor quality. It was clear to Hercule Poirot that Cecilia Williams lived very near the bone. There was no roast beef here. This was the little pig that had none.

Clear, incisive and insistent, the voice of Miss Williams repeated its demand: "You want my recollections of the Crale case? May I ask why?"

It has been said of Hercule Poirot by some of his friends and associates, at moments when he has maddened them most, that he prefers lies to truth and will go out of his way to gain his ends by means of elaborate false statements, rather than trust to the simple truth.

But in this case he proffered no specious explanation of a book to be written on bygone crimes. Instead he narrated simply the circumstances in which Carla Lemarchant had sought him out.

The small, elderly lady in the neat, shabby dress listened attentively. She said, "It interests me very much to have news of that child—to know how she has turned out."

"She is a very charming and attractive young woman, with plenty of courage and a mind of her own."

"Good," said Miss Williams briefly.

"And she is, I may say, a very persistent person. She is not a person whom it is easy to refuse or put off."

The ex-governess nodded thoughtfully. She asked, "Is she artistic?"

"I think not."

Miss Williams said dryly, "That's one thing to be thankful for!"

The tone of the remark left Miss Williams' views as to artists in no doubt whatever. She added, "From your account of her I should imagine that she takes after her mother rather than after her father."

"Very possibly. That you can tell me when you have seen her. You would like to see her?"

"I should like to see her very much indeed. It is always interesting to see how a child you have known has developed."

"She was, I suppose, very young when you last saw her?"

"She was five and a half. A very charming child—a little overquiet, perhaps. Thoughtful. Given to playing her own little games and not inviting outside co-operation. Natural and unspoiled."

Poirot said, "It was fortunate she was so young."

"Yes, indeed. Had she been older the shock of the tragedy might have had a very bad effect."

"Nevertheless," said Poirot, "one feels that there *was* a handicap—however little the child understood or was allowed to know, there would have been an atmosphere of mystery and evasion and an abrupt uprooting. These things are not good for a child."

Miss Williams replied thoughtfully, "They may have been less harmful than you think."

Poirot said, "Before we leave the subject of Carla Lemarchant—little Carla Crale that was—there is something I would like to ask you. If anyone can explain it, I think you can."

"Yes?" Her voice was inquiring, noncommittal.

Poirot waved his hands in an effort to express his meaning.

"There is a something—a *nuance* I cannot define—but it seems to me always that the child, when I mention her, is not given her full value. When I mention her, the response comes always with a vague surprise, as though the person to whom I speak had forgotten altogether that there *was* a child. Now surely, mademoiselle, that is not natural. A child, under these circumstances, is a person of importance, not in herself, but as a pivotal point. Amyas Crale may have had reasons for abandoning his wife —or for not abandoning her. But in the usual breakup of a marriage the child forms a very important point. But here the child seems to count for very little. That seems to me—strange."

Miss Williams said quickly: "You have put your finger on a vital point, M. Poirot. You are quite right. And that is partly why I said what I did just now—that Carla's transportation to different surroundings might have been in some respects a good thing for her. When she became older, you see, she might have suffered from a certain lack in her home life."

She leaned forward and spoke slowly and carefully:

"Naturally, in the course of my work, I have seen a good many aspects of the parent-and-child problem. Many children, *most* children, I should say, suffer from overattention on the part of their parents. There is too much love, too much watching over the child. It is uneasily conscious of this brooding, and seeks to free itself, to get away and be unobserved. With an only child this is particularly the case, and of course mothers are the worst offenders.

"The result on the marriage is often unfortunate. The husband resents coming second, seeks consolation—or rather flattery and attention—elsewhere, and a divorce results sooner or later. The best thing for a child, I am convinced, is to have what I should term healthy neglect on the part of both its parents. This happens naturally enough in the case of a large family of children and very little money. They are overlooked because the mother has literally no time to occupy herself with them. They realize quite well that she is fond of them, but they are not worried by too many manifestations of the fact.

"But there is another aspect. One does occasionally find a husband and wife who are so ill-sufficient to each other, so wrapped up in each other, that the child of the marriage hardly seems very real to either of them. And in those circumstances, I think, a child comes to resent that fact, to feel defrauded and left out in the cold. You understand that I am not speaking of *neglect* in any way. Mrs. Crale, for instance, was what is termed an excellent mother, always careful of Carla's welfare, of her health, playing with her at the right times, and always kind and gay. But, for all that, Mrs. Crale was really completely wrapped up in her husband. She existed, one might say, only in him and for him." Miss Williams paused a minute and then said quietly, "That, I think, is the justification for what she eventually did."

"You mean," Hercule Poirot said, "that they were more like lovers than like husband and wife?"

Miss Williams, with a slight frown of distaste for foreign phraseology said, "You could certainly put it that way."

"He was as devoted to her as she was to him?"

"They were a devoted couple. But he, of course, was a man."

Miss Williams contrived to put into that last word a wholly Victorian significance.

"Men—" said Miss Williams, and stopped.

As a rich property owner says, "Bolsheviks," as an earnest Communist says, "Capitalists," as a good housewife says, "Black beetles," so did Miss Williams say, "Men."

From her spinster's, governess' life, there rose up a blast of fierce feminism. Nobody hearing her speak could doubt that, to Miss Williams, Men were the Enemy!

Poirot said, "You hold no brief for men?"

She answered dryly: "Men have the best of this world. I hope that it will not always be so."

Hercule Poirot eyed her speculatively. He could quite easily visualize Miss Williams methodically and efficiently padlocking herself to a railing, and later hunger-striking with resolute endurance.

Leaving the general for the particular, he said, "You did not like Amyas Crale?"

"I certainly did not like Mr. Crale. Nor did I approve of him. If I had been his wife I should have left him. There are things that no woman should put up with."

"But Mrs. Crale did put up with them?"

"Yes."

"You think she was wrong?"

"Yes, I do. A woman should have a certain respect for herself and not submit to humiliation."

"Did you ever say anything of that kind to Mrs. Crale?"

"Certainly not. It was not my place to do so. I was engaged to educate Angela, not to offer unasked advice to Mrs. Crale. To do so would have been most impertinent."

"You liked Mrs. Crale?"

"I was very fond of Mrs. Crale." The efficient voice softened, held warmth and feeling. "Very fond of her and very sorry for her."

"And your pupil—Angela Warren?" Poirot leaned forward, his eyes fixed hard on Miss Williams'.

Chapter VI

"SHE WAS A most interesting girl—one of the most interesting pupils I have had," Miss Williams said. "A really good brain. Undisciplined, quick-tempered, most difficult to manage in many ways, but really a very fine character."

She paused and then went on:

"I always hoped that she would accomplish something worth while. And she has! You have read her book—on the Sahara? And she excavated those very interesting tombs in the Fayum! Yes, I am proud of Angela. I was not at Alderbury very long—two years and a half—but I always cherish the belief that I helped to stimulate her mind and encourage her taste for archaeology."

"I understand," Poirot murmured, "that it was decided to continue her education by sending her to school. You must have resented that decision."

"Not at all, M. Poirot. I thoroughly concurred in it."

She paused and went on: "Let me make the matter clear to you: Angela was a dear girl, really a very dear girl—warm-hearted and impulsive—but she was also what I call a difficult girl. That is, she was at a difficult age. There is always a moment where a girl feels unsure of herself—neither child nor woman. At one minute Angela would be sensible and mature—quite grown-up, in fact—but a minute later she would relapse into being a hoydenish child—playing mischievous tricks and being rude and losing her temper.

"Girls, you know, *feel* difficult at that age—they are terribly sensitive. Everything that is said to them they resent. They are annoyed at being treated like children and then they suddenly feel shy at being treated like adults. Angela was in that state. She had fits of temper, would suddenly resent teasing and flare out, and then she would be sulky for days at a time, sitting about and frowning; then again she would be in wild spirits, climbing trees, rushing about with the garden boys, refusing to submit to any kind of authority.

"When a girl gets to that stage, school is very helpful. She needs the stimulation of other minds—that and the wholesome discipline of a community help her to become a reasonable member of society. Angela's home conditions were not what I would have called ideal. Mrs. Crale spoiled her, for one thing. Angela had only to appeal to her and Mrs. Crale always backed her up. The result was that Angela considered she had first claim upon her sister's time and attention, and it was in these moods of hers that she used to clash with Mr. Crale.

"Mr. Crale naturally thought that *he* should come first and he intended to. He was really very fond of the girl—they were good companions and used to spar together quite amiably, but there were times when Mr. Crale used suddenly to resent Mrs. Crale's preoccupation with Angela. Like all men, he was a spoiled child—he expected everybody to make a fuss over *him.* Then he and Angela used to have a real set-to—and very often Mrs. Crale would take Angela's side. Then he would be furious. On the other hand, if *she* supported *him,* Angela would be furious. It was on these occasions that Angela used to revert to childish ways and play some spiteful trick on him.

"He had a habit of tossing off his drinks, and she once put a lot of salt into his drink. The whole thing, of course, acted as an emetic, and he was inarticulate with fury. But what really brought things to a head was when she put a lot of slugs into his bed. He had a queer aversion for slugs. He lost his temper completely and said that the girl had to be sent away to school. He wasn't going to put up with all this petty nonsense any more.

"Angela was terribly upset—though actually she had once or twice expressed a wish herself to go to a large school, but she chose to make a huge grievance of it. Mrs. Crale didn't want her to go, but allowed herself to be persuaded—largely owing, I think, to what I said to her on the subject. I pointed out to her that it would be greatly to Angela's advantage, and that I thought it would really be a great benefit to the girl. So it was settled that she should go to Helston—a very fine school on the south coast—in the autumn term.

"But Mrs. Crale was till unhappy about it all those holidays. And Angela kept up a grudge against Mr. Crale whenever she remembered. It wasn't really serious, you understand, M. Poirot, but it made a kind of undercurrent that summer to—well—to everything *else* that was going on."

"Meaning—Elsa Greer?" Poirot said.

Miss Williams said sharply, "Exactly."

"What was your opinion of Elsa Greer?"

"I had no opinion of her at all. A thoroughly unprincipled young woman."

"She was very young."

"Old enough to know better. I can see no excuse for her—none at all."

"She fell in love with him, I suppose—"

Miss Williams interrupted with a snort: "Fell in love with him, indeed. I should hope, M. Poirot, that whatever our feelings, we can keep them in decent control. And we can certainly control our actions. That girl had absolutely no morals of any kind. It meant nothing to her that Mr. Crale was a married man. She was absolutely shameless about it all—cool and determined. Possibly she may have been badly brought up, but that's the only excuse I can find for her."

"Mr. Crale's death must have been a terrible shock to her," said Poirot.

"Oh, it was. And she herself was entirely to blame for it. I don't go as far as condoning murder, but all the same, M. Poirot, if ever a woman was driven to the breaking point that woman was Caroline Crale. I tell you frankly, there were moments when I would have liked to murder them both myself. Flaunting the girl in his wife's face, listening to her having to put up with the girl's insolence—and she *was* insolent, M. Poirot. Oh, no, Amyas Crale deserved what he got. No man should treat his wife as he did and not be punished for it. His death was a just retribution."

Hercule Poirot said, "You feel strongly . . ."

The small woman looked at him with those indomitable gray eyes. She said: "I feel *very strongly* about the marriage tie. Unless it is respected and upheld, a country degenerates. Mrs. Crale was a devoted and faithful wife. Her husband deliberately flouted her and introduced Elsa Greer into her home. As I say, he deserved what he got. He goaded her past endurance and I, for one, do not blame her for what she did."

Poirot said slowly: "He acted very badly—that I admit. But he was a great artist, remember."

Miss Williams gave a terrific snort.

"Oh, yes, I know. That's always the excuse nowadays. An artist! An excuse for every kind of loose living, for drunkenness, for brawling, for infidelity. And what kind of an artist was Mr. Crale, when all is said and done? It may be the fashion to admire his pictures for a few years. But they won't last. Why, he couldn't even draw! His perspective was terrible! Even his anatomy was quite incorrect. I know something of what I am talking about, M. Poirot. I studied painting for a time, as a girl, in Florence, and to anyone who knows and appreciates the great masters these daubs of Mr. Crale's are really ludicrous. Just splashing a few colors about on the canvas—no construction, no careful drawing. No," she shook her head, "don't ask me to admire Mr. Crale's painting."

"Two of them are in the Tate Gallery," Poirot reminded her.

Miss Williams sniffed. "Possibly. So is one of Mr. Epstein's statues, I believe."

Poirot perceived that, according to Miss Williams, the last word had been said. He abandoned the subject of art. He said, "You were with Mrs. Crale when she found the body?"

"Yes. She and I went down from the house together after lunch. Angela had left her pull-over on the beach after bathing, or else in the boat. She was always very careless about her things. I parted from Mrs. Crale at the door of the Battery Garden, but she called me back almost at once. I believe Mr. Crale had been dead over an hour. He was sprawled on the bench near his easel."

"Was she terribly upset at the discovery?"

"What exactly do you mean by that, M. Poirot?"

"I am asking you what your impressions were at the time."

"Oh, I see. Yes, she seemed to me quite dazed. She sent me off to telephone for the doctor. After all, we couldn't be absolutely sure he was dead—it might have been a cataleptic seizure."

"Did she suggest such a possibility?"

"I don't remember."

"And you went and telephoned?"

Miss Williams' tone was dry and brusque: "I had gone half up the path when I met Mr. Meredith Blake. I entrusted my errand to him and returned to Mrs. Crale. I thought, you see, she might have collapsed—and men are no good in a matter of that kind."

"And had she collapsed?"

Mrs. Williams said dryly: "Mrs. Crale was quite in command of herself. She was quite different from Miss Greer, who made a hysterical and very unpleasant scene."

"What kind of a scene?"

"She tried to attack Mrs. Crale."

"You mean she realized that Mrs. Crale was responsible for Mr. Crale's death?"

Miss Williams considered for a moment or two.

"No, she could hardly be sure of that. That—er—terrible suspicion had not yet arisen. Miss Greer just screamed out: 'It's all your doing, Caroline. You killed him. It's all your fault.' She did not actually say, 'You've poisoned him,' but I think there is no doubt that she thought so."

"And Mrs. Crale?"

Miss Williams moved restlessly. "Must we be hypocritical, M. Poirot? I cannot tell you what Mrs. Crale really felt or thought at that moment. Whether it was horror at what she had done—"

"Did it seem like that?"

"N-no, n-no, I can't say it did. Stunned, yes—and, I think, frightened. Yes, I am sure, frightened. But that is natural enough."

Hercule Poirot said in a dissatisfied tone: "Yes, perhaps that is natural enough. . . . What view did she adopt officially as to her husband's death?"

"Suicide. She said, very definitely from the first, that it must be suicide."

"Did she say the same when she was talking to you privately, or did she put forward any other theory."

"No. She—she—took pains to impress upon me that it must be suicide."

Miss Williams sounded embarrassed.

"And what did you say to that?"

"Really, M. Poirot, does it matter *what* I said?"

"Yes, I think it does."

"I don't see why—"

But as though his expectant silence hypnotized her, she said reluctantly: "I think I said: 'Certainly, Mrs. Crale. It must have been suicide.' "

"Did you believe your own words?"

Miss Williams raised her head. "No, I did not," she said firmly. "But please understand, M. Poirot, that I was entirely on Mrs. Crale's side, if you like to put it that way. My sympathies were with her, not with the police."

"You would have liked to have seen her acquitted?"

Miss Williams said defiantly, "Yes, I would."

"Then you are in sympathy with her daughter's feelings?"

"I have every sympathy with Carla."

"Would you have any objection to writing out for me a detailed account of the tragedy?"

"You mean for her to read?"

"Yes."

Miss Williams said slowly: "No, I have no objection. She is quite determined to go into the matter, is she?"

"Yes. I dare say it would have been preferable if the truth had been kept from her—"

Miss Williams interrupted him:

"No. It is always better to face the truth. It is no use evading unhappiness by tampering with facts. Carla has had a shock, learning the truth—now she wants to know exactly how the tragedy came about. That seems to me the right attitude for a brave young woman to take. Once she knows all about it she will be able to forget it again and go on with the business of living her own life."

"Perhaps you are right," said Poirot.

"I'm quite sure I'm right."

"But, you see, there is more to it than that. She not only wants to know —she wants to prove her mother innocent."

Miss Williams said, "Poor child."

"That is what you say, is it?"

Miss Williams said: "I see now why you said that it might be better if she had never known. All the same, I think it is best as it is. To wish to find her mother innocent is a natural hope—and, hard though the actual revelation may be, I think, from what you say of her, that Carla is brave enough to learn the truth and not flinch from it."

"You are sure it *is* the truth?" Poirot asked.

"I don't understand you."

"You see no loophole for believing that Mrs. Crale was innocent?"

"I don't think that possibility has ever been seriously considered."

"And yet she herself clung to the theory of suicide?"

Miss Williams said dryly, "The poor woman had to say *something.*"

"Do you know that when Mrs. Crale was dying she left a letter for her daughter in which she solemnly swears that she is innocent?"

Miss Williams stared. "That was very wrong of her," she said sharply.

"You think so?"

"Yes, I do. Oh, I dare say you are a sentimentalist like most men—"

Poirot interrupted indignantly, "I am *not* a sentimentalist."

"But there is such a thing as false sentiment. Why write that—a lie—at such a solemn moment? To spare your child pain? Yes, many women would do that. But I should not have thought it of Mrs. Crale. She was a brave woman and a truthful woman. I should have thought it far more like her to have told her daughter not to judge."

Poirot said with slight exasperation, "You will not even consider, then, the possibility that what Caroline Crale wrote was the truth?"

"Certainly not!"

Miss Williams looked at Poirot in a very odd way. "It doesn't matter my saying this now—so long afterward. You see, I happen to *know* that Caroline Crale was guilty!"

"What?"

"It's true. Whether I did right in withholding what I knew at the time I cannot be sure, but I *did* withhold it. But you must take it from me, quite definitely, that I *know* Caroline Crale was guilty. . . ."

Angela Warren's flat overlooked Regent's Park. Here, on this spring day, a soft air wafted in through the open window and one might have had the illusion that one was in the country if it had not been for the steady menacing roar of the traffic passing below.

Poirot turned from the window as the door opened and Angela Warren came into the room.

It was not the first time he had seen her. He had availed himself of the opportunity to attend a lecture she had given at the Royal Geographical. It had been, he considered, an excellent lecture. Dry, perhaps, from the view of popular appeal. Miss Warren had an excellent delivery: she neither paused nor hesitated for a word. She did not repeat herself. The tones of her voice were clear and not unmelodious. She made no concessions to romantic appeal or love of adventure. There was very little human interest in the lecture. It was an admirable recital of concise facts, adequately illustrated by excellent slides, and with intelligent deductions from the facts recited. Dry, precise, clear, lucid, highly technical.

The soul of Hercule Poirot approved. Here, he considered, was an orderly mind.

Now that he saw her at close quarters he realized that Angela Warren might easily have been a very handsome woman. Her features were regular, though severe. She had finely marked dark brows; clear, intelligent brown eyes; a fine, pale skin. She had very square shoulders and a slightly mannish walk.

There was certainly about her no suggestion of the little pig who cried "Wee-wee." But on the right cheek, disfiguring and puckering the skin, was that healed scar. The right eye was slightly distorted, the corner pulled downward by it, but no one would have realized that the sight of that eye was destroyed. It seemed to Hercule Poirot almost certain that she had lived with that disability so long that she was now completely unconscious of it. And it occurred to him that of the five people in whom he had become interested as a result of his investigations, those who might have been said to start with the fullest advantages were not those who had actually wrested the most success and happiness from life.

Elsa, who might have been said to have started with all advantages— youth, beauty, riches—had done worst. She was like a flower overtaken by untimely frost—still in bud but without life. Cecilia Williams, to outward appearances, had no assets of which to boast. Nevertheless, to Poirot's eye, there was no despondency there and no sense of failure. Miss Williams' life had been interesting to her—she was still interested in people and events. She had that enormous mental and moral advantage of a strict Victorian upbringing, denied to us in these days—she had done her duty in that station of life to which it had pleased God to call her, and that assurance encased her in an armor impregnable to the slings and darts of envy, discontent and regret. She had her memories, her small pleasures, made possible by stringent economies, and sufficient health and vigor to enable her still to be interested in life.

Now, in Angela Warren—that young creature handicapped by disfigurement and its consequent humiliations—Poirot believed he saw a spirit strengthened by its necessary fight for confidence and assurance. The undisciplined schoolgirl had given place to a vital and forceful woman, a woman of considerable mental power and gifted with abundant energy to accomplish ambitious purposes. She was a woman, Poirot felt sure, both happy and successful. Her life was full and vivid and eminently enjoyable.

She was not, incidentally, the type of woman that Poirot really liked. Though admiring the clear-cut precision of her mind, she had just a sufficient *nuance* of the *femme formidable* about her to alarm him as a mere man. His taste had always been for the flamboyant and extravagant.

With Angela Warren it was easy to come to the point of his visit. There was no subterfuge. He merely recounted Carla Lemarchant's interview with him.

Angela Warren's severe face lighted up appreciatively.

"Little Carla? She is over here? I would like to see her so much."

"You have not kept in touch with her?"

"Hardly as much as I should have done. I was a schoolgirl at the time she went to Canada, and I realized, of course, that in a year or two she would have forgotten me. Of late years an occasional present at Christmas has been the only link between us. I imagined that she would, by now, be completely immersed in the Canadian atmosphere and that her future would lie over there. Better so, under the circumstances."

Poirot said: "One might think so, certainly. A change of name—a change of scene. A new life. But it was not to be so easy as that." And he then told of Carla's engagement, the discovery she had made upon coming of age and her motive in coming to England.

Angela Warren listened quietly, her disfigured cheek resting on one hand. She betrayed no emotion during the recital, but as Poirot finished, she said quietly, "Good for Carla."

Hercule Poirot was startled. It was the first time that he had met with this reaction. He said, "You approve, Miss Warren?"

"Certainly. I wish her every success. Anything I can do to help, I will. I feel guilty, you know, that I haven't attempted anything myself."

"Then you think that there is a possibility that she is right in her views?"

Angela Warren said sharply: "Of course she's right. Caroline didn't do it. I've always known that."

"You surprise me very much indeed, mademoiselle," Poirot murmured. "Everybody else I have spoken to—"

She cut in sharply:

"You mustn't go by that. I've no doubt that the circumstantial evidence is overwhelming. My own conviction is based on knowledge—knowledge of my sister. I just know quite simply and definitely that Caro *couldn't* have killed anyone."

"Can one say that with certainty of any human creature?"

"Probably not in most cases. I agree that the human animal is full of curious surprises. But in Caroline's case there were special reasons—reasons which I have a better chance of appreciating than anyone else could."

She touched her damaged cheek.

"You see this? You've probably heard about it?" Poirot nodded. "Caroline did that. That's why I'm sure—I *know*—that she did not do murder."

"It would not be a convincing argument to most people."

"No, it would be the opposite. It was actually used in that way, I believe. As evidence that Caroline had a violent and ungovernable temper! Because she had injured me as a baby, learned men argued that she would be equally capable of poisoning an unfaithful husband."

Poirot said: "I, at least, appreciated the difference. A sudden fit of ungovernable rage does not lead you to abstract a poison first and then use it deliberately on the following day."

Angela Warren waved an impatient hand.

"That's not what I mean at all. I must try and make it plain to you. Supposing that you are a person of normally affectionate and kindly disposition, but that you are also liable to intense jealousy. And supposing that during the years of your life, when control is most difficult, you do, in a fit of rage, come near to committing what is, in effect, murder. Think of the awful shock, the horror, the remorse that seizes upon you.

"If you are a sensitive person like Caroline that horror and remorse will never quite leave you. It never left her. I don't suppose I was consciously aware of it at the time, but looking back I recognize it perfectly. Caro was haunted, continually haunted, by the fact that she had injured me. That knowledge never left her in peace. It colored all her actions. It explained her attitude to me. Nothing was too good for me. In her eyes, I must always come first. Half the quarrels she had with Amyas were on my account."

Miss Warren paused, then went on:

"It was very bad for me, of course. I got horribly spoiled. But that's neither here nor there. We're discussing the effect on Caroline. The result of that impulse to violence was a life-long abhorrence of any further act of the same kind. Caro was always watching herself, always in fear that something of that kind might happen again. And she took her own ways of guarding against it. One of those ways was a great extravagance of language. She felt (and I think, psychologically quite truly) that if she were violent enough in speech she would have no temptation to violence in action. She found by experience that the method worked.

"That's why I've heard Caro say things like, 'I'd like to cut so and so in pieces and boil him slowly in oil.' And she'd say to me, or to Amyas, 'If you go on annoying me I shall murder you.' In the same way she quarreled easily and violently. She recognized, I think, the impulse to violence that there was in her nature, and she deliberately gave it an outlet that way. She and Amyas used to have the most fantastic and lurid quarrels."

Hercule Poirot nodded. "Yes, there was evidence of that. They quarreled like cat and dog, it was said."

Angela Warren said:

"Exactly. That's what is so stupid and misleading about evidence. Of course, Caro and Amyas quarreled! Of course, they said bitter and outrageous and cruel things to each other! What nobody appreciates is that they *enjoyed* quarreling. But they did! Amyas enjoyed it too. They were that kind of couple. They both of them liked drama and emotional scenes. Most men don't. They like peace. But Amyas was an artist. He liked shouting and threatening and generally being outrageous. It was like letting off steam to him. He was the kind of man who when he loses his collar stud bellows the house down. It sounds very odd, I know, but living that way with continual rows and makings up was Amyas' and Caroline's idea of fun!"

She made an impatient gesture.

"If they'd only not hustled me away and let me give evidence, I'd have told them that." Then she shrugged her shoulders. "But I don't suppose they would have believed me. And, anyway, then it wouldn't have been as clear in my mind as it is now. It was the kind of thing I knew but hadn't thought about and certainly had never dreamed of putting into words."

She looked across at Poirot.

"You do see what I mean?"

He nodded vigorously. "I see perfectly, and I realize the absolute rightness of what you have said. There are people to whom agreement is monotony. They require the stimulant of dissension to create drama in their lives."

"Exactly."

"May I ask you, Miss Warren, what were your own feelings at the time?"

Angela Warren sighed.

"Mostly bewilderment and helplessness, I think. It seemed a fantastic nightmare. Caroline was arrested very soon—about three days afterward, I think. I can still remember my indignation, my dumb fury—and, of course, my childish faith that it was just a silly mistake, that it would be all right. Caro was chiefly perturbed about me—she wanted me kept right away from it all as far as possible. She got Miss Williams to take me away to some relations almost at once. The police had no objection. And then, when it was decided that my evidence would not be needed, arrangements were made for me to go to school abroad.

"I hated going, of course. But it was explained to me that Caro had me terribly on her mind and that the only way I could help her was by going."

She paused. Then she said: "So I went to Munich. I was there when—when the verdict was given. They never let me go to see Caro. Caro wouldn't have it. That's the only time, I think, when she failed in understanding."

"You cannot be sure of that, Miss Warren. To visit someone dearly loved in a prison might make a terrible impression on a young, sensitive girl."

"Possibly."

Angela Warren got up. She said: "After the verdict, when she had been condemned, my sister wrote me a letter. I have never shown it to anyone. I think I ought to show it to you now. It may help you to understand the kind of person Caroline was. If you like, you may take it to show to Carla also."

She went to the door, then turning back she said: "Come with me. There is a portrait of Caroline in my room."

For the second time, Poirot stood gazing up at a portrait.

As a painting, Caroline Crale's portrait was mediocre. But Poirot looked at it with interest—it was not its artistic value that interested him.

He saw a long, oval face, a gracious line of jaw and a sweet, slightly timid expression. It was a face uncertain of itself, emotional, with a withdrawn hidden beauty. It lacked the forcefulness and vitality of her daughter's face—that energy and joy of life Carla Lemarchant had doubtless inherited from her father. This was a less positive creature. Yet, looking at the painted face, Hercule Poirot understood why an imaginative man, like Quentin Fogg had not been able to forget her.

Angela Warren stood at his side again—a letter in her hand. She said quietly, "Now that you have seen what she was like, read her letter."

He unfolded it carefully and read what Caroline Crale had written sixteen years ago:

"My darling little Angela:

"You will hear bad news and you will grieve, but what I want to impress upon you is that it is all, all right. I have never told you lies and I don't now when I say that I am actually happy—that I feel an essential rightness and a peace that I have never known before. It's all right, darling; it's all right. Don't look back and regret and grieve for me—go on with your life and succeed. You can, I know. It's all, all right, darling, and I'm going to Amyas. I haven't the least doubt that we shall be together. I couldn't have lived without him. . . . Do this one thing for me—be happy. I've told you—*I'* m happy. One has to pay one's debts. It's lovely to feel peaceful.

"Your loving sister,
"Caro."

Hercule Poirot read it through twice. Then he handed it back. He said: "That is a very beautiful letter, mademoiselle—and a very remarkable one. A *very* remarkable one."

"Caroline," said Angela Warren, "was a very remarkable person."

"Yes, an unusual mind. . . . You take it that this letter indicates innocence?"

"Of course it does!"

"It does not say so explicitly."

"Because Caro would know that I'd never dream of her being guilty!"

"Perhaps—perhaps. . . . But it might be taken another way. In the sense that she was guilty and that in expiating her crime she will find peace."

It fitted in, he thought, with the description of her in court. And he experienced in this moment the strongest doubts he had yet felt of the course to which he had committed himself. Everything so far had pointed unswervingly to Caroline Crale's guilt. Now even her own words testified against her.

On the other side was only the unshaken conviction of Angela Warren. Angela had known her well, undoubtedly, but might not her certainty be the fanatical loyalty of an adolescent girl, up in arms for a dearly loved sister?

As though she had read his thoughts Angela said, "No, M. Poirot—I *know* Caroline wasn't guilty."

Poirot said briskly: "The *bon Dieu* knows I do not want to shake you on that point. But let us be practical. You say your sister was not guilty. Very well, then, *what really happened?*"

Angela nodded thoughtfully. "That is difficult, I agree," she said. "I suppose that, as Caroline said, Amyas committed suicide."

"Is that likely from what you know of his character?"

"Very unlikely."

"But you do not say, as in the first case, that you *know* it is impossible?"

"No, because, as I said just now, most people *do* do impossible things—

that is, to say things that seem out of character. But I presume, if you know them intimately, it wouldn't be out of character."

"You knew your brother-in-law well?"

"Yes, but not like I knew Caro. It seems to me quite fantastic that Amyas should have killed himself, but I suppose he *could* have done so. In fact, he *must* have done so."

"You cannot see any other explanation?"

Angela accepted the suggestion calmly, but not without a certain stirring of interest.

"Oh, I see what you mean. . . . I've never really considered that possibility. You mean one of the other people killed him? That it was a deliberate cold-blooded murder? . . ."

"It might have been, might it not?"

"Yes, it might have been. . . . But it certainly seems very unlikely."

"More unlikely than suicide?"

"That's difficult to say. . . . On the face of it, there was no reason for suspecting anybody else. There isn't now when I look back. . . ."

"All the same, let us consider the possibility. Who of those intimately concerned would you say was—shall we say the most likely person?"

"Let me think. Well, I didn't kill him. And the Elsa creature certainly didn't. She was mad with rage when he died. Who else was there? Meredith Blake? He was always very devoted to Caroline, quite a tame cat about the house. I suppose that *might* give him a motive in a way. In a book he might have wanted to get Amyas out of the way so that he himself could marry Caroline. But he could have achieved that just as well by letting Amyas go off with Elsa and then in due time consoling Caroline. Besides, I really can't *see* Meredith as a murderer. Too mild and too cautious. Who else was there?"

"Miss Williams? Philip Blake?" Poirot suggested.

Angela's grave face relaxed into a smile. "Miss Williams? One can't really make oneself believe that one's governess could commit a murder! Miss Williams was always so unyielding and so full of rectitude."

She paused a minute and then went on: "She was devoted to Caroline, of course. Would have done anything for her. And she hated Amyas. She was a great feminist and disliked men. Is that enough for murder? Surely not."

"It would hardly seem so," agreed Poirot.

Angela went on: "Philip Blake?" She was silent for some few moments. Then she said quietly, "I think, you know, if we're just talking of *likelihoods* he's the most likely person."

Poirot said, "You interest me very much, Miss Warren. May I ask why you say that?"

"Nothing at all definite. But from what I remember of him, I should say he was a person of rather limited imagination."

"And a limited imagination predisposes you to murder?"

"It might lead you to take a crude way of settling your difficulties. Men of that type get a certain satisfaction from action of some kind or other. Murder is a very crude business, don't you think so?"

"Yes—I think you are right. . . . It is definitely a point of view, that. But, all the same, Miss Warren, there must be more to it than that. What motive could Philip Blake possibly have had?"

Angela Warren did not answer at once. She stood frowning down at the floor.

Hercule Poirot said, "He was Amyas Crale's best friend, was he not?"

She nodded.

"But there is something in your mind, Miss Warren. Something that you have not yet told me. Were the two men rivals, perhaps, over the girl —over Elsa?"

Angela Warren shook her head. "Oh, no, not Philip."

"What is there then?"

Angela Warren said slowly:

"Do you know the way that things suddenly come back to you—after years, perhaps. I'll explain what I mean: Somebody told me a story once, when I was eleven. I saw no point in that story whatsoever. It didn't worry me—it just passed straight over my head. I don't believe I ever, as they say, thought of it again. But about two years ago, sitting in the stalls at a revue, that story came back to me, and I was so surprised that I actually said aloud, 'Oh, *now* I see the point of that silly story about the rice pudding.' And yet there had been no direct allusion on the same lines— only some fun sailing rather near the wind."

Poirot said, "I understand what you mean, mademoiselle."

"Then you will understand what I am going to tell you. I was once staying at a hotel. As I walked along a passage one of the bedroom doors opened and a woman I knew came out. It was not her bedroom—and she registered the fact plainly on her face when she saw me.

"And I knew then the meaning of the expression I had once seen on Caroline's face when at Alderbury she came out of Philip Blake's room one night."

She leaned forward, stopping Poirot's words:

"I had no idea at the *time,* you understand. I *knew* things—girls of the age I was usually do—but I didn't connect them with reality. Caroline coming out of Philip Blake's bedroom was just Caroline coming out of Philip Blake's bedroom to me. It might have been Miss Williams' room or my room. But what I *did* notice was the expression on her face—a queer expression that I didn't know and couldn't understand. I didn't understand it until, as I have told you, the night in Paris when I saw that same expression on another woman's face."

Poirot said slowly: "But what you tell me, Miss Warren, is sufficiently astonishing. From Philip Blake himself I got the impression that he disliked your sister and always had."

"I know," Angela said. "I can't explain it, but there it is."

Poirot nodded slowly. Already, in his interview with Philip Blake, he had felt vaguely that something did not ring true. That overdone animosity against Caroline; it had not, somehow, been natural.

And words and phrases from his conversation with Meredith Blake came back to him: "Very upset when Amyas married—did not go near them for over a year. . . ."

Had Philip, then, always been in love with Caroline? And had his love, when she chose Amyas, turned to bitterness and hate?

Yes, Philip had been too vehement, too biased. Poirot visualized him thoughtfully—the cheerful, prosperous man with his golf and his comfortable house. What had Philip Blake really felt sixteen years ago?

Angela Warren was speaking:

"I don't understand it. You see, I've no experience in love affairs—they haven't come my way. I've told you this for what it's worth in case—in case it might have a bearing on what happened."

Chapter VII

THE NARRATIVE OF PHILIP BLAKE

(Covering letter received with manuscript)

"DEAR M. POIROT:

"I am fulfilling my promise and herewith find enclosed an account of the events relating to the death of Amyas Crale. After such a lapse of time I am bound to point out that my memories may not be strictly accurate, but I have put down what occurred to the best of my recollection.

"Yours truly,
"PHILIP BLAKE."

NOTES ON PROGRESS OF EVENTS LEADING
UP TO MURDER OF AMYAS CRALE ON 18TH SEPT. 19—

My friendship with deceased dates back to a very early period. His home and mine were next door to each other in the country and our families were friends. Amyas Crale was a little over two years older than I was. We played together as boys, in the holidays, though we were not at the same school.

From the point of view of my long knowledge of the man I feel myself particularly qualified to testify as to his character and general outlook on life. And I will say this straightaway—to anyone who knew Amyas Crale well, the notion of his committing suicide is quite ridiculous. Crale would *never* have taken his own life. He was far too fond of living! The contention of the defense at the trial that Crale was obsessed by conscience, and took poison in a fit of remorse is utterly absurd.

Crale, I should say, had very little conscience, and certainly not a morbid one. Moreover, he and his wife were on bad terms and I don't think he would have had any undue scruples about breaking up what was, to him, a very unsatisfactory married life. He was prepared to look after her financial welfare and that of the child of the marriage, and I am sure would have done so generously. He was a very generous man, and altogether a warmhearted and lovable person. Not only was he a great painter, but he was also a man whose friends were devoted to him. As far as I know he had no enemies.

I had also known Caroline Crale for many years. I knew her before her marriage, when she used to come and stay at Alderbury. She was then a somewhat neurotic girl, subject to uncontrollable outbursts of temper, not without attraction, but unquestionably a difficult person to live with.

She showed her devotion to Amyas almost immediately. He, I think, was not really very much in love with her. But they were frequently thrown together. She was, as I say, attractive, and they eventually became engaged. Crale's friends were apprehensive about the marriage, as they felt that Caroline was quite unsuited to him.

This caused a certain amount of strain in the first few years between Crale's wife and Crale's friends, but Amyas was a loyal friend and was not disposed to give up his old friends at the bidding of his wife. After a few years he and I were on the same old terms and I was a frequent visitor at Alderbury. I may add that I stood godfather to the little girl, Carla. This proves, I think, that Amyas considered me his best friend, and it gives me authority to speak for a man who can no longer speak for himself.

To come to the actual events of which I have been asked to write, I arrived down at Alderbury (so I see by an old diary) five days before the crime. That is, on September 13th. I was conscious at once of a certain tension in the atmosphere. There was also staying in the house Miss Elsa Greer, whom Amyas was painting at the time.

It was the first time I had seen Miss Greer in the flesh, but I had been aware of her existence for some time. Amyas had raved about her to me a month previously. He had met, he said, a marvelous girl. He talked about her so enthusiastically that I said to him jokingly, "Be careful, old boy, or you'll be losing your head again." He told me not to be a bloody fool. He was painting the girl; he'd no personal interest in her. I said, "Tell that to the marines! I've heard you say that before." He said, "This time it's different," to which I answered somewhat cynically, "It always is!" Amyas then looked quite worried and anxious. He said, "You don't understand. She's just a girl. Not much more than a child." He added that she had very modern views and was absolutely free from old-fashioned prejudices. He said, "She's honest and natural and absolutely fearless!"

I thought to myself, though I didn't say so, that Amyas had certainly got it badly this time. A few weeks later I heard comments from other people. It was said that the "Greer girl was absolutely infatuated." Somebody else said that it was a bit thick of Amyas, considering how young the girl was, whereupon somebody else snickered and said that Elsa Greer knew her way about all right.

There was a question as to what Crale's wife thought about it, and the significant reply that she must be used to that sort of thing by now, to which someone demurred by saying they'd heard that she was jealous as hell and led Crale such an impossible life that any man would be justified in having a fling from time to time.

I mention all this because I think it is important that the state of affairs before I got down there should be fully realized.

I was interested to see the girl. She was remarkably good-looking and very attractive, and I was, I must admit, maliciously amused to note that Caroline was cutting up very rough indeed.

Amyas Crale himself was less lighthearted than usual. Though to anyone who did not know him well, his manner would have appeared much as usual. I, who knew him so intimately, noted at once various signs of strain, uncertain temper, fits of moody abstraction, general irritability of manner.

Although he was always inclined to be moody when painting, the picture he was at work upon did not account entirely for the strain he showed. He was pleased to see me and said as soon as we were alone, "Thank goodness you've turned up, Phil. Living in a house with four women is enough to send any man clean off his chump. Between them all, they'll send me into a lunatic asylum."

It was certainly an uncomfortable atmosphere. Caroline, as I said, was obviously cutting up rough about the whole thing. In a polite, well-bred way, she was ruder to Elsa than one would believe possible—without a single actually offensive word. Elsa herself was openly and flagrantly rude to Caroline. She was top dog and she knew it, and no scruples of good breeding restrained her from overt bad manners.

The result was that Crale spent most of his time scrapping with the girl Angela when he wasn't painting. They were usually on affectionate terms, though they teased and fought a good deal. But on this occasion there was an edge in everything Amyas said or did, and the two of them really lost their tempers with each other. The fourth member of the party was the governess. "A sour-faced hag," Amyas called her. "She hates me like poison. Sits there with her lips set together, disapproving of me without stopping."

It was then that he said: "Damn all women! If a man is to have any peace he must steer clear of women!"

"You oughtn't to have married," I said. "You're the sort of man who ought to have kept clear of domestic ties."

He replied that it was too late to talk about that now. He added that no doubt Caroline would be only too glad to get rid of him. That was the first indication I had that something unusual was in the wind.

I said: "What's all this? Is this business with the lovely Elsa serious then?" He said with a sort of groan: "She *is* lovely, isn't she? Sometimes I wish I'd never seen her."

I said: "Look here, old boy, you must take a hold on yourself. You don't want to get tied up with any more women." He looked at me and laughed. He said: "It's all very well for you to talk. I can't let women alone—simply can't do it—and if I could they wouldn't let me alone!" Then he shrugged those great shoulders of his, grinned at me and said: "Oh, well, it will all pan out in the end, I expect. And you must admit the picture is good!"

He was referring to the portrait he was doing of Elsa, and, although I had very little technical knowledge of painting, even I could see that it was going to be a work of especial power.

While he was painting, Amyas was a different man. Although he would growl, groan, frown, swear extravagantly and sometimes hurl his brushes away, he was really intensely happy.

It was only when he came back to the house for meals that the hostile atmosphere between the women got him down. That hostility came to a head on September 17th. We had had an embarrassing lunch. Elsa had been particularly—really, I think *insolent* is the only word for it! She had ignored Caroline pointedly, persistently addressing the conversation to Amyas as though he and she were alone in the room. Caroline had talked lightly and gaily to the rest of us, cleverly contriving so that several perfectly innocent-sounding remarks should have a sting. She hadn't Elsa Greer's scornful honesty—with Caroline everything was oblique, suggested rather than said.

Things came to a head after lunch in the drawing room just as we were finishing coffee. I had commented on a carved head in highly polished beechwood—a very curious thing—and Caroline said, "That is the work of a young Norwegian sculptor. Amyas and I admire his work very much. We hope to go and see him next summer." That calm assumption of possession was too much for Elsa. She was never one to let a challenge pass. She waited a minute or two and then she spoke in her clear, rather over-emphasized voice.

She said: "This would be a lovely room if it were properly fixed. It's got far too much furniture in it. When I'm living here I shall take all the rubbish out and just leave one or two good pieces. And I shall have copper-colored curtains, I think—so that the setting sun will just catch them through that big western window." She turned to me and said, "Don't you think that would be rather lovely?"

I didn't have time to answer. Caroline spoke and her voice was soft and

silky and what I can only describe as dangerous. She said, "Are you thinking of buying this place, Elsa?"

Elsa said, "It won't be necessary for me to buy it."

Caroline said, "What do you mean?" And there was no softness in her
voice now. It was hard and metallic. Elsa laughed. She said, "Must we
pretend? Come now, Caroline, you know very well what I mean!"

Caroline said, "I've no idea."

Elsa said to that: "Don't be such an ostrich. It's no good pretending you
don't see and know all about it. Amyas and I care for each other. This isn't
your home. It's his. And after we're married I shall live here with him!"

Caroline said, "I think you're crazy."

Elsa said: "Oh, no, I'm not, my dear, and you know it. It would be
much simpler if we were honest with each other. Amyas and I love each
other; you've seen that clearly enough. There's only one decent thing for
you to do. You've got to give him his freedom."

Caroline said, "I don't believe a word of what you are saying."

But her voice was unconvincing. Elsa had got under her guard all right.

And at that minute Amyas Crale came into the room and Elsa said with
a laugh, "If you don't believe me, ask him."

And Caroline said, "I will."

She didn't pause at all. She said, "Amyas, Elsa says you want to marry
her. Is this true?"

Poor old Amyas. I felt sorry for him. It makes a man feel a fool to have
a scene of that kind forced upon him. He went crimson and started blustering. He turned on Elsa and asked her why the devil she couldn't have held
her tongue.

Caroline said, "Then it *is* true?"

He didn't say anything, just stood there passing his finger round inside
the neck of his shirt. He used to do that as a kid when he got into a jam of
any kind. He said—and he tried to make the words sound dignified and
authoritative—and of course couldn't manage it, poor devil:

"I don't want to discuss it."

Caroline said, "But we're going to discuss it!"

Elsa chipped in and said, "I think it's only fair to Caroline that she
should be told."

"Is it true, Amyas?" Caroline said very quietly.

He looked a bit ashamed of himself. Men do when women pin them
down in a corner.

She said, "Answer me, please. I've got to know."

He flung up his head then, rather the way a bull does in the bull ring.
He snapped out, "It's true enough, but I don't want to discuss it now."

And he turned and strode out of the room. I went after him. I didn't want to be left with the women. I caught up with him on the terrace. He was swearing. I never knew a man to swear more heartily. Then he raved:

"Why couldn't she hold her tongue? Why the devil couldn't she hold her tongue? Now the fat's in the fire. And I've got to finish that picture—do you hear, Phil? It's the best thing I've done. The best thing I've ever done in my *life*. And a couple of fool women want to muck it up between them!"

Then he calmed down a little and said women had no sense of proportion.

I couldn't help smiling a little. I said, "Well, dash it all, old boy, you have brought this on yourself."

"Don't I know it?" he said, and groaned. Then he added: "But you must admit, Phil, that a man couldn't be blamed for losing his head about her. Even Caroline ought to understand that."

I asked him what would happen if Caroline got her back up and refused to give him a divorce.

But by now he had gone off into a fit of abstraction. I repeated the remark and he said absently: "Caroline would never be vindictive. You don't understand, old boy."

"There's the child," I pointed out.

He took me by the arm. "Phil, old boy, you mean well, but don't go on croaking like a raven. I can manage my affairs. Everything will turn out all right. You'll see if it doesn't."

That was Amyas all over—an absolutely unjustified optimist. He said now, cheerfully, "To hell with the whole pack of them!"

I don't know whether we would have said anything more, but a few minutes later Caroline swept out on the terrace. She had a hat on—a queer, flopping, dark brown hat, rather attractive.

She said in an absolutely ordinary, everyday voice: "Take off that paint-stained coat, Amyas. We're going over to Meredith's to tea—don't you remember?"

He stared, stammered a bit as he said: "Oh, I'd forgotten. Yes, of c-c-course we are."

"Then," she said, "go and try and make yourself look less like a rag-and-bone man."

Although her voice was quite natural, she didn't look at him. She moved over toward a bed of dahlias and began picking off some of the overblown flowers.

Amyas turned around slowly and went into the house.

Caroline talked to me. She talked a good deal. About the chances of the weather lasting. And whether there might be mackerel about and, if so,

Amyas and Angela and I might like to go fishing. She was really amazing. I've got to hand it to her.

But I think, myself, that that showed the sort of woman she was. She had enormous strength of will and complete command over herself. I don't know whether she'd made up her mind to kill him then, but I shouldn't be surprised. And she was capable of making her plans carefully and unemotionally, with an absolutely clear and ruthless mind.

Caroline Crale was a very dangerous woman. I ought to have realized then that she wasn't prepared to take this thing lying down. But, like a fool, I thought that she had made up her mind to accept the inevitable—or else possibly she thought that if she carried on exactly as usual Amyas might change his mind.

Presently the others came out. Elsa looking defiant, but at the same time triumphant. Caroline took no notice of her. Angela really saved the situation. She came out arguing with Miss Williams that she wasn't going to change her skirt for anyone. It was quite all right—good enough for darling old Meredith, anyway—*he* never noticed anything.

We got off at last. Caroline walked with Angela. And I walked with Amyas. And Elsa walked by herself, smiling.

I didn't admire her myself—too violent a type—but I have to admit that she looked incredibly beautiful that afternoon. Women do when they've got what they want.

I can't remember the events of that afternoon clearly at all. It's all blurred. I remember old Merry coming out to meet us. I think we walked around the garden first. I remember having a long discussion with Angela about the training of terriers for ratting. She ate an incredible lot of apples, too, and tried to persuade me to do so too.

When we got back to the house, tea was going on under the big cedar tree. Merry, I remember, was looking very upset. I suppose either Caroline or Amyas had told him something. He was looking doubtfully at Caroline, and then he stared at Elsa. The old boy looked thoroughly upset. Of course, Caroline liked to have Meredith on a string more or less—the devoted, platonic friend who would never, never go too far. She was that kind of woman.

After tea Meredith had a hurried word with me. He said, "Look here, Phil, Amyas *can't* do this thing!"

I said, "Make no mistake, he's going to do it."

"He can't leave his wife and child and go off with this girl. He's years older than she is. She can't be more than eighteen."

I said to him that Miss Greer was a fully sophisticated twenty. He said: "Anyway, that's under age. She can't know what she's doing."

Poor old Meredith. Always the chivalrous pucka sahib.

I said, "Don't worry, old boy. *She* knows what she's doing *and* she likes it!"

That's all we had the chance of saying. I thought to myself that probably Merry felt disturbed at the thought of Caroline's being a deserted wife. Once the divorce was through she might expect her faithful Dobbin to marry her. I had an idea that hopeless devotion was really far more in his line. I must confess that that side of it amused me.

Curiously enough, I remember very little about our visit to Meredith's stink room. He enjoyed showing people his hobby. Personally I always found it very boring. I suppose I was in there with the rest of them when he gave a dissertation on the efficacy of coniine, but I don't remember it. And I didn't see Caroline pinch the stuff. As I've said, she was a very adroit woman. I do remember Meredith reading aloud the passage from Plato describing Socrates' death. Very boring, I thought it. Classics always did bore me.

There's nothing much more I can remember about that day. Amyas and Angela had a first-class row, I know, and the rest of us rather welcomed it. It avoided other difficulties. Angela rushed off to bed with a final vituperative outburst. She said, A, she'd pay him out. B, she wished he were dead. C, she hoped he'd die of leprosy—it would serve him right. D, she wished a sausage would stick to his nose, like in the fairy story, and never come off. When she'd gone we all laughed—we couldn't help it, it was such a funny mixture.

Caroline went up to bed immediately afterward. Miss Williams disappeared after her pupil. Amyas and Elsa went off together into the garden. It was clear that I wasn't wanted. I went for a stroll by myself. It was a lovely night.

I came down late the following morning. There was no one in the dining room. Funny, the things you do remember. I remember the taste of the kidneys and bacon I ate quite well. They were very good kidneys. Deviled.

Afterward I wandered out looking for everybody. I went outside, didn't see anybody, smoked a cigarette, encountered Miss Williams running about looking for Angela, who had played truant as usual when she ought to have been mending a torn frock. I went back into the hall and realized that Amyas and Caroline were having a set-to in the library. They were talking very loud. I heard her say:

"You and your women! I'd like to kill you. Some day I will kill you." Amyas said, "Don't be a fool, Caroline." And she said, "I mean it, Amyas."

Well, I didn't want to overhear any more. I went out again. I wandered along the terrace the other way and came across Elsa.

She was sitting on one of the long seats. The seat was directly under the library window, and the window was open. I should imagine that there wasn't much she had missed of what was going on inside. When she saw me she got up as cool as a cucumber and came toward me. She was smiling.

She took my arm and said, "Isn't it a lovely morning?"

It was a lovely morning for her all right! Rather a cruel girl. No, I think merely honest and lacking in imagination. What she wanted herself was the only thing that she could see.

We'd been standing on the terrace talking for about five minutes when I heard the library door bang and Amyas Crale came out. He was very red in the face.

He caught hold of Elsa unceremoniously by the shoulder. He said: "Come on; time for you to sit. I want to get on with that picture."

She said: "All right. I'll just go up and get a pull-over. There's a chilly wind."

She went into the house.

I wondered if Amyas would say anything to me, but he didn't say much. Just, "These women!"

I said, "Cheer up, old boy!"

Then neither of us said anything till Elsa came out of the house again.

They went off together down to the Battery Garden. I went into the house. Caroline was standing in the hall. I don't think she even noticed me. It was a way of hers at times. She'd seem to go right away—to get inside herself as it were. She just murmured something. Not to me—to herself. I caught the words:

"It's too cruel . . ."

That's what she said. Then she walked past me and upstairs, still without seeming to see me—like a person intent on some inner vision. I think myself (I've no authority for saying this, you understand) that she went up to get the stuff, and that it was then she decided to do what she did do.

And just at that moment the telephone rang. In some houses one would wait for the servants to answer it, but I was so often at Alderbury that I acted more or less as one of the family. I picked up the receiver.

It was my brother Meredith's voice that answered. He was very upset. He explained that he had been into his laboratory and that the coniine bottle was half empty.

I don't need to go again over all the things I know now I ought to have done. The thing was so startling, and I was foolish enough to be taken aback. Meredith was dithering a good bit at the other end. I heard someone on the stairs and I just told him sharply to come over at once.

I myself went down to meet him. In case you don't know the lay of the land, the shortest way from one estate to the other was by rowing across a small creek. I went down the path to where the boats were kept by a small jetty. To do so I passed under the wall of the Battery Garden. I could hear Elsa and Amyas talking together as he painted. They sounded very cheerful and carefree.

Amyas said it was an amazingly hot day (so it was, very hot for September), and Elsa said that sitting where she was, poised on the battlements, there was a cold wind blowing in from the sea. And then she said: "I'm horribly stiff from posing. Can't I have a rest, darling?" And I heard Amyas cry out: "Not on your life! Stick it! You're a tough girl. And this is going good, I tell you." I just heard Elsa say, "Brute," and laugh, as I went out of earshot.

Meredith was just rowing himself across from the other side. I waited for him. He tied up the boat and came up the steps. He was looking very white and worried. He said to me: "Your head's better than mine, Philip. What ought I to do? That stuff's dangerous."

I said, "Are you absolutely sure about this?" Meredith, you see, was always rather a vague kind of chap. Perhaps that's why I didn't take it as seriously as I ought to have done. And he said he was quite sure. The bottle had been full yesterday afternoon.

I said, "And you've absolutely *no* idea who pinched it?"

He said none whatever and asked me what *I* thought. Could it have been one of the servants? I said I supposed it might have been, but it seemed unlikely to me. He always kept the door locked, didn't he? Always, he said, and then began a rigmarole about having found the window a few inches open at the bottom. Someone might have got in that way.

"A chance burglar?" I asked. "It seems to me, Meredith, that there are some very nasty possibilities."

He asked what did I really think? And I said, if he was sure he wasn't making a mistake, that probably Caroline had taken it to poison Elsa with —or that, alternatively, Elsa had taken it to get Caroline out of the way and straighten the path of true love.

Meredith twittered a bit. He said it was absurd and melodramatic and couldn't be true. I said: "Well, the stuff's gone. What *your* explanation?" He hadn't any, of course. Actually thought just as I did, but didn't want to face the fact.

He said again, "What are we to do?"

I said, stupid fool that I was: "We must think it over carefully. Either you'd better announce your loss, straight out when everybody's there. Or else you'd better get Caroline alone and tax her with it. If you're convinced *she* has nothing to do with it, adopt the same tactics for Elsa." He said: "A girl like that! She couldn't have taken it." I said I wouldn't put it past her.

We were walking up the path to the house as we talked. As we were rounding the Battery Garden again I heard Caroline's voice.

I thought perhaps a three-handed row was going on, but actually it was Angela that they were discussing. Caroline was protesting. She said: "It's very hard on the girl." And Amyas made some impatient rejoinder. Then the door to the garden opened just as we came abreast of it. Amyas looked a little taken aback at seeing us. Caroline was just coming out. She said: "Hullo, Meredith. We've been discussing the question of Angela's going to school. I'm not at all sure it's the right thing for her." Amyas said: "Don't fuss about the girl. She'll be all right. Good riddance."

Just then Elsa came running down the path from the house. She had some sort of scarlet jumper in her hand. Amyas growled, "Come along! Get back into the pose! I don't want to waste time."

He went back to where his easel was standing. I noticed that he staggered a bit and I wondered if he had been drinking. A man might easily be excused for doing so with all the fuss and the scenes.

He grumbled: "The beer here is red-hot. Why can't we keep some ice down here?"

And Caroline Crale said: "I'll send you down some beer just off the ice."

Amyas grunted out: "Thanks."

Then Caroline shut the door of the Battery Garden and came up with us to the house. We sat down on the terrace and she went into the house. About five minutes later Angela came along with a couple of bottles of beer and some glasses. It was a hot day and we were glad to see it. As we were drinking it Caroline passed us. She was carrying another bottle and said she would take it down to Amyas. Meredith said he'd go, but she was quite firm that she'd go herself. I thought—fool that I was—that it was just her jealousy. She couldn't stand those two being alone down there. That was what had taken her down there once already with the weak pretext of arguing about Angela's departure.

She went off down that zigzag path, and Meredith and I watched her go. We'd still not decided anything, and now Angela clamored that I should come bathing with her. It seemed impossible to get Meredith alone. I just said to him, "After lunch." And he nodded.

Then I went off bathing with Angela. We had a good swim—across the creek and back—and then we lay out on the rocks, sun-bathing. Angela was a bit taciturn, and that suited me. I made up my mind that directly after lunch I'd take Caroline aside and accuse her point-blank of having stolen the stuff. No use letting Meredith do it—he'd be too weak. No, I'd tax her with it outright. After that she'd have to give it back or, even if she didn't, she wouldn't dare use it.

I was pretty sure it must be her on thinking things over. Elsa was far too sensible and hard-boiled a young woman to risk tampering with poisons. She had a hard head and would take care of her own skin. Caroline was made of more dangerous stuff—unbalanced, carried away by impulses and definitely neurotic. And still, you know, at the back of my mind, was the feeling that Meredith *might* have made a mistake. Or some servant might have been poking about in there and spilled the stuff and then not dared to own up. You see, poison seems such a melodramatic thing—you can't believe in it.

Not till it happens.

It was quite late when I looked at my watch, and Angela and I fairly raced up to lunch. They were just sitting down—all but Amyas, who had remained down in the Battery painting. Quite a usual thing for him to do, and privately I thought him very wise to elect to do it today. Lunch was likely to have been an awkward meal.

We had coffee on the terrace. I wish I could remember better how Caroline looked and acted. She didn't seem excited in any way. Quiet and rather sad is my impression. What a devil that woman was!

For it is a devilish thing to do—to poison a man in cold blood. If there had been a revolver about and she'd caught it up and shot him—well, that might have been understandable. But this cold, deliberate, vindictive poisoning . . . and so calm and collected.

She got up and said, in the most natural way possible, that she'd take his coffee to him. And yet she knew—she must have known—that by now she'd find him dead. Miss Williams went with her. I don't remember if that was at Caroline's suggestion or not. I rather think it was.

The two women went off together. Meredith strolled away shortly afterward. I was just making an excuse to go after him when he came running up the path again. His face was gray. He gasped out, "We must get a doctor—quick—Amyas—"

I sprang up. "Is he ill—dying?"

Meredith said, "I'm afraid he's dead. . . ."

We'd forgotten Elsa for a minute. But she let out a sudden cry. It was like the wail of a banshee.

She cried, "Dead? Dead? . . ." And then she ran. I didn't know anyone could move like that—like a deer, like a stricken thing, and like an avenging fury too.

Meredith panted out: "Go after her. I'll telephone. Go after her. You don't know what she'll do."

I did go after her—and it's as well I did. She might quite easily have killed Caroline. I've never seen such grief and such frenzied hate. All the veneer of refinement and education was stripped off. Deprived of her lover, she was just elemental woman. She'd have clawed Caroline's face, torn her hair, hurled her over the parapet if she could. She thought for some reason or other that Caroline had knifed him. She'd got it all wrong—naturally.

I held her off and then Miss Williams took charge. She was good, I must say. She got Elsa to control herself in under a minute—told her she'd got to be quiet and that we couldn't have this noise and violence going on. She was a tartar, that woman. But she did the trick. Elsa was quiet—just stood there gasping and trembling.

As for Caroline, as far as I was concerned, the mask was right off. She stood there perfectly quiet—you might have said dazed. But she wasn't dazed. It was her eyes gave her away. They were watchful—fully aware and quietly watchful. She'd begun, I suppose, to be afraid. . . .

I went up to her and spoke to her. I said it quite low. I don't think either of the two women overheard. I said, "You damned murderess, you've killed my best friend."

She shrank back. She said, "No—oh, no—he—he did it himself. . . ."

I looked her full in the eyes. I said, "You can tell that story—to the police."

She did, and they didn't believe her.

(End of Philip Blake's Statement)

Narrative of Meredith Blake

Dear M. Poirot:

As I promised you, I have set down in writing an account of all I can remember relating to the tragic events that happened sixteen years ago. First of all, I would like to say that I have thought over carefully all you said to me at our recent meeting. And on reflection I am more convinced than I was before that it is in the highest degree unlikely that Caroline Crale poisoned her husband. It always seemed incongruous, but the absence of any other explanation and her own attitude led me to follow, sheeplike, the opinion of other people, and to say with them—that if she didn't do it, what explanation could there be?

Since seeing you I have reflected very carefully on the alternative solution presented at the time and brought forward by the defense at the trial. That is, that Amyas Crale took his own life. Although from what I knew of him that solution seemed quite fantastic at the time, I now see fit to modify my opinion. To begin with, and highly significant, is the fact that Caroline believed it. If we are now to take it that that charming and gentle lady was unjustly convicted, then her own frequently reiterated belief must carry great weight. She knew Amyas better than anyone else. If *she* thought suicide possible, then suicide *must have been possible* in spite of the skepticism of his friends.

I will advance the theory, therefore, that there was in Amyas Crale some core of conscience, some undercurrent of remorse, and even despair at the excesses to which his temperament led him, of which only his wife was aware. This, I think, is a not impossible supposition. He may have shown that side of himself only to her.

Though it is inconsistent with anything I ever heard him say, yet it is nevertheless a truth that in most men there *is* some unsuspected and inconsistent streak which often comes as a surprise to people who have known them intimately. A respected and austere man is discovered to have had a coarser side to his life hidden. A vulgar moneymaker has, perhaps, a secret appreciation of some delicate work of art. Hard and ruthless people have been convicted of unsuspected hidden kindnesses. Generous and jovial men have been shown to have a mean and cruel side to them.

So it may be that in Amyas Crale there ran a strain of morbid self-accusation, and that the more he blustered out his egoism and his right to do as he pleased the more strongly that secret conscience of his worked. It is improbable, on the face of it, but I now believe that it must have been so. And I repeat again, Caroline herself held steadfastly to that view. That, I insist, is significant!

And now to examine *facts,* or rather my memory of facts, in the light of that new belief.

I think that I might with relevance include here a conversation I held with Caroline some weeks before the actual tragedy. It was during Elsa Greer's first visit to Alderbury.

Caroline, as I have told you, was aware of my deep affection and friendship for her. I was, therefore, the person in whom she could most easily confide. She had not been looking very happy. Nevertheless, I was surprised when she suddenly asked me one day whether I thought Amyas really cared very much for this girl he had brought down.

I said: "He's interested in painting her. You know what Amyas is."

She shook her head and said, "No, he's in love with her."

"Well—perhaps a little."

"A great deal, I think."

I said: "She is unusually attractive, I admit. And we both know that Amyas is susceptible. But you must know by now, my dear, that Amyas really only cares for one person—and that is you. He has these infatuations, but they don't last. You are the one person to him, and, though he behaves badly, it does not really affect his feeling for you."

She said: "But this time, Merry, I'm afraid. That girl is so—so terribly sincere. She's so young and so intense I have a feeling that this time it's serious."

I said: "But the very fact that she *is* so young and, as you say, so sincere, will protect her. On the whole, women are fair game to Amyas, but in the case of a girl like this it will be different."

She said, "Yes, that's what I'm afraid of—it will be different."

I said, "But you know, Caroline, you *know* that Amyas is really devoted to you?"

She said to that, "Does one ever know with men?" And then she laughed a little ruefully and said, "I'm a very primitive woman, Merry. I'd like to take a hatchet to that girl."

Chapter VIII

I TOLD HER that the child probably didn't understand in the least what she was doing. She had a great admiration and hero worship for Amyas and she probably didn't realize at all that Amyas was falling in love with her.

Caroline just said to me, "Dear Merry!" and began to talk about the garden. I hoped that she was not going to worry any more about the matter.

Shortly afterward Elsa went back to London. Amyas was away too for several weeks. I had really forgotten all about the business. In fact, I thought there wasn't anything to worry about. And then I heard that Elsa was back again at Alderbury in order that Amyas might finish the picture.

I was a little disturbed by the news. But Caroline, when I saw her, was not in a communicative mood. She seemed quite her usual self—not worried or upset in any way. I imagined that everything was all right.

That's why it was such a shock to me to learn how far the thing had gone.

I have told you of my conversations with Crale and with Elsa. I had no opportunity of talking to Caroline. We were only able to exchange those few words about which I have already told you.

I can see her face now—the wide, dark eyes and the restrained emotion. I can still hear her voice as she said, *"Everything's finished. . . ."*

I can't describe to you the infinite desolation she conveyed in those words. They were a literal statement of truth. With Amyas' defection everything was finished for her. That, I am convinced, was why she took the coniine. It was a way out. A way suggested to her by my stupid dissertation on the drug. And the passage I read from the Phaedo gives a gracious picture of death.

Here is my present belief: She took the coniine, resolved to end her own life when Amyas left her. He may have seen her take it or he may have discovered that she had it later.

That discovery acted upon him with terrific force. He was horrified at what his actions had led her to contemplate. But, notwithstanding his horror and remorse, he still felt himself incapable of giving up Elsa. I can understand that. Anyone who had fallen in love with her would find it almost impossible to tear himself away.

He could not envisage life without Elsa. He realized that Caroline could not live without *him*. He decided there was only one way out—to use the coniine himself.

All this, alas, is not what you asked me for—which was an account of the happenings as I remember them. Let me now repair that omission. I have already told you fully what happened on the day preceding Amyas' death. We now come to the day itself.

I had slept very badly—worried by the disastrous turn of events for my friends. After a long wakeful period, while I vainly tried to think of something helpful I could do to avert the catastrophe, I fell into a heavy sleep about 6 A.M. The bringing of my early tea did not awaken me, and I finally woke up, heavy-headed and unrefreshed, about half past nine. It was shortly after that that I thought I heard movements in the room below, which was the room I used as a laboratory.

I may say here that actually those sounds were probably caused by a cat getting in. I found the window sash raised a little way, as it had carelessly been left from the day before. It was just wide enough to admit the passage of a cat. I merely mention the sounds to explain how I came to enter the laboratory.

I went in there as soon as I had dressed and, looking along the shelves, I noticed that the bottle containing the preparation of coniine was slightly out of line with the rest. Having had my eye drawn to it in this way, I was startled to see that a considerable quantity of it was gone. The bottle had been nearly full the day before, now it was nearly empty.

I shut and locked the window and went out, locking the door behind me. I was considerably upset and also bewildered. When startled, my mental processes are, I am afraid, somewhat slow.

I was first disturbed, then apprehensive, and finally definitely alarmed. I questioned the household, and they all denied having entered the laboratory at all. I thought things over a little while longer and then decided to ring up my brother and get his advice.

Philip was quicker than I was. He saw the seriousness of my discovery and urged me to come over at once and consult with him.

I went out, encountering Miss Williams, who was looking for a truant pupil. I assured her that I had not seen Angela and that she had not been to the house.

I think that Miss Williams noticed there was something amiss. She looked at me rather curiously. I had no intention, however, of telling her what had happened. I suggested she should try the kitchen garden—Angela had a favorite apple tree there—and I myself hurried down to the shore and rowed myself across to the Alderbury side.

My brother was already there waiting for me.

We walked up to the house together by the way you and I went the other day. Having seen the topography, you can understand that in passing underneath the wall of the Battery Garden we were bound to overhear anything being said inside it.

Beyond the fact that Caroline and Amyas were engaged in a disagreement of some kind, I did not pay much attention to what was said.

Certainly I overheard no threat of any kind uttered by Caroline. The subject of discussion was Angela, and I presume Caroline was pleading for a respite from the fiat of school. Amyas, however, was adamant, shouting out irritably that it was all settled—he'd see to her packing.

The door of the Battery opened just as we drew abreast of it and Caroline came out. She looked disturbed, but not unduly so. She smiled rather absently at me, and said they had been discussing Angela. Elsa came down the path at that minute and, as Amyas clearly wanted to get on with the sitting without interruption from us, we went on up the path.

Philip blamed himself severely afterward for the fact that we did not take immediate action. But I myself cannot see it the same way. We had no earthly right to assume that such a thing as murder was being contemplated. (Moreover, I now believe that it was *not* contemplated.) It was clear that we should have to adopt *some* course of action, but I still maintain that we were right to talk the matter over carefully first. It was necessary to find the right thing to do, and once or twice I found myself wondering if I had not, after all, made a mistake. Had the bottle really been full the day before as I thought?

I am not one of these people (like my brother Philip) who can be cocksure of everything. One's memory does play tricks on one. How often, for instance, one is convinced one has put an article in a certain place, later to find that he has put it somewhere quite different. The more I tried to recall the state of the bottle on the preceding afternoon the more uncertain and doubtful I became. This was very annoying to Philip, who began completely to lose patience with me.

We were not able to continue our discussion at the time and tacitly agreed to postpone it until after lunch. (I may say that I was always free to drop in for lunch at Alderbury if I chose.)

Later, Angela and Caroline brought us beer. I asked Angela what she had been up to, playing truant, and told her Miss Williams was on the warpath, and she said she had been bathing, and added that she didn't see why she should have to mend her horrible old skirt when she was going to have all new things to go to school with.

Since there seemed no chance of further talk with Philip alone, and since I was really anxious to think things out by myself, I wandered off down the path toward the Battery. Just above the Battery, as I showed you, there is a clearing in the trees where there used to be an old bench. I sat there smoking and thinking, and watching Elsa as she sat posing for Amyas.

I shall always think of her as she was that day: Rigid in the pose, with her yellow shirt and dark blue trousers and a red pull-over slung round her shoulders for warmth.

Her face was so alight with life and health and radiance. And that gay voice of hers reciting plans for the future.

This sounds as though I was eavesdropping, but that is not so. I was perfectly visible to Elsa. Both she and Amyas knew I was there. She waved her hand at me and called up that Amyas was a perfect bear that morning —he wouldn't let her rest. She was stiff and aching all over.

Amyas growled out that she wasn't as stiff as he was. He was stiff all over—muscular rheumatism. Elsa said mockingly, "Poor old man!" And he said she'd be taking on a creaking invalid.

It shocked me, you know, their light-hearted acquiescence in their future together while they were causing so much suffering. And yet I couldn't hold it against her. She was so young, so confident, so very much in love. And she didn't really know what she was doing. She didn't understand suffering. She just assumed with the naïve confidence of a child that Caroline would be "all right," that "she'd soon get over it." She saw nothing, you see, but herself and Amyas—happy together. She'd already told me my point of view was old-fashioned. She had no doubts, no qualms, no pity either. But can one expect pity from radiant youth? It is an older, wiser emotion.

They didn't talk very much, of course. No painter wants to be chattering when he is working. Perhaps every ten minutes or so Elsa would make an observation and Amyas would grunt a reply. Once she said:

"I think you're right about Spain. That's the first place we'll go to. And you must take me to see a bullfight. It must be wonderful! Only I'd like the bull to kill the man—not the other way about. I understand how Roman women felt when they saw a man die. Men aren't much, but animals are splendid."

I suppose she was rather like an animal herself—young and primitive and with nothing yet of man's sad experience and doubtful wisdom. I don't believe Elsa had begun to *think*—she only *felt*. But she was very much alive—more alive than any person I have ever known. . . .

That was the last time I saw her radiant and assured—on top of the world. Fey is the word for it, isn't it?

The bell sounded for lunch, and I got up and went down the path and in at the Battery door, and Elsa joined me. It was dazzlingly bright there coming in out of the shady trees. I could hardly see. Amyas was sprawled back on the seat, his arms flung out. He was staring at the picture. I've so often seen him like that. How was I to know that already the poison was working, stiffening him as he sat?

He so hated and resented illness. He would never own to it. I dare say he thought he had got a touch of the sun—the symptoms are much the same—but he'd be the last person to complain about it.

Elsa said, "He won't come up to lunch."

Privately I thought he was wise. I said, "So long, then."

He moved his eyes from the picture until they rested on me. There was a queer—how shall I describe it?—it looked like malevolence. A kind of malevolent glare.

Naturally I didn't understand it then—if his picture wasn't going as he liked he often looked quite murderous. I thought *that* was what it was. He made a sort of grunting sound.

Neither Elsa nor I saw anything unusual in him—just artistic temperament.

So we left him there and she and I went up to the house laughing and talking. If she'd known—poor child—that she'd never see him alive again . . . Oh, well, thank God she didn't. She was able to be happy a little longer.

Caroline was quite normal at lunch—a little preoccupied, nothing more. And doesn't that show that she had nothing to do with it? She *couldn't* have been such an actress.

She and the governess went down afterward and found him. I met Miss Williams as she came up. She told me to telephone a doctor and went back to Caroline.

That poor child!—Elsa, I mean. She had that frantic unrestrained grief that children have. They can't believe that life can do these things to them. Caroline was quite calm. Yes, she was quite calm. She was able, of course, to control herself better than Elsa. She didn't seem remorseful—then. Just said he must have done it himself. And we couldn't believe that. Elsa burst out and accused her to her face.

Of course, she may have realized, already, that she herself would be suspected. Yes, that probably explains her manner.

Philip was quite convinced that she *had* done it.

The governess was a great help and stand-by. She made Elsa lie down and gave her a sedative and she kept Angela out of the way when the police came. Yes, she was a tower of strength, that woman.

The whole thing became a nightmare. The police, searching the house and asking questions, and then the reporters, swarming about the place like flies and clicking cameras and wanting interviews with members of the family.

A nightmare, the whole thing. . . .

It's still a nightmare, after all these years. Please God, once you've convinced little Carla what really happened, we can forget it all and never remember it again.

Amyas *must* have committed suicide—however unlikely it seems.

(End of Meredith Blake's Narrative)

NARRATIVE OF LADY DITTISHAM

I have set down here the full story of my meeting with Amyas Crale, up to the time of his tragic death.

I saw him first at a studio party. He was standing, I remember, by a window and I saw him as I came in at the door. I asked who he was. Someone said, "That's Crale, the painter." I said at once that I'd like to meet him.

We talked on that occasion for perhaps ten minutes. When anyone makes the impression on you that Amyas Crale made on me, it's hopeless to attempt to describe it. If I say that when I saw Amyas Crale everybody else seemed to grow very small and fade away, that expresses it as well as anything can.

Immediately after that meeting I went to look at as many of his pictures as I could. He had a show on in Bond Street at the moment and there was one of his pictures in Manchester and one in Leeds and two in public galleries in London. I went to see them all. Then I met him again. I said, "I've been to see all your pictures. I think they're wonderful."

He just looked amused. He said: "Who said you were any judge of painting? I don't believe you know anything about it."

I said, "Perhaps not. But they are marvelous, all the same."

He grinned at me and said, "Don't be a gushing little fool."

I said, "I'm not; I want you to paint me."

Crale said, "If you've any sense at all, you'll realize that I don't paint portraits of pretty women."

I said, "It needn't be a portrait, and I'm not a pretty woman."

He looked at me then as though he'd begun to see me. He said, "No, perhaps you're not."

I said, "Will you paint me, then?"

He studied me for some time with his head on one side. Then he said, "You're a strange child, aren't you?"

I said, "I'm quite rich, you know; I can afford to pay well for it."

He said, "Why are you so anxious for me to paint you?"

I said, "Because I want it!"

He said, "Is that a reason?"

And I said, "Yes. I always get what I want."

He said then, "Oh, my poor child, how young you are!"

I said, "Will you paint me?"

He took me by the shoulders and turned me toward the light and looked me over. Then he stood away from me a little. I stood quite still, waiting.

He said, "I've sometimes wanted to paint a flight of impossibly colored Australian macaws alighting on St. Paul's Cathedral. If I painted you against a nice traditional bit of outdoor landscape I believe I'd get exactly the same result."

I said, "Then you will paint me?"

He said, "You're one of the loveliest, crudest, most flamboyant bits of exotic coloring I've ever seen. I'll paint you!"

I said, "Then that's settled."

He went on, "But I'll warn you, Elsa Greer. If I do paint you, I shall probably make love to you."

I said, "I hope you will. . . ."

I said it quite steadily and quietly. I heard him catch his breath and I saw the look that came into his eyes.

You see, it was as sudden as all that.

A day or two later we met again. He told me that he wanted me to come down to Devonshire—he'd got the very place there that he wanted for a background. He said, "I'm married, you know, and I'm very fond of my wife."

I said if he was fond of her she must be very nice.

He said she was extremely nice. "In fact," he said, "she's quite adorable —and I adore her. So put that in your pipe, young Elsa, and smoke it."

I told him that I quite understood.

He began the picture a week later. Caroline Crale welcomed me very pleasantly. She didn't like me much, but, after all, why should she? Amyas was very circumspect. He never said a word to me that his wife couldn't have overheard and I was polite and formal to him. Underneath, though, we both knew.

After ten days he told me I was to go back to London.

I said, "The picture isn't finished."

He said, "It's barely begun. The truth of the matter is that I can't paint you, Elsa."

I said, "Why?"

He said, "You know well enough why, Elsa. And that's why you've got to clear out. I can't think about the painting—I can't think about anything but you."

I knew it would be no good my going back to London, but I said, "Very well, I'll go if you say so."

Amyas said, "Good girl."

So I went. I didn't write to him.

He held out for ten days and then he came. He was so thin and haggard and miserable that it shocked me.

He said, "I warned you, Elsa. Don't say I didn't warn you."

I said, "I've been waiting for you. I knew you'd come."

He gave a sort of groan and said, "There are things that are too strong for any man. I can't eat or sleep or rest for wanting you."

I said I knew that, and that it was the same with me and had been from the first moment I'd seen him.

We were made for each other and we'd found each other—and we both knew we had to be together always.

But something else happened, too. The unfinished picture began to haunt Amyas. He said to me, "Damned funny, I couldn't paint you before —you yourself got in the way of it. But I *want* to paint you, Elsa. I want to paint you so that that picture will be the finest thing I've ever done. I'm itching and aching now to get at my brushes and to see you sitting there on that hoary old chestnut of a battlement wall with the conventional blue sea and the decorous English trees—and you—you—sitting there like a discordant shriek of triumph."

He said, "And I've got to paint you that way! And I can't be fussed and bothered while I'm doing it. When the picture's finished I'll tell Caroline the truth and we'll get the whole messy business cleaned up."

I said, "Will Caroline make a fuss about divorcing you?"

He said he didn't think so. But you never knew with women.

I said I was sorry if she was going to be upset; but, after all, I said, these things did happen.

He said: "Very nice and reasonable, Elsa. But Caroline isn't reasonable, never has been reasonable, and certainly isn't going to feel reasonable. She loves me, you know."

I said I understood that, but if she loved him she'd put his happiness first, and, at any rate, she wouldn't want to keep him if he wanted to be free.

He said, "Life can't really be solved by admirable maxims out of modern literature. Nature's red in tooth and claw, remember."

I said, "Surely we are all civilized people nowadays!" and Amyas laughed. He said, "Civilized people my foot! Caroline would probably like to take a hatchet to you. She might do it, too."

I said, "Then don't tell her."

He said, "No. The break's got to come. You've got to belong to me properly, Elsa. Before all the world. Openly mine."

I said, "Suppose she won't divorce you?"

He said, "I'm not afraid of that."

I said, "What are you afraid of then?"

And he said slowly, "I don't know. . . ."

You see, he knew Caroline. While I didn't.

If I'd had any idea . . .

We went down again to Alderbury. Things were difficult this time. Caroline had got suspicious. I didn't like it; I didn't like it a bit. I've always hated deceit and concealment. I thought we ought to tell her. Amyas wouldn't hear of it.

The funny part of it was that he didn't really care at all. In spite of being fond of Caroline and not wanting to hurt her, he just didn't care about the honesty or dishonesty of it all. He was painting with a kind of frenzy, and nothing else mattered. I hadn't seen him in one of his working spells before. I realized now what a really great genius he was. It was natural for him to be so carried away that all the ordinary decencies didn't matter. But it was different for me. I was in a horrible position. Caroline resented me—and quite rightly. The only thing to put the position quite straight was to be honest and tell her the truth.

But all Amyas would say was that he wasn't going to be bothered with scenes and fusses until he'd finished the picture. I said there probably wouldn't be a scene. Caroline would have too much dignity and pride for that.

I said, "I want to be honest about it all. We've *got* to be honest!"

Amyas said, "To hell with honesty. I'm painting a picture!"

I did see his point of view, but he wouldn't see mine.

And in the end I broke down. Caroline had been talking of some plan she and Amyas were going to carry out next autumn. She talked about it quite confidently. And I suddenly felt it was too abominable what we were doing—letting her go on like this—and perhaps, too, I was angry, because she was really being very unpleasant to me in a clever sort of way that one couldn't take hold of.

And so I came out with the truth. In a way, I still think I was right.

Though, of course, I wouldn't have done it if I'd had the faintest idea what was to come of it.

The clash came right away. Amyas was furious with me for telling Caroline, but he had to admit that what I had said was true.

I didn't understand Caroline at all. We all went over to Meredith Blake's to tea, and Caroline played up marvelously—talking and laughing. Like a fool, I thought she was taking it well. It was awkward, my not being able to leave the house, but Amyas would have gone up in smoke if I had. I thought perhaps Caroline would go. It would have made it much easier for us if she had.

I didn't see her take the coniine. I want to be honest, so I think that it's just possible that she may have taken it as she said she did—with the idea of suicide in her mind.

But I don't *really* think so. I think she was one of those intensely jealous and possessive women who won't let go of anything that they think belongs to them. Amyas was her property. I think she was quite prepared to kill him rather than to let him go, completely and finally, to another woman. I think she right away made up her mind to kill him. And I think that Meredith's happening to discuss coniine so freely just gave her the means to do what she'd already made up her mind to do. She was a very bitter and revengeful woman—vindictive. Amyas knew all along that she was dangerous. I didn't.

The next morning she had a final showdown with Amyas. I heard most of it from outside on the terrace. He was splendid—very patient and calm. He implored her to be reasonable. He said he was very fond of her and the child, and always would be. He'd do everything he could to assure their future. Then he hardened up and said, "But understand this: I'm damned well going to marry Elsa, and nothing shall stop me. You and I always agreed to leave each other free. These things happen."

Caroline said to him, "Do as you please. I've warned you."

Her voice was very quiet, but there was a queer note in it.

Amyas said, "What do you mean, Caroline?"

She said, "You're mine and *I don't mean to let you go.* Sooner than let you go to that girl *I'll kill you. . . .*"

Just at that minute Philip Blake came along the terrace. I got up and went to meet him. I didn't want him to overhear.

Presently Amyas came out and said it was time to get on with the picture. We went down together to the Battery. He didn't say much. Just said that Caroline was cutting up rough—but not to talk about it. He wanted to concentrate on what he was doing. Another day, he said, would about finish the picture.

He said. "And it'll be the best thing I've done, Elsa, even if it is paid for in blood and tears."

A little later I went up to the house to get a pull-over. There was a chilly wind blowing. When I came back again, Caroline was there. I suppose she had come down to make one last appeal to Amyas. Philip and Meredith Blake were there too.

It was then that Amyas said he was thirsty and wanted a drink. He said there was beer but it wasn't iced.

Caroline said she'd send him down some iced beer. She said it quite naturally, in an almost friendly tone. She was an actress, that woman. She must have known then what she meant to do.

She brought it down about ten minutes later. Amyas was painting. She poured it out and set the glass down beside him. Neither of us was watching her. Amyas was intent on what he was doing and I had to keep the pose.

Amyas drank it down the way he always drank beer—just pouring it down his throat in one draught. Then he made a face and said it tasted foul; but, at any rate, it was cold.

And even then, when he said that, no suspicion entered my head. I just laughed and said, "Liver."

When she'd seen him drink it Caroline went away.

It must have been about forty minutes later that Amyas complained of stiffness and pains. He said he thought he must have got a touch of muscular rheumatism. Amyas was always intolerant of any ailment, and he didn't like being fussed over. After saying that he turned it off with a light "Old age, I suppose. You've taken on a creaking old man, Elsa."

I played up to him. But I noticed that his legs moved stiffly and queerly and that he grimaced once or twice. I never dreamed that it wasn't rheumatism. Presently he drew the bench along and sat sprawled on that, occasionally stretching up to put a touch of paint here and there on the canvas. He used to do that sometimes when he was painting. Just sit staring at me and then at the canvas. Sometimes he'd do it for half an hour at a time. So I didn't think it specially queer.

We heard the bell go for lunch and he said he wasn't coming up. He'd stay where he was and he didn't want anything. That wasn't unusual either and it would be easier for him than facing Caroline at the table.

He was talking in rather a queer way—grunting out his words. But he sometimes did that when he was dissatisfied with the progress of the picture.

Meredith Blake came in to fetch me. He spoke to Amyas, but Amyas only grunted at him.

We went up to the house together and left him there. We left him there

—to die alone. I'd never seen much illness, I didn't know much about it; I thought Amyas was just in a painter's mood. If I'd known—if I'd realized, perhaps a doctor could have saved him. . . . Oh, why didn't I— It's no good thinking of that now. I was a blind fool, a blind, stupid fool.

There isn't much more to tell.

Caroline and the governess went down there after lunch. Meredith followed them. Presently he came running up. He told us Amyas was dead.

Then I knew! Knew, I mean, that it was Caroline. I still didn't think of poison. I thought she'd gone down that minute and either shot or stabbed him.

I wanted to get at her—to kill her. . . .

How *could* she do it? How *could* she? He was so alive, so full of life and vigor. To put all that out—to make him limp and cold. Just so that I shouldn't have him.

Horrible woman! . . . Horrible, scornful, cruel, vindictive woman! . . . I hate her! I still hate her!

They didn't even hang her.

They ought to have hanged her. . . . Even hanging was too good for her. . . .

I hate her! . . . I hate her! . . . I hate her! . . .

(End of Lady Dittisham's Narrative)

NARRATIVE OF CECILIA WILLIAMS

Dear M. Poirot:

I am sending you an account of those events in September, 19—, actually witnessed by myself.

I have been absolutely frank and have kept nothing back. You may show it to Carla Crale. It may pain her, but I have always been a believer in truth. Palliatives are harmful. One must have the courage to face reality. Without that courage, life is meaningless. The people who do us most harm are the people who shield us from reality.

Believe me, yours sincerely,

CECILIA WILLIAMS.

My name is Cecilia Williams. I was engaged by Mrs. Crale as governess to her half sister, Angela Warren, in 19—. I was then forty-eight.

I took up my duties at Alderbury, a very beautiful estate in South Devon which had belonged to Mr. Crale's family for many generations. I knew that Mr. Crale was a well-known painter but I did not meet him until I took up residence at Alderbury.

The household consisted of Mr. and Mrs. Crale, Angela Warren (then a girl of thirteen) and three servants, who had been with the family many years.

I found my pupil an interesting and promising character. She had very marked abilities and it was a pleasure to teach her. She was somewhat wild and undisciplined, but these faults arose mainly through high spirits, and I have always preferred my girls to show spirit. An excess of vitality can be trained and guided into paths of real usefulness and achievement.

On the whole, I found Angela amenable to discipline. She had been somewhat spoiled—mainly by Mrs. Crale, who was far too indulgent where she was concerned. Mr. Crale's influence was, I considered, unwise. He indulged her absurdly one day and was unnecessarily peremptory on another occasion. He was very much a man of moods, possibly owing to what is styled the artistic temperament.

I have never seen, myself, why the possession of artistic ability should be supposed to excuse a man from a decent exercise of self-control. I did not myself admire Mr. Crale's paintings. The drawing seemed to me faulty and the coloring exaggerated, but, naturally, I was not called upon to express any opinion on these matters.

I soon formed a deep attachment to Mrs. Crale. I admired her character and her fortitude in the difficulties of her life. Mr. Crale was not a faithful husband, and I think that that fact was the source of much pain to her. A stronger-minded woman would have left him, but Mrs. Crale never seemed to contemplate such a course. She endured his infidelities and forgave him for them, but I may say that she did not take them meekly. She remonstrated—and with spirit!

It was said at the trial that they led a cat-and-dog life. I would not go as far as that—Mrs. Crale had too much dignity for that term to apply—but they *did* have quarrels. And I consider that that was only natural under the circumstances.

I had been with Mrs. Crale just over two years when Miss Elsa Greer appeared upon the scene. She arrived down at Alderbury in the summer of 19—. Mrs. Crale had not met her previously. She was Mr. Crale's friend, and she was said to be there for the purpose of having her portrait painted.

It was apparent at once that Mr. Crale was infatuated with this girl, and that the girl herself was doing nothing to discourage him. She behaved, in my opinion, quite outrageously, being abominably rude to Mrs. Crale and openly flirting with Mr. Crale.

Naturally Mrs. Crale said nothing to me, but I could see that she was disturbed and unhappy and I did everything in my power to distract her mind and lighten her burden. Miss Greer sat every day for Mr. Crale, but I noticed that the picture was not getting on very fast. They had, no doubt, other things to talk about.

My pupil, I am thankful to say, noticed very little of what was going on. Angela was in some ways young for her age. Though her intellect was well developed, she was not at all what I may term precocious. She seemed to have no wish to read undesirable books and showed no signs of morbid curiosity such as girls often do at her age.

She, therefore, saw nothing undesirable in the friendship between Mr. Crale and Miss Greer. Nevertheless, she disliked Miss Greer and thought her stupid. Here she was quite right. Miss Greer had had, I presume, a proper education, but she never opened a book and was quite unfamiliar with current literary allusions. Moreover, she could not sustain a discussion on any intellectual subject.

She was entirely taken up with her personal appearance, her clothes, and men.

Angela, I think, did not even realize that her sister was unhappy. She was not at that time a very perceptive person. She spent a lot of time in hoydenish pastimes, such as tree climbing and wild feats of bicycling. She was also a passionate reader and showed excellent taste in what she liked and disliked.

Mrs. Crale was always careful to conceal any signs of unhappiness from Angela, and exerted herself to appear bright and cheerful when the girl was about.

Miss Greer went back to London—at which, I can tell you, we were all very pleased! The servants disliked her as much as I did. She was the kind of person who gives a lot of unnecessary trouble and forgets to say thank you.

Mr. Crale went away shortly afterward, and of course I knew that he had gone after the girl. I was very sorry for Mrs. Crale. She felt these things very keenly. I felt extremely bitter toward Mr. Crale. When a man has a charming, gracious, intelligent wife he has no business to treat her badly.

However, she and I both hoped the affair would soon be over. Not that we mentioned the subject to each other—we did not—but she knew quite well how I felt about it.

Unfortunately, after some weeks, the pair of them reappeared. It seemed the sittings were to be resumed.

Mr. Crale was now painting with absolute frenzy. He seemed less preoccupied with the girl than with his picture of her. Nevertheless, I realized that this was not the usual kind of thing we had gone through before. This girl had got her claws into him and she meant business. He was just like wax in her hands.

The thing came to a head on the day before he died—that is, on September 17th. Miss Greer's manner had been unbearably insolent the last few days. She was feeling sure of herself and she wanted to assert her importance. Mrs. Crale behaved like a true gentlewoman. She was icily polite but she showed the other clearly what she thought of her.

On this day, September 17th, as we were sitting in the drawing room after lunch, Miss Greer came out with an amazing remark as to how she was going to redecorate the room when she was living at Alderbury.

Naturally, Mrs. Crale couldn't let that pass. She challenged her and Miss Greer had the impudence to say, before us all, that she was going to marry Mr. Crale. She actually talked about marrying a married man—and she said it to his wife!

Chapter IX

I WAS VERY, very angry with Mr. Crale. How dared he let this girl insult his wife in her own drawing room? If he wanted to run away with the girl he should have gone off with her, not brought her into his wife's house and backed her up in her insolence.

In spite of what she must have felt, Mrs. Crale did not lose her dignity. Her husband came in just then and she immediately demanded confirmation from him.

He was, not unnaturally, annoyed with Miss Greer for her unconsidered forcing of the situation. Apart from anything else, it made *him* appear at a disadvantage, and men do not like appearing at a disadvantage. It upsets their vanity.

He stood there, a great giant of a man, looking as sheepish and foolish as a naughty schoolboy. It was his wife who carried off the honors of the situation. He had to mutter foolishly that it was true, but that he hadn't meant her to learn it like this.

I have never seen anything like the look of scorn she gave him. She went out of the room with her head held high. She was a beautiful woman—much more beautiful than that flamboyant girl—and she walked like an empress.

I hoped, with all my heart, that Amyas Crale would be punished for the cruelty he had displayed and for the indignity he had put upon a long-suffering and noble woman.

For the first time I tried to say something of what I felt to Mrs. Crale, but she stopped me.

She said, "We must try and behave as usual. It's the best way. We're all going over to Meredith Blake's to tea."

I said to her then, "I think you are wonderful, Mrs. Crale."

She said, "You don't know. . . ."

Then, as she was going out of the room, she came back and kissed me. She said, "You're such a great comfort to me."

She went to her room then and I think she cried. I saw her when they all started off. She was wearing a big-brimmed hat that shaded her face—a hat she very seldom wore.

Mr. Crale was uneasy but was trying to brazen things out. Mr. Philip Blake was trying to behave as usual. That Miss Greer was looking like a cat who has got at the cream jug—all self-satisfaction and purrs!

They all started off. They got back about six. I did not see Mrs. Crale again alone that evening. She was very quiet and composed at dinner and she went to bed early. I don't think that anyone but I knew how she was suffering.

The evening was taken up with a kind of running quarrel between Mr. Crale and Angela. They brought up the old school question again. He was irritable and on edge and she was unusually trying. The whole matter was settled and her outfit had been bought and there was no sense in starting up an argument again, but she suddenly chose to make a grievance of it. I have not doubt she sensed the tension in the air and that it reacted on her as much as on everybody else. I am afraid I was too preoccupied with my own thoughts to try to check her, as I should have done. It all ended with her flinging a paperweight at Mr. Crale and dashing wildly out of the room.

I went after her and told her sharply that I was ashamed of her behaving like a baby, but she was still very uncontrolled and I thought it best to leave her alone.

I hesitated as to whether to go to Mrs. Crale's room, but I decided in the end that it would, perhaps, annoy her. I wish since that I had overcome my diffidence and insisted on her talking to me. If she had done so, it might possibly have made a difference. She had no one, you see, in whom she could confide. Although I admire self-control, I must regretfully admit that sometimes it can be carried too far. A natural outlet to the feelings is better.

I met Mr. Crale as I went along to my room. He said good night, but I did not answer.

The next morning was, I remember, a beautiful day. One felt when waking that surely with such peace all around even a man must come to his senses.

I went into Angela's room before going down to breakfast, but she was already up and out. I picked up a torn skirt which she had left lying on the floor and took it down with me for her to mend after breakfast.

She had, however, obtained bread and marmalade from the kitchen and gone out. After I had had my own breakfast I went in search of her. I mention this to explain why I was not more with Mrs. Crale on that morning as perhaps I should have been. At the time, however, I felt it was my duty to look for Angela. She was very naughty and obstinate about mending her clothes and I had no intention of allowing her to defy me in the matter.

Her bathing dress was missing and I accordingly went down to the beach. There was no sign of her in the water or on the rocks so I conceived it possible that she had gone over to Mr. Meredith Blake's. She and he were great friends. I accordingly rowed myself across and resumed my search. I did not find her and eventually returned. Mrs. Crale, Mr. Blake and Mr. Philip Blake were on the terrace.

It was very hot that morning if one was out of the wind, and the house and terrace were sheltered. Mrs. Crale suggested they might like some iced beer.

There was a little conservatory which had been built onto the house in Victorian days. Mrs. Crale disliked it, and it was not used for plants, but it had been made into a kind of bar, with various bottles of gin, vermouth, lemonade, ginger beer, etc., on shelves, and a small refrigerator which was filled with ice every morning and in which some beer and ginger beer were always kept.

Mrs. Crale went there to get the beer and I went with her. Angela was at the refrigerator and was just taking out a bottle of beer.

Mrs. Crale went in ahead of me. She said, "I want a bottle of beer to take down to Amyas."

It is so difficult now to know whether I ought to have suspected anything. Her voice, I feel almost convinced, was perfectly normal. But I must admit that at that moment I was intent, not on her, but on Angela. Angela was by the refrigerator and I was glad to see that she looked red and rather guilty.

I was rather sharp with her, and to my surprise she was quite meek. I asked her where she had been and she said she had been bathing. I said, "I didn't see you on the beach." And she laughed. Then I asked her where her jersey was, and she said she must have left it down on the beach.

I mention these details to explain why I let Mrs. Crale take the beer down to the Battery Garden.

The rest of the morning is quite blank in my mind. Angela fetched her needle book and mended her skirt without any more fuss. I rather think that I mended some of the household linen. Mr. Crale did not come up for lunch. I was glad that he had at least *that* much decency.

After lunch, Mrs. Crale said she was going down to the Battery. I wanted to retrieve Angela's jersey from the beach. We started down together. She went into the Battery; I was going on when her cry called me back. As I told you when you came to see me, she asked me to go up and telephone. On the way up I met Mr. Meredith Blake and I went back to Mrs. Crale.

That was my story as I told it at the inquest and later at the trial.

What I am about to write down I have never told to any living soul. I was not asked any question to which I returned an untrue answer. Nevertheless, I *was* guilty of withholding certain facts. I do not repent of that. I would do it again. I am fully aware that in revealing this I may be laying myself open to censure, but I do not think that after this lapse of time anyone will take the matter very seriously, especially since Caroline Crale was convicted without my evidence.

This, then, is what happened:

I met Mr. Meredith Blake as I said and I ran down the path again as quickly as I could. I was wearing sand shoes and I have always been light on my feet. I came to the open Battery door and this is what I saw:

Mrs. Crale was busily polishing the beer bottle on the table with her handkerchief. Having done so, she took her dead husband's hand and pressed the fingers of it on the beer bottle. All the time she was listening and on the alert. It was the fear I saw on her face that told me the truth.

I knew then, beyond any possible doubt, that Caroline Crale had poisoned her husband. And I, for one, do not blame her. He drove her to a point beyond human endurance, and he brought his fate upon himself.

I never mentioned the incident to Mrs. Crale and she never knew that I had seen it take place. I would never have mentioned it to anybody, but there is one person who I think has a right to know.

Caroline Crale's daughter must not bolster up her life with a lie. However much it may pain her to know the truth, truth is the only thing that matters.

Tell her, from me, that her mother is not to be judged. She was driven beyond what a loving woman can endure. It is for her daughter to understand and forgive.

(End of Cecilia Williams' Narrative)

NARRATIVE OF ANGELA WARREN

Dear M. Poirot:

I am keeping my promise to you and have written down all I can remember of that terrible time sixteen years ago. But it was not until I started that I realized how very little I *did* remember. Until the thing actually happened, you see, there is nothing to fix anything by.

The very first intimation I had of the whole thing was what I overheard from the terrace where I had escaped after lunch one day. Elsa said she

was going to marry Amyas! It struck me as just ridiculous. I remember
tackling Amyas about it. In the garden at Handcross it was. I said to him:
    "Why does Elsa say she's going to marry you? She couldn't. People
can't have two wives—it's bigamy and they go to prison."
    Amyas got very angry and said, "How the devil did you hear that?"
    I said I'd heard it through the library window.
    He was angrier than ever then and said it was high time I went to
school and got out of the habit of eavesdropping.
    I still remember the resentment I felt when he said that. Because it was
so *unfair*. Absolutely and utterly unfair.
    I stammered out angrily that I hadn't been listening—and, anyhow, I
said, why did Elsa say a silly thing like that?
    Amyas said it was just a joke.
    That ought to have satisfied me. It did—almost, but not quite.
    I said to Elsa when we were on the way back, "I asked Amyas what you
meant when you said you were going to marry him and he said it was just
a joke."
    I felt that ought to snub her. But she only smiled.
    I didn't like that smile of hers. I went up to Caroline's room. It was
when she was dressing for dinner. I asked her then outright if it were
possible for Amyas to marry Elsa.
    I remember Caroline's answer as though I heard it now. She must have
spoken with great emphasis. "Amyas will marry Elsa only after I am
dead," she said.
    That reassured me completely. Death seemed ages away from us all.
    I don't remember much about the afternoon at Meredith Blake's, al-
though I *do* remember his reading aloud the passage from the Phaedo,
describing Socrates' death. I had never heard it before. I thought it was the
loveliest, most beautiful thing I had ever heard.
    I don't remember much that happened the next morning either, though
I have thought and thought. I've a vague feeling that I must have bathed,
and I think I remember being made to mend something.
    But it's all very vague and dim till the time when Meredith came pant-
ing up the path from the terrace and his face was all gray and queer. I
remember a coffee cup falling off the table and being broken—Elsa did
that. And I remember her running—suddenly running for all she was
worth down the path—and the awful look there was on her face.
    I kept saying to myself, "Amyas is dead." But it just didn't seem real.
    I remember Dr. Faussett coming and his grave face. Miss Williams was
busy looking after Caroline. I wandered about rather forlornly, getting in
people's way. I had a nasty, sick feeling.

Miss Williams took me into Caroline's room later. Caroline was on the sofa. She looked very white and ill.

She kissed me and said she wanted me to go away as soon as I could, and it was all horrible, but I wasn't to worry or think about it any more than I could help. I was to join Carla at Lady Tressilian's, because this house was to be kept as empty as possible.

I clung to Caroline and said I didn't want to go away. I wanted to stay with her. She said she knew I did, but it was better for me to go away and would take a lot of worry off her mind. And Miss Williams chipped in and said, "The best way you can help your sister, Angela, is to do what she wants you to do without making a fuss about it."

So I said I would do whatever Caroline wished. And Caroline said, "That's my darling, Angela." And she hugged me and said there was nothing to worry about.

I had to go down and talk to a police superintendent. He was very kind, asked me when I had last seen Amyas, and a lot of other questions which seemed to me quite pointless at the time, but which, of course, I see the point of now. He satisfied himself that there was nothing that I could tell him which he hadn't already heard from the others. So he told Miss Williams that he saw no objection to my going over to Ferrilby Grange to Lady Tressilian's.

I went there and Lady Tressilian was very kind to me. But, of course, I soon had to know the truth. They arrested Caroline almost at once. I was so horrified and dumfounded that I became quite ill.

I heard afterward that Caroline was terribly worried about me. It was at her insistence that I was sent out of England before the trial came on. But that I have told you already.

As you see, what I have to put down is pitiably meager. Since talking to you I have gone over the little I remember painstakingly, racking my memory for details of this or that person's expression or reaction. I can remember nothing consistent with guilt. Elsa's frenzy, Meredith's gray worried face, Philip's grief and fury—they all seem natural enough. I suppose, though, someone *could* have been playing a part.

I only know this, *Caroline did not do it.*

I am quite certain on this point and always shall be, but I have no evidence to offer except my own intimate knowledge of her character.

(End of Angela Warren's Narrative)

Carla Lemarchant looked up. Her eyes were full of fatigue and pain. She pushed back the hair from her forehead in a tired gesture.

She said, "It's so bewildering, all this." She touched the pile of manuscripts. "Because the angle's different every time! Everybody sees my mother differently. But the facts are the same. Everyone agrees on the facts."

"It has discouraged you, reading them?"

"Yes. Hasn't it discouraged you?"

"No, I have found those documents very valuable—very informative." He spoke slowly and reflectively.

Carla said, "I wish I'd never read them!"

Poirot looked across at her. "Ah—so it makes you feel that way?"

Carla said bitterly, "They all think she did it—all of them except Aunt Angela, and what she thinks doesn't count. She hasn't got any reason for it. She's just one of those loyal people who'll stick to a thing through thick and thin. She just goes on saying, 'Caroline couldn't have done it.' "

"It strikes you like that?"

"How else should it strike me? I've realized, you know, that if my mother didn't do it, then one of these five people must have done it. I've even had theories as to why."

"Ah? That is interesting. Tell me."

"Oh, they were only theories. Philip Blake, for instance. He's a stockbroker, he was my father's best friend—probably my father trusted him. And artists are usually careless about money matters. Perhaps Philip Blake was in a jam and used my father's money. He may have got my father to sign something. Then the whole thing may have been on the point of coming out—and only my father's death could have saved him. That's one of the things I thought of."

"Not badly imagined at all. What else?"

"Well, there's Elsa. Philip Blake says here she had her head screwed on too well to meddle with poison, but I don't think that's true at all. Supposing my mother had gone to her and told her that she wouldn't divorce my father—that nothing would induce her to divorce him. You may say what you like but I think Elsa had a bourgeois mind—she wanted to be respectably married. I think that then Elsa would have been perfectly capable of pinching the stuff—she had just as good a chance that afternoon—and might have tried to get my mother out of the way by poisoning her. I think that would be quite *like* Elsa. And then, possibly, by some awful accident, Amyas got the stuff instead of Caroline."

"Again it is not badly imagined. What else?"

Carla said slowly, "Well, I thought—perhaps—*Meredith!*"

"Ah! Meredith Blake?"

"Yes. You see, he sounds to me just the sort of person who would do a murder. I mean, he was the slow, dithering one the others laughed at, and underneath, perhaps, he resented that. Then my father married the girl he wanted to marry. And my father was successful and rich. And Meredith did make all those poisons! Perhaps he really made them because he liked the idea of being able to kill someone one day. He had to call attention to the stuff being taken so as to divert suspicion from himself. But he himself was far the most likely person to have taken it. He might, even, have liked getting Caroline hanged—because she turned him down long ago. I think, you know, it's rather fishy what he says in his account of it all—how people do things that aren't characteristic of them. Supposing he meant *himself* when he wrote that?"

Hercule Poirot said: "You are at least right in this—not to take what has been written down as necessarily a true narrative. What has been written may have been written deliberately to mislead."

"Oh, I know. I've kept that in mind."

"Any other ideas?"

Carla said slowly: "I wondered—before I'd read this—about Miss Williams. She lost her job, you see, when Angela went to school. And if Amyas had died suddenly, Angela probably wouldn't have gone after all. I mean, if it passed off as a natural death—which it easily might have done, I suppose, if Meredith hadn't missed the coniine. I read up on coniine and it hasn't any distinctive postmortem appearances. It might have been thought to be sunstroke. I know that just losing a job doesn't sound a very adequate motive for murder. But murders have been committed again and again for what seem ridiculously inadequate motives. Tiny sums of money sometimes. And a middle-aged, perhaps rather incompetent governess might have got the wind up and just seen no future ahead of her.

"As I say, that's what I thought before I read this. But Miss Williams doesn't sound like that at all. She doesn't sound in the least incompetent—"

"Not at all. She is still a very efficient and intelligent woman."

"I know. One can see that. And she sounds absolutely trustworthy, too. That's what has upset me really. Oh, you know—*you* understand. You don't mind, of course. All along you've made it clear it was the truth you wanted. I suppose now we've *got* the truth! Miss Williams is quite right. One must accept truth. It's no good basing your life on a lie because it's what you want to believe. All right, then—I can take it! My mother wasn't innocent! She wrote me that letter because she was weak and unhappy and wanted to spare me. I don't judge her. Perhaps I should feel like that, too. I don't know what prison does to you. And I don't blame her either—if she felt so desperately about my father, I suppose she couldn't help herself. But I don't blame my father altogether, either. I understand—just a little —how *he* felt. So alive and so full of wanting everything. . . . He couldn't help it—he was made that way. And he was a great painter. I think that excuses a lot."

She turned her flushed, excited face to Hercule Poirot with her chin raised defiantly.

"So you are satisfied?" Poirot said.

"Satisfied?" said Carla Lemarchant. Her voice broke on the word.

Poirot leaned forward and patted her paternally on the shoulder. "Listen," he said. "You give up the fight at the moment when it is most worth fighting. At the moment when I, Hercule Poirot, have a very good idea of what really happened."

Carla stared at him. She said: "Miss Williams loved my mother. She saw her—with her own eyes—faking that suicide evidence. If you believe what she says—"

Hercule Poirot got up. "Mademoiselle," he said, "because Cecilia Williams says she saw your mother faking Amyas Crale's fingerprints on the beer bottle—on the beer *bottle,* mind—that is the one thing I need to tell me definitely, once for all, that your mother did not kill your father."

He nodded his head several times and went out of the room, leaving Carla staring after him.

"Well, M. Poirot?"

Philip Blake's tone was impatient.

Poirot said, "I have to thank you for your admirable and lucid account of the Crale tragedy."

Philip Blake looked rather self-conscious. "Very kind of you," he murmured. "Really surprising how much I remembered when I got down to it."

Poirot said, "It was an admirably clear narrative, but there were certain omissions, were there not?"

"Omissions?" Philip Blake frowned.

Hercule Poirot said, "Your narrative, shall we say, was not entirely frank." His tone hardened. "I have been informed, Mr. Blake, that on at least one night during the summer Mrs. Crale was seen coming out of your room at a somewhat compromising hour."

There was a silence broken only by Philip Blake's heavy breathing. He said at last, "Who told you that?"

Hercule Poirot shook his head. "It is no matter who told me. That I *know,* that is the point."

Again there was a silence, then Philip Blake made up his mind. He said, "By accident, it seems, you have stumbled upon a purely private matter. I admit that it does not square with what I have written down. Nevertheless, it squares better than you might think. I am forced now to tell you the truth.

"I *did* entertain a feeling of animosity toward Caroline Crale. At the same time I was always strongly attracted by her. Perhaps the latter fact induced the former. I resented the power she had over me and tried to stifle the attraction she had for me by constantly dwelling on her worst points. I never *liked* her, if you understand. But it would have been easy at any moment for me to make love to her. I had been in love with her as a boy and she had taken no notice of me. I did not find that easy to forgive.

"My opportunity came when Amyas lost his head so completely over the Greer girl. Quite without meaning to, I found myself telling Caroline I loved her. She said quite calmly, 'Yes, I have always known that.' The insolence of the woman!

"Of course, I knew that she didn't love me, but I saw that she was disturbed and disillusioned by Amyas' present infatuation. That is a mood when a woman can very easily be won. She agreed to come to me that night. And she came."

Blake paused. He found now a difficulty in getting the words out. "She came to my room. And then, with my arms around her, she told me quite coolly that it was no good! After all, she said, she was a one-man woman. She was Amyas Crale's, for better or worse. She agreed that she had treated me very badly, but she said she couldn't help it. She asked me to forgive her.

"And she left me. *She left me!* Do you wonder, M. Poirot, that my hatred of her was heightened a hundredfold? Do you wonder that I have never forgiven her? For the insult she did me, as well as for the fact that she killed the friend I loved better than anyone in the world!"

Trembling violently, Philip Blake exclaimed:

"I don't want to speak of it, do you hear? You've got your answer. Now go! And never mention the matter to me again!"

"I want to know, Mr. Blake, the order in which your guests left the laboratory that day."

Meredith Blake protested: "But, my dear M. Poirot—after sixteen years! How can I possibly remember? I've told you that Caroline came out last."

"You are *sure* of that?"

"Yes—at least—I think so. . . ."

"Let us go there now. We must be *quite* sure, you see."

Still protesting, Meredith Blake led the way. He unlocked the door and swung back the shutters. Poirot spoke to him authoritatively: "Now then, my friend. You have showed your visitors your interesting preparations of herbs. Shut your eyes and think."

Meredith Blake did so obediently. Poirot drew a handkerchief from his pocket and gently passed it to and fro. Blake murmured, his nostrils twitching slightly: "Yes, yes—extraordinary how things come back to one! Caroline, I remember, had on a pale coffee-colored dress. Phil was looking bored. . . . He always thought my hobby was quite idiotic."

"Reflect now," Poirot said. "You are about to leave the room. You are going to the library, where you are going to read the passage about the death of Socrates. Who leaves the room first—do you?"

"Elsa and I—yes. She passed through the door first. I was close behind her. We were talking. I stood there waiting for the others to come, so that I could lock the door again. Philip—yes, Philip came out next. And Angela —she was asking him what bulls and bears were. They went on through the hall. Amyas followed them. I stood there waiting still—for Caroline, of course."

"So you are quite sure Caroline stayed behind. Did you see what she was doing?"

Blake shook his head. "No, I had my back to the room, you see. I was talking to Elsa—boring her, I expect—telling her how certain plants must be gathered at the full of the moon, according to old superstition. And then Caroline came out—hurrying a little—and I locked the door."

He stopped and looked at Poirot, who was replacing a handkerchief in his pocket. Meredith Blake sniffed disgustedly and thought, "Why, the fellow actually uses *scent!*" Aloud he said: "I am quite sure of it. That was the order: Elsa, myself, Philip, Angela and Caroline. Does that help you at all?"

Poirot said: "It all fits in. Listen: I want to arrange a meeting here. It will not, I think, be difficult. . . ."

"Well?"

Elsa Dittisham said it almost eagerly—like a child.

Poirot said, "I want to ask you a question, madame."

"Yes?"

Poirot said, "After it was all over—the trial, I mean—did Meredith Blake ask you to marry him?"

Elsa stared. She looked contemptuous, almost bored. "Yes—he did. Why?"

"Were you surprised?"

"Was I? I don't remember."

"What did you say?"

Elsa laughed. She said, "What do you think I said? After *Amyas—*

Meredith? It would have been ridiculous! It was stupid of him. He always was rather stupid."

She smiled suddenly.

"He wanted, you know, to protect me—to 'look after me,' that's how he put it! He thought, like everybody else, that the assizes had been a terrible ordeal for me. And the reporters! And the booing crowds! And all the mud that was slung at me."

She brooded a minute. Then she said, "Poor old Meredith! Such an ass!" And laughed again.

Once again Hercule Poirot encountered the shrewd, penetrating glance of Miss Williams, and once again felt the years falling away and himself a meek and apprehensive little boy.

There was, he explained, a question he wished to ask.

Miss Williams intimated her willingness to hear what the question was.

Poirot said slowly, picking his words carefully:

"Angela Warren was injured as a very young child. Mrs. Crale threw a paperweight at her. Is that right?"

Miss Williams replied, "Yes."

"Who was your informant?"

"Angela herself. She volunteered the information quite early."

"What did she say exactly?"

"She touched her cheek and said: 'Caroline did this when I was a baby. She threw a paperweight at me. Never refer to it—will you?—because it upsets her dreadfully.'"

"Did Mrs. Crale herself ever mention the matter to you?"

"Only obliquely. She assumed that I knew the story. I remember her saying once, 'I know you think I spoil Angela, but, you see, I always feel there is nothing I can do to make up to her for what I did.' And on another occasion she said, 'To know you have permanently injured another human being is the heaviest burden anyone could have to bear.'"

"Thank you, Miss Williams. That is all I wanted to know."

Poirot slowed up a little as he approached the big block of flats overlooking Regent's Park. Really, when he came to think of it, he did not want to ask Angela Warren any questions at all. The only question he did want to ask her could wait. . . .

No, it was really only his insatiable passion for symmetry that was bringing him here. Five people—there should be five questions! It was neater so. It rounded off the thing better.

Angela Warren greeted him with something closely approaching eagerness. She said: "Have you found out anything? Have you got anywhere?"

Slowly Poirot nodded his head in his best China mandarin manner. "At last I make progress," he said.

"Philip Blake?" It was halfway between statement and a question.

"Mademoiselle, I do not wish to say anything at present. The moment has not yet come. What I will ask of you is to be so good as to come down to Handcross Manor. The others have consented."

She said, with a slight frown: "What do you propose to do? Reconstruct something that happened sixteen years ago?"

"See it, perhaps, from a clearer angle. You will come?"

"Oh, yes, I'll come," Angela Warren said slowly. "It will be interesting to see all those people again. I shall see *them* now, perhaps, from a clearer angle (as you put it) than I did then."

"And you will bring with you the letter that you showed me?"

Angela Warren frowned. "That letter is my own. I showed it to you for a good and sufficient reason, but I have no intention of allowing it to be read by strange and unsympathetic persons."

"But you will allow yourself to be guided by me in the matter?"

"I will do nothing of the kind. I will bring the letter with me, but I shall use my own judgment, which I venture to think is quite as good as yours."

Poirot spread out his hands in a gesture of resignation. He got up to go. He said, "You permit that I ask one little question?"

"What is it?"

"At the time of the tragedy, you had lately read—had you not?—a life of the painter Gaugin."

Angela stared at him. Then she said, "I believe—why, yes, that is quite true." She looked at him with frank curiosity. "How did you know?"

"I want to show you, mademoiselle, that even in a small, unimportant matter I am something of a magician. There are things I know without having to be told."

The afternoon sun shone into the laboratory at Handcross Manor. Some easy chairs and a settee had been brought into the room, but they served more to emphasize its forlorn aspect than to furnish it.

Slightly embarrassed, pulling at his mustache, Meredith Blake talked to Carla in a desultory way. He broke off once to say, "My dear, you are very like your mother—and yet unlike her too."

Carla asked, "How am I like her and how unlike?"

"You have her coloring and her way of moving, but you are—how shall I put it—more *positive* than she ever was."

Philip Blake, a scowl creasing his forehead, looked out of the window and drummed impatiently on the pane. He said: "What's the sense of all this? A perfectly fine Saturday afternoon—"

Hercule Poirot hastened to pour oil on troubled waters:

"Ah, I apologize—it is, I know, unpardonable to disarrange the golf. But, M. Blake, this is the daughter of your best friend. You will stretch a point for her, will you not?"

The butler announced, "Miss Warren."

Meredith went to welcome her. He said: "It's good of you to spare the time, Angela. You're busy, I know."

He led her over to the window.

Carla said, "Hullo, Aunt Angela! I read your article in the *Times* this morning. It's nice to have a distinguished relative." She indicated the tall, square-jawed young man with the steady gray eyes. "This is John Rattery. He and I—hope—to be married."

Angela Warren said: "Oh!—I didn't know . . ."

Meredith went to greet the next arrival.

"Well, Miss Williams, it's a good many years since we met."

Thin, frail and indomitable, the elderly governess advanced up the room. Her eyes rested thoughtfully on Poirot for a minute, then they went to the tall, square-shouldered figure in the well-cut tweeds.

Angela Warren came forward to meet her and said with a smile, "I feel like a schoolgirl again."

"I'm very proud of you, my dear," said Miss Williams. "You've done me credit. This is Carla, I suppose? She won't remember me. She was too young. . . ."

Philip Blake said fretfully, "What *is* all this? Nobody told me—"

Hercule Poirot said: "I call it—me—an excursion into the past. Shall we not all sit down? Then we shall be ready when the last guest arrives. And when she is here we can proceed to our business—to lay the ghosts."

Philip Blake exclaimed: "What tomfoolery is this? You're not going to hold a *séance,* are you?"

"No, no. We are only going to discuss some events that happened long ago—to discuss them and, perhaps, to see more clearly the course of them. As to the ghosts, they will not materialize, but who is to say they are not here, in this room, although we cannot see them. Who is to say that Amyas and Caroline Crale are not here—listening?"

Philip Blake said, "Absurd nonsense—" and broke off as the door opened again and the butler announced Lady Dittisham.

Chapter X

ELSA DITTISHAM CAME in with that faint, bored insolence that was a characteristic of hers. She gave Meredith a slight smile, stared coldly at Angela and Philip, and went over to a chair by the window a little apart from the others. She loosened the rich pale furs round her neck and let them fall back. She looked for a minute or two about the room, at Carla, and the girl stared back, thoughtfully appraising the woman who had wrought the havoc in her parents' lives. There was no animosity in her young, earnest face, only curiosity.

Elsa said, "I am sorry if I am late, M. Poirot."

"It was very good of you to come, madame."

Cecilia Williams snorted ever so slightly. Elsa met the animosity in her eyes with a complete lack of interest. She said: "I wouldn't have known *you*, Angela. How long is it? Sixteen years?"

Hercule Poirot seized his opportunity: "Yes, it is sixteen years since the events of which we are to speak, but let me first tell you why we are here." And in a few simple words he outlined Carla's appeal to him and his acceptance of the task.

He went on quickly, ignoring the gathering storm visible on Philip's face and the shocked distaste on Meredith's.

"I accepted that commission. I set to work to find out—the truth."

Carla Lemarchant, in the big grandfather chair, heard Poirot's words dimly, from a distance. With her hand shielding her eyes she studied five faces surreptitiously. Could she see any of these people committing murder?

Could she—if she tried hard—visualize one of them killing someone? Yes, perhaps; but it wouldn't be the right kind of murder. She could picture Philip Blake, in an outburst of fury, strangling some woman—yes, she *could* picture that. . . . And she could picture Meredith Blake threatening a burglar with a revolver—and letting it off by accident. . . . And she could picture Angela Warren, also firing a revolver, but not by accident. With no personal feeling in the matter—the safety of the expedition depended on it! And Elsa, in some fantastic castle, saying from her couch of Oriental silks, "Throw the wretch over the battlements!"

All wild fancies—and not even in the wildest flight of fancy could she imagine little Miss Williams killing anybody at all!

Hercule Poirot was talking:

"That was my task—to put myself in reverse gear, as it were, and go back through the years and discover what really happened."

Philip Blake said, "We all know what happened. To pretend anything else is a swindle—that's what it is, a barefaced swindle. You're getting money out of this girl on false pretenses."

Poirot did not allow himself to be angered. He said:

"You say, *we all know what happened.* You speak without reflection. The accepted version of certain facts is not necessarily the true one. On the face of it, for instance, you, Mr. Blake, disliked Caroline Crale. That is the accepted version of your attitude. But anyone with the least flair for psychology can perceive at once that the exact opposite was the truth. You were always violently attracted toward Caroline Crale. You resented the fact, and tried to conquer it by steadfastly telling yourself her defects and reiterating your dislike.

"In the same way, Mr. Meredith Blake had a tradition of devotion to Caroline Crale lasting over many years. In his story of the tragedy he represents himself as resenting Amyas Crale's conduct on *her* account, but you have only to read carefully between the lines and you will see that the devotion of a lifetime had worn itself thin and that it was the young, beautiful Elsa Greer that was occupying *his* mind and thoughts."

There was a splutter from Meredith, and Lady Dittisham smiled.

Poirot went on:

"I mention these matters only as illustrations, though they have their bearing on what happened. And I learned these facts:

"That at no time did Caroline Crale protest her innocence (except in that one letter written to her daughter).

"That Caroline Crale showed no fear in the dock; that she showed, in fact, hardly any interest; that she adopted throughout a thoroughly defeatist attitude. That in prison she was quiet and serene. That in a letter she wrote to her sister immediately after the verdict she expressed herself as acquiescent in the fate that had overtaken her. And in the opinion of everyone I talked to (with one notable exception) *Caroline Crale was guilty.*"

Philip Blake nodded his head. "Of course she was!"

Hercule Poirot said:

"But it was not my part to accept the verdict of *others.* I had to examine the evidence for *myself.* To examine the facts and to satisfy myself that the psychology of the case accorded itself with them. To do this I went over the police files carefully and I also succeeded in getting the five people who were on the spot to write me out their own accounts of the tragedy. These accounts were very valuable, for they contained certain matter which the police files could not give me—that is to say: A, certain conversations and incidents which, from the police point of view, were not relevant; B, the opinions of the people themselves as to what Caroline Crale was thinking and feeling (not admissible legally as evidence); C, certain facts which had been deliberately withheld from the police.

"I was in a position now to judge the case for *myself*. There seems no doubt whatever that Caroline Crale had ample motive for the crime. She loved her husband, he had publicly admitted that he was about to leave her for another woman, and by her own admission she was a jealous woman.

"To come from motives to means—an empty scent bottle that had contained coniine was found in her bureau drawer. There were no fingerprints upon it but hers. When asked about it by the police she admitted taking it from this room we are in now. The coniine bottle here also had her fingerprints upon it. I questioned Mr. Meredith Blake as to the order in which the people left this room on that day, for it seemed to me hardly conceivable that *anyone* should be able to help himself to the poison while five people were in the room.

"The people left the room in this order: Elsa Greer, Meredith Blake, Angela Warren and Philip Blake, Amyas Crale, and lastly Caroline Crale. Moreover, Mr. Meredith Blake had his back to the room while he was waiting for Mrs. Crale to come out, so that it was impossible for him to see what she was doing. She had, that is to say, the opportunity. I am therefore satisfied that she did take the coniine. There is indirect confirmation of it.

"Mr. Meredith Blake said to me the other day: 'I can remember standing here and smelling the jasmine through the open window.' But the month was September, and the jasmine creeper outside that window would have finished flowering. It is the ordinary jasmine which blooms in June and July. But the scent bottle found in her room and which contained the dregs of coniine had originally contained jasmine scent. I take it as certain, then, that Mrs. Crale decided to steal the coniine, and surreptitiously emptied out the scent from a bottle she had in her bag.

"I tested that a second time the other day when I asked Mr. Blake to shut his eyes and try and remember the order of leaving the room. A whiff of jasmine scent stimulated his memory immediately. We are all more influenced by smell than we know.

"So we come to the morning of the fatal day. So far the facts are not in dispute. Miss Greer's sudden revealing of the fact that she and Mr. Crale contemplate marriage, Amyas Crale's confirmation of that, and Caroline Crale's deep distress. None of these things depend on the evidence of one witness only.

"On the following morning there is a scene between husband and wife in the library. The first thing that is overheard is Caroline Crale saying, 'You and your women!' in a bitter voice and finally going on to say, 'Some day I'll kill you.' Philip Blake overheard this from the hall. And Miss Greer overheard it from the terrace outside.

"She then heard Mr. Crale ask his wife to be reasonable. And she heard Mrs. Crale say, 'Sooner than let you go to that girl—I'll kill you.' Soon after this, Amyas comes out and brusquely tells Elsa Greer to come down and pose for him. She gets a pull-over and accompanies him.

"There is nothing so far that seems psychologically incorrect. Everyone has behaved as he or she might be expected to behave. But we come now to something that *is* incongruous.

"Meredith Blake discovers his loss, telephones his brother. They meet down at the landing stage and they come up past the Battery Garden, where Caroline Crale is having a discussion with her husband on the subject of Angela's going to school. Now, that does strike me as very odd. Husband and wife have a terrific scene, ending in a distinct threat on Caroline's part, and yet, twenty minutes or so later, she goes down and starts a trivial domestic argument."

Poirot turned to Meredith Blake: "You speak in your narrative of certain words you overheard Crale say. These were: 'It's all settled—I'll see to her packing.' That is right?"

Meredith Blake said, "It was something like that—yes."

Poirot turned to Philip Blake. "Is your recollection the same?"

The latter frowned. "I didn't remember it till you say so, but I do remember now. Something *was* said about packing!"

"Said by Mr. Crale—not Mrs. Crale?"

"Amyas said it. All I heard Caroline say was something about its being very hard on the girl. Anyway, what does all this matter? We all know Angela was off to school in a day or two."

Poirot said: "You do not see the force of my objection. Why should *Amyas Crale* pack for the girl? It is absurd, that! There was Mrs. Crale, there was Miss Williams, there was a housemaid. It is a woman's job to pack—not a man's."

"What does it matter?" Philip Blake said impatiently. "It has nothing to do with the crime."

"You think not? For me, it was the first point that struck me as suggestive. And it is immediately followed by another. Mrs. Crale, a desperate woman, brokenhearted, who has threatened her husband a short while before and who is certainly contemplating either suicide or murder, now offers in the most amicable manner to bring her husband down some iced beer."

Meredith Blake said slowly: "That isn't odd if she was contemplating murder. Then, surely, it is just what she *would* do. Dissimulate!"

"You think so? She has decided to poison her husband; she has already got the poison. Her husband keeps a supply of beer down in the Battery Garden. Surely, if she has any intelligence at all she will put the poison in one of *those* bottles at a moment when there is no one about."

Meredith Blake objected: "She couldn't have done that. Somebody else might have drunk it."

"Yes, Elsa Greer. Do you tell me that having made up her mind to murder her husband, Caroline Crale would have scruples against killing the girl too?

"But let us not argue the point. Let us confine ourselves to facts. Caroline Crale says she will send her husband down some iced beer. She goes up to the house, fetches a bottle from the conservatory, where it was kept, and takes it down to him. She pours it out and gives it to him. Amyas Crale drinks it off and says, 'Everything tastes foul today.'

"Mrs. Crale goes up again to the house. She has lunch and appears much as usual. It has been said of her that she looks a little worried and preoccupied. That does not help us, for there is no criterion of behavior for a murderer. There are calm murderers and excited murderers.

"After lunch she goes down again to the Battery. She discovers her husband dead, and does, shall we say, the obviously expected things. She registers emotion and she sends the governess to telephone for a doctor. We now come to a fact which has previously not been known." He looked at Miss Williams. "You do not object?"

Miss Williams was rather pale. She said, "I did not pledge you to secrecy."

Quietly, but with telling effect, Poirot recounted what the governess had seen.

Elsa Dittisham moved her position. She stared at the drab little woman in the big chair. She said incredulously, "You actually saw her do *that?*"

Philip Blake sprang up. "But that settles it!" he shouted. "That settles it once and for all."

Hercule Poirot looked at him mildly. He said, "Not necessarily."

Angela Warren said sharply, "I don't believe it." There was a quick, hostile glint in the glance she shot at the little governess.

Meredith Blake was pulling at his mustache, his face dismayed. Alone, Miss Williams remained undisturbed. She sat very upright and there was a spot of color in each cheek.

She said, "That is what I saw."

Poirot said slowly, "There is, of course, only your word for it. . . ."

"There is only my word for it." The indomitable gray eyes met his. "I am not accustomed, M. Poirot, to having my word doubted."

Hercule Poirot bowed his head. He said: "I do not doubt your word, Miss Williams. What you saw took place exactly as you say it did, and because of what you saw I realized that Caroline Crale was not guilty— could not possibly be guilty."

For the first time, that tall, anxious-faced young man, John Rattery, spoke. He said, "I'd be interested to know *why* you say that, M. Poirot."

Poirot turned to him.

"Certainly. I will tell you. What did Miss Williams see? She saw Caroline Crale very carefully and anxiously wiping off fingerprints and subsequently imposing her dead husband's fingerprints on the beer bottle. On the beer *bottle*, mark. But the coniine was in the glass—not in the bottle. The police found no traces of coniine in the bottle. There had never been any coniine in the bottle. *And Caroline Crale didn't know that.*

"She, who is supposed to have poisoned her husband, didn't know *how* he had been poisoned. She thought the poison was in the bottle."

Meredith objected. "But why—"

Poirot interrupted him in a flash: "Yes—*why?* Why did Caroline Crale try so desperately to establish the theory of suicide. The answer is—must be—quite simple. Because she knew who *had* poisoned him and she was willing to do anything—endure anything—rather than let that person be suspected.

"There is not far to go now. Who could that person be? Would she have shielded Philip Blake? Or Meredith? Or Elsa Greer? Or Cecilia Williams? No, there is only one person whom she would be willing to protect at all costs."

He paused.

"Miss Warren, if you have brought your sister's last letter with you, I should like to read it aloud."

Angela Warren said, "No."

"But, Miss Warren—"

Angela got up. Her voice rang out, cold as steel: "I realize very well what you are suggesting. You are saying—are you not?—that I killed Amyas Crale and that my sister knew it. I deny that allegation utterly."

Poirot said, "The letter . . ."

"That letter was meant for my eyes alone."

Poirot looked to where the two youngest people in the room stood together.

Carla Lemarchant said, "Please, Aunt Angela, won't you do as M. Poirot asks?"

Angela Warren said bitterly: "Really, Carla! Have you no sense of decency? She was your mother—you—"

Carla's voice rang out clear and fierce: "Yes, she was my mother. That's why I've a right to ask you. I'm speaking for *her*. I *want* that letter read."

Slowly Angela Warren took out the letter from her bag and handed it to Poirot. She said bitterly, "I wish I had never shown it to you."

Turning away from them she stood looking out of the window.

As Hercule Poirot read aloud Caroline Crale's last letter, the shadows were deepening in the corners of the room. Carla had a sudden feeling of someone in the room, gathering shape, listening, breathing, waiting. She thought: *"She's* here—my mother's here. Caroline—Caroline Crale is *here* in this room!"

Hercule Poirot's voice ceased. He said:

"You will all agree, I think, that that is a very remarkable letter. A beautiful letter, too, but certainly remarkable. For there is one striking omission in it—it contains no protestation of innocence."

Angela Warren said without turning her head, "That was unnecessary."

"Yes, Miss Warren, it was unnecessary. Caroline Crale had no need to tell her sister that she was innocent, because she thought her sister knew that fact already—knew it for the best of all reasons. All Caroline Crale was concerned about was to comfort and reassure and to avert the possibility of a confession from Angela. She reiterates again and again—*'It's all right, darling; it's all, all right.'* "

Angela Warren said: "Can't you understand? She wanted me to be happy, that is all."

"Yes, she wanted you to be happy, that is abundantly clear. It is her one preoccupation. She has a child, but it is not that child of whom she is thinking—that is to come later. No, it is her sister who occupies her mind to the exclusion of everything else. Her sister must be reassured, must be encouraged to live her life, to be happy and successful. And so that the burden of acceptance may not be too great, Caroline includes that one very significant phrase: *'One must pay one's debts.'*

"That one phrase explains everything. It refers explicitly to the burden that Caroline has carried for so many years, ever since, in a fit of uncontrolled adolescent rage, she hurled a paperweight at her baby sister and injured that sister for life. Now, at last, she has the opportunity to pay the debt she owes. And if it is any consolation, I will say to you all that I earnestly believe that in the payment of that debt Caroline Crale did achieve a peace and serenity greater than any she had ever known. Because of her belief that she was paying that debt, the ordeal of trial and condemnation could not touch her. It is a strange thing to say of a condemned murderess—but she had everything to make her happy. Yes, more than you imagine, as I will show you presently.

"See how, by this explanation, everything falls into its place where Caroline's own reactions are concerned. Look at the series of events from her point of view. To begin with, on the preceding evening, an event occurs which reminds her forcibly of her own undisciplined girlhood. Angela throws a *paperweight* at Amyas Crale. That, remember, is what she herself did many years ago. Angela shouts out that she wishes Amyas was dead.

"Then, on the next morning, Caroline comes into the little conservatory and finds Angela tampering with the beer. Remember Miss Williams' words: 'Angela was there. She looked guilty. . . .' Guilty of playing truant was what Miss Williams meant; but to Caroline, Angela's guilty face, as she was caught unawares, would have a different meaning. Remember that on at least one occasion before Angela had put things in Amyas' drink. It was an idea which might readily occur to her.

"Caroline takes the bottle *that Angela gives her* and goes down with it to the Battery. And there she pours it out and gives it to Amyas, and he makes a face as he tosses it off and utters those significant words: 'Everything tastes foul today.'

"Caroline has no suspicions then, but after lunch she goes down to the Battery and finds her husband dead—and she has no doubts at all but that he has been poisoned. *She* has not done it. Who, then, has? And the whole thing comes over her with a rush: Angela's threats, Angela's face stooping over the beer and caught unawares—guilty—guilty—guilty. Why has the child done it? As a revenge on Amyas, perhaps not meaning to kill, just to make him ill or sick? Or has she done it for her, Caroline's sake? Has she realized and resented Amyas' desertion of her sister?

"Caroline remembers—oh, so well—her own undisciplined violent emotions at Angela's age. And only one thought springs to her mind: How can she protect Angela? Angela handled that bottle—Angela's fingerprints will be on it. She quickly wipes it and polishes it. If only everybody can be got to believe it is suicide. If Amyas' fingerprints are the only ones found. She tries to fit his dead fingers round the bottle—working desperately, listening for someone to come. . . .

"Once take that assumption as true and everything from then on fits in. Her anxiety about Angela all along, her insistence on getting her away, keeping her out of touch with what was going on. Her fear of Angela's being questioned unduly by the police. Finally her overwhelming anxiety to get Angela out of England before the trial comes on. Because she is always terrified that Angela might break down and confess."

Slowly, Angela Warren swung around. Her eyes, hard and contemptuous, ranged over the faces turned toward her.

She said: "You blind fools—all of you. Don't you know that if I had done it I *would* have confessed? I'd never have let Caroline suffer for what I'd done. Never!"

"But you did tamper with the beer," Poirot said.

"I? Tamper with the beer?"

Poirot turned to Meredith Blake. "Listen, monsieur. In your account here of what happened you describe having heard sounds in this room, which is below your bedroom, on the morning of the crime."

Blake nodded. "But it was only a cat."

"How do you know it was a cat?"

"I—I can't remember. But it was a cat. I am quite sure it was a cat. The window was open just wide enough for a cat to get through."

"But it was not fixed in that position. The sash moves freely. It could have been pushed up and a human being could have got in and out."

"Yes, but I know it was a cat."

"You did not *see* a cat?"

Blake said perplexedly and slowly, "No, I did not see it—" He paused, frowning, "And yet I know."

"I will tell you *why* you know presently. In the meantime I put this point to you: Someone could have come up to the house that morning, have got into your laboratory, taken something from the shelf and gone again without your seeing him or her. Now, if that someone had come over from Alderbury it could not have been Philip Blake, nor Elsa Greer, nor Amyas Crale, nor Caroline Crale. We know quite well what all those four were doing. That leaves Angela Warren and Miss Williams.

"Miss Williams was over here—you actually met her as you went out. She told you then that she was looking for Angela. Angela had gone bathing early, but Miss Williams did not see her in the water, nor anywhere on the rocks. She could swim across to this side easily—in fact, she did so later in the morning when she was bathing with Philip Blake. I suggest that she swam across here, came up to the house, got in through the window and took something from the shelf."

Angela Warren said, "I did nothing of the kind—not at least—"

"Ah!" Poirot gave a yelp of triumph, *"You have remembered.* You told me—did you not?—that to play a malicious joke on Amyas Crale you pinched some of what you called 'the cat stuff'—that is how you put it—"

Meredith Blake said sharply, "Valerian! Of course."

"Exactly. *That* is what made you sure in your mind that it was a cat who had been in the room. Your nose is very sensitive. You smelled the faint, unpleasant odor of valerian without knowing, perhaps, that you did so, but it suggested to your subconscious mind 'cat.' Cats love valerian and will go anywhere for it. Valerian is particularly nasty to taste, and it was your account of it the day before which made mischievous Miss Angela plan to put some in her brother-in-law's beer, which she knew he always tossed down his throat in a draught."

Angela Warren said wonderingly: "Was it really that day? I remember taking it perfectly—yes, and I remember putting it in the beer and Caroline coming in and nearly catching me! Of course I remember. . . . But I've never connected it with that particular day."

"Of course not, because there was no connection *in your mind.* The two events were entirely dissimilar to you. One was on a par with other mischievous pranks, the other was a bombshell of tragedy arriving without warning and succeeding in banishing all lesser incidents from your mind. But me, I noticed when you spoke of it that you said, 'I pinched, etc., etc., *to put* it in Amyas' drink.' You did not say you had actually *done* so."

"No, because I never did. Caroline came in just when I was unscrewing the bottle. Oh!" It was a cry. "And Caroline thought—she thought it was *me!*"

She stopped. She looked around. She said quietly in her usual cool tones, "I suppose you all think so too."

She paused and then said, *"I didn't kill Amyas.* Not as the result of a malicious joke nor in any other way. If I had I would never have kept silence."

Miss Williams said sharply, "Of course you wouldn't, my dear." She looked at Hercule Poirot. "Nobody but a *fool* would think so."

"I am not a fool," Poirot said mildly, "and I do not think so. *I know quite well who killed Amyas Crale.*"

He paused.

"There is always a danger of accepting facts as proved which are really nothing of the kind. Let us take the situation at Alderbury. A very old situation. Two women and one man. We have taken it for granted that Amyas Crale proposed to leave his wife for the other woman. But I suggest to you now *that he never intended to do anything of the kind.*

"He had had infatuations for women before. They obsessed him while they lasted, but they were soon over. The women he had fallen in love with were usually women of a certain experience—they did not expect too much of him. But this time the woman did. She was not, you see, a woman at all. She was a girl and, in Caroline Crale's words, she was terribly sincere. . . . She may have been hard-boiled and sophisticated in speech, but in love she was frighteningly single-minded. *Because* she herself had a deep and overmastering passion for Amyas Crale she assumed that he had the same for her. She assumed without any question that their passion was for life. She assumed without asking him that he was going to leave his wife.

"But why, you will say, did Amyas Crale not undeceive her? And my answer is—the picture. He wanted to finish his picture.

"To some people that sounds incredible, but not to anybody who knows about artists. And we have already accepted that explanation in principle. That conversation between Crale and Meredith Blake is more intelligible now. Crale is embarrassed—pats Blake on the back, assures him optimistically the whole thing is going to pan out all right. To Amyas Crale, you see, everything is simple. He is painting a picture, slightly encumbered by what he describes as a couple of jealous, neurotic women, but neither of them is going to be allowed to interfere with what to him is the most important thing in life.

"If he were to tell Elsa the truth it would be all up with the picture. Perhaps in the first flush of his feelings for her he did talk of leaving Caroline. Men do say these things when they are in love. Perhaps he merely let it be assumed, as he is letting it be assumed now. He doesn't care what Elsa assumes. Let her think what she likes. Anything to keep her quiet for another day or two.

"Then he will tell her the truth—that things between them are over. He has never been a man to be troubled with scruples.

"He did, I think, make an effort not to get embroiled with Elsa to begin with. He warned her what kind of man he was, but she would not take warning. She rushed on to her fate. And to a man like Crale, women were fair game. If you had asked him, he would have said easily that Elsa was young—she'd soon get over it. That was the way Amyas Crale's mind worked.

"His wife was actually the only person he cared about at all. He wasn't worrying much about her. She only had to put up with things for a few days longer. He was furious with Elsa for blurting out things to Caroline, but he still optimistically thought it would be 'all right.' Caroline would forgive him as she had done so often before, and Elsa—Elsa would just have to 'lump it.' So simple are the problems of life to a man like Amyas Crale.

"But I think that that last evening he became really worried. About Caroline, not about Elsa. Perhaps he went to her room and she refused to speak to him. At any rate, after a restless night he took her aside after breakfast and blurted out the truth. He had been infatuated with Elsa, but it was all over. Once he'd finished the picture he'd never see her again.

"And it was in answer to that that Caroline Crale cried out indignantly, 'You and your women!' That phrase, you see, put Elsa in a class with others—those others who had gone their way. And she added indignantly, 'Some day I'll kill you.'

"She was angry, revolted by his callousness and by his cruelty to the girl. When Philip Blake saw her in the hall and heard her murmur to herself, 'It's too cruel!' it was of Elsa she was thinking.

"As for Crale, he came out of the library, found Elsa with Philip Blake and brusquely ordered her down to go on with the sitting. What he did not know was that Elsa Greer had been sitting just outside the library window and had overheard everything. And the account she gave later of that conversation was not the true one. There is only her word for it, remember.

"Imagine the shock it must have been to her to hear the truth, brutally spoken!

"On the previous afternoon Meredith Blake has told us that while he was waiting for Caroline to leave this room he was standing in the doorway with his back to the room. He was talking to Elsa Greer. That means that she would have been *facing* him and that *she* could see exactly what Caroline was doing over his shoulder—and that she *was the only person who could do so.*

"She saw Caroline take that poison. She said nothing, but she remembered it as she sat outside the library window.

"When Amyas Crale came out she made the excuse of wanting a pullover and went up to Caroline Crale's room to look for that poison. Women know where other women are likely to hide things. She found it and, being careful not to obliterate any fingerprints or to leave her own, she drew off the fluid into a fountain-pen filler.

"Then she came down again and went off with Crale to the Battery Garden. And presently, no doubt, she poured him out some beer and he tossed it down in his usual way.

"Meanwhile, Caroline Crale was seriously disturbed. When she saw Elsa come up to the house (this time really to fetch a pull-over), Caroline slipped quickly down to the Battery Garden and tackled her husband. What he is doing is shameful! She won't stand for it! It's unbelievably cruel and hard on the girl! Amyas, irritable at being interrupted, says it's all settled—when the picture is done he'll send the girl packing! *'It's all settled —I'll send her packing, I tell you!'*

"And then they hear the footsteps of the two Blakes, and Caroline comes out and, slightly embarrassed, murmurs something about Angela and school and having a lot to do, and by a natural association of ideas the two men judge the conversation they have overheard refers to *Angela* and 'I'll send her packing' becomes 'I'll see to her packing.'

"And Elsa, pull-over in hand, comes down the path, cool and smiling, and takes up the pose once more.

"She has counted, no doubt, upon Caroline's being suspected and the coniine bottle being found in her room. But Caroline now plays into her hands completely. She brings down some iced beer and pours it out for her husband.

"Amyas tosses if off, makes a face and says, 'Everything tastes foul today.'

"Do you not see how significant that remark is? *Everything tastes* foul? Then there has been something else *before* that beer that has tasted unpleasant and the taste of which is *still in his mouth*. And one other point: Philip Blake speaks of Crale's staggering a little and wonders 'if he has been drinking.' But that slight stagger was the *first sign of the coniine working,* and that means *that it had already been administered to him some time before Caroline brought him the iced bottle of beer.*

"And so Elsa Greer sat on the gray wall and posed and, since she must keep him from suspecting until it was too late, she talked to Amyas Crale brightly and naturally. Presently she saw Meredith on the bench above and waved her hand to him and acted her part even more thoroughly for his behalf.

"And Amyas Crale, a man who detested illness and refused to give in to it, painted doggedly on till his limbs failed and his speech thickened, and he sprawled there on that bench, helpless, but with his mind still clear.

"The bell sounded from the house and Meredith left the bench to come down to the Battery. I think in that brief moment Elsa left her place and ran across to the table and dropped the last few drops of the poison into the beer glass that held that last innocent drink. (She got rid of the dropper on the path up to the house, crushing it to powder.) Then she met Meredith in the doorway.

"There is a glare there coming in out of the shadows. Meredith did not see very clearly—only his friend sprawled in a familiar position and saw his eyes turn from the picture in what he described as a malevolent glare.

"How much did Amyas know or guess? How much his conscious mind knew we cannot tell, but his hand and his eye were faithful."

Hercule Poirot gestured toward the picture on the wall.

"I should have known when I first saw that picture. For it is a very remarkable picture. It is the picture of a murderess painted by her victim —it is the picture of a girl watching her lover die. . . ."

In the silence that followed—a horrified, appalled silence—the sunset slowly flickered away, the last gleam left the window where it had rested on the dark head and pale furs of the woman sitting there.

Elsa Dittisham moved and spoke. She said: "Take them away, Meredith. Leave me with M. Poirot."

She sat there motionless until the door shut behind them. Then she said, "You are very clever, aren't you?"

Poirot did not answer.

She said, "What do you expect me to do? Confess?"

He shook his head.

"Because I shall do nothing of the kind!" Elsa said. "And I shall admit nothing. But what we say here, together, does not matter. Because it is only your word against mine."

"Exactly."

"I want to know what you are going to do."

Hercule Poirot said, "I shall do everything I can to induce the authorities to grant a posthumous free pardon to Caroline Crale."

Elsa laughed. "How absurd!" she said. "To be given a free pardon for something you didn't do." Then she said, "What about me?"

"I shall lay my conclusions before the necessary people. If they decide there is the possibility of making out a case against you, then they may act. I will tell you in my opinion there is not sufficient evidence—there are only inferences, not facts. Moreover, they will not be anxious to proceed against anyone in your position unless there is ample justification for such a course."

"I shouldn't care," Elsa said. "If I were standing in the dock, fighting for my life, there might be something in that—something alive—exciting. I might—enjoy it."

"Your husband would not."

"Do you think I care in the least what my husband would feel?"

"No, I do not. I do not think you have ever in your life cared about what any other person would feel. If you had, you might be happier."

She said sharply, "Why are you sorry for me?"

"Because, my child, you have so much to learn."

"What have I got to learn?"

"All the grown-up emotions—pity, sympathy, understanding. The only things you know—have ever known—are love and hate."

Elsa said:

"I saw Caroline take the coniine. I thought she meant to kill herself. That would have simplified things. And then, the next morning, I found out. He told her that he didn't care a button about me—he *had* cared, but it was all over. Once he'd finished the picture he'd send me packing. She'd nothing to worry about, he said.

"And she—was sorry for me. . . . Do you understand what that did to me? I found the stuff and I gave it to him and I sat there watching him die.

I've never felt so alive, so exultant, so full of power. I watched him die. . . ."

She flung out her hands.

"I didn't understand that I was killing *myself*—not him. Afterward I saw her caught in a trap—and that was no good either. I couldn't hurt her —she didn't care—she escaped from it all—half the time she wasn't there. She and Amyas both escaped—they went somewhere where I couldn't get at them. But they didn't die. *I* died."

Elsa Dittisham got up. She went across to the door. She said again, *"I died. . . ."*

In the hall she passed two young people whose life together was just beginning.

The chauffeur held open the door of the car. Lady Dittisham got in and the chauffeur wrapped the fur rug around her knees.

THIRTEEN AT DINNER

TO

DR. AND MRS. CAMPBELL THOMPSON

CONTENTS

Contents

Chapter I

A THEATRICAL PERFORMANCE

THE MEMORY OF the public is short. Already the intense interest and excitement aroused by the murder of George Alfred St. Vincent Marsh, fourth Baron Edgware, is a thing past and forgotten. Newer sensations have taken its place.

My friend, Hercule Poirot, was never openly mentioned in connection with the case. This, I may say, was entirely in accordance with his own wishes. He did not choose to appear in it. The credit went elsewhere—and that is how he wished it to be. Moreover, from Poirot's own peculiar private point of view, the case was one of his failures. He always swears that it was the chance remark of a stranger in the street that put him on the right track.

However that may be, it was his genius that discovered the truth of the affair. But for Hercule Poirot I doubt if the crime would have been brought home to its perpetrator.

I feel, therefore, that the time has come for me to set down all I know of the affair in black and white. I know the ins and outs of the case thoroughly, and I may also mention that I shall be fulfilling the wishes of a very fascinating lady in so doing.

I have often recalled that day in Poirot's prim, neat little sitting-room when, striding up and down a particular strip of carpet, my little friend gave us his masterly and astounding résumé of the case. I am going to begin my narrative where he did on that occasion—at a London theatre in June of last year.

Carlotta Adams was quite the rage in London at that moment. The year before she had given a couple of matinées which had been a wild success. This year she had had a three weeks season of which this was the last night but one.

Carlotta Adams was an American girl, with the most amazing talent for single-handed sketches, unhampered by make-up or scenery. She seemed to speak every language with ease. Her sketch of an evening in a foreign hotel was really wonderful. In turn, American tourists, German tourists, middle-class English families, questionable ladies, impoverished Russian aristocrats and weary, discreet waiters all flitted across the scene.

Her sketches went from grave to gay and back again. Her dying Czechoslovakian woman in hospital brought a lump to the throat. A minute later we were rocking with laughter as a dentist plied his trade and chatted amiably with his victims.

Her program closed with what she announced as "Some Imitations." Here again, she was amazingly clever. Without make-up of any kind, her features seemed to dissolve suddenly and re-form themselves into those of a famous politician, or a well-known actress, or a society beauty. In each character she gave a short, typical speech. These speeches, by the way, were remarkably clever. They seemed to hit off every weakness of the subject selected.

One of her last impersonations was Jane Wilkinson—a talented young American actress well known in London. It was really very clever. Inanities slipped off her tongue, charged with some powerful emotional appeal so that, in spite of yourself, you felt that each word was uttered with some potent and fundamental meaning. Her voice, exquisitely toned, with a deep, husky note in it, was intoxicating. The restrained gestures, each strangely significant, the slightly swaying body, the impression, even, of strong physical beauty—how she did it, I cannot think!

I had always been an admirer of the beautiful Jane Wilkinson. She had thrilled me in her emotional parts, and I had always maintained, in face of those who admitted her beauty but declared she was no actress, that she had considerable histrionic powers.

It was a little uncanny to hear that well-known, slightly husky voice, with the fatalistic drop in it that had stirred me so often, and to watch that seemingly poignant gesture of the slowly closing and unclosing hand and the sudden throw back of the head, with the hair shaken back from the face, that I realized she always gave at the close of a dramatic scene.

Jane Wilkinson was one of those actresses who had left the stage on her marriage, only to return to it a couple of years later. Three years ago she had married the wealthy but slightly eccentric Lord Edgware. Rumour went that she left him shortly afterward. At any rate, eighteen months after the marriage, she was acting for the films in America and had this season appeared in a successful play in London.

Watching Carlotta Adams' clever but perhaps slightly malicious imitation, it occurred to me to wonder how such imitations were regarded by the subjects selected. Were they pleased at the notoriety—at the advertisement it afforded? Or were they annoyed at what was, after all, a deliberate exposing of the tricks of their trade? Was not Carlotta Adams in the position of the rival conjuror who says: "Oh! this is an old trick! Very simple. I'll show you how this one's done!"

I decided that if *I* were the subject in question, I should be very much annoyed. I should, of course, conceal my vexation, but decidedly I should not like it. One would need great broad-mindedness and a distinct sense of humour to appreciate such a merciless exposé.

I had just arrived at these conclusions when the delightful husky laugh from the stage was echoed from behind me. I turned my head sharply. In the seat immediately behind mine, leaning forward with her lips slightly parted, was the subject of the present imitation—Lady Edgware, better known as Jane Wilkinson. I realized immediately that my deductions had been all wrong. She was leaning forward, her lips parted, with an expression of delight and excitement in her eyes.

As the "imitation" finished, she applauded loudly, laughing and turning to her companion, a tall, extremely good-looking man, of the Greek god type, whose face I recognized as one better known on the screen than on the stage. It was Bryan Martin, the hero of the screen most popular at the moment. He and Jane Wilkinson had been starred together in several screen productions.

"Marvellous, isn't she?" Lady Edgware was saying.

He laughed.

"Jane—you look all excited."

"Well, she really is too wonderful! Heaps better than I thought she'd be."

I did not catch Bryan Martin's amused rejoinder. Carlotta Adams had started on a fresh improvisation. What happened later is, I shall always think, a very curious coincidence.

After the theatre, Poirot and I went on to supper at the Savoy. At the very next table to ours were Lady Edgware, Bryan Martin, and two other people whom I did not know. I pointed them out to Poirot and, as I was doing so, another couple came and took their place at the table beyond that again. The woman's face was familiar; and yet, strangely enough, for the moment I could not place it. Then suddenly I realized that it was Carlotta Adams at whom I was staring! The man I did not know. He was well groomed, with a cheerful, somewhat vacuous face. Not a type that I admire.

Carlotta Adams was dressed very inconspicuously in black. Hers was not a face to command instant attention or recognition. It was one of those mobile, sensitive faces that pre-eminently lend themselves to the art of mimicry. It could take on an alien character easily, but it had no very recognizable character of its own.

I imparted these reflections of mine to Poirot. He listened attentively, his egg-shaped head cocked slightly to one side while he darted a sharp glance at the two tables in question.

"So that is Lady Edgware? Yes, I remember—I have seen her act. She is *belle femme.*"

"And a fine actress too."

"Possibly."

"You don't seem convinced."

"I think it would depend on the setting, my friend. If she is the centre of the play, if all revolves round her—yes, then she could play her part. I doubt if she could play a small part adequately, or even what is called a character part. The play must be written *about* her and *for* her. She appears to me of the type of women who are interested only in themselves." He paused and then added, rather unexpectedly, "Such people go through life in great danger."

"Danger?" I said, surprised.

"I have used a word that surprises you, I see, *mon ami.* Yes, danger. Because, you see, a woman like that sees only one thing—herself. Such women see nothing of the dangers and hazards that surround them—the million conflicting interests and relationships of life. No, they see only their own forward path. And so—sooner or later—disaster."

I was interested. I confessed to myself that such a point of view would not have struck me.

"And the other?" I asked.

"Miss Adams?"

His gaze swept to her table.

"Well?" he said, smiling. "What do you want me to say about her?"

"Only how she strikes you."

"*Moncher,* am I tonight the fortune teller who reads the palm and tells the character?"

"You could do it better than most," I rejoined.

"It is a very pretty faith that you have in me, Hastings. It touches me. Do you not know, my friend, that each one of us is a dark mystery, a maze of conflicting passions and desires and aptitudes? *Mais oui, c'est vrai.* One makes one's little judgments—but nine times out of ten, one is wrong."

"Not Hercule Poirot," I said, smiling.

"Even Hercule Poirot! Oh! I know very well that you have always a little idea that I am conceited, but indeed, I assure you, I am really a very humble person."

I laughed.

"You—humble!"

"It is so. Except—I confess it—that I am a little proud of my moustaches. Nowhere in London have I observed anything to compare with them."

"You're quite safe," I said dryly. "You won't. So you are not going to risk judgment on Carlotta Adams."

"Elle est artiste!" said Poirot simply. "That covers nearly all, does it not?"

"Anyway, you don't consider that she walks through life in peril?"

"We all do that, my friend," said Poirot gravely. "Misfortune may always be waiting to rush out upon us. But, as to your question—Miss Adams, I think, will succeed. She is shrewd and she is ambitious.

"These make for success. Though there is still one avenue of danger— since it is of danger we are talking."

"You mean?"

"Love of the money that comes with success. Love of money might lead such a one from the prudent and cautious path."

"It might do that to all of us," I said.

"That is true, but at any rate you or I would see the danger involved. We could weigh the pros and cons. If you care for money too much, it is only the money you see; everything else is in shadow."

I laughed at his serious manner.

"Esmeralda, the gipsy queen, is in good form," I remarked teasingly.

"The psychology of character is interesting," returned Poirot, unmoved. "One cannot be interested in crime without being interested in psychology. It is not the mere act of killing; it is what lies *behind* it that appeals to the expert. You follow me, Hastings?"

I said that I followed him perfectly.

"I have noticed that, when we work on a case together, you are always urging me on to physical action, Hastings. You wish me to measure footprints, to analyze cigarette ash, to prostrate myself on my stomach for the examination of detail. You never realize that by lying back in an armchair, with the eyes closed, one can come nearer to the solution of any problem. One sees then with the eyes of the mind."

"I don't," I said. "When I lie back in an armchair with my eyes closed one thing happens to me and one thing only!"

"I have noticed it!" said Poirot. "It is strange. At such moments the brain should be working feverishly, not sinking into sluggish repose. The mental activity—it is so interesting, so stimulating! The employment of the little grey cells is a mental pleasure. They and they only can be trusted to lead one through fog to the truth."

I am afraid that I have got into the habit of averting my attention whenever Poirot mentions his little grey cells. I have heard it all so often before. In this instance my attention wandered to the four people sitting at the next table. When Poirot's monologue drew to a close I remarked with a chuckle:

"You have made a hit, Poirot. The fair Lady Edgware can hardly take her eyes off you."

"Doubtless she has been informed of my identity," said Poirot, trying to look modest, and failing.

"I think it is the famous moustaches," I said. "She is carried away by their beauty."

Poirot caressed them surreptitiously.

"It is true that they are unique," he admitted. "Oh, my friend—the 'toothbrush' as you call it, that you wear—it is a horror—an atrocity—a wilful stunting of the bounties of nature. Abandon it, my friend, I pray of you."

"By Jove," I said, disregarding Poirot's appeal, "the lady's getting up. I believe she's coming to speak to us. Bryan Martin is protesting, but she won't listen to him."

Sure enough, Jane Wilkinson swept impetuously from her seat and came over to our table. Poirot rose to his feet, bowing, and I rose also.

"M. Hercule Poirot, isn't it?" said the soft, husky voice.

"At your service."

"M. Poirot, I want to talk to you. I must talk to you."

"But certainly, madame, will you not sit down?"

"No, no, not here. I want to talk to you privately. We'll go right up-stairs to my suite."

Bryan Martin had joined her. He spoke now with a deprecating laugh.

"You must wait a little, Jane. We're in the middle of supper. So is M. Poirot."

But Jane Wilkinson was not so easily turned from her purpose.

"Why, Bryan, what does that matter? We'll have supper sent up to the suite. Speak to them about it, will you? And, Bryan—"

She went after him as he was turning away and appeared to urge some course upon him. He stood out about it, I gathered, shaking his head and frowning. But she spoke even more emphatically, and finally, with a shrug of the shoulders, he gave way.

Once or twice during her speech to him she had glanced at the table where Carlotta Adams sat, and I wondered if what she was suggesting had anything to do with the American girl.

Her point gained, Jane came back, radiant.

"We'll go right up now," she said, and included me in a dazzling smile.

The question of our agreeing or not agreeing to her plan did not seem to occur to her mind. She swept us off without a shade of apology.

"It's the greatest luck just seeing you here this evening, M. Poirot," she said as she led the way to the lift. "It's wonderful how everything seems to turn out right for me. I'd just been thinking and wondering what on earth I was going to do, and I looked up and there you were at the next table, and I said to myself: 'M. Poirot will tell me what to do!' "

She broke off to say "Second floor" to the lift boy.

"If I can be of aid to you—" began Poirot.

"I'm sure you can. I've heard you're just the most marvellous man that ever existed. Somebody's got to get me out of the tangle I'm in, and I feel you're just the man to do it."

We got out at the second floor, and she led the way along the corridor, paused at a door and entered one of the most opulent of the Savoy suites.

Casting her white fur wrap on one chair, and her small jewelled bag on the table, the actress sank onto a chair and exclaimed:

"M. Poirot, somehow or other I've just *got* to get rid of my husband!"

Chapter II

AFTER A MOMENT'S astonishment Poirot recovered himself!

"But, madame," he said, his eyes twinkling. "Getting rid of husbands is not my speciality."

"Well, of course, I know that."

"It is a lawyer you require."

"That's just where you're wrong. I'm just about sick and tired of lawyers. I've had straight lawyers and crooked lawyers, and not one of them's done me any good. Lawyers just know the law; they don't seem to have any kind of natural sense."

"And you think I have?"

She laughed.

"I've heard that you're the cat's whiskers, M. Poirot."

"Comment? The cat's whiskers? I do not understand."

"Well—that you're *It.*"

"Madame, I may or may not have brains—as a matter of fact I have—why pretend? But your little affair, it is not my *genre.*"

"I don't see why not. It's a problem."

"Oh! a problem!"

"And it's difficult," went on Jane Wilkinson. "I should say you weren't the man to shy at difficulties."

"Let me compliment you on your insight, madame. But all the same, me, I do not make the investigations for divorce. It is not pretty—*ce métier là.*"

"My dear man, I'm not asking you to do spying work. It wouldn't be any good. But I've just got to get rid of the man, and I'm sure you could tell me how to do it."

Poirot paused awhile before replying. When he did, there was a new note in his voice.

"First tell me, madame, why you are so anxious to 'get rid' of Lord Edgware?"

There was no delay or hesitation about her answer. It came swift and pat.

"Why, of course. I want to get married again. What other reason could there be?"

Her great blue eyes opened ingenuously.

"But surely a divorce should be easy to obtain?"

"You don't know my husband, M. Poirot. He's—he's—" She shivered. "I don't know how to explain it. He's a queer man—he's not like other people." She paused and then went on: "He should never have married—anyone. I know what I'm talking about. I just can't describe him, but he's —queer. His first wife, you know, ran away from him—left a baby of three months behind. He never divorced her and she died miserably abroad somewhere. Then he married me. Well—I couldn't stick it. I was frightened. I left him and went to the States. I've no grounds for a divorce; and, if I've given him grounds for one, he won't take any notice of them. He's—he's a kind of fanatic."

"In certain American States you could obtain a divorce, madame."

"That's no good to me—not if I'm going to live in England."

"You want to live in England?"

"Yes."

"Who is the man you want to marry?"

"That's just it. The Duke of Merton."

I drew in my breath sharply. The Duke of Merton had so far been the despair of matchmaking mammas. A young man of monkish tendencies, a violent Anglo-Catholic, he was reported to be completely under the thumb of his mother, the redoubtable dowager duchess. His life was austere in the extreme. He collected Chinese porcelain and was reputed to be of aesthetic tastes. He was supposed to care nothing for women.

"I'm just crazy about him," said Jane sentimentally. "He's unlike anyone I ever met, and Merton Castle is too wonderful. The whole thing is the most romantic business that ever happened. He's so good-looking too—like a dreamy kind of monk."

She paused.

"I'm going to give up the stage when I marry. I just don't seem to care about it any more."

"In the meantime," said Poirot dryly, "Lord Edgware stands in the way of these romantic dreams."

"Yes, and it's driving me to distraction." She leaned back thoughtfully. "Of course if we were only in Chicago I could get him bumped off quite easily, but you don't seem to run to gunmen over here."

"Over here," said Poirot, smiling, "we consider that every human being has the right to live."

"Well, I don't know about that. I guess you'd be better off without some of your politicians; and knowing what I do of Edgware, I think he'd be no loss—rather the contrary."

There was a knock at the door and a waiter entered with supper dishes. Jane Wilkinson continued to discuss her problem, with no appreciation of his presence.

"But I don't want you to kill him for me, M. Poirot."

"*Merci,* madame."

"I thought perhaps you might argue with him in some clever way. Get him to give in to the idea of divorce. I'm sure you could."

"I think you overrate my persuasive powers, madame."

"Oh! but you can surely think of *something*, M. Poirot." She leaned forward. Her blue eyes opened wide again. "You'd like me to be happy, wouldn't you?"

Her voice was soft, low and deliciously seductive.

"I should like everybody to be happy," said Poirot cautiously.

"Yes, but I wasn't thinking of everybody. I was thinking of just me."

"I should say you always do that, madame." He smiled.

"You think I'm selfish?"

"Oh! I did not say so, madame."

"I dare say I am. But you see I do so hate being unhappy. It affects my acting, even. And I'm going to be ever so unhappy unless he agrees to a divorce—or dies."

"On the whole," she continued thoughtfully, "it would be much better if he died. I mean, I'd feel more finally quit of him."

She looked at Poirot for sympathy.

"You *will* help me, won't you, M. Poirot?" She rose, picking up the white wrap, and stood looking appealingly into his face. I heard the noise of voices outside in the corridor. The door was ajar. "If you don't—" she went on.

"If I don't, madame?"

She laughed.

"I'll have to call a taxi and go round and bump him off myself."

Laughing, she disappeared through a door to an adjoining room just as Bryan Martin came in with the American girl, Carlotta Adams and her escort, and the two people who had been supping with him and Jane Wilkinson. They were introduced to me as Mr. and Mrs. Widburn.

"Hello!" said Bryan. "Where's Jane? I want to tell her I've succeeded in the commission she gave me."

Jane appeared in the doorway of the bedroom. She held a lipstick in one hand.

"Have you got her? How marvellous! Miss Adams, I do admire your performance so. I felt I just had to know you. Come in here and talk to me while I fix my face. It's looking too perfectly frightful."

Carlotta Adams accepted the invitation. Bryan Martin flung himself down in a chair.

"Well, M. Poirot," he said, "you were duly captured. Has our Jane persuaded you to fight her battles? You might as well give in sooner as later. She doesn't understand the word 'No.'"

"She has not come across it, perhaps."

"A very interesting character, Jane," said Bryan Martin. He lay back in his chair and puffed cigarette smoke idly towards the ceiling. "Taboos have no meaning for her. No morals whatever. I don't mean she's exactly immoral—she isn't. Amoral is the word, I believe. Just sees one thing only in life—what Jane wants."

He laughed.

"I believe she'd kill somebody quite cheerfully—and feel injured if they caught her and wanted to hang her for it. The trouble is that she *would* be caught. She hasn't any brains. Her idea of a murder would be to drive up in a taxi, sail in under her own name and shoot."

"Now I wonder what makes you say that?" murmured Poirot.

"Eh?"

"You know her well, monsieur?"

"I should say I did."

He laughed again, and it struck me that his laugh was unusually bitter.

"You agree, don't you?" he flung out to the others.

"Oh! Jane's an egoist," agreed Mrs. Widburn. "An actress has got to be, though. That is, if she wants to express her personality."

Poirot did not speak. His eyes were resting on Bryan Martin's face, dwelling there with a curious speculative expression that I could not quite understand.

At that moment Jane sailed in from the next room, Carlotta Adams behind her. I presume that Jane had now "fixed her face," whatever that term denoted, to her own satisfaction. It looked to me exactly the same as before and quite incapable of improvement.

The supper party that followed was quite a merry one, yet I sometimes had the feeling that there were undercurrents which I was incapable of appreciating.

Jane Wilkinson I acquitted of any subtleties. She was obviously a young woman who saw only one thing at a time. She had desired an interview with Poirot, and had carried her point and obtained her desire without delay. Now she was obviously in high good humour. Her desire to include Carlotta Adams in the party had been, I decided, a mere whim. She had been highly amused, as a child might be amused, by the clever counterfeit of herself.

No, the undercurrents that I sensed were nothing to do with Jane Wilkinson. In what direction did they lie? I studied the guests in turn. Bryan Martin? He was certainly not behaving quite naturally. But that, I told myself, might be merely characteristic of a film star, the exaggerated self-consciousness of a vain man, too accustomed to playing a part to lay it aside easily.

Carlotta Adams, at any rate, was behaving naturally enough. She was a quiet girl, with a pleasant low voice. It studied her with some attention, now that I had the chance to do so at close quarters. She had, I thought, distinct charm, but charm of a somewhat negative order. I consisted in an absence of any jarring or strident note. She was a kind of personified soft agreement. Her very appearance was negative. Soft, dark hair, eyes a rather colourless pale blue, pale face, and a mobile, sensitive mouth. A face that you liked but that you would find it hard to know again, if you were to meet her, say, in different clothes.

She seemed pleased at Jane's graciousness and complimentary sayings. Any girl would be, I thought—and then, just at that moment, something occurred that caused me to revise that rather too hasty opinion.

Carlotta Adams looked across the table at her hostess, who was at that moment turning her head to talk to Poirot. There was a curious scrutinizing quality in the girl's gaze—it seemed a deliberate summing up, and at the same time it struck me that there was a very definite hostility in those pale blue eyes.

Fancy, perhaps. Or possibly professional jealousy. Jane was a successful actress who had definitely arrived. Carlotta was merely climbing the ladder.

I looked at the three other members of the party. Mr. and Mrs. Widburn, what about them? He was a tall, cadaverous man; she, a plump, fair, gushing soul. They appeared to be wealthy people with a passion for everything connected with the stage. They were, in fact, unwilling to talk on any other subject. Owing to my recent absence from England they found me sadly ill-informed, and finally Mrs. Widburn turned a plump shoulder on me and remembered my existence no more.

The last member of the party was the dark young man with the round, cheerful face, who was Carlotta Adams' escort. I had had my suspicions from the first that the young man was not quite so sober as he might have been. As he drank more champagne, this became even more clearly apparent.

He appeared to be suffering from a profound sense of injury. For the first half of the meal he sat in gloomy silence. Towards the latter half he unbosomed himself to me, apparently under the impression that I was one of his oldest friends.

"What I mean to say," he said. "It isn't. No, dear old chap, it isn't—"

I omit the slight slurring together of the words.

"I mean to say," he went on, "I ask you? I mean, if you take a girl— well, I mean—butting in. Going round upsetting things. Not as though I'd ever said a word to her I shouldn't have done. She's not the sort. You know—Puritan Fathers—the *Mayflower*—all that. Dash it—the girl's straight. What I mean is—what was I saying?"

"That it was hard lines," I said soothingly.

"Well, dash it all, it is. Dash it, I had to borrow the money for this beano from my tailor. Very obliging chap, my tailor. I've owed him money for years. Makes a sort of bond between us. Nothing like a bond, is there, dear old fellow. You and I. You and I. Who the devil are you, by the way?"

"My name is Hastings."

"You don't say so. Now I could have sworn you were a chap called Spencer Jones. Dear old Spencer Jones. Met him at the Eton and Harrow and borrowed a fiver from him. What I say is one face is very like another face—that's what I say. If we were a lot of Chinks we wouldn't know each other apart."

He shook his head sadly, then cheered up suddenly and drank off some more champagne.

"Anyway," he said, "I'm not a damned foreigner."

This reflection seemed to cause him such elation that he presently made several remarks of a hopeful character.

"Look on the bright side, my boy," he adjured me. "What I say is, look on the bright side. One of these days—when I'm seventy-five or so—I'm going to be a rich man. When my uncle dies. Then I can pay my tailor."

He sat smiling happily at the thought. There was something strangely likable about the young man. He had a round face and an absurdly small black moustache that gave one the impression of being marooned in the middle of a dent.

Carlotta Adams, I noticed, had an eye on him, and it was after a glance in his direction that she rose and broke up the party.

"It was just sweet of you to come up here," said Jane. "I do so love doing things on the spur of the moment, don't you?"

"No," said Miss Adams. "I'm afraid I always plan a thing out very carefully before I do it. It saves—worry."

There was something faintly disagreeable in her manner.

"Well, at any rate the results justify you," laughed Jane. "I don't know when I enjoyed anything so much as I did your show tonight."

The American girl's face relaxed.

"Well, that's very sweet of you," she said warmly, "and I appreciate your telling me so. I need encouragement. We all do."

"Carlotta," said the young man with the black moustache, "shake hands and say thank you for the party to Aunt Jane and come along."

The way he walked straight through the door was a miracle of concentration. Carlotta followed him quickly.

"Well," said Jane, "what was that that blew in and called me Aunt Jane? I hadn't noticed him before."

"My dear," said Mrs. Widburn, "you mustn't take any notice of him. Most brilliant as a boy in the O.U.D.S. You'd hardly think so now, would you? I hate to see early promise come to nothing. But Charles and I positively must toddle."

The Widburns duly toddled, and Bryan Martin went with them.

"Well, M. Poirot?"

He smiled at her.

"*Eh bien*, Lady Edgware?"

"For goodness sake, don't call me that. Let me forget it! If you aren't the hardest-hearted little man in Europe!"

"But no, but no, I am not hard-hearted."

Poirot, I thought, had had quite enough champagne—possibly a glass too much.

"Then you'll go and see my husband? And make him do what I want?"

"I will go and see him," Poirot promised cautiously.

"And if he turns you down—as he will—you'll think of a clever plan. They say you're the cleverest man in England, M. Poirot."

"Madame, when I am hard-hearted, it is Europe you mention. But for cleverness you say only England."

"If you put this through I'll say the Universe."

Poirot raised a deprecating hand.

"Madame, I promise nothing. In the interests of the psychology I will endeavour to arrange a meeting with your husband."

"Psychoanalyze him as much as you like. Maybe it would do him good. But you've got to pull it off—for my sake. I've got to have my romance, M. Poirot."

She added dreamily: "Just think of the sensation it will make."

Chapter III

THE MAN WITH THE GOLD TOOTH

IT WAS A few days later, when we were sitting at breakfast, that Poirot flung across to me a letter that he had just opened.

"Well, *mon ami,*" he said. "What do you think of that?"

The note was from Lord Edgware, and in stiff, formal language it made an appointment for the following day at eleven.

I must say that I was very much surprised. I had taken Poirot's words as uttered lightly in a convivial moment, and I had had no idea that he had actually taken steps to carry out his promise.

Poirot, who was very quick-witted, read my mind, and his eyes twinkled a little.

"But yes, *mon ami,* it was not solely the champagne."

"I didn't mean that."

"But yes—but yes—you thought to yourself: 'The poor old one, he has the spirit of the party, he promises things that he will not perform—that he has no intention of performing.' But, my friend, the promises of Hercule Poirot are sacred."

He drew himself up in a stately manner as he said the last words.

"Of course. Of course. I know that," I said hastily. "But I thought that perhaps your judgment was slightly—what shall I say?—influenced."

"I am not in the habit of letting my judgment be 'influenced' as you call it, Hastings. The best and driest of champagne, the most golden-haired and seductive of women—nothing influences the judgment of Hercule Poirot. No, *mon ami,* I am interested—that is all."

"In Jane Wilkinson's love affair?"

"Not exactly that. Her love affair, as you call it, is a very commonplace business. It is a step in the successful career of a very beautiful woman. If the Duke of Merton had neither a title nor wealth, his romantic likeness to a dreamy monk would no longer interest the lady. No, Hastings, what intrigues me is the psychology of the matter, the interplay of character. I welcome the chance of studying Lord Edgware at close quarters."

"You do not expect to be successful in your mission?"

"*Pourquoi pas?* Every man has his weak spot. Do not imagine, Hastings, that, because I am studying the case from a psychological standpoint, I shall not try my best to succeed in the commission entrusted to me. I always enjoy exercising my ingenuity."

I had feared an allusion to the little grey cells and was thankful to be spared it.

"So we go to Regent Gate at eleven tomorrow," I said.

"We?" Poirot raised his eyebrows quizzically.

"Poirot!" I cried. "You are not going to leave me behind. I always go with you."

"If it were a crime, a mysterious poisoning case, an assassination—ah! those are the things your soul delights in. But a mere matter of social adjustment?"

"Not another word," I said determinedly. "I'm coming."

Poirot laughed gently, and at that moment we were told that a gentleman had called. To our great surprise our visitor proved to be Bryan Martin.

The actor looked older by daylight. He was still handsome but it was a kind of ravaged handsomeness. It flashed across my mind that he might conceivably take drugs. There was a kind of nervous tension about him that suggested the possibility.

"Good morning, M. Poirot," he said in a cheerful manner. "You and Captain Hastings breakfast at a reasonable hour, I am glad to see. By the way, I suppose you are very busy just now?"

Poirot smiled at him amiably.

"No," he said. "At the moment I have practically no business of importance on hand."

"Come now," laughed Bryan. "Not called in by Scotland Yard? No delicate matters to investigate for Royalty? I can hardly believe it."

"You confound fiction with reality, my friend," said Poirot, smiling. "I am, I assure you, at the moment completely out of work, though not yet on the dole. *Dieu merci.*"

"Well, that's luck for me," said Bryan with another laugh. "Perhaps you'll take on something for me."

Poirot considered the young man thoughtfully.

"You have a problem for me—yes?" he said in a minute or two.

"Well—it's like this. I have and I haven't."

This time his laugh was rather nervous. Still considering him thoughtfully, Poirot indicated a chair. The young man took it. He sat facing us, for I had taken a seat by Poirot's side.

"And now," said Poirot, "let us hear all about it."

Bryan Martin still seemed to have a little difficulty in getting under way.

"The trouble is that I can't tell you quite as much as I'd like to." He hesitated. "It's difficult. You see the whole business started in America."

"In America? Yes?"

"A mere incident first drew my attention to it. As a matter of fact I was travelling by train and I noticed a certain fellow—ugly little chap, clean-shaven, glasses, and a gold tooth."

"Ah! a gold tooth."

"Exactly. That's really the crux of the matter."

Poirot nodded his head several times.

"I begin to comprehend. Go on."

"Well, as I say, I just noticed the fellow. I was travelling, by the way, to New York. Six months later, I was in Los Angeles, and I noticed the fellow again. Don't know why I should have—but I did. Still, nothing in that."

"Continue."

"A month afterward, I had occasion to go to Seattle; and shortly after I got there, whom should I see but my friend again, *only this time he wore a beard.*"

"Distinctly curious."

"Wasn't it? Of course I didn't fancy it had anything to do with me at that time, but when I saw the man again in Los Angeles, beardless, in Chicago with a moustache and different eyebrows, and in a mountain village disguised as a hobo—well, I began to wonder."

"Naturally."

"And at last—well, it seemed odd, but not a doubt about it. I was being what you call shadowed."

"Most remarkable."

"Wasn't it? After that I made sure of it. Wherever I was, there, some-where near at hand, was my shadow, made up in different disguises. Fortu-nately, owing to the gold tooth, I could always spot him."

"Ah! that gold tooth; it was a very fortunate occurrence."

"It was."

"Pardon me, M. Martin, but did you never speak to the man? Question him as to the reason of his persistent shadowing?"

"No, I didn't." The actor hesitated. "I thought of doing so once or twice, but I always decided against it. It seemed to me that I should merely put the fellow on his guard and learn nothing. Possibly, once they had discovered that I had spotted him, they would have put someone else on my track—someone whom I might not recognize."

"*En effet*—someone without that useful gold tooth."

"Exactly. I may have been wrong, but that's how I figured it out."

"Now, M. Martin, you referred to 'they' just now. Whom did you mean by 'they'?"

"It was a mere figure of speech, used for convenience. I assumed—I don't know why—a nebulous 'they' in the background."

"Have you any reason for that belief?"

"None."

"You mean you have no conception of who could want you shadowed or for what purpose?"

"Not the slightest. At least—"

"Continuez," said Poirot encouragingly.

"I *have* an idea," said Bryan Martin slowly. "It's a mere guess on my part, mind."

"A guess may be very successful sometimes, Monsieur."

"It concerns a certain incident that took place in London about two years ago. It was a slight incident, but an inexplicable and an unforgettable one. I've often wondered and puzzled over it. Just because I could find no explanation of it at the time. I am inclined to wonder if this shadowing business might not be connected in some way with it—but for the life of me I can't see why or how."

"Perhaps I can."

"Yes, but you see—" Bryan Martin's embarrassment returned. "The awkward thing is that I can't tell you about it—not now, that is. In a day or so I might be able to."

Stung into further speech by Poirot's inquiring glance he continued desperately:

"You see—a girl was concerned in it."

"Ah! parfaitement! An English girl?"

"Yes. At least— Why?"

"Very simple. You cannot tell me now, but you hope to do so in a day or two. That means that you want to obtain the consent of the young lady. Therefore, she is in England. Also she must have been in England during the time you were shadowed, for if she had been in America you would have sought her out then and there. Therefore since she has been in England for the last eighteen months, she is probably, though not certainly, English. It is good reasoning that, eh?"

"Rather. Now tell me, M. Poirot; if I get her permission, will you look into the matter for me?"

There was a pause. Poirot seemed to be debating the matter in his mind. Finally he said:

"Why have you come to me before going to her?"

"Well, I thought—" He hesitated. "I wanted to persuade her to—to clear things up—I mean to let things be cleared up by you. What I mean is, if *you* investigate the affair, nothing need be made public, need it?"

"That depends," said Poirot calmly.

"What do you mean?"

"If there is any question of crime—"

"Oh! there's no crime concerned."

"You do not know. There may be."

"But you would do your best for her—for us?"

"That, naturally."

He was silent for a moment and then said:

"Tell me, this follower of yours—this shadow—of what age was he?"

"Oh! quite youngish. About thirty."

"Ah!" said Poirot. "That is indeed remarkable. Yes, that makes the whole thing very much more interesting."

I stared at him. So did Bryan Martin. This remark of his was, I am sure, equally inexplicable to us both. Bryan questioned me with a lift of his eyebrows. I shook my head.

"Yes," murmured Poirot. "It makes the whole story very interesting."

"He *may* have been older," said Bryan doubtfully, "but I don't think so."

"No, no, I am sure your observation is quite accurate, M. Martin. Very interesting—extraordinary interesting."

Rather taken aback by Poirot's enigmatical words, Bryan Martin seemed at a loss what to say or do next. He started making desultory conversation.

"An amusing party the other night," he said. "Jane Wilkinson is the most high-handed woman that ever existed."

"She has the single vision," said Poirot, smiling. "One thing at a time."

"She gets away with it too," said Martin. "How people stand it, I don't know!"

"One will stand a good deal from a beautiful woman, my friend," said Poirot with a twinkle. "If she had the pug dog nose, the sallow skin, the greasy hair, then—ah! then she would not 'get away with it' as you put it."

"I suppose not," conceded Bryan. "But it makes me mad sometimes. All the same, I'm devoted to Jane, though in some ways, mind you, I don't think she's quite all there."

"On the contrary, I should say she was very much on the spot."

"I don't mean that, exactly. She can look after her interests all right. She's got plenty of business shrewdness. No, I meant morally."

"Ah! morally."

"She's what they call amoral. Right and wrong don't exist for her."

"Ah! I remember you said something of the kind the other evening."

"We were talking of crime just now—"

"Yes, my friend?"

"Well, it would never surprise me if Jane committed a crime."

"And you should know her well," murmured Poirot thoughtfully. "You have acted much with her, have you not?"

"Yes. I suppose I know her through and through, and up and down. I can see her killing anybody quite easily."

"Ah! she has the hot temper, yes?"

"No, no, not at all. Cool as a cucumber. I mean if anyone were in her way she'd just remove them—without a thought. And one couldn't really blame her—morally, I mean. She'd just think that anyone who interfered with Jane Wilkinson had got to go."

There was a bitterness in his last words that had been lacking heretofore. I wondered what memory he was recalling.

"You think she would do—murder?"

Poirot watched him intently. Bryan drew a deep breath.

"Upon my soul, I do. Perhaps, one of these days, you'll remember my words. I *know* her, you see. She'd kill as easily as she'd drink her morning tea. *I mean it, M. Poirot.*"

He had risen to his feet.

"Yes," said Poirot quietly. "I can see you mean it."

"I know her," said Bryan Martin again, "through and through."

He stood frowning for a minute, then with a change of tone, he said:

"As to this business we've been talking about—I'll let you know, M. Poirot, in a few days. You will undertake it, won't you?"

Poirot looked at him for a moment or two without replying.

"Yes," he said at last. "I will undertake it. I find it—interesting." There was something queer in the way he said the last word.

I went downstairs with Bryan Martin. At the door he said to me:

"Did you get the hang of what he meant about that fellow's age? I mean why was it interesting that he should be about thirty? I didn't get the hang of that at all."

"No more did I," I admitted.

"It doesn't seem to make sense. Perhaps he was just having a game with me."

"No," I said. "Poirot is not like that. Depend upon it, the point has significance, since he says so."

"Well, blessed if I can see it. Glad you can't either. I'd hate to feel I was a complete mutt."

He strode away. I rejoined my friend.

"Poirot," I said. "What was the point about the age of the shadower?"

"You do not see? My poor Hastings!" He smiled and shook his head. Then he asked: "What did you think of our interview on the whole?"

"There's so little to go upon. It seems difficult to say. If we knew more—"

"Even without knowing more, do not certain ideas suggest themselves to you, *mon ami?*"

The telephone ringing at that moment saved me from the ignominy of admitting that no ideas whatever suggested themselves to me. I took up the receiver.

A woman's voice spoke, a crisp, clear, efficient voice.

"This is Lord Edgware's secretary speaking. Lord Edgware regrets that he must cancel the appointment with M. Poirot for tomorrow morning. He has to go over to Paris tomorrow, unexpectedly. He could see M. Poirot for a few minutes at a quarter past twelve this morning, if that would be convenient."

I consulted Poirot.

"Certainly, my friend, we will go there this morning."

I repeated this into the mouthpiece.

"Very good," said the crisp businesslike voice. "A quarter past twelve this morning."

She rang off.

Chapter IV

AN INTERVIEW

I ARRIVED WITH Poirot at Lord Edgware's house in Regent Gate in a very pleasant state of anticipation. Though I had not Poirot's devotion to "the psychology," yet the few words in which Lady Edgware had referred to her husband had aroused my curiosity. I was anxious to see what my own judgment would be.

The house was an imposing one—well built, handsome and slightly gloomy. There were no window boxes or such frivolities.

The door was opened to us promptly, and by no aged, white-haired butler, such as would have been in keeping with the exterior of the house. On the contrary, it was opened by one of the handsomest young men I have ever seen. Tall, fair, he might have posed to a sculptor for Hermes or Apollo. Despite his good looks, there was something vaguely effeminate that I disliked about the softness of his voice. Also, in a curious way, he reminded me of someone—someone, too, whom I had met quite lately; but who it was I could not for the life of me remember.

We asked for Lord Edgware.

"This way, sir."

He led us along the hall, past the staircase, to a door at the rear of the hall. Opening it, he announced us in that same soft voice which I instinctively distrusted.

The room into which we were shown was a kind of library. The walls were lined with books; the furnishings were dark and sombre but handsome; the chairs were formal and not too comfortable.

Lord Edgware, who rose to receive us, was a tall man of about fifty. He had dark hair streaked with grey, a thin face and a sneering mouth. He looked bad-tempered and bitter. His eyes had a queer, secretive look about them. There was something, I thought, distinctly odd about those eyes. His manner was stiff and formal.

"M. Hercule Poirot? Captain Hastings? Please be seated."

We sat down. The room felt chilly. There was little light coming in from the one window, and the dimness contributed to the cold atmosphere.

Lord Edgware had taken up a letter which I saw to be in my friend's handwriting.

"I am familiar, of course, with your name, M. Poirot. Who is not?" Poirot bowed at the compliment. "But I cannot quite understand your position in this matter. You say that you wish to see me on behalf of—" he paused—"my wife."

He said the last two words in a peculiar way—as though it were an effort to get them out.

"That is so," said my friend.

"I understood that you were an investigator of—crime, M. Poirot?"

"Of problems, Lord Edgware. There are problems of crime, certainly. There are other problems."

"Indeed. And what may this one be?"

The sneer in his words was palpable by now. Poirot took no notice of it.

"I have the honour to approach you on behalf of Lady Edgware," he said. "Lady Edgware, as you may know, desires—a divorce."

"I am quite aware of that," said Lord Edgware coldly.

"Her suggestion was that you and I should discuss the matter."

"There is nothing to discuss."

"You refuse, then?"

"Refuse? Certainly not."

Whatever else Poirot had expected, he had not expected this. It is seldom that I have seen my friend utterly taken aback, but I did on this occasion. His appearance was ludicrous. His mouth fell open, his hands flew out, his eyebrows rose. He looked like a cartoon in a comic paper.

"Comment?" he cried. "What is this? You do not refuse?"

"I am at a loss to understand your astonishment, M. Poirot."

"Ecoutez. You are willing to divorce your wife?"

"Certainly I am willing. She knows that perfectly well. I wrote and told her so."

"You wrote and told her so?"

"Yes. Six months ago."

"But I do not understand. I do not understand at all."

Lord Edgware said nothing.

"I understood that you were opposed to the principle of divorce."

"I do not see that my principles are your business, M. Poirot. It is true that I did not divorce my first wife. My conscience would not allow me to do so. My second marriage, I will admit frankly, was a mistake. When my wife suggested a divorce, I refused point-blank. Six months ago she wrote to me again, urging the point. I have an idea she wanted to marry again—

some film actor or fellow of that kind. My views had, by this time, undergone modification. I wrote to her at Hollywood telling her so. Why she has sent you to me I cannot imagine. I suppose it is a question of money."

His lips sneered again as he said the last words.

"Extremely curious," murmured Poirot. "Extremely curious. There is something here I do not understand at all."

"As regards money," went on Lord Edgware. "I have no intention of making any financial arrangement. My wife deserted me of her own accord. If she wishes to marry another man, I can set her free to do so, but there is no reason why she should receive a penny from me, and she will not do so."

"There is no question of any financial arrangement."

Lord Edgware raised his eyebrows.

"Jane must be marrying a rich man," he murmured cynically.

"There is something here that I do not understand," said Poirot. His face was perplexed and wrinkled with the effort of thought. "I understood from Lady Edgware that she had approached you repeatedly through lawyers?"

"She did," replied Lord Edgware dryly. "English lawyers, American lawyers, every kind of lawyer, down to the lowest kind of scallywag. Finally, as I say, she wrote to me herself."

"You having previously refused?"

"That is so."

"But, on receiving her letter, you changed your mind. Why did you change your mind, Lord Edgware?"

"Not on account of anything in that letter," he said sharply. "My views happened to have changed, that is all."

"The change was somewhat sudden."

Lord Edgware did not reply.

"What special circumstance brought about your change of mind, Lord Edgware?"

"That, really, is my own business, M. Poirot. I cannot enter into that subject. Shall we say that gradually I had perceived the advantages of severing what—you will forgive my plain speaking—I considered a degrading association. My second marriage was a mistake."

"Your wife says the same," said Poirot softly.

"Does she?"

There was a queer flicker for a moment in his eyes, but it was gone almost at once. He rose with an air of finality and, as we said good-bye, his manner became more unbending.

"You must forgive my altering the appointment. I have to go over to Paris tomorrow."

"Perfectly—perfectly."

"A sale of works of art as a matter of fact. I have my eye on a little statuette—a perfect thing in its way—a *macabre* way, perhaps. But I enjoy the *macabre*. I always have. My taste is peculiar."

Again that queer smile. I had been looking at the books in the shelves near. There were the Memoirs of Casanova, also a volume on the Comte de Sade, another on mediaeval tortures.

I remembered Jane Wilkinson's little shudder as she spoke of her husband. That had not been acting. That had been real enough. I wondered exactly what kind of a man George Alfred St. Vincent Marsh, fourth Baron Edgware, was.

Very suavely he bade us farewell, touching the bell as he did so. We went out of the door. The Greek god of a butler was waiting in the hall. As I closed the library door behind me, I glanced back into the room. I almost uttered an exclamation as I did so.

That suave, smiling face was transformed. The lips were drawn back from the teeth in a snarl, the eyes were alive with fury and an almost insane rage.

I wondered no longer that two wives had left Lord Edgware. What I did marvel at was the iron self-control of the man. To have gone through that interview with such frozen self-control, such aloof politeness!

Just as we reached the front door, a door on the right opened. A girl stood at the doorway of the room, shrinking back a little as she saw us. She was a tall, slender girl, with dark hair and a white face. Her eyes, dark and startled, looked for a moment into mine. Then, like a shadow, she shrank back into the room again, closing the door.

A moment later, we were out in the street. Poirot hailed a taxi. We got in and he told the man to drive to the Savoy.

"Well, Hastings," he said with a twinkle. "That interview did not go at all as I figured to myself it would."

"No, indeed. What an extraordinary man Lord Edgware is."

I related to him how I had looked back before closing the door of the study and what I had seen. He nodded his head slowly and thoughtfully.

"I fancy that he is very near the border line of madness, Hastings. I should imagine he practises many curious vices and that beneath his frigid exterior he hides a deep-rooted instinct of cruelty."

"It is no wonder both his wives left him."

"As you say."

"Poirot, did you notice a girl as we were coming out? A dark girl with a white face."

"Yes, I noticed her, *mon ami*. A young lady who was frightened and not happy."

His voice was grave.

"Who do you think she was?"

"Probably his daughter. He has one."

"She did look frightened," I said slowly. "That house must be a gloomy place for a young girl."

"Yes, indeed. Ah! here we are, *mon ami.* Now to acquaint her ladyship with the good news."

Jane was in, and, after telephoning, the clerk informed us that we were to go up. A page boy took us to the door.

It was opened by a neat middle-aged woman, with glasses and primly arranged grey hair. From the bedroom, Jane's voice, with its husky note, called to her.

"Is that M. Poirot, Ellis? Make him sit right down. I'll find a rag to put on and be there in a moment."

Jane Wilkinson's idea of a rag was a gossamer negligee which revealed more than it hid. She came in eagerly, saying: "Well?"

Poirot rose and bowed over her hand.

"Exactly the word, madame; it *is* well."

"Why—how do you mean?"

"Lord Edgware is perfectly willing to agree to a divorce."

"What?"

Either the stupefaction on her face was genuine, or else she was indeed a most marvellous actress.

"M. Poirot! You've managed it! At once! Like that! Why, you're a genius. How in mercy's name did you set about it?"

"Madame, I cannot take compliments where they are not earned. Six months ago, your husband wrote to you withdrawing his opposition."

"What's that you say? *Wrote* to *me?* Where?"

"It was when you were at Hollywood, I understand."

"I never got it. Must have gone astray, I suppose. And to think I've been thinking and planning and fretting and going nearly crazy all these months."

"Lord Edgware seemed to be under the impression that you wished to marry an actor."

"Naturally. That's what I told him." She gave a pleased child's smile. Suddenly it changed to a look of alarm. "Why, M. Poirot, you didn't go and tell him about me and the Duke?"

"No, no; reassure yourself. I am discreet. That would not have done, eh?"

"Well, you see he's got a queer mean nature. Marrying Merton, he'd feel, was perhaps a kind of leg up for me—so then naturally he'd queer the pitch. But a film actor's different. Though all the same I'm surprised. Yes, I am. Aren't you surprised, Ellis?"

I had noticed that the maid had come to and fro from the bedroom tidying away various outdoor garments which were lying flung over the backs of chairs. It had been my opinion that she had been listening to the conversation. Now it seemed that she was completely in Jane's confidence.

"Yes, indeed, m'lady. His lordship must have changed a good deal since we knew him," said the maid spitefully.

"Yes, he must."

"You cannot understand his attitude. It puzzles you?" suggested Poirot.

"Oh! It does. But anyway we needn't worry about that. What does it matter what made him change his mind, so long as he has changed it?"

"It may not interest you but it interests me, Madame."

Jane paid no attention to him.

"The thing is that I'm free—at last."

"Not yet, madame."

She looked at him impatiently.

"Well, going to be free. It's the same thing."

Poirot looked as though he did not think it was.

"The Duke is in Paris," said Jane. "I must cable him right away. My— won't his old mother be wild!"

Poirot rose.

"I am glad, madame, that all is turning out as you wish."

"Good-bye, M. Poirot, and thanks awfully."

"I did nothing."

"You brought me the good news, anyway, M. Poirot, and I'm ever so grateful. I *really* am."

"And that is that," said Poirot to me, as we left the suite. "The single idea—herself! She has no speculation, no curiosity as to why that letter never reached her. You observe, Hastings, she is shrewd beyond belief in the business sense, but she has absolutely no intellect. Well, well, the good God cannot give everything."

"Except to Hercule Poirot," I said slyly.

"You mock yourself at me, my friend," he replied serenely. "But come, let us walk along the Embankment. I wish to arrange my ideas with order and method."

I maintained a discreet silence until such time as the oracle should speak.

"That letter," he resumed, when we were pacing along by the river. "It intrigues me. There are four solutions of that problem, my friend."

"Four?"

"Yes. First it was lost in the post. That *does* happen, you know. But not very often. No, not very often. Incorrectly addressed, it would have been returned to Lord Edgware long before this. No, I am inclined to rule out that solution—though of course it may be the true one.

"Solution two; our beautiful lady is lying when she says she never received it. That, of course, is quite possible. That charming lady is capable of telling any lie to her advantage, with the most childlike candour. But I cannot see, Hastings, how it could be to her advantage. If she knows that he will divorce her, why send me to ask him to do so? It does not make sense.

"Solution three. Lord Edgware is lying. And if anyone is lying it seems more likely that it is he than his wife. But I do not see much point in such a lie. Why invent a fictitious letter sent six months ago? Why not simply agree to my proposition? No, I am inclined to think that he *did* send that letter—though what the motive was for his sudden change of attitude I cannot guess.

"So we come to the fourth solution—that someone suppressed that letter. And there, Hastings, we enter on a very interesting field of speculation, because that letter could have been suppressed at either end—in America or England.

"Whoever suppressed it was someone who did not want that marriage dissolved. Hastings, I would give a great deal to know what is behind that affair. There is *something*— I swear there is something."

He paused and then added slowly:

"Something of which as yet I have only been able to get a glimpse."

Chapter V

MURDER

THE FOLLOWING DAY was the thirtieth of June. It was just half past nine when we were told that Inspector Japp was below and anxious to see us. It was some years since we had seen anything of the Scotland Yard Inspector.

"Ah! ce bon Japp," said Poirot. "What does he want, I wonder?"

"Help," I snapped. "He's out of his depth over some case, and he's come to you."

I had not the indulgence for Japp that Poirot had. It was not so much that I minded his picking Poirot's brains. After all, Poirot enjoyed the process, it was a delicate flattery. What did annoy me was Japp's hypocritical pretence that he was doing nothing of the kind. I liked people to be straightforward. I said so, and Poirot laughed.

"You are the dog of the bulldog breed, eh, Hastings? But you must remember that the poor Japp, he has to save his face. So he makes his little pretence. It is very natural."

I thought it merely foolish and said so. Poirot did not agree.

"The outward form—it is a *bagatelle*—but it matters to people. It enables them to keep the *amour propre.*"

Personally I thought a dash of inferiority complex would do Japp no harm, but there was no point in arguing the matter. Besides I was anxious to learn what Japp had come about.

He greeted us both heartily.

"Just going to have breakfast, I see. Not got the hens to lay square eggs for you yet, M. Poirot?"

This was an illusion to a complaint from Poirot as to the varying sizes of eggs which had offended his sense of symmetry.

"As yet, no," said Poirot, smiling. "And what brings you to see us so early, my good Japp?"

"It's not early—not for me. I've been up and at work for a good two hours. As to what brings me to see you—well, it's murder."

"Murder?"

Japp nodded.

"Lord Edgware was killed at his house in Regent Gate last night. Stabbed in the neck by his wife."

"By his wife?" I cried.

In a flash, I remembered Bryan Martin's words on the previous morning. Had he had a prophetic knowledge of what was going to happen? I remembered, too, Jane's easy reference to "bumping him off." Amoral, Bryan Martin had called her. She was the type, yes. Callous, egoistical and stupid. How right he had been in his judgment.

All this passed through my mind while Japp went on:

"Yes. Actress, you know. Well known. Jane Wilkinson. Married him three years ago. They didn't get on. She left him."

Poirot was looking puzzled and serious.

"What makes you believe that it was she who killed him?"

"No belief about it. She was recognized. Not much concealment about it, either. She drove up in a taxi—"

"A taxi—" I echoed involuntarily, her words at the Savoy that night coming back to me.

"Rang the bell, asked for Lord Edgware. It was ten o'clock. Butler said he'd see. 'Oh!' she says, cool as a cucumber. 'You needn't. I am Lady Edgware. I suppose he's in the library.' And with that she walks along and opens the door and goes in and shuts it behind her.

"Well, the butler thought it was queer, but all right. He went downstairs again. About ten minutes later he heard the front door shut. So anyway she hadn't stayed long. He locked up for the night about eleven. He opened the library door, but it was dark, so he thought his master had gone to bed. This morning the body was discovered by a housemaid. Stabbed in the back of the neck just at the roots of the hair."

"Was there no cry? Nothing heard?"

"They say not. That library's got pretty well sound-proof doors, you know. And there's traffic passing, too. Stabbed in that way, death results amazing quick. Straight through the cistern into the medulla, that's what the doctor said—or something very like it. If you hit on exactly the right spot, it kills a man instantaneously."

"That implies a knowledge of exactly where to strike. It almost implies medical knowledge."

"Yes—that's true. A point in her favour as far as it goes. But ten to one it was a chance. She just struck lucky. Some people do have amazing luck, you know."

"Not so lucky if it results in her being hanged, *mon ami,*" observed Poirot.

"No. Of course she was a fool—sailing in like that and giving her name and all."

"Indeed very curious."

"Possibly she didn't intend mischief. They quarrelled and she whipped out a penknife and jabbed him one."

"Was it a penknife?"

"Something of that kind, the doctor says. Whatever it was, she took it away with her. It wasn't left in the wound."

Poirot shook his head in a dissatisfied manner.

"No, no, my friend, it was not like that. I know the lady. She would be quite incapable of such a hot-blooded, impulsive action. Besides she would be most unlikely to have a penknife with her. Few women have—and assuredly not Jane Wilkinson."

"You know her, you say, M. Poirot?"

"Yes. I know her."

He said no more for the moment. Japp was looking at him inquisitively.

"Got something up your sleeve, M. Poirot?" he ventured at last.

"Ah!" said Poirot. "That reminds me. What has brought you to me? Eh? It is not merely to pass the time of day with an old comrade? Assuredly not. You have here a nice straightforward murder. You have the criminal. You have the motive. What exactly is the motive, by the way?"

"Wanted to marry another man. She was heard to say so not a week ago. Also heard to make threats. Said she meant to call round in a taxi and bump him off."

"Ah!" said Poirot. "You are very well informed—very well informed. Someone has been very obliging."

I thought his eyes looked a question; but, if so, Japp did not respond.

"We get to hear things, M. Poirot," he said stolidly.

Poirot nodded. He had reached out for the daily paper. It had been opened by Japp, doubtless while he was waiting, and had been cast impatiently aside on our entry. In a mechanical manner, Poirot folded it back at the middle page, smoothed and arranged it. Though his eyes were on the paper, his mind was deep in some kind of puzzle.

"You have not answered," he said presently. "Since all goes in the swimming fashion, why come to me?"

"Because I heard you were at Regent Gate yesterday morning."

"I see."

"Now as soon as I heard that, I said to myself, 'Something here.' His lordship sent for M. Poirot. Why? What did he suspect? What did he fear? Before doing anything definite, I'd better go round and have a word with him."

"What do you mean by 'anything definite'? Arresting the lady, I suppose?"

"Exactly."

"You have not seen her yet?"

"Oh! yes, I have. Went round to the Savoy first thing. Wasn't going to risk her giving us the slip?"

"Ah!" said Poirot. "So you—"

He stopped. His eyes, which had been fixed thoughtfully and up to now unseeingly on the paper in front of him, now took on a different expression. He lifted his head and spoke in a changed tone of voice.

"And what did she say? Eh! my friend. What did she say?"

"I gave her the usual stuff, of course, about wanting a statement and cautioning her. You can't say the English police aren't fair."

"In my opinion, foolishly so. But proceed. What did milady say?"

"Took hysterics—that's what she did. Rolled herself about, threw up her arms and finally flopped down on the ground. Oh! she did it well—I'll say that for her. A pretty bit of acting."

"Ah!" said Poirot blandly. "You formed then, the impression that the hysterics were not genuine?"

Japp winked vulgarly.

"What do you think? I'm not to be taken in with those tricks. *She* hadn't fainted—not she! Just trying it on, she was. I'll swear she was enjoying it."

"Yes," said Poirot thoughtfully. "I should say that was perfectly possible. What next?"

"Oh! well, she came to—pretended to, I mean. And moaned, *and* groaned, and carried on; and that sour-faced maid of hers doped her with smelling salts; and at last she recovered enough to ask for her solicitor. Wasn't going to say anything without her solicitor. Hysterics one moment, solicitor the next, now I ask you, is that natural behaviour, sir?"

"In this case quite natural, I should say," said Poirot calmly.

"You mean because she's guilty and knows it."

"Not at all, I mean because of her temperament. First she gives you her conception of how the part of a wife suddenly learning of her husband's death should be played. Then, having satisfied her histrionic instinct, her native shrewdness makes her send for a solicitor. That she creates an artificial scene, and enjoys it, is no proof of her guilt. It merely indicates that she is a born actress."

"Well, she can't be innocent. That's sure."

"You are very positive," said Poirot. "I suppose that it must be so. She made no statement, you say? No statement at all?"

Japp grinned.

"Wouldn't say a word without her solicitor. The maid telephoned for him. I left two of my men there and came along to you. I thought it just as well to get put wise to whatever there was going on before I went on with things."

"And yet you are sure?"

"Of course I'm sure. But I like as many facts as possible. You see there's going to be a big splash made about this. No hole-and-corner business. All the papers will be full of it. And you know what papers are."

"Talking of papers," said Poirot, "how do you account for this, my dear friend? You have not read your morning paper very carefully."

He leant across the table, his finger on a paragraph in the Society news. Japp read the item aloud.

"Sir Montagu Corner gave a very successful dinner-party last night at his house on the river at Chiswick. Among those present were Sir George and Lady du Fisse, Mr. James Blunt, the well-known dramatic critic, Sir Oscar Hammerfeldt of the Overton Film Studios, Miss Jane Wilkinson (Lady Edgware) and others."

For a moment Japp looked taken aback. Then he rallied.

"What's that got to do with it? This thing was sent to the press beforehand. You'll see. You'll find that our lady wasn't there, or that she came in late—eleven o'clock or so. Bless you, sir, you mustn't believe everything you see in the press to be gospel. You of all people ought to know better than that."

"Oh! I do, I do. It only struck me as curious, that was all."

"These coincidences do happen. Now, M. Poirot, close as an oyster I know you to be by bitter experience. But you'll come across with things, won't you? You'll tell me why Lord Edgware sent for you?"

Poirot shook his head.

"Lord Edgware did not send for me. It was I who requested him to give me an appointment."

"Really? And for what reason?"

Poirot hesitated a minute.

"I will answer your question," he said slowly, "but I should like to answer it in my own way."

Japp groaned. I felt a sneaking sympathy with him. Poirot can be intensely irritating at times.

"I will request," went on Poirot, "that you permit me to ring up a certain person and ask him to come here."

"What person?"

"Mr. Bryan Martin."

"The film star? What's he got to do with it?"

"I think," said Poirot, "that you may find what he has got to say interesting—and possibly helpful. Hastings, will you be so good?"

I took up the telephone book. The actor had a flat in a big block of buildings near St. James' Park.

"Victoria 49499."

The somewhat sleepy voice of Bryan Martin spoke after a few minutes.

"Hello—who's speaking?"

"What am I to say?" I whispered, covering the mouthpiece with my hand.

"Tell him," said Poirot, "that Lord Edgware has been murdered, and that I should esteem it a favour if he would come round here and see me immediately."

I repeated this meticulously. There was a startled exclamation at the other end.

"My God," said Martin. "So she's done it then! I'll come at once."

"What did he say?" asked Poirot.

I told him.

"Ah!" said Poirot. He seemed pleased. " 'So she's done it then.' That is what he said? Then it is as I thought; it is as I thought."

Japp looked at him curiously.

"I can't make you out, M. Poirot. First you sound as though you thought the woman might not have done it after all. And now you make out that you knew it all along."

Poirot only smiled.

Chapter VI

THE WIDOW

BRYAN MARTIN WAS as good as his word. In less than ten minutes he had joined us. During the time that we awaited his arrival, Poirot would talk only of extraneous subjects and refused to satisfy Japp's curiosity in the smallest degree.

Evidently our news had upset the young actor terribly. His face was white and drawn.

"Good heavens, M. Poirot," he said as he shook hands, "this is a terrible business. I'm shocked to the core—and yet I can't say I'm surprised. I've always half suspected that something of this kind might happen. You may remember I was saying so yesterday."

"Mais oui, mais oui," said Poirot. "I remember perfectly what you said to me yesterday. Let me introduce you to Inspector Japp who is in charge of the case."

Bryan Martin shot a glance of reproach at Poirot.

"I had no idea," he murmured. "You should have warned me."

He nodded coldly to the inspector.

He sat down, his lips pressed tightly together.

"I don't see," he objected, "why you asked me to come round. All this has nothing to do with me."

"I think it has," said Poirot gently. "In a case of murder one must put one's private repugnances behind one."

"No, no. I've acted with Jane. I know her well. Dash it all, she's a friend of mine."

"And yet the moment that you hear Lord Edgware is murdered, you jump to the conclusion that it is she who has murdered him," remarked Poirot dryly.

The actor started.

"Do you mean to say—?" His eyes seemed starting out of his head. "Do you mean to say that I'm wrong? That she had nothing to do with it?"

Japp broke in.

"No, no, Mr. Martin. She did it right enough."

The young man sank back again in his chair.

"For a moment," he murmured, "I thought I'd made the most ghastly mistake."

"In a matter of this kind friendship must not be allowed to influence you," said Poirot decisively.

"That's all very well, but—"

"My friend, do you seriously wish to range yourself on the side of a woman who has murdered? Murder—the most repugnant of human crimes."

Bryan Martin sighed.

"You don't understand. Jane is not an ordinary murderess. She—she has no sense of right or wrong. Honestly she's not responsible."

"That'll be a question for the jury," said Japp.

"Come, come," said Poirot kindly. "It is not as though you were accusing her. She is already accused. You cannot refuse to tell us what you know. You have a duty to society, young man."

Bryan Martin sighed.

"I suppose you're right," he said. "What do you want me to tell you?"

Poirot looked at Japp.

"Have you ever heard Lady Edgware—or perhaps I'd better call her Miss Wilkinson—utter threats against her husband?" asked Japp.

"Yes, several times."

"What did she say?"

"She said that if he didn't give her her freedom she'd have to 'bump him off.' "

"And that was not a joke, eh?"

"No. I think she meant it seriously. Once she said she'd take a taxi and go round and kill him—you heard that, M. Poirot?"

He appealed pathetically to my friend. Poirot nodded. Japp went on with his questions.

"Now, Mr. Martin, we've been informed that she wanted her freedom in order to marry another man. Do you know who that man was?"

Bryan nodded.

"Who?"

"It was—the Duke of Merton."

"The Duke of Merton! Whew!" The detective whistled. "Flying at high game, eh? Why, he's said to be one of the richest men in England."

Bryan nodded more dejectedly than ever.

I could not quite understand Poirot's attitude. He was lying back in his chair, his fingers pressed together, and the rhythmic motion of his head suggested the complete approval of a man who has put a chosen record on the gramophone and is enjoying the result.

"Wouldn't her husband divorce her?"

"No, he refused absolutely."

"You know that for a fact?"

"Yes."

"And now," said Poirot, suddenly taking part once more in the proceedings, "you see where I come in, my good Japp. I was asked by Lady Edgware to see her husband and try to get him to agree to a divorce. I had an appointment for this morning."

Bryan Martin shook his head.

"It would have been of no use," he declared confidently. "Edgware would never have agreed."

"You think not?" said Poirot, turning an amiable glance on him.

"Sure of it. Jane knew that in her heart of hearts. She'd no real confidence that you'd succeed. She'd given up hope. The man was a monomaniac on the subject of divorce."

Poirot smiled. His eyes grew suddenly very green.

"You are wrong, my dear young man," he said gently. "I saw Lord Edgware yesterday, and he agreed to a divorce."

There was no doubt that Bryan Martin was completely dumbfounded by this piece of news. He stared at Poirot with his eyes almost starting out of his head.

"You—you saw him yesterday?" he spluttered.

"At a quarter past twelve," said Poirot in his methodical manner.

"And he agreed to a divorce?"

"He agreed to a divorce."

"You should have told Jane at once," cried the young man reproachfully.

"I did, M. Martin."

"You did?" cried Martin and Japp together.

Poirot smiled.

"It impairs the motive a little, does it not?" he murmured. "And now, M. Martin, let me call your attention to this."

He showed him the newspaper paragraph.

Bryan read it, but without much interest.

"You mean this makes an alibi?" he said. "I suppose Edgware was shot some time yesterday evening?"

"He was stabbed, not shot," said Poirot.

Martin laid the paper down slowly.

"I'm afraid this does no good," he said regretfully. "Jane didn't go to that dinner."

"How do you know?"

"I forget. Somebody told me."

"That is a pity," said Poirot thoughtfully.

Japp looked at him curiously.

"I can't make you out, moosior. Seems now as though you don't want the young woman to be guilty."

"No, no, my good Japp. I am not the partisan you think. But frankly, the case as you present it, revolts the intelligence."

"What do you mean, revolts the intelligence? It doesn't revolt mine."

I could see words trembling on Poirot's lips. He restrained them.

"Here is a young woman who wishes, you say, to get rid of her husband. That point I do not dispute. She told me so frankly. *Eh bien,* how does she set about it? She repeats several times in the loud clear voice before witnesses that she is thinking of killing him. She then goes out one evening, calls at his house, has herself announced, stabs him and goes away. What do you call that, my good friend? Has it even the common sense?"

"It was a bit foolish, of course."

"Foolish? It is the imbecility!"

"Well," said Japp, rising. "It's all to the advantage of the police when criminals lose their heads. I must go back to the Savoy now."

"You permit that I accompany you?"

Japp made no demur, and we set out. Bryan Martin took a reluctant leave of us. He seemed to be in a great state of nervous excitement. He begged earnestly that any further development might be reported to him.

"Nervy sort of chap," was Japp's comment on him. Poirot agreed.

At the Savoy we found an extremely legal-looking gentleman who had just arrived, and we proceeded all together to Jane's suite. Japp spoke to one of his men.

"Anything?" he inquired laconically.

"She wanted to use the telephone!"

"Who did she telephone to?" inquired Japp eagerly.

"Jay's. For mourning."

Japp swore under his breath. We entered the suite.

The widowed Lady Edgware was trying on hats in front of the glass. She was dressed in a filmy creation of black and white. She greeted us with a dazzling smile.

"Why, M. Poirot, how good of you to come along. Mr. Moxon" (this was to the solicitor), "I'm so glad you've come. Just sit right by me and tell me what questions I ought to answer. This man here seems to think that I went out and killed George this morning."

"Last night, madam," said Japp.

"You said this morning. Ten o'clock."

"I said ten P.M."

"Well, I can never tell which is which—A.M.'s and P.M.'s."

"It's only just about ten o'clock now," added the inspector severely.

Jane's eyes opened very wide.

"Mercy," she murmured. "It's years since I've been awake as early as this. Why, it must have been early dawn when you came along."

"One moment, Inspector," said Mr. Moxon in his ponderous legal voice. "When am I to understand that this—er—regrettable—most shocking—occurrence took place?"

"Round about ten o'clock last night, sir."

"Why, that's all right," said Jane sharply. "I was at a party— Oh!" she covered her mouth up suddenly. "Perhaps I oughtn't to have said that."

Her eyes sought the solicitor's in timid appeal.

"If, at ten o'clock last night, you were—er—at a party, Lady Edgware, I—er—I can see no objection to your informing the inspector of the fact— no objection whatever."

"That's right," said Japp. "I only asked you for a statement of your movements yesterday evening."

"You didn't. You said ten something M. And anyway you gave me the most terrible shock. I fainted dead away, Mr. Moxon."

"About this party, Lady Edgware?"

"It was at Sir Montagu Corner's—at Chiswick."

"What time did you go there?"

"The dinner was for eight-thirty."

"You left here—when?"

"I started about eight o'clock. I dropped in at the Piccadilly Palace for a moment, to say good-bye to an American friend who was leaving for the States—Mrs. Van Dusen. I got to Chiswick at a quarter to nine."

"What time did you leave?"

"About half past eleven."

"You came straight back here?"

"Yes."

"In a taxi?"

"No. In my own car. I hire it from the Daimler people."

"And while you were at the dinner party you didn't leave it?"

"Well—I—"

"So you did leave it?"

It was like a terrier pouncing on a rat.

"I don't know what you mean. I was called to the telephone when we were at dinner."

"Who called you?"

"I guess it was some kind of hoax. A voice said, 'Is that Lady Edgware?' And I said, 'Yes, that's right,' and then they just laughed and rang off."

"Did you go outside the house to telephone?"

Jane's eyes opened wide in amazement.

"Of course not."

"How long were you away from the dinner table?"

"About a minute and a half."

Japp collapsed after that. I was fully convinced that he did not believe a word she was saying, but, having heard her story, he could do no more until he had confirmed or disproved it.

Having thanked her coldly, he withdrew. We also took our leave, but she called Poirot back.

"M. Poirot. Will you do something for me?"

"Certainly, madame."

"Send a cable for me to the Duke in Paris. He's at the Crillon. He ought to know about this. I don't like to send it myself. I guess I've got to look the bereaved widow for a week or two."

"It is quite unnecessary to cable, madame," said Poirot gently. "It will be in the papers over there."

"Why, what a headpiece you've got! Of course it will. Much better not to cable. I feel it's up to me to keep up my position, now everything's gone right. I want to act the way a widow should. Sort of dignified, you know. I thought of sending a wreath of orchids. They're about the most expensive things going. I suppose I shall have to go to the funeral. What do you think?"

"You will have to go to the inquest first, madame."

"Why, I suppose that's true." She considered for a moment or two. "I don't like that Scotland Yard inspector at all. He just scared me to death. M. Poirot?"

"Yes?"

"Seems it's kind of lucky I changed my mind and went to that party after all."

Poirot had been going towards the door. Suddenly, at these words, he wheeled round.

"What is that you say, madame? You changed your mind?"

"Yes. I meant to give it a miss. I had a frightful headache yesterday afternoon."

Poirot swallowed once or twice. He seemed to have a difficulty in speaking.

"Did you—say so to anyone?" he asked at last.

"Certainly I did. There was quite a crowd of us having tea and they wanted me to go on to a cocktail party and I said 'No.' I said my head was aching fit to split and that I was going right home and that I was going to cut the dinner too."

"And what made you change your mind, madame?"

"Ellis went on at me. Said I couldn't afford to turn it down. Old Sir Montagu pulls a lot of strings, you know, and he's a crotchety creature— takes offence easily. Well, I didn't care. Once I marry Merton I'm through with all this. But Ellis is always on the cautious side. She said there's many a slip, et cetera, and after all I guess she's right. Anyway, off I went."

"You owe Ellis a debt of gratitude, madame," said Poirot seriously.

"I suppose I do. That inspector had got it all taped out, hadn't he?"

She laughed. Poirot did not. He said in a low voice:

"All the same—this gives one furiously to think. Yes, furiously to think."

"Ellis," called Jane.

The maid came in from the next room.

"M. Poirot says it's very lucky you made me go to that party last night."

Ellis barely cast a glance at Poirot. She was looking grim and disapproving.

"It doesn't do to break engagements, m'lady. You're much too fond of doing it. People don't always forgive it. They turn nasty."

Jane picked up the hat she had been trying on when we came in. She tried it again.

"I hate black," she said disconsolately. "I never wear it. But, I suppose, as a correct widow, I've just got to. All those hats are too frightful. Ring up the other hat place, Ellis. I've got to be fit to be seen."

Poirot and I slipped quietly from the room.

Chapter VII

THE SECRETARY

WE HAD NOT seen the last of Japp. He reappeared about an hour later, flung down his hat on the table and said he was eternally blasted.

"You have made the inquiries?" asked Poirot sympathetically.

Japp nodded gloomily.

"And unless fourteen people are lying, she didn't do it," he growled. He went on: "I don't mind telling you, M. Poirot, that I expected to find a put-up job. On the face of it, it didn't seem likely that anyone else could have killed Lord Edgware. She's the only person who's got the ghost of a motive."

"I would not say that. *Mais continuez.*"

"Well, as I say, I expected to find a put-up job. You know what these theatrical crowds are—they'd all hang together to screen a pal. But this is rather a different proposition. The people there last night were all big guns; they were none of them close friends of hers, and some of them didn't know each other. Their testimony is independent and reliable. I hoped then to find that she'd slipped away for half an hour or so. She could easily have done that—powdering her nose or some excuse. But no. She did leave the dinner table, as she told us, to answer a telephone call, but the butler was with her—and by the way it was just as she told us. He heard what she said. 'Yes, quite right. This is Lady Edgware.' And then the other side rang off. It's curious, that, you know. Not that it's got anything to do with it."

"Perhaps not—but it is interesting. Was it a man or a woman who rang up?"

"A woman, I think she said."

"Curious," said Poirot thoughtfully.

"Never mind that," said Japp impatiently. "Let's get back to the important part. The whole evening went exactly as she said. She got there at a quarter to nine, left at half past eleven and got back here at a quarter to twelve. I've seen the chauffeur who drove her—he's one of Daimler's regular people. And the people at the Savoy saw her come in, and confirm the time."

"*Eh! bien,* that seems very conclusive."

"Then what about those two in Regent Gate? It isn't only the butler. Lord Edgware's secretary saw her too. They both swear by all that's holy that it was Lady Edgware who came there at ten o'clock."

"How long has the butler been there?"

"Six months. Handsome chap, by the way."

"Yes, indeed. *Eh bien,* my friend, if he has only been there six months he cannot have recognized Lady Edgware, since he had not seen her before."

"Well, he knew her from her pictures in the papers. And anyway, the secretary knew her. She's been with Lord Edgware five or six years, and she's the only one who's absolutely positive."

"Ah!" said Poirot. "I should like to see the secretary."

"Well, why not come along with me now?"

"Thank you, *mon ami,* I should be delighted to do so. You include Hastings in your invitation, I hope?"

Japp grinned.

"What do you think? Where the master goes, there the dog follows," he added, in what I could not think was the best of taste.

"Reminds me of the Elizabeth Canning Case," said Japp. "You remember? How at least a score of witnesses on either side swore they had seen the gipsy, Mary Squires, in two different parts of England. Good reputable witnesses, too. And she with such a hideous face there couldn't be two like it. That mystery was never cleared up. It's very much the same here. Here's a separate lot of people prepared to swear a woman was in two different places at the same time. Which of 'em is speaking the truth?"

"That ought not to be difficult to find out?"

"So you say—but this woman, Miss Carroll, really *knew* Lady Edgware. I mean she'd lived in the house with her day after day. She wouldn't be likely to make a mistake."

"We shall soon see."

"Who comes into the title?" I asked.

"A nephew, Captain Ronald Marsh. Bit of a waster, I understand."

"What does the doctor say as to the time of death?" asked Poirot.

"We'll have to wait for the autopsy, to be exact, you know. See where the dinner had got to." Japp's way of putting things was, I am sorry to say, far from refined. "But ten o'clock fits in well enough. He was last seen alive at a few minutes past nine, when he left the dinner table and the butler took whisky and soda into the library. At eleven o'clock, when the butler went up to bed, the light was out—so he must have been dead then. He wouldn't have been sitting in the dark."

Poirot nodded thoughtfully. A moment or two later we drew up to the house, the blinds of which were now down. The door was opened to us by the handsome butler.

Japp took the lead and went in first. Poirot and I followed. The door opened to the left, so that the butler stood against the wall on that side. Poirot was on my right and, since he is smaller than I am, it was only just as we stepped into the hall that the butler saw him. Being close to him, I heard the sudden intake of his breath and looked sharply at the man to find him staring at Poirot with a kind of startled fear visible on his face. I put the fact away in my mind for what it might be worth.

Japp marched into the dining-room, which lay on our right, and called the butler in after him.

"Now then, Alton, I want to go into this again very carefully. It was ten o'clock when this lady came?"

"Her ladyship? Yes, sir."

"How did you recognize her?" asked Poirot.

"She told her name, sir; and besides I've seen her portrait in the papers. I've seen her act, too."

Poirot nodded.

"How was she dressed?"

"In black, sir. Black walking dress, and a small black hat. A string of pearls and grey gloves."

Poirot looked a question at Japp.

"White taffeta evening dress and ermine wrap," said the latter succinctly.

The butler proceeded. His tale tallied exactly with that which Japp had already passed on to us.

"Did anybody else come to see your master that evening?" asked Poirot.

"No, sir."

"How was the front door fastened?"

"It has a Yale lock, sir. I usually draw the bolts when I go to bed, sir. At eleven, that is. But last night Miss Geraldine was at the opera so it was left unbolted."

"How was it fastened this morning?"

"It was bolted, sir. Miss Geraldine had bolted it when she came in."

"When did she come in? Do you know?"

"I think it was about a quarter to twelve, sir."

"Then during the evening, until a quarter to twelve, the door could not be opened from outside without a key? From the inside it could be opened by simply drawing back the handle."

"Yes, sir."

"How many latchkeys were there?"

"His lordship had his, sir, and there was another key in the hall drawer, which Miss Geraldine took last night. I don't know if there were any others."

"Does nobody else in the house have a key?"

"No, sir. Miss Carroll always rings."

Poirot intimated that that was all he wished to ask, and we went in search of the secretary. We found her busily writing at a large desk.

Miss Carroll was a pleasant, efficient-looking woman of about forty-five. Her fair hair was turning grey, and she wore pince-nez, through which a pair of shrewd blue eyes gleamed out on us. When she spoke I recognized the clear, businesslike voice that had spoken to me through the telephone.

"Ah! M. Poirot," she said as she acknowledged Japp's introduction. "Yes. It was with you I made that appointment for yesterday morning."

"Precisely, mademoiselle."

I thought that Poirot was favourably impressed by her. Certainly she was neatness and precision personified.

"Well, Inspector Japp?" said Miss Carroll. "What more can I do for you?"

"Just this. Are you absolutely certain that it was Lady Edgware who came here last night?"

"That's the third time you've asked me. Of course, I'm sure. I saw her."

"Where did you see her, mademoiselle?"

"In the hall. She spoke to the butler for a minute, then she went along the hall and in at the library door."

"And where were you?"

"On the first floor—looking down."

"And you are positive you were not mistaken."

"Absolutely. I saw her face distinctly."

"You could not have been misled by a resemblance?"

"Certainly not. Jane Wilkinson's features are quite unique. It was her."

Japp threw a glance at Poirot as much as to say: "You see."

"Had Lord Edgware any enemies?" asked Poirot suddenly.

"Nonsense," said Miss Carroll.

"How do you mean—nonsense, mademoiselle?"

"Enemies! People in these days don't have *enemies.* Not English people!"

"Yet Lord Edgware was murdered."

"That was his wife," said Miss Carroll.

"A wife is not an enemy—no?"

"I'm sure it was a most extraordinary thing to happen. I've never heard of such a thing happening—I mean to anyone in our class of life."

It was clearly Miss Carroll's idea that murders were only committed by drunken members of the lower classes.

"How many keys are there to the front door?"

"Two," replied Miss Carroll promptly. "Lord Edgware always carried one. The other was kept in the drawer in the hall, so that anybody who was going to be late in could take it. There was a third one, but Captain Marsh lost it. Very careless."

"Did Captain Marsh come much to the house?"

"He used to live here until three years ago."

"Why did he leave?" asked Japp.

"I don't know. He couldn't get on with his uncle, I suppose."

"I think you know a little more than that, mademoiselle," said Poirot gently.

She darted a quick glance at him.

"I am not one to gossip, M. Poirot."

"But you can tell us the truth concerning the rumours of a serious disagreement between Lord Edgware and his nephew."

"It wasn't so serious as all that. Lord Edgware was a difficult man to get on with."

"Even you found that?"

"I'm not speaking of myself. I never had any disagreements with Lord Edgware. He always found me perfectly reliable."

"But as regards Captain Marsh—"

Poirot stuck to it, gently continuing to goad her into further revelations.

Miss Carroll shrugged her shoulders.

"He was extravagant. Got into debt. There was some other trouble—I don't know exactly what. They quarrelled. Lord Edgware forbade him the house. That's all."

Her mouth closed firmly. Evidently she intended to say no more.

The room we had interviewed her in was on the first floor. As we left it, Poirot took me by the arm.

"A little minute. Remain here if you will, Hastings. I am going down with Japp. Watch till we have gone into the library, then join us there."

I have long ago given up asking Poirot questions beginning "Why?" Like the Light Brigade, "Mine not to reason why, mine but to do or die," though fortunately it has not yet come to dying! I thought that possibly he suspected the butler of spying on him and wanted to know if such were really the case.

I took up my stand looking over the banisters. Poirot and Japp went first to the front door—out of my sight. Then they reappeared, walking slowly along the hall. I followed their backs with my eye until they had gone into the library. I waited a minute or two, in case the butler appeared, but there was no sign of anyone, so I ran down the stairs and joined them.

The body had, of course, been removed. The curtains were drawn and the electric light was on. Poirot and Japp were standing in the middle of the room looking round them.

"Nothing here," Japp was saying.

And Poirot replied with a smile:

"Alas! not the cigarette ash—nor the footprint—nor a lady's glove— nor even a lingering perfume! Nothing that the detective of fiction so conveniently finds."

"The police are always made out to be as blind as bats in detective stories," said Japp with a grin.

"I found a clue once," said Poirot dreamily. "But since it was four feet long instead of four centimetres no one would believe in it."

I remembered the circumstance and laughed. Then I remembered my mission.

"It's all right, Poirot," I said. "I watched, but no one was spying upon you as far as I could see."

"The eyes of my friend Hastings," said Poirot in a kind of gentle mockery. "Tell me, my friend, did you notice the rose between my lips?"

"The rose between your lips?" I asked in astonishment. Japp turned aside spluttering with laughter.

"You'll be the death of me, M. Poirot," he said. "The death of me. A rose. What next?"

"I had the fancy to pretend I was Carmen," said Poirot quite undisturbed.

I wondered if they were going mad or if I was.

"You did not observe it, Hastings?" There was reproach in Poirot's voice.

"No," I said, staring. "But then I couldn't see your face."

"No matter." He shook his head gently.

Were they making fun of me?

"Well," said Japp. "No more to do here, I fancy. I'd like to see the daughter again if I could. She was too upset before for me to get anything out of her."

He rang the bell for the butler.

"Ask Miss Marsh if I can see her for a few moments?"

The man departed. It was not he, however, but Miss Carroll who entered the room a few minutes later.

"Geraldine is asleep," she said. "She's had a terrible shock, poor child.

After you left I gave her something to make her sleep, and she's fast asleep now. In an hour or two, perhaps."

Japp agreed.

"In any case there's nothing she can tell you that I can't," said Miss Carroll firmly.

"What is your opinion of the butler?" asked Poirot.

"I don't like him much, and that's a fact," replied Miss Carroll. "But I can't tell you why."

We had reached the front door.

"It was up there that you stood, was it not, last night, mademoiselle?" said Poirot suddenly, pointing with his hand up the stairs.

"Yes. Why?"

"And you saw Lady Edgware go along the hall into the study?"

"Yes."

"And you saw her face distinctly?"

"Certainly."

"But you could not have seen her face, mademoiselle. You can only have seen the back of her head from where you were standing."

Miss Carroll flushed angrily. She seemed taken aback.

"Back of her head, her voice, her walk! It's all the same thing. Absolutely unmistakable! I tell you I *know* it was Jane Wilkinson—a thoroughly bad woman if there ever was one."

And turning away she flounced upstairs.

Chapter VIII

POSSIBILITIES

JAPP HAD TO leave us. Poirot and I turned into Regent's Park and found a quiet seat.

"I see the point of your rose between the lips now," I said, laughing. "At the moment I thought you had gone mad."

He nodded without smiling.

"You observe, Hastings, that the secretary is a dangerous witness. Dangerous because inaccurate. You notice that she stated positively that she saw the visitor's *face?* At the time I thought that impossible. Coming *from* the study—yes, but not going *to* the study. So I made my little experiment, which resulted as *I* thought, and then sprung my trap upon her. She immediately changed her ground."

"Her belief was quite unaltered, though," I argued. "And, after all, a voice and a walk are just as unmistakable."

"No, no."

"Why, Poirot, I think a voice and the general gait are about the most characteristic things about a person."

"I agree. And therefore they are the most easily counterfeited."

"You think—"

"Cast your mind back a few days. Do you remember one evening as we sat in the stalls of a theatre—"

"Carlotta Adams? Ah! but then she is a genius."

"A well-known person is not so difficult to mimic. But I agree she has unusual gifts. I believe she could carry a thing through without the aid of footlights and distance—"

A sudden thought flashed into my mind.

"Poirot," I cried. "You don't think that possibly—no, that would be too much of a coincidence."

"It depends how you look at it, Hastings. Regarded from one angle it would be no coincidence at all."

"But why should Carlotta Adams wish to kill Lord Edgware? She did not even know him."

"How do you know she did not know him? Do not assume things, Hastings. There may have been some link between them of which we know nothing. Not that that is precisely my theory."

"Then you have a theory?"

"Yes. The possibility of Carlotta Adams being involved struck me from the beginning."

"But, Poirot—"

"Wait, Hastings. Let me put together a few facts for you. Lady Edgware, with a complete lack of reticence, discusses the relations between her and her husband, and even goes so far as to talk of killing him. Not only you and I hear this. A waiter hears it, her maid probably has heard it many times, Bryan Martin hears it, and I imagine Carlotta Adams herself hears it. And there are the people to whom these people repeat it. Then, on that same evening, the excellence of Carlotta Adams' imitation of Jane is commented upon. Who had a motive for killing Lord Edgware? His wife.

"Now supposing that someone else wishes to do away with Lord Edgware. Here is a scapegoat ready to his hand. On the day when Jane Wilkinson announces that she has a headache and is going to have a quiet evening—the plan is put into operation.

"Lady Edgware must be seen to enter the house in Regent Gate. Well, she is seen. She even goes so far as to announce her identity. *Ah! c'est un peu trop, ça!* It would awaken suspicion in an oyster.

"And another point—a small point I admit. The woman who came to the house last night wore black. *Jane Wilkinson never wears black.* We heard her say so. Let us assume, then, that the woman who came to the house last night was *not* Jane Wilkinson—that it was a woman impersonating Jane Wilkinson. Did that woman kill Lord Edgware?

"Did a third person enter that house and kill Lord Edgware? If so, did the person enter before or after the supposed visit of Lady Edgware? If after, what did the woman say to Lord Edgware? How did she explain her presence? She might deceive the butler, who did not know her, and the secretary, who did not see her at close quarters, but she could not hope to deceive a husband. Or was there only a dead body in the room? Was Lord Edgware killed *before* she entered the house—some time between nine and ten?"

"Stop, Poirot!" I cried. "You are making my head spin."

"No, no, my friend. We are only considering possibilities. It is like trying on the clothes. Does this fit? No, it wrinkles on the shoulder? This one? Yes, that is better—but not quite large enough. This other one is too small. So on and so on, until we reach the perfect fit—the truth."

"Whom do you suspect of such a fiendish plot?" I asked.

"Ah! that is too early to say. One must go into the question of who has a motive for wishing Lord Edgware dead. There is, of course, the nephew who inherits. A little obvious, that, perhaps. And then, in spite of Miss Carroll's dogmatic pronouncement, there is the question of enemies. Lord Edgware struck me as a man who very easily might make enemies."

"Yes," I agreed. "That is so."

"Whoever it was must have fancied himself pretty safe. Remember, Hastings, but for her change of mind at the last minute, Jane Wilkinson would have had no alibi. She might have been in her room at the Savoy, and it would have been difficult to prove it. She would have been arrested, tried—probably hanged."

I shivered.

"But there is one thing that puzzles me," went on Poirot. "The desire to incriminate her is clear—but what then of the telephone call? Why did someone ring her up at Chiswick and, once satisfied of her presence there, immediately ring off? It looks, does it not, as if someone wanted to be sure of her presence there before proceeding to—what? That was at nine-thirty, almost certainly before the murder. The intention then seems—there is no other word for it—*beneficent.* It *cannot* be the murderer who rings up— the murderer has laid all his plans to incriminate Jane. Who, then, was it? It looks as though we have here two entirely different sets of circumstances."

I shook my head, utterly fogged.

"It might be just a coincidence," I suggested.

"No, no, everything cannot be a coincidence. Six months ago, a letter was suppressed. Why? There are too many things here unexplained. There must be some reason linking them together."

He sighed. Presently he went on:

"That story that Bryan Martin came to tell us—"

"Surely, Poirot, that has got no connection with this business."

"You are blind, Hastings, blind and wilfully obtuse. Do you not see that the whole thing makes a pattern? A pattern confused at present but which will gradually become clear."

I felt Poirot was being over optimistic. I did not feel that anything would ever become clear. My brain was frankly reeling.

"It's no good," I said suddenly. "I can't believe it of Carlotta Adams. She seemed such a—well, such a thoroughly nice girl."

Yet, even as I spoke, I remembered Poirot's words about love of money. Love of money! Was that at the root of the seemingly incomprehensible? I felt that Poirot had been inspired that night. He had seen Jane in danger—

the result of her strange, egoistical temperament. He had seen Carlotta led astray by avarice.

"I do not think she committed the murder, Hastings. She is too cool and level-headed for that. Possibly she was not even told that murder would be done. She may have been used innocently. But then—"

He broke off, frowning.

"Even so, she's an accessory after the fact now. I mean, she will see the news today. She will realize—"

A hoarse sound broke from Poirot.

"Quick, Hastings. Quick! I have been blind—imbecile. A taxi. At once."

I stared at him.

He waved his arms.

"A taxi—at once."

One was passing. He hailed it and we jumped in.

"Do you know her address?"

"Carlotta Adams, do you mean?"

"*Mais oui, mais oui.* Quickly, Hastings, quickly. Every minute is of value."

"No," I said, "I don't."

Poirot swore under his breath.

"The telephone book? No, she would not be in it. The theatre."

At the theatre they were not disposed to give Carlotta's address, but Poirot managed it. It was a flat in a block of mansions near Sloane Square. We drove there, Poirot in a fever of impatience.

"If I am not too late, Hastings. If I am not too late."

"What is all this haste? I don't understand. What does it mean?"

"It means that I have been slow. Terribly slow to realize the obvious. Ah! *mon Dieu,* if only we may be in time."

Chapter IX

THE SECOND DEATH

THOUGH I DID not understand the reason for Poirot's agitation, I knew him well enough to be sure that he had a reason for it.

We arrived at Rosedew Mansions. Poirot sprang out, paid the driver and hurried into the building. Miss Adams' flat was on the first floor, as a visiting card stuck on a board informed us.

Poirot hurried up the stairs not waiting to summon the lift which was at one of the upper floors. He knocked and rang. There was a short delay; then the door was opened by a neat, middle-aged woman with hair drawn tightly back from her face. Her eyelids were reddened as though with weeping.

"Miss Adams?" demanded Poirot eagerly.

The woman looked at him.

"Haven't you heard?"

"Heard? Heard what?"

His face had gone deadly pale, and I realized that this, whatever it was, was what he had feared.

The woman continued slowly to shake her head.

"She's dead. Passed away in her sleep. It's terrible."

Poirot leaned against the doorpost.

"Too late," he murmured.

His agitation was so apparent that the woman looked at him with more attention.

"Excuse me, sir, but are you a friend of hers? I do not remember seeing you come here before?"

Poirot did not reply to this directly. Instead he said:

"You have had a doctor? What did he say?"

"Took an overdose of a sleeping draught. Oh! the pity of it! Such a nice young lady. Nasty dangerous things—these drugs. Veronal, he said it was."

Poirot suddenly stood upright. His manner took on a new authority.

"I must come in," he said.

The woman was clearly doubtful and suspicious.

"I don't think—" she began.

But Poirot meant to have his way. He took probably the only course that would have obtained the desired result.

"You must let me in," he said. "I am a detective and I have got to inquire into the circumstances of your mistress's death."

The woman gasped. She stood aside and we passed into the flat. From there on Poirot took command of the situation.

"What I have told you," he said authoritatively, "is strictly confidential. It must not be repeated. Everyone must continue to think that Miss Adams' death was accidental. Please give me the name and address of the doctor you summoned."

"Dr. Heath, Seventeen Carlisle Street."

"And your own name?"

"Bennett—Alice Bennett."

"You were attached to Miss Adams, I can see, Miss Bennett."

"Oh! yes, sir. She were a nice young lady. I worked for her last year when she were over here. It wasn't as though she were one of those actresses. She were a real young lady. Dainty ways she had and liked everything just so."

Poirot listened with attention and sympathy. He had now no signs of impatience. I realized that to proceed gently was the best way of extracting the information he wanted.

"It must have been a great shock to you," he observed gently.

"Oh! it was, sir. I took her in her tea—at half past nine as usual—and there she was lying, asleep I thought. And I put the tray down. And I pulled the curtains. One of the rings caught, sir, and I had to jerk it hard. Such a noise it made. I was surprised when I looked round to see she hadn't woken. And then all of a sudden something seemed to take hold of me. Something not quite natural about the way she lay. And I went to the side of the bed, and I touched her hand. Icy cold it was, sir, and I cried out."

She stopped, tears coming into her eyes.

"Yes, yes," said Poirot sympathetically. "It must have been terrible for you. Did Miss Adams often take stuff to make her sleep?"

"She'd take something for a headache now and again, sir—some little tablets in a bottle—but it was some other stuff she took last night, or so the doctor said."

"Did anyone come to see her last night? A visitor?"

"No, sir. She was out yesterday evening, sir."

"Did she tell you where she was going?"

"No, sir. She went out about seven o'clock."

"Ah! How was she dressed?"

"She had on a black dress, sir. A black dress and a black hat."

Poirot looked at me.

"Did she wear any jewellery?"

"Just the string of pearls she always wore, sir."

"And gloves—grey gloves?"

"Yes, sir. Her gloves were grey."

"Ah! Now describe to me, if you will, what her manner was. Was she gay? Excited? Sad? Nervous?"

"It seemed to me she was pleased about something, sir. She kept smiling to herself, as though there were some kind of joke on."

"What time did she return?"

"A little after twelve o'clock, sir."

"And what was her manner then? The same?"

"She was terribly tired, sir."

"But not upset? Or distressed?"

"Oh! no, sir. I think she was pleased about something, but just done up, if you know what I mean. She started to ring someone up on the telephone, and then she said she couldn't bother. She'd do it tomorrow morning."

"Ah!" Poirot's eyes gleamed with excitement. He leaned forward and spoke in a would-be indifferent voice.

"Did you hear the name of the person she rang up?"

"No, sir. She just asked for the number and waited and then the Exchange must have said, 'I'm trying to get them,' as they do, sir, and she said, 'All right,' and then suddenly she yawned and said, 'Oh! I can't bother. I'm too tired,' and she put the receiver back and started undressing."

"And the number she called? Do you recollect that? Think. It may be important."

"I'm sorry I can't say, sir. It was a Victoria number, and that's all I can remember I wasn't paying special heed, you see."

"Did she have anything to eat or drink before she went to bed?"

"A glass of hot milk, sir, like she always did."

"Who prepared it?"

"I did, sir."

"And nobody came to the flat that evening?"

"Nobody, sir."

"And earlier in the day?"

"Nobody came that I can remember, sir. Miss Adams was out to lunch and tea. She came in at six o'clock."

"When did the milk come? The milk she drank last night?"

"It was the new milk she had, sir. The afternoon delivery. The boy leaves it outside the door at four o'clock. But oh! sir, I'm sure there wasn't nothing wrong with the milk. I had it myself for tea this morning. And the doctor he said positive as she'd taken the nasty stuff herself."

"It is possible that I am wrong," said Poirot. "Yes, it is possible that I am entirely wrong. I will see the doctor. But, you see, Miss Adams had enemies. Things are very different in America—"

He hesitated, but the good Alice leapt at the bait.

"Oh! I know, sir, I've read about them gunmen and all that. It must be a wicked country; and what the police can be about, I can't think. Not like our policemen."

Poirot left it thankfully at that, realizing that Alice Bennett's insular proclivities would save him the trouble of explanations.

His eye fell on a small suitcase, more of an attaché case, that was lying on a chair.

"Did Miss Adams take that with her when she went out last night?"

"In the morning she took it, sir. She didn't have it when she came back at tea time, but she brought it back last thing."

"Ah! you permit that I open it?"

Alice Bennett would have permitted anything. Like most canny and suspicious women, once she had overcome her distrust she was child's play to manipulate. She would have assented to anything Poirot suggested.

The case was not locked. Poirot opened it. I came forward and looked over his shoulder.

"You see, Hastings, you see?" he murmured excitedly.

The contents were certainly suggestive.

There was a box of make-up materials, two objects which I recognized as elevators to place in shoes and raise the height an inch or so, there was a pair of grey gloves and, folded in tissue paper, an exquisitely made wig of golden hair, the exact shade of gold of Jane Wilkinson's, and dressed like hers, with a centre parting and curls in the back of the neck.

"Do you doubt now, Hastings?" asked Poirot.

I believe I had up to that moment. But now I doubted no longer.

Poirot closed the case again and turned to the maid.

"You do not know with whom Miss Adams dined yesterday evening?"

"No, sir."

"Do you know with whom she had lunch or tea?"

"I know nothing about tea, sir. I believe she lunched with Miss Driver."

"Miss Driver?"

"Yes, her great friend. She has a hat shop in Moffatt Street, just off Bond Street. Genevieve, it's called."

Poirot noted the address in his notebook, just below that of the doctor.

"One thing more, madame. Can you remember anything—*anything at all*—that Mademoiselle Adams said or did, after she came in at six o'clock, that strikes you as at all unusual or significant?"

The maid thought for a moment or two.

"I really can't say that I do, sir," she said at last. "I asked her if she would have tea and she said she'd had some."

"Oh! she said she had had it," interrupted Poirot. "Pardon. Continue."

"And after that she was writing letters till just on the time she went out."

"Letters, eh? You do not know to whom?"

"Yes, sir. It was just one letter—to her sister in Washington. She wrote her sister twice a week regular. She took the letter out with her to post because of catching the mail. But she forgot to post it."

"Then it is here still?"

"No, sir. I posted it. She remembered last night just as she was getting into bed. And I said I'd run out with it. By putting an extra stamp on it and putting it in the late fee box it would go all right."

"Ah! And is that far?"

"No, sir, the post office is just round the corner."

"Did you shut the door of the flat behind you?"

Bennett stared.

"No, sir. I just left it to—as I always do when I go out to post."

Poirot seemed about to speak. Then he checked himself.

"Would you like to look at her, sir?" asked the maid tearfully. "Looks beautiful she does."

We followed her into the bedroom.

Carlotta Adams looked strangely peaceful and much younger than she had appeared that night at the Savoy. She looked like a tired child asleep.

There was a strange expression on Poirot's face as he stood looking down on her. I saw him make the sign of the Cross.

"*J'ai fait un serment,* Hastings," he said as we went down the stairs.

I did not ask him what his vow was. I could guess. A minute or two later he said:

"There is one thing off my mind at least. I could not have saved her. By the time I heard of Lord Edgware's death she was already dead. That comforts me. Yes, that comforts me very much."

Chapter X

JENNY DRIVER

OUR NEXT PROCEEDING was to call upon the doctor whose address the maid had given us.

He turned out to be a fussy elderly man somewhat vague in manner. He knew Poirot by repute and expressed a lively pleasure at meeting him in the flesh.

"And what can I do for you, M. Poirot?" he asked after this opening preamble.

"You were called this morning, M. le docteur, to the bedside of a Miss Carlotta Adams."

"Ah! yes, poor girl. Clever actress too. I've been twice to her show. A thousand pities it's ended this way. Why these girls must have drugs, I can't think."

"You think she was addicted to drugs, then?"

"Well, professionally, I should hardly have said so. At all events she didn't take them hypodermically. No marks of the needle. Evidently always took it by the mouth. Maid said she slept well naturally, but then maids never know. I don't suppose she took veronal every night, but she'd evidently taken it for some time."

"What makes you think so?"

"This. Dash it—where did I put the thing?"

He was peering into a small case.

"Ah! here it is."

He drew out a small black morocco handbag.

"There's got to be an inquest, of course. I brought this away so that the maid shouldn't meddle with it."

Opening the pochette he took out a small gold box. On it were the initials C. A. in rubies. It was a valuable and expensive trinket. The doctor opened it. It was nearly full of a white powder.

"Veronal," he explained briefly. "Now look what's written inside."

On the inside of the lid of the box was engraved:

C. A. from D.   Paris, Nov. 10th.
Sweet Dreams.

"November 10th," said Poirot thoughtfully.

"Exactly, and we're now in June. That seems to show that she's been in the habit of taking the stuff for at least six months; and, as the year isn't given, it might be eighteen months or two years and a half—or any time."

"Paris. D," said Poirot, frowning.

"Yes. Convey anything to you? By the way, I haven't asked you what your interest is in the case. I'm assuming you've got good grounds. I suppose you want to know if it's suicide? Well, I can't tell you. Nobody can. According to the maid's account, she was perfectly cheerful yesterday. That looks like accident, and in my opinion accident it is. Veronal's very uncertain stuff. You can take a devil of a lot and it won't kill you, and you can take very little and off you go. It's a dangerous drug for that reason. I've no doubt they'll bring it in accidental death at the inquest. I'm afraid I can't be of any more help to you."

"May I examine the little bag of mademoiselle?"

"Certainly. Certainly."

Poirot turned out the contents of the pochette. There was a fine handkerchief with C. M. A. in the corner, a powder puff, a lipstick, a pound note and a little change, and a pair of pince-nez.

These last Poirot examined with interest. They were gold-rimmed and rather severe and academic in type.

"Curious," said Poirot. "I did not know that Miss Adams wore glasses. But perhaps they are for reading?"

The doctor picked them up.

"No, these are outdoor glasses," he affirmed. "Pretty powerful too. The person who wore these must have been very short-sighted."

"You do not know if Miss Adams—"

"I never attended her before. I was called in once to see a poisoned finger of the maid's. Otherwise I have never been in the flat. Miss Adams, whom I saw for a moment on that occasion, was certainly not wearing glasses then."

Poirot thanked the doctor and we took our leave.

Poirot wore a puzzled expression.

"It can be that I am mistaken," he admitted.

"About the impersonation?"

"No, no. That seems to me proved. No, I mean as to her death. Obviously she had veronal in her possession. It is possible that she was tired and strung up last night and determined to ensure herself a good night's rest."

Then he suddenly stopped dead—to the great surprise of the passers-by —and beat one hand emphatically on the other.

"No, no, no, no!" he declared emphatically. "Why should that accident happen so conveniently? It was no accident. It was not suicide. No, she played her part and in doing so she signed her death warrant. Veronal may have been chosen simply because it was known that she occasionally took it and that she had that box in her possession. But if so, the murderer must have been someone who knew her well. Who is D, Hastings? I would give a good deal to know who D was."

"Poirot," I said, as he remained wrapt in thought, "hadn't we better go on? Everyone is staring at us."

"Eh? Well, perhaps you are right. Though it does not incommode me that people should stare. It does not interfere in the least with my train of thought."

"People were beginning to laugh," I murmured.

"That has no importance."

I did not quite agree. I have a horror of doing anything conspicuous. The only thing that affects Poirot is the possibility of the damp or the heat affecting the set of his famous moustache.

"We will take a taxi," said Poirot, waving his stick.

One drew up by us, and Poirot directed it to go to Genevieve in Moffatt Street.

Genevieve turned out to be one of those establishments where one non-descript hat and a scarf display themselves in a glass box downstairs and where the real centre of operations is one floor up a flight of musty-smelling stairs.

Having climbed the stairs we came to a door with "Genevieve. Please Walk In" on it, and, having obeyed this command, we found ourselves in a small room full of hats while an imposing blonde creature came forward with a suspicious glance at Poirot.

"Miss Driver?" asked Poirot.

"I do not know if modom can see you. What is your business, please?"

"Please tell Miss Driver that a friend of Miss Adams would like to see her."

The blonde beauty had no need to go on this errand. A black velvet curtain was violently agitated and a small vivacious creature with flaming red hair emerged.

"What's that?" she demanded.

"Are you Miss Driver?"

"Yes. What's that about Carlotta?"

"You have heard the sad news?"

"What sad news?"

"Miss Adams died in her sleep last night. An overdose of veronal."

The girl's eyes opened wide.

"How awful!" she exclaimed. "Poor Carlotta. I can hardly believe it. Why, she was full of life yesterday."

"Nevertheless it is true, mademoiselle," said Poirot. "Now see—it is just on one o'clock. I want you to do me the honour of coming out to lunch with me and my friend. I want to ask you several questions."

The girl looked him up and down. She was a pugilistic little creature. She reminded me in some ways of a fox terrier.

"Who are you?" she demanded bluntly.

"My name is Hercule Poirot. This is my friend Captain Hastings."

I bowed.

Her glance travelled from one to the other of us.

"I've heard of you," she said abruptly. "I'll come."

She called to the blonde:

"Dorothy?"

"Yes, Jenny."

"Mrs. Lester's coming in about that Rose Descartes model we're making for her. Try the different feathers. By by, shan't be long, I expect."

She picked up a small black hat, affixed it to one ear, powdered her nose furiously, and then looked at Poirot.

"Ready," she said abruptly.

Five minutes afterward, we were sitting in a small restaurant in Dover Street. Poirot had given an order to the waiter and cocktails were in front of us.

"Now," said Jenny Driver. "I want to know the meaning of all this? What has Carlotta been getting herself mixed up in?"

"She had been getting herself mixed up in something then, mademoiselle?"

"Now then, who is going to ask the questions, you or me?"

"My idea was that I should," said Poirot, smiling. "I have been given to understand that you and Miss Adams were great friends."

"Right."

"Eh bien, then I ask you, mademoiselle, to accept my solemn assurance that, what I do, I am doing in the interests of your dead friend. I assure you that that is so."

There was a moment's silence while Jenny Driver considered this question. Finally she gave a quick assenting nod of the head.

"I believe you. Carry on. What do you want to know?"

"I understand, mademoiselle, that your friend lunched with you yesterday."

"She did."

"Did she tell you what her plans were for last night?"

"She didn't exactly mention last night."

"But she said something?"

"Well, she mentioned something that maybe is what you're driving at. Mind you, she spoke in confidence."

"That is understood."

"Well, let me see now. I think I'd better explain things in my own words."

"If you please, mademoiselle."

"Well, then. Carlotta was excited. She isn't often excited. She's not that kind. She wouldn't tell me anything definite, said she'd promised not to, but she'd got something on—something, I gathered, in the nature of a gigantic hoax."

"A hoax?"

"That's what she said. She didn't say how or when or where. Only—" She paused, frowning. "Well—you see—Carlotta's not the kind of person who enjoys practical jokes or hoaxes or things of that kind. She's one of those serious, nice-minded, hard-working girls. What I mean is somebody had obviously put her up to this stunt. And I think—she didn't say so, mind—"

"No, no, I quite understand. What was it that you thought?"

"I thought—I was sure—that in some way money was concerned. Nothing really ever excited Carlotta except money. She was made that way. She'd got one of the best heads for business I've ever met. She wouldn't have been so excited and so pleased unless money—quite a lot of money—had been concerned. My impression was that she'd taken on something for a bet, and that she was pretty sure of winning. And yet that isn't quite true. I mean, Carlotta didn't bet. I've never known her make a bet. But anyway, somehow or other, I'm sure money was concerned."

"She did not actually say so?"

"N-n-o. Just said that she'd be able to do this, that and the other in the near future. She was going to get her sister over from America to meet her in Paris. She was crazy about her little sister. Very delicate, I believe, and musical. Well, that's all I know. Is that what you want?"

Poirot nodded his head.

"Yes. It confirms my theory. I had hoped, I admit, for more. I had anticipated that Miss Adams would have been bound to secrecy. But I hoped that, being a woman, she would not have counted revealing the secret to her best friend."

"I tried to make her tell me," admitted Jenny, "but she only laughed and said she'd tell me all about it some day."

Poirot was silent for a moment. Then he said:

"You know the name of Lord Edgware?"

"What? The man who was murdered? On a poster half an hour ago."

"Yes. Do you know if Miss Adams was acquainted with him?"

"I don't think so. I'm sure she wasn't. Oh! wait a minute."

"Yes, mademoiselle?" said Poirot eagerly.

"What was it now?" she frowned, knitting her brow as she tried to remember. "Yes, I've got it now. She mentioned him once. Very bitterly."

"Bitterly?"

"Yes. She said—what was it?—that men like that shouldn't be allowed to ruin other people's lives by their cruelty and lack of understanding. She said—why, so she did—that he was the kind of man whose death would probably be a good thing for everybody."

"When was it she said this, mademoiselle?"

"Oh! about a month ago, I think it was."

"How did the subject come up?"

Jenny Driver racked her brains for some minutes and finally shook her head.

"I can't remember," she confessed. "His name cropped up or something. It might have been in the newspaper. Anyway, I remember thinking it odd that Carlotta should be so vehement all of a sudden when she didn't even know the man."

"Certainly it is odd," agreed Poirot thoughtfully. Then he asked:

"Do you know if Miss Adams was in the habit of taking veronal?"

"Not that I knew. I never saw her take it or mention taking it."

"Did you ever see in her bag a small gold box with the initials C. A. on it in rubies?"

"A small gold box—no, I am sure I didn't."

"Do you happen to know where Miss Adams was last November?"

"Let me see. She went back to the States in November, I think—towards the end of the month. Before that she was in Paris."

"Alone?"

"Alone of course! Sorry—perhaps you didn't mean that! I don't know why any mention of Paris always suggests the worst. And it's such a nice respectable place really. But Carlotta wasn't the week-ending sort, if that's what you're driving at."

"Now, mademoiselle, I am going to ask you a very important question. Was there any man Miss Adams was specially interested in?"

"The answer to that is 'No,' " said Jenny slowly. "Carlotta, since I've known her, has been wrapped up in her work and in her delicate sister. She's had the 'head of the family all depends on me' attitude very strongly. So the answer's No—strictly speaking."

"Ah! and not speaking so strictly?"

"I shouldn't wonder if—lately—Carlotta hadn't been getting interested in some man."

"Ah!"

"Mind you, that's entirely guesswork on my part. I've gone simply by her manner. She's been—different—not exactly dreamy, but abstracted. And she's looked different somehow. Oh! I can't explain. It's the sort of thing that another woman just feels, and of course may be quite wrong about."

Poirot nodded.

"Thank you, mademoiselle. One thing more. Is there any friend of Miss Adams whose initial is D?"

"D," said Jenny Driver thoughtfully. "D? No, I'm sorry, I can't think of anyone."

Chapter XI

I DO NOT think Poirot had expected any other answer to his question. All the same he shook his head sadly. He remained lost in thought. Jenny Driver leant forward, her elbows on the table.

"And now," she said, "am I going to be told anything?"

"Mademoiselle," said Poirot, "first of all let me compliment you. Your answers to my questions have been singularly intelligent. Clearly you have brains, mademoiselle. You ask whether I am going to tell you anything. I answer—not very much. I will tell you just a few bare facts, mademoiselle."

He paused, and then said quietly:

"Last night Lord Edgware was murdered in his library. At ten o'clock yesterday evening a lady, whom I believe to have been your friend Miss Adams, came to the house, asked to see Lord Edgware, and announced herself as Lady Edgware. She wore a golden wig and was made up to resemble the real Lady Edgware who, as you probably know, is Miss Jane Wilkinson the actress. Miss Adams (if it were she) only remained a few moments. She left the house at five minutes past ten but she did not return home till after midnight. She went to bed, having taken an overdose of veronal. Now, mademoiselle, you see the point, perhaps, of some of the questions I have been asking you."

Jenny drew a deep breath.

"Yes," she said. "I see now. I believe you're right, M. Poirot. Right about its having been Carlotta, I mean. For one thing she bought a new hat off me yesterday."

"A new hat?"

"Yes. She said she wanted one to shade the left side of her face."

Here I must insert a few words of explanation, as I do not know when these words will be read. I have seen many fashions of hats in my time— the cloche that shaded the face so completely that one gave up in despair the task of recognizing one's friends. The tilted forward hat, the hat attached airily to the back of the head, the beret, and many other styles. In this particular June the hat of the moment was shaped like an inverted soup plate and was worn attached (as if by suction) over one ear, leaving the other side of the face and hair open to inspection.

"These hats are usually worn on the right side of the head?" asked Poirot.

The little modiste nodded.

"But we keep a few to be worn on the opposite side," she explained, "because there are people who much prefer their right profile to the left or who have a habit of parting the hair on one side only. Now would there be any special reason for Carlotta's wanting that side of her face to be in shadow?"

I remembered that the door of the house in Regent Gate opened to the left, so that anyone entering would be in full view of the butler that side. I remembered also that Jane Wilkinson (so I had noticed the other night) had a tiny mole at the corner of the left eye. I said as much, excitedly. Poirot agreed, nodding his head vigorously.

"It is so. It is so. *Vous avez parfaitement raison,* Hastings. Yes, that explains the purchase of the hat."

"M. Poirot?" Jenny sat suddenly bolt upright. "You don't think—you don't for one moment think—that Carlotta did it? Killed him, I mean. You can't think that? Not just because she spoke so bitterly about him."

"I do not think so, but it is curious all the same—that she should have spoken so, I mean. I would like to know the reason for it. What had he done—what did she know of him to make her speak in such a fashion?"

"I don't know, but she didn't kill him. She's—oh! she was—well—too refined."

Poirot nodded approvingly.

"Yes, yes. You put that very well. It is a point psychological. I agree. This was a scientific crime, but not a refined one."

"Scientific?"

"The murderer knew exactly where to strike so as to reach the vital nerve centres at the base of the skull where it joins the spinal cord."

"Looks like a doctor," said Jenny thoughtfully.

"Did Miss Adams know any doctors? I mean was any particular doctor a friend of hers?"

Jenny shook her head.

"Never heard of one. Not over here, anyway."

"Another question. Did Miss Adams wear pince-nez?"

"Glasses? Never."

"Ah!" Poirot frowned.

A vision rose in my mind. A doctor, smelling of carbolic, with short-sighted eyes magnified by powerful lenses. Absurd!

"By the way, did Miss Adams know Bryan Martin, the film actor?"

"Why, yes. She used to know him as a child, she told me. I don't think she saw much of him, though. Just once in a while. She told me she thought he'd got very swollen headed."

She looked at her watch and uttered an exclamation.

"Goodness, I must fly. Have I helped you at all, M. Poirot?"

"You have. I shall ask you for further help by and by."

"It's yours. Someone staged this deviltry. We've got to find out who it is."

She gave us a quick shake of the hand, flashed her white teeth in a sudden smile and left us with characteristic abruptness.

"An interesting personality," said Poirot as he paid the bill.

"I like her," I said.

"It is always a pleasure to meet a quick mind."

"A little hard, perhaps," I reflected. "The shock of her friend's death did not upset her as much as I should have thought it would have done."

"She is not the sort that weeps, certainly," agreed Poirot dryly.

"Did you get what you hoped from the interview?"

He shook his head.

"No. I hoped—very much I hoped—to get a clue to the personality of D, the person who gave her the little gold box. There I have failed. Unfortunately Carlotta Adams was a reserved girl. She was not one to gossip about her friends or her possible love affairs. On the other hand, the person who suggested the hoax may not have been a friend at all. It may have been a mere acquaintance who proposed it—doubtless for some 'sporting' reason—on a money basis. This person may have seen the gold box she carried about with her and made some opportunity to discover what it contained."

"But how on earth did they get her to take it? And when?"

"Well, there was the time during which the flat door was open, when the maid was out posting a letter. Not that that satisfies me. It leaves too much to chance. But now—to work. We have still two possible clues."

"Which are?"

"The first is the telephone call to a Victoria number. It seems to me quite a probability that Carlotta Adams would ring up on her return to announce her success. On the other hand, where was she between five minutes past ten and midnight? She may have had an appointment with the instigator of the hoax. In that case the telephone call may have been merely one to a friend."

"What is the second clue?"

"Ah! that I do have hopes of. The letter, Hastings. The letter to the sister. It is possible—I only say possible—that in that she may have described the whole business. She would not regard it as a breach of faith, since the letter would not be read till a week later and in another country at that."

"Amazing, if that is so!"

"We must not build too much upon it, Hastings. It is a chance, that is all. No, we must work now from the other end."

"What do you call the other end?"

"A careful study of those who profit in any degree by Lord Edgware's death."

I shrugged my shoulders.

"Apart from his nephew and his wife—"

"And the man the wife wanted to marry," added Poirot.

"The Duke? He is in Paris."

"Quite so. But you cannot deny that he is an interested party. Then there are the people in the house—the butler, the servants. Who knows what grudges they may have had? But I think myself our first point of attack should be a further interview with Mademoiselle Jane Wilkinson. She is shrewd. She may be able to suggest something."

Once more we made our way to the Savoy. We found the lady surrounded by boxes and tissue paper, while exquisite black draperies were strewn over the back of every chair. Jane had a rapt and serious expression and was just trying on yet another small black hat before the glass.

"Why, M. Poirot. Sit down. That is, if there's anything to sit on. Ellis, clear something, will you?"

"Madame, you look charming."

Jane looked serious.

"I don't want exactly to play the hypocrite, M. Poirot, but one must observe appearances, don't you think? I mean, I think I ought to be careful. Oh! by the way, I've had the sweetest telegram from the Duke."

"From Paris?"

"Yes, from Paris. Guarded, of course, and supposed to be condolences but put so that I can read between the lines."

"My felicitations, madame."

"M. Poirot." She clasped her hands; her husky voice dropped. She looked like an angel about to give event to thoughts of exquisite holiness. "I've been thinking. It all seems so *miraculous,* if you know what I mean. Here I am—all my troubles over. No tiresome business of divorce. No bothers. Just my path cleared and all plain sailing. It makes me feel almost religious—if you know what I mean."

I held my breath. Poirot looked at her, his head a little on one side. She was quite serious.

"That is how it strikes you, madame, eh?"

"Things happen right for me," said Jane in a sort of awed whisper. "I've thought and I've thought lately—if Edgware was to die. And there—he's dead! It's—it's almost like an answer to prayer."

Poirot cleared his throat.

"I cannot say I look at it quite like that, madame. Somebody killed your husband."

She nodded.

"Why of course."

"Has it not occurred to you to wonder who that someone was?"

She stared at him.

"Does it matter? I mean—what's that to do with it? The Duke and I can be married in about four or five months."

With difficulty Poirot controlled himself.

"Yes, madame, I know that. But apart from that has it not occurred to you to ask yourself *who killed your husband?*"

"No." She seemed quite surprised by the idea. We could see her thinking about it.

"Does it not interest you to know?" asked Poirot.

"Not very much, I'm afraid," she admitted. "I suppose the police will find out. They're very clever, aren't they?"

"So it is said. I, too, am going to make it my business to find out."

"Are you? How funny."

"Why funny?"

"Well, I don't know." Her eyes strayed back to the clothes. She slipped on a satin coat and studied herself in the glass.

"You do not object, eh?" said Poirot, his eyes twinkling.

"Why, of course not, M. Poirot. I should just love you to be clever about it all. I wish you every success."

"Madame, I want your more than wishes. I want your opinion."

"Opinion?" said Jane absently, as she twisted her head over her shoulder. "What on?"

"Who do you think likely to have killed Lord Edgware?"

Jane shook her head.

"I haven't any idea."

She wriggled her shoulders experimentally and took up the hand glass.

"Madame!" said Poirot in a loud emphatic voice. "WHO DO *YOU* THINK KILLED YOUR HUSBAND?"

This time it got through. Jane threw him a startled glance.

"Geraldine, I expect," she said.

"Who is Geraldine?"

But Jane's attention had gone again.

"Ellis, take this up a little on the right shoulder. So. What, M. Poirot? Geraldine's his daughter. No, Ellis, the *right* shoulder. That's better. Oh! must you go, M. Poirot? I'm terribly grateful for everything. I mean, for the divorce, even though it isn't necessary after all. I shall always think you were wonderful."

I saw Jane Wilkinson only twice again—once on the stage, once when I sat opposite her at a luncheon party. I always think of her as I saw her then, absorbed heart and soul in clothes, her lips carelessly throwing out the words that were to influence Poirot's further actions, her mind concentrated firmly and beatifically on herself.

"*Épatant,*" said Poirot with reverence as we emerged into the Strand.

Chapter XII

THERE WAS A letter sent by hand lying on the table when we got back to our rooms. Poirot picked it up, slit it open with his usual neatness and then laughed.

"What is it you say—'Talk of the devil'? See here, Hastings."

I took the note from him.

The paper was stamped 17 Regent Gate and was written in very upright, characteristic handwriting which looked easy to read and curiously enough was not.

Dear Sir, [it ran]

I hear you were at the house this morning with the Inspector. I am sorry not to have had the opportunity of speaking to you. If convenient to yourself I should be much obliged if you could spare me a few minutes any time this afternoon.

Yours truly,
Geraldine Marsh.

"Curious," I said. "I wonder why she wants to see you?"

"Is it curious that she should want to see me? You are not polite, my friend."

Poirot has the most irritating habit of joking at the wrong moment.

"We will go round at once, my friend," he said; and, lovingly brushing an imagined speck of dust from his hat, he put it on his head.

Jane Wilkinson's careless suggestion that Geraldine might have killed her father seemed to me particularly absurd. Only a particularly brainless person could have suggested it. I said as much to Poirot.

"Brains. Brains. What do we really mean by the term? In your idiom you would say that Jane Wilkinson has the brains of the rabbit. That is a term of disparagement. But consider the rabbit for a moment. He exists and multiplies, does he not? That, in nature, is a sign of mental superiority.

The lovely Lady Edgware she does not know history, or geography, or the classics *sans doute*. The name of Lao Tse would suggest to her a prize Pekingese dog, the name of Molière a *maison de couture*. But when it comes to choosing clothes, to making rich and advantageous marriages, and to getting her own way—her success is phenomenal. The opinion of a philosopher as to who murdered Lord Edgware would be no good to me; the motive for murder, from a philosopher's point of view, would be the greatest good of the greatest number, and, as that is difficult to decide, few philosophers are murderers. But a careless opinion from Lady Edgware *might* be useful to me, because her point of view would be materialistic and based on a knowledge of the worst side of human nature."

"Perhaps there's something in that," I conceded.

"Nous voici," said Poirot. "I am curious to know why the young lady wishes so urgently to see me."

"It is a natural desire," I said, getting my own back. "You said so a quarter of an hour ago. The natural desire to see something unique at close quarters."

"Perhaps it is you, my friend, who made an impression on her heart the other day," replied Poirot as he rang the bell.

I recalled the startled face of the girl who had stood in the doorway. I could still see those burning dark eyes in the white face. That momentary glimpse had made a great impression on me.

We were shown upstairs to a big drawing-room and in a minute or two Geraldine Marsh came to us there. The impression of intensity which I had noticed before was heightened on this occasion. This tall, thin, white-faced girl, with her big haunting black eyes, was a striking figure. She was extremely composed—in view of her youth, remarkably so.

"It is very good of you to come so promptly, M. Poirot," she said. "I am sorry to have missed you this morning."

"You were lying down?"

"Yes. Miss Carroll—my father's secretary, you know—insisted. She has been very kind."

There was a queer grudging note in the girl's voice that puzzled me.

"In what way can I be of service to you, mademoiselle?" asked Poirot.

She hesitated a minute and then said:

"On the day before my father was killed you came to see him?"

"Yes, mademoiselle."

"Why? Did he—send for you?"

Poirot did not reply for a moment. He seemed to be deliberating. I believe, now, that it was a cleverly calculated move on his part. He wanted to goad her into further speech. She was, he realized, of the impatient type. She wanted things in a hurry.

"Was he afraid of something? Tell me! Tell me! I must know. Who was he afraid of? Why? What did he say to you? Oh! why can't you speak?"

I had thought that that forced composure was not natural. It had soon broken down. She was leaning forward now, her hands twisting themselves nervously on her lap.

"What passed between Lord Edgware and myself was in confidence," said Poirot slowly.

His eyes never left her face.

"Then it was about—I mean, it must have been something to do with—the family. Oh! you sit there and torture me. Why won't you tell me? It's necessary for me to know. It's necessary, I tell you."

Again, very slowly, Poirot shook his head, apparently a prey to deep perplexity.

"M. Poirot." She drew herself up. "I'm his daughter. It is my right to know—what my father dreaded on the last day but one of his life. It isn't fair to leave me in the dark. It isn't fair to him—not to tell me."

"Were you so devoted to your father, then, mademoiselle?" asked Poirot gently.

She drew back as though stung.

"Fond of him?" she whispered. "Fond of him. I—I—"

And suddenly her self-control snapped. Peals of laughter broke from her. She lay back in her chair and laughed and laughed.

"It's so funny," she gasped. "It's so funny—to be asked that."

That hysterical laughter had not passed unheard. The door opened and Miss Carroll came in. She was firm and efficient.

"Now, now, Geraldine, my dear, that won't do. No, no. Hush, now. I insist. No. Stop it! I mean it. Stop it at once!"

Her determined manner had its effect. Geraldine's laughter grew fainter. She wiped her eyes and sat up.

"I'm sorry," she said in a low voice. "I've never done that before."

Miss Carroll was still looking at her anxiously.

"I'm all right now, Miss Carroll. It was idiotic."

She smiled suddenly, a queer bitter smile that twisted her lips. She sat up very straight in her chair and looked at no one.

"He asked me," she said in a cold, clear voice, "if I had been very fond of my father."

Miss Carroll made a sort of indeterminate cluck. It denoted irresolution on her part. Geraldine went on, her voice high and scornful:

"I wonder if it is better to tell lies or the truth? The truth, I think. I wasn't fond of my father. I hated him!"

"Geraldine dear."

"Why pretend? You didn't hate him, because he couldn't touch you!

You were one of the few people in the world that he couldn't get at. You saw him as the employer who paid you so much a year. His rages and his queernesses didn't interest you. You ignored them. I know what you'd say: 'Everyone has got to put up with something.' You were cheerful and uninterested. You're a very strong woman. You're not really human. But then you could have walked out of the house any minute. I couldn't. I belonged."

"Really, Geraldine, I don't think it's necessary going into all this. Fathers and daughters often don't get on, but the less said in life the better, I've found."

Geraldine turned her back on her. She addressed herself to Poirot.

"M. Poirot, I *hated* my father! I am glad he is dead! It means freedom for me—freedom and independence. I am not in the least anxious to find his murderer. For all we know the person who killed him may have had reasons—ample reasons—justifying that action."

Poirot looked at her thoughtfully.

"That is a dangerous principle to adopt, mademoiselle."

"Will hanging someone else bring Father back to life?"

"No," said Poirot dryly, "but it may save other innocent people from being murdered."

"I don't understand."

"A person who has once killed, mademoiselle, nearly always kills again —sometimes again and again."

"I don't believe it. Not—not a real person."

"You mean—not a homicidal maniac? But yes, it is true. One life is removed—perhaps after a terrific struggle with the murderer's conscience. Then—danger threatens. The second murder is morally easier. At the slightest threatening of suspicion, a third follows. And little by little an artistic pride arises; it is a *métier*—to kill. It is done at last almost for pleasure."

The girl had hidden her face in her hands.

"Horrible! Horrible! It isn't true."

"And supposing I told you that it *had already happened?* That already —to save himself—*the murderer has killed a second time?*"

"What's that, M. Poirot?" cried Miss Carroll. "Another murder? Where? Who?"

Poirot gently shook his head.

"It was an illustration only. I ask pardon."

"Oh! I see. For a moment I really thought— Now, Geraldine, if you've finished talking arrant nonsense—"

"You are on my side, I see," said Poirot with a little bow.

"I don't believe in capital punishment," said Miss Carroll briskly. "Otherwise I am certainly on your side. Society must be protected."

Geraldine got up. She smoothed back her hair.

"I am sorry," she said. "I am afraid I have been making rather a fool of myself. You still refuse to tell me why my father called you in?"

"Called him in?" said Miss Carroll in lively astonishment.

"You misunderstand, Miss Marsh. I have not refused to tell you."

Poirot was forced to come out into the open.

"I was only considering how far that interview might have been said to be confidential. Your father did not call me in. *I* sought an interview with *him* on behalf of a client. That client was Lady Edgware."

"Oh! I see."

An extraordinary expression came over the girl's face. I thought at first it was disappointment. Then I saw it was relief.

"I have been very foolish," she said slowly. "I thought my father had perhaps thought himself menaced by some danger. It was stupid."

"You know, M. Poirot, you gave me quite a turn just now," said Miss Carroll, "when you suggested that woman had done a second murder."

Poirot did not answer her. He spoke to the girl.

"Do you believe Lady Edgware committed the murder, mademoiselle?"

She shook her head.

"No, I don't. I can't see her doing a thing like that. She's much too—well, artificial."

"I don't see who else can have done it," said Miss Carroll, "and I don't think women of that kind have got any moral sense."

"It needn't have been her," argued Geraldine. "She may have come here and just had an interview with him and gone away, and the real murderer may have been some lunatic who got in afterward."

"All murderers are mentally deficient—of that I am assured," said Miss Carroll. "Internal gland secretion."

At that moment the door opened and a man came in—then stopped awkwardly.

"Sorry," he said. "I didn't know anyone was in here."

Geraldine made a mechanical introduction.

"My cousin, Lord Edgware. M. Poirot. It's all right, Ronald. You're not interrupting."

"Sure, Dina? How do you do, M. Poirot? Are your grey cells functioning over our particular family mystery?"

I cast my mind back trying to remember. That round, pleasant, vacuous face, the eyes with slight pouches underneath them, the little moustache marooned like an island in the middle of the expanse of face.

Of course! It was Carlotta Adams' escort on the night of the supper party in Jane Wilkinson's suite.

Captain Ronald Marsh. Now Lord Edgware.

Chapter XIII

THE NEPHEW

THE NEW LORD Edgware's eye was a quick one. He noticed the slight start I gave.

"Ah! you've got it," he said amiably. "Aunt Jane's little supper party. Just a shade bottled, wasn't I? But I fancied it passed quite unperceived."

Poirot was saying good-bye to Geraldine Marsh and Miss Carroll.

"I'll come down with you," said Ronald genially.

He led the way down the stairs talking as he went.

"Rum thing—life. Kicked out one day, lord of the manor the next. My late unlamented uncle kicked me out, you know, three years ago. But I expect you know all about that, M. Poirot?"

"I had heard the fact mentioned, yes," replied Poirot composedly.

"Naturally. A thing of that kind is sure to be dug up. The earnest sleuth can't afford to miss it."

He grinned. Then he threw open the dining-room door.

"Have a spot before you go."

Poirot refused; so did I, but the young man mixed himself a drink and continued to talk.

"Here's to murder," he said cheerfully. "In the space of one short night I am converted from the creditor's despair to the tradesman's hope. Yesterday ruin stared me in the face, today all is affluence. God bless Aunt Jane."

He drained his glass. Then, with a slight change of manner, he spoke to Poirot.

"Seriously, though, M. Poirot, what *are* you doing here? Four days ago Aunt Jane was dramatically declaiming; 'Who will rid me of this insolent tyrant?' and lo and behold she is ridded! Not by your agency, I hope? The perfect crime, by Hercule Poirot, ex-sleuth hound."

Poirot smiled.

"I am here this afternoon in answer to a note from Miss Geraldine Marsh."

"A discreet answer, eh? No, M. Poirot, what are you really doing here? For some reason or other you are interesting yourself in my uncle's death."

"I am always interested in murder, Lord Edgware."

"But you don't commit it. Very cautious. You should teach Aunt Jane caution. Caution and a shade more camouflage. You'll excuse me calling her Aunt Jane. It amuses me. Did you see her blank face when I did it the other night? Hadn't the foggiest notion who I was."

"En verité?"

"No. I was kicked out of here three months before she came along."

The fatuous expression of good-nature on his face failed for a moment. Then he went on lightly:

"Beautiful woman. But no subtlety. Methods rather crude, eh?"

Poirot shrugged his shoulders.

"It is possible."

Ronald looked at him curiously.

"I believe you think she didn't do it. So she's got round you too, has she?"

"I have a great admiration for beauty," said Poirot evenly. "But also for —evidence."

He brought the last word out very quietly.

"Evidence?" said the other sharply.

"Perhaps you do not know, Lord Edgware, that Lady Edgware was at a party at Chiswick last night at the time she was supposed to have been seen here."

Ronald swore.

"So she went after all! How like a woman! At six o'clock she was throwing her weight about, declaring that nothing on earth would make her go, and I suppose about ten minutes after she'd changed her mind! When planning a murder never depend upon a woman doing what she says she'll do. That's how the best laid plans of murder gang agley. No, M. Poirot, I'm not incriminating myself. Oh! yes, don't think I can't read what's passing through your mind. Who is the Natural Suspect? The well-known Wicked Ne'er-do-Well Nephew."

He leaned back in his chair chuckling.

"I'm saving your little grey cells for you, M. Poirot. No need for you to hunt round for someone who saw me in the offing when Aunt Jane was declaring she never, never, never would go out that night, et cetera. I was there. So you ask yourself, did the wicked nephew in very truth come here last night disguised in a fair wig and a Paris hat?"

Seemingly enjoying the situation, he surveyed us both. Poirot, his head a little on one side, was regarding him with close attention. I felt rather uncomfortable.

"I had a motive—oh! yes, motive admitted. And I'm going to give you a present of a very valuable and significant piece of information. I called to see my uncle yesterday morning. Why? To ask for money. Yes, lick your lips over that. TO ASK FOR MONEY. And I went away without getting any. And that same evening—that very same evening—Lord Edgware dies. Good title that, by the way. Lord Edgware Dies. Look well on a bookstall."

He paused. Still Poirot said nothing.

"I'm really flattered by your attention, M. Poirot. Captain Hastings looks as though he had seen a ghost—or were going to see one any minute. Don't get so strung up, my dear fellow. Wait for the anticlimax. Well, where were we? Oh! yes, case against the Wicked Nephew. Guilt is to be thrown on the hated Aunt by Marriage. Nephew, celebrated at one time for acting female parts, does his supreme histrionic effort. In a girlish voice he announces himself as Lady Edgware and sidles past the butler with mincing steps. No suspicions are aroused. 'Jane,' cries my fond Uncle. 'George,' I squeak. I fling my arms about his neck and neatly insert the penknife. The next details are purely medical and can be omitted. Exit the spurious lady. And so to bed at the end of a good day's work."

He laughed and, rising, poured himself out another whisky and soda. He returned slowly to his chair.

"Works out well, doesn't it? But you see, here comes the crux of the matter. The disappointment! The annoying sensation of having been led up the garden. For now, M. Poirot, we come to the alibi!"

He finished off his glass.

"I always find alibis very enjoyable," he remarked. "Whenever I happen to be reading a detective story I sit up and take notice when the alibi comes along. This is a remarkably good alibi. Three strong. In plainer language, Mr., Mrs., and Miss Dortheimer. Extremely rich and extremely musical. They have a box at Covent Garden. Into that box they invite young men with prospects. I, M. Poirot, am a young man with prospects. Do I like the opera? Frankly, no. But I enjoy the excellent dinner in Grosvenor Square first, and I also enjoy an excellent supper somewhere else afterward, even if I do have to dance with Rachel Dortheimer and have a stiff arm for two days afterward. So, you see, M. Poirot, there you are. When Uncle's life blood is flowing, I am whispering cheerful nothings into the diamond-encrusted ears of the fair Rachel in a box at Covent Garden. And so you see, M. Poirot, why I can afford to be so frank."

He leaned back in his chair.

"I hope I have not bored you. Any questions to ask?"

"I can assure you that I have not been bored," said Poirot. "Since you are so kind, there is one little question that I would like to ask."

"Delighted."

"How long, Lord Edgware, have you known Miss Carlotta Adams?"

Whatever the young man had expected, it certainly had not been this. He sat up sharply with an entirely new expression on his face.

"Why on earth do you want to know that? What's that got to do with what we've been talking about?"

"I was curious, that was all. For the other, you have explained so fully everything there is to explain that there is no need for me to ask questions."

Ronald shot a quick glance at him. It was almost as though he did not care for Poirot's amiable acquiescence. He would, I thought, have preferred him to be more suspicious.

"Carlotta Adams? Let me see. About a year. A little more. I got to know her last year when she gave her first show."

"You knew her well?"

"Pretty well. She's not the sort of girl you ever get to know frightfully well. Reserved and all that."

"But you liked her?"

Ronald stared at him.

"I wish I knew why you are so interested in the lady. Is it because I was with her the other night? Yes, I like her very much. She's sympathetic—listens to a chap and makes him feel he's something of a fellow after all."

Poirot nodded.

"I comprehend. Then you will be sorry."

"Sorry? What about?"

"Sorry to hear the news."

"What news?"

"That she is dead?"

"What?" Ronald sprang up in astonishment. "Carlotta dead?"

He looked absolutely dumbfounded by the news.

"You're pulling my leg, M. Poirot. Carlotta was perfectly well the last time I saw her."

"When was that?" asked Poirot quickly.

"Day before yesterday, I think. I can't remember."

"*Tout de même,* she is dead."

"It must have been frightfully sudden. What was it? A street accident?"

Poirot looked at the ceiling.

"No. She took an overdose of veronal."

"Oh! I say. Poor kid. How frightfully sad."

"*N'est ce pas?*"

"I *am* sorry. And she was getting on so well. She was going to get her kid sister over and had all sorts of plans. Dash it, I'm more sorry than I can say."

"Yes," said Poirot. "It is sad to die when you are young—when you do not want to die—when all life is open before you and you have everything to live for."

Ronald looked at him curiously.

"I don't think I quite get you, M. Poirot?"

"No?"

Poirot rose and held out his hand.

"I express my thoughts a little strongly perhaps, for I do not like to see youth deprived of its right to live, Lord Edgware. I feel—very strongly about it. I wish you good-day."

"Oh!—er— Good-bye."

He looked rather taken aback.

As I opened the door I almost collided with Miss Carroll.

"Ah! M. Poirot, they told me you hadn't gone yet. I'd like a word with you if I may. Perhaps you wouldn't mind coming up to my room."

"It's about that child, Geraldine," she said when we had entered her sanctum and she had closed the door.

"Yes, mademoiselle?"

"She talked a lot of nonsense this afternoon. Now don't protest. Nonsense! That's what I call it and that's what it was. She broods."

"I could see that she was suffering from over strain," said Poirot gently.

"Well—to tell the truth—she hasn't had a very happy life. No, one can't pretend she has. Frankly, M. Poirot, Lord Edgware was a peculiar man— not the sort of man who ought to have had anything to do with the upbringing of children. Quite frankly, he terrorized Geraldine."

Poirot nodded.

"Yes, I should imagine something of the kind."

"He was a peculiar man. He—I don't quite know how to put it—but he enjoyed seeing anyone afraid of him. It seemed to give him a morbid kind of pleasure."

"Quite so."

"He was an extremely well-read man, and a man of considerable intellect; but in some ways—well, I didn't come across that side of him myself, but it was there. I'm not really surprised his wife left him. This wife, I mean. I didn't approve of her, mind. I've no opinion of that young woman at all, but in marrying Lord Edgware she got all and more than she deserved. Well, she left him—and no bones broken, as they say. But Geraldine couldn't leave him. For a long time he'd forget all about her, and then, suddenly, he'd remember. I sometimes think—though perhaps I shouldn't say it—"

"Yes, yes, mademoiselle, say it."

"Well, I sometimes thought he revenged himself on the mother—his first wife—that way. She was a gentle creature, I believe, with a very sweet disposition. I've always been sorry for her. I shouldn't have mentioned all this, M. Poirot, if it hadn't been for that very foolish outburst of Geraldine's just now. The things she said—about hating her father—they might sound peculiar to anyone who didn't know."

"Thank you very much, mademoiselle. Lord Edgware, I fancy, was a man who would have done much better not to marry."

"Much better."

"He never thought of marrying for a third time?"

"How could he? His wife was alive."

"By giving her her freedom, he would have been free himself."

"I should think he had had enough trouble with two wives as it was," said Miss Carroll grimly.

"So you think there would have been no question of a third marriage. There was no one? Think, mademoiselle. No one?"

Miss Carroll's colour rose.

"I cannot understand the way you keep harping on the point. Of course there was no one."

Chapter XIV

FIVE QUESTIONS

"WHY DID YOU ask Miss Carroll about the possibility of Lord Edgware's wanting to marry again?" I asked with some curiosity as we were driving home.

"It just occurred to me that there was the possibility of such a thing, *mon ami.*"

"Why?"

"I have been searching in my mind for something to explain Lord Edgware's sudden *volte face* regarding the matter of divorce. There is something curious there, my friend."

"Yes," I said thoughtfully. "It is rather odd."

"You see, Hastings, milor', he confirmed what madame had told us. She had employed the lawyers of all kinds, but he refused to budge the inch. No, he would not agree to the divorce. And then, all of a sudden, he yields!"

"Or so he says," I reminded him.

"Very true, Hastings. It is very just, the observation you make there. *So he says.* We have no proof, whatever, that that letter was written. *Eh bien,* on one part, *ce monsieur* is lying. For some reason he tells us the fabrication, the embroidery. Is it not so? Why, we do not know. But, on the hypothesis that he *did* write that letter, there must have been a *reason* for so doing. Now the reason that presents itself most naturally to the imagination is that he has suddenly met someone whom he desires to marry. That explains perfectly his sudden change of face. And so, naturally, I make the inquiries."

"Miss Carroll turned the idea down very decisively," I said.

"Yes. Miss Carroll," said Poirot in a meditative voice.

"Now what are you driving at?" I asked in exasperation.

Poirot is an adept at suggesting doubts by the tone of his voice.

"What reason should she have for lying about it?" I asked.

"Aucune—aucune. But, you see, Hastings, it is difficult to trust her evidence."

"You think she's lying? But why? She looks a most upright person."

"That is just it. Between the deliberate falsehood and the disinterested inaccuracy it is very hard to distinguish sometimes."

"What *do* you mean?"

"To deceive deliberately—that is one thing. But to be so sure of your facts, of your ideas, and of their essential truth, that the details do not matter—that, my friend, is a special characteristic of particularly honest persons. Already, mark you, she has told us one lie. She said she saw Jane Wilkinson's face when she could not possibly have done so. Now how did that come about? Look at it this way. She looks down and sees Jane Wilkinson in the hall. No doubt enters her head that it *is* Jane Wilkinson. She *knows* it is. She says she saw her face distinctly because—being so sure of her facts—exact details do not matter! It is pointed out to her that she could not have seen her face. Is that so? Well, what does it matter if she saw her face or not—it *was* Jane Wilkinson. And so with any other question. She *knows.* And so she answers questions in the light of her knowledge, not by reason of remembered facts. The positive witness should always be treated with suspicion, my friend. The uncertain witness, who doesn't remember, isn't sure, will think a minute—ah! yes, that's how it was—is infinitely more to be depended upon!"

"Dear me, Poirot," I said. "You upset all my preconceived ideas about witnesses."

"In reply to my question as to Lord Edgware's marrying again she ridicules the idea—simply because it has never occurred to her. She will not take the trouble to remember whether any infinitesimal signs may have pointed that way. Therefore we are exactly where we were before."

"She certainly did not seem at all taken aback when you pointed out that she could not have seen Jane Wilkinson's face," I remarked thoughtfully.

"No. That is why I decided that she was one of those honestly inaccurate persons, rather than a deliberate liar. I can see no motive for deliberate lying unless—true, that is an idea!"

"What is?" I asked eagerly.

But Poirot shook his head.

"An idea suggested itself to me, but it is too impossible—yes, much too impossible."

And he refused to say more.

"She seems very fond of the girl," I said.

"Yes. She certainly was determined to assist at our interview. What was your impression of Miss Geraldine Marsh, Hastings?"

"I was sorry for her—deeply sorry for her."

"You have always the tender heart, Hastings. Beauty in distress upsets you every time."

"Didn't you feel the same?"

He nodded gravely.

"Yes. She has not had a happy life. That is written very clearly on her face."

"At any rate," I said warmly, "you realize how preposterous Jane Wilkinson's suggestion was—that she should have had anything to do with the crime, I mean."

"Doubtless her alibi is satisfactory, but Japp has not communicated it to me as yet."

"My dear Poirot, do you mean to say that, even after seeing her and talking to her, you are still not satisfied and want an alibi?"

"*Eh bien,* my friend, what is the result of seeing and talking to her? We perceive that she has passed through great unhappiness; she admits that she hated her father and is glad that he is dead, and she is deeply uneasy about what he may have said to us yesterday morning. And after that you say—no alibi is necessary!"

"Her mere frankness proves her innocence," I said warmly.

"Frankness is a characteristic of the family. The new Lord Edgware— with what a gesture he laid his cards on the table."

"He did indeed," I said, smiling at the remembrance. "Rather an original method."

Poirot nodded.

"He—what do you say?—cuts the ground before our feet."

"From under," I corrected. "Yes, it made us look rather foolish."

"What a curious idea. You may have looked foolish. I did not feel foolish in the least, and I do not think I looked it. On the contrary, my friend, I put him out of countenance."

"Did you?" I said doubtfully, not remembering having seen signs of anything of the kind.

"*Si, si.* I listen—and listen, and at last I ask a question about something quite different; and that, you may have noticed, disconcerts our brave monsieur very much. You do not observe, Hastings."

"I thought his horror and astonishment at hearing of Carlotta Adams' death was genuine," I said. "I suppose you will say it was a piece of clever acting."

"Impossible to tell. I agree it *seemed* genuine."

"Why do you think he flung all those facts at our head in that cynical way? Just for amusement?"

"That is always possible. You English, you have the most extraordinary notions of humour. But it may have been policy. Facts that are concealed acquire a suspicious importance. Facts that are frankly revealed tend to be regarded as less important than they really are."

"The quarrel with his uncle that morning, for instance?"

"Exactly. He knows that the fact is bound to leak out. *Eh bien,* he will parade it."

"He is not so foolish as he looks."

"Oh! he is not foolish at all. He has plenty of brains when he cares to use them. He sees exactly where he stands and, as I said, he lays his cards on the table. You play the bridge, Hastings. Tell me, when does one do that?"

"You play bridge yourself," I said, laughing. "You know well enough— when all the rest of the tricks are yours and you want to save time and get on to a new hand."

"Yes, *mon ami,* that is all very true. But occasionally there is another reason. I have remarked it once or twice when playing with *les dames.* There is perhaps a little doubt. *Eh bien, la dame,* she throws down the cards, says 'and all the rest are mine' and gathers up the cards and cuts the new pack. And possibly the other players agree—especially if they are a little inexperienced. The thing is not obvious, mark you. It requires to be followed out. Half way through dealing the next hand, one of the players thinks: 'Yes, but she would have to have taken over that fourth diamond in dummy whether she wanted to or not, and then she would have had to lead a little club and my nine would have made.' "

"So you think?"

"I think, Hastings, that too much bravado is a very interesting thing. And I also think that it is time we dined. *Une petite omelette, n'est ce pas?* And after that, about nine o'clock, I have one more visit I wish to make."

"Where is that?"

"We will dine first, Hastings, and, until we drink our coffee, we will not discuss the case further. When engaged in eating, the brain should be the servant of the stomach."

Poirot was as good as his word. We went to a little restaurant in Soho where he was well known, and there we had a delicious omelette, a sole, a chicken and a baba au rhum of which Poirot was inordinately fond.

Then, as we sipped our coffee, Poirot smiled affectionately across the table at me.

"My good friend," he said. "I depend upon you more than you know."

I was confused and delighted by these unexpected words. He had never said anything of the kind to me before. Sometimes, secretly, I had felt slightly hurt. He seemed almost to go out of his way to disparage my mental powers.

Although I did not think his own powers were flagging, I did realize suddenly that perhaps he had come to depend on my aid more than he knew.

"Yes," he said dreamily, "you may not always comprehend just how it is so—but you do often and often point the way."

I could hardly believe my ears.

"Really, Poirot," I stammered, "I'm awfully glad. I suppose I've learnt a good deal from you one way or another—"

He shook his head.

"*Mais non, ce n'est pas ça.* You have learnt nothing."

"Oh!" I said, rather taken aback.

"That is as it should be. No human being should learn from another. Each individual should develop his own powers to the uttermost, not try to imitate those of someone else. I do not wish you to be a second and inferior Poirot. I wish you to be the supreme Hastings. And you are the supreme Hastings. In you, Hastings, I find the normal mind almost perfectly illustrated."

"I'm not abnormal, I hope," I said.

"No, no. You are beautifully and perfectly balanced. In you sanity is personified. Do you realize what that means to me? When the criminal sets out to do a crime his first effort is to deceive. Whom does he seek to deceive? The image in his mind is that of the normal man. There is probably no such thing actually—it is a mathematical abstraction. But you come as near to realizing it as is possible. There are moments when you have flashes of brilliance, when you rise above the average, moments (I hope you will pardon me) when you descend to curious depths of obtuseness, but, take it all for all, you are amazingly normal. *Eh bien,* how does this profit me? Simply in this way. As in a mirror I see reflected in your mind exactly what the criminal wishes me to believe. That is terrifically helpful and suggestive."

I did not quite understand. It seemed to me that what Poirot was saying was hardly complimentary. However, he quickly disabused me of that impression.

"I have expressed myself badly," he said quickly. "You have an insight into the criminal mind, which I myself lack. You show me what the criminal wishes me to believe. It is a great gift."

"Insight," I said thoughtfully. "Yes, perhaps I have got insight."

I looked across the table at him. He was smoking his tiny cigarettes and regarding me with great kindliness.

"*Ce cher Hastings,*" he murmured. "I have indeed much affection for you."

I was pleased but embarrassed and hastened to change the subject.

"Come," I said in a businesslike manner. "Let us discuss the case."

"Eh bien." Poirot threw his head back, his eyes narrowed. He slowly puffed out smoke.

"Je me pose de questions," he said.

"Yes?" I said eagerly.

"You, too, doubtless?"

"Certainly," I said. And also leaning back and narrowing my own eyes I threw out:

"Who killed Lord Edgware?"

Poirot immediately sat up and shook his head vigorously.

"No, no. Not at all. Is it a question, that? You are like someone who reads the detective story and who starts guessing each of the characters in turn without rhyme or reason. Once, I agree, I had to do that myself. It was a very exceptional case. I will tell you about it one of these days. It was a feather in my cap. But of what were we speaking?"

"Of the questions you were 'posing' to yourself," I replied dryly. It was on the tip of my tongue to suggest that my real use to Poirot was to provide him with a companion to whom he could boast, but I controlled myself. If he wished to instruct, then let him.

"Come on," I said. "Let's hear them."

That was all that the vanity of the man wanted. He leaned back again and resumed his former attitude.

"The first question we have already discussed. *Why did Lord Edgware change his mind on the subject of divorce?* One or two ideas suggest themselves to me on that subject. One of them you know.

"The second question I ask myself is *What happened to that letter?* To whose interest was it that Lord Edgware and his wife should continue to be tied together?

"Three, *What was the meaning of the expression on his face that you saw when you looked back yesterday morning on leaving the library?* Have you any answer to that, Hastings?"

I shook my head.

"I can't understand it."

"You are sure that you didn't imagine it? Sometimes, Hastings, you have the imagination *un peu vif.* "

"No, no." I shook my head vigorously. "I'm quite sure I wasn't mistaken."

"Bien. Then it is a fact to be explained. My fourth question concerns those pince-nez. Neither Jane Wilkinson nor Carlotta Adams wore glasses. *What, then, are the glasses doing in Carlotta Adams' bag?*

"And for my fifth question. *Why did someone telephone to find out if Jane Wilkinson were at Chiswick and who was it?*

"Those, my friend, are the questions with which I am tormenting myself. If I could answer those, I should feel happier in my mind. If I could even evolve a theory that explained them satisfactorily, my *amour propre* would not suffer so much."

"There are several other questions," I said.

"Such as?"

"Who incited Carlotta Adams to this hoax? Where was she that evening before and after ten o'clock? Who is D, who gave her the golden box?"

"Those questions are self-evident," Said Poirot. "There is no subtlety about them. They are simply things we do not know. They are questions of *fact.* We may get to know them any minute. My questions, *mon ami,* are psychological. The little grey cells of the brain—"

"Poirot," I said desperately. I felt that I must stop him at all costs. I could not bear to hear it all over again. "You spoke of making a visit tonight?"

Poirot looked at his watch.

"True," he said. "I will telephone and find out if it is convenient."

He went away and returned a few minutes later.

"Come," he said. "All is well."

"Where are we going?" I asked.

"To the house of Sir Montagu Corner at Chiswick. I would like to know a little more about that telephone call."

Chapter XV

IT WAS ABOUT ten o'clock when we reached Sir Montagu Corner's house on the river at Chiswick. It was a big house standing back in its own grounds. We were admitted into a beautifully panelled hall. On our right, through an open door, we saw the dining-room, with its long polished table lit with candles.

"Will you come this way, please?"

The butler led the way up a broad staircase and into a long room on the first floor overlooking the river.

"M. Hercule Poirot," announced the butler.

It was a beautifully proportioned room, and had an old-world air with its carefully shaded dim lamps. In one corner of the room was a bridge table, set near the open window, and round it sat four people. As we entered the room one of the four rose and came towards us.

"It is a great pleasure to make your acquaintance, M. Poirot."

I looked with some interest at Sir Montagu Corner. He had very small, intelligent black eyes and a carefully arranged toupee. He was a short man —five foot eight at most, I should say. His manner was affected to the last degree.

"Let me introduce you. Mr. and Mrs. Widburn."

"We've met before," said Mrs. Widburn brightly.

"And Mr. Ross."

Ross was a young fellow of about twenty-two, with a pleasant face and fair hair.

"I disturb your game. A million apologies," said Poirot.

"Not at all. We have not started. We were commencing to deal the cards only. Some coffee, M. Poirot?"

Poirot declined, but accepted an offer of old brandy. It was brought us in immense goblets.

As we sipped it, Sir Montagu discoursed. He spoke of Japanese prints, of Chinese lacquer, of Persian carpets, of the French impressionists, of modern music and of the theories of Einstein. Then he sat back and smiled at us beneficently. He had evidently thoroughly enjoyed his performance. In the dim light he looked like some genie of mediaeval days. All round the room were exquisite examples of art and culture.

"And now, Sir Montagu," said Poirot. "I will trespass on your kindness no longer but will come to the object of my visit."

Sir Montagu waved a curious clawlike hand.

"There is no hurry. Time is infinite."

"One always feels that in this house," sighed Mrs. Widburn. "So wonderful."

"I would not live in London for a million pounds," said Sir Montagu. "Here one is in the old-world atmosphere of peace that, alas, we have put behind us in these jarring days."

A sudden impish fancy flashed over me that, if someone were really to offer Sir Montagu a million pounds, old-world peace might go to the wall, but I trod down such heretical sentiments.

"What is money, after all?" murmured Mrs. Widburn.

"Ah!" said Mr. Widburn thoughtfully and rattled some coins absent-mindedly in his trousers pocket.

"Archie," said Mrs. Widburn reproachfully.

"Sorry," said Mr. Widburn and stopped.

"To speak of crime in such an atmosphere is, I feel, unpardonable," began Poirot apologetically.

"Not at all." Sir Montagu waved a gracious hand. "A crime can be a work of art. A detective can be an artist. I do not refer, of course, to the police. An inspector has been here today. A curious person. He had never heard of Benvenuto Cellini, for instance."

"He came about Jane Wilkinson, I suppose," said Mrs. Widburn with instant curiosity.

"It was fortunate for that lady that she was at your house last night," said Poirot.

"So it seems," said Sir Montagu. "I asked her here knowing that she was beautiful and talented and hopping that I might be able to be of use to her. She was thinking of going into management. But it seems that I was fated to be of use to her in a very different way."

"Jane's got luck," said Mrs. Widburn. "She's been dying to get rid of Edgware, and here's somebody gone and saved her the trouble. She'll marry the young Duke of Merton now. Everyone says so. His mother's wild about it."

"I was favourably impressed by her," said Sir Montagu graciously. "She made several most intelligent remarks about Greek art."

I smiled to myself, picturing Jane saying, "Yes," and "No," "Really, how wonderful," in her magical husky voice. Sir Montagu was the type of man to whom intelligence consisted of the faculty of listening to his own remarks with suitable attention.

"Edgware was a queer fish by all accounts," said Widburn. "I dare say he had a good few enemies."

"Is it true, M. Poirot," asked Mrs. Widburn, "that somebody ran a penknife into the back of his brain?"

"Perfectly true, madame. It was very neatly and efficiently done—scientific, in fact."

"I note your artistic pleasure, M. Poirot," said Sir Montagu.

"And now," said Poirot, "let me come to the object of my visit. Lady Edgware was called to the telephone when she was here at dinner. It is about that telephone call that I seek information. Perhaps you will allow me to question your domestics on the subject?"

"Certainly. Certainly. Just press that bell, will you, Ross?"

The butler answered the bell. He was a tall, middle-aged man of ecclesiastical appearance. Sir Montagu explained what was wanted. The butler turned to Poirot with polite attention.

"Who answered the telephone when it rang?" began Poirot.

"I answered it myself, sir. The telephone is in a recess leading out of the hall."

"Did the person calling ask to speak to Lady Edgware or to Miss Jane Wilkinson?"

"To Lady Edgware, sir."

"What did they say exactly?"

The butler reflected for a moment.

"As far as I remember, sir, I said, 'Hello.' A voice then asked if I was Chiswick 43434. I replied that that was so. It then asked me to hold the line. Another voice then asked if that was Chiswick 43434 and on my replying, 'Yes,' it said, 'Is Lady Edgware dining there?' I said her ladyship *was* dining here. The voice said, 'I would like to speak to her please.' I went and informed her ladyship, who was at the dinner table. Her ladyship rose, and I showed her where the phone was."

"And then?"

"Her ladyship picked up the receiver and said: 'Hello—who's speaking?' Then she said, 'Yes—that's all right. Lady Edgware speaking.' I was just about to leave her ladyship when she called to me and said they had cut her off. She said someone had laughed and evidently hung up the receiver. She asked me if the person ringing up had given any name. They had not done so. That was all that occurred, sir."

Poirot frowned to himself.

"Do you really think the telephone call has something to do with the murder, M. Poirot?" asked Mrs. Widburn.

"Impossible to say, madame. It is just a curious circumstance."

"People do ring up for a joke sometimes. It's been done to me."

"C'est toujours possible, madame."

He spoke to the butler again.

"Was it a man's voice or a woman's who rang up?"

"A lady's, I think, sir."

"What kind of a voice, high or low?"

"Low, sir. Careful and rather distinct." He paused. "It may be my fancy, sir, but it sounded like a *foreign* voice. The R's were very noticeable."

"As far as that goes, it might have been a Scotch voice, Donald," said Mrs. Widburn, smiling at Ross.

Ross laughed.

"Not guilty," he said. "I was at the dinner table."

Poirot spoke once again to the butler.

"Do you think," he asked, "that you would recognize that voice if you were to hear it any time?"

The butler hesitated.

"I couldn't quite say, sir. I might do so. I think it is possible that I should do so."

"I thank you, my friend."

"Thank you, sir."

The butler inclined his head and withdrew, pontifical to the last.

Sir Montagu Corner continued to be very friendly and to play his rôle of old-world charm. He persuaded us to remain and play bridge. I excused myself—the stakes were bigger than I cared about. Young Ross seemed relieved also at the prospect of someone taking his hand. He and I sat looking on while the other four played. The evening ended in a heavy financial gain to Poirot and Sir Montagu.

Then we thanked our host and took our departure. Ross came with us.

"A strange little man," said Poirot as we stepped out into the night.

The night was fine and we had decided to walk until we picked up a taxi, instead of having one telephoned for.

"Yes, a strange little man," said Poirot again.

"A very rich little man," said Ross with feeling.

"I suppose so."

"He seems to have taken a fancy to me," said Ross. "Hope it will last. A man like that behind you means a lot."

"You are an actor, Mr. Ross?"

Ross said that he was. He seemed sad that his name had not brought instant recognition. Apparently he had recently won marvellous notices in some gloomy play translated from the Russian. When Poirot and I between us had soothed him down again, Poirot asked casually:

"You knew Carlotta Adams, did you not?"

"No. I saw her death announced in the paper tonight. Overdose of some drug or other. Idiotic the way all these girls dope."

"It is sad, yes. She was clever, too."

"I suppose so."

He displayed a characteristic lack of interest in anyone else's performance but his own.

"Did you see her show at all?" I asked.

"No. That sort of thing's not much in my line. Kind of craze for it at present, but I don't think it will last."

"Ah!" said Poirot. "Here is a taxi."

He waved a stick.

"Think I'll walk," said Ross. "I get a tube straight home from Hammersmith."

Suddenly he gave a nervous laugh.

"Odd thing," he said. "That dinner last night."

"Yes?"

"We were thirteen. Some fellow failed at the last minute. We never noticed it till just the end of dinner."

"And who got up first?" I asked.

He gave a queer little nervous cackle of laughter.

"I did," he said.

Chapter XVI

MAINLY DISCUSSION

WHEN WE GOT home we found Japp waiting for us.

"Thought I'd just call round and have a chat with you before turning in, M. Poirot," he said cheerfully.

"*Eh bien,* my good friend, how goes it?"

"Well, it doesn't go any too well, and that's a fact." He looked depressed. "Got any help for me, M. Poirot?"

"I have one or two little ideas I should like to present to you," said Poirot.

"You and your ideas! In some ways, you know, you're a caution. Not that I don't want to hear them. I do. There's some good stuff in that funny shaped head of yours."

Poirot acknowledged the compliment somewhat coldly.

"Have you any ideas about the double lady problem? That's what I want to know. Eh, M. Poirot? What about it? Who was she?"

"That is exactly what I wish to talk to you about."

He asked Japp if he had ever heard of Carlotta Adams.

"I've heard the name. For the moment I can't just place it."

Poirot explained.

"Her! Does imitations, does she? Now what made you fix on her? What have you got to go on?"

Poirot related the steps we had taken and the conclusion we had drawn.

"By the Lord, it looks as though you were right. Clothes, hat, gloves, and the fair wig. Yes, it must be. I will say, you're the goods, M. Poirot. Smart work, that! Not that I think there's anything to show she was put out of the way. That seems a bit far fetched. I don't quite see eye to eye with you there. Your theory is a bit fantastical for me. I've more experience than you have. I don't believe in this villain-behind-the-scenes motif. Carlotta Adams was the woman all right, but I should put it one of two ways. She went there for purposes of her own—blackmail, maybe, since she hinted she was going to get money. They had a bit of a dispute. He turned nasty, she turned nasty, and she finished him off. And I should say that when she got home she went all to pieces. She hadn't meant murder. It's my belief she took an overdose on purpose, as the easiest way out."

"You think that covers all the facts?"

"Well, naturally there are a lot of things we don't know yet. It's a good working hypothesis to go on with. The other explanation is that the hoax and the murder had nothing to do with each other. It's just a damned queer coincidence."

Poirot did not agree, I knew, but he merely said noncommittally:

"*Mais oui, c'est possible.*"

"Or, look here, how's this? The hoax is innocent enough. Someone gets to hear of it and thinks it will suit their purpose jolly well. That's not a bad idea?" He paused, then went on: "But personally I prefer idea number one. What the link was between his lordship and the girl we'll find out somehow or other."

Poirot told him of the letter to America, posted by the maid, and Japp agreed that that might possibly be of great assistance.

"I'll get on to that at once," he said, making a note of it in his little book.

"I'm the more in favour of the lady being the killer because I can't find anyone else," he said, as he put the book away. "Captain Marsh now, his lordship as now is. He's got a motive sticking out a yard. A bad record too. Hard up and none too scrupulous over money. What's more he had a row with his uncle yesterday morning. He told me that himself, as a matter of fact, which rather takes the taste out of it. Yes, he'd be a likely customer. But he's got an alibi for yesterday evening. He was at the opera with the Dortheimers. Grosvenor Square. I've looked into that and it's all right. He dined with them, went to the opera and they went on to supper at Sobrani's. So that's that."

"And mademoiselle?"

"The daughter, you mean? She was out of the house too. Dined with some people called Carthew West. They took her to the opera and saw her home afterward. Quarter to twelve she got in. That disposes of *her*. The secretary woman seems all right—very efficient, decent woman. Then there's the butler. I can't say I take to him much. It isn't natural for a man to have good looks like that. There's something fishy about him, and something odd about the way he came to enter Lord Edgware's service. Yes, I'm checking up on him all right. I can't see any motive for murder, though."

"No fresh facts have come to light?"

"Yes, one or two. It's hard to say whether they mean anything or not. For one thing Lord Edgware's key's missing."

"The key to the front door?"

"Yes."

"That is interesting, certainly."

"As I say, it may mean a good deal or nothing at all. Depends. What *is* a bit more significant to my mind is this. Lord Edgware cashed a cheque yesterday—not a particularly large one—a hundred pounds, as a matter of fact. He took the money in French notes. That's why he cashed the cheque, because of his journey to Paris today. Well, that money has disappeared."

"Who told you of this?"

"Miss Carroll. She cashed the cheque and obtained the money. She mentioned it to me, and then I found that it had gone."

"Where was it yesterday evening?"

"Miss Carroll doesn't know. She gave it to Lord Edgware about half past three. It was in a bank envelope. He was in the library at the time. He took it and laid it down beside him on a table."

"That certainly gives one to think. It is a complication."

"Or a simplification. By the way—the wound."

"Yes?"

"The doctor says it wasn't made by an ordinary penknife. Something of that kind but a different shaped blade. And it was amazingly sharp."

"Not a razor?"

"No, no. Much smaller."

Poirot frowned thoughtfully.

"The new Lord Edgware seems to be fond of his joke," remarked Japp. "He seems to think it amusing to be suspected of murder. He made sure we *did* suspect him of murder, too. Looks a bit queer, that."

"It might be merely intelligence."

"More likely guilty conscience. His uncle's death came very pat for him. He's moved into the house, by the way."

"Where was he living before?"

"Martin Street, St. George's Road. Not a very swell neighbourhood."

"You might make a note of that, Hastings."

I did so, though I wondered a little. If Ronald had moved to Regent Gate, his former address was hardly likely to be needed.

"*I* think the Adams girl did it," said Japp, rising. "A fine bit of work on your part, M. Poirot, to tumble to that. But there, of course you go about to theatres and amusing yourself. Things strike you that don't get the chance of striking me. Pity there's no apparent motive, but a little spade work will soon bring it to light, I expect."

"There is one person with a motive to whom you have given no attention," remarked Poirot.

"Who's that, sir?"

"The gentleman who is reputed to have wanted to marry Lord Edgware's wife. I mean the Duke of Merton."

"Yes, I suppose there is a motive." Japp laughed. "But a gentleman in his position isn't likely to do murder. And anyway, he's over in Paris."

"You do not regard him as a serious suspect, then?"

"Well, M. Poirot, do you?"

And laughing at the absurdity of the idea, Japp left us.

Chapter XVII

THE BUTLER

THE FOLLOWING DAY was one of inactivity for us, and activity for Japp. He came round to see us about tea time. He was red and wrathful.

"I've made a bloomer."

"Impossible, my friend," said Poirot soothingly.

"Yes, I have. I've let that (here he gave way to profanity) . . . of a butler slip through my fingers."

"He has disappeared?"

"Yes. Hooked it. What makes me kick myself for a double-dyed idiot is that I didn't particularly suspect him."

"Calm yourself—but calm yourself then."

"All very well to talk. *You* wouldn't be calm if you'd been hauled over the coals at headquarters. Oh! he's a slippery customer. It isn't the first time he's given anyone the slip. He's an old hand."

Japp wiped his forehead and looked the picture of misery. Poirot made sympathetic noises, somewhat suggestive of a hen laying an egg. With more insight into the English character, I poured out a stiff whisky and soda and placed it in front of the gloomy inspector. He brightened a little.

"Well," he said. "I don't mind if I do."

Presently he began to talk more cheerfully.

"I'm not so sure even now that he's the murderer! Of course it looks bad his bolting this way, but there might be other reasons for that. I'd begun to get on to him, you see. Seems he's mixed up with a couple of rather disreputable night clubs. Not the usual thing. Something a great deal more recherché and nasty. In fact, he's a real bad hat."

"*Tout de même,* that does not necessarily mean that he is a murderer."

"Exactly! He may have been up to some funny business or other, but not necessarily murder. No, I'm more than ever convinced it was the Adams girl. I've got nothing to prove it as yet, though. I've had men going all through her flat today, but we've found nothing that's helpful. She was a canny one. Kept no letters except a few business ones about financial contracts. They're all neatly docketed and labelled. Couple of letters from her sister in Washington. Quite straight and above board. One or two pieces of good old-fashioned jewellery—nothing new or expensive. She didn't keep a diary. Her pass book and cheque book don't show anything helpful. Dash it all, the girl doesn't seem to have had any private life at all!"

"She was of a reserved character," said Poirot thoughtfully. "From our point of view that is a pity."

"I've talked to the woman who did for her. Nothing there. I've been and seen that girl who keeps a hat shop and who, it seems, was a friend of hers."

"Ah! and what do you think of Miss Driver?"

"She seems a smart, wide-awake bit of goods. She couldn't help me, though. Not that that surprises me. The amount of missing girls I've had to trace, and their family and their friends always say the same things. 'She was of a bright and affectionate disposition and had no men friends.' That's never true. It's unnatural. Girls ought to have men friends. If not there's something wrong about them. It's the muddle-headed loyalty of friends and relations that makes a detective's life so difficult."

He paused for want of breath, and I replenished his glass.

"Thank you, Captain Hastings, I don't mind if I do. Well, there you are. You've got to hunt and hunt about. There's about a dozen young men she went out to supper and danced with, but nothing to show that one of them meant more than another. There's the present Lord Edgware; there's Mr. Bryan Martin, the film star, there's half a dozen others, but nothing special and particular. Your man-behind idea is all wrong. I think you'll find that she played a lone hand, M. Poirot. I'm looking now for the connection between her and the murdered man. That must exist. I think I'll have to go over to Paris. There was Paris written in that little gold box, and the late Lord Edgware ran over to Paris several times last autumn, so Miss Carroll tells me, attending sales and buying curios. Yes, I think I must go over to Paris. Inquest's tomorrow. It'll be adjourned, of course. After that I'll take the afternoon boat."

"You have a furious energy, Japp. It amazes me."

"Yes, you're getting lazy. You just sit here and *think!* What you call employing the little grey cells. No good; you've got to go out to things. They won't come to you."

The little maid servant opened the door.

"Mr. Bryan Martin, sir. Are you busy or will you see him?"

"I'm off, M. Poirot." Japp hoisted himself up. "All the stars of the theatrical world seem to consult you."

Poirot shrugged a modest shoulder, and Japp laughed.

"You must be a millionaire by now, M. Poirot. What do you do with the money? Save it?"

"Assuredly I practise the thrift. And talking of the disposal of money, how did Lord Edgware dispose of his?"

"Such property as wasn't entailed he left to his daughter. Five hundred to Miss Carroll. No other bequests. Very simple will."

"And it was made—when?"

"After his wife left him, just over two years ago. He expressly excludes her from participation, by the way."

"A vindictive man," murmured Poirot to himself.

With a cheerful "So long," Japp departed.

Bryan Martin entered. He was faultlessly attired and looked extremely handsome, yet I thought that he looked haggard and not too happy.

"I am afraid I have been a long time coming, M. Poirot," he said apologetically, "and, after all, I have been guilty of taking up your time for nothing."

"En verité?"

"Yes. I have seen the lady in question. I've argued with her, pleaded with her, but all to no purpose. She won't hear of my interesting you in the matter. So I'm afraid we'll have to let the thing drop. I'm very sorry—very sorry to have bothered you—"

"Du tout, du tout," said Poirot genially. "I expected this."

"Eh?" The young man seemed taken aback.

"You expected this?" he asked in a puzzled way.

"Mais oui. When you spoke of consulting your friend, I could have predicted that all would have arrived as it has done."

"You have a theory, then?"

"A detective, M. Martin, always has a theory. It is expected of him. I do not call it a theory myself. I say that I have a little idea. That is the first stage."

"And the second stage?"

"If the little idea turns out to be right, then I *know!* It is quite simple, you see."

"I wish you'd tell me what your theory—or your little idea—is?"

Poirot shook his head gently.

"That is another rule. The detective never tells."

"Can't you suggest it even?"

"No. I will only say that I formed my theory as soon as you mentioned a gold tooth."

Bryan Martin stared at him.

"I'm absolutely bewildered," he declared. "I can't make out what you are driving at. If you'd just give me a hint."

Poirot smiled and shook his head.

"Let us change the subject."

"Yes, but first, your fee—you must let me."

Poirot waved an imperious hand.

"*Pas un sou!* I have done nothing to aid you."

"I took up your time—"

"When a case interests me, I do not touch money. Your case interested me very much."

"I'm glad," said the actor uneasily. He looked supremely unhappy.

"Come," said Poirot kindly. "Let us talk of something else."

"Wasn't that the Scotland Yard man whom I met on the stairs?"

"Yes, Inspector Japp."

"The light was so dim, I wasn't sure. By the way, he came round and asked me some questions about that poor girl, Carlotta Adams, who died of an overdose of veronal."

"You knew her well, Miss Adams?"

"Not very well. I knew her as a child in America. I came across her here once or twice, but I never saw very much of her. I was very sorry to hear of her death."

"You liked her?"

"Yes. She was extraordinary easy to talk to."

"A personality very sympathetic. Yes, I found the same."

"I suppose they think it might be suicide? I knew nothing that could help the inspector. Carlotta was always very reserved about herself."

"I do not think it was suicide," said Poirot.

"Far more likely to be an accident, I agree."

There was a pause. Then Poirot said with a smile:

"The affair of Lord Edgware's death becomes intriguing, does it not?"

"Absolutely amazing. Do you know, have they any idea who did it—now that Jane is definitely out of it?"

"*Mais oui,* they have a very strong suspicion."

Bryan Martin looked excited.

"Really? Who?"

"The butler has disappeared. You comprehend—flight is as good as a confession."

"The butler! Really, you surprise me."

"A singularly good-looking man. *Il vous ressemble un peu.*" He bowed in a complimentary fashion.

Of course! I realized now why the butler's face had struck me as being faintly familiar when I first saw it.

"You flatter me," said Bryan Martin with a laugh.

"No, no, no. Do not all the young girls, the servant girls, the flappers, the typists, the girls of society, do they not all adore M. Bryan Martin? Is there one who can resist you?"

"A lot, I should think," said Martin. He got up abruptly.

"Well, thank you very much, M. Poirot. Let me apologize again for having troubled you."

He shook hands with us both. Suddenly, I noticed, he looked much older. The haggard look was more apparent.

I was devoured with curiosity, and as soon as the door closed behind him, I burst out with what I wanted to know.

"Poirot, did you really expect him to come back and relinquish all idea of investigating those queer things that happened to him in America?"

"You heard me say so, Hastings."

"But then—" I followed the thing out logically.

"Then you must know who this mysterious girl is that he had to consult?"

He smiled.

"I have a little idea, my friend. As I told you, it started from the mention of the gold tooth; and, if my little idea is correct, I know who the girl is; I know why she will not let M. Martin consult me; I know the truth of the whole affair. And so could you know it if you would only use the brains the good God has given you. Sometimes, I really am tempted to believe that by inadvertence he passed you by."

Chapter XVIII

THE OTHER MAN

I DO NOT propose to describe either the inquest on Lord Edgware or that on Carlotta Adams. In Carlotta's case the verdict was death by misadventure. In the case of Lord Edgware the inquest was adjourned, after evidence of identification and the medical evidence had been given. As a result of the analysis of the stomach, the time of death was fixed as having occurred not less than an hour after the completion of dinner, with possible extension to an hour after that. This put it as between ten and eleven o'clock with the probability in favour of the earlier time.

None of the facts concerning Carlotta's impersonation of Jane Wilkinson were allowed to leak out. A description of the butler was published in the press and the general impression seemed to be that the butler was the man wanted. His story of Jane Wilkinson's visit was looked upon as an impudent fabrication. Nothing was said of the secretary's corroborating testimony. There were columns concerning the murder in all the papers, but little real information.

Meanwhile Japp was actively at work, I knew. It vexed me a little that Poirot adopted such an inert attitude. The suspicion that approaching old age had something to do with it flashed across me—not for the first time. He made excuses to me which did not ring very convincingly.

"At my time of life one saves oneself the trouble," he explained.

"But, Poirot, my dear fellow, you mustn't think of yourself as old," I protested. I felt that he needed bracing. Treatment by suggestion—that, I know, is the modern idea.

"You are as full of vigour as ever you were," I said earnestly. "You're in the prime of life, Poirot, at the height of your powers. You could go out and solve this case magnificently if you only would."

Poirot replied that he preferred to solve it sitting at home.

"But you can't do that, Poirot."

"Not entirely, it is true."

"What I mean is, we are doing nothing! Japp is doing everything."

"Which suits me admirably."

"It doesn't suit me at all. I want you to be doing things."

"So I am."

"What are you doing?"

"Waiting."

"Waiting for what?"

"Pour que mon chien de chasse me rapporte le gibier," replied Poirot with a twinkle.

"What *do* you mean?"

"I mean the good Japp. Why keep a dog and bark yourself? Japp brings us here the result of the physical energy you admire so much. He has various means at his disposal which I have not. He will have news for us very soon, I do not doubt."

By dint of persistent inquiry, it was true that Japp was slowly getting together material. He had drawn a blank in Paris, but a couple of days later he came in looking pleased with himself.

"It's slow work," he said, "but we're getting somewhere at last."

"I congratulate you, my friend. What has happened?"

"I've discovered that a fair-haired lady deposited an attaché case in the cloak room at Euston at nine o'clock that night. They've been shown Miss Adams' case and identify it positively. It's of American make and so just a little different."

"Ah! Euston. Yes, the nearest of the big stations to Regent Gate. She went there doubtless, made herself up in the lavatory, and then left the case. When was it taken out again?"

"At half past ten. The clerk says by the same lady."

Poirot nodded.

"And I've come on something else too. I've reason to believe that Carlotta Adams was in Lyons Corner House in the Strand at eleven o'clock."

"Ah! c'est très bien ça! How did you come across that?"

"Well, really more or less by chance. You see, there's been a mention in the papers of the little gold box with the ruby initials. Some reporter wrote it up. He was doing an article on the prevalence of dope-taking among young actresses. Sunday paper romantic stuff. The fatal little gold box with its deadly contents—pathetic figure of a young girl with all the world before her! And just a wonder expressed as to where she passed her last evening and how she felt and so on and so on.

"Well, it seems a waitress at the Corner House read this, and she remembered that a lady she had served that evening had had such a box in her hand. She remembered the C. A. on it. And she got excited and began talking to all her friends. Perhaps a paper would give her something?

"A young newspaper man soon got onto it, and there's going to be a good sobstuff article in tonight's *Evening Shriek*. The last hours of the talented actress. Waiting—for the man who never came—and a good bit about the waitress's sympathetic intuition that something was not well with her sister woman. You know the kind of bilge, M. Poirot?"

"And how has it come to your ears so quickly?"

"Oh, well, we're on very good terms with the *Evening Shriek*. It got passed on to me while their particular bright young man tried to get some news out of me about something else. So I rushed along to the Corner House straight away—"

Yes, that was the way things ought to be done. I felt a pang of pity for Poirot. Here was Japp getting all this news at first hand—quite possibly missing valuable details—and here was Poirot placidly content with stale news.

"I saw the girl, and I don't think there's much doubt about it. She couldn't pick out Carlotta Adams' photograph, but then she said she didn't notice the lady's face particularly. She was young and dark and slim, and very well dressed, the girl said. Had got on one of the new hats. I wish women looked at faces a bit more and hats a bit less."

"The face of Miss Adams was not an easy one to observe," said Poirot. "It had the mobility, the sensitiveness, the fluid quality."

"I dare say you're right. I don't go in for analyzing these things. Dressed in black the lady was, so the girl said, and she had an attaché case with her. The girl noticed that particularly, because it struck her as odd that a lady so well dressed should be carrying a case about. She ordered some scrambled eggs and some coffee, but the girl thinks she was putting in time and waiting for someone. She'd got a wrist watch on, and she kept looking at it. It was when the girl came to give her the bill that she noticed the box. The lady took it out of her handbag and had it on the table looking at it. She opened the lid and shut it down again. She was smiling in a pleased, dreamy sort of way. The girl noticed the box particular because it was such a lovely thing. 'I'd like to have a gold box with my initials in rubies on it!' she said.

"Apparently Miss Adams sat there some time after paying her bill. Then, finally, she looked at her watch once more, seemed to give it up, and went out."

Poirot was frowning.

"It was a rendezvous," he murmured. "A rendezvous with someone who did not turn up. Did Carlotta Adams meet that person afterward? Or did she fail to meet him and go home and try to ring him up? I wish I knew—oh! how I wish I knew."

"That's *your* theory, M. Poirot. Mysterious Man-in-the-Background. That Man-in-the-Background's a myth. I don't say she mayn't have been waiting for someone; that's possible. She may have made an appointment to meet someone there after her business with his lordship was settled satisfactorily. Well, we know what happened. She lost her head and stabbed him. But she's not one to lose her head for long. She changes her appearance at the station, gets out her case, goes to the rendezvous, and then what they call the 'reaction' gets her. Horror of what she's done. And when her friend doesn't turn up, that finishes her. He may be someone who knew she was going to Regent Gate that evening. She feels the game's up, so she takes out her little box of dope. An overdose of that and it'll be all over. At any rate she won't be hanged. Why, it's as plain as the nose on your face."

Poirot's hand strayed doubtfully to his nose, then his fingers dropped to his moustaches. He caressed them tenderly with a proud expression.

"There was no evidence at all of a mysterious Man-in-the-Background," said Japp, pursuing his advantage doggedly. "I haven't got evidence yet of a conversation between her and his lordship, but I shall do—it's only a question of time. I must say I'm disappointed about Paris, but nine months ago is a long time. I've still got someone making inquiries over there. Something may come to light yet. I know you don't think so. You're a pig-headed old boy, you know."

"You insult first my nose and then my head!"

"Figure of speech, that's all," said Japp soothingly. "No offence meant."

"The answer to that," I said, "is 'Nor taken.'"

Poirot looked from one to the other of us completely puzzled.

"Any orders?" inquired Japp facetiously from the door.

Poirot smiled forgivingly at him.

"An order, no. A suggestion, yes."

"Well, what is it? Out with it."

"A suggestion that you circularize the taxicabs. Find one that took a fare—or more probably two fares—yes, two fares—from the neighbourhood of Covent Garden to Regent Gate on the night of the murder. As to time it would probably be about twenty minutes to eleven."

Japp cocked an eye alertly. He had the look of a smart terrier dog.

"So that's the idea, is it?" he said. "Well, I'll do it. Can't do any harm, and you sometimes know what you're talking about."

No sooner had he left than Poirot arose and, with great energy, began to brush his hat.

"Ask me no questions, my friend. Instead bring me the benzine. A morsel of omelette this morning descended on my waistcoat."

I brought it to him.

"For once," I said, "I do not think I need to ask questions. It seems fairly obvious. But do you think it really is so?"

"*Mon ami,* at the moment I concern myself solely with the toilet. If you will pardon me saying so your tie does not please me."

"It's a jolly good tie," I said.

"Possibly—once. It feels the old age as you have been kind enough to say I do. Change it, I beseech you, and also brush the right sleeve."

"Are we proposing to call on King George?" I inquired sarcastically.

"No. But I saw in the newspaper this morning that the Duke of Merton had returned to Merton House. I understand he is a premier member of the English aristocracy. I wish to do him all honour."

There is nothing of the Socialist about Poirot.

"Why are we going to call on the Duke of Merton?"

"I wish to see him."

That was all I could get out of him. When my attire was at last handsome enough to please Poirot's critical eye, we started out.

At Merton House, Poirot was asked by a footman if he had an appointment. Poirot replied in the negative. The footman bore away the card and returned shortly to say that His Grace was very sorry but he was extremely busy this morning. Poirot immediately sat down in a chair.

"*Très bien,*" he said. "I wait. I will wait several hours if need be."

This, however, was not necessary. Probably as the shortest way of getting rid of the importunate caller, Poirot was bidden to the presence of the gentleman he desired to see.

The Duke was about twenty-seven years of age. He was hardly prepossessing in appearance, being thin and weakly. He had nondescript hair, going bald at the temples, a small, bitter mouth and vague, dreamy eyes. There were several crucifixes in the room and various religious works of art. A wide shelf of books seemed to contain nothing but theological works. He looked far more like a weedy young haberdasher than like a duke.

He had, I knew, been educated at home, having been a terribly delicate child. He had succeeded to the dukedom as a boy of eight years old, and had grown up under the thumb of a strong-willed mother. This was the man who had fallen an immediate prey to Jane Wilkinson! It was really ludicrous in the extreme. His manner was priggish and his reception of us just short of courteous.

"You may, perhaps, know my name," began Poirot.

"I have no acquaintance with it."

"I study the psychology of crime."

The Duke was silent. He was sitting at a writing-table, an unfinished letter before him. He tapped impatiently on the desk with his pen.

"For what reason did you wish to see me?" he inquired coldly.

Poirot was sitting opposite him. His back was to the window. The Duke was facing it.

"I am at present engaged on investigating the circumstances connected with Lord Edgware's death."

Not a muscle of the weak yet obstinate face moved.

"Indeed? I was not acquainted with him."

"But you are, I think, acquainted with his wife—with Miss Jane Wilkinson?"

"That is so."

"You are aware that she is supposed to have had a strong motive for desiring the death of her husband?"

"I am really not aware of anything of the kind."

"I should like to ask you outright, your Grace, are you shortly going to marry Miss Jane Wilkinson?"

"When I am engaged to marry anyone the fact will be announced in the newspapers. I consider your question an impertinence." He stood up. "Good-morning."

Poirot stood up also. He looked awkward. He hung his head. He stammered.

"I did not mean—I— *Je vous demande pardon—*"

"Good-morning," repeated the Duke, a little louder.

This time Poirot gave it up. He made a characteristic gesture of hopelessness, and we left. It was an ignominious dismissal.

I felt rather sorry for Poirot. His usual bombast had not gone well. To the Duke of Merton a great detective was evidently lower than a black beetle.

"That didn't go too well," I said sympathetically. "What a stiff-necked tartar the man is. What did you really want to see him for?"

"I wanted to know whether he and Jane Wilkinson are really going to marry."

"She said so."

"Ah! she said so; but, you realize, she is of those who say anything that suits their purpose. She might have decided to marry him and he—poor man—might not yet be aware of the fact."

"Well, he certainly sent you away with a flea in the ear."

"He gave me the reply he would give to a reporter—yes." Poirot chuckled. "But I know! I know exactly how the case stands."

"How do you know? By his manner?"

"Not at all. You saw he was writing a letter?"

"Yes."

"*Eh bien,* in my early days in the police force in Belgium I learned that it was very useful to read handwriting upside down. Shall I tell you what he was saying in that letter? '*My dearest, I can hardly bear to wait through the long months. Jane, my adored, my beautiful angel, how can I tell you what you are to me? You who have suffered so much! Your beautiful nature—*' "

"Poirot!" I cried, scandalized, stopping him.

"That was as far as he had got, '*Your beautiful nature—only I know it.*' "

I felt very upset. He was so naïvely pleased with his performance.

"Poirot," I cried. "You can't do a thing like that, overlook a private letter."

"You say the imbecilities, Hastings. Absurd to say I 'cannot do' a thing which I have just done!"

"It's not—not playing the game."

"I do not play games. You know that. Murder is not a game. It is serious. And anyway, Hastings, you should not use that phrase, playing the game. It is not said any more. I have discovered that. It is dead. Young people laugh when they hear it. *Mais oui*, young beautiful girls will laugh at you if you say 'playing the game' and 'not cricket.' "

I was silent. I could not bear this thing that Poirot had done so light-heartedly.

"It was so unnecessary," I said. "If you had only told him that you had gone to Lord Edgware at Jane Wilkinson's request, then he would have treated you very differently."

"Ah! but I could not do that. Jane Wilkinson was my client. I cannot speak of my client's affairs to another. I undertake a mission in confidence. To speak of it would not be honourable."

"Honourable!"

"Precisely."

"But she's going to marry him?"

"That does not mean that she has no secrets from him. Your ideas about marriage are very old-fashioned. No, what you suggest, I couldn't possibly have done. I have my honour as a detective to think of. The honour, it is a very serious thing."

"Well, I suppose it takes all kinds of honour to make a world."

Chapter XIX

A GREAT LADY

THE VISIT THAT we received on the following morning was to my mind one of the most surprising things about the whole affair. I was in my room when Poirot slipped in with his eyes shining.

"Mon ami, we have a visitor."

"Who is it?"

"The Dowager Duchess of Merton."

"How extraordinary! What does she want?"

"If you accompany me downstairs, *mon ami,* you will know."

I hastened to comply. We entered the room together.

The Duchess was a small woman with a high-bridged nose and autocratic eyes. Although she was short, one would not have dared to call her dumpy. Dressed though she was in unfashionable black, she was yet every inch a *grande dame.* She also impressed me as having an almost ruthless personality. Where her son was negative, she was positive. Her will power was terrific. I could almost feel waves of force emanating from her. No wonder this woman had always dominated all those with whom she came in contact!

She put up a lorgnette and studied first me and then my companion. Then she spoke to him. Her voice was clear and compelling, a voice accustomed to command and to be obeyed.

"You are M. Hercule Poirot?"

My friend bowed.

"At your service, Madame la Duchesse."

She looked at me.

"This is my friend, Captain Hastings. He assists me in my cases."

Her eyes looked momentarily doubtful. Then she bent her head in acquiescence. She took the chair that Poirot offered.

"I have come to consult you on a very delicate matter, M. Poirot, and I must ask that what I tell you shall be understood to be entirely confidential."

"That without saying, madame."

"It was Lady Yardly who told me about you. From the way in which she spoke of you, and the gratitude she expressed, I felt that you were the only person likely to help me."

"Rest assured, I will do my best, madame."

Still she hesitated. Then, at last, with an effort, she came to the point, came to it with a simplicity that reminded me in an odd way of Jane Wilkinson on that memorable night at the Savoy.

"M. Poirot, I want to ensure that my son does not marry the actress, Jane Wilkinson."

If Poirot felt astonishment, he refrained from showing it. He regarded her thoughtfully and took his time about replying.

"Can you be a little more definite, madame, as to what you want me to do?"

"That is not easy. I feel that such a marriage would be a great disaster. It would ruin my son's life."

"Do you think so, madame?"

"I am sure of it. My son has very high ideals. He knows really very little of the world. He has never cared for the young girls of his own class. They have struck him as empty headed and frivolous. But as regards this woman —well, she is very beautiful, I admit that, and she has the power of enslaving men. She has bewitched my son. I have hoped that the infatuation would run its course. Mercifully she was not free. But now that her husband is dead—"

She broke off.

"They intend to be married in a few months' time. The whole happiness of my son's life is at stake." She spoke more peremptorily. "It must be stopped, M. Poirot."

Poirot shrugged his shoulders.

"I do not say that you are not right, madame. I agree that the marriage is not a suitable one. But what can one do?"

"It is for you to do something."

Poirot slowly shook his head.

"Yes, yes, you must help me."

"I doubt if anything would avail, madame. Your son, I should say, would refuse to listen to anything against the lady! And also, I do not think there is very much against her to say! I doubt if there are any discreditable incidents to be raked up in her past. She has been—shall we say—careful?"

"I know," said the Duchess grimly.

"Ah! So you have already made the inquiries in that direction."

She flushed a little under his keen glance.

"There is nothing I would not do, M. Poirot, to save my son from this marriage." She reiterated the word emphatically: *"Nothing!"*

She paused, then went on:

"Money is nothing in this matter. Name any fee you like. But the marriage must be stopped. You are the man to do it."

Poirot slowly shook his head.

"It is not a question of money. I can do nothing—for a reason which I will explain to you presently. But also, I may say, I do not see there is anything to be done. I cannot give you help, Madame la Duchesse. Will you think me impertinent if I give you advice?"

"What advice?"

"Do not antagonize your son! He is of an age to choose for himself. Because his choice is not your choice, do not assume that you must be right. If it is a misfortune, then accept misfortune. Be at hand to aid him when he needs aid. But do not turn him against you."

"You hardly understand."

She rose to her feet. Her lips were trembling.

"But, yes, Madame la Duchesse, I understand very well. I comprehend the mother's heart. No one comprehends it better than I, Hercule Poirot. And I say to you with authority, be patient. Be patient and calm, and disguise your feelings. There is yet a chance that the matter may break itself. Opposition will merely increase your son's obstinacy."

"Good-bye, M. Poirot," she said coldly. "I am disappointed."

"I regret infinitely, madame, that I cannot be of service to you. I am in a difficult position. Lady Edgware, you see, has already done me the honour to consult me herself."

"Oh! I see." Her voice cut like a knife. "You are in the opposite camp. That explains, no doubt, why Lady Edgware has not yet been arrested for her husband's murder."

"Comment, Madame la Duchesse?"

"I think you heard what I said. Why is she not arrested? She was there that evening. She was seen to enter the house—to enter his study. No one else went near him, and he was found dead. And yet she is not arrested! Our police force must be corrupt through and through."

With shaking hands she arranged the scarf round her neck; then, with the slightest of bows, she swept out of the room.

"Whew!" I said. "What a tartar! I admire her, though, don't you?"

"Because she wishes to arrange the universe to her manner of thinking?"

"Well, she's only got her son's welfare at heart."

Poirot nodded his head.

"That is true enough, and yet, Hastings, will it really be such a bad thing for M. le Duc to marry Jane Wilkinson?"

"Why, you don't think she is really in love with him?"

"Probably not. Almost certainly not. But she is very much in love with his position. She will play her part carefully. She is an extremely beautiful woman and very ambitious. It is not such a catastrophe. The Duke might very easily have married a young girl of his own class who would have accepted him for the same reasons, but no one would have made the song and the dance about that."

"That is quite true, but—"

"And suppose he marries a girl who loves him passionately, is there such a great advantage in that? Often I have observed that it is a great misfortune for a man to have a wife who loves him. She creates the scenes of jealousy, she makes him look ridiculous, she insists on having all his time and attention. Ah! *non,* it is not the bed of roses."

"Poirot," I said, "you're an incurable old cynic."

"Mais non, mais non, I only make the reflections. See you, really, I am on the side of the good mamma."

I could not refrain from laughing at hearing the haughty Duchess described in this way.

Poirot remained quite serious.

"You should not laugh. It is of great importance, all this. I must reflect. I must reflect a great deal."

"I don't see what you can do in the matter," I said.

Poirot paid no attention.

"You observed, Hastings, how well informed the Duchess was? And how vindictive. She knew all the evidence there was against Jane Wilkinson."

"The case for the prosecution but not the case for the defence," I said, smiling.

"How did she come to know of it?"

"Jane told the Duke. The Duke told her," I suggested.

"Yes, that is possible. Yet I have—"

The telephone rang sharply. I answered it.

My part consisted of saying "Yes" at varying intervals. Finally I put down the receiver and turned excitedly to Poirot.

"That was Japp. Firstly, you're 'the goods,' as usual. Secondly, he's had a cable from America. Thirdly, he's got the taxi driver. Fourthly, would you like to come round and hear what the taxi driver says? Fifthly, you're 'the goods' again, and all along he's been convinced that you'd hit the nail on the head when you suggested that there was some man behind all this! I omitted to tell him that we'd just had a visitor here who says the police force is corrupt."

"So Japp is convinced at last," murmured Poirot. "Curious that the Man-in-the-Background theory should be proved just at the moment when I was inclining to another possible theory."

"What theory?"

"The theory that the motive for the murder might have nothing to do with Lord Edgware himself. Imagine someone who hated Jane Wilkinson, hated her so much that they would have even had her hanged for murder. *C'est une idee, ça!*"

He sighed, then he roused himself.

"Come, Hastings, let us hear what Japp has to say."

Chapter XX

WE FOUND JAPP interrogating an old man with a ragged moustache and spectacles. He had a hoarse, self-pitying voice.

"Ah! there you are," said Japp. "Well, things are all plain sailing, I think. This man—his name's Jobson—picked up two people in Long Acre on the night of June twenty-ninth.

"That's right," assented Jobson hoarsely. "Lovely night it were. Moon and all. The young lady and gentleman were by the tube station and hailed me."

"They were in evening dress?"

"Yes, gent in white waistcoat and the young lady all in white with birds embroidered on it. Come out of the Royal Opera, I guess."

"What time was this?"

"Sometime afore eleven."

"Well, what next?"

"Told me to go to Regent Gate—they'd tell me which house when they got there. And told me to be quick, too. People always says that. As though you wanted to loiter. Sooner you get there and get another fare the better for you. They never think of that. And, mind you, if there's an accident you'll get the blame for dangerous driving!"

"Cut it out," said Japp impatiently. "There wasn't an accident this time, was there?"

"No—no," agreed the man as though unwilling to abandon his claim to such an occurrence. "No, as a matter of fact, there weren't. Well, I got to Regent Gate—not above seven minutes it didn't take me—and there the gentleman rapped on the glass, and I stopped. About at Number Eight that were. Well, the gentleman and lady got out. The gentleman stopped where he was and told me to do the same. The lady crossed the road, and began walking back along the houses the other side. The gentleman stayed by the cab, standing on the sidewalk with his back to me, looking after her. Had his hands in his pockets. It was about five minutes when I heard him say something—kind of exclamation under his breath—and then off he goes too. I looks after him because I wasn't going to be bilked. It's been done afore to me, so I kept my eye on him. He went up the steps of one of the houses on the other side and went in."

"Did he push the door open?"

"No, he had a latchkey."

"What number was the house?"

"It would be Seventeen or Nineteen, I fancy. Well, it seemed odd to me my being told to stay where I was. So I kept watching. About five minutes later him and the young lady came out together. They got back into the cab and told me to drive back to Covent Garden Opera House. They stopped me just before I got there and paid me. Paid me handsome, I will say, though I expect I've got into trouble over it. Seems there's nothing but trouble."

"You're all right," said Japp. "Just run your eye over these, will you, and tell me if the young lady is among them."

There were half a dozen photographs, all fairly alike as to type. I looked with some interest over his shoulder.

"That were her," said Jobson. He pointed a decisive finger at one of Geraldine Marsh in evening dress.

"Sure?"

"Quite sure. Pale she was and dark."

"Now the man."

Another sheaf of photographs was handed to him.

He looked at them attentively and then shook his head.

"Well, I couldn't say—not for sure. Either of these two might be him."

The photographs included one of Ronald Marsh, but Jobson had not selected it. Instead he indicated two other men not unlike Marsh in type.

Jobson then departed and Japp flung the photographs on the table.

"Good enough. Wish I could have got a clearer identification of his lordship. Of course it's an old photograph, taken seven or eight years ago. The only one I could get hold of. Yes, I'd like a clearer identification, although the case is clear enough. Bang go a couple of alibis. Clever of you to think of it, M. Poirot."

Poirot looked modest.

"When I found that she and her cousin were both at the opera it seemed to me possible that they might have been together during one of the intervals. Naturally the parties they were with would assume that they had not left the Opera House. But a half hour interval gives plenty of time to get to Regent Gate and back. The moment the new Lord Edgware laid such stress upon his alibi, I was sure something was wrong with it."

"You're a nice suspicious sort of fellow, aren't you?" said Japp affectionately. "Well, you're about right. Can't be too suspicious in a world like this. His lordship is our man all right. Look at this."

He produced a paper.

"Cable from New York. They got into touch with Miss Lucie Adams. The letter was in the mail delivered to her this morning. She was not willing to give up the original unless absolutely necessary, but she willingly allowed the officer to take a copy of it and cable it to us. Here it is and it's as damning as you could hope for."

Poirot took the cable with great interest. I read it over his shoulder.

Following is text letter to Lucie Adams dated June 29th 8 Rosedew Mansions London. S.W.3 Begins Dearest little Sister, I'm sorry I wrote you such a scrappy bit last week but things were rather busy and there was a lot to see to. Well, darling, it's been ever such a success! Notices splendid, box office good, and everybody most kind. I've got some real good friends over here and next year I'm thinking of taking a theatre for two months. The Russian dancer sketch went very well and the American woman in Paris too, but the Scenes at a Foreign Hotel are still the favourites, I think. I'm so excited that I hardly know what I'm writing, and you'll see why in a minute, but first I must tell you what people have said. Mr. Hergsheimer was ever so kind and he's going to ask me to lunch to meet Sir Montagu Corner who might do great things for me. The other night I met Jane Wilkinson and she was ever so sweet about my show and my take off of her which brings me round to what I am going to tell you. I don't really like her very much because I've been hearing a lot about her lately from someone I know and she's behaved cruelly, I think, and in a very underhand way—but I won't go into that now. You know that she really is Lady Edgware? I've heard a lot about him too lately and he's no beauty, I can tell you. He treated his nephew, the Captain Marsh I have mentioned to you, in the most shameful way—literally turned him out of the house and discontinued his allowance. He told me all about it and I felt awfully sorry for him. He enjoyed my show very much, he said, "I believe it would take in Lord Edgware himself. Look here, will you take something on for a bet?" I laughed and said. "How much?" Lucie, darling, the answer fairly took my breath away. Ten thousand dollars. Ten thousand dollars, think of it—just to help someone win a silly bet. "Why," I said, "I'd play a joke on the King in Buckingham Palace and risk lèse majesté for that." Well then, we laid our heads together and got down to details.

I'll tell you all about it next week—whether I'm spotted or not. But anyway, Lucie darling, whether I succeed or fail, I'm to have the ten thousand dollars. Oh! Lucie, little sister, what that's going to mean to us. No time for more—just going off to do my "hoax." Lots and lots and lots of love, little sister mine.

Yours,

Carlotta

Poirot laid down the letter. It had touched him, I could see.

Japp, however, reacted in quite a different way.

"We've got him," said Japp exultantly.

"Yes," said Poirot.

His voice sounded strangely flat.

Japp looked at him curiously.

"What is it, M. Poirot?"

"Nothing," said Poirot. "It is not, somehow, just as I thought. That is all."

He looked acutely unhappy.

"But still it must be so," he said as though to himself. "Yes, it must be so."

"Of course it is so. Why, you've said so all along!"

"No, no. You misunderstood me."

"Didn't you say there was someone back of all this who got the girl into doing it innocently?"

"Yes, yes."

"Well, what more do you want?"

Poirot sighed and said nothing.

"You are an odd sort of cove. Nothing ever satisfies you. I say, it was a piece of luck the girl wrote this letter."

Poirot agreed with more vigour than he had yet shown.

"*Mais oui,* that is what the murderer did not expect. When Miss Adams accepted that ten thousand dollars she signed her death warrant. The murderer thought he had taken all precautions—and yet in sheer innocence she outwitted him. The dead speak. Yes, sometimes the dead speak."

"I never thought she'd done it off her own bat," said Japp unblushingly.

"No, no," said Poirot absently.

"Well, I must get on with things."

"You are going to arrest Captain Marsh—Lord Edgware, I mean?"

"Why not? The case against him seems proved up to the hilt."

"True."

"You seem very despondent about it, M. Poirot. The truth is you like things to be difficult. Here's your own theory proved, and even that does not satisfy you. Can you see any flaw in the evidence we've got?"

Poirot shook his head.

"Whether Miss Marsh was accessory or not, I don't know," said Japp.

"Seems as though she must have known about it, going there with him from the opera. If she wasn't, why did he take her? Well, we'll hear what they've both got to say."

"May I be present?"

Poirot spoke almost humbly.

"Certainly you can. I owe the idea to you!"

He picked up the telegram on the table.

I drew Poirot aside.

"What is the matter, Poirot?"

"I am very unhappy, Hastings. This seems the plain sailing and the above board. But there is something wrong. Somewhere or other, Hastings, there is a fact that escapes us. It all fits together, it is as I imagined it, and yet, my friend, there is something wrong."

He looked at me piteously. I was at a loss what to say.

Chapter XXI

RONALD'S STORY

I FOUND IT hard to understand Poirot's attitude. Surely this was what he had predicted all along?

All the way to Regent Gate, he sat perplexed and frowning, paying no attention to Japp's self-congratulations. He came out of his reverie at last with a sigh.

"At all events," he murmured, "we can see what he has to say."

"Next to nothing, if he's wise," said Japp. "There's any amount of men that have hanged themselves by being too eager to make a statement. Well, no one can say as we don't warn them! It's all fair and above board. And the more guilty they are, the more anxious they are to pipe up and tell you the lies they've thought out to meet the case. They don't know that you should always submit your lies to a solicitor first."

He sighed and said:

"Solicitors and coroners are the worst enemies of the police. Again and again I've had a perfectly clear case messed up by the coroner fooling about and letting the guilty party get away with it. Lawyers you can't object to so much, I suppose. They're paid for their artfulness and twisting things this way and that."

On arrival at Regent Gate we found that our quarry was at home. The family were still at the luncheon table. Japp proffered a request to speak to Lord Edgware privately. We were shown into the library.

In a minute or two the young man came to us. There was an easy smile on his face which changed a little as he cast a quick glance over us. His lips tightened.

"Hello, Inspector," he said. "What's all this about?"

Japp said his little piece in the classic fashion.

"So that's it, is it?" said Ronald.

He drew a chair towards him and sat down. He pulled out a cigarette case.

"I think, Inspector, I'd like to make a statement."

"That's as you please, my lord."

"Meaning that it's damned foolish on my part. All the same, I think I will. 'Having no reason to fear the truth,' as the heroes in books always say."

Japp said nothing. His face remained expressionless.

"There's a nice handy table and chair," went on the young man. "Your minion can sit down and take it all down in shorthand."

I don't think that Japp was used to having his arrangements made for him so thoughtfully. Lord Edgware's suggestion was adopted.

"To begin with," said the young man. "Having some grains of intelligence I strongly suspect that my beautiful alibi has bust. Gone up in smoke. Exit the useful Dortheimers. Taxi driver, I suppose?"

"We know all about your movements on that night," said Japp woodenly.

"I have the greatest admiration for Scotland Yard. All the same, you know, if I had really been planning a deed of violence I shouldn't have hired a taxi and driven straight to the place and kept the fellow waiting. Have you thought of that? Ah! I see M. Poirot has."

"It had occurred to me, yes," said Poirot.

"Such is not the manner of premeditated crime," said Ronald. "Put on a red moustache and horn-rimmed glasses and drive to the next street and pay the man off. Take the tube—well—well, I won't go into it all. My counsel, at a fee of several thousand guineas will do it better than I can. Of course I see the answer. Crime was a sudden impulse. There was I, waiting in the cab, et cetera. It occurs to me, 'Now, my boy, up and doing.'

"Well, I'm going to tell you the truth. I was in a hole for money. That's been pretty clear, I think. It was rather a desperate business. I had to get it by the next day or drop out of things. I tried my uncle. He'd no love for me, but I thought he might care for the honour of his name. Middle-aged men sometimes do. My uncle proved to be lamentably modern in his cynical indifference.

"Well—it looked like just having to grin and bear it. I was going to try and have a shot at borrowing from Dortheimer, but I knew there wasn't a hope. And marry his daughter I couldn't. She's much too sensible a girl to take me, anyway. Then, by chance, I met my cousin at the opera. I don't often come across her, but she was always a decent kid when I lived in the house. I found myself telling her all about it. She'd heard something from her father, anyway. Then she showed her mettle. She suggested I should take her pearls. They'd belonged to her mother."

He paused. There was something like real emotion, I think, in his voice. Or else he suggested it better than I could have believed possible.

"Well—I accepted the blessed child's offer. I could raise the money I wanted on them, and I swore I'd turn to and redeem them, even if it meant working to manage it. But the pearls were at home in Regent Gate. We decided that the best thing to do would be to go and fetch them at once. We jumped in a taxi and off we went.

"We made the fellow stop on the opposite side of the street, in case anyone should hear the taxi draw up at the door. Geraldine got out and went across the road. She had her latchkey with her. She would go in quietly, get the pearls and bring them out to me. She didn't expect to meet anyone except possibly a servant. Miss Carroll, my uncle's secretary, usually went to bed at half past nine. He, himself, would probably be in the library.

"So off Dina went. I stood on the pavement smoking a cigarette. Every now and then I looked over towards the house to see if she was coming. And now I come to the part of the story that you may believe or not as you like. A man passed me on the sidewalk. I turned to look after him. To my surprise he went up the steps and let himself in to number Seventeen. At least I thought it was number Seventeen, but of course I was some distance away. That surprised me very much, for two reasons. One was that the man had let himself in with a key, and the second was that I thought I recognized in him a certain well-known actor.

"I was so surprised that I determined to look into matters. I happened to have my own key of Number Seventeen in my pocket. I'd lost it, or thought I'd lost it three years ago, had come across it unexpectedly a day or two ago and had been meaning to give it back to my uncle this morning. However, in the heat of our discussion, it had slipped my memory. I had transferred it with the other contents of my pockets when I changed.

"Telling the taxi man to wait, I strode hurriedly along the pavement, crossed the road, went up the steps of Number Seventeen and opened the door with my key. The hall was empty. There was no sign of any visitor having just entered. I stood for a minute looking about me. Then I went towards the library door. Perhaps the man was in with my uncle. If so, I should hear the murmur of voices. I stood outside the library door, but I heard nothing.

"I suddenly felt I had made the most abject fool of myself. Of course the man must have gone into some other house—the house beyond probably. Regent Gate is rather dimly lighted at night. I felt an absolute idiot. What on earth had possessed me to follow the fellow, I could not think. It had landed me here, and a pretty fool I should look if my uncle were to come suddenly out of the library and find me. I should get Geraldine into trouble and altogether the fat would be in the fire. All because something in the man's manner had made me imagine that he was doing something that he didn't want known. Luckily no one had caught me. I must get out of it as soon as I could.

"I tiptoed back towards the front door and at the same moment Geraldine came down the stairs with the pearls in her hand. She was very startled at seeing me, of course. I got her out of the house, and then explained."

He paused.

"We hurried back to the opera, got there just as the curtain was going up. No one suspected that we'd left it. It was a hot night and several people went outside to get a breath of air."

He paused.

"I know what you'll say: Why didn't I tell you this right away? And now I put it to you: Would you, with a motive for murder sticking out a yard, admit light-heartedly that you'd actually been at the place the murder was committed on the night in question?

"Frankly, I funked it! Even if we were believed, it was going to be a lot of worry for me and for Geraldine. We'd had nothing to do with the murder; we'd seen nothing; we'd heard nothing. Obviously, I thought, Aunt Jane had done it. Well, why bring myself in? I told you about the quarrel and my lack of money, because I knew you'd ferret it out; and, if I'd tried to conceal all that, you'd be much more suspicious and you'd probably examine that alibi much more closely. As it was, I thought that if I bucked enough about it it would almost hypnotize you into thinking it all right. The Dortheimers were, I know, honestly convinced that I'd been at Covent Garden all the time. That I spent one interval with my cousin wouldn't strike them as suspicious. And she could always say she'd been with me there and that we hadn't left the place."

"Miss Marsh agreed to this—concealment?"

"Yes. Soon as I got the news, I got onto her and cautioned her for her life not to say anything about her excursion here last night. She'd been with me and I'd been with her during the last interval at Covent Garden. We'd walked in the street a little, that was all. She understood and she quite agreed."

He paused.

"I know it looks bad, coming out with this afterward, but the story's true enough. I can give you the name and address of the man who let me have the cash on Geraldine's pearls this morning. And if you ask her, she'll confirm every word I've told you."

He sat back in his chair and looked at Japp. Japp continued to look expressionless.

"You say you thought Jane Wilkinson had committed the murder, Lord Edgware?" he said.

"Well, wouldn't you have thought so? After the butler's story?"

"What about your wager with Miss Adams?"

"Wager with Miss Adams? With Carlotta Adams, do you mean? What has she got to do with it?"

"Do you deny that you offered her the sum of ten thousand dollars to impersonate Miss Jane Wilkinson at the house that night?"

Ronald stared.

"Offered her ten thousand dollars? Nonsense. Someone's been pulling your leg. I haven't got ten thousand dollars to offer. You've got hold of a mare's nest. Does *she* say so? Oh! dash it all—I forgot. She's dead, isn't she?"

"Yes," said Poirot quietly. "She is dead."

Ronald turned his eyes from one to the other of us. He had been debonair before. Now his face had whitened. His eyes looked frightened.

"I don't understand all this," he said. "It's true what I told you. I suppose you don't believe me—any of you."

And then to my amazement, Poirot stepped forward.

"Yes," he said. "I believe you."

Chapter XXII

STRANGE BEHAVIOUR OF HERCULE POIROT

WE WERE IN our rooms.

"What on earth—" I began.

Poirot stopped me with a gesture more extravagant than any gesture I had ever seen him make. Both arms whirled in the air.

"I implore of you, Hastings! Not now! Not now!"

And upon that, he seized his hat, clapped it on his head as though he had never heard of order and method, and rushed headlong from the room. He had not returned when, about an hour later, Japp appeared.

"Little man gone out?" he inquired.

I nodded.

Japp sank into a seat. He dabbed his forehead with a handkerchief. The day was warm.

"What the devil took him?" he inquired. "I can tell you, Captain Hastings, you could have knocked me over with a feather when he stepped up to the man and said: 'I believe you,' for all the world as though he were acting in a romantic melodrama. It beats me."

It beat me also, and I said so.

"And then he marches out of the house," said Japp. "What did he say about it to you?"

"Nothing," I replied.

"Nothing at all?"

"Absolutely nothing. When I was going to speak to him he waved me aside. I thought it best to leave him alone. When we got back here I started to question him. He waved his arms, seized his hat and rushed out again."

We looked at each other. Japp tapped his forehead significantly.

"Must be," he said.

For once I was disposed to agree. Japp had often suggested before that Poirot was what he called "touched." In those cases he had simply not understood what Poirot was driving at. Here, I was forced to confess, I could not understand Poirot's attitude. If not touched, he was, at any rate,

suspiciously changeable. Here was his own private theory triumphantly
confirmed, and straight away he went back on it. It was enough to dismay
and distress his warmest supporters. I shook my head in a discouraged
fashion.

"He's always been what I call peculiar," said Japp. "Got his own particular angle of looking at things—and a very queer one it is. He's a kind of
genius, I admit that. But they always say that geniuses are very near the
border line and liable to slip over any minute. He's always been fond of
having things difficult. A straightforward case is never good enough for
him. No, it's got to be tortuous. He's got away from real life. He plays a
game of his own. It's like an old lady playing patience. If it doesn't come
out, she cheats. Well, it's the other way round with him. If it's coming out
too easily, he cheats to make it more difficult! That's the way I look at it."

I found it difficult to answer him. I was too perturbed and distressed to
be able to think clearly. I, also, found Poirot's behaviour unaccountable;
and, since I was very attached to my strange little friend, it worried me
more than I cared to express.

In the middle of a gloomy silence, Poirot walked into the room. He was,
I was thankful to see, quite calm now. Very carefully, he removed his hat,
placed it with his stick on a table and sat down in his accustomed chair.

"So you are here, my good Japp. I am glad. It was on my mind that I
must see you as soon as possible."

Japp looked at him without replying. He saw that this was only the
beginning. He waited for Poirot to explain himself. This my friend did,
speaking slowly and carefully.

"*Ecoutez,* Japp. We are wrong. We are all wrong. It is grievous to admit
it, but we have made a mistake."

"That's all right," said Japp confidently.

"But it is not all right. It is deplorable. It grieves me to the heart."

"You needn't be grieved about that young man. He richly deserves all
he gets."

"It is not he I am grieving about; it is you."

"Me? You needn't worry about me."

"But I do. See you, who was it set you on this course? It was Hercule
Poirot. *Mais oui,* I set you on the trail. I direct your attention to Carlotta
Adams, I mention to you the matter of the letter to America. Every step of
the way it is I who point it!"

"I was bound to get there anyway," said Japp coldly. "You got a bit
ahead of me, that's all."

"*Cela ce peut.* But it does not console me. If harm, if loss of prestige
comes to you through listening to my little ideas, I shall blame myself
bitterly."

Japp merely looked amused. I think he credited Poirot with motives that were none too pure. He fancied that Poirot grudged him the credit resulting from the successful elucidation of the affair.

"That's all right," he said. "I shan't forget to let it be known that I owe something to you over this business."

He winked at me.

"Oh! it is not that at all." Poirot clicked his tongue with impatience. "I want no credit. And what is more, I tell you there will be no credit. It is a fiasco that you prepare for yourself, and I, Hercule Poirot, am the cause."

Suddenly, at Poirot's expression of extreme melancholy, Japp shouted with laughter. Poirot looked affronted.

"Sorry, M. Poirot." He wiped his eyes. "But you did look for all the world like a dying duck in a thunderstorm. Now look here, let's forget all this. I'm willing to shoulder the credit or the blame of this affair. It will make a big noise; you're right there. Well, I'm going out to get a conviction. It may be that a clever counsel will get his lordship off; you never know with a jury. But even so, it won't do me any harm. It will be known that we caught the right man, even if we couldn't get a conviction. And if, by any chance, the third housemaid has hysterics and owns up she did it—well, I'll take my medicine and I won't complain you led me up the garden. That's fair enough."

Poirot gazed at him mildly and sadly.

"You have the confidence—always the confidence! You never stop and say to yourself: 'Can it be so?' You never doubt—or wonder. You never think: 'This is too easy!' "

"You bet your life I don't. And that's just where, if you'll excuse me saying so, you go off the rails every time. Why shouldn't a thing be easy? What's the harm in a thing being easy?"

Poirot looked at him, sighed, half threw up his arms, then shook his head.

"C'est fini! I will say no more."

"Splendid," said Japp heartily. "Now let's get down to brass tacks. You'd like to hear what I've been doing?"

"Assuredly."

"Well, I saw Miss Marsh, and her story tallied exactly with his lordship's. They may both be in it together, but I think not. It's my opinion he bluffed her. She's three parts sweet on him anyway. Took on terribly when she found he was arrested."

"Did she now? And the secretary—Miss Carroll?"

"Wasn't too surprised, I fancy. However, that's only my idea."

"What about the pearls?" I asked. "Was that part of the story true?"

"Absolutely. He raised the money on them early the following morning.

But I don't think that touches the main argument. As I see it, the plan came into his head when he came across his cousin at the opera. It came to him in a flash. He was desperate—here was a way out. I fancy he'd been meditating something of the kind; that's why he had the key with him. I don't believe that story of suddenly coming across it. Well, as he talks to his cousin, he sees that, by involving her, he gains additional security for himself. He plays on her feelings, hints at the pearls; she plays up, and off they go. As soon as she's in the house he follows her in and goes along to the library. Maybe his lordship had dozed off in his chair. Anyway, in two seconds he's done the trick and he's out again. I don't fancy he meant the girl to catch him in the house. He counted on being found pacing up and down near the taxi. And I don't think the taxi man was meant to see him go in. The impression was to be that he was walking up and down smoking while he waited for the girl. The taxi was facing the opposite direction, remember.

"Of course, the next morning, he has to pledge the pearls. He must still seem to be in need of the money. Then, when he hears of the crime, he frightens the girl into concealing their visit to the house. They will say that they spent that interval together at the Opera House."

"Then why did they not do so?" asked Poirot sharply.

Japp shrugged his shoulders.

"Changed his mind. Or judged that she wouldn't be able to go through with it. She's a nervous type."

"Yes," said Poirot meditatively. "She is a nervous type."

After a minute or two, he said:

"It does not strike you that it would have been easier and simpler for Captain Marsh to have left the opera during the interval by himself, to have gone in quietly with his key, killed his uncle, and returned to the opera—instead of having a taxi outside and a nervous girl coming down the stairs any minute who might lose her head and give him away."

Japp grinned.

"That's what you and I would have done. But then we're a shade brighter than Captain Ronald Marsh."

"I am not so sure. He strikes me as intelligent."

"But not so intelligent as M. Hercule Poirot! Come now, I'm sure of that!" Japp laughed.

Poirot looked at him coldly.

"If he isn't guilty, why did he persuade the Adams girl to take on that stunt?" went on Japp. "There can be only one reason for that stunt—to protect the real criminal."

"There I am of accord with you absolutely."

"Well, I'm glad we agree about something."

"It might be he who actually spoke to Mademoiselle," mused Poirot, "while really—no, that is an imbecility."

Then, looking suddenly at Japp, he rapped out a quick question.

"What is your theory as to her death?"

Japp cleared his throat.

"I'm inclined to believe accident. A convenient accident, I admit. I can't see that he could have had anything to do with it. His alibi is straight enough after the opera. He was at Sobranis' with the Dortheimers till after one o'clock. Long before that she was in bed and asleep. No, I think that was an instance of the infernal luck criminals sometimes have. Otherwise, if that accident hadn't happened, I think he had his plans for dealing with her. First, he'd put the fear of the Lord into her—tell her she'd be arrested for murder if she confessed the truth. And then he'd square her with a fresh lot of money."

"Does it strike you—" Poirot stared straight in front of him—"does it strike you that Miss Adams would let another woman be hanged when she herself held evidence that would acquit her?"

"Jane Wilkinson wouldn't have been hanged. The Montagu Corner party evidence was too strong for that."

"But the murderer did not know that. He would have had to count on Jane Wilkinson being hanged and Carlotta Adams keeping silence."

"You love talking, don't you, M. Poirot? And you're positively convinced now that Ronald Marsh is a white-headed boy who can do no wrong. Do you believe that story of his about seeing a man sneak surreptitiously into the house?"

Poirot shrugged his shoulders.

"Do you know who he says he thought it was?"

"I could guess, perhaps."

"He says he thought it was the film star, Bryan Martin. What do you think of that? A man who'd never even met Lord Edgware."

"Then it would certainly be curious if one saw such a man entering that house with a key."

"Chah!" said Japp. A rich noise expressive of contempt. "And now I suppose it will surprise you to hear that Mr. Bryan Martin wasn't in London that night. He took a young lady to dine down at Molesey. They didn't get back to London till midnight."

"Ah!" said Poirot mildly. "No, I am not surprised. Was the young lady also a member of the profession?"

"No. Girl who keeps a hat shop. As a matter of fact it was Miss Adams' friend, Miss Driver. I think you'll agree her testimony is past suspicion."

"I am not disputing it, my friend."

"In fact, you're done down and you know it, old boy," said Japp, laughing. "Cock and bull story trumped up on the moment, that's what it was. Nobody entered Number Seventeen—and nobody entered either of the houses either side—so what does that show? That his lordship's a liar."

Poirot shook his head sadly.

Japp rose to his feet, his spirits restored.

"Come now, we're right, you know."

"Who was D, Paris, November?"

Japp shrugged his shoulders.

"Ancient history, I imagine. Can't a girl have a souvenir six months ago without its having something to do with this crime? We must have a sense of proportion."

"Six months ago," murmured Poirot, a sudden light in his eyes. "*Dieu, que je suis bête!*"

"What's he saying?" inquired Japp of me.

"Listen." Poirot rose and tapped Japp on the chest. "Why does Miss Adams' maid not recognize that box? Why does Miss Driver not recognize it?"

"What do you mean?"

"Because the box was *new!* It had only just been given to her. Paris, November—that is all very well—doubtless that is the date of which the box is to be a souvenir. But it was given to her *now,* not *then.* It has just been bought! Only just been bought! Investigate that, I implore you, my good Japp. It is a chance, decidedly a chance. It was bought not here, but abroad. Probably Paris. If it had been bought here, some jeweller would have come forward. It has been photographed and described in the papers. Yes, yes, Paris. Possibly some other foreign town, but I think Paris. Find out, I implore you. Make the inquiries. I want—I so badly want to know who is this mysterious D."

"It will do no harm," said Japp good-naturedly. "Can't say I'm very excited about it myself, but I'll do what I can. The more we know the better."

Nodding cheerfully to us he departed.

Chapter XXIII

"AND NOW," SAID Poirot, "we will go out to lunch."

He put his hand through my arm. He was smiling at me.

"I have hope," he explained.

I was glad to see him restored to his old self, though I was none the less convinced myself of young Ronald's guilt. I fancied that Poirot himself had perhaps come round to this view, convinced by Japp's arguments. The search for the purchaser of the box was, perhaps, a last sally to save his face.

We went amicably to lunch together. Somewhat to my amusement, at a table the other side of the room, I saw Bryan Martin and Jenny Driver lunching together. Remembering what Japp had said, I suspected a possible romance. They saw us and Jenny waved a hand.

When we were sipping coffee, Jenny left her escort and came over to our table. She looked as vivid and dynamic as ever.

"May I sit here and talk to you a minute, M. Poirot?"

"Assuredly, mademoiselle. I am charmed to see you. Will not M. Martin join us also?"

"I told him not to. You see, I wanted to talk to you about Carlotta."

"Yes, mademoiselle?"

"You wanted to get a line onto some man friend of hers. Isn't that so?"

"Yes, yes."

"Well, I've been thinking and thinking. Sometimes you can't get at things straight away. To get them clear, you've got to think back—remember a lot of little words and phrases that perhaps you didn't pay much attention to at the time. Well, that's what I've been doing, thinking and thinking and remembering just what she said. And I've come to a certain conclusion."

"Yes, mademoiselle?"

"I think the man that she cared about—or was beginning to care about

—was Ronald Marsh—you know, the one who has just succeeded to the title."

"What makes you think it was he, mademoiselle?"

"Well, for one thing, Carlotta was speaking in a general sort of way one day, about a man having hard luck, and how it might affect character. That a man might be a decent sort really and yet go down the hill. More sinned against than sinning—you know the idea. The first thing a woman kids herself with when she's getting soft about a man. I've heard the old wheeze so often! Carlotta had plenty of sense, yet here she was coming out with this stuff just like a complete ass who knew nothing of life. 'Hello,' I said to myself. 'Something's up.' She didn't mention a name; it was all general, but almost immediately after that she began to speak of Ronald Marsh and that she thought he'd been badly treated. She was very impersonal and off-hand about it. I didn't connect the two things at the time. But now, I wonder. It seems to me that it was Ronald she meant. What do you think, M. Poirot?"

Her face looked earnestly up into his.

"I think, mademoiselle, that you have perhaps given me some very valuable information."

"Good," Jenny clapped her hands.

Poirot looked kindly at her.

"Perhaps you have not heard; the gentleman of whom you speak—Ronald Marsh, Lord Edgware—has just been arrested."

"Oh!" Her mouth flew open in surprise. "Then my bit of thinking comes rather late in the day."

"It is never too late," said Poirot. "Not with me, you understand. Thank you, mademoiselle."

She left us to return to Bryan Martin.

"There, Poirot," I said. "Surely that shakes your belief."

"No, Hastings. On the contrary it strengthens it."

Despite that valiant assertion I believed myself that secretly he had weakened.

During the days that followed he never once mentioned the Edgware case. If I spoke of it, he answered monosyllabically and without interest. In other words, he had washed his hands of it. Whatever idea he had had lingering in his fantastic brain, he had now been forced to admit himself that it had not materialized—that his first conception of the case had been the true one, and that Ronald Marsh was only too truly accused of the crime. Only, being Poirot, he could not admit openly that such was the case! Therefore he pretended to have lost interest.

Such, I say, was my interpretation of his attitude. It seemed borne out by the facts. He took no faintest interest in the police court proceedings, which in any case were purely formal. He busied himself with other cases and, as I say, displayed no interest when the subject was mentioned.

It was nearly a fortnight later than the events mentioned in my last chapter when I came to realize that my interpretation of his attitude was entirely wrong. It was breakfast time. The usual heavy pile of letters lay by Poirot's plate. He sorted through them with nimble fingers. Then he uttered a quick exclamation of pleasure and picked up a letter with an American stamp on it. He opened it with his little letter opener. I looked on with interest, since he seemed so moved to pleasure about it. There was a letter and a fairly thick enclosure.

Poirot read the former through twice, then he looked up.

"Would you like to see this, Hastings?"

I took it from him. It ran as follows:

Dear M. Poirot, I was much touched by your kind—your very kind letter. I have been feeling so bewildered by everything. Apart from my terrible grief, I have been so affronted by the things that seem to have been hinted about Carlotta—the dearest, sweetest sister that a girl ever had. No, M. Poirot, she did not take drugs. I'm sure of it. She had a horror of that kind of thing. I've often heard her say so. If she played a part in that poor man's death, it was an entirely innocent one—but of course her letter to me proves that. I am sending you the actual letter itself, since you ask me to do so. I hate parting with the last letter she ever wrote, but I know you will take care of it and let me have it back; and if it helps you to clear up some of the mystery about her death, as you say it may do, why, then, of course it must go to you.

You ask whether Carlotta mentioned any friend specially in her letters. She mentioned a great many people, of course, but nobody in a very outstanding way. Bryan Martin whom we used to know years ago, a girl called Jenny Driver, and a Captain Ronald Marsh were, I think, the ones she saw most of.

I wish I could think of something to help you. You write so kindly and with such understanding, and you seem to realize what Carlotta and I were to each other.

Gratefully yours,

Lucie Adams.

P.S. An officer has just been here for the letter. I told him that I had already mailed it to you. This, of course, was not true, but I felt, somehow or other, that it was important you should see it first. It seems Scotland Yard need it as evidence against the murderer. You will take it to them. But Oh!

please be sure they let you have it back again some day. You see, it is Carlotta's last words to me.

"So you wrote yourself to her," I remarked as I laid the letter down. "Why did you do that, Poirot? And why did you ask for the original of Carlotta Adams' letter?"

He was bending over the enclosed sheets of the letter I mentioned.

"In verity I could not say, Hastings, unless it is that I hoped against hope that the original letter might in some way explain the inexplicable."

"I don't see how you can get away from the text of that letter. Carlotta Adams gave it herself to the maid to post. There was no hocus pocus about it, and certainly it reads as a perfectly genuine ordinary epistle."

Poirot sighed.

"I know. I know. And that is what makes it so difficult, because, Hastings, as it stands, that letter is *impossible.*"

"Nonsense."

"*Si, si,* it is so. See you, as I have reasoned it out, certain things *must* be; they follow each other with method and order in an understandable fashion. But then comes this letter. It does not accord. Who, then, is wrong? Hercule Poirot or the letter?"

"You don't think it possible that it could be Hercule Poirot?" I suggested as delicately as I was able.

Poirot threw me a glance of reproof.

"There are times when I have been in error, but this is not one of them. Clearly then, since the letter seems impossible, it *is* impossible. There is some fact about the letter which escapes us. I seek to discover what that fact is."

And thereupon he resumed his study of the letter in question, using a small pocket microscope. As he finished perusing each page, he passed it across to me. I, certainly, could find nothing amiss. It was written in a firm, fairly legible handwriting, and it was word for word as it had been telegraphed across.

Poirot sighed deeply.

"There is no forgery of any kind here. No, it is all written in the same hand. And yet, since, as I say, it is impossible—"

He broke off. With an impatient gesture he demanded the sheets from me. I passed them over, and once again he went slowly through them.

Suddenly he uttered a cry. I had left the breakfast table and was standing looking out of the window. At this sound, however, I turned sharply.

Poirot was literally quivering with excitement. His eyes were green like a cat's. His pointing finger trembled.

"See you, Hastings? Look here—quickly—come and look."

I ran to his side. Spread out before him was one of the middle sheets of the letter. I could see nothing unusual about it.

"See you not? All these other sheets they have the clean edge; they are single sheets. But this one—see—one side of it is ragged; it has been torn. Now do you see what I mean? *This was a double sheet*, and so, you comprehend, *one page of the letter is missing.*"

I stared stupidly no doubt.

"But how can it be? It makes sense."

"Yes, yes, it makes sense. That is where the cleverness of the idea comes in. Read—and you will see."

I think I cannot do better than to append a facsimile of the page in question.

"You see it now?" said Poirot. "The letter breaks off where she is talking of Captain Marsh. She is sorry for him, and then she says: 'He enjoyed my show very much.' Then on the new sheet she goes on 'he said—' But *mon ami, a page is missing.* The 'he' of the new page may not be the 'he' of the old page. *In fact it is not the he of the old page.* It is another man altogether who proposed that hoax. Observe; nowhere after that is the name mentioned. Ah! *c'est épatant!* Somehow or other our murderer gets hold of this letter. It gives him away. No doubt he thinks to suppress it altogether, and then—reading it over—he sees another way of dealing with it. Remove one page, and the letter is capable of being twisted into a damning accusation of another man, a man, too, who has a motive for Lord Edgware's death. Ah! it was a gift! The money for the *confiture* as you say! He tears the sheet off and replaces the letter."

I looked at Poirot in some admiration. I was not perfectly convinced of the truth of his theory. It seemed to me highly possible that Carlotta had used an odd half sheet that was already torn, but Poirot was so transfigured with joy that I simply had not the heart to suggest this prosaic possibility. After all, he *might* be right.

I did, however, venture to point out one or two difficulties in the way of his theory.

"But how did the man, whoever he was, get hold of the letter? Miss Adams took it straight from her handbag and gave it herself to the maid to post. The maid told us so."

"Therefore we must assume one of two things. Either the maid was lying, or else, during that evening, Carlotta Adams met the murderer."

I nodded.

"It seems to me that that last possibility is the most likely one. We still do not know where Carlotta Adams was between the time she left her flat and nine o'clock when she left her suitcase at Euston station. During that time, I believe myself that she met the murderer in some appointed spot.

She said I believe it
would rate in land
Edgware himself. Look
here, will you take some
thing on for a bet?"
I laughed and said
"How much?"

Lu cie darling —
the answer family took
my breath away

Ten thousand dollars!

They probably had some food together. He gave her some last instructions. What happened exactly in regard to the letter we do not know. One can make a guess. She may have been carrying it in her hand, meaning to post it. She may have laid it down on the table in the restaurant. He sees the address and scents a possible danger. He may have picked it up adroitly, made an excuse for leaving the table, opened it, read it, torn out the sheet, and then either replaced it on the table or perhaps given it to her as she left, telling her that she had dropped it without noticing. The exact way of it is not important, but one thing does seem clear—that Carlotta Adams met the murderer that evening, either before the murder of Lord Edgware or afterward (there was time after she left the Corner House for a brief interview). I have a fancy, though there I am perhaps wrong, that it was the murderer who gave her the gold box. It was possibly a sentimental memento of their first meeting. *If so the murderer is D.*"

"I don't see the point of the gold box."

"Listen, Hastings; Carlotta Adams was not addicted to veronal. Lucie Adams says so, and I, too, believe it to be true. She was a clear-eyed, healthy girl with no predilection for such things. None of her friends nor her maid recognized the box. Why, then, was it found in her possession after she died? To create the impression that she *did* take veronal and that she had taken it for a considerable time—that is to say, at least six months. Let us say that she met the murderer after the murder, if only for a few minutes. They had a drink together, Hastings, to celebrate the success of their plan, and in the girl's drink he put sufficient veronal to ensure that there should be no waking for her on the following morning."

"Horrible," I said with a shudder.

"Yes, it was not pretty," said Poirot dryly.

"Are you going to tell Japp all this?" I asked after a minute or two.

"Not at the moment. What have I got to tell? He would say, the excellent Japp, 'Another nest of the mare! The girl wrote on an odd sheet of paper!' *C'est tout.*"

I looked guiltily at the ground.

"What can I say to that? Nothing. It is a thing that might have happened. I only know it did not happen because *it is necessary that it should not have happened.*"

He paused. A dreamy expression stole across his face.

"Figure to yourself, Hastings; if only that man had had the order and the method, he would have cut that sheet, not torn it. And we should have noticed nothing. But nothing!"

"So we deduce that he is a man of careless habits," I said, smiling.

"No, no. He might have been in a hurry. You observe it is very carelessly torn. Oh! assuredly he was pressed for time."

He paused and then said:

"One thing you do remark, I hope. This man—this D—he must have had a very good alibi for that evening."

"I can't see how he could have had any alibi at all, if he spent his time first at Regent Gate doing a murder and then with Carlotta Adams."

"Precisely," said Poirot. "That is what I mean. He is badly in need of an alibi, so no doubt he prepared one. Another point: Does his name really begin with D? Or does D stand for some nickname by which he was known to her?"

He paused and then said softly:

"A man whose initial or whose nickname is D. We have got to find him, Hastings. Yes, we have got to find him."

Chapter XXIV

ON THE FOLLOWING day we had an unexpected visit. Geraldine Marsh was announced. I felt sorry for her as Poirot greeted her and set a chair for her. Her large dark eyes seemed wider and darker than ever. There were black circles round them, as though she had not slept. Her face looked extraordinarily haggard and weary for one so young—little more, really, than a child.

"I have come to see you, M. Poirot, because I don't know how to go on any longer. I am so terribly worried and upset."

"Yes, mademoiselle?"

His manner was gravely sympathetic.

"Ronald told me what you said to him that day. I mean that dreadful day when he was arrested." She shivered. "He told me that you came up to him suddenly, just when he had said that he supposed no one would believe him, and that you said to him: 'I believe you.' Is that true, M. Poirot?"

"It is true, mademoiselle; that is what I said."

"I know, but I meant not was it true you said it, but were the words really true. I mean, *did* you believe his story?"

Terribly anxious she looked, leaning forward there, her hands clasped together.

"The words were true, mademoiselle," said Poirot quietly. "I do not believe your cousin killed Lord Edgware."

"Oh!" The colour came into her face, her eyes opened big and wide. "Then you must think—that someone else did it!"

"*Evidement,* mademoiselle." He smiled.

"I'm stupid. I say things badly. What I mean is—you think you know who that somebody is?"

She leaned forward eagerly.

"I have my little ideas, naturally, my suspicions, shall we say?"

"Won't you tell me? Please—please."

Poirot shook his head.

"It would be, perhaps, unfair."

"Then you *have* got a definite suspicion of somebody?"

Poirot merely shook his head noncommittally.

"If only I knew a little more," pleaded the girl, "it would make it so much easier for me. And I might perhaps be able to help you. Yes, really I might be able to help you."

Her pleading was very disarming, but Poirot continued to shake his head.

"The Duchess of Merton is still convinced it was my stepmother," said the girl thoughtfully. She gave a slight questioning glance at Poirot. He showed no reaction.

"But I hardly see how that can be."

"What is your opinion of her? Of your stepmother?"

"Well—I hardly know her. I was at school in Paris when my father married her. When I came home, she was quite kind. I mean, she just didn't notice I was there. I thought her very empty-headed and—well, mercenary."

Poirot nodded.

"You spoke of the Duchess of Merton. You have seen much of her?"

"Yes. She has been very kind to me. I have been with her a great deal during the last fortnight. It has been terrible, with all the talk, and the reporters, and Ronald in prison and everything." She shivered. "I feel I have no real friends, but the Duchess has been wonderful, and he has been nice too—her son, I mean."

"You like him?"

"He is shy, I think, stiff and rather difficult to get on with. But his mother talks a lot about him, so that I feel that I know him better than I really do."

"I see. Tell me, mademoiselle, you are fond of your cousin?"

"Of Ronald? Of course. He—I haven't seen much of him the last two years, but before that he used to live in the house. I—I always thought he was wonderful, always joking and thinking of mad things to do. Oh! in that gloomy house of ours it made all the difference."

Poirot nodded sympathetically, but he went on to make a remark that shocked me in its crudity.

"You do not want to see him hanged then?"

"No, no." The girl shivered violently. "Not that. Oh! if only it were her —my stepmother. It *must* be her. The Duchess says it must."

"Ah!" said Poirot. "If only Captain Marsh had stayed in the taxi, eh?"

"Yes—at least, what do you mean?" Her brow wrinkled. "I don't understand."

"If he had not followed that man into the house. Did you hear anyone come in, by the way?"

"No, I didn't hear anything."

"What did you do when you came into the house?"

"I ran straight upstairs, to fetch the pearls, you know."

"Of course. It took you some time to fetch them."

"Yes. I couldn't find the key of my jewel-case all at once."

"So often is that the case. The more in haste, the less the speed. It was some time before you came down, and then—you found your cousin in the hall?"

"Yes, coming from the library." She swallowed.

"I comprehend. It gave you quite the turn."

"Yes, it did." She looked grateful for his sympathetic tone. "It startled me, you see."

"Quite, quite."

"Ronnie just said: 'Hello, Dina, got them?' from behind me, and it made me jump."

"Yes," said Poirot gently. "As I said before it is a pity he did not stay outside. Then the taxi driver would have been able to swear he never entered the house."

She nodded. Her tears began to fall, splashing unheeded on her lap. She got up. Poirot took her hand.

"You want me to save him for you. Is that it?"

"Yes, yes—oh! please, yes. You don't know—"

She stood there striving to control herself, clenching her hands.

"Life has not been easy for you, mademoiselle," said Poirot gently. "I appreciate that. No, it has not been easy. Hastings, will you get mademoiselle a taxi?"

I went down with the girl and saw her into the taxi. She had composed herself by now and thanked me very prettily.

I found Poirot walking up and down the room, his brows knitted in thought. He looked unhappy. I was glad when the telephone bell rang to distract him.

"Who is that? Oh! it is Japp. *Bonjour, mon ami.*"

"What's he got to say?" I asked, drawing nearer the telephone.

Finally, after various ejaculations, Poirot spoke.

"Yes, and who called for it? Do they know?"

Whatever the answer, it was not what he expected. His face dropped ludicrously.

"Are you sure?"

". . . . ."

"No, it is a little upsetting, that is all."

"Yes, I must rearrange my ideas."

". . . . ."

"Comment?"

". . . . ."

"All the same, I was right about it. Yes, a detail, as you say."

". . . . ."

"No, I am still of the same opinion. I would pray of you to make still further inquiries of the restaurants in the neighbourhood of Regent Gate and Euston, Tottenham Court Road and perhaps Oxford Street."

". . . . ."

"Yes, a woman and a man. And also in the neigbourhood of the Strand just before midnight. *Comment?"*

". . . . ."

"But, yes, I know that Captain Marsh was with the Dortheimers. But there are other people in the world besides Captain Marsh."

". . . . ."

"To say I have the head of the pig is not pretty. *Tout de même,* oblige me in this matter, I pray of you."

". . . . ."

He replaced the receiver.

"Well?" I asked impatiently.

"Is it well? I wonder. Hastings, that gold box *was* bought in Paris. It was ordered by letter and it comes from a well-known Paris shop which specializes in such things. The letter was supposedly from a Lady Ackerley —Constance Ackerley the letter was signed. Naturally there is no such person. The letter was received two days before the murder. It ordered the initials of (presumably) the writer in rubies and the inscription inside. It was a rush order—to be called for the following day. That is the day before the murder."

"And it was called for?"

"Yes, it was called for and paid for in notes."

"Who called for it?" I asked excitedly. I felt we were getting near to the truth.

"A woman called for it, Hastings."

"A woman?" I said, surprised.

"Mais oui. A woman—short, middle-aged and *wearing pince-nez."*

We looked at each other completely baffled.

Chapter XXV

A LUNCHEON PARTY

IT WAS, I think, on the day after that that we went to the Widburns' luncheon party at Claridge's. Neither Poirot nor I was particularly anxious to go. It was, as a matter of fact, about the sixth invitation we had received. Mrs. Widburn was a persistent woman and she liked celebrities. Undaunted by refusals, she finally offered such a choice of dates that capitulation was inevitable. Under those circumstances the sooner we went and got it over the better.

Poirot had been very uncommunicative ever since the news from Paris. To my remarks on the subject he returned always the same answer:

"There is something here I do not comprehend." And once or twice he murmured to himself: "Pince-nez. Pince-nez in Paris. Pince-nez in Carlotta Adams' bag."

I really felt glad of the luncheon party as a means of distraction.

Young Donald Ross was there and came up and greeted me cheerily. There were more men than women, and he was put next to me at table. Jane Wilkinson sat almost opposite us, and next to her, between her and Mrs. Widburn, sat the young Duke of Merton.

I fancied—of course it may have been only my fancy—that he looked slightly ill at ease. The company in which he found himself was, so I should imagine, little to his liking. He was a strictly conservative and somewhat reactionary young man, the kind of character that seemed to have stepped out of the Middle Ages by some regrettable mistake. His infatuation for the extremely modern Jane Wilkinson was one of those anachronistic jokes that Nature so loves to play.

Seeing Jane's beauty and appreciating the charm that her exquisite husky voice lent to the most trite utterances, I could hardly wonder at his capitulation. But one can get used to perfect beauty and an intoxicating voice! It crossed my mind that perhaps even now a ray of common sense was dissipating the mists of intoxicated love. It was a chance remark, a rather humiliating *gaffe* on Jane's part, that gave me that impression.

Somebody—I forget who—had uttered the phrase "judgment of Paris," and straight away Jane's delightful voice was uplifted.

"Paris?" she said. "Why, Paris doesn't cut any ice nowadays. It's London and New York that count."

As sometimes happens, the words fell in a momentary lull of conversation. It was an awkward moment. On my right I heard Donald Ross draw in his breath sharply. Mrs. Widburn began to talk violently about Russian opera. Everyone hastily said something to somebody else. Jane alone looked serenely up and down the table without the least consciousness of having said anything amiss.

It was then I noticed the Duke. His lips were drawn tightly together, he had flushed, and it seemed to me as though he drew slightly away from Jane. He must have had a foretaste of the fact that for a man of his position to marry a Jane Wilkinson might lead to some awkward contretemps.

As so often happens, I made the first remark that came into my head to my left hand neighbour, a stout, titled lady who arranged children's matinées. I remember that the remark in question was: "Who is that extraordinarily got-up woman in purple at the other end of the table?" It was, of course, the lady's sister! Having stammered apologies I turned and chatted to Ross, who answered in monosyllables.

It was then, rebuffed on both sides, that I noticed Bryan Martin. He must have come late, for I had not seen him before. He was a little way further down the table on my side and was leaning forward and chatting with great animation to a pretty blonde woman.

It was some time since I had seen him at close quarters, and I was struck at once by the great improvement in his looks. The haggard lines had almost disappeared. He looked younger and in every way more fit. He was laughing and chaffing his vis-à-vis and seemed in first rate spirits.

I did not have time to observe him further, for at that moment my stout neighbour forgave me and graciously permitted me to listen to a long monologue on the beauties of a children's matinée which she was organizing for charity.

Poirot had to leave early, as he had an appointment. He was investigating the strange disappearance of an ambassador's boots, and had a rendezvous fixed for half-past two. He charged me to make his adieus to Mrs. Widburn. While I was waiting to do so—not an easy matter, for she was at the moment closely surrounded by departing friends all breathing out "Darlings" at a great rate—somebody touched me on the shoulder. It was young Ross.

"Isn't M. Poirot here? I wanted to speak to him."

I explained that Poirot had just departed. Ross seemed taken aback.

Looking more closely at him, I saw that something seemed to have upset him. He looked white and strained and he had a queer uncertain look in his eyes.

"Did you want to see him particularly?" I asked.

He answered slowly:

"I—don't know."

It was such a queer answer that I stared at him in surprise. He flushed.

"It sounds odd, I know. The truth is that something rather queer has happened, something that I can't make out. I—I'd like M. Poirot's advice about it, because, you see, I don't know what to do. I don't want to bother him, but—"

He looked so puzzled and unhappy that I hastened to reassure him.

"Poirot has gone to keep an appointment," I said, "but I know he means to be back at five o'clock. Why not ring him up then, or come and see him?"

"Thanks. Do you know, I think I will. Five o'clock?"

"Better ring up first," I said, "and make sure before coming round."

"All right, I will. Thanks, Hastings. You see I think it might—just might—be very important."

I nodded and turned again to where Mrs. Widburn was dispensing honied words and limp handshakes. My duty done, I was turning away when a hand was slipped through my arm.

"Don't cut me," said a merry voice. It was Jenny Driver—looking extremely chic, by the way.

"Hello," I said. "Where have you sprung from?"

"I was lunching at the next table to you."

"I didn't see you. How is business?"

"Booming, thank you."

"The soup plates going well?"

"Soup plates, as you rudely call them, are going very well. When everybody has got thoroughly laden up with them, there's going to be dirty work done. Something like a blister with a feather attached is going to be worn bang in the middle of the forehead."

"Unscrupulous," I said.

"Not at all. Somebody must come to the rescue of the ostriches. They're all on the dole."

She laughed and moved away.

"Good-bye. I'm taking an afternoon off from business. Going for a spin in the country."

"And very nice too," I said approvingly. "It's stifling in London to-day."

I myself walked leisurely through the Park. I reached home about four o'clock. Poirot had not yet come in. It was twenty minutes to five when he returned. He was twinkling and clearly in a good humour.

"I see, Holmes," I remarked, "that you have tracked the ambassadorial boots."

"It was a case of cocaine smuggling. Very ingenious. For the last hour I have been in a ladies' beauty parlour. There was a girl there with auburn hair who would have captured your susceptible heart at once."

Poirot always has the impression that I am particularly susceptible to auburn hair. I do not bother to argue about it.

The telephone ran.

"That's probably Donald Ross," I said as I went across to the instrument.

"Donald Ross?"

"Yes. The young man we met at Chiswick. He wants to see you about something."

I took down the receiver.

"Hello. Captain Hastings speaking."

It was Ross.

"Oh! is that you, Hastings? Has M. Poirot come in?"

"Yes, he's here now. Do you want to speak to him or are you coming round?"

"It's nothing much. I can tell him just as well over the telephone."

"Right. Hold on."

Poirot came forward and took the receiver. I was so close that I could hear, faintly, Ross's voice.

"Is that M. Poirot?" The voice sounded eager, excited.

"Yes, it is I."

"Look here, I don't want to bother you, but there's something that seems to me a bit odd. It's in connection with Lord Edgware's death."

I saw Poirot's figure go taut.

"Continue, continue."

"It may seem just nonsense to you—"

"No, no. Tell me, all the same."

"It was Paris set me off. You see—" Very faintly I heard a bell trilling.

"Half a second," said Ross.

There was the sound of the receiver being laid down.

We waited, Poirot at the mouthpiece, I standing beside him.

I say we waited.

Two minutes passed—three minutes—four minutes—five minutes.

Poirot shifted his feet uneasily. He glanced up at the clock. Then he moved the hook up and down and spoke to the Exchange. He turned to me.

"The receiver is still off at the other end, but there is no reply. They cannot get an answer. Quick, Hastings, look up Ross's address in the telephone book. We must go there at once."

Chapter XXVI

PARIS?

A FEW MINUTES later we were jumping into a taxi. Poirot's face was very grave.

"I am afraid, Hastings," he said. "I am afraid."

"You don't mean—" I said and stopped.

"We are up against somebody who has already struck twice. That person will not hesitate to strike again. He is twisting and turning like a rat, fighting for his life. Ross is a danger. Then Ross will be eliminated."

"Was what he had to tell so important?" I asked doubtfully. "He did not seem to think so."

"Then he was wrong. Evidently what he had to tell was of supreme importance."

"But how could anyone know?"

"He spoke to you, you say. There, at Claridge's. With people all round. Madness—utter madness. Ah! why did you not bring him back with you—guard him—let no one near him till I had heard what he had to say?"

"I never thought—I never dreamt—" I stammered.

Poirot made a quick gesture.

"Do not blame yourself. How could you know? I—I would have known. The murderer, see you, Hastings, is as cunning as a tiger and as relentless. Ah! shall we never arrive?"

We were there at last. Ross lived in a maisonnette on the first floor of a house in a big square in Kensington. A card stuck in a little slot by the doorbell gave us the information. The hall door was open. Inside was a big flight of stairs.

"So easy to come in. None to see," murmured Poirot as he sprang up the stairs.

On the first floor was a kind of partition and a narrow door with a Yale lock. Ross's card was stuck in the centre of the door.

We paused there. Everywhere there was dead silence.

I pushed the door—to my surprise it yielded. We entered.

There was a narrow hall and an open door one side, another in front of us opening into what was evidently the sitting-room.

Into this sitting-room we went. It was the divided half of a big front drawing-room. It was cheaply but comfortably furnished, and it was empty. On a small table was the telephone; the receiver stood down beside the instrument.

Poirot took a swift step forward, looked round, then shook his head.

"Not here. Come, Hastings."

We retraced our steps and, going out into the hall, we passed through the other door. The room was a tiny dining-room. At one side of the table, fallen sideways from a chair and sprawled across the table, was Ross.

Poirot bent over him.

He straightened up. His face was white.

"He's dead. Stabbed at the base of the skull."

For long afterward the events of that afternoon remained like a nightmare in my mind. I could not rid myself of a dreadful feeling of responsibility.

Much later, that evening, when we were alone together, I stammered out to Poirot my bitter self-reproachings. He responded quickly:

"No, no, do not blame yourself. How could you have suspected? The good God has not given you a suspicious nature to begin with."

You would have suspected?"

"That is different. All my life, see you, I have tracked down murderers. I know how, each time, the impulse to kill becomes stronger, till, at last, for a trivial cause—" He broke off.

He had been very quiet ever since our ghastly discovery. All through the arrival of the police, the questioning of the other people in the house, the hundred and one details of the dreadful routine following upon a murder, Poirot had remained aloof—strangely quiet—a far-away, speculative look in his eyes. Now, as he broke off his sentence, that same far-away, speculative look returned.

"We have no time to waste in regrets, Hastings," he said quietly. "No time to say 'If.' The poor young man who is dead had something to tell us, and we know now that that something must have been of great importance —otherwise he would not have been killed. Since he can no longer tell us, we have got to guess. We have got to guess, with only one little clue to guide us."

"Paris," I said.

"Yes, Paris." He got up and began to stroll up and down.

"There have been several mentions of Paris in this business, but unluckily in different connections. There is the word Paris engraved in the gold box. Paris in November last. Miss Adams was there then; perhaps Ross was there also. Was there someone else there whom Ross knew, whom he saw with Miss Adams under somewhat peculiar circumstances?"

"We can never know," I said.

"Yes, yes, we can know. We *shall* know! The power of the human brain, Hastings, is almost unlimited. What other mentions of Paris have we in connection with the case? There is the short woman with the pince-nez who called for the box at the jeweller's there. Was she known to Ross? The Duke of Merton was in Paris when the crime was committed. Paris, Paris, Paris. Lord Edgware was going to Paris— Ah! possibly we have something there. Was he killed to prevent him going to Paris?"

He sat down again, his brows drawn together. I could almost feel the waves of his furious concentration of thought.

"What happened at that luncheon?" he murmured. "Some casual word or phrase must have shown to Donald Ross the significance of knowledge which was in his possession but which up to then he had not known was significant. Was there some mention of France? Of Paris? Up your end of the table, I mean."

"The word Paris was mentioned but not in that connection."

I told him about Jane Wilkinson's *"gaffe."*

"That probably explains it," he said thoughtfully. "The word Paris would be sufficient—taken in conjunction with something else. But what was that something else? At what was Ross looking? Or of what had he been speaking when that word was uttered?"

"He'd been talking about Scottish superstitions."

"And his eyes were where?"

"I'm not sure. I think he was looking up towards the head of the table where Mrs. Widburn was sitting."

"Who sat next to her?"

"The Duke of Merton, then Jane Wilkinson, then some fellow I didn't know."

"M. le Duc. It is possible that he was looking at M. le Duc when the word Paris was spoken. The Duke, remember, was in Paris, or was supposed to be in Paris, at the time of the crime. Suppose Ross suddenly remembered something which went to show that Merton was *not* in Paris."

"My dear Poirot!"

"Yes, you consider that an absurdity. So does everyone. Had M. le Duc a motive for the crime? Yes, a very strong one. But to suppose that he committed it—oh! absurd. He is so rich, of so assured a position, of such a well-known lofty character. No one will scrutinize his alibi too carefully. And yet to fake an alibi in a big hotel is not so difficult. To go across by the afternoon service—to return—it *could* be done. Tell me, Hastings, did

Ross not say anything when the word Paris was mentioned. Did he show no emotion?"

"I do seem to remember that he drew in his breath rather sharply."

And his manner when he spoke to you afterward. Was it bewildered? Confused?"

"That absolutely describes it."

"*Précisément.* An idea has come to him. He thinks it preposterous! Absurd! And yet— He hesitates to voice it. First he will speak to me. But alas! when he has made up his mind, I am already departed."

"If he had only said a little more to me," I lamented.

"Yes. If only— Who was near you at the time?"

"Well, everybody, more or less. They were saying good-bye to Mrs. Widburn. I didn't notice particularly."

Poirot got up again.

"Have I been all wrong?" he murmured as he began once more to pace the floor. "All the time, have I been wrong?"

I looked at him with sympathy. Exactly what the ideas were that passed through his head I did not know. "Close as an oyster," Japp had called him, and the Scotland Yard inspector's words were truly descriptive. I only knew that now, at this moment, he was at war with himself.

"At any rate," I said, "this murder cannot be put down to Ronald Marsh."

"It is a point in his favour," my friend said absent-mindedly. "But that does not concern us for the moment."

Abruptly, as before, he sat down.

"I cannot be entirely wrong. Hastings, do you remember that I once posed to myself five questions?"

"I seem to remember dimly something of the sort."

"They were: Why did Lord Edgware change his mind on the subject of divorce? What is the explanation of the letter he said he wrote to his wife and which she said she never got? Why was there that expression of rage on his face when we left his house that day? What were a pair of pince-nez doing in Carlotta Adams' handbag? Why did someone telephone to Lady Edgware at Chiswick and immediately ring off?"

"Yes, these were the questions," I said. "I remember now."

"Hastings, I have had in my mind all along a certain little idea. An idea as to who the man was—*the man behind.* Three of those questions I have answered, and the answers accord with my little idea. But two of the questions, Hastings, I cannot answer.

"You see what that means. Either I am wrong as to the person—*and it cannot be that reason*—or else the answer to the two questions that I cannot answer is there all the time. Which is it, Hastings? Which is it?"

Rising, he went to his desk, unlocked it and took out the letter Lucie Adams had sent him from America. He had asked Japp to let him keep it a day or two, and Japp had agreed. Poirot laid it on the table in front of him and pored over it.

The minutes went by. I yawned and picked up a book. I did not think that Poirot would get much result from his study. We had already gone over and over the letter. Granted that it was not Ronald Marsh who was referred to, there was nothing whatever to show who else it might be.

I turned the pages of my book. Possibly I dozed off.

Suddenly Poirot uttered a low cry. I sat up abruptly. He was looking at me with an indescribable expression, his eyes green and shining.

"Hastings, Hastings."

"Yes, what is it?"

"Do you remember I said to you that if the murderer had been a man of order and method he would have cut this page, not torn it."

"Yes?"

"I was wrong. There is order and method throughout this crime. The page had to be torn, not cut. Look for yourself."

I looked.

"Eh bien, you see?"

I shook my head.

"You mean he was in a hurry?"

"Hurry or no hurry, it would be the same thing. Do you not see, my friend. *The page had to be torn."*

I shook my head.

In a low voice Poirot said:

"I have been foolish. I have been blind. But *now—now—*we shall get on!"

Chapter XXVII

CONCERNING PINCE-NEZ

A MINUTE LATER his mood had changed. He sprang to his feet. I also sprang to mine—completely uncomprehending but willing.

"We will take a taxi. It is only nine o'clock, not too late to make a visit."

I hurried after him down the stairs.

"Whom are we going to visit?"

"We are going to Regent Gate."

I judged it wisest to hold my peace. Poirot, I saw, was not in the mood for being questioned. That he was greatly excited I could see. As we sat side by side in the taxi, his fingers drummed on his knee with a nervous impatience most unlike his usual calm.

I went over in my mind every word of Carlotta Adams' letter to her sister. By this time I almost knew it by heart. I repeated again and again to myself Poirot's words about the torn page. But it was no good. As far as I was concerned, Poirot's words simply did not make sense. Why had a page *got* to be torn? No, I could not see it.

A new butler opened the door to us at Regent Gate. Poirot asked for Miss Carroll and, as we followed the butler up the stairs, I wondered for the fiftieth time where the former "Greek god" could be. So far the police had failed utterly to run him to earth. A sudden shiver passed over me as I reflected that perhaps he, too, was dead.

The sight of Miss Carroll, brisk and neat and eminently sane, recalled me from the fantastic speculations. She was clearly very much surprised to see Poirot.

"I am glad to find you still here, mademoiselle," said Poirot as he bowed over her hand. "I was afraid you might be no longer in the house."

"Geraldine would not hear of my leaving," said Miss Carroll. "She begged me to stay on. And really, at a time like this, the poor child needs someone. If she needs nothing else, she needs a buffer. And I can assure you, when need be, I make a very efficient buffer, M. Poirot."

Her mouth took on a grim line. I felt that she would have a short way with reporters or news hunters.

"Mademoiselle, you have always seemed to me the pattern of efficiency. The efficiency, I admire it very much. It is rare. Mademoiselle Marsh now, she has not got the practical mind."

"She's a dreamer," said Miss Carroll. "Completely impractical. Always has been. Lucky she hasn't got her living to get."

"Yes, indeed."

"But I don't suppose you came here to talk about people being practical or impractical. What can I do for you, M. Poirot?"

I do not think Poirot quite liked to be recalled to the point in this fashion. He was somewhat addicted to the oblique approach. With Miss Carroll, however, such a thing was not practicable. She blinked at him suspiciously through her strong glasses.

"There are a few points on which I should like definite information. I know I can trust your memory, Miss Carroll."

"I wouldn't be much use as a secretary if you couldn't," said Miss Carroll grimly.

"Was Lord Edgware in Paris last November?"

"Yes."

"Can you tell me the date of his visit?"

"I shall have to look it up."

She rose, unlocked a drawer, took out a small bound book, turned the pages and finally announced:

"Lord Edgware went to Paris on November third and returned on the seventh. He also went over on November twenty-ninth and returned on December fourth. Anything more?"

"Yes. For what purpose did he go?"

"On the first occasion he went to see some statuettes which he thought of purchasing and which were to be auctioned later. On the second occasion he had no definite purpose in view so far as I know."

"Did Mademoiselle Marsh accompany her father on either occasion?"

"She never accompanied her father on any occasion, M. Poirot. Lord Edgware would never have dreamed of such a thing. At that time she was at a convent in Paris, but I do not think her father went to see her or took her out—at least it would surprise me very much if he had."

"You yourself did not accompany him?"

"No."

She looked at him curiously and then said abruptly:

"Why are you asking me these questions, M. Poirot? What is the point of them?"

Poirot did not reply to this question. Instead he said:

"Miss Marsh is very fond of her cousin, is she not?"

"Really, M. Poirot, I don't see what that has got to do with you."

"She came to see me the other day. You knew that?"

"No, first I've heard of it." She seemed startled. "What did she say?"

"She told me—though not in actual words—that she was very fond of her cousin."

"Well, then, why ask me?"

"Because I seek your opinion."

This time Miss Carroll decided to answer.

"Much too fond of him in my opinion. Always has been."

"You do not like the present Lord Edgware?"

"I don't say that. I've no use for him, that's all. He's not serious. I don't deny he's got a pleasant way with him. He can talk you round. But I'd rather see Geraldine getting interested in someone with a little more backbone."

"Such as the Duke of Merton."

"I don't know the Duke. At any rate he seems to take the duties of his position seriously. But he's running after that woman—that precious Jane Wilkinson."

"His mother—"

"Oh! I dare say his mother would prefer him to marry Geraldine. But what can mothers do? Sons never want to marry the girls their mothers want them to marry."

"Do you think that Miss Marsh's cousin cares for her?"

"Doesn't matter whether he does or doesn't, in the position he's in."

"You think, then, that he will be condemned?"

"No, I don't. I don't think he did it."

"But he might be condemned all the same?"

Miss Carroll did not reply.

"I must not detain you." Poirot rose. "By the way, did you know Carlotta Adams?"

"I saw her act. Very clever."

"Yes, she was clever." He seemed lost in meditation. "Ah! I have put down my gloves."

Reaching forward to get them from the table where he had laid them, his cuff caught the chain of Miss Carroll's pince-nez and jerked them off. Poirot retrieved them and the gloves which he had dropped, uttering confused apologies.

"I must apologize also once more for disturbing you," he ended, "but I fancied there might be some clue in a dispute Lord Edgware had with someone last year. Hence my questions about Paris. A forlorn hope, I fear, but Mademoiselle seemed so very positive she was. Well, good-night, mademoiselle, and a thousand pardons for disturbing you."

We had reached the door when Miss Carroll's voice recalled us.

"M. Poirot, these aren't my glasses. I can't see through them."

"*Comment?*" Poirot stared at her in amazement. Then his face broke up into smiles.

"Imbecile that I am! My own glasses fell out of my pocket as I stooped to get the gloves and pick up yours. I have mixed the two pairs. They look very alike, you see."

An exchange was made, with smiles on both sides, and we took our departure.

"Poirot," I said when we were outside. "You don't wear glasses."

He beamed at me.

"Penetrating! How quickly you see the point."

"Those were the pince-nez found in Carlotta Adams' handbag?"

"Correct."

"Why did you think they might be Miss Carroll's?"

Poirot shrugged his shoulders.

"She is the only person connected with the case who wears glasses."

"However, they are not hers," I said thoughtfully.

"So she affirms."

"You suspicious old devil."

"Not at all, not at all. Probably she spoke the truth. I think she did speak the truth. Otherwise I doubt if she would have noticed the substitution. I did it very adroitly, my friend."

We were strolling through the streets more or less at random. I suggested a taxi but Poirot shook his head.

"I have need to think, my friend. Walking aids me."

I said no more. The night was a close one and I was in no hurry to return home.

"Were your questions about Paris mere camouflage?" I asked curiously.

"Not entirely."

"We still haven't solved the mystery of the initial D," I said thoughtfully. "It's odd that nobody to do with the case has an initial D—either surname or Christian name—except—oh! yes, that's odd—except Donald Ross himself. And he's dead."

"Yes," said Poirot in a sombre voice. "He is dead."

I remembered another evening when three of us had walked at night, remembered something else, too, and drew my breath in sharply.

"By Jove, Poirot," I said. "Do you remember?"

"Remember what, my friend?"

"What Ross said about thirteen at table. *And he was the first to get up.*"

Poirot did not answer. I felt a little uncomfortable as one always does when superstition is proved justified.

"It is queer," I said in a low voice. "You must admit it is queer."

"Eh?"

"I said it was queer—about Ross and thirteen. Poirot, what are you thinking about?"

To my utter amazement and, I must admit, somewhat to my disgust, Poirot began suddenly to shake with laughter. He shook and he shook. Something was evidently causing him to most exquisite mirth.

"What the devil are you laughing at?" I said sharply.

"Oh! Oh! Oh!" gasped Poirot. "It is nothing. It is that I think of a riddle I hear the other day. I will tell it to you. What is it that has two legs, feathers, and barks like a dog?"

"A chicken, of course," I said wearily. "I knew that in the nursery."

"You are too well-informed, Hastings. You should say I do not know. And then me, I say, 'A chicken,' and then you say, 'But a chicken does not bark like a dog,' and I say, 'Ah! I put that in to make it more difficult.' Supposing, Hastings, that there we have the explanation of the letter D?"

"What nonsense!"

"Yes, to most people, but to a certain type of mind— Oh! if I had only someone I could ask—"

We were passing a big cinema. People were streaming out of it, discussing their own affairs, their servants, their friends of the opposite sex, and, occasionally, the picture they had just seen.

With a group of them we crossed the Euston Road.

"I loved it," a girl was sighing. "I think Bryan Martin's just wonderful. I never miss any picture he's in. The way he rode down that cliff and got there in time with the papers."

Her escort was less enthusiastic.

"Idiotic story. If they'd just had the sense to ask Ellis right away, which anyone with sense would have done—"

The rest was lost. Reaching the pavement I turned back to see Poirot standing in the middle of the road with buses bearing down on him from either side. Instinctively I put my hands over my eyes. There was a jarring of brakes, and some rich bus driver language. In a dignified manner Poirot walked to the curb. He looked like a man walking in his sleep.

"Poirot," I said. "Were you mad?"

"No, *mon ami.* It was just that—something came to me. There, at that moment."

"A damned bad moment," I said, "and very nearly your last one."

"No matter. Ah! *mon ami*—I have been blind, deaf, insensible. Now I see the answers to all those questions—yes, all five of them. Yes, I see it all —so simple, so childishly simple."

Chapter XXVIII

WE HAD A curious walk home. Poirot was clearly following out some train of thought in his own mind. Occasionally he murmured a word under his breath. I heard one or two of them. Once he said "Candles" and another time he said something that sounded like *"douzaine."* I suppose if I had been really bright I should have seen the line his thoughts were taking. It was really such a clear trail. However, at the time, it sounded to me mere gibberish.

No sooner were we at home than he flew to the telephone. He rang up the Savoy and asked to speak to Lady Edgware.

"Not a hope, old boy," I said with some amusement.

Poirot, as I have often told him, is one of the worst informed men in the world.

"Don't you know?" I went on. "She's in a new play. She'll be at the theatre. It's only half past ten."

Poirot paid no attention to me. He was speaking to the hotel clerk who was evidently telling him exactly what I had just told him.

"Ah! is that so? I should like then to speak to Lady Edgware's maid."

In a few minutes the connection was made.

"Is that Lady Edgware's maid? This is M. Poirot speaking. M. Hercule Poirot. You remember me, do you not?"

". . . . ."

"Très bien. Now, you understand, something of importance has arisen. I would like you to come and see me at once."

". . . . ."

"But, yes, very important. I will give you the address. Listen carefully."

He repeated it twice, then hung up the receiver with a thoughtful face.

"What is the idea?" I asked curiously. "Have you really got a piece of information?"

"No, Hastings, it is she who will give me the information."

"What information?"

"Information about a certain person."

"Jane Wilkinson?"

"Oh! as to her, I have all the information I need. I know her back side before as you say."

"Who then?"

Poirot gave me one of his supremely irritating smiles and told me to wait and see. He then busied himself in tidying up the room in a fussy manner.

Ten minutes later the maid arrived. She seemed a little nervous and uncertain. A small, neat figure, dressed in black, she peered about her doubtfully.

Poirot bustled forward.

"Ah! you have come. That is most kind. Sit here, will you not, Mademoiselle—Ellis, I think?"

"Yes, sir. Ellis."

She sat down on the chair Poirot had drawn forward for her.

She sat with her hands folded on her lap looking from one to the other of us. Her small, bloodless face was quite composed, and her thin lips were pinched together.

"To begin with, Miss Ellis, you have been with Lady Edgware how long?"

"Three years, sir."

"That is as I thought. You know her affairs well."

Ellis did not reply. She looked disapproving.

"What I mean is, you should have a good idea of who her enemies are likely to be."

Ellis compressed her lips more tightly.

"Most women have tried to do her a spiteful turn, sir. Yes, they've been all against her. Nasty jealousy."

"Her own sex did not like her?"

"No, sir. She's too good-looking. And she always gets what she wants. There's a lot of nasty jealousy in the theatrical profession."

"What about men?"

Ellis allowed a sour smile to appear on her withered countenance.

"She can do what she likes with the gentlemen, sir, and that's a fact."

"I agree with you," said Poirot, smiling. "Yet, even allowing that, I can imagine circumstances arising—" He broke off.

Then he said in a different voice:

"You know Mr. Bryan Martin, the film actor?"

"Oh! yes, sir."

"Very well?"

"Very well indeed."

"I believe I am not mistaken in saying that a little less than a year ago, Mr. Bryan Martin was very deeply in love with your mistress."

"Head over ears, sir. And it's 'is' not 'was,' if you ask me."

"He believed at that time she would marry him, eh?"

"Yes, sir."

"Did she ever seriously consider marrying him?"

"She thought of it, sir. If she could have got her freedom from his lordship, I believe she would have married him."

"And then, I suppose, the Duke of Merton appeared on the scene?"

"Yes, sir. He was doing a tour through the States. Love at first sight it was with him."

"And so good-bye to Bryan Martin's chances."

Ellis nodded.

"Of course Mr. Martin made an enormous amount of money," she explained, "but the Duke of Merton had position as well, and her ladyship is very keen on position. Married to the Duke, she'd have been one of the first ladies in the land."

The maid's voice held a smug complacency. It amused me.

"So Mr. Bryan Martin was—how do you say—turned down? Did he take it badly?"

"He carried on something awful, sir."

"Ah!"

"He threatened her with a revolver once. And the scenes he made! It frightened me, it did. He was drinking a lot, too. He went all to pieces."

"But in the end he calmed down."

"So it seemed, sir, but he still hung about, and I didn't like the look in his eye. I've warned her ladyship about it, but she only laughed. She's one who enjoys feeling her power, if you know what I mean."

"Yes," said Poirot thoughtfully. "I think I know what you mean."

"We've not seen so much of him just lately, sir. A good thing in my opinion. He's beginning to get over it, I hope."

"Perhaps."

Something in Poirot's utterance of the word seemed to strike her. She asked anxiously:

"You don't think she's in danger, sir?"

"Yes," said Poirot gravely. "I think she is in great danger, but she has brought it on herself."

His hand, running aimlessly along the mantelshelf, caught a vase of roses and it toppled over. The water fell on Ellis's face and head. I had seldom known Poirot clumsy, and I could deduce from it that he was in a great state of mental perturbation. He was very upset—rushed for a towel

—tenderly assisted the maid to dry her face and neck and was profuse in apologies.

Finally a treasury note changed hands and he escorted her towards the door thanking her for her goodness in coming.

"But it is still early," he said, glancing at the clock. "You will be back before your mistress returns."

"Oh! that is quite all right, sir. She is going out to supper, I think, and anyway she never expects me to sit up for her unless she says so special."

Suddenly Poirot flew off at a tangent.

"Mademoiselle, pardon me, but you are limping."

"That's nothing, sir. My feet are a little painful."

"The corns?" murmured Poirot in the confidential voice of one sufferer to another.

Corns, apparently it was. Poirot expatiated upon a certain remedy which according to him worked wonders.

Finally Ellis departed.

I was full of curiosity.

"Well, Poirot," I said. "Well?"

He smiled at my eagerness.

"Nothing more this evening, my friend. Tomorrow morning, early, we will ring up Japp. We will ask him to come round. We will also ring up Mr. Bryan Martin. I think he will be able to tell us something interesting. Also, I wish to pay him a debt that I owe him."

"Really?"

I looked at Poirot sideways. He was smiling to himself in a curious way.

"At any rate," I said, "you can't suspect *him* of killing Lord Edgware, especially after what we've heard tonight. That would be playing Jane's game with a vengeance. To kill off the husband so as to let the lady marry someone else is a little too disinterested for any man."

"What profound judgment!"

"Now don't be sarcastic," I said with some annoyance. "And what on earth are you fiddling with all the time?"

Poirot held the object in question up.

"With the pince-nez of the good Ellis, my friend. She left them behind."

"Nonsense, she had them on her nose when she went out."

He shook his head gently.

"Wrong! Absolutely wrong! What she had on, my dear Hastings, was the pair of pince-nez we found in Carlotta Adams' handbag."

I gasped.

Chapter XXIX

POIROT SPEAKS

IT FELL TO me to ring up Inspector Japp the following morning. His voice sounded rather depressed.

"Oh! it's you, Captain Hastings. Well, what's in the wind now?"

I gave him Poirot's message.

"Come round at eleven? Well, I dare say I could. He's not got anything to help us over young Ross's death, has he? I don't mind confessing that we could do with something. There's not a clue of any kind. Most mysterious business."

"I think he's got something for you," I said noncommittally. "He seems very pleased with himself, at all events."

"That's more than I am, I can tell you. All right, Captain Hastings. I'll be there."

My next task was to ring up Bryan Martin. To him I said what I had been told to say: that Poirot had discovered something rather interesting which he thought Mr. Martin would like to hear. When asked what it was, I said that I had no idea. Poirot had not confided in me. There was a pause.

"All right," said Bryan at last. "I'll come."

He rang off.

Presently, somewhat to my surprise, Poirot rang up Jenny Driver and asked her, also, to be present. He was quiet and rather grave. I asked him no questions.

Bryan Martin was the first to arrive. He looked in good health and spirits, but—or it might have been my fancy—a shade uneasy. Jenny Driver arrived almost immediately afterward. She seemed surprised to see Bryan, and he seemed to share her surprise.

Poirot brought forward two chairs and urged them to sit down. He glanced at his watch.

"Inspector Japp will be here in one moment, I expect."

"Inspector Japp?" Bryan seemed startled.

"Yes. I have asked him to come here—informally—as a friend."

"I see."

He relapsed into silence. Jenny gave a quick glance at him, then glanced away. She seemed rather preoccupied about something this morning.

A moment later, Japp entered the room. He was, I think, a trifle surprised to find Bryan Martin and Jenny Driver there, but he made no sign. He greeted Poirot with his usual jocularity.

"Well, M. Poirot, what's it all about? You've got some wonderful theory or other, I suppose."

Poirot beamed at him.

"No, no, nothing wonderful. Just a little story, quite simple; so simple that I am ashamed not to have seen it at once. I want, if you permit, to take you with me through the case from the beginning."

Japp sighed and looked at his watch.

"If you won't be more than an hour—" he said.

"Reassure yourself," said Poirot. "It will not take as long as that. See here, you want to know, do you not, who it was killed Lord Edgware, who it was killed Miss Adams, who it was killed Donald Ross?"

"I'd like to know the last," said Japp cautiously.

"Listen to me and you shall know everything. See, I am going to be humble." (Not likely! I thought unbelievingly.) "I am going to show you every step of the way. I am going to reveal how I was hoodwinked, how I displayed the gross imbecility, how it needed the conversation of my friend Hastings and a chance remark by a total stranger to put me on the right track."

He paused and then, clearing his throat, he began to speak in what I called his "lecture" voice.

"I will begin at the supper party at the Savoy. Lady Edgware accosted me and asked for a private interview. She wanted to get rid of her husband. At the close of our interview she said—somewhat unwisely, I thought— that she might have to go round in a taxi and kill him herself. Those words were heard by Mr. Bryan Martin who came in at that moment."

He wheeled round.

"Eh? That is so, is it not?"

"We all heard," said the actor. "The Widburns, Marsh, Carlotta—all of us."

Oh! I agree. I agree perfectly. Eh bien, I did not have a chance to forget those words of Lady Edgware's. Mr. Bryan Martin called on me the following morning for the express purpose of driving those words home."

"Not at all," cried Bryan Martin angrily; "I came—"

Poirot held up a hand.

"You came, ostensibly, to tell me a cock and bull story about being shadowed, a tale that a child might have seen through. You probably took it from an out-of-date film. A girl whose consent you had to obtain—a man whom you recognized by a gold tooth. *Mon ami,* no young man would have a gold tooth; it is not done in these days, and especially in America. The gold tooth, it is a hopelessly old-fashioned piece of dentistry. Oh! it was all of a piece—absurd! Having told your cock and bull story, you get down to the real purpose of your visit—to poison my mind against Lady Edgware. To put it clearly, you prepare the ground for the moment when she murders her husband."

"I don't know what you're talking about," muttered Bryan Martin. His face was deathly pale.

"You ridicule the idea that he will agree to a divorce! You think I am going to see him the following day, but actually the appointment is changed. I go to see him that morning and he *does* agree to a divorce. Any motive for a crime on Lady Edgware's part is gone. Moreover he tells me that he has already written to Lady Edgware to that effect.

"But Lady Edgware declares that she never got that letter. Either she lies, her husband lies, or somebody has suppressed it—who?

"Now I ask myself *why* does M. Bryan Martin give himself the trouble to come and tell me all these lies? What inner power drives him on? And I form the idea, monsieur, that you have been frantically in love with that lady. Lord Edgware says that his wife told him she wanted to marry an actor. Well, supposing that is so, but that the lady changes her mind. By the time Lord Edgware's letter agreeing to the divorce arrives, it is someone else she wants to marry—not you! There would be a reason, then, for your suppressing that letter."

"I never—"

"Presently you shall say all you want to say. Now you will attend to me.

"What then would be your frame of mind—you, a spoilt idol who has never known a rebuff? As I see it, a kind of baffled fury, a desire to do Lady Edgware as much harm as possible. And what greater harm could you do her than to have her accused—perhaps hanged—for murder."

"Good Lord!" said Japp.

Poirot turned to him.

"But yes, that was the little idea that began to shape itself in my mind. Several things came to support it. Carlotta Adams had two principal men friends—Captain Marsh and Bryan Martin. It was possible, then, that Bryan Martin, a rich man, was the one who suggested the hoax and offered her ten thousand dollars to carry it through. It has seemed to me unlikely all along that Miss Adams could ever have believed Ronald Marsh would have the ten thousand dollars to give her. She knew him to be extremely hard up. Bryan Martin was a far more likely solution."

"I didn't—I tell you I didn't—" came hoarsely from the film actor's lips.

"When the substance of Miss Adams' letter to her sister was wired from Washington— Oh! *là là!* I was very upset. It seemed that my reasoning was wholly wrong. But later I made a discovery. The actual letter itself was sent to me, and, instead of being continuous, a sheet of the letter was missing. *So 'he' might refer to someone who was not Captain Marsh.*

"There was one more piece of evidence. Captain Marsh, when he was arrested, distinctly stated that he thought he saw Bryan Martin enter the house. Coming from an accused man, that carried no weight. Also M. Martin had an alibi. That naturally! It was to be expected. If M. Martin did the murder, to have an alibi was absolutely necessary.

"That alibi was vouched for by one person only—Miss Driver."

"What about it?" said the girl sharply.

"Nothing, mademoiselle," said Poirot, smiling, "except that that same day I noticed you lunching with M. Martin and that you presently took the trouble to come over and try and make me believe that your friend Miss Adams was specially interested in Ronald Marsh, not, as I was sure was the case, in Bryan Martin."

"Not a bit of it," said the film star stoutly.

"You may have been unaware of it, monsieur," said Poirot quietly, "but I think it was true. It explains, as nothing else could, her feeling of dislike towards Lady Edgware. That dislike was on your behalf. You had told her all about your rebuff, had you not?"

"Well—yes—I felt I must talk to someone and she—"

"Was sympathetic. Yes, she was sympathetic; I noticed it myself. *Eh bien,* what happens next? Ronald Marsh, he is arrested. Immediately your spirits improve. Any anxiety you may have had is over. Although your plan has miscarried, owing to Lady Edgware's change of mind about going to a party at the last minute, yet somebody else has become the scapegoat and relieved you of all anxiety on your own account. And then—at a luncheon party—you hear Donald Ross—that pleasant but rather stupid young man—say something to Hastings that seems to show that you are not so safe after all."

"It isn't true," the actor howled. The perspiration was running down his face. His eyes looked wild with terror. "I tell you I heard nothing—nothing—I did nothing."

Then, I think, came the greatest shock of the morning.

"That is quite true," said Poirot quietly, "and I hope you have now been sufficiently punished for coming to me—*me,* Hercule Poirot, with a cock and bull story."

We all gasped. Poirot continued dreamily.

"You see—I am showing you all my mistakes. There were five questions I had asked myself. Hastings knows them. The answer to three of them fitted in very well. Who had suppressed that letter? Clearly Bryan Martin answered that question very well. Another question was what had induced Lord Edgware suddenly to change his mind and agree to a divorce? Well, I had an idea as to that. Either he wanted to marry again—but I could find no evidence pointing to that—or else some kind of blackmail was involved. Lord Edgware was a man of peculiar tastes. It was possible that facts about him had come to light which, while not entitling his wife to an English divorce, might yet be used by her as a lever, coupled with the threat of publicity. I think that is what happened. Lord Edgware did not want an open scandal attached to his name. He gave in, though his fury at having to do so was expressed in the murderous look on his face when he thought himself unobserved. It also explains the suspicious quickness with which he said, 'Not because of anything in the letter,' before I had even suggested that that might be the case.

"Two questions remained. The question of an odd pair of pince-nez in Miss Adams' bag, which did not belong to her, and the question of why Lady Edgware was rung up on the telephone while she was at dinner at Chiswick. In no way could I fit in M. Bryan Martin with either of those questions.

"So I was forced to the conclusion that either I was wrong about M. Martin, or wrong about the questions. In despair I once again read that letter of Miss Adams' through very carefully, and I found something! Yes, I found something!

"See for yourselves. Here it is. You see the sheet is torn? Unevenly, as often happens. Supposing now that before the 'h' at the top there was an 's.'

"Ah! you have it! You see. Not *he*—but *she!* It was a *woman* who suggested this hoax to Carlotta Adams.

"Well, I made a list of all the women who had been even remotely connected with the case. Besides Jane Wilkinson, there were four—Geraldine Marsh, Miss Carroll, Miss Driver and the Duchess of Merton.

"Of those four, the one that interested me most was Miss Carroll. She wore glasses, she was in the house that night, she had already been inaccurate in her evidence, owing to her desire to incriminate Lady Edgware, and she was also a woman of great efficiency and nerve who could have carried out such a crime. The motive was more obscure, but after all she had worked with Lord Edgware some years, and some motive might exist of which we were totally unaware.

"I also felt that I could not quite dismiss Geraldine Marsh from the case. She hated her father—she had told me so. She was a neurotic, highly strung type. Suppose when she went into the house that night she had deliberately stabbed her father and then coolly proceeded upstairs to fetch the pearls. Imagine her agony when she found that her cousin, whom she loved devotedly, had not remained outside in the taxi but had entered the house!

"Her agitated manner could be well explained on these lines. It could equally well be explained by her own innocence but by her fear that her cousin really had done the crime. There was another small point. The gold box found in Miss Adams' bag had the initial D in it. I had heard Geraldine addressed by her cousin as 'Dina.' Also she was in a Pensionnat in Paris last November and *might* possibly have met Carlotta Adams in Paris.

"You may think if fantastic to add the Duchess of Merton to the list. But she had called upon me and I recognized in her a fanatical type. The love of her whole life was centred on her son, and she might have worked herself up to contrive a plot to destroy the woman who was about to ruin her son's life.

"Then there was Miss Jenny Driver—"

He paused, looking at Jenny. She looked back at him, an impudent head on one side.

"And what have you got on me?" she asked.

"Nothing, mademoiselle, except that you were a friend of Bryan Martin's—and that your surname begins with D."

"That's not very much."

"There's one thing more. You have the brains and the nerve to commit such a crime. I doubt if anyone else had."

The girl lit a cigarette.

"Continue," she said cheerfully.

"Was M. Martin's alibi genuine or was it not? That was what I had to decide. If it was, who was it Ronald Marsh had seen go into the house? And suddenly I remembered something. The good-looking butler at Regent Gate bore a very marked resemblance to M. Martin. It was he whom Captain Marsh had seen, and I formed a theory as to that. It is my idea that he discovered his master killed. Beside his master was an envelope containing French banknotes to the value of a hundred pounds. He took these notes, slipped out of the house, left them in safe keeping with some rascally friend, and returned, letting himself in with Lord Edgware's key. He let the crime be discovered by the housemaid on the following morning. He felt in no danger himself, as he was quite convinced that Lady Edgware had done the murder, and the notes were out of the house and already changed before their loss was noticed. However, when Lady

Edgware had an alibi and Scotland Yard began investigating his antecedents, he got the wind up and decamped."

Japp nodded approvingly.

"I still have the question of the pince-nez to settle. If Miss Carroll was
the owner, then the case seemed settled. She could have suppressed the
letter, and, in arranging details with Carlotta Adams, or in meeting her on
the evening of the murder, the pince-nez might have inadvertently found
their way into Carlotta Adams' bag.

"But the pince-nez were apparently nothing to do with Miss Carroll. I
was walking home with Hastings here, somewhat depressed, trying to arrange things in my mind with order and method. And then the miracle
happened!

"First Hastings spoke of things in a certain order. He mentioned Donald Ross having been one of thirteen at table at Sir Montagu Corner's and
having been the first to get up. I was following out a train of thought of my
own and did not pay much attention. It just flashed through my mind that,
strictly speaking, that was not true. He may have got up first at the end of
dinner, but actually Lady Edgware had been the first to get up, since she
was called to the telephone. Thinking of her, a certain riddle occurred to
me—a riddle that I fancied accorded well with her somewhat childish
mentality. I told it to Hastings. He was, like Queen Victoria, not amused. I
next fell to wondering whom I could ask for details about M. Martin's
feeling for Jane Wilkinson. She herself would not tell me, I knew. And
then a passer-by, as we were all crossing the road, uttered a simple sentence.

"He said to his girl companion that somebody or other 'should have
asked Ellis.' And immediately the whole thing came to me in a flash!"

He looked round.

"Yes, yes, the pince-nez, the telephone call, the short woman who called
for the gold box in Paris. *Ellis*, of course, Jane Wilkinson's maid. I followed every step of it—the candles—the dim light—Miss Van Dusen—
everything. I *knew!"*

Chapter XXX

THE STORY

HE LOOKED ROUND at us.

"Come, my friends," he said gently. "Let me tell you the real story of what happened that night.

"Carlotta Adams leaves her flat at seven o'clock. From there she takes a taxi and goes to the Piccadilly Palace."

"What?" I exclaimed.

"To the Piccadilly Palace. Earlier in the day she has taken a room there as Mrs. Van Dusen. She wears a pair of strong glasses which, as we all know, alters the appearance very much. As I say, she books a room, saying that she is going by the night boat train to Liverpool and that her luggage has gone on. At eight-thirty Lady Edgware arrives and asks for her. She is shown up to her room. There they change clothes. Dressed in a fair wig, a white taffeta dress and ermine wrap, *Carlotta Adams and not Jane Wilkinson leaves the hotel and drives to Chiswick*. Yes, yes, it is perfectly possible. I have been to the house in the evening. The dinner table is lit only with candles, the lamps are dim, no one there knows Jane Wilkinson very well. There is the golden hair, the well-known husky voice and manner. Oh! it was quite easy. And if it had not been successful—if someone had spotted the fake—well, that was all arranged for, too. Lady Edgware, wearing a dark wig, Carlotta's clothes and the pince-nez, pays her bill, has her suitcase put on a taxi, and drives to Euston. She removes the dark wig in the lavatory; she puts her suitcase in the cloakroom. Before going to Regent Gate she rings up Chiswick and asks to speak to Lady Edgware. This has been arranged between them. If all has gone well and Carlotta has not been spotted, she is to answer simply: 'That's right.' I need hardly say Miss Adams was ignorant of the real reason for the telephone call. Having heard the words, Lady Edgware goes ahead. She goes to Regent Gate, asks for Lord Edgware, proclaims her individuality, goes into the library, and commits the first murder. Of course she did not know that Miss Carroll was watching her from above. As far as she is aware it will be the butler's word (and he has never seen her, remember—and also she wears a hat which shields her from his gaze) against the word of twelve well-known and distinguished people.

"She leaves the house, returns to Euston, changes from fair to dark again and picks up her suitcase. She has now to put in time till Carlotta Adams returns from Chiswick. They have agreed as to the approximate time. She goes to the Corner House, occasionally glancing at her watch, for the time passes slowly. Then she prepares for the second murder. She puts the small gold box she has ordered from Paris in Carlotta Adams' bag which, of course, she is carrying. Perhaps it is then she finds the letter. Perhaps it was earlier. Anyway, as soon as she sees the address, she scents danger. She opens it—her suspicions are justified.

"Perhaps her first impulse is to destroy the letter altogether. But she soon sees a better way. By removing one page of the letter she makes it read like an accusation of Ronald Marsh—a man who had a powerful motive for the crime. Even if Ronald has an alibi, it will still read as an accusation of a man so long as she tears off the s of 'she.' So that is what she does, then replaces it in the envelope and the envelope back in the bag.

"Then, the time having come, she walks in the direction of the Savoy Hotel. As soon as she sees the car pass, with (presumably) herself inside, she quickens her pace, enters at the same time and goes straight up the stairs. She is inconspicuously dressed in black. It is unlikely that anyone will notice her.

"Upstairs, she goes to her room. Carlotta Adams has just reached it. The maid has been told to go to bed—a perfectly usual proceeding. They again change clothes, and then, I fancy, Lady Edgware suggests a little drink—to celebrate. In that drink is the veronal. She congratulates her victim, says she will send her the cheque tomorrow. Carlotta Adams goes home. She is very sleepy—tries to ring up a friend—possibly M. Martin or Captain Marsh, for both have Victoria numbers—but gives it up. She is too tired. The veronal is beginning to work. She goes to bed, and she never wakes again. The second crime has been carried through successfully.

"Now for the third crime. It is at a luncheon party. Sir Montagu Corner makes a reference to a conversation he had with Lady Edgware on the night of the murder. That is easy. She has only to murmur some flattering phrase. But Nemesis comes upon her later. There is a mention of the 'judgment of Paris' and she takes Paris to be the only Paris she knows—the Paris of fashions and frills!

"But opposite her is sitting a young man who was at that dinner at Chiswick—a young man who heard the Lady Edgware of that night discussing Homer and Greek civilization generally. Carlotta Adams was a cultured, well-read girl. He cannot understand. He stares. And suddenly it comes to him. *This is not the same woman.* He is terribly upset. He is not sure of himself. He must have advice. He thinks of me. He speaks to Hastings.

"But the lady overhears him. She is quick enough and shrewd enough to realize that in some way or other she has given herself away. She hears Hastings say that I will not be in till five. At twenty to five she goes to Ross's maisonnette. He opens the door, is very surprised to see her, but it does not occur to him to be afraid. A strong, able-bodied young man is not afraid of a woman. He goes with her into the dining-room. She pours out some story to him. Perhaps she goes on her knees and flings her arms round his neck. And then, swift and sure, she strikes—as before. Perhaps he gives a choked cry—no more. He, too, is silenced."

There was a silence. Then Japp spoke hoarsely.

"You mean—she did it all the time?"

Poirot bowed his head.

"But why, if he was willing to give her a divorce?"

"Because the Duke of Merton is a pillar of the Anglo-Catholics. Because he would not dream of marrying a woman whose husband was alive. He was a young man of fanatical principles. As a widow, she was pretty certain of being able to marry him. Doubtless she had tentatively suggested divorce but he had not risen to the bait."

"Then why send you to Lord Edgware?"

"*Ah! parbleu.*" Poirot from having been very correct and English, suddenly relapsed into his natural self. "To pull the cotton-wool over my eyes! To make me a witness to the fact that there was no motive for the murder! Yes, she dared to make me, Hercule Poirot, her cat's paw! *Ma foi,* she succeeded too! Oh! that strange brain—childlike and cunning. She can act! How well she acted surprise at being told of the letter her husband had written her which she swore she had never received. Did she feel the slightest pang of remorse for any of her three crimes? I can swear she did not."

"I told you what she was like," cried Bryan Martin. "I told you. I knew she was going to kill him. I felt it. And I was afraid that somehow she'd get away with it. She's clever—devilish clever in a kind of half-wit way. And I wanted her to suffer. I wanted her to suffer. I wanted her to hang for it."

His face was scarlet. His voice came thickly.

"Now, now," said Jenny Driver.

She spoke exactly as I have heard nursemaids speak to a small child in the Park.

"And the gold box with the initial D and Paris November inside?" said Japp.

"She ordered that by letter and sent Ellis, her maid, to fetch it. Naturally Ellis just called for a parcel which she paid for. She had no idea what was inside. Also, Lady Edgware borrowed a pair of Ellis's pince-nez to help in the Van Dusen impersonation. She forgot about them and left them in Carlotta Adams' handbag—her one mistake.

"Oh! it came to me—it all came to me as I stood in the middle of the road. It was not polite what the bus driver said to me, but it was worth it. Ellis! Ellis's pince-nez. Ellis calling for the box in Paris. Ellis, and therefore Jane Wilkinson. Very possibly, she borrowed something else from Ellis besides the pince-nez."

"What?"

"A corn knife."

I shivered. There was a momentary silence. Then Japp said with a strange reliance in the answer:

"M. Poirot. Is this *true?*"

"It is true, *mon ami.*"

Then Bryan Martin spoke, and his words were, I thought, very typical of him.

"But look here," he said peevishly. "What about *me?* Why bring *me* here today? Why nearly frighten me to death?"

Poirot looked at him coldly.

"To punish you, monsieur, for being impertinent! How dare you try and make the games with Hercule Poirot?"

And then Jenny Driver laughed. She laughed and laughed.

"Serves you right, Bryan," she said at last.

She turned to Poirot.

"I'm glad as I can be that it wasn't Ronnie Marsh," she said. "I've always liked him. And I'm glad, glad, *glad* that Carlotta's death won't go unpunished! As for Bryan here, well, I'll tell you something, M. Poirot. I'm going to marry him, and if he thinks he can get divorced and married every two or three years, in the approved Hollywood fashion, well, he never made a bigger mistake in his life. He's going to marry me and stick to me."

Poirot looked at her—looked at her determined chin and at her flaming hair.

"It is very possible, mademoiselle," he said, "that that may be so. I said that you had sufficient nerve for anything. Even to marry a film 'star.' "

Chapter XXXI

A HUMAN DOCUMENT

A DAY OR two after that I was suddenly recalled to the Argentine, so it happened that I never saw Jane Wilkinson again and only read in the paper of her trial and condemnation. Unexpectedly, at least unexpectedly to me, she went completely to pieces when charged with the truth. So long as she was able to be proud of her cleverness and act her part, she made no mistakes; but once her self-confidence failed her, owing to someone having found her out, she was as incapable as a child would be of keeping up a deception. Cross-examined, she went completely to pieces.

So, as I said before, that luncheon party was the last time I saw Jane Wilkinson. But when I think of her, I always see her the same way—standing in her room at the Savoy, trying on expensive black clothes with a serious, absorbed face. I am convinced that that was no pose. She was being completely natural. Her plan had succeeded, and therefore she had no further qualms and doubts. Neither do I think that she ever suffered one pang of remorse for the three crimes she had committed.

I reproduce here a document which she had directed was to be sent to Poirot after her death. It is, I think, typical of that very lovely and completely conscienceless lady.

Dear M. Poirot, I have been thinking things over and I feel that I should like to write this for you. I know that you sometimes publish reports of your cases. I don't really think that you've ever published a document by the person themselves. I feel, too, that I would like everyone to know just exactly how I did it all. I still think it was all very well planned. If it hadn't been for you everything would have been quite all right. I've felt rather bitter about that, but I suppose you couldn't help it. I'm sure, if I send you this, you'll give it plenty of prominence. You will, won't you? I should like to be remembered. And I do think I am really a unique person. Everybody here seems to think so.

It began in America when I got to know Merton. I saw at once that if only

I were a widow he would marry me. Unfortunately he has got a queer sort of prejudice against divorce. I tried to overcome it but it was no good, and I had to be careful, because he was a very kinky sort of person.

I soon realized that my husband simply had got to die, but I didn't know how to set about it. You can manage things like that ever so much better in the States. I thought and I thought—but I couldn't see how to arrange it. And then, suddenly, I saw Carlotta Adams do her imitation of me and at once I began to see a way. With her help I could get an alibi. That same evening I saw you, and it suddenly struck me that it would be a good idea to send you to my husband to ask him for a divorce. At the same time I would go about talking of killing my husband, because I've always noticed that if you speak the truth in a rather silly way nobody believes you. I've often done it over contracts. And it's also a good thing to seem stupider than you are. At my second meeting with Carlotta Adams I broached the idea. I said it was a bet—and she fell for it at once. She was to pretend to be me at some party and if she got away with it she was to have ten thousand dollars. She was very enthusiastic and several of the ideas were hers—about changing clothes and all that. You see we couldn't do it here because of Ellis, and we couldn't do it at her place because of her maid. She, of course, didn't see why we couldn't. It was a little awkward. I just said "No." She thought me rather stupid about it, but she gave in and we thought of the hotel plan. I took a pair of Ellis's pince-nez.

Of course I realized quite soon that she would have to be got out of the way too. It was a pity, but, after all, those imitations of hers really were very impertinent. If mine hadn't happened to suit me I'd have been angry about it. I had some veronal myself, though I hardly ever take it, so that was quite easy. And then I had quite a brain wave. You see, it would be so much better if it could seem that she was in the habit of taking it. I ordered a box—the duplicate of one I'd been given—and I had her initials put on it and an inscription inside. I thought if I put some odd initial and Paris, November, inside it, it would make it all much more difficult. I wrote for the box from the Ritz when I was in there lunching one day. And I sent Ellis over to fetch it. She didn't know what it was, of course.

Everything went off quite well on the night. I took one of Ellis's corn knives, while she was over in Paris, because it was nice and sharp. She never noticed, because I put it back afterward. It was a doctor in San Francisco who showed me just where to stick it in. He'd been talking about lumbar and cistern punctures, and he said one had to be very careful, otherwise one went through the cistertia magna and into the medulla oblongata where all the vital nerve centres are and that that would cause immediate death. I made him show me the exact place several times. I thought it might perhaps come in useful one day. I told him I wanted to use the idea in a film.

It was very dishonourable of Carlotta Adams to write to her sister. She'd promised me to tell nobody. I do think it was clever of me to see what a good thing it would be to tear off that one page and leave he instead of she. I thought of that all by myself. I think I'm more proud of that than anything else. Everyone always says I haven't got brains—but I think it needed real brains to think of that.

I'd thought things out very carefully and I did exactly what I'd planned when the Scotland Yard man came. I rather enjoyed that part of it. I had thought, perhaps, that he'd really arrest me. I felt quite safe because I knew they'd have to believe all those people at the dinner and I didn't see how they could find out about me and Carlotta changing clothes.

After that I felt so happy and contented. My luck had held and I really felt everything was going to go right. The old Duchess was beastly to me, but Merton was sweet. He wanted to marry me as soon as possible and hadn't the least suspicion.

I don't think I've ever been so happy as I was those few weeks. My husband's nephew being arrested made me feel just as safe as anything. And I was more proud of myself than ever for having thought of tearing that page out of Carlotta Adams' letter.

The Donald Ross business was just sheer bad luck. I'm not quite sure now just how it was he spotted me. Something about Paris being a person and not a place. Even now I don't know who Paris was—and I think it's a silly name for a man, anyway.

It's curious how when luck starts going against you, it keeps on going. I had to do something about Donald Ross quickly, and that did go all right. It mightn't have, because I hadn't time to be clever or think of making an alibi. I did think I was safe after that.

Of course Ellis told me you had sent for her and questioned her, but I gathered it was all something to do with Bryan Martin. I couldn't think what you were driving at. You didn't ask her whether she had called for the parcel in Paris. I suppose you thought if she repeated that to me I should smell a rat. As it was, it came as a complete surprise. I couldn't believe it. It was just uncanny the way you seemed to know everything I'd done.

I just felt it was no good. You can't fight against luck. It was bad luck, wasn't it? I wonder if you are ever sorry for what you did. After all, I only wanted to be happy in my own way. And if it hadn't been for me you would never have had anything to do with the case. I never thought you'd be so horribly clever. You didn't look clever.

It's funny, but I haven't lost my looks a bit. In spite of all that dreadful trial and the horrid things that man on the other side said to me, and the way he battered me with questions.

I look much paler and thinner, but it suits me somehow. They all say I'm wonderfully brave. They don't hang you in public any more, do they? I think that's a pity.

I'm sure there's never been a murderess like me before.
I suppose I must say Good-bye now. It's very queer. I don't seem to realize things a bit. I'm going to see the chaplain tomorrow.

Yours forgivingly (because I must forgive my enemies, mustn't I?)
Jane Wilkinson.

P.S. Do you think they will put me in Madame Tussaud's?